Wilbur Smith

Wilbur Smith

Eagle in
the Sky

Shout at
the Devil

CHANCELLOR
PRESS

Eagle in the Sky first published in Great Britain
in 1974 by William Heinemann Limited
Shout at the Devil first published in Great Britain
in 1968 by William Heinemann Limited

This edition first published in Great Britain in 1983 by

Chancellor Press
an imprint of the Octopus Publishing Group p.l.c.
59 Grosvenor Street
London, W.1.

in association with

William Heinemann Limited
10 Upper Grosvenor Street
London, W.1.

and

Martin Secker & Warburg Limited
54 Poland Street
London, W.1.

ISBN: 0 907486 42 8

Printed and Bound in Great Britain by Collins, Glasgow

Wilbur Smith

Contents

Eagle in the Sky

Shout at the Devil

Wilbur
Smith

Eagle in
the Sky

While writing this story I had valuable help
from a number of people. Major Dick Lord
and Lieutenant Peter Cooke gave me advice
on the technique and technicalities of
modern fighter combat. Dr Robin Sandell
and Dr David Davies provided me with the
medical details. A brother angler, the Rev.
Bob Redrup, helped with the choice of the
title. To them all I am sincerely grateful.
While in Israel many of the citizens of that
state gave help and hospitality in generous
measure. It grieves me that I may not
mention their names.
As always my faithful research assistant gave
comfort, encouragement and criticism when
it was most needed. This book is dedicated
to her son – my stepson – Dieter Schmidt.

There was snow on the mountains of the Hottentots' Holland and the wind came off it, whimpering like a lost animal. The instructor stood in the doorway of his tiny office and hunched down into his flight jacket, thrusting his fists deeply into the fleece-lined pockets.

He watched the black chauffeur-driven Cadillac coming down between the cavernous iron-clad hangars, and he frowned sourly. For the trappings of wealth Barney Venter had a deeply aching gut-envy.

The Cadillac swung in and parked in a visitors' slot against the hangar wall, and a boy sprang from the rear door with boyish enthusiasm, spoke briefly with the coloured chauffeur, then hurried towards Barney.

He moved with a lightness that was strange for an adolescent. There was no stumbling over feet too big for his body, and he carried himself tall. Barney's envy curdled as he watched the young princeling approach. He hated these pampered darlings, and it was his particular fate that he must spend so much of his working day in their company. Only the very rich could afford to instruct their children in the mysteries of flight.

He was reduced to this by the gradual running down of his body, the natural attrition of time. Two years previously, at the age of forty-five, he had failed the strict medical on which his position of senior airline captain depended, and now he was going down the other side of the hill, probably to end as a typical fly-bum, steering tired and beaten-up heaps on unscheduled and shady routes for unlicensed and unprincipled charter companies.

The knowledge made him growl at the child who stood before him. 'Master Morgan, I presume?'

'Yes, sir, but you may call me David.' The boy offered his hand and instinctively Barney took it—immediately wishing he had not. The hand was slim and dry, but with a hard grip of bone and sinew.

'Thank you, David.' Barney was heavy on irony. 'And you may continue to call me "sir".'

He knew the boy was fourteen years old, but he stood almost level with Barney's five-foot-seven. David smiled at him and Barney was struck almost as by a physical force by the boy's beauty. It seemed as though each detail of his features had been wrought with infinite care by a supreme artist. The total effect was almost unreal, theatrical. It seemed indecent that hair should curl and glow so darkly, that skin should be so satiny and delicately tinted, or that eyes possess such depth and fire.

Barney became aware that he was staring at the boy, that he was falling under the spell that the child seemed so readily to weave—and he turned away abruptly.

'Come on.' He led the way through his office with its flyblown nude calendars and handwritten notices carrying terse admonitions against asking for credit, or making right-hand circuits.

'What do you know about flying?' he asked the boy as they passed through the cool gloom of the hangar where gaudily coloured aircraft stood in long rows, and out again through the wide doors into the bright mild winter sunshine.

'Nothing, sir.' The admission was refreshing, and Barney felt his mood sweeten slightly.

'But you want to learn?'

'Oh, yes sir!' The reply was emphatic and Barney glanced at him. The boy's eyes were so dark as to be almost black, only in the sunlight did they turn deep indigo blue.

'All right then—let's begin.' The aircraft was waiting on the concrete apron.

'This is a Cessna 150 high-wing monoplane.' Barney began the walk-around check with David following attentively, but when he started a brief explanation of the control surfaces and the principle of lift and wing-loading, he became aware that the boy knew more than he had owned up to. His replies to Barney's rhetorical questions were precise and accurate.

'You've been reading,' Barney accused.

'Yes, sir,' David admitted, grinning. His teeth were of peculiar whiteness and symmetry and the smile was irresistible. Despite himself, Barney realized he was beginning to like the boy.

'Right, jump in.'

Strapped into the cramped cockpit shoulder to shoulder, Barney explained the controls and instruments, then led into the starting procedure.

'Master switch on.' He flipped the red button. 'Right, turn that key—same as in a car.'

David leaned forward and obeyed. The prop spun and the engine fired and kicked, surged, then settled into a satisfying healthy growl. They taxied down the apron with David quickly developing his touch on the rudders, and paused for the final checks and radio procedure before swinging wide on to the runway.

'Right, pick an object at the end of the runway. Aim for it and open the throttle gently.'

Around them the machine became urgent, and it buzzed busily towards the far-off fence markers.

'Ease back on the wheel.'

And they were airborne, climbing swiftly away from earth.

'Gently,' said Barney. 'Don't freeze on to the controls. Treat her like—' he broke off. He had been about to liken the aircraft to a woman, but realized the unsuitability of the simile. 'Treat her like a horse. Ride her light.'

Instantly he felt David's death-grip on the wheel relax, the touch repeated through his own controls.

'That's it, David.' He glanced sideways at the boy, and felt a flare of disappointment. He had felt deep down in his being that this one might be bird, one of the very rare ones like himself whose natural element was the blue. Yet here in the first few moments of flight the child was wearing an expression of frozen terror. His lips and nostrils were trimmed with marble white and there were shadows in the dark blue eyes like the shape of sharks moving beneath the surface of a summer sea.

'Left wing up,' he snapped, disappointed, trying to shock him out of it. The wing came up and held rock steady, with no trace of over-correction.

'Level her out.' His own hands were off the controls as the nose sank to find the horizon.

'Throttle back.' The boy's right hand went unerringly to the throttle. Once more Barney glanced at him. His expression had not altered, and then with a sudden revelation Barney recognized it not as fear, but as ecstasy.

'He is bird.' The thought gave him a vast satisfaction, and while they flew on through the basic instruction in trim and attitude, Barney's mind went back thirty years to a battered old yellow Tiger Moth and another child in his first raptures of flight.

They skirted the harsh blue mountains, wearing their mantles of sun-blazing snow, and rode the tail of the wild winds that came down off them. 'Wind is like the sea, David. It breaks and swirls around high ground. Watch for it.' David nodded as he listened to his first fragment of flying lore, but his eyes were fixed ahead savouring each instant of the experience.

They turned north over the bleak bare land, the earth naked pink and smoky brown, stripped by the harvest of its robes of golden wheat.

'Wheel and rudder together, David,' Barney told him. 'Let's try a steep turn now.' Down went the wing and boldly the nose swept around holding its attitude to the horizon.

Ahead of them the sea broke in long lines of cream on the white beaches. The Atlantic was cold green and ruffled by the wind, flecked with dancing white.

South again, following the coastline where small figures on the white sand paused to look up at them from under shading hands, south towards the great flat mountain that marked the limit of the land, its shape unfamiliar from this approach. The shipping lay thick in the bay and the winter sunshine flashed from the windows of the white buildings huddling below the steep wooded sides of the mountain.

Another turn, confident and sure, Barney sitting with his hands in his lap, and his feet off the rudder bars, and they ran in over the Tygerberg towards the airfield.

'Okay,' said Barney. 'I've got her. And he took them in for the touch-down and taxied back to the concrete apron beside the hangars. He pulled the mixture control fully lean and let the engine starve and die.

They sat silent for a moment, neither of them moving or speaking, both of them unwinding but still aware that something important and significant had happened and that they had shared it.

'Okay?' Barney asked at last.

'Yes, sir,' David nodded, and they unstrapped and climbed down on to the concrete stiffly. Without speaking they walked side by side through the hangar and office. At the door they paused.

'Next Wednesday?' Barney asked.

'Yes, sir.' David left him and started towards the waiting Cadillac, but after a dozen steps he stopped, hesitated, then turned back.

'That was the most beautiful thing that has ever happened to me,' he said shyly. 'Thank you, sir.' And he hurried away leaving Barney staring after him.

The Cadillac pulled off, gathering speed, and disappeared round a bend amongst the trees beyond the last buildings. Barney chuckled, shook his head ruefully and turned back into his office. He dropped into the ancient swivel chair and crossed his ankles on the desk. He fished a crumpled cigarette from the pack, straightened and lit it.

'Beautiful?' he grunted, grinning. 'Crap!' He flicked the match at the waste bin and missed it.

The telephone woke Mitzi Morgan and she crept out from under her pillows groping blindly for it.

''Lo.'

'Mitzi?'

'Hi, Dad, are you coming up?' She came half-awake at her father's voice, remembering that this was the day he would fly up to join the family at their holiday home.

'Sorry, baby. Something has broken here. I won't be up until next week.'

'Oh, Dad!' Mitzi expressed her disappointment.

'Where's Davey?' her father went on quickly to forestall any recriminations.

'You want him to call you back?'

'No, I'll hold on. Call him, please, baby.'

Mitzi stumbled out of bed to the mirror, and with her fingers tried to comb some order into her hair. It was off-blonde and wiry, and fuzzed at the first touch of sun or salt or wind. The freckles were even more humiliating, she decided, looking at herself disapprovingly.

'You look like a Pekinese,' she spoke aloud, 'a fat little Pekinese–with freckles,' and gave up the effort of trying to change it. David had seen her like this a zillion times. She pulled a silk gown over her nudity and went into the passage, pass the door to her parents' suite where her mother slept alone, and into the living area of the house.

The house was stacked in a series of open planes and galleries, glass and steel and white pine, climbing out of the dunes along the beach, part of sea and sky, only glass separating it from the elements, and now the dawn filled it with a strange glowing light and made a feature of the massive headland of the Robberg that thrust out into the sea across the bay.

The Playroom was scattered with the litter of last night's party, twenty house guests and as many others from the big holiday homes along the dunes had left their mark–spilled beer, choked ashtrays and records thrown carelessly from their covers.

Mitzi picked her way through the debris and climbed the circular staircase to the guest rooms. She checked David's door, found it open, and went in. The bed was untouched, but his denims and sweat shirt were thrown across the chair and his shoes had been kicked off carelessly.

Mitzi grinned, and went through on to the balcony. It hung high above the beach, level with the gulls which were already dawn-winging for the scraps that the sea had thrown up during the night.

Quickly Mitzi hoisted her gown up around her waist, climbed up on to the rail of the balcony and stepped over the drop to the rail of the next balcony in line. She jumped down, drew the curtains aside and went into Marion's bedroom.

Marion was her best friend. Secretly she knew that this happy state of affairs existed chiefly because she, Mitzi, provided a foil for Marion's petite little body and wide-eyed doll-like beauty–and was a source of never-ending gifts and parties, free holidays and other good things.

She looked so pretty now in sleep, her hair golden and soft as it fanned out across David's chest. Mitzi transferred all her attention to her cousin, and felt that sliding sensation in her breast as she looked at him. He was seventeen years old now, but already he had the body of a grown man.

He was her most favourite person in all the world, she thought. He's so beautiful, so tall and straight and beautiful, and his eyes can break your heart.

The couple on the bed had thrown aside their covering in the warmth of the night, and there was hair on David's chest now, thick and dark and curly, there was muscle in arm and leg, and breadth across the shoulders.

'David,' she called softly, and touched his shoulder. 'Wake up.'

His eyes opened, and he was awake instantly, his gaze focused and aware.

'Mitz? What is it?'

'Get your pants on, warrior. My papa's on the line.'

'God.' David sat up, dropping Marion's head on to the pillow. 'What time is it?'

'Late,' Mitzi told him. 'You should set the alarm when you go visiting.'

Marion mumbled a protest and groped for the sheets as David jumped from the bed.

'Where's the phone?'

'In my room—but you can take it on the extension in yours.'

She followed him across the balcony railing, and curled up on David's bed while he picked up the receiver and with the extension cord trailing behind him began pacing the thick carpet restlessly.

'Uncle Paul?' David spoke. 'How are you?'

Mitzi groped in the pocket of her gown and found a Gauloise. She lit it with her gold Dunhill, but at the third puff David turned aside from his pacing, grinned at her, took the cigarette from between her lips and drew deeply upon it.

Mitzi pulled a face at him to disguise the turmoil that his nakedness stirred within her, and selected another cigarette for herself.

'He'd die if he knew what I was thinking,' she told herself, and derived a little comfort from the thought.

David finished his conversation and cradled the receiver before turning to her.

'He's not coming.'

'I know.'

'But he is sending Barney up in the Lear to fetch me. Big pow-wow.'

'It figures,' Mitzi nodded, then began a convincing imitation of her father. 'We have to start thinking about your future now, my boy. We have to train you to meet the responsibilities with which destiny has entrusted you.'

David chuckled and rummaged for his running shorts in the drawer of his bureau.

'I suppose I'll have to tell him now.'

'Yes,' Mitzi agreed. 'You sure will have to do that.'

David pulled up his shorts and turned for the door.

'Pray for me, doll.'

'You'll need more than prayer, warrior,' said Mitzi comfortably.

The tide had swept the beach smooth and firm, and no other feet had marked it this early. David ran smoothly, long strides leaving damp footsteps in a chain behind him.

The sun came up casting a soft pink sheen on the sea, and touching the Outeniqua mountains with flame—but David ran unseeing. His thoughts were on the impending interview with his guardian.

It was a time of crisis in his life, high school completed and many roads open. He knew the one he had chosen would draw violent opposition, and he used these last few hours of solitude to gather and strengthen his resolve.

A conclave of gulls, gathered about the body of a stranded fish, rose in cloud as he ran towards them, their wings catching the low sun as they hovered then dropped again when he passed.

He saw the Lear coming before he heard it. It was low against the dawn, rising and dropping over the towering bulk of the Robberg. Then swiftly, coming in on a muted shriek, it streaked low along the beach towards him.

David stopped, breathing lightly even after the long run, and raised both arms above his head in salute. He saw Barney's head through the Perspex canopy turned towards him, the flash of his teeth as he grinned and the hand raised, returning his salute as he went by.

The Lear turned out to sea, one wingtip almost touching the wave crests, and it came back to him. David stood on the exposed beach and steeled himself as the long sleek nose dropped lower and lower, aimed like a javelin at him.

Like some fearsome predatory bird it swooped at him and at the last possible instant David's nerve broke and he flung himself on the wet sand. The jet blast lashed him as the Lear rose and turned inland for the airfield.

'Son of a bitch,' muttered David as he stood up brushing damp sand from his bare chest, and imagined Barney's amused chuckle.

'I taught him good,' thought Barney, sprawled in the co-pilot's seat of the Lear as he watched David ride the delicate line of altitude where skill gave way to chance.

Barney had put on weight since he had been eating Morgan bread, and his paunch peeked shyly over his belt. The beginning of jowls bracketed the wide down-turned mouth that gave him the air of a disgruntled toad, and the cap of hair that covered his skull was sparser and speckled with salt.

Watching David fly, he felt the small warmth of his affection for him that his sour expression belied. Three years he had been chief pilot of the Morgan group and he knew well to whose intervention he owed the post. It was security he had now, and prestige. He flew great men in the most luxuriously fitted machines, and when the time came for him to go out to pasture he knew the grazing would be lush. The Morgan group looked after its own.

This knowledge sat comfortably on his stomach as he watched his protégé handle the jet.

Extended low flying like this required enormous concentration, and Barney watched in vain for any relaxation of it in his pupil.

The long golden beaches of Africa streamed steadily beneath them, punctuated by rock promontories and tiny resorts and fishing villages. Delicately the Lear followed the contours of the coastine, for they had spurned the direct route for the exhilaration of this flight.

Ahead of them stretched another strip of beach but as they howled low along it they saw that this one was occupied.

A pair of tiny feminine figures left the frothy surf and ran panic-stricken to where towels and discarded bikinis lay above the high-water mark. White buttocks constrasted sharply with a coffee-brown tan, and they laughed delightedly.

'Nice change for you to see them running away, David,' Barney grinned as they left the tiny figures far behind and bore onwards into the south.

From Cape Agulhas they turned inland, climbing steeply over the mountain ranges, then David eased back on the throttles and they sank down beyond the crests towards the city, nestling under its mountain.

As they walked side by side towards the hangar, Barney looked up at David who now topped him by six inches.

'Don't let him stampede you, boy,' he warned. 'You've made your decision. See you stick to it.'

David took his British racing green M.G. over De Waal Drive, and from the lower slopes of the mountains looked down to where the Morgan building stood four-square amongst the other tall monuments to power and wealth.

David enjoyed its appearance, clean and functional like an aircraft's wing—but he knew that the soaring freedom of its lines was deceptive. It was a prison and fortress.

He swung off the freeway at an interchange and rode down to the foreshore, glancing up at the towering bulk of the Morgan building again before entering the ramp that led to the underground garages beneath it.

When he entered the executive apartments on the top floor, he passed along the row of desks where the secretaries, hand-picked for their looks as well as their skill with a typewriter, sat in a long row. Their lovely faces opened into smiles like a garden of exotic blooms as David greeted each of them. Within the Morgan building he was treated with the respect due the heir apparent.

Martha Goodrich, in her own office that guarded the inner sanctum, looked up from her typewriter, severe and business-like.

'Good morning, Mister David. Your uncle is waiting—and I do think you could have worn a suit.'

'You're looking good, Martha. You've lost weight and I like your hair like that.' It worked, as it always did. Her expression softened.

'Don't you try buttering me up,' she warned him primly. 'I'm not one of your floozies.'

Paul Morgan was at the picture window looking down over the city spread below him like a map, but he turned quickly to greet David.

'Hello, Uncle Paul. I'm sorry I didn't have time to change. I thought it best to come directly.'

'That's fine, David.' Paul Morgan flicked his eyes over David's floral shirt open to the navel, the wide tooled leather belt, white slacks and open sandals. On him they looked good, Paul admitted reluctantly. The boy wore even the most outlandish modern clothes with a furious grace.

'It's good to see you.' Paul smoothed the lapels of his own dark conservatively-cut suit and looked up at his nephew. 'Come in. Sit down, there, the chair by the fireplace.' As always, he found that David standing emphasized his own lack of stature. Paul was short and heavily built in the shoulders, thick muscular neck and square thrusting head. Like his daughter, his hair was coarse and wiry and his features squashed and puglike.

All the Morgans were built that way. It was proper course of things, and David's exotic appearance was outside the natural order. It was from his mother's side, of course. All that dark hair and flashing eyes, and the temperament that went with it.

'Well, David. First off, I want to congratulate you on your final results. I was most gratified,' Paul Morgan told him gravely, and he could have added—'I was also mightily relieved.' David Morgan's scholastic career had been a tempestuous affair. Pinnacles of achievement followed immediately by depths of disgrace from which only the Morgan name and wealth had rescued him.

There had been the business with the games master's young wife. Paul never did find out the truth of the matter, but had thought it sufficient to smooth it over by donating a new organ to the school chapel and arranging a teaching scholarship for the games master to a foreign university. Immediately thereafter David had won the coveted Wessels prize for mathematics, and all was forgiven—until he decided to test his housemaster's new sports car, without that gentleman's knowledge, and took it into a tight bend at ninety miles an hour. The car was unequal to the test, and David picked himself up out of the wreckage and limped away with a nasty scratch on his calf. It had taken all Paul Morgan's weight to have the housemaster agree not to cancel David's appointment as head of house. His prejudices had finally been overcome by the replacement of his wrecked car with a more expensive model, and the Morgan group had made a grant to rebuild the ablution block of East House.

The boy was wild, Paul knew it well, but he knew also that he could tame him. Once he had done that he would have forged a razor-edged tool. He possessed all the attributes that Paul Morgan wanted in his successor. The verve and confidence, the bright quick mind and adventurous spirit—but above all he possessed the aggressive attitude, the urge to compete that Paul defined as the killer instinct.

'Thank you, Uncle Paul,' David accepted his uncle's congratulations warily. They were silent, each assessing the other. They had never been easy in the other's company, they were too different in many ways—and yet in others too much alike. Always it seemed that their interests were in conflict.

Paul Morgan moved across to the picture windows, so that the daylight back-lit him. It was an old trick of his to put the other person at a disadvantage.

'Not that we expected less of you, of course,' he laughed, and David smiled to acknowledge the fact that his uncle had come close to levity.

'And now we must consider your future.' David was silent.

'The choice open to you is wide,' said Paul Morgan, and then went on swiftly to narrow it. 'Though I do feel business science and law at an American University is what it should be. With this obvious goal in mind I have used my influence to have you enrolled in my old college—'

'Uncle Paul, I want to fly,' said David softly, and Paul Morgan paused. His expression changed fractionally.

'We are making a career decision, my boy, not expressing preferences for different types of recreation.'

'No, sir. I mean I want to fly—as a way of life.'

'Your life is here, with the Morgan group. It is not something in which you have freedom of action.'

'I don't agree with you, sir.'

Paul Morgan left the window and crossed to the fireplace. He selected a cigar from the humidor on the mantel, and while he prepared it he spoke softly, without looking at David.

'Your father was a romantic, David. He got it out of his system by charging around the desert in a tank. It seems you have inherited this romanticism from him.' He made it sound like some disgusting disease. He came back to where David sat.

'Tell me what you propose.'

'I have enlisted in the air force, sir.'

'You've done it? You've signed?'

'Yes, sir.'

'How long?'

'Five years. Short service commission.'

'Five years–' Paul Morgan whispered, 'well, David, I don't know what to say. You know that you are the last of the Morgans. I have no son. It will be sad to see this vast enterprise without one of us at the helm. I wonder what your father would have thought of this–'

'That's hitting low, Uncle Paul.'

'I don't think so, David. I think you are the one who is cheating. Your trust fund is a huge block of Morgan shares, and other assets given to you, on the unstated understanding that you assume your duties and responsibilities–'

'If only he would bawl me out,' thought David fiercely, knowing that he was being stampeded as Barney had warned him. 'If only he would order me to do it–so I could tell him to shove it.' But he knew he was being manipulated by a man skilled in the art, a man whose whole life was the manipulation of men and money, in whose hands a seventeen-year-old boy was as soft as dough.

'You see, David, you are born to it. Anything else is cowardice, self indulgence–' the Morgan Group reached out its tentacles, like some grotesque flesh-eating plant, to suck him in and digest him, '–we can have your enlistment papers annulled. It will be the matter of a single phone call–'

'Uncle Paul,' David almost shouted, trying to shut out the all-pervasive flow of words. 'My father. He did it. He joined the army.'

'Yes, David. But it was different at that time. One of us had to go. He was the younger–and, of course there were other personal considerations. Your mother–' he let the rest of it hang for a moment then went on, '–and when it was over he came back and took his rightful place here. We miss him now, David. No one else has been able to fill the gap he left. I have always hoped that you might be the one.'

'But I don't want to.' David shook his head. 'I don't want to spend my life in here.' He gestured at the mammoth structure of glass and concrete that surrounded them. 'I don't want to spend each day poring over piles of paper–'

'It's not like that, David. It's exciting, challenging, endlessly variable–'

'Uncle Paul.' David raised his voice again. 'What do you call a man who fills his belly with rich food–and then goes on eating?'

'Come now, David.' The first edge of irritation showed in Paul Morgan's voice, and he brushed the question aside impatiently.

'What do you call him?' David insisted.

'I expect that you would call him a glutton,' Paul Morgan answered.

'And what do you call a man with many millions–who spends his life trying to make more?'

Paul Morgan froze into stillness. He stared at his ward for long seconds before he spoke.

'You become insolent,' he said at last.

'No, sir. I did not mean it so. You are not the glutton–but I would be.'

Paul Morgan turned away and went to his desk. He sat in the high-backed leather chair and lit the cigar at last. They were silent again for a long time until at last Paul Morgan sighed.

'You'll have to get it out of your system, the way your father did. But how I grudge you five wasted years.'

'Not wasted, Uncle Paul. I will come out with a Bachelor of Science degree in aeronautical engineering.'

'I suppose we'll just have to be thankful for little things like that.'
David went and stood beside his chair.

'Thank you. This is very important to me.'

'Five years, David. After that I want you,' then he smiled slightly to signal a witticism, 'at least they will make you cut your hair.'

Four miles above the warm flesh-coloured earth, David Morgan rode the high heavens like a young god. The sun visor of his helmet was closed, masking with its dark cyclops eye the rapt, almost mystic expression with which he flew. Five years had not dulled the edge of his appetite for the sensation of power and isolation that flight in a Mirage interceptor awoke in him.

The unfiltered sunlight blazed ferociously upon the metal of his craft, clothing him in splendour—while far below the very clouds were insignificant against the earth, scattered and flying like a sheep flock before the wolf of the wind.

Today's flight was tempered by a melancholy, a sense of impending loss. The morrow was the last day of his enlistment. At noon his commission expired and if Paul Morgan prevailed he would become Mister David—new boy at Morgan Group.

He thrust the thought aside, and concentrated on the enjoyment of these last precious minutes; but too soon the spell was broken.

'Zulu Striker One, this is Range Control. Report your position.'

'Range Control, this is Zulu Striker One holding up range fifty miles.'

'Striker One, the range is clear. Your target-markers are figures eight and twelve. Commence your run.'

The horizon revolved abruptly across the nose of the Mirage, as the wing came over and he went down under power, falling from the heights, a controlled plunge, purposeful and precise as the stoop of a falcon.

David's right hand moved swiftly across the weapon selector panel, locking in the rocket circuit.

The earth flattened out ahead, immense and featureless, speckled with a low bush that blurred past his wing-tips as he let the Mirage sink lower. At this height the awareness of speed was breathtaking, and as the first marker came up ahead it seemed at the same instant to flash away below the silvery nose.

Five, six, seven—the black numerals on their glaring white grounds flickered by.

A touch of left rudder and stick, both adjustments made without conscious effort—and ahead was the circular layout of the rocket range, the concentric rings shrinking in size around the central mound—the 'coke' of flight jargon, which was the bull's-eye of the target.

David brought the deadly machine in fast and low, his mach meter recording a speed that was barely sub-sonic. He was running off the direct line of track, judging his moment with frowning concentration. When it came he pulled the Mirage's nose in to the 'pitch up' and went over on to the target with his gloved right finger curled about the trigger lever.

The shrieking silver machine achieved her correct slightly nose-down attitude for rocket launch at the precise instant of time that the white blob of 'coke' was centred in the diamond patterns of the reflector sight.

It was an evolution executed with subtle mastery of many diverse skills, and David pressed against the spring-loaded resistance of the trigger. There was no change in the feel of the aircraft, and the hiss of the rocket launch was almost lost beneath the howl of the great jet, but from beneath his wings the brief smoke lines reached out ahead towards the target, and in certainty of a fair strike David pushed his throttle to the gate and waited for the rumbling ignition of his after-burners, giving him power for the climb out of range of enemy flak.

'What a way to go,' he grinned to himself as he lay on his back with the Mirage's nose pointed into the bright blue, and gravity pressing him into the padding of his seat.

'Hello, Striker One. This is Range Control. That was right on the nose. Give the man a coke. Nice shooting. Sorry to lose you, Davey.' The break in hallowed range discipline touched David. He was going to miss them—all of them. He pressed the transmit button on the moulded head of his joystick, and spoke into the microphone of his helmet, 'From Striker One, thanks and farewell,' David said. 'Over and out.'

His ground crew were waiting for him also. He shook hands with each of them, the awkward handshakes and rough jokes masking the genuine affection that the years had built between them. Then he left them and went down the vast metal-skinned cavern, redolent with the smell of grease and oil along which the gleaming rows of needle-nosed interceptors stood, even in repose their forward lines giving them speed and thrust.

David paused to pat the cold metal of one of them, and the orderly found him there peering up at the emblem of the Flying Cobra upon the towering tailplane.

'C.O.'s compliments, sir, and will you report to him right away.'

Colonel 'Rastus' Naude was a dried-out stick of a man, with a wizened monkey face, who wore his uniform and medal ribbons with a casually distracted air. He had flow Hurricanes in the Battle of Britain, Mustangs in Italy, Spitfires and Messerschmitt 109's in Palestine and Sabres in Korea—and he was too old for his present command—but nobody could muster the courage to tell him that, especially as he could out-fly and out-gun most of the young bucks on the squadron.

'So we are getting rid of you at last, Morgan,' he greeted David.

'Not until after the mess party, sir.'

'Ja,' Rastus nodded. 'You've given me enough hardship these last five years. You owe me a bucket of whisky.' He gestured to the hard-backed chair beside his desk. 'Sit down, David.'

It was the first ime he had used David's given name, and David placed his flying helmet on the corner of the desk and lowered himself into the chair, clumsy in the constricting grip of his G-suit.

Rastus took his time filling his pipe with the evil black Magaliesberg shag and he studied the young man opposite him intently. He recognized the same qualities in him that Paul Morgan had prized, the aggressive and competitive drive that gave him a unique value as an interceptor pilot.

He lit the pipe at last, puffing thick rank clouds of blue smoke as he slid a sheaf of documents across the desk to David.

'Read and sign,' he said. 'That's an order.' David glanced rapidly through the papers, then he looked up and grinned.

'You don't give in easily, sir,' he admitted.

One document was a renewal of his short service contract for an additional five years, the other was a warrant of promotion—from captain to major.

'We have spent a great deal of time and money in making you what you are. You have been given an exceptional talent, and we have developed it until now you are—I'll not mince words—one hell of a pilot.'

'I'm sorry, sir,' David told him sincerely.

'Damn it,' said Rastus angrily. 'Why the hell did you have to be born a Morgan. All that money—they'll clip your wings, and chain you to a desk.'

'It's not the money.' David denied it swiftly. He felt his own anger stir at the accusation.

Rastus nodded cynically. 'Ja!' he said. 'I hate the stuff also.' He picked up the documents David had rejected, and grunted. 'Not enough to tempt you, hey?'

'Colonel, it's hard to explain. I just feel that there is more to do, something important that I have to find out about—and it's not here. I have to go look for it.'

Rastus nodded heavily. 'All right then,' he said. 'I had a good try. Now you can take your long-suffering commanding officer down to the mess and spend some of the Morgan millions on filling him up with whisky.' He stood up and clapped his uniform hat at a rakish angle over his cropped grey head. 'You and I will get drunk together this night—for both of us are losing something, I perhaps more than you.'

It seemed that David had inherited his love of beautiful and powerful machines from his father. Clive Morgan had driven himself, his wife, and his brand new Ferrari sports car into the side of a moving goods train at an unlit level crossing. The traffic police estimated that the Ferrari was travelling at one hundred and fifty miles an hour at the moment of impact.

Clive Morgan's provision for his eleven-year-old son was detailed and elaborate. The child became a ward of his uncle Paul Morgan, and his inheritance was arranged in a series of trust funds.

On his majority he was given access to the first of the funds which provided an income equivalent to that of, say, a highly successful surgeon. On that day the old green M.G. had given way to a powder-blue Maserati, in true Morgan tradition.

On his twenty-third birthday, control of the sheep ranches in the Karroo, the cattle ranch in South West Africa and Jubulani, the sprawling game ranch in the Sabi-Sand block, passed to him, their management handled smoothly by his trustees.

On his twenty-fifth birthday the number two fund interest would divert to him, in addition to a large block of negotiable paper and title in two massive urban holdings—office and supermarket complexes, and a high-rise housing project.

At age thirty the next fund opened for him, as large as the previous two combined, and transfer to him of the first of five blocks of Morgan stock would begin.

From then onwards, every five years until age fifty further funds opened, further blocks of Morgan stock would be transferred. It was a numbing procession of wealth that stretched ahead of him, daunting in its sheer magnitude; like a display of too much rich food, it seemed to depress appetite.

David drove fast southwards, with the Michelin metallics hissing savagely on the tarmac, and he thought about all that wealth, the great golden cage, the insatiable maw of Morgan Group yawning open to swallow him so that, like the cell of a jelly fish, he would become part of the whole, a prisoner of his own abundance.

The prospect appalled him, adding a hollow sensation in his belly to the pulse of pain that beat steadily behind his eyes—testimony to the foolhardiness of trying to drink level with Colonel Rastus Naude.

He pushed the Maserati harder, seeking the twin opiates of power and speed, finding comfort and escape in the rhythms and precision of driving very fast, and the hours flew past as swiftly as the miles so it was still daylight when he let himself into Mitzi's apartment on the cliffs that overlooked Clifton beach and the clear green Atlantic.

Mitzi's apartment was chaos, that much had not changed. She kept open house for a string of transitory guests who drank her liquor, ate her food and vied with each other as to who could create the most spectacular shambles.

In the first bedroom that David tried there was a strange girl with dark hair curled on the bed in boys' pyjamas, sucking her thumb in sleep.

With the second room he was luckier, and he found it deserted, although the bed was unmade and someone had left breakfast dishes smeared with congealed egg upon the side table.

David slung his bag on the bed and fished out his bathing costume. He changed quickly and went out by the side stairs that spiralled down to the beach and began to run—a trot at first, and then suddenly he sprinted away, racing blindly as though from some terrible monster that pursued him. At the end of Fourth beach where the rocks began, he plunged into the icy surf and swam out to the edge of the kelp at Bakoven point, driving overarm through the water and the cold lanced him to the bone, so that when he came out he was blue and shuddering. But the hunted feeling was gone and he warmed a little as he jogged back to Mitzi's apartment.

He had to remove the forest of pantihose and feminine underwear that festooned the bathroom before he could draw himself a bath. He filled it to the overflow, and as he settled into it the front door burst open and Mitzi came in like the north wind.

'Where are you, warrior?' She was banging the doors. 'I saw your car in the garage—so I know you're here!'

'In here, doll,' he called, and she stood in the doorway and they grinned at each other. She had put on weight again, he saw, straining the seam of her skirt, and her bosom was bulky and amorphous under the scarlet sweater. She had finally given up her struggle with myopia and the metal-framed spectacles sat on the end of her little nose, while her hair fuzzed out at unexpected angles.

'You're beautiful,' she cried, coming to kiss him and getting soap down her sweater as she hugged him.

'Drink or coffee?' she asked, and David winced at the thought of alcohol.

'Coffee will be great, doll.'

She brought it to him in a mug, then perched on the toilet seat.

'Tell all!' she commanded and while they chatted the pretty dark-haired girl wandered in, still in her pyjamas and bug-eyed from sleep.

'This is my coz, David. Isn't he beautiful?' Mitzi introduced them. 'And this is Liz.'

The girl sat on the dirty linen basket in the corner and fixed David with such an awed and penetrating gaze that Mitzi warned her. 'Cool it, darling. Even from here I can hear your ovaries bouncing around like ping-pong balls.'

But she was such a silent, ethereal little thing that they soon forgot her and talked as if they were alone. It was Mitzi who said suddenly, without preliminaries, 'Papa is waiting for you, licking his lips like an ivy-league ogre. I ate with them Saturday night–he must have brought your name up one zillion times. It's going to be strange to have you sitting up there on Top Floor, in a charcoal suit, being bright at Monday morning conference–'

David stood up suddenly in the bath, cascading suds and steaming water, and began soaping his crotch vigorously. They watched him with interest, the dark-haired girl's eyes widening until they seemed to fill her face.

David sat down again, slopping water over the edge.

'I'm not going!' he said, and there was a long heavy silence.

'What do you mean–you're not going?' Mitzi asked timorously.

'Just that,' said David. 'I'm not going to Morgan Group.'

'But you have to!'

'Why?' asked David.

'Well, I mean it's decided–you promised Daddy that when you finished with the airforce.'

'No,' David said, 'I made no promise. He just took it. When you said a moment ago–being bright at Monday morning conference–I knew I couldn't do it. I guess I've known all along.'

'What you going to do, then?' Mitzi had recovered from the first shock, and her plump cheeks were tinged with excitement.

'I don't know. I just know I am not going to be a caretaker for other men's achievements. Morgan Group isn't me. It's something that Gramps, and Dad and Uncle Paul made. It's too big and cold–'

Mitzi was flushed, bright-eyes, nodding her agreement, enchanted by this prospect of rebellion and open defiance.

David was warming to it also. 'I'll find my own road to go. There's more to it. There has to be something more than this.'

'Yes,' Mitzi nodded so that she almost shook her spectacles from her nose. 'You're not like them. You would shrivel and die up there on executive suite.'

'I've got to find it, Mitzi. It's got to be out there somewhere.'

David came out of the bath, his body glowing dull red-brown from the scalding water and steam rising from him in light tendrils. He pulled on a Terry robe as he talked and the two girls followed him through to the bedroom and sat side by side on the edge of the bed, eagerly nodding their encouragement as David Morgan made his formal declaration of independence. Mitzi spoiled it, however.

'What are you going to tell Daddy?' she asked. The question halted David's flow of rhetoric, and he scratched the hair on his chest as he considered it. The girls waited attentively.

'He's not going to let you get away again,' Mitzi warned. 'Not without a stand-up, knock-down, drag-em-out fight.'

In this moment of crisis David's courage deserted him. 'I've told him once, I don't have to tell him again.'

'You just going to cut and run?' Mitzi asked.

'I'm not running,' David replied with frosty dignity as he picked up the pigskin folder which held his thick sheaf of credit cards from the bedside table. 'I am merely reserving the right to determine my own future.' He crossed to the telephone and began dialling.

'Who are you calling?'

'The airline.'

'Where are you heading?'

'The same place as their first flight out.'

'I'll cover for you,' declared Mitzi loyally, 'you're doing the right thing, warrior.'

'You bet I am,' David agreed. 'My way—and screw the rest of them.'

'Do you have time for that?' Mitzi giggled, and the dark-haired girl spoke for the first time in a husky intense voice without once taking her eyes off David. 'I don't know about the rest of them, but may I be first, please?'

With the telephone receiver to his ear David glanced at her, and realized with only mild surprise that she was in deadly earnest.

David came out into the impersonal concrete and glass arrivals hall of Schipol Airport, and he paused to gloat on his escape and to revel at this sense of anonymity in the uncaring crowd. There was a touch at his elbow, and he turned to find a tall, smiling Dutchman quizzing him through rimless spectacles.

'Mr David Morgan, I think?' and David gaped at him.

'I am Frederick Van Gent of Holland and Indonesian Stevedoring. We have the honour to act on behalf of Morgan Shipping Lines in Holland. It is a great pleasure to make your acquaintance.'

'God, no!' David whispered wearily.

'Please?'

'No. I'm sorry. It's nice to meet you.' David shook the hand with resignation.

'I have two urgent Telex messages for you, Mr Morgan.' Van Gent produced them with a flourish. 'I have driven out from Amsterdam especially to deliver same.'

The first was from Mitzi who had sworn to cover for him.

'Abject apologies your whereabouts extracted with rack and thumbscrew stop be brave as a lion stop be ferocious as an eagle Love Mitzi.'

David said, 'Traitorous bitch!' and opened the second envelope.

'Your doubts understood, your action condoned stop confident your good sense will lead you eventually on to path of duty stop your place here always open affectionately Paul Morgan.'

David said, 'Crafty old bastard,' and stuffed both messages into his pocket.

'Is there a reply?' Van Gent asked.

'Thank you, no. It was good of you to take this trouble.'

'No trouble, Mr Morgan. Can I help you in any way? Is there anything you require?'

'Nothing, but thanks again.' They shook hands and Van Gent bowed and left him. David went to the Avis counter and the girl smiled brightly at him.

'Good evening, sir.'

David slipped his Avis card across the desk. 'I want something with a little jump to it, please.'

'Let me see, we have a Mustang Mach I?' She was pure blonde with a cream and pink unlined face.

'That will do admirably,' David assured her, and as he began filling the form in, she asked, 'Your first visit to Amsterdam, sir?'

'They tell me it's the city with the most action in Europe, is that right?'

'If you know where to go,' she murmured.

'You could show me?' David asked and she looked up at him with calculating eyes behind a neutral expression, made a decision and resumed her writings.

'Please sign here, sir. Your account will be charged,' then she dropped her voice. 'If you have any queries on this contract, you can contact me at this number–after hours. My name is Gilda.'

Gilda shared a walk-up over the outer canal with three other girls who showed no surprise, and made no objection when David carried his single Samsonite case up the steep staircase. However, the action that Gilda provided was in a series of discotheques and coffee bars where lost little people gathered to talk revolution and guru babble. In two days David discovered that pot tasted terrible and made him nauseous, and that Gilda's mind was as bland and unmarked as her exterior. He felt the stirrings of uneasiness when he studied the others that had been drawn to this city by the news that it was wide open, with the most understanding police force in the world. In them he saw symptoms of his own restlessness, and he recognized them as fellow seekers. Then the damp chill of the lowlands seemed to rise up out of the canals like the spirits of the dead on doomsday, and when you have been born under the sun of Africa the wintry effusions of the north are a pale substitute.

Gilda showed no visible emotion when she said goodbye, and with the heaters blasting hot air into the cab of the Mustang, David sent it booming southwards. On the outskirts of Namur there was a girl standing beside the road. In the cold her legs were bare and brown, protruding sweetly from the short faded blue denim pants she wore. She tilted her golden head and cocked a thumb.

David hit the stick down, and braked with the rubber squealing protest. He reversed back to where she stood. She had flat-planed slavic features and her hair was white blonde and hung in a thick plait down her back. He guessed her age at nineteen.

'You speak English?' he asked through the window. The cold was making her nipples stand out like marbles through the thin fabric of her shirt.

'No,' she said. 'But I speak American–will that do?'

'Right on!' David opened the passenger door, and she threw her pack and rolled sleeping bag into the back seat.

'I'm Philly,' she said.

'David.'

'You in show biz?'

'God, no–what makes you ask?'

'The car–the face–the clothes.'

'The car is hired, the clothes are stolen and I'm wearing a mask.'

'Funny man,' she said and curled up on the seat like a kitten and went to sleep.

He stopped in a village where the forests of the Ardennes begin and bought a long roll of crisp bread, a slab of smoked wild boar meat and a bottle of Möet Chandon. When he got back to the car Philly was awake.

'You hungry?' he asked.

'Sure.' She stretched and yawned.

He found a loggers' track going off into the forest and they followed it to a clearing where a long golden shaft of sunlight penetrated the green cathedral gloom.

Philly climbed out and looked around her. 'Keen, Davey, keen!' she said.

David poured the champagne into paper cups and sliced the meat with a penknife while Philly broke the bread into hunks. They sat side by side on a fallen log and ate.

'It's so quiet and peaceful—not at all like a killing ground. This is where the Germans made their last big effort—did you know that?'

Philly's mouth was full of bread and meat which didn't stop her reply. 'I saw the movie, Henry Fonda, Robert Ryan—it was a complete crock.'

'All that death and ugliness, we should do something beautiful in this place,' David said dreamily, and she swallowed the bread, took a sip of wine, before she stood up languidly and went to the Mustang. She fetched her sleeping bag and spread it on the soft bed of leaf mould.

'Some things are for talking about—others are for doing,' she told him.

For a while in Paris it looked as though it might be significant, as though they might have something for each other of importance. They found a room with a shower in a clean and pleasant little pension near the Gare St Lazare, and they walked through the streets all that day, from Concorde to Etoile, then across to the Eiffel Tower and back to Notre Dame. They ate supper at a sidewalk café on the 'Boul Mich', but half-way through the meal they reached an emotional dead end. Suddenly they ran out of conversation, they sensed it at the same time, each aware that they were strangers in all but the flesh and the knowledge chilled them both. Still they stayed together that night, even going through the mechanical and empty motions of love, but in the morning, when David came out of the shower, she sat up in the bed and said, 'You are splitting.'

It was a statement and not a question, and it needed no reply.

'Are you all right for bread?' he asked, and she shook her head. He peeled off a pair of thousand-franc notes and put them on the side table.

'I'll pay the bill downstairs.' He picked up his bag. 'Stay loose,' he said.

Paris was spoiled for him now, so he took the road south again towards the sun for the sky was filled with swollen black cloud and it rained before he passed the turn-off to Fontainebleau. It rained as he believed was only possible in the tropics, a solid deluge that flooded the concrete of the highway and blurred his windscreen so that the flogging of the wipers could not clear it swiftly enough for safe vision.

David was alone and discomforted by his inability to sustain communication with another human being. Although the other traffic had moderated its pace in the rain, he drove fast, feeling the drift and skate of his tyres on the slick surface. This time the calming effect of speed was ineffective and when he ran out of the rain south of Beaune it seemed that the wolf pack of loneliness ran close behind him.

However, the first outpouring of sunshine lightened his mood, and then far over the stone walls and rigid green lines of the vineyards he saw a wind-sock floating like a soft white sausage from its pole. He found the exit from the highway half a mile farther on, and the sign 'Club Aeronautique de Provence'. He followed it to a neat little airfield set among the vineyards, and one of the aircraft on the hard-stand was a Marchetti Aerobatic type F260. David climbed out of the Mustang and stared at it like a drunkard contemplating his first whisky of the day.

The Frenchman in the club office looked like an unsuccessful undertaker, and even when David showed him his logbook and sheafs of licences, he resisted the temptation of hiring him the Marchetti. David could take his pick from the others—but the Marchetti was not for hire. David added a 500-franc note to the pile of documents, and it disappeared miraculously into the Frenchman's pocket. Still he would not let David take the Marchetti solo, and he insisted on joining him in the instructor's seat.

David executed a slow and stately four-point roll before they had crossed the boundary fence. It was an act of defiance, and he made the stops crisp and exaggerated. The Frenchman cried 'Sacré bleu!' with great feeling and froze in his seat, but he had the good sense not to interfere with the controls. David completed the manœuvre and then immediately rolled in the opposite direction with the wing-tip a mere fifty feet above the tips of the vines. The Frenchman relaxed visibly, recognizing the masterly touch, and when David landed an hour later he grinned mournfully at him.

'*Formidable!*' he said, and shared his lunch with David—garlic polony, bread and a bottle of rank red wine. The good feeling of flight and the aroma of garlic lasted David all the way to Madrid.

In Madrid suddenly it began to happen, almost as though it had been arranged long before, as though his frantic flight across half of Europe was a pre-knowledge that something of importance awaited him in Madrid.

He reached the city in the evening, hurrying the last day's journey to be in time for the first running of the bulls that season. He had read Hemingway and Conrad and much of the other romantic literature of the bullring. He wondered if there might not be something for him in this way of life. It read so well in the books—the beauty, the glamour and excitement—the courage and trial and the final moment of truth. He wanted to evaluate it, to see it here in the great Plaza Des Torros, and then, if it still intrigued him, go on to the festival at Pamplona later in the season.

David checked in at the Gran Via with its elegance faded to mere comfort, and the porter arranged tickets for the following day. He was tired from the long drive and he went to bed early, waking refreshed and eager for the day. He found his way out to the ring and parked the Mustang amongst the tourist buses that already crowded the parking lot so early in the season.

The exterior of the ring was a surprise, sinister as the temple of some pagan and barbaric religion, unrelieved by the fluted tiers of balconies and encrustations of ceramic tiles—but the interior was as he knew it would be from film and photograph. The sanded ring smooth and clean, the flags against the cloud-flecked sky, the orchestra pouring out its jerky, rousing refrain—and the excitement.

The excitement amongst the crowd was more intense than he had known at prize fights or football internationals, they hummed and swarmed, rank upon rank of white eager faces and the music goaded them on.

David was sitting amongst a group of young Australians who wore souvenir sombreros and passed goat-skins of bad wine about, the girls squealing and chittering like sparrows. One of them picked on David, leaning forward to tug his shoulder and offer him the wine-skin. She was pretty enough in a kittenish way and her eyes made it clear that the offer was for more than cheap wine, but he refused both invitations brusquely and went to fetch a can of beer from one of the vendors. His chilly experience with the girl in Paris was still too fresh. When he returned to his seat the Aussie girl eyed the beer he carried reproachfully and then turned brightly and smiling to her companions.

The late arrivals were finding their seats now and the excitement was escalating sharply. Two of them climbed the stairs of the aisle towards where David sat. A striking young couple in their early twenties, but what first drew

David's attention was the good feeling of companionship and love that glowed around them, like an aura setting them apart.

They climbed arm in arm, passed where David sat, and took seats a row behind and across the aisle. The girl was tall with long legs clad in short black boots and dark pants over which she wore an apple-green suède jacket that was not expensive but of good cut and taste. In the sun her hair glittered like coal newly cut from the face and it hung to her shoulders in a sleek soft fall. Her face was broad and sun-browned, not beautiful for her mouth was too big and her eyes too widely spaced, but those eyes were the colour of wild honey, dark brown and flecked with gold. Like her, her companion was tall and straight, dark and strong-looking. He guided her to her seat with a brown muscled arm and David felt a sharp stab of anger and envy for him.

'Big cocky son of a gun,' he thought. They leaned their heads together and spoke secretly, and David looked away, his own loneliness accentuated by their closeness.

The parade of the toreadors began, and they came out with the sunlight glittering on the sequins and embroidery of their suits, as though they were the scales of some flamboyant reptile. The orchestra blared, and the keys to the bull pens were thrown down on to the sand. The toreadors' capes were spread on the *barrera* below their favourites and they retired from the ring.

In the pause that followed David glanced at the couple again. He was startled to find that they were both watching him and the girl was discussing him. She was leaning on her companion's shoulder, her lips almost touching his ear as she spoke and David felt his stomach clench under the impact of those honey golden eyes. For an instant they stared at each other and then the girl jerked away guiltily and dropped her gaze—but her companion held David's eyes openly, smiling easily, and it was David who looked away.

Below them in the ring the bull came out at full charge, head high, and hooves skidding in the sand.

He was beautiful and black and glossy, muscle in the neck and shoulder bunching as he swung his head from side to side and the crowd roared as he spun and burst into a gallop, pursuing an elusive flutter of pink across the ring. They took him on a circuit, passing him smoothly from cape to cape, letting him show off his bulk and high-stepping style, and the perfect sickle of his horns with their creamy points, before they brought in the horse.

The trumpets ushered in the horse, and they were a mockery—a brave greeting for the wretched nag, with scrawny neck and starting coat, one rheumy old eye blinkered so he could not see the fearsome creature he was going to meet.

Clownish in his padding, seeming too frail to carry the big armoured man on his back, they led him out and placed him in the path of the bull—and here any semblance of beauty ended.

The bull went into him head down, sending the gawky animal reeling against the *barrera* and the man leaned over the broad black back and ripped and tore into the hump with the lance, worrying the flesh, working in the steel with all his weight until the blood poured out in a slick tide, black as crude oil, and dripped from the bull's legs into the sand.

Raging at the agony of the steel, the bull hooked and butted at the protective pads that covered the horse's flanks. They came up as readily as a theatre curtain and the bull was into the scrawny roan body, hacking with the terrible horns, and the horse screamed as its belly split open and the purple and pink entrails spilled out and dangled into the sand.

David was dry-mouthed with horror as around him the crowd blood-roared, and the horse went down in a welter of equipment and its own guts.

They drew the bull away and flogged the fallen horse, twisting its tail and prodding its testicles, forcing it to rise at last and stand quivering and forlorn. Then beating it to make it move again they led it from the ring stumbling over its own entrails.

Then they went to work on the bull, slowly, torturously, reducing it from a magnificent beast to a blundering hunk of sweating and bleeding flesh, splattered with the creamy froth blown from its agonized lungs.

David wanted to scream at them to stop it, but sick to the stomach, frozen by guilt for his own part in this obscene ritual, he sat through it in silence until the bull stood in the centre of the ring, the sand about him ploughed and riven by his dreadful struggles. He stood with his head down, muzzle almost touching the sand and the blood and froth dripped from his nostrils and gaping mouth. The hoarse sawing of his breathing carried to David even above the crazed roaring crowd. The bull's legs shuddered and he passed a dribble of loose liquid yellow dung that fouled his back legs. It seemed to David that this was the final humiliation, and he found he was whispering aloud.

'No! No! Stop it! Please, stop it!'

Then the man in the glittering suit and ballet shoes came to end it, and the point of the sword struck bone and the blade arced then spun away in the sunlight, and the bull heaved and threw back thick droplets of blood, before he stood again.

They picked up the sword from the sand and gave it to the man and he sighted over the quiescent, dying beast and again the thrust was deflected by bone and David found that at last he had power in his voice, and he screamed:

'Stop it! You filthy bastards.'

Twelve times the man in the centre tried with sword, and each time the sword flicked out of his hand, and then at last the bull fell of its own accord, weak from the slow loss of much blood and with its heart broken by the torture and the striving. It tried to rise, lunging weakly, but the strength was not there and they killed it where it lay, with a dagger in the back of the neck, and they dragged it out with a team of mules—its legs waggling ridiculously in the air and its blood leaving a long brown smudge across the sand.

Stunned with the monstrous cruelty of it, David turned slowly to look at the girl. Her companion was leaning over her solicitously, whispering to her, trying to comfort her.

She was shaking her head slowly, in a gesture of incomprehension, and her honey-coloured eyes were blinded with weeping. Her lips were apart, quivering with grief, and her cheeks were awash, shiny with her tears.

Her companion helped her to her feet, and gently took her down the steps, leading her away blindly like a new widow from her husband's grave.

Around him the crowd was laughing and exhilarated, high on the blood and the pain—and David felt himself rejected, cut off from them. His heart went out to the weeping girl, she of all of them was the only one who seemed real to him. He had seen enough also, and he knew he would never get to Pamplona. He stood up and followed the girl out of the ring, he wanted to speak to her, to tell her that he shared her desolation, but when he reached the parking lot they were already climbing into a battered old Citroen CV.100, and although he broke into a run, the car pulled away—blowing blue smoke and clattering like a lawn-mower, and turned into the traffic leading east.

David watched it go with a sense of loss that effectively washed away the good feeling of the last few days, but he saw the old Citroen again two days later, when he had abandoned all idea of the Pamplona Festival and headed south. The Citroen looked even sicker than before, under a layer of pale dust and with the canvas showing on a rear tyre. The suspension seemed to have sagged on the one side, giving it a rakishly drunken aspect.

It was parked at a filling station on the outskirts of Zaragoza on the road to Barcelona, and David pulled off the road and park beyond the gasoline pumps. An attendant in greasy overalls was filling the tank of the Citroen under the supervision of the muscular young man from the bullring. David looked quickly for the girl—but she was not in thé car. Then he saw her.

She was in a *cantina* across the street, haggling with the elderly woman behind the counter. Her back was turned towards him, but David recognized the mass of dark hair now piled on top of her head. He crossed the road quickly and went into the shop behind her. He was not certain what he was going to do, acting only on impulse.

The girl wore a short floral dress which left her back and shoulders bare, and her feet were thrust into open sandals. But in concession to the ice in the air she wore a shawl over her shoulders. Close to, her skin had a plastic smoothness and elasticity, as though it had been lightly oiled and polished, and down the back of her naked neck the hair was fine and soft, growing in a whorl in the nape.

David moved closer to her as she completed her purchase of dried figs and counted her change. He smelt her, a light summery perfume that seemed to come from her hair. He resisted the temptation to press his face into the dense pile of it.

She turned smiling and saw him standing close behind her. She recognized him instantly, his was not a face a girl would readily forget. She was startled. The smile flickered out on her face and she stood very still looking at him, her expression completely neutral, but her lips slightly parted and her eyes soft and glowing golden. This peculiar stillness of hers was a quality he would come to know so well in the time ahead.

'I saw you in Madrid,' he said, 'at the bulls.'

'Yes,' she nodded, her voice neither welcoming nor forbidding.

'You were crying.'

'So were you.' Her voice was low and clear, her enunciation flawless, too perfect not to be foreign.

'No,' David denied it.

'You were crying,' she insisted softly. 'You were crying inside.' And he inclined his head in agreement. Suddenly she proffered the paper bag of figs.

'Try one,' she said and smiled. It was a warm friendly smile. He took one of the fruits and bit into the sweet flesh as she moved towards the door, somehow conveying an invitation for him to join her. He walked with her and they looked across the street at the Citroen. The attendant had finished filling the tank, and the girl's companion was waiting for her, leaning against the bonnet of the weary old car. He was lighting a cigarette, but he looked up and saw them. He evidently recognized David also, and he straightened up quickly and flicked away the burning match.

There was a soft whooshing sound and the heavy thump of concussion in the air, as fire flashed low across the concrete from a puddle of spilled gasoline. In an instant the flames had closed over the rear of the Citroen, and were drumming hungrily at the coachwork.

David left the girl and sprinted across the road.

'Get it away from the pumps, you idiot,' he shouted, and the driver started out of frozen shock.

It was happy fifth of November, a spectacular pyrotechnic display—but David got the handbrake off and the gearbox into neutral, and he and the driver pushed it into an open parking area alongside the filling station while a crowd materialized, seeming to appear out of the very earth, to scream hysterical encouragement and suggestions while keeping at a discreet distance.

They even managed to rescue the baggage from the rear seat before the flames engulfed it entirely—and belatedly the petrol attendant arrived with an enormous scarlet fire extinguisher. To the delighted applause of the crowd, he drenched the pathetic little vehicle in a great cloud of foam, and the excitement was over. The crowd drifted away, still laughing and chattering and congratulating the amateur firefighter on his virtuoso performance with the extinguisher—while the three of them regarded the scorched and blackened shell of the Citroen ruefully.

'I suppose it was a kindness really—the poor old thing was very tired,' the girl said at last. 'It was like shooting a horse with a broken leg.'

'Are you insured?' David asked, and the girl's companion laughed.

'You're joking—who would insure that? I only paid a hundred U.S. dollars for her.'

They assembled the small pile of rescued possessions, and she spoke quickly to her companion in foreign, slightly guttural language which touched a deep chord in David's memory. He understood what she was saying, so it was no surprise when she looked at him.

'We've got to meet somebody in Barcelona this evening. It's important.'

'Let's go,' said David.

They piled the luggage into the Mustang and the girl's companion folded up his long legs and piled into the back seat. His name was Joseph—but David was advised by the girl to call him Joe. She was Debra, and surnames didn't seem important at that stage. She sat in the seat beside David, with her knees pressed together primly and her hands in her lap. With one sweeping glance, she assessed the Mustang and its contents. David watched her check the expensive luggage, the Nikon camera and Zeiss binoculars in the glove compartment and the cashmere jacket thrown over the seat. Then she glanced sideways at him, seeming to notice for the first time the raw silk shirt with the slim gold Piaget under the cuff.

'Blessed are the poor,' she murmured, 'but still it must be pleasant to be rich.'

David enjoyed that. He wanted her to be impressed, he wanted her to make a few comparisons between himself and the big muscular buck in the back seat.

'Let's go to Barcelona,' he laughed.

David drove quietly through the outskirts of the town, and Debra looked over her shoulder at Joe.

'Are you comfortable?' she asked in the guttural language she had used before.

'If he's not—he can run behind,' David told her in the same language, and she gawked at him a moment in surprise before she let out a small exclamation of pleasure.

'Hey! You speak Hebrew!'

'Not very well,' David admitted. 'I've forgotten most of it,' and he had a vivid picture of himself as a ten-year-old, wrestling unhappily with a strange and mysterious language with back-to-front writing, an alphabet that was squiggly tadpoles and in which most sounds were made in the back of the throat, like gargling.

'Are you Jewish?' she asked, turning in the seat to confront him. She was no longer smiling; the question was clearly of significance to her.

David shook his head. 'No,' he laughed at the notion. 'I'm a half-convinced non-practising monotheist, raised and reared in the Protestant Christian tradition.'

'Then why did you learn Hebrew?'

'My mother wanted it,' David explained, and felt again the stab of an old guilt. 'She was killed when I was a kid. I just let it drop. It didn't seem important after she had gone.'

'Your mother—' Debra insisted, leaning towards him, '—she was Jewish?'

'Yeah. Sure,' David agreed. 'But my father was a Protestant. There was all sorts of hell when Dad married her. Everyone was against it—but they went ahead and did it anyway.'

Debra turned in the seat to Joe. 'Did you hear that—he's one of us.'

'Oh, come on!' David protested, still laughing.

'Mazaltov,' said Joe. 'Come and see us in Jerusalem some time.'

'You're Israeli?' David asked, with new interest.

'Sabras, both of us,' said Debra, with a note of pride and deep satisfaction. 'We are only on holiday here.'

'It must be an interesting country,' David hazarded.

'Like Joe just said, why don't you come and find out some time,' she suggested offhandedly. 'You have the right of return.' Then she changed the subject. 'Is this the fastest this machine will go? We have to be in Barcelona by seven.'

There was a relaxed feeling between them now, as though some invisible barrier had been lowered, as though she had made some weighty judgement. They were out of the city and ahead the open road wound down into the valley of the Ebro towards the sea.

'Kindly extinguish cigarettes and fasten your seat belts,' David said, and let the Mustang go.

She sat very still beside him with her hands folded in her lap and she stared ahead when the bends leapt at them, and the straights streamed in a soft blue blur beneath the body of the Mustang. There was a small rapturous smile on her mouth and the golden lights danced in her eyes, and David was moved to know that speed affected her the way it did him.

He forgot everything else but the girl in the seat beside him and the need to keep the mighty roaring machine on the ribbon of tarmac.

Once when they went twisting down into a dry dusty valley in a series of tight curves and David snaked the Mustang down into it with his hands darting from wheel to gear lever, and his feet dancing heel and toe on the foot pedals—she laughed aloud with the thrill of it.

They bought cheese and bread and a bottle of white wine at a village *cantina* and ate lunch sitting on the parapet of a stone bridge while the water swirled below them, milky with snow melt from the mountains.

David's thigh touched Debra's, as they sat side by side. He could feel the warmth and resilience of her flesh through the stuff of their clothing and she made no move to pull away. Her cheeks were flushed a little brighter than seemed natural, even in the chill little wind that nagged at them.

David was puzzled by Joe's attitude. He seemed to be completely oblivious of David's bird dogging his girl, and he was deriving a childlike pleasure out of tossing pebbles at the trout in the waters below them. Suddenly David wished he would put up a better resistance, it would make his conquest a lot more enjoyable—for conquest was what David had decided on.

He leaned across Debra for another chunk of the white, tangy cheese and he let his arm brush lightly against the tantalizing double bulge of her bosom. Joe seemed not to notice.

'Come on you big ape,' David thought scornfully. 'Fight for it. Don't just sit there.'

He wanted to test himself against this buck. He was big, and strong, and David could tell from the way he moved and held himself that he was well co-ordinated and self-assured. His face was chunky and half ugly, but he knew that some women liked them that way, and he was not fooled by Joe's slow and lazy grin—the eyes were quick and sharp.

'You want to drive, Joe?' he asked suddenly, and the slow grin spread like a puddle of spilled oil on Joe's face—but the eyes glittered with anticipation.

'Don't mind if I do,' said Joe, and David regretted the gesture as he found himself hunched in the narrow back seat. For the first five minutes Joe drive sedately, touching the brakes to test for grab and pull, flicking through the gears to feel the travel and bite of the stick, taking a burst of power through a bend to establish stability and detect any tendency for the tail to break out.

'Don't be scared of her,' David told him, and Joe grunted with a little frown of concentration creasing his broad forehead. Then he nodded to himself and his hands settled firmly, taking a fresh grip, and Debra whooped as he changed down to get the revs peaking. He slid the car through the first bend and David's right foot stabbed instinctively at a non-existent brake pedal and he felt his breathing jam in his throat.

When Joe parked them in the lot outside the airport at Barcelona and switched off the engine, all of them were silent for a few seconds and then David said softly,

'Son of a gun!'

Then they were all laughing. David felt a tinge of regret that he was going to have to take the girl away from him, for he was beginning to like him, despite himself, beginning to enjoy the slow deliberation of his speech and movements that was so clearly a put on and finding pleasure in the big slow smile that took so long to reach its full bloom. David had to harden his resolve.

They were an hour early for the plane they were meeting and they found a table in the restaurant overlooking the runways. David ordered an earthen-ware jug of Sangria, and Debra sat next to Joe and put her hand on his arm while she chatted, a gesture that tempered David's new-found liking for him.

A private flight landed as the waiter brought the Sangria, and Joe looked up.

'One of the new executive Gulfstreams. They tell me she is a little beauty.' And he went on to list the aircraft's specifications in technical language that Debra seemed to follow intelligently.

'You know anything about aircraft?' David challenged him.

'Some,' admitted Joe, but Debra took the question.

'Joe is in the airforce,' she said proudly, and David stared at them.

'So is Debs,' Joe laughed, and David switched his attention to her. 'She's a lieutenant in signals.'

'Only the reserve,' Debra demurred, 'but Joe is a flier. A fighter pilot.'

'A flier,' David repeated stupidly. He should have known from Joe's clear and steady gaze that was the peculiar mark of the fighter pilot. He should have known by the way he handled the Mustang. If he was an Israeli flier–then he would have flown a formidable number of operations. Hell, every time they took off, they were operational. He felt a vast tide of respect rising within him.

'What squadron are you on–Phantoms?'

'Phantoms!' Joe curled his lip. 'That isn't flying. That's operating a computer. No, we really fly. You ever heard of a Mirage?'

David blinked, and then nodded.

'Yeah,' said David, 'I've heard of them.'

'Well, I fly a Mirage.'

David began to laugh, shaking his head.

'What's wrong?' Joe demanded, his smile fading. 'What's funny about that?'

'I do too,' said David. 'I fly a Mirage.' It was no use trying to get hot against this buck, he decided. 'I've got over a thousand hours on Mirages.' And it was Joe's turn to stare, then suddenly they were both talking at once–Debra's head turning quickly from one to the other.

David ordered another jug of Sangria, but Joe would not let him pay. He repeated for the fiftieth time, 'Well, that beats all,' and punched David's shoulder. 'How about that, Debs?'

Half-way through the second jug, David interrupted the talk which had been exclusively on aviation.

'Who are we meeting, anyway? We've driven across half of Spain and I don't even know who the guy is.'

'This guy is a girl,' Joe laughed, and Debra filled in.

'Hannah,' and she grinned at Joe, 'his fiancée. She is a nursing sister at Hadassah Hospital, and she could only get away for a week.'

'Your fiancée?' David whispered.

'They are getting married in June.' Debra turned to Joe. 'It's taken him two years to make up his mind.'

Joe chuckled with embarrassment, and Debra squeezed his arm.

'Your fiancée?' asked David again.

'Why do you keep saying that?' Debra demanded. David pointed at Joe, and then at Debra.

'What,' he started, 'I mean, who–what the hell?'

Debra realized suddenly and gasped. She covered her mouth with both hands, her eyes sparkling. 'You mean–you thought–? Oh, no,' she giggled. She pointed at Joe and then at herself. 'Is that what you thought?' David nodded.

'He is my brother,' Debra hooted. 'Joe is my brother, you idiot! Joseph Israel Mordecai and Debra Ruth Mordecai–brother and sister.'

Hannah was a rangy girl with bright copper hair and freckles like sovereigns. She was only an inch or two shorter than Joe but he lifted her as she came through the customs gate, swung her off her feet and then engulfed her in an enormous embrace.

It seemed completely natural that the four of them should stay together. By a miracle of packing they got all their luggage and themselves into the Mustang with Hannah perched on Joe's lap in the rear.

'We've got a week,' said Debra. 'A whole week! What are we going to do with it?'

They agreed that Torremolinos was out. It was far south, and since Michener had written *The Drifters*, it had become a hangout for all the bums and freaks.

'I was talking to someone on the plane. There is a place called Colera up the coast. Near the border.'

They reached it in the middle of the next morning and it was still so early in the season that they had no trouble finding pleasant rooms at a small hotel off the winding main street.

The girls shared, and David insisted on a room of his own. He had certain plans for Debra that made privacy desirable.

Debra's bikini was blue and brief, hardly sufficient to restrain a bosom that was more exuberant than David had guessed. Her skin was satiny and tanned to a deep mahogany, although a strip of startling white peeped over the back of her costume when she stooped to pick up her towel. She was long in the waist, and leg, and a strong swimmer—pacing David steadily through the cool blue water when they set out for a rocky islet half a mile off shore.

They had the tiny island to themselves and they found a pitch of flat smooth rock out of the wind and full in the sun. They lay side by side with their fingers entwined and the salt water had sleeked Debra's hair to her shoulders, like the coat of an otter.

They lay in the sun and they talked away the afternoon. There was so much they had to learn about each other.

Her father had been one of the youngest colonels in the American Airforce during World War II, but afterwards he had gone on to Israel. He had been there ever since, and was now a Major-General. They lived in a house in an old part of Jerusalem which was five hundred years old, but was a lot of fun.

She was a senior lecturer in English at the Hebrew University in Jerusalem and, this shyly as though it were a rather special secret, she wanted to write. A small volume of her poetry had already been published. That impressed David, and he came up on one elbow and looked at her with new respect, and a twinge of envy, for someone who saw the way ahead clearly.

She lay with her eyes closed against the sun, and droplets of water sparkling like gems on her thick dark eyelashes. She wasn't beautiful, he decided carefully, but very handsome and very, very sexy. He was going to have her, of course. There was no doubt in David's mind about this, but there seemed little urgency in it now. He was enjoying listening to her talk, she had a quaint way of expressing herself, once she was in full flight, and her accent was strangely neutral—although there were faint echoes of her American background now he knew to look for them. She told him that the poetry was merely a beginning. She was going to write a novel about being young and living in Israel. She had the outline worked out, and it seemed like a pretty interesting story to David. Then she started to talk about her land and the people who lived in it. David felt something move within him as he listened—a nostalgia, a deep race memory. Again his envy stirred. She was so certain where she was from and where she was going—she knew where she belonged, and what her destiny was, and this made her strong. Beside her he felt suddenly insignificant and without purpose.

She opened her eyes suddenly, squinting a little in the sunlight and looked up at him.

'Oh dear,' she smiled. 'We are so sad, David. Do I talk too much?' He shook his head but did not answer her smile, and she became solemn also.

She studied his face carefully, with minute attention. The sun had dried his hair and fluffed it out, and it was soft and fine and very dark. The bone of his cheek and jaw was sculptured and finely balanced, the eyes very clear and slightly Asiatic in cast, the lips full and firm, and the nose delicately fluted with wide nostrils and a straight graceful line.

She reached up and touched his cheek.

'You are very beautiful, David. You are the most beautiful human being I have ever seen.'

He did not move, she ran the finger down his neck on to his chest, twirling it slowly in the dark body hair.

Slowly he leaned forward and placed his mouth over hers. Her lips were warm and soft and tasted of sea salt. Her arms came up around the back of his head and folded around him. They kissed until he reached behind her and unfastened the clasp of her costume between the smooth brown shoulder blades. She stiffened immediately and tried to pull away from him.

David held her gently but firm, murmuring little soothing noises as he kissed her again. Slowly she relaxed and he went on gentling her until her hands went to the back of his neck again, and she sighed and shuddered.

His hands were skilled and expert, masterful enough to prevent rebellion, not rough enough to panic her. He pushed up the thin material of her costume top and was surprised and enchanted with the firm rubbery weight of her breasts and the big husky rose-brown nipples which were pebble hard to his touch.

It was shocking, completely foreign to his experience, for David was not accustomed to check or denial, but Debra placed her hands on his shoulders and shoved him with such force that he lost his balance and slid down the rock, grazing his elbow and ending in a heap at the water's edge.

He scrambled angrily to his feet as Debra came up with a fluid explosive movement, fastening her costume as she did so. A single bound of her long brown legs carried her to the edge of the rocks and she dived outwards, hitting the water flat and surfacing to call back to him.

'I'll race you to the beach.'

David would not accept the challenge and followed her at his own dignified pace. When he emerged unsmilingly from the low surf, she studied his face a moment and then grinned.

'When you sulk you look about ten years old,' she told him, which was no great exercise of tact and David stalked back to his room.

He was still being extremely dignified and aloof that evening when they discovered a discotheque named '2001 A.D.' run by a couple of English boys down on the sea-front. They crowded round a table at which there were already two B.E.A. hostesses and a couple of raggedy-looking beards. The music was loud enough and the rhythm hard enough to jar the spine and loosen the bowels, and when the two hostesses gazed at David with almost religious awe Debra forsook her attitude of cool amusement and suggested to David that they dance. Mollified by this little feminine by-play, David dropped his impersonation of the Ice King.

They moved well together, sharing the gut rhythms of the harsh music, executing the primeval movements that reeked of Africa with a grace that drew the attention of the other dancers.

When the music changed Debra came to him and lay her body against his. David felt some force flowing from her that seemed to charge every nerve of his body—and he knew that no relationship he had with this woman would ever run calmly. It was too deeply felt for that, too volatile and triggered for momentary explosion.

When the record ended they left Joe and Hannah huddled over a carafe of red wine and they went out into the silent street and down to the beach.

There was a moon in the sky that lit the dark cliffs crowding in above the beach, and reflected off the sea in multiple yellow images. The low surf hissed and coughed on the pebble beach and they took off their shoes and walked along it, letting the water wash around their ankles.

In an angle of the cliff, they found a hidden place amongst the rocks and they stopped to kiss again, and David mistakenly took her new soft mood as an invitation to continue from where he had left off that afternoon.

Debra pulled away again, but this time with determination and said angrily, 'Damn you! Don't you ever learn? I don't want to do that. Do we have to go through this every time we are alone?'

'What's the matter?' David was immediately stung by her tone, and furious with this fresh check. 'This is the twentieth century, darling. The simpering virgin is out of style this season—hadn't you heard?'

'And spoilt little boys should grow up before they come out on their own,' she flashed back at him.

'Thanks!' he snarled. 'I don't have to stay around taking insults from any professional virgin.'

'Well, why don't you move out then?' she challenged him.

'Hey, that's a great idea!' He turned his back on her and walked away up the beach. She had not expected that, and she started to run after him—but her pride checked her. She stopped and leaned against the rock.

He shouldn't have rushed me, she thought miserably. I want him, I want him very much, but he will be the first since Dudu. If he will just give me time it will be all right, but he mustn't rush me. If he could only go at my speed, help me to do it right.

It is funny, she thought, how little I remember about Dudu now. It's only three years, but his memory is fading so swiftly, I wonder if I really did love him. Even his face is hazy in my mind, while I know every detail of David's—every plane and line of it.

Perhaps I should go after him and tell him about Dudu, and ask him to be patient and to help me a little. Perhaps I should do that, she thought, but she did not and slowly she walked up the beach, through the silent town to the hotel.

Hannah's bed across the room was empty. She would be with Joe, lying with him, loving with him. I should be with David also, she thought. Dudu is dead, and I'm alive, and I want David and I should be with him—but she undressed slowly and climbed into the bed and lay without sleeping.

David stood in the doorway of '2001 A.D.' and peered through the weirdly flashing lights and the smog, the warm palpable emanation from a hundred straining bodies. The B.E.A. hostesses were still at the table, but Joe and Hannah had gone.

David made his way through the dancers. The one hostess was tall and blonde, with high English colour and china-doll eyes. She looked up and saw David, glanced around for Debra, made sure she was missing before she smiled.

They danced one cut of the record without touching each other and then David leaned close to her and placed both hands on her hips. She strained towards him with her lips parting.

'Have you got a room?' he asked, and she nodded, running the tip of her tongue lewdly around her lips.

'Let's go,' said David.

It was light when David got back to his own room. He shaved and packed his bag, surprised at the strength of his residual anger. He lugged the bag down to the proprietor's office and paid his bill with his Diners Club card.

Debra came out of the breakfast room with Joe and Hannah. They were all dressed for the beach with Terry robes over their bathing gear, and they were gay and laughing—until they saw David.

'Hey!' Joe challenged him. 'Where are you going?'

'I've had enough of Spain,' David told them. 'I'm taking some good advice, and I'm moving out,' and he felt a flare of savage triumph as he saw the quick shadow of pain in Debra's eyes. Both Joe and Hannah glanced at her, and quickly she controlled the quiver of her lips. She smiled then, a little too brightly and stepped forward, holding out her hand.

'Thank you for all your help, David. I'm sorry you have to go. It was fun.' Then her voice dropped slightly and there was a tiny quaver in it. 'I hope you find what you are looking for. Good luck.'

She turned quickly and hurried away to her room. Hannah's expression was steely, and she gave David a curt nod before following Debra.

'So long, Joe.'

'I'll carry your bag.'

'Don't bother.' David tried to stop him.

'No trouble.' Joe took it out of his hand and carried it out to the Mustang. He dumped it on the rear seat.

'I'll ride up to the top of the hills with you and walk back.' He climbed into the passenger seat and settled comfortably. 'I need the exercise.'

David drove swiftly, and they were silent as Joe deliberately lit a cigarette and flicked the match out the window.

'I don't know what went wrong, Davey, but I can guess.'

David didn't reply, he concentrated on the road.

'She's had a bad time. These last few days she has been different. Happy, I guess, and I thought it was going to work out.'

Still David was silent, not giving him any help. Why didn't the big bonehead mind his own business.

'She's a pretty special sort of person, Davey, not because she's my sister. She really is, and I think you should know about her—just so you don't think too badly about her.'

They had reached the top of the hills above the town and the bay. David pulled on to the verge but kept the engine running. He looked down on the brilliant blue of the sea, where it met the cliffs and the pine-covered headlands.

'She was going to be married,' said Joe softly. 'He was a nice guy, older than she was, they worked together at the University. He was a tank driver in the reserve and he took a hit in the Sinai and burned with his tank.'

David turned and looked at him, his expression softening a little.

'She took it badly,' Joe went on doggedly. 'These last few days were the first time I've seen her truly happy and relaxed.' He shrugged, and grinned like a big St Bernard dog. 'Sorry to give you the family history, Davey. Just thought

it might help.' He held out a huge brown hand. 'Come and see us. It's your
country also, you know. I'd like to show it to you.'

David took the hand. 'I might do that,' he said.

'Shalom.'

'Shalom, Joe. Good luck.' Joe climbed out of the car and when David pulled
away he watched him standing on the side of the road with his hands on his
hips. He waved and the first bend in the road hid him.

There was a school for aspiring Formula I racing drivers on a neglected
concrete circuit near Ostia, on the road from Rome. The course lasted three
weeks and cost $500 U.S.

David stayed at the Excelsio in the Via Veneto, and commuted each day to
the track. He completed the full course, but after the first week knew it was not
what he wanted. The physical limitation of the track was constricting after
flying the high heavens, and even the crackling snarling power of a Tyrell Ford
could not match the thrust from the engine of a jet interceptor. Although he
lacked the dedication and motivation of others in his class his natural talent for
speed and his co-ordination brought him out high in the finishing order–and
he had an offer to drive on the works team of a new and struggling company
that was building and fielding a production team of Formula I racing
machines. Of course, the salary was starvation, and it was a measure of his
desperation that he came close to signing a contract for the season, but at the
last moment he changed his mind and went on.

In Athens he spent a week hanging around the yacht basins of Piraeus and
Glyfada. He was investigating the prospects of buying a motor yacht and
running it out on charter to the islands. The prospect of sun and sea and pretty
girls seemed appealing and the craft themselves were beautiful in their snowy
paint and varnished teakwork. In one week he learned that charter work was
merely running a sea-going boarding house for a bunch of bored, sunburned
and seasick tourists.

On the seventh day the American Sixth Fleet dropped anchor in the bay of
Athens. David sat at a table of one of the beach-front cafés and drank *ouzo* in
the sun, while he studied the anchored aircraft carriers through his binoculars.
On the great flat tops the rows of Crusaders and Phantoms were grouped with
their wings folded. Watching them he felt a consuming hunger, a need that was
almost spiritual. He had searched the earth, it seemed, and there was nothing
for him upon its face. He laid the binoculars aside, and he looked up into the
sky. The clouds were high, a brilliant silver against the blue.

He picked up the glass of milky *ouzo* that the sun had warmed and rolled its
sweet liquorice taste about his tongue.

'East, west, home is best.'

He spoke aloud, and had a mental image of Paul Morgan sitting in his high
office of glass and steel. Like a patient fisherman he tended his lines laid across
the world. Right now the one to Athens was beginning to twitch. He could
imagine the quiet satisfaction as he began to reel it in, drawing David
struggling feebly back to the centre. What the hell, I could still fly Impalas as a
reserve officer, he thought, and there was always the Lear–if he could get it
away from Barney.

David drained the glass and stood up abruptly, feeling the fading glow of his
defiance. He flagged a cab and was driven back to his room at the Grande
Bretagne on Syndagma Square.

His defiance was dying so swiftly that one of his companions for dinner that night was John Dinopoulos, Morgan Group's agent for Greece, a slim elegant sophisticate with an unlined sun-tanned face, silver wings in his hair and an elegantly casual way of dressing.

John had selected for David's table companion the female star of a number of Italian spaghetti westerns. A young lady of ample bosom and dark flashing eye whose breathing and bosom had become agitated when John introduced David as a diamond millionaire from Africa.

Diamonds were the most glamorous, although not the most significant of Morgan Group's interests.

They sat upon the terrace of Dionysius, for the evening was mild. The restaurant was carved into the living rock of the hill-top of Lycabettus, under the church of St Paul.

Down the zig-zag path from the church, the Easter procession of worshippers unwound in a flickering stream of candle flames through the pine forest below them, and the singing carried sweetly on the still night air. On its far hill-top the stately columns of the Acropolis were flood-lit so that they glowed as creamily as ancient ivory, and beyond that again on the midnight waters of the bay the American fleet wore gay garlands of fairy lights.

'The glory that was Greece—' murmured the star of Italian westerns, as though she voiced the wisdom of the ages, and placed one heavily jewelled hand on David's thigh while with the other she raised a glass of red Samos wine to him and cast him a look under thick eyelashes that was fraught with significance.

Her restraint was impressive, and it was only after they had eaten the main course of savoury meats wrapped in vine leaves and swimming in creamy lemon sauce that she suggested that David might like to finance her next movie.

'Let's find some place where we can talk about it—' she murmured, and what better place than her suite?

John Dinopoulos waved them away with a grin and a knowing wink, a gesture that annoyed David for it made him see the whole episode for the emptiness that it was.

The star's suite was pretentious, with thick white carpets and bulky black leather furniture. David poured himself a drink while she went to change into clothing more suitable for a discussion of high finance. David tasted the drink, realized that he did not want it and left it on the bar counter.

The star came out of the bedroom in a bedrobe of white satin which was cut back from arm and bosom, and was so sheer that her flesh gleamed with a pearly pink sheen through the material. Her hair was loose, a great wild mane of swirling curls—and suddenly David was sick of the whole business.

'I'm sorry,' he said. 'John was joking—I'm not a millionaire, and I really prefer boys.'

He heard his untouched glass shatter against the door of the suite as he closed it behind him.

Back at his own hotel he ordered coffee from room service, and then on an impulse he picked up the telephone again and placed a Cape Town call. It came through with surprising speed, and the girl's voice on the other end was thickened with sleep.

'Mitzi,' he laughed. 'How's the girl?'

'Where are you, warrior? Are you home?'

'I'm in Athens, doll.'

'Athens—God! How's the action?'

'It's a drag.'

'Yeah! I bet,' she scoffed. 'The Greek girls are never going to be the same again.'

'How are you, Mitzi?'

'I'm in love, Davey. I mean really in love, it's far out. We are going to be married. Isn't that just something else?' David felt a spur of anger, jealous of the happiness in her voice.

'That's great, doll. Do I know him?'

'Cecil Lawley, you know him. He's one of Daddy's accountants.' David recalled a large, pale-faced, bespectacled man with a serious manner.

'Congratulations,' said David. He felt very much alone again. Far from home, and aware that life there flowed on without his presence.

'You want to talk to him?' Mitzi asked. 'I'll wake him up.' There was murmur and mutter on the other end, then Cecil came on.

'Nice work,' David told him, and it really was. Mitzi's share of Morgan Group would be considerably larger than David's. Cecil had drilled himself an oil well in a most unconventional manner.

'Thanks, Davey.' Cecil's embarrassment at being caught tending his oil well carried clearly over five thousand miles of telephone cable.

'Listen, lover. You do anything to hurt that girl, I'll personally tear out your liver and stuff it down your throat, okay?'

'Okay,' said Cecil, and his alarm was brittle in his tone. 'I'll put you back to Mitzi.'

She prattled on for another fifty dollars' worth before hanging up. David lay on the bed with his hands behind his head and thought about his dumpy soft-hearted cousin and her new happiness. Then quite suddenly he made the decision which had been lurking at the edge of his consciousness all these weeks since leaving Spain. He picked up the phone again and asked for the porter's desk.

'I'm sorry to trouble you at this time of the morning,' he said, 'but I should like to get on a flight to Israel as soon as possible, will you please arrange that.'

The sky was filled with a soft golden haze that came off the desert. The gigantic T.W.A. 747 came down through it, and David had a glimpse of dark green citrus orchards before the solid jolt of the touch-down. Lod was like any other airport in the world but beyond its doors was a land like no other he had ever known. The crowd who fought him for a seat in one of the big black sheruts, communal taxis plastered with stickers and hung with gew-gaws, made even the Italians seem shining towers of restrained good manners.

Once aboard, however, it was as though they were on a family outing—and he a member of that family. On one side of him a paratrooper in beret and blouse with his winged insignia on the breast and an Uzzi submachine-gun slung about his neck offered him a cigarette, on the other a big strapping lass also in khaki uniform and with the dark gazelle eyes of an Israeli, which became even darker and more soulful when she looked at David, which was often, shared a sandwich of unleavened bread and balls of fried chick-peas, the ubiquitous pita and falafel, with him and practised her English upon him. All the occupants of the front seat turned around to join the conversation, and this included the driver who nevertheless did not allow his speed to diminish in the slightest and who punctuated his remarks with fierce blasts of his horn and cries of outrage at pedestrians and other drivers.

The perfume of orange blossom lay as heavily as sea mist upon the coastal lowlands, and always afterwards it would be for David the smell of Israel.

Then they climbed into the Judaean hills, and David felt a sense of nostalgia as they followed the winding highway through pine forests and across the pale shining slopes where the white stone gleamed like bone in the sunlight and the silver olive trees twisted their trunks in graceful agony upon the terraces which were the monuments to six thousand years of man's patient labour.

It was so familiar and yet subtly different from those fair and well-beloved hills of the southern cape he called home. There were flowers he did not recognize, crimson blooms like spilled blood, and bursts of sunshine-yellow blossoms upon the slopes—then suddenly a pang that was like a physical pain as he glimpsed the bright flight of chocolate and white wings amongst the trees, and he recognized the crested head of an African hoopoe—a bird which was a symbol of home.

He felt a sense of excitement building within him, unformed and undirected as yet but growing, as he drew closer to the women he had come to see—and to something else of which he was as yet uncertain.

There was, at last, a sense of belonging. He felt in sympathy with the young persons who crowded close to him in the cab.

'See,' cried the girl, touching his arm and pointing to the wreckage of war still strewn along the roadside, the burned-out carapaces of trucks and armoured vehicles, preserved as a memorial to the men who died on the road to Jerusalem. 'There was fighting here.'

David turned in the seat to study her face, and he saw again the strength and certainty that he had so admired in Debra. These were a people who lived each day to its limit, and only at its close did they consider the next.

'Will there be more fighting?' he asked.

'Yes,' she answered him without hesitation.

'Why?'

'Because—if it is good—you must fight for it,' and she made a wide gesture that seemed to embrace the land and all its people, 'and this is ours, and it is good,' she said.

'Right on, doll,' David agreed with her, and they grinned at each other.

So they came to Jerusalem with its tall, severe apartment blocks of custard-yellow stone, standing like monuments upon the hills, grouped about the massive walled citadel that was its heart.

T.W.A. had reserved a room at the Intercontinental Hotel for David while on board the inward flight. From his window he looked across the garden of Gethsemane at the old city, at its turrets and spires and the blazing golden Dome of the Rock—centre of Christianity and Judaism, holy place of the Moslems, battleground for two thousand years, ancient land reborn—and David felt a sense of awe. For the first time in his life, he recognized and examined that portion of himself that was Jewish, and he thought it was right that he should have come to this city.

'Perhaps,' he said aloud, 'it's just possible that this is where it's all at.'

It was early evening when David paid off the cab in the car park of the University and submitted to a perfunctory search by a guard at the main gate. Here body search was a routine that would soon become so familiar as to pass unnoticed. He was surprised to find the campus almost deserted, until he remembered it was Friday–and that the whole tempo was slowing for the Sabbath.

The red-bud trees were in full bloom around the main plaza and the ornamental pool, as David crossed to the admin block and asked for her at the inquiries desk where the porter was on the point of leaving his post.

'Miss Mordecai–' the porter checked his list. 'Yes. English Department. On the second floor of the Lauterman building.' He pointed out through the glass doors. 'Third building on your right. Go right on in.'

Debra was in a students' tutorial, and while he waited for her, he found a seat on the terrace in the warmth of the sun. It was as well, for suddenly he felt a breath of uncertainty cooling his spine. For the first time since leaving Athens, he wondered if he had much cause to expect a hearty welcome from Debra Mordecai. Even at this remove in time, David had difficulty in judging his own behaviour towards her. Self-criticism was an art which David had never seriously practised; with a face and fortune such as his, it was seldom necessary. In this time of waiting he found it novel and uncomfortable to admit that it was just possible that his behaviour may have been, as Debra had told him, that of a spoiled child. He was still exploring this thought, when a burst of voices and the clatter of heels upon the flags distracted him and a group of students came out on to the terrace, hugging their books to their chests, and most of the girls glanced at him with quick speculative attention as they passed.

There was a pause then before Debra came. She carried books under her arm and a sling bag over one shoulder, and her hair was pulled back severely at the nape of her neck; she wore no make-up, but her skirt was brightly coloured in big summery whorls of orange. Her legs were bare and her feet were thrust into leather sandals. She was in deep conversation with the two students who flanked her, and she did not see David until he stood up from the parapet. Then she froze into that special stillness he had first noticed in the *cantina* at Zaragoza.

David was surprised to find how awkward he felt, as though his feet and hands had grown a dozen sizes. He grinned and made a shrugging, self-deprecatory gesture.

'Hello, Debs.' His voice sounded gruff in his own ears, and Debra stirred and made a panicky attempt to brush back the wisps of hair at her temples, but the books hampered her.

'David–' She started towards him, a pace before she hesitated and stopped, glancing at her students. They sensed her confusion and melted, and she swung back at him.

'David–' she repeated, and then her expression crumbled into utter desolation. 'Oh God, and I haven't even a shred of lipstick on.'

David laughed with relief and went towards her, spreading his arms, and she flew at him and it was all confusion with books and sling bag muddled, and Debra making breathless exclamations of frustration before she could divest herself of them. Then at last they embraced.

'David,' she murmured with both arms wound tightly around his neck. 'You beast–what on earth took you so long? I had almost given you up.'

Debra had a motor scooter which she drove with such murderous abandon that she frightened even the Jerusalem taxi-drivers who crossed her path–men with a reputation for steel nerves and disregard for danger.

Perched on the pillion David clung to her waist and remonstrated with her gently as she overtook a solid line of traffic and then cut smartly across a stream coming in the opposite direction with her exhaust popping merrily.

'I'm happy,' she explained over her shoulder.

'Fine! Then let's live to enjoy it.'

'Joe will be surprised to see you.'

'If we ever get there.'

'What's happened to your nerve?'

'I've just this minute lost it.'

She went down the twisting road into the valley of Ein Karem, as though she was driving a Mirage, and called a travelogue back to him as she went.

'That's the Monastery of Mary's Well where she met the mother of John the Baptist—according to the Christian tradition in which you are a professed expert.'

'Hold the history,' pleaded David. 'There's a bus around that bend.'

The village was timeless amongst the olive trees, dug into the slope with its churches and monasteries and high-walled gardens, an oasis of the picturesque, while the skyline above it was cluttered with the high-rise apartments of modern Jerusalem.

From the main street Debra scooted into the mouth of a narrow lane, where high walls of time-worn stone rose on each hand, and braked to a halt outside a forbidding iron gate.

'Home,' she said, and wheeled the scooter into the gatehouse and locked it away before letting them in through a side gate hidden in a corner of the wall.

They came out into a large garden court enclosed by the high rough plastered walls which were lime-washed to glaring white. There were olive trees growing in the court with thick twisted trunks. Vines climbed the walls and spread their boughs overhead; already there were bunches of green grapes forming upon them.

'The Brig is a crazy keen amateur archaeologist,' Debra indicated the Roman and Greek statues that stood amongst the olive trees, the exhibits of pottery amphorae arranged around the walls, and the ancient mosaic tiles which paved the pathway to the house. 'It's strictly against the law, of course, but he spends all his spare time digging around in the old sites.'

The kitchen was cavernous with an enormous open fireplace in which a modern electric stove looked out of place, but the copper pots were burnished until they glowed and the tiled floor was polished and sweet-smelling.

Debra's mother was a tall slim woman with a quiet manner, who looked like Debra's older sister. The family resemblance was striking and, as she greeted them, David thought with pleasure that this was how Debra would look at the same age. Debra introduced them and announced that David was a guest for dinner, a fact of which he had been unaware until that moment.

'Please,' he protested quickly, 'I don't want to intrude.' He knew that Friday was a special night in the Jewish home.

'You don't intrude. We will be honoured,' she brushed aside his protest. 'This house is home for most of the boys on Joe's squadron, we enjoy it.'

Debra fetched David a Goldstar beer and they were sitting on the terrace together when her father arrived. He came in through the wicket gate, stooping his tall frame under the stone lintel and taking off his uniform cap as he entered the garden.

He wore uniform casually cut, and open at the throat with cloth insignia of rank and wings at the breast pocket. He was slightly round-shouldered, probably from cramming his lanky body into the cramped cockpits of fighter aircraft, and his head was brown and bald with a monk's fringe of hair and a fierce spiky moustache through which a gold tooth gleamed richly. His nose was big and hooked, the nose of a biblical warrior, and his eyes were dark and snapping with the same golden lights as Debra's. He was a man of such presence that he commanded David's instant respect. He stood to shake the General's hand and called him 'sir' completely naturally.

The Brig subjected David to a rapid, raking scrutiny and reserved his judgement, showing neither pleasure nor disdain.

Later David would learn that the nickname 'The Brig' was a shortened version of 'The Brigand', a name the British had given him before 1948 when he was smuggling warplanes and arms into Palestine for the *Haganah*. Everyone, even his children called him that and only his wife used his given name, Joshua.

'David is sharing the Sabbath meal with us tonight,' Debra explained to him.

'You are welcome,' said the Brig, and turned to embrace his women with love and laughter, for he had seen neither of them since the previous Sabbath, his duties keeping him at air bases and control rooms scattered widely across the land.

When Joe arrived, he was also in uniform, the casual open-necked khaki of summer, and when he saw David he dropped his slow manner and hurried to him, laughing, and enfolded him in a bear hug, speaking over his shoulder to Debra.

'Was I right?'

'Joe said you would come,' Debra explained.

'It looks like I was the only one who didn't know,' David protested.

There were fifteen at dinner, and the candlelight gleamed on the polished wood of the huge refectory table and the silver Sabbath goblets. The Brig said a short prayer, the satin and gold embroidered *yamulka* looking slightly out of place on his wicked bald head, then he filled the wine goblets with his own hand murmuring a greeting to each of his guests. Hannah was with Joe, her copper hair glowing handsomely in the candlelight, and she greeted David with reserve. There were two of the Brig's brothers with their wives and children and grandchildren, and the talk was loud and confusing as the children vied with their elders for a hearing and the language changed at random from Hebrew to English. The food was exotic and spicy, although the wine was too sweet for David's taste. He was content to sit quietly beside Debra and enjoy the sense of belonging in this happy group. He was startled then when one of Debra's cousins leaned across her to speak to him.

'This must be very confusing for you—your first day in such an unusual country as Israel, and not understanding Hebrew, you not being Jewish—'

The words were not meant unkindly, but all conversation stopped abruptly and the Brig looked up, frowning swiftly, quick to sense an unkindness to a guest at his board.

David was aware of Debra staring at him intently, as if to will words from him, and suddenly he thought how three denials finalized any issue—in the New Testament, in Mohammedan law, and perhaps in that of Moses as well. He did not want to be excluded from this household, from these people. He didn't want to be alone again. It was good here.

He smiled at the cousin and shook his head. 'It's strange, yes–but not as bad as you think. I understand Hebrew, though I don't speak it very well. You see, I am Jewish also.'

Beside him Debra gave a soft gasp of pleasure and exchanged quick glances with Joe.

'Jewish?' the Brig demanded. 'You don't look it,' and David explained, and when he was through the Brig nodded. It seemed that his manner had thawed a little.

'Not only that, but he is a flier also,' Debra boasted, and the Brig's moustache twitched like a living thing so that he had to soothe it with his napkin while he reappraised David carefully.

'What experience?' he demanded brusquely.

'Twelve hundred hours, sir, almost a thousand on jets.'

'Jets?'

'Mirages.'

'Mirages!' The Brig's gold tooth gleamed secretly.

'What squadron?'

'Cobra Squadron.'

'Rastus Naude's bunch?' The Brig stared at David as he asked.

'Do you know Rastus?' David was startled.

'We flew in the first Spitfires from Czechoslovakia together–back in '48. We used to call him Butch Ben Yok–Son of a Gentile–in those days. How is he, he must be getting on now? He was no spring chick even then.'

'He's as spry as ever, sir,' David answered tactfully.

'Well, if Rastus taught you to fly–you must be half good,' the Brig conceded.

As a general rule the Israeli Airforce would not refuse foreign pilots, but here was a Jew with all the marks of a first-class fighter pilot. The Brig had noticed the marvellous *élan* and thrust which that other consummate judge of young men, Paul Morgan, had recognized also and valued so highly. Unless he had read the signs wrongly, something he seldom did, then here was a rare one. Once more he appraised the young man in the candlelight and noticed that clear and steady gaze that seemed to seek a distant horizon. It was the eye of the gunfighter, and all his pilots were gunfighters.

To train an interceptor pilot took many years and nearly a million dollars. Time and money were matters of survival in his country's time of trial–and rules could be bent.

He picked up the wine bottle and carefully refilled David's goblet. 'I will place a telephone call to Rastus Naude,' he decided silently, 'and find out a bit more about this youngster.'

Debra watched her father as he began to question David searchingly on his reasons, or lack of them, for coming to Israel–and on his future plans.

She knew precisely how the Brig's mind was working, for she had anticipated it. Her reasons for inviting David to dinner and for exposing him to the Brig were devious and calculated.

She switched her attention back to David, feeling the tense warm sensation in the pit of her stomach and the electric prickle of the skin upon her forearms as she looked at him.

'Yes, you big cocky stallion,' she thought comfortably, 'you aren't going to find it easy to escape again. This time I'm playing for keeps, and I've got the Brig on to you also.'

She lifted her goblet to him, smiling sweetly at him over the rim.

'You're going to get exactly what you're after, but in trumps and with bells on,' she threatened silently, and aloud she said, '*Lechaim!* To life!' and David echoed the toast.

'This time I'm not going to be put off so easily,' he promised himself firmly as he watched the candlelight explode in tiny golden sparks in her eyes. 'I'm going to have you, my raven-haired beauty, no matter how long it takes or what it costs.'

The telephone beside his bed woke David in the dawn, and the Brig's voice was crisp and alert, as though he had already completed a day's work.

'If you have no urgent plans for today, I'm taking you to see something,' he said.

'Of course, sir.' David was taken off balance.

'I will fetch you from your hotel in forty-five minutes, that will give you time to breakfast. Please wait for me in the lobby.'

The Brig drove a small nondescript compact with civilian plates, and he drove it fast and efficiently. David was impressed with his reaction time and co-ordination—after all the Brig must be well into his fifties, and David allowed himself to contemplate such immense age with awe.

They took the main highway west towards Tel Aviv, and the Brig broke a long silence.

'I spoke with your old C.O. last night. He was surprised to hear where you were. He tells me that you were offered promotion to staff rank before you left—'

'It was a bribe,' said David, and the Brig nodded and began to talk. David listened to him quietly while he watched with pleasure the quickly changing landscape as they came down out of the hills and turned southwards through the low rolling plains towards Beersheba and the desert.

'I am taking you to an airforce base, and I might add that I am flouting all sorts of security regulations to do so. Rastus assured me that you can fly, and I want to see if he was telling me the truth.'

David looked at him quickly.

'We are going to fly?' and he felt a deep and pleasurable excitement when the Brig nodded.

'We are at war here, so you will be flying a combat sortie, and breaking just about every regulation in the book. But you'll find we don't go by the book very much.'

He went on quietly, explaining his own particular view of Israel, its struggle and its chances of success, and David remembered odd phrases he used.

'—We are building a nation, and the blood we have been forced to mix into the foundations has strengthened them—'

'—We don't want to make this merely a sanctuary for all the beaten-up Jews of the world. We want the strong bright Jews also—'

'—There are three million of us, and one hundred and fifty million enemies, sworn to our total annihilation—'

'—If they lose a battle, they lose a few miles of desert, if we lose one we cease to exist—'

'—We'll have to give them one more beating. They won't accept the others. They believe their ammunition was faulty in 1948, after Suez the lines were restored so they lost nothing, and in '67 they think they were cheated. We'll have to beat them one more time before they'll leave us alone—'

He talked as to a friend or an ally and David was warmed by his trust, and enlivened by the prospect of flying again.

A plantation of eucalyptus trees grew as a heavy screen alongside the road, and the Brig slowed to a gate in the barbed wire fence and a sign that proclaimed in both languages: 'Chaim Weissmann Agricultural Experimental Centre.'

They turned on to the side road through the plantation, and there was a secondary fence and a guard post amongst the trees.

A guard at the gate checked the Brig's papers briefly, they clearly knew him well. Then they drove on, emerging from the plantation into neatly laid-out blocks of different cereal crops. David recognized oats, barley, wheat and maize—all of it flourishing in the warm spring sunshine. The roads between each field were surveyed long and straight and paved with concrete that had been tinted to the colour of the surrounding earth. There was something unnatural in these smooth two-mile-long fairways bisecting each other at right angles, and to David they were familiar. The Brig saw his interest and nodded, 'Yes,' he said, 'runways. We are digging in—not to be taken by the same tactics we used in '67.'

David pondered it while they drove rapidly towards a giant concrete grain silo that stood tall in the distance. In the fields, scarlet tractors were at work, and overhead irrigation equipment threw graceful glittering ostrich feathers of spray into the air.

They reached the concrete silo and the Brig drove the compact through the wide doors of the barn-like building that abutted it. David was startled to see the lines of buses and automobiles parked in neat lines along the length of the barn. There was transport here for many hundreds of men—and yet he had noticed less than a score of tractor-drivers.

There were guards here again, in paratrooper uniform, and when the Brig led David to the rounded bulk of the silo, he realized suddenly that it was a dummy. A massive bomb-proof structure of solid concrete, housing all the sophisticated communications and radar equipment of a modern fighter base. It was combined control tower and plot for four full squadrons of Mirage fighters, the Brig explained briefly as they entered an elevator and sank below the earth.

They emerged into a reception area where again the Brig's papers were examined, and a paratrooper major was called to pass David through, a duty he performed reluctantly and at the Brig's insistence. Then the Brig led David along a carpeted and air-conditioned underground tunnel to the pilots' dressing-room. It was tiled and spotless, with showers and toilets and lockers like a country club changing-room.

The Brig had ordered clothing for David, guessing his size and doing so accurately. The orderly corporal had no trouble fitting him out in overalls, boots, G-suit, gloves and helmet.

The Brig dressed from his own locker and both of them went through into the ready room, moving stiffly in the constricting grip of the G-suits and carrying their helmets under their arms.

The duty pilots looked up from chess games and magazines as they entered, recognized the general and stood to greet him, but the atmosphere was easy and informal. The Brig made a small witticism and they all laughed and relaxed, while he led David through into the briefing-room.

Swiftly, but without overlooking a detail, he outlined the patrol that they would fly, and checked David out on radio procedure, aircraft identification, and other parochial details.

'All clear?' he asked at last, and when David nodded, he went on, 'Remember what I told you, we are at war. Anything we find that doesn't belong to us we hit it, hard! All right?'

'Yes, sir.'

'It's been nice and quiet the last few weeks, but yesterday we had a little trouble down near Ein Yahav, a bit of nastiness with one of our border patrols. So things are a little sensitive at the moment.' He picked up his helmet and map case then turned to face David, leaning close to him and fixing him with those fierce brown and golden eyes.

'It will be clear up there today, and when we get to forty thousand, you will be able to see it all, every inch of it from Rosh Hanikra to Suez, from Mount Hermon to Eilat, and you will see how small it is and how vulnerable to the enemies that surround us. You said you were looking for something worthwhile—I want you to decide whether guarding the fate of three million people might not be a worthwhile job for a man.'

They rode on a small electric personnel carrier down one of the long underground passages, and they entered the concrete bunker dispersed at one point of a great star whose centre was the concrete silo, and they climbed down from the cart.

The Mirages stood in a row, six of them, sleek and needle-nosed, crouching like leashed and impatient animals, so well remembered in outline, but vaguely unfamiliar in their desert brown and drab green camouflage with the blue Star of David insignia on the fuselage.

The Brig signed for two machines, grinning as he wrote 'Butch Ben Yok' under David's numeral.

'As good a name as any to fly under,' he grunted. 'This is the land of the pseudonym and alias.'

David settled into the tiny cockpit with a sense of homecoming. In here it was all completely familiar and his hands moved over the massed array of switches, instruments and controls like those of a lover as he began his pre-flight check.

In the confined space of the bunkers the jet thunder assaulted the eardrums, their din only made bearable by the perforated steel baffles set into the rear of the structure.

The Brig looked across at David, his head enclosed in the garishly painted helmet, and gave him the high sign. David returned it and reached up to pull the Perspex canopy closed. Ahead of them, the steel blast doors rolled swiftly upwards, and the ready lamps above them switched from red to green.

There was no taxiing to take-off areas; no needless ground exposure. Wing-tip to wing-tip they came up the ramp out of the bunker into the sunlight. Ahead of them stretched one of the long brown runways, and David pushed open his throttle to the gate, and then ignited his afterburners, feeling the thrust of the mighty jet through the cushioning of his seat. Down between the fields of green corn they tore, and then up, with the swooping sensation in the guts and the rapier nose of the Mirage pointed at the sapphire of the sky that arched unbroken and unsullied above them, and once again David experienced the euphoria of jet-powered flight.

They levelled out a little under forty thousand feet avoiding even altitudes or orderly flight patterns, and David placed his machine under the Brig's tail and eased back on the throttles to cruising power, his hands delighting in the familiar rituals of flight which his helmeted head revolved restlessly in the search routine, sweeping every quarter of the sky about him, weaving the Mirage to clear the blind spot behind his own tail.

The air had an unreal quality of purity, a crystalline clarity that made even the most distant mountain ranges stand out in crisp silhouette, hardly shaded with the blue of distance. In the north the Mediterranean blazed like a pool of molten silver in the sunlight, while the sea of Galilee was soft cool green, and farther south the Dead Sea was darker, forbidding in its sunken bed of tortured desert.

They flew north over the ridge of Carmel and the flecked white buildings of Haifa with its orange gold beaches on which the sea broke in soft ripples of creamy lacework. Then they turned together easing back on the power and sinking slowly to patrol altitude at twenty thousand feet as they passed the peak of Mount Hermon where the last snows still lingered in the gullies and upon the high places, streaking the great rounded mountain like an old man's pate.

The softly dreaming greens and pastels delighted David who was accustomed to the sepia monochromes of Africa. The villages clung to the hill-tops, their white walls shining like diamonds above the terraced slopes and the darker areas of cultivated land.

They turned south again, booming down the valley of the Jordan, over the Sea of Galilee with its tranquil green waters enclosed by the thickets of date palm and the neatly tended fields of the Kibbutzim, losing altitude as the land forsook its gentle aspect and the hills were riven and tortured, rent by the wadis as though by the claws of a dreadful predator.

On the left hand rose the mountains of Edom, hostile and implacable, and beneath them Jericho was a green oasis in the wilderness. Ahead lay the shimmering surface of the Dead Sea. The Brig dropped down, and they thundered so low across the salt-thickened water that the jet blast ruffled the surface behind them.

The Brig's voice chuckled in David's earphones, 'That's the lowest you are ever going to fly—twelve hundred feet below sea level.'

They were climbing again as they crossed the mineral works at the southern end of the sea, and faced the blasted and mountainous deserts of the south.

'Hello, Cactus One, this is Desert Flower,' again the radio silence was broken, but this time David recognized the call sign of command net. They were being called directly from the Operation Centre of Airforce Command, situated in some secret underground bunker at a location that David would never learn. On the command plot their position being accurately relayed by the radar repeaters.

'Hello, Desert Flower,' the Brig acked, and immediately the exchange became as informal as two old friends chatting, which was precisely what it was.

'Brig, this is Motti. We've just had a ground support request in your area,' he gave the co-ordinates quickly, 'a motorized patrol of border police is under sneak low-level attack by an unidentified aircraft. See to it, will you.'

'Beseder, Motti, okay.' The Brig switched to flight frequency. 'Cactus Two, I'm going to interception power, confirm to me,' he told David, and they turned together on to the new heading.

'No point in trying a radar scan,' the Brig grumbled aloud. 'He'll be down in the ground clutter. We'll not pick the swine off amongst those mountains. Just keep your eyes open.'

'Beseder.' David had already picked up the word. The favourite Hebrew word in a land where very little was really 'okay'.

David spotted it first, a slim black column of smoke beginning to rise like a pencil line drawn slowly against the windless and dazzling cobalt blue of the horizon.

'Ground smoke,' he said into his helmet microphone. 'Eleven o'clock low.'

The Brig squinted ahead silently, searching for it, and then saw it on the extreme limit of his vision range. He grunted, Rastus had been right in one thing at least. The youngster had eyes like a hawk.

'Going to attack speed now,' he said and David acked and lit his afterburners. The upholstery of the seat smacked into his back under the mighty increase in thrust and David felt the drastic alteration in trim as the Mirage went shooting through the sonic barrier.

Near the base of the smoke column, something flashed briefly against the drab brown earth, and David narrowed his eyes and made out the tiny shape, flitting as a sunbird, its camouflage blending naturally into the backdrop of desert, so it was ethereal as a shadow.

'Bandit turning to port of the smoke,' he called the sighting.

'I have him,' said the Brig, and switched to command net.

'Hello, Desert Flower, I'm on an intruder. Call strike, please.' The decision to engage must be made to command level, and the answering voice was laconic, and flat.

'Brig, this is Motti. Hit him!'

While they spoke they were rushing down so swiftly that the details of the little drama being played out below sprang into comprehension.

Along a dusty border track three patrol vehicles of the border police were halted. They were camouflaged half tracks, tiny as children's toys in the vastness of the desert.

One of the half tracks was burning. The smoke was greasy black and rose straight into the air, the beacon that had drawn them. Lying spread-eagled in the road was a human body, flung down carelessly in death, and the sight of it stirred in David a deeply bitter feeling of resentment such as he had last felt in the bullring at Madrid.

The other vehicles were pulled off the track at abandoned angles, and David could see their crews crouching amongst the scrub and rock. Some of them were firing with small arms at their attacker who was circling for his next run down upon them.

David had never seen the type before, but knew it instantly from the recognition charts that he had studied so often. It was a Russian MIG 17 of the Syrian airforce. The high tailplane was unmistakable. The dappled brown desert camouflage was brightened by the red, white and black roundels with their starred green centres on the fuselage and the stubby swept wings.

The MIG completed its turn, settling swiftly down and levelling off for its next strafing run upon the parked vehicles. The pilot's attention was concentrated on the helpless men cowering amongst the rocks and he was unaware of the terrible vengeance that was bearing down upon him from on high.

The Brig lined up for his pass, turning slightly to bring himself down on the Syrian's tail, attacking in classic style from behind and above, and David dropped back to weave across his rear, covering him and backing up to press in a supporting attack if the first failed.

The Syrian opened fire again and the cannon bursts twinkled like fairy lights amongst the men and trucks. Another truck exploded in a dragon's breath of smoke and flame.

'You bastard,' David whispered as he levelled out behind the Brig, and saw the havoc that was being wrought amongst his people. It was the first time he had thought of them as that, his people, and he felt the cold anger of the shepherd whose flock is under attack.

A line of poetry popped up in his mind 'The Assyrian came down like a wolf on the fold,' and his hands went purposefully to the chore of locking in his cannons-selectors and flicking the trigger forward out of its recess in the moulded grip of the joystick. The soft green glow lit his gunsight as it came alive and he squinted through it.

The Brig was pressing his attack in to close range, rapidly overhauling the slower clumsy-looking MIG, and at that moment that he knew he would open fire David saw the Syrian's wing-shape alter. At the fatal instant he had become aware of his predicament, and he had done what was best in the circumstances. He had pulled on full flap and while his speed fell sharply he dropped one wing in a slide towards the earth a hundred feet below.

The Brig was committed and he loosed his salvo of cannon fire at the instant that the Syrian dropped, ducking under it like a boxer avoiding a heavy punch. David saw the blaze of shot pass high, rending the air above the sand-coloured aircraft. Then the Brig was through, missing with every shell, spiralling up and around in a great flashing circle, raging internally at his failure.

At the instant that David recognized the MIG's manœuvre, he reacted with a rapidity that was purely reflexive. He closed down his power, and hit his air brakes to punch a little of the speed off the Mirage.

The MIG turned steeply away to port, standing on one wing-tip that seemed to be pegged into the bleak desert earth. David released his air brakes, to give his wings lift for the next evolution, and then he dropped his own wing-tip and went sweeping round to follow the Syrian's desperate twists with the Mirage hovering on the edge of the stall.

The Syrian was turning inside him, slower and more manœuvrable; David could not bring his sights to bear, his right forefinger was curled around the trigger but always the dark shape of the MIG was out of centre in the illuminated circle of the sight as the aiming pipper dipped and rose to the pull of gravity.

Ahead of the two circling aircraft rose a steep and forbidding line of cliffs, rent by deep defiles and gullies.

The MIG made no attempt to climb above them, but selected a narrow pass through the hills and went into it like a ferret into its run, a desperate attempt to shake off the pursuit.

The Mirage was not designed for this type of flying, and David felt the urge to hit his afterburners and ride up over the jagged fangs of rock—but to do so was to let the MIG escape, and his anger was still strong upon him.

He followed the Syrian into the rock pass, and the walls of stone on either hand seemed to brush his wing-tips, the gully turned sharply to starboard and David dropped his wing and followed its course. Back upon itself the rock turned, and David swung the needle nose from maximum rate turn starboard to port, and the stall warning device winked amber and red at him as he abused the Mirage's delicate flying capabilities.

Ahead of him the MIG clawed its way through the tunnel of rock. The pilot looked back over his shoulder and he saw the Mirage following him, creeping slowly up on him, and he turned back to his controls and forced his machine lower still, hugging the rugged walls of stone.

The air in the hills was hot and turbulent, and the Mirage bucked and fought against restraint wanting to be free and high, while ahead of it the Syrian drifted tantalizingly off-centre in David's gunsight.

Now the valley turned again and narrowed, before climbing and ending abruptly against a solid dark purple wall of smooth rock.

The Syrian was trapped, he levelled out and climbed steeply upwards, his flight path dictated by the rocks on each side and ahead.

David pushed his throttle to the gate and lit his afterburners, and the mighty engine rumbled, thrusting him powerfully forward, up under the Syrian's stern.

The eternal micro-seconds of mortal combat dragged by, as the Syrian floated lazily into the circle of the gunsight, expanding it to fill it as the Mirage's nose seemed to touch the other's tailplane and David felt the buffeting of the Syrian's slip-stream.

He pressed the cannon trigger and the Mirage lurched as she hurled her deadly load into the other machine in a clattering double stream of cannon fire and an eruption of incendiary shells.

The Syrian disintegrated, evaporating in a gush of silvery smoke, rent through with bright white lightning, and the ejecting pilot's body was blown clear of the fuselage. For an instant it was outlined ahead of David's screen, cruciform in shape with arms and legs thrown wide, the helmet still on the head, and the clothing ballooning in the rush of air. Then it flickered past the Mirage's canopy as David climbed swiftly up out of the valley and into the open sky.

The soldiers were moving about amongst their vehicles, tending their wounded and covering their dead, but they all looked up as David flew back low along the road. He passed so close that he could see their faces clearly. They were sun-browned, some with beards or moustaches, strong young faces, their mouths open as they cheered him, waving their thanks.

My people, he thought. He was still high on the adrenalin that had poured into his blood, and he felt a fierce elation. He grinned wolfishly at the men below him and lifted one gloved hand in salute before climbing up to where the Brig was circling, waiting for him.

The artificial lights of the bunkers were dim after the brilliance of the sun. An engineer helped David from the cockpit as his mates swarmed over the Mirage to refuel and rearm it. This was one of the vital skills of this tiny airforce, the ability to ready a warplane for combat in a fraction of the time usually required for the task. Thus in emergency the machine could return to the battle long before its adversary.

Moving stiffly from the confines of the cockpit, David crossed to where the Brig was already in conversation with the flight controller.

He stood with the gaudy helmet tucked under one arm as he stripped off his gloves, but as David came up he turned to him and his wintry smile exposed the gold tooth in its nest of fur.

Lightly he punched David's arm 'Ken! Yes!' said Major-General Joshua Mordecai. 'You'll do.'

David was late to fetch Debra for dinner that evening, but she had already learned the reason from her father.

They went to the Select behind David's Tower, inside the Jaffa Gate of the old city. Its unpretentious interior, decorated with patterns of rope upon the walls, did not fully prepare David for the excellent meal that the Arab proprietor served them with the minimum of delay—mousakha chicken, with nuts and spices on a bed of kouskous.

They ate almost in silence, Debra quickly recognizing and respecting David's mood. He was in the grip of post-combat *tristesse,* the adrenalin hangover of stress and excitement, but slowly the good food in his belly and the heavy Carmel wine relaxed him, until over the thimble-sized cups of Turkish coffee, black and powerfully reeking of cardamom seed, Debra could ask, 'What happened today, David?'

He sipped the coffee before replying.

'I killed a man.' She set down her cup and studied his face solemnly, and he began to speak, telling her the details of it, the chase and the kill, until he ended lamely, 'I felt only satisfaction at the time. A sense of achievement. I knew I had done what was right.'

'And now?' she prompted him.

'Now I am sad,' he shrugged. 'I am saddened that I had to do it.'

'My father, who has always been a soldier, says that only those who do the actual fighting can truly know what it is to hate war.'

David nodded. 'Yes, I understand that now. I love to fly, but I hate to destroy.'

They were silent again, both of them considering their own personal vision of war, both of them trying to find words to express it.

'And yet it is necessary,' Debra broke the silence. 'We must fight—there is no other way.'

'There is no other way—with the sea at our backs and the Arabs at our throats.'

'You speak like an Israeli,' Debra challenged him softly.

'I made a decision today—or rather I was press-ganged by your father. He has given me three weeks to brush up my Hebrew, and complete the immigration formalities.'

'And then?' Debra leaned towards him.

'A commission in the airforce. That was the only point I scored on, I had just enough strength to hold out for the equivalent rank I would have had back home. He haggled like a secondhand clothes dealer, but I had him, and he knew it. So he gave in at last. Acting major, with confirmation of rank at the end of twelve months.'

'That's wonderful, Davey, you'll be one of the youngest majors in the service.'

'Yeah,' David agreed, 'and after I've paid my taxes I'll have a salary a little less than a bus-driver back home.'

'Never mind,' Debra smiled for the first time. 'I'll help you with your Hebrew.'

'I was going to talk to you about that,' he answered her smile. 'Come on, let's get out of here. I'm restless tonight—and I want to walk.'

They strolled through the Christian quarter. The open stalls on each side were loaded with garish and exotic clothes, and leather work and jewellery, and the smell of spices and food and drains and stale humanity was almost solid in the narrow lanes where the arches met overhead.

Debra drew him into one of the antique stores in the Via Dolorosa, and the proprietor came to them, almost wriggling with pleasure.

'Ah, Miss Mordecai—and how is your dearly esteemed father?' Then he rushed into the back room to brew more coffee for them.

'He's one of the half-honest ones, and he lives in mortal fear of the Brig.'

Debra selected an antique solid gold Star of David on a slim golden neck chain, and though he had never before worn personal jewellery, David bowed his head and let her place it about his neck. The golden star lay against the coarse dark curls of his chest.

'That's the only decoration you'll ever get—we don't usually give medals,' she told him laughingly. 'But welcome to Israel anyway.'

'It's beautiful,' David was touched and embarrassed by the gift, 'thank you.' And he buttoned his shirt over it and then reached awkwardly to kiss her—but she drew away and warned him.

'Not in here. He's a Moslem, and he'd be very offended.'

'All right,' said David. 'Let's go and find some place where we won't hurt anybody's sensibilities.'

They went out through the Lion Gate in the great wall and found a stone bench in a quiet place amongst the olive trees of the Moslem cemetery. There was half a moon in the sky, silver and mysterious, and the night was warm and waiting, seemingly as expectant as a new bride.

'You can't stay on at the Intercontinental,' Debra told him, and they both looked up at its arched and lighted silhouette across the valley.

'Why not?'

'Well, first of all it's too expensive. On your salary you just can't afford it.'

'You don't really expect me to live on my salary?' David protested, but Debra ignored him and went on.

'And what is more important, you aren't a tourist any more. So you can't live like one.'

'What do you suggest?'

'We could find you an apartment.'

'Who would do the housework, and the laundry, and the cooking?' he protested vehemently. 'I haven't had much practice at that sort of thing.'

'I would,' said Debra, and he froze for an instant and then turned slowly on the seat to look at her.

'What did you say?'

'I said, I would,' she repeated firmly, and then her voice quavered. 'That's if you want me to.' He was silent for a long moment.

'See here, Debs. And you talking about living together? I mean, playing house-house on a full-time basis—the whole bit?'

'That's precisely what I am talking about.'

'But—' He could think of nothing further to say. The idea was novel, breathtaking, and alive with enchanting possibilities. All David's previous experiences with the opposite sex had been profuse rather than deep, and he found himself on the frontiers of unexplored territory.

'Well?' Debra asked at last.

'Do you want to get married?' his voice cracked on the word, and he cleared his throat.

'I'm not sure that you are the finest marriage material in the market, my darling David. You are as beautiful as the dawn, and fun to be with—but you are also selfish, immature and spoiled stupid.'

'Thank you kindly.'

'Well, there is no point in me mincing words now, David, not when I am about to throw all caution aside and become your mistress.'

'Wow!' he exclaimed, with all the frost thawing from his voice. 'When you say it straight out like that—it almost blows my mind.'

'Me too,' Debra confessed. 'But one condition is that we wait until we have our own special place, you may recall that I'm not so high on public beaches or rocky islands.'

'I'll never forget,' David agreed. 'Does this mean that you *don't* want to marry me?' He found his mortal terror of matrimony fading under this slur on his potential marriage worth.

'I didn't say that either,' Debra demurred. 'But let's make that decision when both of us are ready for it.'

'Right on, doll,' said David, with an almost idiot grin of happiness spreading over his face.

'And now, Major Morgan, you may kiss me,' she said. 'But do try and help me remember the conditions.'

A long while later, they drew a little apart to breathe and a sudden thought made David frown with worry.

'My God,' he exclaimed, 'what will the Brig say!'

'He won't be joining us,' she told him, and they both laughed together, excited by their own wickedness.

'Seriously, what will you tell your parents?'

'I'll lie to them graciously, and they'll pretend to believe me. Let me worry about that.'

'Beseder,' he agreed readily.

'You are learning,' she applauded. 'Let's just try that kiss again—but this time in Hebrew, please.'

'I love you,' he said in that language.

'Good boy,' she murmured. 'You are going to make a prize pupil.'

There was one more doubt to be set at rest, and Debra voiced it at the iron gate to the garden, when at last he took her home.

'Do you know what the Bris, the Covenant, is?'

'Sure,' he grinned, and made scissors out of his fist and second finger. It seemed in the uncertain light that she blushed, and her voice was only just audible.

'Well, what about you?'

'That,' David told her severely, 'is a highly personal question, the answer to which little girls should find out for themselves,' and his expression became lascivious, 'the hard way.'

'All knowledge is precious as gold,' she said in a small voice, 'and be sure that I will seek the answer diligently.'

David discovered that the acquisition of an apartment in Jerusalem was a task much like the quest for the Holy Grail. Although the high-rise blocks were being thrown up with almost reckless energy, the demand for accommodation far outweighed the supply.

The father of one of Debra's students was an estate agent and the poor man took their problem to his heart; the waiting-list for the new blocks was endless, but an occcassional apartment in one of the older buildings fell vacant, and he used all his influence for them.

At unexpected moments of the day, Debra would send out an urgent signal, and David would fetch her in a taxi at the University and they would hell across town, urging on the driver, to inspect the latest offering.

The last of these reminded David of a movie set from *Lawrence of Arabia* complete with a dispirited palm tree out front, a spectacular display of bright laundry hanging from every balcony and window, and all the sounds and smells of an Arab camel market and a nursery-school playground at recess from the courtyard.

There were two rooms and an alleged bathroom. The roses and wreaths of the wallpaper had faded, except in patches where hangings had protected their original pristine virulent colouring.

David pushed open the door of the bathroom and, without entering, inspected the raggedy linoleum floor-covering and the stained and chipped bath tub; then pushing the door further he discovered the toilet bowl festering quietly in the gloom with its seat at a rakish angle like the halo of a drunken angel.

'You and Joe could work on it,' Debra suggested uncertainly. 'It's not really *that* bad.'

David shuddered, and closed the door as though it were the lid of a coffin.

'You're joking—of course,' he said, and Debra's determinedly bright smile cracked and her lip quivered.

'Oh, David, we are never going to find a place.'

'And I can't wait much longer.'

'Nor can I,' admitted Debra.

'Right,' David rubbed his hands together briskly' 'It's time to send in the first team.'

He was not sure what form the presence of Morgan Group would take in Jerusalem, but he found it listed in the business directory under 'Morgan Industrial Finance' and the Managing Director was a large mournful-looking gentleman named Aaron Cohen who had a suite of offices in the Leumi Bank building opposite the main post office. He was overcome with emotion to discover that one of the Morgan family had been ten days in Jerusalem without his knowledge

David told him what he wanted, and in twenty hours he had it signed and paid for. Paul Morgan picked his executives with care, and Cohen was an example of this attention. The price David must pay for this service was that Paul Morgan would have a full report of David's transaction, present whereabouts and future plans on his desk the next morning—but it was worth it.

Above the Hinnom canyon, facing Mount Zion with its impressive array of spires, the Montefiore quarter was being rebuilt as an integrated whole by some entrepreneur. All of it was clad in the lovely golden Jerusalem stone, and the designs of the houses were traditional and ageless. However, the interiors were lavishly modernized with tall cool rooms, mosaic-tiled bathrooms, and ceilings arched like those of a crusader church. Most of them had their own walled and private terraces. The one that Aaron Cohen procured for David was the pick of those that fronted Malik Street. The price was astronomical. That was the first question that Debra asked, once she had recovered her voice. She stood stunned upon the terrace beneath the single olive tree. The stone of the terrace had been cut and polished until it resembled old ivory, and she ran her fingers lightly over the carved front door. Her voice was hushed and her expression bemused.

'David! David! How much is this going to cost?'

'That's not important. What is important is whether you like it.'

'It's too beautiful. It's too much, David. We can't afford this.'

'It's paid for already.'

'Paid for?' She stared at him. 'How much, David?'

'If I said half a million Israeli pounds or a million, what difference would it make? It's only money.'

She clapped her hands over her ears. 'No!' she cried. 'Don't tell me! I'd feel so guilty I wouldn't be able to live in it.'

'Oh, so! You are actually consenting to live in it.'

'Try me,' she said with emphasis. 'You just try me, lover!'

They stood in the central room that opened on to the terrace, and although it was light and airy enough for the savage heat of summer that was coming, it smelled of new paint and varnished woodwork.

'What are we going to do about furniture?' David asked.

'Furniture?' Debra repeated. 'I hadn't thought that far ahead.'

'For what I have in mind, we'll need at least one king-size bed.'

'Sex maniac,' she said, and kissed him.

No modern furniture looked at home under the domed roof, or upon the stone-flagged doors. So they began to furnish from the bazaars and antique shops.

Debra solved the main problem with the discovery in a junk yard of an enormous brass bedstead from which they scraped the accumulated dirt; they polished it until it glowed, fitting it with a new inner-spring mattress, and covered it with a cream-coloured lace bedspread from Debra's bottom drawer.

They purchased *kelim* and woven woollen rugs by the bale from the Arab dealers in the old city, and scattered them thickly upon the stone floors, with leather cushions to sit upon and a low olive-wood table, inlaid with ebony and mother of pearl, to eat off. The rest of the furniture would come when they could find it for sale, or, failing that, have it custom-made by an Arab cabinet-maker that Debra knew of. Both the bed and the table were enormously heavy, and they needed muscle to move them, so they called for Joe. He and Hannah arrived in his tiny Japanese compact, and after they had recovered from the impact of the Morgan palace they fell to work enthusiastically with David supervising. Joe grunted and heaved, while Hannah disappeared with Debra into the modern American kitchen to exclaim with envy and admiration over the washing-machine, dryer, dish-washer and all the other appliances that went with the house. She helped to cook the first meal.

David had laid in a case of Goldstar beer, and after their labours they all gathered about the olive-wood table to warm the house and wet the roof.

David had expected Joe to be a little reserved, after all it was his baby sister who was being set up in a fancy house; but Joe was as natural as ever and enjoyed the beer and the company so well that Hannah had to intervene at last.

'It's late,' she said firmly.

'Late?' asked Joe. 'It's only nine o'clock.'

'On a night like tonight, that's late.'

'What do you mean?' Joe looked puzzled.

'Joseph Mordecai, diplomat extraordinary,' Hannah said with heavy sarcasm, and suddenly Joe's expression changed as he glanced from Debra to David guiltily, swallowed his beer in a single gulp, and hoisted Hannah to her feet by one arm.

'Come on,' he said. 'What are we sitting here for?'

David left the terrace lights burning, and they shone through the slats of the shuttered windows, so the room was softly lit, and the sounds from the outside world were so muted by distance and stone walls as to be a mere murmur that drifted from afar, and seemed rather to accentuate their aloneness than to spoil it.

The brass of the bedstead gleamed softly in the gloom, and the ivory lacework of the bedspread smelled of lavender and moth balls.

He lay upon the bed and watched her undress slowly, conscious of his eyes upon her and shy now as she had never been before.

Her body was slim and with a flowing line of waist and leg, young and tender-looking, with a child's awkward grace, and yet with womanly thrust of hip and bosom.

She came to sit upon the edge of the bed, and he marvelled once again at the lustre and plasticity of her skin, at the subtlety of colouring where the sun had darkened it from soft cream to burned honey, and at the contrast of her dusky rose-tipped breasts and the dark thick bush of curls at the base of her softly curving stomach.

She leaned over him, still shyly, and touched his cheek with one finger, running down his throat on to his chest where the gold star lay upon the hard muscle.

'You are beautiful,' she whispered, and she saw it was true. For he was tall and straight with muscled shoulders and lean flanks and belly. The planes of his face were pure and perfect, perhaps its only fault lying in its very perfection. It was almost unreal, as though she were lying with some angel or god from out of mythology.

She twisted her legs up on to the bed, stretching out beside him upon the lace cover, and they lay on their sides facing each other, not touching but so close that she could feel the warmth of his belly upon her own like a soft desert wind, and his breath stirred the dark soft hair upon her cheek.

She sighed then, with happiness and contentment, like a traveller reaching the end of a long lonely journey.

'I love you,' she said for the first time, and reaching out she took his head, her fingers twining in the thick springing hair at the nape of his neck, and drew it tenderly to her breast.

Long afterwards the chill of night oozed into the room, and they came half-awake and crept together beneath the covers.

As they began drifting back into sleep she murmured sleepily, 'I'm so glad that surgery won't be necessary, after all,' and he chuckled softly.

'Wasn't it better finding out for yourself?'

'Much better, lover. Much, much better,' she admitted.

Debra spent one entire evening explaining to David that a high-performance sports car was not a necessity for travel between his base and the house on Malik Street, for she knew her man's tastes by then. She pointed out that this was a country of young pioneers, and that extravagance and ostentation were out of place. David agreed vehemently, secure in the knowledge that Aaron Cohen and his minions were scouring the country for him.

Debra suggested a Japanese compact similiar to Joe's, and David told her that he would certainly give that his serious consideration.

Aaron Cohen's henchman tracked down a Mercedes Benz 350 SL belonging to the German Charge d'Affaires in Tel Aviv. This gentleman was returning to

Berlin and wished to dispose of his auto, for a suitable consideration in negotiable cash. A single phone call was sufficient to arrange payment through the Crédit Suisse in Zurich.

It was golden bronze in colour, with a little under twenty thousand kilometres on the clock, and it had clearly been maintained with the loving care of an enthusiast.

Debra, returning on her motor scooter from the University, found this glorious machine parked at the top end of Malik Street, where a heavy chain denied access by all motor-driven vehicles to the village.

She took one look at it, and knew beyond all reasonable doubt who it belonged to. She was really quite angry when she stormed on to the terrace, but she pretended to be angrier than that.

'David Morgan, you really are absolutely impossible.'

'You catch on fast,' David agreed amiably; he was sun-bathing on the terrace.

'How much did you pay for it?'

'Ask me another question, doll. That one is becoming monotonous.'

'You are really—' Debra paused and searched frantically for a word of sufficient force. She found it and delivered it with relish, 'decadent!'

'You don't know the meaning of the word,' David told her gently as he rose from the cushions in the sun and drifted lazily in her direction. Though she had been his lover for only a mere three days she recognized the look in his eye and she began backing away.

'I will teach you the meaning,' he said. 'I am about to give you a practical demonstration of decadence in such a sensitive spot that you are likely to remember it for a long time.'

She ducked behind the olive tree as he lunged, and her books spilled across the terrace.

'Leave me! Hands off, you beast.'

He feinted right, and caught her as she fell for it. He picked her up easily across his chest.

'David Morgan, I warn you, I shall scream if you don't put me down this instant.'

'Let's hear it. Go ahead!' and she did, but in a ladylike fashion so as not to alarm the neighbours.

Joe, on the other hand, was delighted with the 350. The four of them took it on a trial run down the twisting road through the Wilderness of Judaea to the shores of the Dead Sea. The road challenged the car's suspension and David's driving skill, and they whooped with excitement through the bends. Even Debra was able to overcome her initial disapproval, and finally admitted it was beautiful—but still decadent.

They swam in the cool green waters of the oasis of Ein Gedi where they formed a deep rock pool before overflowing and running down into the thick saline water of the sea itself.

Hannah had brought her camera and she photographed Debra and David sitting together on the rocks beside the pool.

They were in their bathing costumes, Debra's brief bikini showing off her fine young body as she half-turned to laugh into David's face. He smiled back at her, his face in profile and the dark sweep of his hair falling on to his forehead. The desert light picked out the pure features and the boldly stated facets of his beauty.

Hannah had a print of the photograph made for each of them, and later those squares of glossy photographic paper were all they had left of it, all that remained of the joy and the laughter of those days, like a lovely flower taken from the growing tree of life and pressed and dried, flattened and desiccated, deprived of its colour and perfume.

But the future threw no shadow over their happiness on that bright day, and with Joe driving this time they ran back for Jerusalem. Debra insisted that they stop for a group of tank corps boys hitch-hiking home on leave, and although David protested it was impossible, they squeezed three of them into the small cab. It was Debra's sop to her feelings of guilt, and she sat in the back seat with her arms around David's neck and they all sang the song that was that year a favourite with the young people of Israel, 'Let there be peace'.

In the last few days while David waited to enter the airforce, he loafed shamelessly, frittering the time away in small chores like having his uniforms tailored. He resisted Debra's suggestion that if regulation issue were good enough for her father, a general officer, then they might be good enough for David. Aaron Cohen supplied him with an introduction to his own tailor. Aaron was beginning to develop a fine respect for David's style.

Debra had arranged membership for David at the University Athletic Club, and he worked out in the first-class modern gym every day, and finished with twenty lengths of the Olympic-size swimming pool to keep himself in shape.

However, at other times, David merely lay sunbathing on the terrace, or fiddled with electrical plugs or other small tasks Debra had asked him to see to about the house.

As he moved through the cool and pleasant rooms, he would find an item belonging to Debra, a book or a brooch perhaps, and he would pick it up and fondle it briefly. Once a robe of hers thrown carelessly across the foot of the bed and redolent of her particular perfume gave him a physical pang as it reminded him sharply of her, and he held the silkiness to his face and breathed the scent of her, and grudged the hours until her return.

However, it was amongst her books that he discovered more about her than years of study would have revealed. She had crates of these piled in the unfurnished second bedroom which they were using as a temporary store-room until they could find shelves and cupboards. One afternoon David began digging around in the crates. It was a literary mixed grill–Gibbon and Vidal, Shakespeare and Mailer, Solzhenitsyn and Mary Stewart, among other strange bedfellows. There was fiction and biography, history and poetry, Hebrew and English, softbacks and leather-bound editions–and a thin green-jacketed volume which he almost discarded before the author's name caught his attention. It was by D. Mordecai and with a feeling of discovery he turned to the flyleaf. *This year, in Jerusalem,* a collection of poems, by Debra Mordecai.

He carried the book through to the bedroom, remembering to kick off his shoes before lying on the lace cover–she was very strict about that–and he turned to the first page.

There were five poems. The first was the title piece, the two-thousand-year promise of Jewry 'Next year in Jerusalem' had become reality. It was a patriotic tribute to her land and even David, whose taste in writing ran to Maclean and Robbins, recognized that it had a superior quality. There were lines of startling beauty, evocative phrasing and penetrative glimpses. It was good, really good, and David felt a strange proprietary pride–and a sense of awe. He had not guessed at these depths within her, these hidden areas of the mind.

When he came to the last poem, he found it was the shortest of the five, and it was a love poem—or rather it was a poem to someone dearly loved who was gone—and suddenly David was aware of the difference between that which was good and that which was magic.

He found himself shivering to the music of her words, felt the hair on his forearms standing erect with the haunting beauty of it, and then at last he felt himself choking on the sadness of it, the devastation of total loss, and the words swam as his eyes flooded, and he had to blink rapidly as the last terrible cry of the poem pierced him to the heart.

He lowered the book on to his chest, remembering what Joe had told him about the soldier who had died in the desert. A movement attracted his attention and he made a guilty effort to hide the book as he sat up. It was such a private thing, this poetry, that he felt like a thief.

Debra stood in the doorway of the bedroom watching him, leaning against the jamb with her hands clasped in front of her, studying him quietly.

He sat up on the bed and weighed the book in his hands. 'It's lovely,' he said at last, his voice was gruff with the emotions that her words had evoked.

'I'm glad you like it,' she said, and he realized that she was shy.

'Why did you not show it to me before?'

'I was afraid you might not like it.'

'You must have loved him very much?' he asked softly.

'Yes, I did,' she said, 'but now I love you.'

Then, finally, his posting came through and the Brig's hand was evident in it all, though Joe admitted that he had used his own family connections to influence the orders.

He was ordered to report to Mirage squadron 'Lance' which was a crack interceptor outfit based at the same hidden airfield from which he had first flown. Joe Mordecai was on the same squadron, and when he called at Malik Street to tell David the news, he showed no resentment that David would out-rank him, but instead he was confident that they would be able to fly together as a regular team. He spent the evening briefing David on squadron personnel, from 'Le Dauphin' the commanding officer, a French immigrant, down to the lowest mechanic. In the weeks ahead David would find Joe's advice and help invaluable, as he settled into his niche amongst this tightly-knit team of fliers.

The following day the tailor delivered his uniforms, and he wore one to surprise Debra when she backed in through the kitchen door, laden with books and groceries, using her bottom as a door buffer, her hair down behind and her dark glasses pushed up on top of her head.

She dropped her load by the sink, and circled him with her hands on her hips, her head cocked at a critical angle.

'I should like you to wear that, and come to pick me up at the University tomorrow afternoon, please,' she said at last.

'Why?'

'Because there are a few little bitches that lurk around the Lauterman Building. Some of them my students and some my colleagues. I want them to get a good look at you—and eat their tiny hearts out.'

He laughed. 'So you aren't ashamed of me?'

'Morgan, you are too beautiful for one person, you should have been born twins.'

It was their last day together, so he indulged her whimsy and wore his uniform to fetch her at the English Literature Department, and he was surprised to find how the dress affected the strangers he passed on the street—the girls smiled at him, the old ladies called *shalom,* even the guard at the University gates waved him through with a grin and a joke. To them he was a guardian angel, one of those that had swept death from the very sky above them.

Debra hurried to meet and kiss him, and then walked beside him, her hand tucked proudly and possessively into the crook of his elbow. She took him to eat an early dinner at the staff dining-room in the rounded glass Belgium building.

While they ate, a casual question of his revealed the subterfuge she had used to protect her reputation.

'I'll probably not get off the base for the first few weeks, but I'll write to you at Malik Street—'

'No,' she said quickly, 'I won't be staying there. It would be too lonely without you in that huge bed.'

'Where then? At your parents' home?'

'That would be a dead give-away. Every time you arrive back in town, I leave home! No, they think I am staying at the hostel here at the University. I told them I wanted to be closer to the department—'

'You've got a room here?' He stared at her.

'Of course, Davey. I have to be a little discreet. I couldn't tell my relatives, friends and employers to contact me care of Major David Morgan. This may be the twentieth century, and modern Israel, but I am still a Jewess, with a tradition of chastity and modesty behind me.'

For the first time David began to appreciate the magnitude of Debra's decision to come to him. He had taken it lightly compared to her.

'I'm going to miss you,' he said.

'And I you,' she replied.

'Let's go home.'

'Yes,' she agreed, laying aside her knife and fork. 'I can eat any old time.'

However, as they left Belgium House she exclaimed with exasperation: 'Damn, I have to have these books back by today. Can we go by the library? I'm sorry, Davey, it won't take a minute.'

So they climbed again to the main terrace and passed the brightly-lit plate-glass windows of the Students' Union Restaurant, and went on towards the solid square tower of the library whose windows were lighted already against the swiftly falling darkness. They had climbed the library steps and reached the glass doors when a party of students came pouring out, and they were forced to stand aside.

They were facing back the way they had come, across the plaza with its terraces and red-bud trees, towards the restaurant.

Suddenly the dusk of evening was lit by the searing white furnace glare of an explosion, and the glass windows of the restaurant were blown out in a glittering cloud of flying glass. It was as though a storm surf had burst upon a rock cliff, flinging out its shining droplets of spray, but this was a lethal spray that scythed down two girl students who were passing the windows at that moment.

Immediately after the flash of the explosion the blast swept across the terrace, a draught of violence that shook the red-bud trees and sent David and Debra reeling against the pillars of the library veranda. The air was driven in upon them so that their eardrums ached with the blow, and the breath was sucked from their lungs.

David caught her to him and held her for the moments of dreadful silence that followed the blast. As they stared so, a soft white fog of phosphorus smoke billowed from the gutted windows of the restaurant and began to roll and drift across the terrace.

Then the sounds reached them through their ringing eardrums, the small tinkle and crunch of glass, the patter and crack of falling plaster and shattered furniture. A woman began to scream, and it broke the spell of horror.

There were shouts and running feet. One of the students near them began in a high hysterical voice, 'A bomb. They've bombed the cafe.'

One of the girls who had fallen under the storm of glass fragments staggered up and began running in small aimless circles, screaming in a thin passionless tone. She was white with plaster dust through which the blood poured in dark rivulets, drenching her skirt.

In David's arms Debra began to tremble. 'The swine,' she whispered, 'oh, the filthy murdering swine.'

From the smoking destruction of the shattered building another figure shambled with slow deliberation. The blast had torn his clothing from his body, and it hung from him in tatters, making him a strange scarecrow figure. He reached the terrace and sat down slowly, removed from his face the spectacles that were miraculously still in place and began fumbling to clean them on the rags of his shirt. Blood dripped from his chin.

'Come on,' grated David, 'we must help.' And they ran down the steps together.

The explosion had brought down part of the roof, trapping and crushing twenty-three of the students who had come here to eat and talk over the evening meal.

Others had been hurled about the large low hall, like the toys of a child in tantrum, and their blood turned the interior into a reeking charnel house. Some of them were crawling, creeping, or moving spasmodically amongst the tumbled furniture, broken crockery and spilled food. Some lay contorted as though in silent laughter at death's crude joke.

Afterwards they would learn that two young female members of El Fatah had enrolled in the university under false papers, and they had daily smuggled small quantities of explosive on to the campus until they had accumulated sufficient for this outrage. A suitcase with a timing device had been left under a table and two terrorists had walked out and got clean away. A week later they were on Damascus television, gloating over their success.

Now, however, there was no reason nor explanation for this sudden burst of violence. It was as undirected, and yet as dreadfully effective as some natural cataclysm. Chilling in its insensate enormity, so that they, the living, worked in a kind of terrified frenzy, to save the injured and to carry from the shambles the broken bodies of the dead.

They laid them upon the lawns beneath the red-bud trees and covered them with sheets brought hurriedly from the nearest hostel. The long white bundles in a neat row upon the green grass was a memory David knew he would have for ever.

The ambulances came, with their sirens pulsing and roof-lights flashing, to carry away death's harvest and the police cordoned off the site of the blast before David and Debra left and walked slowly down to where the Mercedes was parked in the lot. Both of them were filthy with dust and blood, and wearied with the sights and sounds of pain and mutilation. They drove in silence to Malik Street and showered off the smell and the dirt. Debra soaked David's uniform in cold water to remove the blood. Then she made coffee for them and they drank it, sitting side by side in the brass bed.

'So much that was good and strong died there tonight,' Debra said.

'Death is not the worst of it. Death is natural, it's the logical conclusion to all things. It was the torn and broken flesh that still lived which appalled me. Death has a sort of dignity, but the maimed are obscene.'

She looked at him with almost fear in her eyes. 'That's cruel, David.'

'In Africa there is a beautiful and fierce animal called the sable antelope. They run together in herds of up to a hundred, but when one of them is hurt—wounded by a hunter or mauled by a lion—the lead bulls turn upon him and drive him from the herd. I remember my father telling me about that, he would say that if you want to be a winner then you must avoid the company of the losers for their despair is contagious.'

'God, David, that's a terribly hard way to look at life.'

'Perhaps,' David agreed, 'but then, you see, life *is* hard.'

When they made love, there was for the first time a quality of desperation in it, for it was the eve of parting and they had been reminded of their mortality.

In the morning David went to join his squadron and Debra locked the house on Malik Street.

Each day for seventeen days David flew two, and sometimes three, sorties. In the evenings, if they were not flying night interceptions, there were lectures and training films, and after that not much desire for anything but a quick meal and then sleep.

The Colonel, le Dauphin, had flown one sortie with David. He was a small man with a relaxed manner and quick, shrewd eyes. He had made his judgement quickly.

After that first day, David and Joe flew together, and David moved his gear into the locker across from Joe in the underground quarters that the crews on standby used.

In those seventeen days the last links in an iron friendship were forged. David's flare and dash balanced perfectly with Joe's rock-solid dependability.

David would always be the star while Joe seemed destined to be the accompanist, the straight guy who was a perfect foil, the wingman without personal ambition for glory whose talent was to put his number one into the position for the strike.

Quickly they developed into a truly formidable team, so perfectly in accord that communication in the air was almost extra-sensory, similar to the instantaneous reaction of the bird flock or the shoal of fish.

Joe sitting out there behind him was for David like a million dollars in insurance. His tail was secure and he could concentrate on the special task that his superior eyesight and lightning reactions were so suited to. David was the gunfighter, in a service where the gunfighter was supreme.

The I.A.F. had been the first to appreciate the shortcomings of the air-to-air missile, and to revert to the classic type of air combat. A missile could be induced to 'run stupid'. It was possible to make its computer think in a set pattern and then sucker it with a break in the pattern. For every three hundred missile launches in air-to-air combat, a single strike could be expected.

However, if you had a gunfighter coming up into your six o'clock position with his finger on the trigger of twin 30-mm. cannons, capable of pouring twelve thousand shells a minute into you, then your chances were considerably lighter than three hundred to one.

Joe also had his own special talent. The forward scanning radar of the Mirage was a complicated and sophisticated body of electronics, that required firstly a high degree of manual dexterity. The mechanism was operated entirely by the left hand, and the fingers of that hand had to move like those of a concert pianist. However, more important was the 'feel' for the instrument, a lover's touch to draw the optimum results from it. Joe had the 'feel', David did not.

They flew training interceptions, day and night, against high-flying and low-altitude practice targets. They flew low-level training strikes, and at other times they went out high over the Mediterranean and engaged each other in plane-to-plane dog-fights.

However, Desert Flower steered them tactfully away from any actual or potential combat situation. They were watching David.

At the end of the period, David's service dossier passed over Major-General Mordecai's desk. Personnel was the Brig's special responsibility and although each officer's dossier was reviewed by him regularly, he had asked particularly to see David's.

The dossier was still slim, compared to the bulky tomes of some of the old salts and the Brig flicked quickly over his own initial recommendation and the documents of David's acting commission. Then he stopped to read the later reports and results. He grinned wolfishly as he saw the gunnery report. He could pick them out of a crowd, he thought with satisfaction.

At last he came to le Dauphin's personal appraisal:

'Morgan is a pilot of exceptional ability. Recommended that acting rank be confirmed and that he be placed on fully operational basis forthwith.'

The Brig picked up the red pen that was his own special prerogative and scrawled 'I agree' at the foot of the report.

That took care of Morgan, the pilot. He could now consider Morgan, the man. His expression became bleak and severe. Debra's sudden desire to leave home almost immediately David arrived in Jerusalem had been too much of a coincidence for a man who was trained to search for underlying motives and meanings.

It had taken him two days and a few phone calls to learn that Debra was merely using the hostel room at the University as an accommodation address, and that her real domestic arrangements were more comfortable.

The Brig did not approve, very definitely not. Yet he knew that it was beyond his jurisdiction. He had learned that his daughter had inherited his own iron will. Confrontations between them were cataclysmic events, that shook the family to its foundations and seldom ended in satisfactory results.

Although he spent much of his time with young people, still he found the new values hard to live with—let alone accept. He remembered the physical agony of his long and chaste engagement to Ruth with pride, like a veteran reviewing an old campaign.

'Well, at the least she has the sense not to flout it, not to bring shame on us all. She has spared her mother that.' The Brig closed the dossier firmly.

Le Dauphin called David into his office and told him of his change in status. He would go on regular 'green' standby, which meant four nights a week on base.

David would now have to undergo his paratrooper training in unarmed combat and weapons. A downed pilot in Arab territory had a much better chance of survival if he was proficient in this type of fighting.

David went straight from le Dauphin's office to the telephone in the crew-room. He caught Debra before she left the Lauterman Building for lunch.

'Warm the bed, wench,' he told her, 'I'll be home tomorrow night.'

He and Joe drove up to Jerusalem in the Mercedes, and he wasn't listening to Joe's low rumbling voice until a thumb like an oar prodded his ribs.

'Sorry, Joe, I was thinking.'

'Well, stop it. Your thoughts are misting up the windows.'

'What did you say?'

'I was talking about the wedding—Hannah and me.'

David realized it was only a month away now, and he expected the excitement amongst the women was heavy as static on a summer's day before the rain. Debra's letters had been filled with news of the arrangements.

'I would be happy if you will stand up with me, and be my witness. You fly as wingman for a change, and I'll take on the target.'

David realized that he was being honoured by the request and he accepted with proper solemnity. Secretly he was amused. Like most young Israelis David had spoken to, both Debra and Joe claimed not to be religious. He had learned that this was a pose. All of them were very conscious of their religious heritage, and well versed in the history and practice of Judaism. They followed all the laws of living that were not oppressive, and which accorded with a modern and busy existence.

To them 'religious' meant dressing in the black robes and wide-brimmed hats of the ultra-orthodox Mea Shearim, or in following a routine for daily living that was crippling in its restrictions.

The wedding would be a traditional affair, complete with all the ceremony and the rich symbolism, complicated only by the security precautions which would have to be most rigorously enforced.

The ceremony was to take place in the Brig's garden, for Hannah was an orphan. Also the secluded garden and fortress-like walls about it, were easier to protect.

Amongst the guests would be many prominent figures in the government and the military.

'At the last count we have five generals and eighteen colonels on the list,' Joe told him, 'to which add most of the cabinet, even Golda has promised to try and be there. So you see, it's going to make a nice juicy target for our friends in Black September.' Joe scowled and lit two cigarettes, passing one to David. 'If it wasn't for Hannah, you know how women feel about weddings, I would just as soon go down to a registry office.'

'You are fooling nobody,' David grinned. 'You are looking forward to it.'

'Sure,' Joe's scowl cleared. 'It's going to be good to have our own place, like you and Debs. I wish Hannah had been sensible. A year of pretending,' he shook his head. 'Thank God it's nearly over.'

He dropped Joe in the lane outside the Brig's house in Ein Karem.

'I won't bother to invite you in,' Joe said. 'I guess you've got plans.'

'Good guess,' David smiled. 'Will we see you and Hannah? Come to dinner tomorrow night.'

Joe shook his head again. 'I'm taking Hannah down to Ashkelon to visit her parents' graves. It's traditional before a wedding. Perhaps we'll see you Saturday.'

'Right then, I'll try and make it. Debra will want to see you. *Shalom,* Joe,'

'*Shalom, shalom,*' said Joe and David pulled away, flicking the gears in a racing change as he put the Mercedes at the hill. Suddenly he was in a hurry.

The terrace door stood open in welcome, and she was waiting for him. Debra was vibrant and tense with expectation, sitting in one of the new leather chairs with her legs curled under her. Her hair was freshly washed and shimmering like a starling's wing. She was dressed in a billowing kaftan of light silk and subtle honey colours that picked out the gold in her eyes.

She came out of the chair in a swirl of silk, and ran bare-footed across the rugs to meet him.

'David! David!' she cried and he caught her up and spun on his heels, laughing with her.

Afterwards she led him proudly about the rooms and showed him the changes and additions that had turned it into a real home during his absence. David had convinced her that cost was not fundamental and they had chosen the designs for the furniture together. These had been made and delivered by Debra's tame Arab and she had arranged them as they had planned it. It was all in soft leather and dark wood, lustrous copper and brass, set off by the bright rugs. However, there was one article he had never seen before—a large oil-painting on canvas, and Debra had hung it unframed on the freshly painted white wall facing the terrace. It was the only decoration upon the wall, and any other would have been insignificant beside it. It was a harsh dominant landscape, a desert scene which captured the soul of the wilderness; the colours were hot and fierce and seemed to pour through the room like the rays of the desert sun itself.

Debra held his hand and watched David's face anxiously for a reaction as he studied it.

'Wow!' he said at last.

'You like it?' She was relieved.

'It's terrific. Where did you get it?'

'A gift from the artist. She's an old friend.'

'She?'

'That's right. We are driving up to Tiberias tomorrow to have lunch with her. I've told her all about you, and she wants to meet you.'

'What's she like?'

'She's one of our leading artists, and her name is Ella Kadesh, but apart from that I can't begin to describe her. All I can do is promise you an entertaining day.'

Debra had prepared a special dish of lamb and olives and they ate it on the terrace under the olive tree. Again the talk turned to Joe's wedding, and in the midst of it David asked abruptly, 'What made you decide to come with me—without marrying?'

She replied after a moment. 'I discovered that I loved you, and I knew that you were too impatient to play the waiting game. I knew that if I didn't, I might lose you again.'

'Until recently, I didn't realize what a big decision it was,' he mused, and she sipped her wine without replying.

'Let's get married, Debs,' he broke the silence.

'Yes,' she nodded. 'That's a splendid idea.'

'Soon,' he said. 'Soon as possible.'

'Not before Hannah. I don't want to steal her day from her.'

'Right,' David agreed, 'but immediately afterwards.'

'Morgan, you have got yourself a date,' she told him.

It was a three-hour drive to Tiberias so they rose as soon as the sun came through the shutters and tiger-striped the wall above the brass bed. To save time, they shared one bath, sitting facing each other, waist-deep in suds.

'Ella is the rudest person you'll ever meet,' Debra warned him. She looked like a little girl this morning with her hair piled on top of her head and secured with a pink ribbon. 'The greater the impression you make on her, the ruder she will be, and you are expected to retaliate in kind. So please, David, don't lose your temper.'

David scooped up a dab of suds with a finger and smeared it on the tip of her nose.

'I promise,' he said.

They drove down to Jericho, and then turned north along the valley of the Jordan, following the high barbed-wire fence of the border with its warning notice boards for the minefields, and the regular motorized patrols grinding deliberately along the winding road.

It was hot in the valley and they drove with the windows open and Debra pulled her skirts high around her waist to cool her long brown legs.

'Better not do that if you want to be in time for lunch,' David warned her, and she smoothed them down hurriedly.

'Nothing is safe with you around,' she protested.

They came at last out of the barren land into the fertile basin of the Kibbutzim below Galilee, and again the smell of orange blossom was so strong on the warm air that it was difficult to breathe.

At last they saw the waters of the lake flashing amongst the date palms and Debra touched his arm.

'Slow down, Davey. Ella's place is a few miles this side of Tiberias. That's the turn-off, up ahead.'

It was a track that led down to the lake shore and it ended against a wall of ancient stone blocks. Five other cars were parked there already.

'Ella's having one of her lunch parties,' Debra remarked and led him to a gate in the wall. Beyond was a small ruined castle. The tumbled walls formed weird shapes and the stone was black with age; over them grew flamboyant creepers of bougainvillaea and the tall palms clattered their fronds in the light breeze that came off the lake. Other exotic flowering shrubs grew upon the green lawns.

Part of the ruins had been restored and renovated into a picturesque and unusual lakeside home, with a wide patio and a stone jetty against which a motor-boat was moored. Across the green waters of the lake rose the dark smooth whale-back of the Golan Heights.

'It was a crusader fortress,' Debra explained. 'One of the guard posts for traffic across the lake and part of the series leading up to the great castle on the Horns of Hittem that the Moslems destroyed when they drove the crusaders out of the Holy Land. Ella's grandfather purchased it during the Allenby administration, but it was a ruin until she did it up after the war of independence.'

The care with which the alterations had been made so as not to spoil the romantic beauty of the site was a tribute to Ella Kadesh's artistic vision, which was completely at odds with the woman herself.

She was enormous; not simply fat or tall, but big. Her hands and feet were huge, her fingers clustered with rings and semi-precious stones and her toenails through the open sandals were painted a glaring crimson, as if to flaunt their size. She stood as tall as David, but the tent-like dress that billowed about her was covered with great explosive designs that enhanced her bulk until she seemed to make up for two of him. She wore a wig of tiered curls, flaming red in colour and dangling earrings. It seemed she must have applied her eye make-up with a spade, and her rouge with a spray gun. She removed the thin black cheroot from her mouth and kissed Debra before she turned to study David. Her voice was gravelly, hoarse with cheroot smoke and brandy.

'I had not expected you to be so beautiful,' she said, and Debra quailed at the expression in David's eyes. 'I do not like beauty. It is so often deceptive, or inconsequential. It usually hides something deadly—like the glittering beauty of the cobra—or like the pretty wrapper of a candy bar, it contains cloying sweetness and a soft centre.' She shook the stiffly lacquered curls of her wig, and fixed David with her shrewd little eyes. 'No, I prefer ugliness to beauty.'

David smiled at her with all his charm upon display. 'Yes,' he agreed, 'having met you, and seen some of your work, I can understand that.'

She let out a cackle of raucous laughter, and clapped the cheroot back in her mouth. 'Well now, at the very least we are not dealing with a chocolate soldier.' She placed a huge masculine arm about David's shoulders and led him to meet the company.

They were a mixed dozen, all intellectuals—artists, writers, teachers, journalists—and David was content to sit beside Debra in the mild sunshine and enjoy the beer and the amusing conversation. However, Ella would not let him relax for long and when they sat down to the gargantuan *alfresco* meal of cold fish and poultry, she attacked him again.

'Your martial airs and affectations, your pomp and finery. A plague on it I say, a pox on your patriotism, and courage—on your fearlessness and your orders of chivalry. It is all sham and pretence, an excuse for you to stink up the earth with piles of carrion.'

'I wonder if you will feel the same when a platoon of Syrian infantry break in here to rape you,' David challenged her.

'My boy, I find it difficult to get laid these days that I should pray for such a heaven-sent opportunity.' She let out a mighty hoot of laughter and her wig slipped forward at an abandoned angle. Nothing was safe from her, and she pushed the wig back into place and streamed straight into the attack again.

'Your male bombast, your selfish arrogance. To you this woman—' and she indicated Debra with a turkey leg, '—to you she is merely a receptacle of your seething careless sperm. It matters not to you that she is a promise for the future, that within her are the seeds of a great writing talent. No, to you she is a rubbing block, a convenient means to a—'

Debra interrupted her. 'That definitely is enough, I will not allow a public debate on my bedroom,' and Ella turned towards her with the battle lust lighting her eyes.

'Your gift is not yours to use as you wish. You hold it in trust for all mankind, and you have a duty to them. That duty is to exercise your gift, to allow it to grow and blossom and give forth fruit.' She used the turkey leg like a judge's gavel, banging the edge of her plate with it, to silence Debra's protests.

'Have you written a word since you took young Mars to your heart? What of the novel we discussed on this very terrace a year ago? Have your animal passions swamped all else? Has the screeching of your ovaries—'

'Stop it, Ella!' Debra was angry now, her cheeks flushed and her brown eyes snapping.

'Yes! Yes!' Ella tossed the bone aside and sucked her fingers noisily. 'Ashamed you should be, angry with yourself—'

'Damn you,' Debra flared at her.

'Damn me if you will—but you are damned yourself if you do not write! Write, woman, write!' She sat back and the wicker chair protested at the movement of her vast body. 'All right, now we will all go for a swim. David has not seen me in a bikini yet—much he will care for that skinny little wench when he does!'

They drove back to Jerusalem in the night, flushed with the sun, and although the Mercedes seats had not been designed for lovers, Debra managed to sit close up against him.

'She's right, you know,' David broke a long contented silence. 'You must write, Debs.'

'Oh, I will,' she answered lightly.

'When?' he persisted, and to distract him she snuggled a little closer.

'One of these days,' she whispered as she made her dark head comfortable on his shoulder.

'One of these days,' he mimicked her.

'Don't bug me, Morgan.' She was already half-asleep.

'Stop being evasive.' He stroked her hair with his free hand. 'And don't go to sleep while I'm talking to you.'

'David, my darling, we have a lifetime—and more,' she murmured. 'You have made me immortal. You and I shall live for a thousand years, and there will be time for everything.'

Perhaps the dark gods heard her boast, and they chuckled sardonically and nudged each other.

On Saturday Joe and Hannah came to the house on Malik Street, and after lunch they decided on a tourist excursion for David and the four of them climbed Mount Zion across the valley. They entered the labyrinth of corridors that led to David's tomb, covered with splendid embroidered cloth and silver crowns and Torah covers. From there it was a few steps to the room of Christ's last supper in the same building, so closely interwoven were the traditions of Judaism and Christianity in this citadel.

Afterwards they entered the old city through the Zion gate and followed the wall around to the centre of Judaism, the tall cliff of massive stone blocks, bevelled in the fashion of Herodian times, which was all that remained of the fabulous second temple of Herod, destroyed two thousand years before by the Romans.

They were searched at the gate and then joined the stream of worshippers flocking down towards the wall. At the barrier they stood for a long time in silence. David felt again the stirring of a deep race memory, a hollow feeling of the soul which longed to be filled.

The men prayed facing the wall, many of them in the long black coats of the

Orthodox Jew with the ringlets dangling against their cheeks as they rocked and swayed in religious ecstasy. Within the enclosure on the right-hand side, the women seemed more reserved in their devotions.

Joe spoke at last, a little embarrassed and in a gruff tone. 'I think I'll just go say a *sh'ma*.'

'Yes,' Hannah agreed. 'Are you coming with me, Debra?'

'A moment.' Debra turned to David, and took something from her handbag. 'I made it for you for the wedding,' she said. 'But wear it now.'

It was a *yamulka*, an embroidered prayer cap of black satin.

'Go with Joe,' she said. 'He will show you what to do.'

The girls moved off to the women's enclosure and David placed the cap upon his head and followed Joe down to the wall.

A *shamash* came to them, an old man with a long silver beard, and he helped David bind upon his right arm a tiny leather box containing a portion of the Torah.

'So you shall lay these words upon your heart and your soul, and you shall bind them upon your right arm—'

Then he spread a *tallit* across David's shoulders, a tasselled shawl of woven wool, and he led him to the wall, and he began to repeat after the *shamash*:

'Hear, O Israel, the Lord our God, the Lord is one—'

His voice grew surer as he remembered the words from long ago, and he looked up at the wall of massive stone blocks that towered high above him. Thousands of previous worshippers had written down their prayers on scraps of paper and wedged them into the joints between the blocks, and around him rose the plaintive voices of spoken prayer. It seemed to David that in his imagination a golden beam of prayer rose from this holy place towards the heavens.

Afterwards they left the enclosure and climbed the stairs into the Jewish quarter, and the good feeling remained with David, glowing warmly in his belly.

That evening they sat together on the terrace drinking Goldstar beer and splitting sunflower seeds for the nutty kernels, and naturally the talk turned to God and religion.

Joe said, 'I'm an Israeli and then a Jew. First my country, and a long way behind that comes my religion.'

But David remembered the expression on his face as he prayed against the wailing wall.

The talk lasted until late, and David glimpsed the vast body of his religious heritage.

'I would like to learn a little more about it all,' he admitted, and Debra said nothing but when she packed for him to go on base that night she placed a copy of Herman Wouk's *This is my God* on top of his clean uniforms.

He read it and when next he returned to Malik Street, he asked for more. She picked them for him, English works at first but then Hebrew, as his grip upon the language became stronger. They were not religious works only, but histories and historical novels that excited his interest on this ancient centre of civilization which for three thousand years had been a crossroads and a battle ground.

He read anything and everything that she put into his case, from Josephus Flavius to Leon Uris.

This led to a desire to see and inspect the ground. It became so that much of the time they were free together was spent in these explorations. They began with the hill-top fortress of Herod at Masada where the zealots had killed each other rather than submit to Rome, and from there they moved off the tourist beat to the lesser-known historical sites.

In those long sunlit days they might eat their basket lunch sitting on the ruins of a Roman aqueduct and watching a falcon working the thermals that rose off the floor of the desert, after they had searched the bed of a dry wadi for coins and arrowheads brought down by the last ruins.

Around them rose the tall cliffs of orange and golden stone, and the light was so clean and stark that it seemed they could see for ever, and the silence so vast that they were the only living things in the world.

They were the happiest days that David had ever known, and they gave point and meaning to the weary hours of squadron standby, and when the day had ended there was always the house on Malik Street with its warmth and laughter and love.

Joe and David arranged leave of absence from the base for the wedding. It was a time of quiet, and le Dauphin let them go without protest, for he would be a guest.

They drove up to Jerusalem the day before and were immediately conscripted to assist with arrangements. David laboured mightily as a taxi-driver and trucker. The Mercedes transported everything from flowers to musical instruments and distant relatives.

The Brig's garden was decorated with palm leaves and coloured bunting. In the centre stood the *huppah*, a canopy worked with religious symbols in blue and gold, the Star of David and the grapes and ears of wheat, the pomegranates and all the other symbols of fertility. Beneath it, the marriage ceremony would take place. Trestle tables covered with gay cloths set with bowls of flowers and dishes of fruit were arranged beneath the olive trees. There were places for three hundred guests, an open space for the dancing, a raised timber stand hung with flags for the band.

The catering was contracted out to a professional firm and the menu had been carefully decided upon by the chef and the women. It would have two high points—an enormous stuffed tuna, again a symbol of fertility, and a lamb dish in the bedouin style served upon enormous copper salvers.

On the Sunday of the wedding, David drove Debra to the home of the chief surgeon of Hadassah Hospital. Hannah was one of his theatre sisters and he had insisted that she use his home to prepare for the wedding. Debra was to assist her, and David left them and drove on to Ein Karem. The lane leading to the house was cordoned off and thick with secret service men and paratroopers.

While he watched Joe dressing, losing and finding the ring, and sweating with nerves, David lay on Joe's bed and gave him bad advice. They could hear the guests gathering on the garden below, and David stood up and went to the window. He watched an airforce colonel being carefully scrutinized and searched at the gates, but taking it all in good part.

'They are being pretty thorough,' David remarked.

'Hannah has asked to have as few as possible of the guards in the garden. So they are being damned careful about who they let in.' Joe had at last completed dressing and already he was beginning to sweat through the armpits of his uniform.

'How do I look?' he asked anxiously.

'God, you handsome beast,' David told him.

'Piss off, Morgan,' Joe grinned at him, crammed his cap on to his head and glanced at his watch. 'Let's go,' he said.

The Chief Rabbi of the army was waiting with the Brig and the others in the Brig's study. The Rabbi was the mild-mannered man who had personally liberated the Tomb of the Patriarchs in the war of '67. During the advance on Hebron, he had driven a jeep through the disintegrating Arab lines, shot open the door to the tomb with a submachine-gun and chased the Arab guards screaming over the rear wall.

Joe sat at the Brig's desk and signed the *ketubbah*, the marriage contract, then the Rabbi handed him a silken cloth which Joe lifted in a formal act of acquisition to a chorus of congratulatory '*Mazal tovs*' from the witnesses.

The bridegroom's party trooped out into the crowded garden now to await the arrival of the bride, and she came accompanied by the chief surgeon standing in for her dead father, and a party of festively dressed women, including Debra and her mother. They all carried lighted candles.

To David, Hannah had never been particularly attractive, she was too tall and severe in body and expression; however, in her white bridal dress and veil she was transformed.

She seemed to float cloudlike upon the billowing white skirts, and her face was softened by the veil and by the inner happiness that seemed to glow through her green eyes. Red-gold hair framed her cheeks, and the freckles were disguised under make-up applied by Debra's cunning hand. She had used it to mute the rather harsh lines of Hannah's bony nose, and the result was as near to beautiful as she would ever come.

Joe, looking big and handsome in his airforce tans, went forward eagerly to meet her at the gate to the garden and to lower the veil over her face in the ceremony of *bedeken dikalle*.

Joe moved to the *chuppah* canopy where the Rabbi waited with a *tallit* over his shoulders. After Joe the women led Hannah, each of them still carrying a burning candle, and the Rabbi chanted a blessing as the women and the bride circled Joe seven times in a magical circle which in olden times would serve to ward off evil spirits. At last bride and groom stood side by side, facing towards the site of the Temple with the guests and witnesses pressed closely about them and the ceremony proper began.

The Rabbi spoke the benediction over a goblet of wine from which bride and groom both drank. Then Joe turned to Hannah, her face still veiled, and he placed the plain gold ring upon her right forefinger.

'Behold you are consecrated unto me by this ring, according to the law of Moses and Israel.'

Then Joe broke the glass under his heel and the sharp crunch was a signal for an outburst of music and song and gaiety. David left Joe's side and worked his way through the joyous crowd of guests to where Debra waited for him.

She wore a gown of yellow and she had fresh flowers in the dark sheen of her hair. David smelled their perfume as he hugged her surreptitiously about the waist and whispered in her ear, 'You next, my beauty!' and she whispered back, 'Yes, please!'

Joe took Hannah on his arm, and they went to the improvised dance floor. The band began with a light bouncy tune and all the younger ones flocked to join them—while the elders spread out at the tables beneath the palm-decked trellis.

Yet amongst all the laughter and the gaiety, the uniforms added a sombre touch; almost every second man was adorned with the trappings of war, and at the golden gate and the entrance to the kitchens were uniformed paratrooper guards each with a Uzzi submachine-gun slung at his shoulder. It was easy to pick out the secret service men. They were the ones in civilian clothes who moved without smiling, alert and vigilant, amongst the guests.

David and Debra danced together, and she was so light and warm and strong in his arms that when the band paused for breath he resented it. He led her to a quiet corner, and they stood together, discussing the other guests in the most disrespectful terms until Debra giggled at some particularly outrageous remark and struck his arm lightly.

'You are terrible.' She leaned against him. 'I'm dying of thirst, won't you get me something to drink?'

'A glass of cold white wine?' he suggested.

'Lovely,' she said, smiling up into his face. For a moment they studied each other, and suddenly David felt something dark welling up from within him, a terrible despair, a premonition of impending loss. It was a physical thing and he could feel the chill of it enclose his chest and squeeze out all the happiness and the joy.

'What is it, David?' Her own expression altered in sympathy with his, and she tightened her grip on his arm.

'Nothing.' Abruptly he pulled away from her, trying to fight off the feeling. 'It's nothing,' he repeated, but it was still strong in his belly, and he felt a wave of nausea from it. 'I'll get you the wine,' he said and turned away.

He made his way towards the bar, pushing gently through the throng. The Brig caught his eye and smiled bleakly across the garden at him. Joe was with his father and he called to David, laughing, with one arm around his bride. Hannah had her veil pushed up and her freckles were beginning to emerge from under the make-up, glowing vividly against the snow-white lace. David waved at them but went towards the open-air bar at the end of the garden, the mood of sadness was still on him and he didn't want to talk to Joe now.

So he was cut off from Debra at the moment when, with a flourish, a procession of white-jacketed waiters came in through the iron gate of the garden. Each of them carried a huge copper salver from which, even in the warm sun, rose tendrils of steam, and the odour of meat and fish and spices filled the garden. There were gasps and cries of appreciation from the guests.

A way opened for them towards the high table on the raised terrace which led to the kitchen doors and the house.

The procession of waiters passed close to David, and suddenly his attention was drawn from the display of fine food to the face of the second waiter in line. He was a man of medium height and dark complexion, a mahogany face with a thickly drooping moustache.

He was sweating. That was what had drawn David's attention, his face was shiny with sweat. Droplets clung in his moustache and slid down his cheeks. The white jacket was sodden at the armpits as he lifted the gigantic platter on high.

At the moment that he drew level with David their eyes met for an instant. David realized that the man was in the grip of some deep emotion—fear, perhaps, or exhilaration. Then the waiter seemed to become aware of David's scrutiny and his eyes slid nervously away.

David felt suspicion begin to chill his arms as the three figures climbed the stone stairs, and filed behind the table.

The waiter glanced again at David, saw that his gaze was still locked upon his face, and then he said something out of the corner of his mouth to one of his companions. He also glanced at David, and caught his stare, and his expression was sufficient to send alarm flaring urgently through David's chest and brain. Something was happening, something dangerous and ugly, he was certain of it.

Wildly he looked about for the guards. There were two of them on the terrace behind the line of waiters, and one near David beside the gate.

David shoved his way desperately towards him, mindless of the outraged comments of those in his way. He was watching the three waiters and so he saw it begin to happen.

It had obviously been carefully rehearsed for as the three waiters placed the salvers upon the table to the laughter and applause of the guests crowded in the garden below them, so they drew the sheets of plastic on which a thin display of food had been arranged to cover the deadly load that each copper salver carried.

The brown-faced waiter lifted a machine pistol from under the plastic sheet, and turned swiftly to fire a traversing burst into the two paratroopers behind him at point-blank range. The clattering thunder of automatic fire was deafening in the walled garden, and the stream of bullets slashed through the bellies of the two guards like a monstrous cleaver, almost cutting them in half.

The waiter on David's left was a wizened monkey-faced man, with bright black berries for eyes. He, too, lifted a machine pistol from his salver, and he crouched over it and fired a burst at the paratrooper by the gate.

They were going for the guards, taking them first. The pistol shook and roared in his fists, and the bullets socked into human flesh with a rubbery thumping sound.

The guard had cleared his Uzzi, and was trying to aim as a bullet hit him in the mouth and snapped his head back, his paratrooper beret spinning high into the air. The machine-gun flew from his arms as he fell, and it slid across the tiles towards David. David dropped flat below the stone steps of the terrace as the Arab gunner turned their pistols on the wedding crowd, hosing the courtyard with a triple stream of bullets, and unleashing a hurricane of screams and shouts and desperate cries to join the roar of the guns.

Across the yard, a security agent had the pistol out of his shoulder holster and he dropped into the marksman crouch, holding the pistol with both arms extended as he aimed. He fired twice and hit the monkey-faced gunman, sending him reeling back against the wall, but he stayed on his feet and returned the agent's fire with the machine pistol, knocking him down and rolling him across the paving stones.

The yard was filled with a panic-stricken mob, a struggling mass of humanity, that screamed and fell and crawled and died beneath the flail of the guns.

Two bullets caught Hannah in the chest, smashing her backwards over a table of glasses and bottles that shattered about her. The bright blood spurted from the wounds, drenching the front of her white wedding gown.

The centre gunman dropped his pistol as it emptied, and he stooped quickly over the copper salver and came up with a grenade in each hand. He hurled them into the struggling, screaming throng and the double blast was devastating, twin bursts of brightest white flame and the terrible sweep of shrapnel. The screams of the women rose louder, seeming as deafening as the gunfire—and the gunman stooped once more and his hands held another load of grenades.

All this had taken only seconds, but a fleeting moment of time to turn festivity into shocking carnage and torn flesh.

David left the shelter of the stone steps. He rolled swiftly across the flags towards the abandoned Uzzi, and he came up on his knees, holding it at the hip. His paratrooper training made his actions automatic.

The wounded gunman saw him, and turned towards him, staggering slightly, pushing himself weakly away from the wall. His one arm was shattered and hung loosely in the tattered, blood-soaked sleeve of his jacket, but he lifted the machine pistol and aimed at David.

David fired first, the bullets struck bursts of plaster from the wall behind the Arab and David corrected his aim. The bullets drove the gunman backwards, pinning him to the wall, while his body jumped and shook and twitched. He slumped down leaving a glistening wet smear of blood down the white plaster.

David swivelled the gun on to the Arab beside the kitchen door. He was poised to throw his next grenade, right arm extended behind him, both fists filled with the deadly steel balls. He was shouting something, a challenge or a war cry, a harsh triumphant screech that carried clearly above the screams of his victims.

Before he could release the grenade, David hit him with a full burst, a dozen bullets that smashed into his chest and belly, and the Arab dropped both grenades at his feet and doubled over clutching at his broken body, trying to stem the flood of his blood with his bare hands.

The grenades were short fused and they exploded almost immediately, engulfing the dying man in a net of fire and shredding his body from the waist down. The same explosion knocked down the third assassin at the end of the terrace, and David came to his feet and charged up the steps.

The third and last Arab was mortally wounded, his head and chest torn by grenade fragments, but he was still alive, thrashing about weakly as he groped for the machine pistol that lay beside him in a puddle of his own blood.

David was consumed by a terrible rage. He found that he was screaming and raging like a maniac, and he crouched at the head of the stairs and aimed at the dying Arab.

The Arab had the machine pistol and was lifting it with the grim concentration of a drunken man. David fired, a single shot that slapped into the Arab's body without apparent effect, and then suddenly the Uzzi in David's hands was empty, the pin falling with a hollow click on an empty chamber.

Across the terrace, beyond range of a quick rush, the Arab's face was streaked with sweat and blood as he frowned heavily, trying to aim the machine pistol as it wavered. He was dying swiftly, the flame fluttering towards extinction, but he was using the last of his strength.

David stood frozen with the empty weapon in his hand, and the blank eye of the pistol sought him out, and fastened upon him. He watched the Arab's eyes narrow, and his sudden murderous grin of achievement as he saw David in his sights, and his finger tightening on the trigger.

At that range the bullets would hit like the solid stream of a fire hose. He began to move, to throw himself down the stairs, but he knew it was too late. The Arab was at the instant of firing, and at the same instant a revolver shot crashed out at David's side.

Half the Arab's head was cut away by the heavy lead slug, and he was flung backwards with the yellow custard contents of his skull splattering the whitewashed wall behind him, and his death grip on the trigger emptied the machine pistol with a shattering roar harmlessly into the grape vines above him.

Dazedly David turned to find the Brig beside him, the dead security guard's pistol in his fist. For a moment they stared at each other, and then the Brig stepped past him and walked to the fallen bodies of the other two Arabs. Standing over each in turn he fired a single pistol shot into their heads.

David turned away and let the Uzzi drop from his hands. He went down the stairs into the garden.

The dead and the wounded lay singly and in piles, pitiful fragments of humanity. The soft cries and the groans of the wounded, the bitter weeping of a child, the voice of a mother, were sounds more chilling than the screaming and the shouting.

The garden was drenched and painted with blood. There were splashes and gouts of it upon the white walls, there were puddles and snakes of it spreading and crawling across the paving, dark slicks of it sinking into the dust, ropes of it dribbling and pattering like rain from the body of a musician as he hung over the rail of the bandstand. The sickly sweetish reek of it mingled with the smell of spice food and spilled wine, with the floury taste of plaster dust and the bitter stench of burned explosive.

The veils of smoke and dust that still drifted across the garden could not hide the terrible carnage. The bark of the olive trees was torn in slabs from the trunks by flying steel, exposing the white wet wood. The wounded and dazed survivors crawled over a field of broken glass and shattered crockery. They swore and prayed, and whispered and groaned and called for succour.

David went down the steps, his feet moving without his bidding; his muscles were numb, his body senseless and only his finger-tips tingled with life.

Joe was standing below one of the torn olive trees. He stood like a colossus, with his thick powerful legs astride, his head thrown back and his face turned to the sky, but his eyes were tight-closed and his mouth formed a silent cry of agony—for he held Hannah's body in his arms.

Her bridal veil had fallen from her head, and the bright copper mane of her hair hung back—almost to the ground. Her legs and one arm hung loosely, also, slack and lifeless. The golden freckles stood out clearly on the milky-white skin of her face—and the bloody wounds bloomed like the petals of the poinsettia tree upon the bosom of her wedding-gown.

David averted his eyes. He could not watch Joe in his anguish, and he walked on slowly across the garden, in terrible dread of what he would find.

'Debra!' he tried to raise his voice, but it was a hoarse raven's croak. His feet slipped in a puddle of thick dark blood, and he stepped over the unconscious body of a woman who lay, face down, in a floral dress, with her arms thrown wide. He did not recognize her as Debra's mother.

'Debra!' He tried to hurry, but his legs would not respond. He saw her then, at the corner of the wall where he had left her.

'Debra!' He felt his heart soar. She seemed unhurt, kneeling below one of the marble Grecian statues, with the flowers in her hair and the yellow silk dress gay and festive.

She knelt, facing the wall, and her head was bowed as though in prayer. The dark wind of her hair hung forward screening her and she held her cupped hands to her face.

'Debra.' He dropped to his knees beside her, and timidly he touched her shoulder.

'Are you all right, my darling?' And she lowered her hands slowly, but still holding them cupped together. A great coldness closed around David's chest as he saw that her cupped hands were filled with blood. Rich red blood, bright as wine in a crystal glass.

'David,' she whispered, turning her face towards him. 'Is that you, darling?'

David gave a small breathless moan of agony as he saw her blood-glutted eye sockets, the dark gelatinous mess that congealed in the thick dark eyelashes and turned the lovely face into a gory mask.

'Is that you, David?' she asked again, her head cocked at a blind listening angle.

'Oh God, Debra.' He stared into her face.

'I can't see, David.' She groped for him. 'Oh David—I can't see.'

And he took her sticky wet hands in his, and he thought that his heart would break.

The stark modern silhouette of Hadassah Hospital stood upon the skyline above the village of Ein Karem. The speed with which the ambulances arrived saved many of the victims whose lives were critically balanced, and the hospital was geared to sudden influxes of war casualties.

The three men—the Brig, Joe and David—kept their vigil together all that night upon the hard wooden benches of the hospital waiting-room. When more was learned of the planning behind the attack, a security agent would come to whisper a report to the Brig.

One of the assassins was a long-term and trusted employee of the catering firm, and the other two were his 'cousins' who had been employed as temporary staff on his recommendation. It was certain that their papers were forged.

The Prime Minister and her cabinet had been delayed by an emergency session, but had been on their way to the wedding when the attack was made. A fortunate chance had saved them, and she sent her personal condolences to the relatives of the victims.

At ten o'clock, Damascus radio gave a report in which El Fatah claimed responsibility for the attack by members of a suicide squad.

A little before midnight, the chief surgeon came from the main theatre, still in his theatre greens and boots, with his mask pulled down to his throat. Ruth Mordecai was out of danger, he told the Brig. They had removed a bullet that had passed through her lung and lodged under her shoulder blade. They had saved the lung.

'Thank God,' murmured the Brig and closed his eyes for a moment, imagining life without his woman of twenty-five years. Then he looked up. 'My daughter?'

The surgeon shook his head. 'They are still working on her in the small casualty theatre.' He hesitated. 'Colonel Halman died in theatre a few minutes ago.'

The toll of the dead was eleven so far, with four others on the critical list.

In the early morning the undertakers arrived for the bodies with their long wicker baskets and black limousines. David gave Joe the keys of the Mercedes, that he might follow the hearse bearing Hannah's body and arrange the details of the funeral.

David and the Brig sat side by side, haggard and with sleepless bruised eyes, drinking coffee from paper cups.

In the late morning the eye surgeon came out to them. He was a smooth-faced, young-looking man in his forties, the greying of his hair seeming incongruous against the unlined skin and clear blue eyes.

'General Mordecai?'

The Brig rose stiffly. He seemed to have aged ten years during the night.

'I am Doctor Edelman. Will you come with me please?'

David rose to follow them, but the doctor paused and looked to the Brig.

'I am her fiancé,' said David.

'It might be best if we spoke alone first, General.' Edelman was clearly trying to pass a warning with his eyes, and the Brig nodded.

'Please, David.'

'But–' David began, and the Brig squeezed his shoulder briefly, the first gesture of affection that had ever passed between them.

'Please, my boy,' and David turned back to the hard bench.

In the tiny cubicle of his office Edelman hitched himself on to the corner of the desk and lit a cigarette. His hands were long and slim as a girl's, and he used the lighter with a surgeon's neat economical movements.

'You don't want it with a sugar coating, I imagine?' He had appraised the Brig carefully, and went on without waiting for a reply. 'Neither of your daughter's eyes are damaged,' but he held up a hand to forestall the rising expression of relief on the Brig's lips, and turned to the scanner on which hung a set of X-ray plates. He switched on the back light.

'The eyes were untouched, there is almost no damage to her facial features—however, the damage is here–' he touched a hard frosty outline in the smoky grey swirls and patterns of the X-ray plates, '–that is a steel fragment, a tiny steel fragment, almost certainly from a grenade. It is no larger than the tip of a lead pencil. It entered the skull through the outer edge of the right temple, severing the large vein which accounted for the profuse haemorrhage, and it travelled obliquely behind the eye-balls without touching them or any other vital tissue. Then, however, it pierced the bony surrounds of the optic chiasma,' he traced the path of the fragment through Debra's head, 'and it seems to have cut through the canal and severed the chiasma, before lodging in the bone sponge beyond.' Edelman drew heavily on the cigarette while he looked for a reaction from the Brig. There was none.

'Do you understand the implications of this, General?' he asked, and the Brig shook his head wearily. The surgeon switched off the light of the X-ray scanner, and returned to the desk. He pulled a scrap pad towards the Brig and took a propelling pencil from his top pocket. Boldly he sketched an optical chart, eyeballs, brain, and optical nerves, as seen from above.

'The optical nerves, one from each eye, run back into this narrow tunnel of bone where they fuse, and then branch again to opposite lobes of the brain.'

The Brig nodded, and Edelman slashed the point of his pencil through the point where the nerves fused. Understanding began to show on the Brig's strained and tired features.

'Blind?' he asked, and Edelman nodded.

'Both eyes?'

'I'm afraid so.'

The Brig bowed his head and gently massaged his own eyes with thumb and forefinger. He spoke again without looking at Edelman.

'Permanently?' he asked.

'She has no recognition of shape, or colour, of light or darkness. The track of the fragment is through the optic chiasma. All indications are that the nerve is severed. There is no technique known to medical science which will restore that.' Edelman paused to draw breath, before going on. 'In a word then, your daughter is permanently and totally blinded in both eyes.'

The Brig sighed, and looked up slowly. 'Have you told her?' and Edelman could not hold his gaze.

'I was rather hoping that you would do that?'

'Yes,' the Brig nodded, 'it would be best that way. Can I see her now? Is she awake?'

'She is under light sedation. No pain, only a small amount of discomfort, the external wound is insignificant—and we shall not attempt to remove the metal fragment. That would entail major neurosurgery.' He stood up and indicated to the door. 'Yes, you may see her now. I will take you to her.'

The corridor outside the row of emergency theatres was lined along each wall with stretchers, and the Brig recognized many of his guests laid out upon them. He stopped briefly to speak with one or two of them, before following Edelman to the recovery room at the end of the corridor.

Debra lay on the tall bed below the window. She was very pale, dry blood was still clotted in her hair and a thick cotton wool and bandage covered her eyes.

'Your father is here, Miss Mordecai,' Edelman told her, and she rolled her head swiftly towards them.

'Daddy?'

'I am here, my child.'

The Brig took the hand she held out, and stooped to kiss her. Her lips were cold, and she smelled strongly of disinfectant and anaesthetic.

'Mama?' she asked anxiously.

'She is out of danger,' the Brig assured her, 'but Hannah—'

'Yes. They told me,' Debra stopped him, her voice choking. 'Is Joe all right?'

'He is strong,' the Brig said. 'He will be all right.'

'David?' she asked.

'He is here.'

Eagerly she struggled up on to one elbow, her face lighting with expectation, the heavily bound eyes turned blindly seeking.

'David,' she called, 'where are you? Damn this bandage. Don't worry, David it's just to rest my eyes.'

'No,' the Brig restrained her with a hand on her arm. 'He is outside, waiting,' and she slumped with disappointment.

'Ask him to come to me, please,' she whispered.

'Yes,' said the Brig, 'in a while, but first there is something we must talk about—something I have to tell you.'

She must have guessed what it was, she must have been warned by the tone of his voice for she went very still. That peculiar stillness of hers, like a frightened animal of the veld.

He was a soldier, with a soldier's blunt ways, and although he tried to soften it, yet even his tone was roughened with his own sorrow, so that it came out brutally. Her hand in his was the only indication that she had heard him, it spasmed convulsively like a wounded thing and then lay still, a small tense hand in the circle of his big bony fist.

She asked no questions and when he had done they sat quietly together for a long time. He spoke first.

'I will send David to you now,' he said, and her response was swift and vehement.

'No.' She gripped his hand hard. 'No, I can't meet him now. I have to think about this first.'

The Brig went back to the waiting-room and David stood up expectantly, the pure lines of his face seemingly carved from pale polished marble, and the dark blue of his eyes in deep contrast.

The Brig forestalled him harshly. 'No visitors.' He took David's arm. 'You will not be allowed to see her until tomorrow.'

'Is something wrong? What is it?' David tried to pull away, but the Brig held him and steered him towards the door.

'Nothing is wrong. She will be all right—but she must have no excitement now. You'll be able to see her tomorrow.'

They buried Hannah that evening in the family plot on the Mountain of Olives. It was a small funeral party attended by the three men and a mere handful of relatives, many of who, had others to mourn from the previous day's slaughter.

There was an official car waiting to take the Brig to a meeting of the high command, where retaliatory measures would certainly be discussed, another revolution in the relentless wheel of violence that rolled across the troubled land.

Joe and David climbed into the Mercedes and sat silently, David making no effort to start the engine, Joe lit cigarettes for them, and they both felt drained of purpose and direction.

'What are you going to do now?' David asked him.

'We had two weeks,' Joe answered him. 'We were going down to Ashkelon–' his voice trailed off. 'I don't know. There isn't anything to do now, is there?'

'Shall we go and have a drink somewhere?'

Joe shook his head. 'I don't feel like drinking,' he said. 'I think I'll go back to the base. They are flying night interceptions tonight.'

'Yes,' David agreed quickly, 'I'll come with you.' He could not see Debra until tomorrow, and the house on Malik Street would be lonely and cold. Suddenly he longed for the peace of the night heavens.

The moon was a brightly curved Saracen blade against the soft darkness of the sky, and the stars were fat and silver and gemlike in their clarity.

They flew high above the earth, remote from its grief and sorrow, wrapped in the isolation of flight and lost in the ritual and concentration of night interception.

The target was a Mirage of their own squadron, and they picked it up on the scanner far out over the Negev. Joe locked on to it and called the track and range while David searched for and at last spotted the moving star of the target's jet blast, burning redly against the velvety blackness of the night.

He took them in on a clean interception creeping up under the target's belly and then pulling steeply up past its wing-tip, the way a barracuda goes for the lure from below and explodes out through the surface of the sea. They shot past so close that the target Mirage broke wildly away to port, unaware of their presence until that moment.

Joe slept that night, exhausted with grief, but David lay in the bunk beneath him and listened to him. In the dawn he rose and showered and left Joe still asleep. He drove into Jerusalem and reached the hospital just as the sun came up and lit the hills with its rays of soft gold and pearly pink.

The night sister at the desk was brusque and preoccupied. 'You shouldn't be here until visiting hours this afternoon,' but David smiled at her with all the charm he could muster.

'I just wanted to know if she was doing well. I have to rejoin my squadron this morning.'

The sister was not immune either to his smile or the airforce uniform, and she went to consult her lists.

'You must be mistaken,' she said at last. 'The only Mordecai we have is Mrs Ruth Mordecai.'

'That's her mother,' David told her, and the sister flipped the sheet on her clipboard.

'No wonder I couldn't find it,' she muttered irritably. 'She was discharged last night.'

'Discharged?' David stared at her uncomprehendingly.

'Yes, she went home last night. I remember her now. Her father came to fetch her just as I came on duty. Pretty girl with eye bandages—'

'Yes,' David nodded. 'Thank you. Thank you very much,' and he ran down the steps to the Mercedes, his feet light with relief, freed at last from the gnawing doubt and dread.

Debra had gone home. Debra was safe and well.

The Brig opened the door to him, and let him into the silent house. He was still in his uniform, and it was wilted and rumpled. The Brig's face was fine-drawn, the lines crudely chiselled around his mouth, and his eyes were swollen and bloodshot from worry and sorrow and lack of sleep.

'Where is Debra?' David demanded eagerly, and the Brig sighed and stood aside for him to enter.

'Where is she?' David repeated, and the Brig led him to his study and waved him to a chair.

'Why don't you answer me?' David was becoming angry, and the Brig slumped into a chair across the large bare room, with its severe monastic furnishings of books and archaeological relics.

'I couldn't tell you yesterday, David, she asked me not to. I'm sorry.'

'What is it?' David was fully alarmed now.

'She had to have time to think—to make up her mind.' The Brig stood up again and began to pace, his footsteps echoing hollowly on the bare wooden floor, pausing every now and then to touch one of the pieces of ancient statuary, caressing it absently as he talked, as though to draw comfort from it.

David listened quietly, occasionally shaking his head, as though to deny that what he was hearing was the truth.

'So you see it is permanent, final, without hope. She is blind, David, totally blind. She has gone into a dark world of her own where nobody else can follow her.'

'Where is she? I want to go to her,' David whispered, but the Brig ignored the request and went on steadily.

'She wanted time to make her decision—and I gave it to her. Last night, after the funeral, I went back to her and she was ready. She had faced it, come to terms with it, and she had decided how it must be.'

'I want to see her,' David repeated. 'I want to talk to her.'

Now the Brig looked at him and the bleakness in his eyes faded, his voice dropped, becoming gruff with compassion.

'No, David. That was her decision. You will not see her again. For you she is dead. Those were her words. Tell him I am dead, but he must only remember me when I was alive—'

David interrupted him, jumping to his feet. 'Where is she, damn you?' His voice was shaking. 'I want to see her now.' He crossed swiftly to the door and jerked it open, but the Brig went on.

'She is not here.'

'Where is she?' David turned back.

'I cannot tell you, I swore a solemn oath to her.'

'I'll find her—'

'You might, if you search carefully—but you will forfeit any respect or love she may have for you,' the Brig went on remorselessly. 'Again I will give you her exact words. "Tell him that I charge him on our love, on all we have ever been to each other, that he will let me be, that he will not come looking for me."'

'Why, but why?' David demanded desperately. 'Why does she reject me?'

'She knows that she is altered beyond all hope or promise. She knows that what was before can never be again. She knows that she can never be to you again what you have a right to expect—' he stopped David's protest with an angry chopping gesture of his hand. 'Listen to me, she knows that it cannot endure. She can never be your wife now. You are too young, too vital, too arrogant—' David stared at him. '—she knows that it will begin to spoil. In a week, a month, a year perhaps, it will have died. You will be trapped, tied to a blind woman. She doesn't want that. She wants it to die now, swiftly—mercifully, not to drag on—'

'Stop it,' David shouted. 'Stop it, damn you. That's enough.' He stumbled to the chair and fell into it. They were silent for a while, David crouched in the chair with his face buried in his hands. The Brig standing before the narrow window casement, the early morning light catching the fierce old warrior's face.

'She asked me to make you promise—' he hesitated, and David looked up at him, '—to promise that you would not try to find her.'

'No.' David shook his head stubbornly.

The Brig sighed. 'If you refused, I was to tell you this—she said you would understand, although I don't—she said that in Africa there is a fierce and beautiful animal called the sable antelope, and sometimes one of them is wounded by a hunter or mauled by a lion.'

The words were as painful as the cut of a whiplash, and David remembered himself saying them to her once when they were both young and strong and invulnerable.

'Very well,' he murmured at last, 'if that's what she wants—then I promise not to try and find her, though I don't promise not to try and convince her she is wrong.'

'Perhaps it would be best if you left Israel,' the Brig told him. 'Perhaps you should go back to where you came from and forget all of this ever happened.'

David paused, considering this a moment, before he answered, 'No, all I have is here. I will stay here.'

'Good.' The Brig accepted the decision. 'You are always welcome in this house.'

'Thank you, sir,' said David and went out to where the Mercedes was parked. He let himself into the house on Malik Street, and saw instantly that someone had been there before him.

He walked slowly into the living-room; the books were gone from the olive-wood table, the Kadesh painting no longer hung over the leather couch. In the bathroom he opened the wall cabinet and all her toilet articles had been removed, the rows of exotic bottles, the tubes and pots, even the slot for her toothbrush beside his was empty.

Her cupboard was bare, the dresses gone, the shelves blank, every trace of her swept away, except the lingering scent of her perfume on the air, and the ivory lace cover upon the bed.

He went to the bed and sat upon it, stroking the fine lacework, remembering how it had been.

There was the hard outline of something thin and square upon the pillow, beneath the cover. He turned back the lace and picked up the thin green book. *This year, in Jerusalem*. It had been left there as a parting gift.

The title swam and went misty before his eyes. It was all he had left of her.

It seemed as though the slaughter at Ein Karem was the signal for a fresh upsurge of hostility and violence throughout the Middle East. A planned escalation of international tensions, as the Arab nations rattled their impressive, oil-purchased, array of weaponry and swore once more to leave not a single Jew in the land they still called Palestine.

There were savage and merciless attacks on soft targets, ill-protected embassies and consulates around the world, letter bombs, and night ambushes on school buses in isolated areas.

Then the provocations grew bolder, more directly aimed at the heart of Israel. Border infringements, commando-style raids, violations of air space, shellings and a threatening gathering and massing of armed might along the long, vulnerable frontiers of the wedge-shaped territories of the tiny land.

The Israelis waited, praying for peace—but girt for war.

Day after day, month after month, David and Joe flew to maintain that degree of expertise, where instinct and instantaneous reaction superseded conscious thought and reasoned action.

At those searing speeds beyond sound, it was only this training that swung the advantage from one combat to another. Even the superior reaction times of these carefully hand-picked young men were unequal to the tasks of bringing their mighty machines into effective action, where latitudes of error were measured in hundredths of a second, until they had attained this extra-sensory perfection.

To seek out, to recognize, to close, to destroy, and to disengage—it was a total preoccupation that blessedly left little time for brooding and sorrow.

Yet the sorrow and anger, that David and Joe shared, seemed doubly to arm them. Their vengeance was all-consuming.

Soon they joined that select half-dozen strike teams that Desert Flower called to undertake the most delicate of sorties. Again and again they were ordered into combat, and each time the confidence that Command had in them was strengthened.

As David sat in his cockpit, dressed from head to foot in the stiff constricting embrace of a full-pressure suit, breathing oxygen from his closed face mask, although the Mirage still crouched upon the ground, there were four black, red and white miniature roundels painted on the fuselage below his cockpit. The scalps of the enemy.

It was a mark of Desert Flower's trust that Bright Lance flight had been selected for high altitude 'Red' standby. With the starter lines plugged ready to blow compressed air into the compressors and whirl the great engines into life, and the ground crew lounging beside the motors, the Mirages were ready to be hurled aloft in a manner of seconds. Both David and Joe were suited to survive the almost pressureless altitudes above sixty thousand feet where an unprotected man's blood would fizzle like champagne.

David had lost count of the weary uncomfortable days and hours he had sat cramped in his cockpit on 'Red' standby with only the regular fifteen-minute checks to break the monotony.

'Checking 11.15 hours—fifteen minutes to stand-down,' David said into the microphone, and heard Joe's breathing in his ears before the reply.

'Two standing by. Beseder.'

Immediately after stand-down, when another crew would assume the arduous waiting of standby, David would change into a track suit and run for five or six miles to get the stiffness out of his body and to have his sweat wash away the staleness. He was looking forward to that, afterwards he would—

There was a sharp crackle in his earphones and a new voice.

'Red standby—Go! Go!'

The command was repeated over loudspeakers in the underground bunker, and the ground crew boiled into action. With all his pre-flight checks and routine long ago completed, David merely pushed his throttle to starting position, and the whine of the starters showed immediate results. The engine caught and he ran up his power to one hundred per cent.

Ahead of him the blast doors were lifting.

'Bright Lance Two, this is leader going to take off power.'

'Two conforming,' said Joe and they went screaming up the ramp and hurled themselves at the sky.

'Hallo, Desert Flower, this is Bright Lance airborne and climbing.'

'Bright Lance, this is the Brig,' David was not surprised to find that he was in charge of command plot. Distinctive voices and the use of personal names would prevent any chance of the enemy confusing the net with false messages. 'David, we have an intruder approach at high level that should enter our air space in four minutes, if it continues on its present course. We are tracking him at seventy-five thousand feet which means it is either an American U.2, which is highly unlikely, or that it is a Russian spy plane coming over to have a look at our latest dispersals.'

'Beseder, sir,' David acked.

'We are going to try for a storm-climb to intercept as soon as the target becomes hostile in our air space.'

'Beseder, sir.'

'Level at twenty thousand feet, turn to 186 and go to maximum speed for storm-climb.'

At twenty thousand, David went to straight and level flight and glanced into his mirror to see Joe's Mirage hanging out on his tail.

'Bright Lance Two, this is leader. Commencing run now.'

'Two conforming.'

David lit his tail and pushed the throttle open to maximum afterburn position. The Mirage jumped away, and David let the nose drop slightly to allow the speed to build up quickly. They went blazing through the sound barrier without a check, and David retrimmed for supersonic flight, thumbing the little top-hat on the end of his stick.

Their speed rocketed swiftly through mach 1·2, mach 1·5.

Their Mirages were stripped of all their essentials, there were no missiles dangling beneath them, no auxiliary fuel tanks to create drag, the only weapons they carried were their two 30 mm. cannons.

Flying lightly, they drove on up the mach scale, streaking from Beersheba to Eilat in the time it would take a man to walk a city block. Their speed stabilized at mach 1·9, just short of the heat barrier.

'David, this is the Brig. We are tracking you. You are on correct course and speed for interception. Prepare to commence climb in sixteen seconds.'

'Beseder, sir.'

'Counting now. Eight, seven, six . . . two, one. Go! Go!'

David tensed his body and as he pulled up the nose of the Mirage, he opened his mouth and screamed to fight off the effects of gravity. But despite these precautions and the constricting grip of his pressure suit, the abrupt change of direction crammed him down into his seat and the blood drained out of his head so that his vision went grey and then black.

The Mirage was standing on her tail flying at very nearly twice the speed of sound and, as his vision returned, David glanced at the G-meter and saw that he had subjected his body to nearly nine times the force of gravity to achieve this attitude of climb without loss of speed.

Now he lay on his back and stared up at the empty sky while the needle of his altimeter raced upwards, and his speed gradually eroded away.

A quick sweep showed Joe's Mirage rock steady in position below him, climbing in concert with him, and his voice came through calm and reassuring.

'Leader, this is Two. I have contact with target.'

Even under the stress of storm-climb, Joe was busy manipulating his beloved radar, and he had picked up the spy plane high above them.

In this manœuvre they were trading speed for height, and as one increased so the other drained away.

They were like a pair of arrows aimed directly upwards. The bowstring could throw them just so far and then they would hang there in space for a few moments, until they were drawn irresistibly back to earth. In those few moments they must find and kill the enemy.

David lay back in his seat and watched with fresh wonder as the sky turned darker blue and then slowly became the midnight black of space, shot through with the fiery prickings of the stars.

They were at the top edge of the stratosphere, high above the highest clouds or signs of weather as known to earth. Outside the cockpit the air was thin and weak, insufficient for life, hardly sufficient to keep the jets of the Mirage's engines burning—and the cold was a fearsome sixty degrees of frost.

The two aircraft slowly ran out of energy, and they came out together at the top of a mighty parabola. The sensation of flight was gone, they swam through the dark forbidding oceans of space and far below them the earth glowed strangely, with a weird unnatural light.

There was no time to admire the view, the Mirage was wallowing in the thin and treacherous air, her control surfaces skidding and sliding without bite.

Joe was on the target, tracking quietly and steadily and they came round carefully on to the heading, with the aircraft staggering mushily and beginning to fall away from these inhospitable heights.

David stared ahead, holding the Mirage's nose up for sustained altitude but already the stall warning device was flicking amber and red at him. He was running out of time and height.

Then suddenly he saw it, seeming startlingly close in the rare air, ghosting along on its immense wings, like a black manta-ray through the sable and silent sea of space—ahead and slightly below them—calmly and silently, it drifted along, its height giving it a false sense of invulnerability.

'Desert Flower, this is Bright Lance visual on the intruder and requesting permission for strike.' David's cool tone hid the sudden gust of his anger and hatred that the sighting had released.

'Report your target,' the Brig was hedging, it was a dangerous decision to call the strike on an unknown target.

'Desert Flower, it's an Ilyushin Mark 17-11. No apparent markings.'

It needed no markings, it could only belong to one nation. David was closing fast, he could fly no slower than this, and he was rapidly overhauling the other machine. Those huge wings were designed to float upon the feeble air of the stratosphere.

'Closing fast,' he warned Desert Flower. 'Opportunity for strike will pass in approximately ten seconds.'

The silence in his headphones hummed quickly, and he readied his cannons and watched the spy plane blowing up rapidly in size as he dropped down upon it.

Suddenly the Brig made the decision, perhaps committing his country to heavy retaliation, but knowing that the spy plane's cameras were steadily recording vital details of their ability to resist aggression, information that would be passed quickly to their enemies.

'David,' his voice was curt and harsh, 'this is the Brig. Hit him!'

'Beseder.' David let the Mirage's nose drop a fraction, and she responded gratefully.

'Two, this is leader attacking.'

'Two conforming.'

He went down on the Ilyushin so fast, that as she came into his sights he knew he had time for only a few seconds of fire.

He pressed the trigger with the aiming pipper on the spy plane's wing roots, and he saw her rear up like a great fish struck by the steel of the harpoon.

For three seconds he poured his cannon shells into her, and watched them flash and twinkle against the massive black silhouette. Then he was through, falling away below the giant's belly, with his power spent, dropping away like the burned-out shell of a rocket.

Joe came down astern of him, backing up the attack, and in his sights the spy plane hung helplessly on its wide wings, its long rounded nose pointing to the black sky with its cold uncaring stars.

He pressed the trigger and the plane broke up amidst the bright flashes of exploding cannon shells. One wing snapped off at its root and the carcass began its long slow tumble down the heavens.

'Hello, Desert Flower, this is Bright Lance leader. Target destroyed.' David tried to keep his voice level, but he found his hands were trembling and his guts were aching cold from the spill-over of his hatred that not even the enemy's death could expunge.

Again he pressed the button to open the flight net. 'Joe, that's one more for

Hannah,' he said, but for once there was no reply, and after he had listened in vain to the throb of the carrier beam for a few seconds he closed it, and activated his doppler gear for a homing signal, and silently Joe followed him back to base.

Debra had been a steadying and maturing influence, but now David reacted so wildly to her going that Joe had to continue his role of wing man, even when they were off base.

They spent much of their leisure time together, for although they seldom mentioned their loss, yet the sharing of it drew them closer.

Often Joe slept over at Malik Street, for his own home was a sad and depressing place now. The Brig was seldom there in these troubled times, Debra gone and his mother was so altered by her terrible experience that she was grey and broken, aged beyond her years. The bullet wound in her body had closed, but there was other damage that would never heal.

David's wildness was a craving for the forgetfulness of constant action. He was only truly at peace when he was in the air, and on the ground he was restless and mercurial. Joe moved, big and calm beside him, steering him tactfully out of trouble with a slow grin and an easy word.

As a consequence of the downed spy plane, the Syrians began a policy of provocative patrols, calculated infringement of Israeli air space, which was discontinued as soon as retaliation was drawn. As the interceptors raced to engage they would swing away, declining combat, and move back within their own borders.

Twice David saw the greenish luminous blur of these hostile patrols on the screen of his scanning radar, and each time he had surprised himself with the icy feeling of anger and hatred that had lain heavy as a rock upon his heart and lungs as he led Joe in on the interception. Each time, however, the Syrians had been warned by their own radar and they had turned away, increasing speed, and withdrawn discreetly and mockingly.

'Bright Lance, this is Desert Flower. Target is no longer hostile. Discontinue attack pattern.' The Syrian MIG21's had crossed their own frontier, and each time David had answered quietly, 'Two, this is leader. Discontinuing attack pattern and resuming scan.'

The tactics were designed to wear on the nerves of the defenders, and in all the interceptor squadrons the tension was becoming explosive. The provocation was pushing them to the edge of restraint. Incidents were only narrowly being averted, as the hot-bloods crowded their interceptions to the very frontiers of war. Finally, however, there had to come intervention from above as Desert Flower tried to hold them on a tighter leash. They sent the Brig to talk to his crews and as he stood on the dais and looked about the crowded briefing room, he realized that it was unfair to train the hawk and then keep the hood over his eyes and the thong upon his leg, to hold him upon the wrist, when the wild duck were flighting overhead.

He started at a philosophical level, taking advantage of the regard that he knew his young pilots had for him.

'—the object of war is peace, the ultimate strategy of any commander is peace—' There was no response from his audience. The Brig caught the level scrutiny of his own son. How could he talk of placation to a trained warrior who had just buried the mutilated body of his bride? The Brig ploughed on manfully.

'Only a fool allows himself to be drawn on to a field of the enemy's choosing,' he was reaching them now, 'I won't have one of you young pups pushing us into something we are not ready for. I don't want to give them an excuse. That is what they want—' They were thawing now, he saw a head nod thoughtfully and heard a murmur of agreement.

'Any of you looking for big trouble, you don't have to go to Damascus, you know my address,' he tried for his first laugh, and got it. They were chuckling now. 'All right, then. We don't want trouble. We are going to lean right over backwards to prevent it—but we are not going to fall on our arses. When the time comes, I'll give you the word and it won't be the soft word, or the other cheek—' they growled then, a fierce little sound, and he ended it, '—but you wait for that word.'

Le Dauphin stood up and took over from the Brig.

'All right, while I've got you all together, I've a little news for you that may help to cool the hot-heads who want to follow the MIGs over the border.' He motioned to the projection box at the end of the briefing-room, the lights went down and there was a shuffling of feet, and an outburst of coughing. A voice protested resignedly.

'Not *another* film show!'

'Yes,' the colonel took it up. '*Another* film show.' Then as the images began to flash upon the screen he went on, 'This is a military intelligence film, and the subject is a new ground-to-air missile system that has been delivered by the Soviet Army to the armies of the Arab Union. The code name for the system is "Serpent" and it updates the existing "Sam III" system. As far as we know, the system has been installed and is operative in the Syrian defensive perimeter, and will shortly be installed by the Egyptians. It is manned at present by Russian instructors.' As the colonel went on talking, the Brig sat back in his chair and watched their faces in the silver reflection from the screen. They were intent and serious, men looking for the first time on the terrible machines that might be the instrument of their own deaths.

'The missile is fired from a tracked vehicle. Here you see aerial reconnaissance shots of a mobile column. Notice that each vehicle carries a pair of missiles, and you will realize that they constitute an enormous threat—'

The Brig picked out the marvellously pure profile of David Morgan as he leaned forward to study the screen, and he felt a pang of sympathy and sorrow for him—and yet this was underlined by a new respect, a realignment of judgement. The boy had proved himself to be constant, capable of embracing an ideal and remaining loyal to it.

'The improvements in design of the "Serpent" are not certain, but it is believed that the missile is capable of greater speeds, probably in the order of mach 2·5, and that the guidance system is a combination of both infra-red heat seeker and computerized radar control.'

Watching the handsome young face, he wondered if Debra had not misjudged his reserves. It was possible that he would have been capable of—no, the Brig shook his head and groped for a cigarette. He was too young, too greedy for life, spoiled by good looks and riches. He would not be capable of it. Debra was right, as so often was the case. She had chosen the correct course. She could never hold him, she must set him free.

'It is expected that the "Serpent" is capable of engaging targets at altitudes between 1,500 ft. and 75,000 ft.'

There was a stir amongst the listeners, as they assessed the threat of this new weapon.

'The warhead delivers a quarter of a ton of explosive and it is armed with a proximity fuse which is set to fire if the target is passed at range less than 150 feet. Within these limits the "Serpent" is lethal.'

The Brig was still watching David. Ruth and he had not seen the boy at their home for many months. He had come with Joe to spend the Sabbath evening with them twice after the outrage. However, the atmosphere had been stiff and artificial, everybody carefully avoiding mention of Debra's name. He had not come again after the second time, nearly six months ago.

'Evasive tactics at this stage will be the same as for "Sam III".'

'Prayer and good luck!' Someone interjected and that raised a laugh.

'–a maximum-rate turn towards the missile, to screen the radiation from your jet blasts, and attempt to force the "Serpent" to overshoot. In the event that the missile continues to track, you should climb into the sun and then make another maximum-rate turn. The missile may then accept the sun's infra-red radiation as a more tempting target–'

'And if that doesn't work?' a voice called, and another answered flippantly, 'Repeat the following: "Hear O Israel, the Lord our God, the Lord is one."' But this time nobody laughed at the old blasphemy.

The Brig timed his departure from the briefing room to fall in beside David.

'When are we going to see you, David? It's been a long time.'

'I'm sorry, sir. I hope Joe made my apologies.'

'Yes, of course. But why don't you come with Joe this evening? God knows, there will be enough food.'

'I'll be very busy tonight, sir,' David declined lamely.

'I understand.' And as they reached the door of the O.C.'s office the Brig paused, 'Remember you are always welcome,' and he turned away.

'Sir!' the Brig stopped and looked back at him. David spoke rapidly–almost guiltily.

'How is she, sir?' and then again, 'how is Debra? Have you seen her–I mean, recently?'

'She is well,' the Brig answered heavily. 'As well as she can be.'

'Will you tell her I asked?'

'No,' answered the Brig, ignoring the pleading in the dark blue eyes. 'No. You know I can't do that.'

David nodded and turned away. For a moment the Brig looked after him and then with a frown he went on into the colonel's office.

David dropped Joe in Ein Karem, at the entrance to the lane, and then he drove on into the main shopping area of East Jerusalem and parked outside the big new supermarket in Melech George V to do his shopping for the weekend ahead.

He was hanging over the freezer tray pondering the delicate choice between lamb cutlets and steak, when he became aware that he was being watched.

David looked up quickly and saw that she was a statuesque woman with a thick mane of blonde curls. She stood beside the shelves farther down the aisle. Her hair was dyed, he could see the dark shadow of the roots, and she was older than he was, with a womanly heaviness in her hips and bosom and tiny lines at the corners of her eyes. She was eyeing him, a steady appraisal so unashamedly sensual that he felt the check in his breathing and the quick stirring of his loins. He looked back at the meat in the freezer, guilty and angry with the treachery of his body. It had been so long, so very long since he had experienced sexual awareness. He had believed that he never would again. He wanted to throw the pack of steak back into the freezer and leave, but he stood rooted with the breathless feeling squeezing his lungs, and he was aware of the woman's presence at his side. He could feel the warmth of her on his arm, and smell her–the flowery perfume mingled with the natural musky odour of the sexually aroused female.

'The steak is very good,' she said. She had a light sweet voice and he recognized the same breathless quality as his own. He looked at her. Her eyes were green, and her teeth were a little crooked but white. She was even older than he had thought, almost forty. She wore her dress low in front, he could see the crêpe effect of the skin between her breasts. The breasts were big and motherly, and suddenly David wanted to lay his head against them. They looked so soft and warm and safe.

'You should cook it rare, with mushrooms and garlic and red wine,' she said. 'It's very good that way.'

'Is it?' he asked hoarsely.

'Yes,' she nodded, smiling. 'Who will cook it for you? Your wife? Your mother?'

'No,' said David. 'I will cook it myself. I live alone,' and she leaned a little closer to him, her breast touching his arm.

David was dizzy and hot with the brandy. He had bought a bottle of it at the supermarket, and he had drunk it mixed with ginger ale to mask the spiritous taste. He had drunk it fast, and now he leaned over the basin in the bathroom and felt the house rock and sway about him. He steadied himself, gripping the edge of the basin.

He splashed cold water on to his face and shook off the drops, then he grinned stupidly at himself in the mirror above the basin. His hair was damp and hung on to his forehead; he closed one eye and the wavering image in the mirror hardened and squinted back at him.

'Hi there, boy,' he muttered and reached for the towel. He had dripped water down his tunic and this annoyed him. He threw the towel over the toilet seat and went back into the living-room.

The woman was gone. The leather couch still carried the indentation of her backside, and the dirty plates were on the olive-wood table. The air was thick with cigarette smoke and her perfume.

'Where are you?' he called thickly, swaying slightly in the doorway.

'Here, big boy.' He went to the bedroom. She lay on the bed, naked, plump and white with huge soft breasts and swelling belly. He stared at her.

'Come on, Davey.' Her clothing was thrown across the dressing-table, and he saw that her corsets were grey and unwashed. Her hair was yellow against the soft ivory lacework.

'Come to Mama,' she whispered hoarsely, opening her limbs languidly in invitation. She was spread upon the brass bed, upon the lace cover which had been Debra's–and David felt his anger surge within him.

'Get up,' he said, slurring the words.

'Come on, baby.'

'Get off that bed,' his voice tightened and she heard the tone and sat up with mild alarm.

'What is it, Davey?'

'Get out of here,' his voice was rising sharply. 'Get out, you bitch. Get out of here!' He was shaking now, his face pale and his eyes savage blue.

Quivering with panic, she climbed hurriedly from the bed, the great white breasts and buttocks wobbling with ridiculous haste as she stuffed them into the grey corset.

When she had gone, David went through into the bedroom and vomited into the toilet bowl. Then he cleaned the house, scouring pans and plates, polishing the glasses until they shone, emptying the ashtrays, opening the shutters to blow out the stench of cigarette and perfume—and finally, going through into the bedroom, he stripped and remade the bed with fresh sheets and smoothed the lace cover carefully until not a crease or wrinkle showed.

He put on a clean tunic and his uniform cap, and drove to the Jaffa gate. He parked the car in the lot outside the gate and walked through the old city to the reconstructed sephardic synagogue in the Jewish quarter.

It was very quiet and peaceful in the high-domed hall and he sat a long time on the hard wooden bench.

Joe sat opposite David with a worried expression creasing his deep forehead as he studied the board. Three or four of the other pilots had hiked their chairs up and were concentrating on the game also. These chessboard conflicts between David and Joe were usually epics and attracted a partisan audience.

David had been stalking Joe's rook for half a dozen moves and now he had it trapped. Two more moves would shatter the kingsize defence, and the third must force a resignation. David grinned smugly as Joe reached a decision and moved a knight out.

'That's not going to save you, dear boy,' David hardly glanced at the knight, and he hit the rook with a white bishop. 'Mate in five,' he predicted, as he dropped the castle into the box, and then—too late—he realized that Joe's theatrical expression of anguish had slowly faded into a beatific grin. Joseph Mordecai used any deception to bait his traps, and David looked with alarm at the innocuous-seeming knight, suddenly seeing the devious plotting in which the castle was merely bait.

'Oh, you bastard,' David moaned. 'you sneaky bastard.'

'Check!' Joe gloated as he put the knight into a forked attack, and David had to leave his queen exposed to the horseman.

'Check,' said Joe again with an ecstatic little sigh as he lifted the white queen off the board, and again the harassed king took the only escape route open to him.

'And mate,' sighed Joe again as his own queen left the back file to join the attack. 'Not in five, as you predicted, but in three.' There was a loud outburst of congratulation and applause from the onlookers and Joe cocked an eye at David.

'Again?' he said, and David shook his head.

'Take on one of these other patsies,' he said. 'I'm going to sulk for an hour.' He vacated his seat and it was filled by another eager victim as Joe reset the board. David crossed to the coffee machine, moving awkwardly in the grip of his G-suit, and drew a mug of the thick black liquid, stirred in four spoons of sugar and found another seat in a quieter corner of the crewroom beside a slim curly-headed young kibbutznik, with whom David had become friendly. He was reading a thick novel.

'*Shalom*, Robert. How you been?'

Robert grunted without looking up from his book, and David sipped the sweet hot coffee. Beside him, Robert moved restlessly in his seat and coughed softly, David was lost in his own thoughts, for the first time in months thinking of home, wondering about Mitzi and Barney Venter, wondering if the yellowtail were running hot in False Bay this season, and remembering how the proteas looked upon the mountains of the Helderberg.

Again Robert stirred in his chair and cleared his throat. David glanced at him, realizing that he was in the grip of a deep emotion as he read, his lips quivering, and his eyes too bright.

'What you reading?' David was amused, and he leaned forward to read the title. The picture on the dust jacket of the book was instantly familiar. It was a deeply felt desert landscape of fierce colours and great space. Two distant figures, man and woman, walked hand in hand through the desert and the effect was mystic and haunting. David realized that only one person could have painted that—Ella Kadesh.

Robert lowered the book. 'This is uncanny,' his voice was muffled with emotion. 'I tell you, Davey, it's beautiful. It must be one of the most beautiful books ever written.'

With a strange feeling of pre-knowledge, with a sense of complete certainty, of what it would be, David took the book out of his hands and turned it to read the title, *A Place of Our Own.*

Robert was still talking. 'My sister made me read it. She works for the publisher. She cried all night when she read it. It is very new, only published last week, but it's got to be the biggest book ever written about this country.'

David hardly heard him, he was staring at the writer's name in small print below the title.

'Debra Mordecai.'

He ran his fingers lightly over the glossy paper of the jacket, stroking the name.

'I want to read it,' he said softly.

'I'll let you have it when I'm finished,' Robert promised.

'I want to read it now!'

'No way!' Robert exclaimed with evident alarm, and almost snatched the book out of David's hands.

'You wait your turn, comrade!'

David looked up. Joe was watching him from across the room, and David glared at him accusingly. Joe dropped his eyes quickly to the chessboard again, and David realized that he had known of the publication. He started up to go to him, to challenge him, but at that moment the tannoy echoed through the bunker.

'All flights Lance Squadron to "Red" standby,' and on the readiness board the red lamps lit beside the flight designations.

'Bright Lance.'

'Red Lance.'

'Fire Lance.'

David snatched up his flying helmet and joined the lumbering rush of G-suited bodies for the electric personnel carrier in the concrete tunnel outside the crew-room door. He forced a place for himself beside Joe.

'Why didn't you tell me?' he demanded.

'I was going to, Davey. I really was.'

'Yeah, I bet,' David snapped sarcastically. 'Have you read it?'

Joe nodded, and David went on, 'What's it about?'

'I couldn't begin to tell you. You'd have to read it yourself.'

'Don't worry about that,' David muttered grimly, 'I will,' and he jumped down as they reached their hangar and strode across to his Mirage.

Twenty minutes later they were airborne and Desert Flower sent them hastening out over the Mediterranean at interception speed to answer a Mayday call from an El Al Caravelle who reported that she was being buzzed by an Egyptian MIG 21 J.

The Egyptian sheered off and raced for the coast and the protection of his own missile batteries as the Mirages approached. They let him go and picked up the airliner. They escorted her into the circuit over Lod before returning to base.

Still in his G-suit and overalls, David stopped off at le Dauphin's office and got himself a twenty-four-hour pass.

Ten minutes before closing time he ran into one of the bookstores in Jaffa Road.

There was a pyramid display of *A Place of Our Own* on the table in the centre of the store.

'It's a beautiful book,' said the salesgirl as she wrapped it.

He opened a Goldstar, and he kicked off his shoes before stretching out on the lace cover of the bed.

He began to read, and paused only once to switch on the overhead lights and fetch another beer. It was a thick book, and he read slowly—savouring every word, sometimes going back to re-read a paragraph.

It was their story, his and Debra's, woven into the plot she had described to him that day on the island off the Costa Brava, and it was rich with the feeling of the land and its people. He recognized many of the secondary characters, and he laughed aloud with the pleasure and the joy of it. Then at the end, he choked on the sadness as the girl of the story lies dying in Hadassah Hospital, with half her face torn away by a terrorist's bomb, and she will not let the boy come to her. Wanting to spare him that, wanting him to remember her as she was.

It was dawn then, and David had not noticed the passage of the night. He rose from the bed, light-headed from lack of sleep, and filled with a sense of wonder that Debra had captured so clearly the way it had been—that she had seen so deeply into his soul, had described emotions for which he had believed there were no words.

He bathed and shaved and dressed in casual clothes and went back to where the book lay upon the bed. He studied the jacket again, and then turned to the flyleaf for confirmation. It was there. 'Jacket design by Ella Kadesh.'

So early in the morning he had the road almost to himself and he drove fast, into the rising morning sun. At Jericho he turned north along the frontier road, and he remembered her sitting in the seat beside him with her skirts drawn high around her long brown legs and her thick dark hair shaking in the wind.

The whisper of the wind against the body of the Mercedes seemed to urge him, 'Hurry, hurry.' And the urgent drumming of the tyres carried him up towards the lake.

He parked the Mercedes beside the ancient crusader wall and went through into the garden on the lake shore.

Ella sat upon the wide patio before her easel. She wore a huge straw hat the size of a wagon wheel adorned with plastic cherries and ostrich feathers, her vast overalls covered her like a circus tent and they were stiff with dried paint in all her typically vivid colours.

Calmly she looked up from her painting with her brush poised.

'Hail, young Mars!' she greeted him. 'Well met indeed, and why do you bring such honour on my humble little home?'

'Piss on it, Ella, you know damn well why I'm here.'

'So sweetly phrased,' she was shifty, he could see it in her bright little eyes. 'Shame on it that such vulgar words pass such fair lips. Would you like a beer, Davey?'

'No, I don't want a beer. I want to know where she is?'

'Just who are we discussing?'

'Come on, I read the book. I saw the cover. You know, damn you, you know.'

She was silent then staring at him. Then slowly the ornate head-dress dipped in acquiescence.

'Yes,' she agreed. 'I know.'

'Tell me where she is.'

'I can't do that, Davey. You and I both made a promise. Yes, I know of yours, you see.'

She watched the bluster go out of him. The fine young body with the arrogant set of shoulders seemed to sag, and he stood uncertainly in the sunlight.

'How about that beer now, Davey?' She heaved herself up from her stool and crossed the terrace with her stately tread. She came back and gave him a tall glass with a head of froth and they took a seat together at the end of the terrace out of the wind, in the mild winter sunlight.

'I've been expecting you for a week now,' she told him. 'Ever since the book was published. I knew it would set you on fire. It's just too damned explosive—even I wept like a leaky faucet for a couple of days,' she giggled shyly. 'You'd hardly believe it possible, would you?'

'That book was us—Debra and me,' David told her. 'She was writing about us.'

'Yes,' Ella agreed, 'but it does not alter the decision she has made. A decision which I think is correct, by the way.'

'She described exactly how I felt, Ella. All the things I felt and still feel—but which I could never have put into words.'

'It's beautiful and it's true, but don't you see that it confirms her position.'

'But I love her, Ella—and she loves me,' he cried out violently.

'She wants it to stay that way. She doesn't want it to die, she doesn't want it to sicken.' He began to protest, but she gripped his arm in a surprisingly powerful grip to silence him. 'She knows that she can never keep pace with you now. Look at you, David, you are beautiful and vital and swift—she must drag you back, and in time you must as certainly resent it.'

Again he tried to interrupt, but she shook his arm in her huge fist. 'You would be shackled, you could never leave her, she is helpless, she would be your charge for all your life—think on it, David.'

'I want her,' he muttered stubbornly. 'I had nothing before I met her, and I have nothing now.'

'That will change. Perhaps she has taught you something and young emotions heal as swiftly as young flesh. She wants happiness for you, David. She loves you so much that her gift to you is freedom. She loves you so much that for your sake she will deny that love.'

'Oh, God,' he groaned. 'If only I could see her, if I could touch her and talk to her for a few minutes.'

She shook her massive head, and her jowls wobbled dolefully.

'She would not agree to that.'

'Why, Ella, tell me why?' His voice was rising again, desperate with his anguish.

'She is not strong enough, she knows that if you came near her, she would waver and bring even greater disaster upon you both.'

They sat silently together then and looked out across the lake. High mountains of cloud rose up beyond the heights of Golan, brilliant white in the winter sunlight, shaded with blue and bruised grey, and range upon range they bore down upon the lake. David shivered as an icy little wind came ferreting across the terrace and sought them out.

He drank the rest of his beer, and then revolved the glass slowly through his fingers.

'Will you give her a message from me, then?' he asked.

'I don't think—'

'Please, Ella. Just one message.'

She nodded.

'Tell her that what she wrote in the book is exactly how much I love her. Tell her that it is big enough to rise above this thing. Tell her that I want the chance to try.'

She listened quietly, and David made a groping gesture with his hands as though to pluck words from the air that might convince her.

'Tell her—' he paused, then shook his head. 'No, that's all. Just tell her that I love her, and want to be with her.'

'All right, David. I'll tell her.'

'And you will give me her answer?'

'Where can I reach you?'

He gave her the number of the telephone in the crew ready room at the base.

'You'll ring me soon, Ella? Don't keep me waiting.'

'Tomorrow,' she promised. 'In the morning.'

'Before ten o'clock. It must be before ten.'

He stood up, and then suddenly he leaned forward and kissed her sagging and raddled cheek.

'Thank you,' he said. 'You are not a bad old bag.'

'Away with you, you and your blarney. You'd have the sirens of the Odyssey themselves come arunning to your bidding.' She sniffed moistly. 'Get away with you now, I think I'm going to cry, and I want to be alone to enjoy it.'

She watched him go up across the lawns under the date palms and at the gate in the wall he paused and looked back. For a second they stared at each other and then he stepped through the gate.

She heard the engine of the Mercedes whirr and pull away slowly up the track, then the note of it rose as it hit the highway and went racing away southwards. Ella rose heavily and crossed the terrace, went down the steps towards the jetty and its stone boathouses screened from the house by part of the ancient wall.

Her speedboat rode at its mooring, restless in the wind and the chop of the lake. She went on down to the farthest and largest of the boathouses and stood in the open doorway.

The interior had been stripped and repainted with clean white. The furniture was simple and functional. The rugs on the stone floor were for warmth, plain woven wool, thick and rough. The large bed was built into a curtained alcove in the wall beside the fireplace.

On the opposite wall was a gas stove with a double cooking ring above which a number of copper cooking pots hung. A door beyond led through to a bathroom and toilet which Ella had added very recently.

The only decoration was the Ella Kadesh painting from the house on Malik Street, which hung on the bare white wall, facing the door. It seemed to lighten and warm the whole room; below it the girl sat at a working table. She was listening intently to her own voice speaking in Hebrew from the tape recorder. Her expression was rapt and intent, and she stared at the blank wall before her.

Then she nodded her head, smiling at what she had just heard. She switched off the recorder and turned in the swivel chair to the second recorder and punched the transmit button. She held the microphone close to her lips as she began to translate the Hebrew into English.

Ella stood in the doorway and watched her work. An American publisher had purchased the English-language rights of *A Place of Our Own*. They had paid Debra an advance of thirty thousand American dollars for the book, and an additional five thousand for her services as translator. She had almost completed the task now.

From where she stood, Ella could see the scar on Debra's temple. It was glazed pinkish white against the deeply tanned skin of her face, a dimple like a child's drawing of a seagull in flight; V-shaped and no bigger than a snowflake, it seemed to enhance her fine looks, almost like a beauty spot, a tiny blemish that gave a focus point for her strong regular features.

She had made no attempt to conceal it for her dark hair was drawn back to the nape of her neck and secured there with a leather thong. She wore no make-up, and her skin looked clean and glowing, tanned and smooth.

Despite the bulky fisherman's jersey and woollen slacks her body appeared firm and slim for she swam each day, even when the snow winds came down from the north.

Ella left the doorway and moved silently closer to the desk, studying Debra's eyes as she so often did. One day she would paint that expression. There was no hint of the damage that lay behind, no hint that the eyes could not see. Rather their calm level gaze seemed to penetrate deeper, to see all. They had a serenity that was almost mystic, a depth and understanding that Ella found strangely disquieting.

Debra pressed the switch of the microphone, ending the recording, and then she spoke again without turning her head.

'Is that you, Ella?'

'How do you do it?' Ella demanded with astonishment.

'I felt the air move when you walked in, and then I smelt you.'

'I'm big enough to blow up a storm, but do I smell so bad?' Ella protested, chuckling.

'You smell of turpentine, and garlic and beer,' Debra sniffed, and laughed with her.

'I've been painting, and I was chopping garlic for the roast, and I was drinking beer with a friend.' Ella dropped into one of the chairs. 'How does it go with the book?'

'Nearly finished. It can go to the typist tomorrow. Do you want some coffee?' Debra stood up and crossed to the gas stove. Ella knew better than to offer her help, even though she gritted her teeth every time she watched Debra working with fire and boiling water. The girl was fiercely independent, utterly determined to live her life without other people's pity or assistance.

The room was laid out precisely, each item in its place where Debra could put her hand to it without hesitation. She could move confidently through her little world, doing her own house-work, preparing her own food and drink, working steadily, and paying her own way.

Once a week, a driver came up from her publisher's office in Jerusalem to collect her tapes and her writing was typed out along with her other correspondence.

Weekly also she would go with Ella in the speedboat up the lake to Tiberias to do their shopping together, and each day she swam for an hour from the stone jetty. Often an old fisherman with whom she had become friendly would row down the lake to fetch her and she would go out with him, baiting her own lines and taking her turn at the oars.

Across the lawns from the jetty, in the crusader castle, there was always Ella's companionship and intelligent conversation—and here in her little cottage there was quietness and safety and work to fill the long hours. And in the night there was the chill of terrible aloneness and silent bitter tears into her solitary pillow, tears which only she knew about.

Debra placed a mug of coffee beside Ella's chair and carried her own back to her work bench.

'Now,' she said, 'you can tell me what is keeping you fidgeting around in your seat, and drumming your fingers on the arm of the chair,' she smiled towards Ella, sensing the surprise. 'You have got something to tell me, and it's killing you.'

'Yes,' Ella spoke after a moment. 'Yes, you are right, my dear.' She took a deep breath and then went on. 'He came, Debra. He came to see me, as we knew he must.'

Debra set the mug down on the table, her hand was steady and her face expressionless.

'I didn't tell him where you were.'

'How is he, Ella? How does he look?'

'He is thinner, a little thinner, I think, and paler than when I last saw him, but it suits him. He is still the most beautiful man I have ever seen.'

'His hair,' Debra asked, 'has he let it grow a little?'

'Yes, I think so. It's soft and dark and thick around his ears and curly down the back.'

Debra nodded, smiling. 'I'm glad he didn't cut it.' They were silent again, and then almost timidly Debra asked, 'What did he say? What did he want?'

'He had a message for you.'

'What was it?'

And Ella repeated it faithfully in his exact words. When she had finished, Debra turned away to face the wall above her desk.

'Please go away now, Ella. I want to be alone.'

'He asked me to give him your reply. I promised to speak to him tomorrow morning.'

'I will come to you later—but please leave me now.' And Ella saw the drop of bright liquid that slid down the smooth brown curve of her cheek.

Mountainously Ella came to her feet and moved towards the door. Behind her she heard the girl sob, but she did not turn back. She went across the stone jetty and up to the terrace. She sat before her canvas and picked up her brush and began to paint. Her strokes were broad and crude and angry.

David was sweating in the stiff shiny skin of his full pressure suit and he waited anxiously beside the telephone, glancing every few minutes at the crew-room clock.

He and Joe would go on high-altitude 'Red' standby at ten o'clock, in seven minutes' time, and Ella had not called him.

David's depression was thunderous and there was black anger and despair in his heart. She had promised to call before ten o'clock.

'Come on, Davey,' Joe called from the doorway and he stood up heavily and followed Joe to the electric carrier. As he took his seat beside Joe he heard it ring in the crew-room.

'Hold it,' he told the driver, and he saw Robert answer the telephone and wave through the glass panel at him.

'It's for you, Davey,' and he ran back into the crew-room.

'I'm sorry, David,' Ella's voice was scratchy and far away. 'I tried earlier but the exchange here—'

'Sure, sure,' David cut her short, his anger was still strong. 'Did you speak to her?'

'Yes, Davey. Yes, I did. I gave her your message.'

'What was her reply?' he demanded.

'There was no reply.'

'What the hell, Ella. She must have said something.'

'She said—' Ella hesitated, '—and these are her exact words—"the dead cannot speak with the living. For David, I died a year ago."'

He held the receiver with both hands but still it shook. After a while she spoke again.

'Are you still there?'

'Yes,' he whispered, 'I'm still here.'

They were silent again, but David broke it at last.

'That's it, then,' he said.

'Yes. I'm afraid that's it, Davey.'

Joe stuck his head around the door.

'Hey, Davey. Cut it short, will you. Time to go.'

'I have to go now, Ella. Thanks for everything.'

'Goodbye, David,' she said, and even over the scratchy connection he could hear the compassion in her tone. It heightened the black anger that gripped him as he rode beside Joe to the Mirage bunker.

For the first time ever, David felt uncomfortable in the cockpit of a Mirage. He felt trapped and restless, sweating and angry, and it seemed hours between each of the fifteen-minute readiness checks.

His ground crew were playing backgammon on the concrete floor below him, and he could see them laughing and joshing each other. It made him angrier than ever to see others happy.

'Tubby!' he barked in to the microphone, and his voice was repeated by the overhead loudspeakers. The plump, serious young man, who was chief engineer for Lance squadron, climbed quickly up beside his cockpit and peered anxiously through the canopy at him.

'There is dirt on my screen,' David snapped at him. 'How the hell do you expect me to pick up a MIG, when I'm looking through a screen you ate your bloody breakfast off?'

The cause of David's distress was a speck of carbon that marred the glistening perfection of his canopy. Tubby himself had supervised the polishing and buffing of it, and the carbon speck was wind-carried since then. Carefully he removed the offending spot, and lovingly he polished the place where it had been with a chamois leather.

The reprimand had been public and unfair, very unlike their top boy Davey. However, they all made allowances for 'Red' standby nerves–and spots on a canopy played hell with a pilot's nerves. Every time it caught his eye it looked exactly like a pouncing MIG.

'That's better,' David gruffed at him, fully aware that he had been grossly unfair. Tubby grinned and gave a high sign as he climbed down.

At that moment there was a click and throb in his earphones and the distinctive voice of the Brig.

'"Red" standby–Go! Go!'

Under full reheat and with the driving thrust of the after-burners hurling him aloft David called, 'Hello, Desert Flower, Bright Lance airborne and climbing.'

'Hello, David, this is the Brig. We have a contact shaping up for intrusion on our air space. It looks like another teaser from the Syrians. They are closing our border at twenty-six thousand and should be hostile in approximately three minutes. We are going to initiate attack plan Gideon. Your new heading is 42° and I want you right down on the deck.'

David acked and immediately rotated the Mirage's nose downwards. Plan Gideon called for a low-level stalk so that the ground clutter would obscure the enemy radar and conceal their approach until such time as they were in position to storm-climb up into an attack vector above and behind the target.

They dropped to within feet of the ground, lifting and falling over the undulating hills, so low that the herds of black Persian sheep scattered beneath them as they shrieked eastwards towards the Jordan.

'Hello, Bright Lance, this is Desert Flower–we are not tracking you.' Good, thought David, then neither is the enemy. 'Target is now hostile in sector'–the Brig gave the co-ordinates–'Scan for your own contact.'

Almost immediately Joe's voice came in. 'Leader, this is Two. I have a contact.'

David dropped his eyes to his own radar screen and manipulated his scan as Joe called range and bearing. It was a dangerous distraction when flying in the sticky phase of high subsonic drag at zero feet, and his own screen was clear of contact.

They raced onwards for many more seconds before David picked up the faint luminous fuzz at the extreme range of his set.

'Contact firming. Range figures nine six nautical miles. Parallel heading and track. Altitude 25,500 feet.'

David felt the first familiar tingle and slither of his anger and hatred, like the cold of a great snake uncoiling in his belly.

'Beseder, Two. Lock to target and go to interception speed.'

They went supersonic and David looked up ahead at the crests of the thunderheads that reared up from the solid banks of cumulo nimbus lower down. These mountainous upthrusts of silver and pale blue were sculptured into wonderful shapes that teased the imagination–towers and turrets embattled and emblazoned, heroic human shapes standing proud or hunched in the attitude of mourning, the rearing horsemen of the chessboard, a great fleecy pack of wolves, and other animal shapes of fantasy–with the deep crevasses between them bridged in splendour by the rainbows. There were hundreds of these, great blazes of colour, that turned and followed their progress across the sky, keeping majestic station upon them. Above them, the sky was a dark unnatural blue, dappled like a Windsor grey by the thin striation of the cirro cumulus, and the sunlight poured down to shimmer upon the two speeding warplanes. As yet there was no sight of the target. It was up there somewhere amongst the cloud mountains. He looked back at his radar screen. He had taken his radar out of scan and locked it into the target, and now as they closed rapidly he could appraise their relative positions.

The target was flying parallel to them, twenty miles out on their starboard side, and it was high above them and moving at a little more than half their speed. The sun was beyond the target, just short of its zenith, and David calculated his approach path to bring him into an attack vector from above and into the target's starboard quarter.

'Turning to starboard now,' he warned Joe, and they came around together, crossing the target's rear to put themselves in the sun. Joe was calling the range and bearing, it showed a leisurely patrol pattern. There was no indication as yet that the target was aware of the hunters behind and far below.

'Two, this is leader. Arm your circuits.'

Without taking his eyes from the radar screen, David pressed the master switch on his weapon console. He activated the two air-to-air sidewinder missiles that hung under each wing-tip, and immediately heard the soft electronic tone cycling in his earphones. That tone indicated that the missiles were dormant, they had not yet detected an infra-red source to excite them. When they did they would increase the volume and rate of cycle, growling with anticipation, clamouring like hunting dogs on the leash. He tuned them down so he could no longer hear them.

Now he selected his cannon switch, readying the twin 30-mm. weapons in their pods just below his seat. The trigger flicked forward out of its recess in the head of the joystick and he curled his forefinger about it to familiarize himself with the feel of it.

'Two, this is leader. I am commencing visual.' It was a warning to Joe to concentrate all his attention on the screen and feed David with directional data.

'Target is now ten o'clock high, range figures two seven nautical miles.'

David searched carefully, raking the billowing walls of blinding white, breaking off the search to look away at a ground point or a pinnacle of cloud to prevent his eyes focusing short, and to sweep the blind spot behind them, lest the hunters become the hunted.

Then he saw them. There were five of them, and they appeared suddenly out of cloud high above and were immediately outlined against it like tiny black fleas on a newly ironed bedsheet. Just then Joe called the range again.

'Figures one three nautical miles,' but the targets were outlined so crisply against their background that David could make out the delta-winged dart shape, and the high tailplane that identified them beyond all doubt as MIG 21 J.

'I have target visual,' he told Joe. 'Five MIG 21's J.' His tone was flat and neutral, but it was a lie, for now at last his anger had something on which to fasten, and it changed its shape and colour, it was no longer black and aching but cold and bright and keen as a rapier's blade.

'Target is still hostile,' Joe confirmed that they were within Israeli territory, but his tone was not as well guarded as David's. David could detect the huskiness in it, and knew that Joe was feeling that anger also.

It would be another fifteen seconds before they had completed their turn across the enemy's stern, and David assessed the relative positions and saw that so far it had been a perfect approach. The formation sailed on serenely, unaware of the enemy beneath their tail, creeping up in the blind spot where the forward scanning radar could not discover them and rapidly moving into a position up sun. Once there, David would go to attack speed and climb steeply up into a position of superior height and tactical advantage over the enemy formation. Looking ahead now, he realized that chance had given him an added bonus; one of the huge tower blocks of cloud was perfectly placed to screen his climb into the sun. He would use it to cover his stalk, the way the Boer huntsman of Africa stalked wild buffalo from behind a herd of domestic oxen.

'Target is altering course to starboard,' Joe warned him. The MIGS were turning away, edging back towards the Syrian border. They had completed their taunting gesture, they had flaunted the colours of Islam in the face of the infidel, and were making for safety.

David felt the blade of anger in his guts burn colder, sting sharper, and with an effort of restraint he waited out the last few seconds before making his climb. The moment came and his voice was still flat and without passion as he called to Joe, 'Two, this is leader, commencing storm-climb.'

'Two conforming.'

David eased back on the controls and they went up in a climb so vicious that it seemed to tear their bowels from their bellies.

Almost immediately, Desert Flower picked up the radar images as they emerged from the ground clutter.

'Hullo both units Bright Lance. We are now tracking you. Show friend or foe.'

Both David and Joe were lying on their backs in the thrust of storm-climb, but at the order they punched in the I.F.F. systems. Identification Friend or Foe would show a distinctive pattern, a bright halo, around their radar images on command plot identifying them positively even while they were locked with the enemy in the close proximity of the dogfight.

'Beseder—we are tracking you in I.F.F.,' said the Brig, and they went plunging into the pillar of cloud and raked upwards through it. David's eyes darted between the boulé that contained his blind-flying instruments and the radar screen on which the enemy images shone bright and with hard outline, so close now that the individual aircraft in the enemy formation stood out clearly.

'Target is increasing speed and tightening starboard turn,' Joe intoned and David compensated for the enemy's manœuvre.

David was certain that they had not detected his approach, the turn away was coincidental. Another glance at the screen showed that he had achieved his height advantage. He was now two miles off their quarter above them, with the sun at his back. It was the ideal approach.

'Turning now into final leg of attack pattern,' he alerted Joe to his intention and they began the pitch in. The last-second strike which would send their speed rocketing as they closed.

The target centred dead ahead, and the gunsight lit up, glowing softly on the screen ahead of him. The sidewinder missiles caught the first faint emanations of infra-red rays from their victims, and they began to growl softly in David's earphones.

Still blinded by thick grey cloud they raced in, and suddenly they burst out into the clear. Ahead and below them opened a deep trough of space, a valley between cloud ranges and close below them the five MIGS sparkled silvery in the sunlight, pretty and toylike, their red, white and green markings festive and gay, the clean geometrical sweeps of wing and tail nicely balanced and the shark-like mouths of the jet intakes gaping, as they sucked in air.

They were in loose V-formation, two stacked back on each flank of the leader and in the fleeting seconds that David had to study them, he had assessed them. The four wingmen were Syrians, there was an indefinable sloppiness in their flying, a looseness of control. They flew with that lack of polish and confidence of the pupil. They were soft targets, easy pickings.

However, it did not need the three red rings about the leader's fuselage to identify him as a Russian instructor. Some leery old veteran with hawk's blood in his veins, tough and canny, and dangerous as an angry black mamba.

'Engage two port targets,' David ordered Joe, reserving the MIG leader and the starboard echelon for his attack. In David's headphones the missiles were growling their anxiety, they had sniffed out the massed jet blasts below them and already they were tracking, howling their eagerness to kill.

David switched to command net. 'Hello, Desert Flower, this is Bright Lance on target and requesting strike.'

Almost instantly the voice came back. 'David, this is the Brig–' he was speaking rapidly, urgently, '–discontinue attack pattern. I repeat, disengage target. They are no longer hostile. Break off attack.'

Shocked by the command, David glanced down the deep valley of cloud and saw the long brown valley of the Jordan falling away behind them. They had crossed over a line on the earth and immediately their roles had changed from defender to aggressor. But they were closing the target rapidly. It was a fair bounce, they were still unaware.

'We are going to hit them,' David made the decision through the cold bright thing that burned within him and he closed command net and spoke to Joe. 'Two, this is leader attacking.'

'Negative! I say again negative!' Joe called urgently. 'Target is no longer hostile!'

'Remember Hannah!' David shouted into his mask. 'Conform to me!' and he curled his finger about the trigger and touched left rudder, yawing fractionally to bring the nearest MIG into the field of his sights. It seemed to balloon in size as he shrieked towards it.

There was a heart-beat of silence from Joe, and then his voice strangled and rough.

'Two conforming.'

'Kill them, Joe,' David yelled and pressed against the spring-loaded tension of the trigger. There was a soft double hiss, hardly discernible above the jet din, and from under each wing-tip the missiles unleashed, they skidded and twisted as they aligned themselves on the targets, leaving darkly etched trails of vapour across David's front, and at that moment the MIGS became aware.

At a shouted warning from their leader, the entire formation burst into its five separate parts, splintering silvery swift like a shoal of sardines before the driving charge of the barracuda.

The rearmost Syrian was slow, he had only just begun to turn away when one of the sidewinders flicked its tail, followed his turn and united with him in an embrace of death.

The shock wave of the explosion jarred David's machine, but the sound of it was muted as the MIG was enveloped in the greenish-tinted cloud of the strike and it shattered into fragments. A wing snapped off and went whirling high and the brief blooming flower of smoke blew swiftly past David's head.

The second missile had chosen the machine with the red rings, the formation leader, but the Russian had reacted so swiftly and pulled his turn so tight that the missile slid past him in an overshoot, and it lost the scent, unable to follow the MIG around. As David hauled the Mirage round after the Russian, he saw the missile destroy itself in a burst of greenish smoke, far out across the valley of clouds.

The Russian was in a hard right-hand turn, and David followed him. Staring across the imaginary circle that separated them, he could see every detail of the enemy machine; the scarlet helmet of the pilot, the gaudy colours of its roundels, the squiggle of Arabic script that was its identification markings—even the individual rivets that stitched the polished metal skin of the MIG.

David pulled back with all his strength against his joystick, for gravity was tightening the loading of his controls, opposing his efforts to place additional stress on the Mirage lest he tear its wings off the fuselage.

Gravity had hold of David also, its insidious force sucked the blood away from his brain so that his vision dimmed, the colour of the enemy's pilot's helmet faded to dull brown, and David felt himself crushed down into his seat.

About his waist and legs his G-suit tightened its coils squeezing brutally like a hungry python, attempting to prevent the drainage of blood from his upper torso.

David tensed every muscle in his body, straining to resist the loss of blood, and he took the Mirage up in a sliding, soaring yo-yo, up the side of an imaginary barrel. Like a motor-cyclist on a wall of death he whirled aloft, trying once more for the advantage of height.

His vision narrowed, greyed out, until his field was reduced to the limits of his cockpit, and he was pinned heavily to his seat, his mouth sagging open, his eyelids dragging downwards; the effort of holding his right hand on the control column was Herculean.

In the corner of his vision the stall indicator blinked its little eye at him, changing from amber to red, warning him that he was on the verge of catastrophe, courting the disaster of supersonic stall.

David filled his lungs and screamed with all his strength, his own voice echoing through the grey mist. The effort forced a little blood back to his brain and his vision cleared briefly, enough to let him see that the MIG had anticipated his yo-yo and had come up under him, sliding up the wall of death towards his unprotected flank and belly.

David had no alternative but to break out of the turn before the MIG's cannons could bear. He rolled the Mirage out, and went instantly into a tight climbing left-hander, his afterburners still thundering at full power, consuming fuel at a prodigious rate and placing a limit upon these desperate manœuvres.

Neatly and gracefully as a ballet dancer, the Russian followed him out of the turn and locked into his next manœuvre. David saw him coming up into an attack position in his rear-view mirror and he rolled out again and went up and right, blacking out with the rate of turn.

Roll and turn, turn for life, David had judged the Russian fairly. He was a deadly opponent, quick and hard, anticipating each of David's turns and twists, riding always within an ace of strike. Turn, and turn again, in great winging parabolas, climbing always, turning always, vapour trails spinning out from their wing-tips in silky arabesque patterns against the hard blue of the sky.

David's arms and shoulders ached as he fought the control dampers and the weight of gravity, sickened by the drainage of blood and the adrenalin in his system. His cold battle rage turned gradually to icy despair as each of his efforts to dislodge the Russian were met and countered, and always the gaping shark's maw of the MIG hung and twisted a point off his shoulder or belly. All David's expertise, all the brilliance of his natural flying gifts were slowly being discounted by the store of combat experience upon which his enemy could draw.

At one stage, when for an instant they flew wing-tip to wing-tip, David glanced across the gap and saw the man's face. Just the eyes and forehead above the oxygen mask; the skin was pale as bone and the eyes were deep socketed like those of a skull—and then David was turning again, turning and screaming and straining against gravity, screaming also against the first enfolding coils of fear.

He rolled half out of the turn and then without conscious thought, reversed the roll. The Mirage shuddered with protest and his speed bled off. The Russian saw it and came down on him from high on his starboard quarter. As David pushed the stick fully forward and left he kicked on full left rudder, ducking under the blast of cannon fire, and the Mirage went down in a spiralling dive. The blood which gravity had sucked from his head was now flung upwards through his body, filling his head and his vision with bright redness, the red-out of inverted gravitational force. A vein in his nose popped under the pressure and suddenly his oxygen mask was filled with a flood of warm choking blood.

The Russian was after him, following him into the dive, lining him up for his second burst.

David screamed with the metallic salty taste of blood in his mouth and hauled back on the stick with all his strength, the nose came up and over, climbing out of the dive, and again the blood drained from his head—going from red-out to black-out in the fraction of a second and he saw the Russian following him up, drawn by the ploy. At the top David kicked it out in a breakaway roll. It caught the Russian, he was one-hundredth of a second slow in countering and he swung giddily through David's gunsight, an almost impossible deflection shot that sluiced cannon fire wildly across the sky, spraying it like water from a garden hose. The MIG was in David's sights for perhaps one-tenth of a second, but in that time David saw a flash of light, a bright wink of it below the pilot's canopy, and then David rolled and turned out, coming around hard and finding the Russian still hanging in the circuit, but losing air space, swaying out with a feather of white vapour streaming back from below his cockpit canopy.

'I've hit him, David exulted, and his fear was gone, become anger again, a fierce triumphant anger. He took the Mirage up in another soaring yo-yo and this time the MIG could not hold station on him and David flick-rolled off the top and came out with the Russian centred in his gunsight.

He fired a one-second burst and saw the incendiary shells lace in and burst in quick little stabbing stars in the silver fuselage of the MIG.

The Russian came out of his turn, in a gentle dive, flying straight, no longer taking evasive action, probably dead at his controls, and David sat on his tail, and settled the pipper of his gunsight.

He fired another one-second burst and the MIG began to break up. Small unidentifiable pieces of wreckage flew back at David, but the Russian stayed with his machine.

Again David hit him with a two-second burst, and now the MIG's nose sank until she was in a vertical dive still under full power and she went down like a silver javelin. David could not follow her without tearing off his own wings. He pulled out and watched the Russian fly into the earth at a speed that must have exceeded mach 2. He burst like a bomb in a tall tower of dust and smoke that stood for long seconds on the brown plains of Syria.

David shut down his afterburner and looked to his fuel gauges. They were all showing only a narrow strip above the empty notch, and David realized that the last screaming dive after the MIG had taken him down to an altitude of five thousand, he was over enemy territory and too low—much too low.

Expending precious fuel he came around on a westerly heading and went to interception speed, climbing swiftly out of range of flak and searching the heavens above him for sign of either Joe or the other MIGs—although he guessed that the Syrians were either with Allah in the garden of the Houris, or back home with mother by this time.

'Bright Lance Two, this is leader. Do you read me?'

'Leader, this is Two,' Joe's voice answered him immediately. 'I have you visual. In the name of God, get out of there!'

'What is my position?'

'We are fifty miles within Syrian territory, our course for base is 250°.'

'How did you go?'

'I took out one of mine. The other one ran for it, after that I was too busy keeping an eye on you—'

David blinked his eyes and was surprised to find that sweat was pouring down his forehead from under his helmet and his mask was slick and sticky with blood from his nose-bleed. His arms and shoulders still ached, and he felt drunken and light-headed from the effects of gravity and combat and his hands on the control column were shaky and weak.

'I got two,' he said, 'two of the swines—one for Debra, and one for Hannah.'

'Shut up, Davey,' Joe's voice was stiff with tension. 'Concentrate on getting out of here. You are within range of both flak and ground missiles. Light your tail—and let's go.'

'Negative,' David answered him. 'I'm low on fuel. Where are you?'

'Six o'clock high at 25,000.' As he answered, Joe sat up in his seat, leaning forward against his shoulder straps to watch the tiny wedge shape of David's machine far below. It was climbing slowly to meet him, slowly—too slowly, and low—too low. David was vulnerable and Joe was afraid for him, frowning heavily into his face mask and searching restlessly, sweeping heaven and earth for the first hint of danger. Two minutes would see them clear, but they would be two long, slow minutes.

He almost missed the first missile. The ground crew must have allowed David to overfly their launch pad before they put it up in pursuit—for Joe picked up its vapour trail as it streaked in from behind David, closing rapidly with him.

'Missile, break left,' Joe yelled into his mask. 'Go! Go! Go!' and he saw David begin his turn instantly, steeply, side-stepping the sizzling attack of the missile.

'It's lost you!' Joe called, as the missile continued its crazy career through space, beginning to yaw from side to side as it hunted for a target and at last bursting in self-destruction.

'Keep going, Davey,' Joe encouraged him, 'but keep awake, there will be more.'

They both saw the next one leave the ground from its camouflaged vehicle. There was a nest of them on a rocky ridge above a sun-blasted plain. The Serpent slid off the rock and lifted into the sky, climbed rapidly towards David's little machine.

'Light your tail,' Joe told him, 'and wait for it!' He watched the missile boring in, converging with dazzling speed on David's Mirage.

'Break right! Go! Go! Go!' Joe yelled and David twisted violently aside. Again the Serpent slid past him, over-shooting, but this time not losing contact and coming around to attack again, its seekers locked on David's machine.

'He's still on you,' Joe was screaming now. 'Go for the sun, Davey. Try for the sun,' and the Mirage pointed its nose at the great blazing orb that burned above the mountain ranges of dark cloud. The Serpent followed him upwards, hunting him with the dreadful single-mindedness of the automaton.

'He's on to you, Davey. Flip out now! Go! Go! Go!'

David flicked the Mirage out of her vertical climb, and fell like a stone—while the Serpent fastened its attention upon the vast infra-red output from the sun and streaked on towards it, losing the Mirage.

'You've lost it. Get out, Davey, get out!' Joe pleaded with him, but for the moment the Mirage was helpless. In her desperate climb for the sun she had lost manoeuvring speed and was wallowing clumsily now. It would be many seconds before she became agile and lithe once more—and by then it would be too late—for Joe saw the third missile become airborne and dart upwards on its feather of flame and smoke aiming at David's Mirage.

Joe did not consciously realize what he was going to do until he had winged over and commenced his dive under full power. He came down with his mach meter indicating twice the speed of sound, and he levelled across David's tail, cutting obliquely across his track under the nose of the oncoming Serpent.

The Serpent saw him with its little cyclops radar eye, and it sensed the heat of his exhausts—fresher, more tantalizing than David's, and it accepted him as an alternative target and swung away after him, leaving David to fly on unscathed.

David saw Joe's aircraft flash past his wing-tip at searing speed, and but an instant behind him followed the Serpent. It took him only a second to realize that Joe had deliberately pulled the missile off him, had accepted the attack that must surely have destroyed David.

He watched with fascinated horror as Joe pulled out of his dive, and used his speed to climb into the sun. The missile followed him smoothly, angling upwards, overhauling Joe's Mirage with effortless ease. Joe was watching the missile in his mirror, and at the last instant he flipped out of the climb—but this time the Serpent was not deceived; as Joe dropped so it swivelled also, and as

earlier David had wallowed helplessly now Joe was in the same predicament.
He had taken his chance and it had not worked for him. The missile found him,
and in a brusque burst of flame, Joe and his Mirage died together.

David flew on alone, his Mirage once more at manœuvring speed and his
throat dry with horror and fear and grief. He found himself talking aloud.

'Joe, no, Joe. Oh God no! You shouldn't have done it.'

Ahead of him through the gaps in the massive cloud bases he saw the Jordan.

'It should be you that's going home, Joe,' he said. 'It should be you, Joe,'
and felt the hard ball of sorrow in his throat.

But the instinct of survival was still strong and David yawed and glanced
back to clear his blind spot—and he saw the last missile coming in on him. It
was just a small black speck far behind, with a little frill of dark smoke around
it, but it was watching him hungrily with its wicked little eye.

As he saw it, he knew beyond doubt that this one was his, the one that the
fates had reserved for him. The attacks he had evaded so far had worn his
nerves and strained his judgement, he felt a sense of fatalistic dismay as he
watched the attacking missile gaining on him, nevertheless he gathered his
scattered reserves for one more supreme effort.

His eyes narrowed to slits, the sweat sliding down his face and drenching his
mask, his left hand holding the throttle fully open and his right gripping the
control column with the strength, of despair, he judged his moment.

The missile was almost upon him and he screamed with all his might and
hurled the Mirage into the turn, but he had misjudged it by the smallest part of
a second. As he turned away the missile slid past him and it was close enough to
pick up the shadow of the Mirage in the photo-electric eye of its fusing device.
The eye winked at him and the missile exploded.

The Mirage was in the critical attitude of its turn, and the cockpit canopy
was exposed entirely to the centre of the blast. It hit the plane with a blow that
sent it tumbling; like a running man tripping it went over, and it lost lift and
flying capability.

The canopy was penetrated by flying steel. A piece struck David's armoured
seat with a clang and then it glanced off and struck his left arm above the elbow,
snapping the bone cleanly so that the arm dropped uselessly and hung into his
lap.

An icy wind raged through the torn canopy as the Mirage hurled itself
through space with suicidal force, whipping its nose through the vicious
motions and flat plane of high-speed spin. David was thrown against his
straps, his ribs bruised and his skin seared from his shoulders, and the broken
arm flailing agonizingly.

He tried to hold himself upright in his seat as he reached up over his head,
caught hold of the handle of the ejector mechanism and hauled the blind down
over his face. He expected to have the charge explode beneath his seat and hurl
him free of the doomed Mirage—but nothing happened.

Desperately he released the handle and strained forward to reach the
secondary firing mechanism under his seat between his feet. He wrenched it
and felt despair as there was no response. The seat was not working, the blast
had damaged some vital part of it. He had to fly the Mirage out of it, with one
arm and very little altitude left to him. He fastened his right fist on to the
moulded grip of the stick, and in the crazy fall and flutter and whirl, David
began to fight for control, flying now by instinct alone, for he was badly hurt,
and sky and horizon, earth and cloud spun giddily across his vision.

He was aware that he was losing height rapidly, for every time the earth swayed through his line of vision it was closer and more menacing, but doggedly he continued his attempts to roll against the direction of spin.

The earth was very close before he felt the first hint of response, and the ferocity of her gyrations abated slightly. Stick and rudder together, he tried again and the Mirage showed herself willing at last. Gently, with the touch of a lover, he wooed her and suddenly she came out and he was flying straight and level, but she was hard hit. The blast of the missile had done mortal damage, and she was heavy and sick in his hands. He could feel the rough vibration of the engine shaking her, and he guessed that the compressor had thrown a blade and was now out of balance. Within minutes or seconds she would begin to tear herself to pieces. He could not try for climbing power on her.

David looked quickly about him and realized with a shock how far he had fallen in that terrible tumble down the sky. He was only two or three hundred feet above the earth. He was not sure of his direction, but when he glanced at his doppler compass, he found with mild surprise that he was still heading in the general direction of home.

The engine vibration increased, and he could hear the shrill screech of rending metal. He wasn't going to make it home—that was certain, and there was insufficient height to jettison the canopy, release his straps and attempt to scramble out of the cockpit. There was only one course still remaining, he must fly the Mirage in.

Even as he made the decision his one good hand was busy implementing it. Holding the stick between his knees, he let down his landing gear; the nose wheel might hold him up long enough to take some of the speed off her and prevent her cartwheeling.

He looked ahead, and saw a low ridge of rocky ground and sparse green vegetation. Disaster lurked for him there—but beyond it were open fields, ploughed land, orderly blocks of orchard, neatly laid-out buildings. That in itself was cheering. Such order and industry could only mean that he had returned across the border to Israel.

David skimmed over the ridge of broken rocks, sucking in his own belly as though to lift the Mirage bodily over the hungry teeth of granite, and ahead of him lay the fields. He could see women working in one of the orchards, stopping and turning to look at him. So close that he could clearly see the expression of surprise and apprehension on their faces.

There was a man on a blue tractor and he jumped from his seat and fell to the earth as David passed only feet above his head.

All fuel cocks closed, all switches off, master switch off—David went into the final ritual for crash-landing.

Ahead of him lay the smooth brown field, open and clear. He might just be lucky enough, it might just come off.

The Mirage was losing flying speed, her nose coming up, the airspeed needle sinking back, 200 miles per hour, 190, 180, dropping back to her stalling speed of 150.

Then suddenly David realized that the field ahead of him was latticed with deep concrete irrigation channels. They were twenty feet wide, and ten deep, a deadly hazard—enough to destroy a Centurion tank.

There was nothing David could do now to avoid their gaping jaws. He flew the Mirage in, touching down smoothly.

'Smooth as a tomcat pissing on a sheet of velvet,' he thought bitterly, aware that all his skill was unavailing now. 'Even Barney would have been proud of me.' The field was rough, but the Mirage settled to it, pitching and lurching, shaking David ruthlessly about the cockpit, but she was up on all three wheels, losing speed handily, her undercart taking the strain. However, she was still travelling at ninety miles an hour when she went into the irrigation ditch.

It snapped her undercart off like pretzel sticks and she nosed in, struck the far bank of concrete that sheered through metal like a scythe, and sent the fuselage cartwheeling across the field with David still strapped within it. The wings broke away and the body slid on across the soft earth to come to rest at last, right way up like a stranded whale.

The whole of David's left side was numb, no feeling in his arm or leg, the straps had mauled him with their rude grasp, and he was stunned and bewildered in the sudden engrossing silence.

For many seconds he sat still, unable to move or think. Then he smelled it, the pervasive reek of Avtur jet fuel from the ruptured tanks and lines. The smell of it galvanized him with the pilot's deadly fear of fire.

With his right hand he grabbed the canopy release lever and heaved at it. He wasted ten precious seconds with it, for it was jammed solid. Then he turned his attention to the steel canopy breaker in its niche below the lever. This was a tool specially designed for this type of emergency. He lifted it, lay back in his seat and attacked the Perspex dome above his head. The stink of jet fuel was overpowering, filling the cockpit, and he could hear the little pinging and tinkling sound made by white-hot metal.

His left arm hampered him, he had no feeling or use in it. The straps bound him tightly to his seat and he had to pause in his assault upon the canopy to loosen them.

Then he began again. He tore an opening in the Perspex, the size of a hand, and as he worked to enlarge it, a ruptured fuel pressure line somewhere in the shattered fuselage sprayed a jet of Avtur high in the air. it fell in a heavy drizzle upon the canopy like a garden sprinkler, poured down the curved sides and dribbled through the hole David was cutting. It fell into his face, icy cold on his cheeks and stinging his eyes, it drenched his shoulders and the front of his pressure suit, and David began to pray. For the first time ever in his life the words took on meaning and he felt his terror receding.

'Hear O Israel, the Lord our God, the Lord is one.'

He prayed aloud, striking up at the softly yielding Perspex and feeling the soft rain of death in his face. He tore at the opening with his hands, bringing away slabs of transparent material, but ripping his gloves and leaving his blood smearing the jagged edges of the opening.

'Blessed be His name, whose glorious kingdom is for ever–'

The opening was large enough. He hauled himself up in the seat, and found himself caught by the oxygen and radio lines attached to his helmet. He could not reach them with his crippled left arm. He stared down at the offending limb, and saw the blood welling out of the torn sleeve of the suit. There was no pain but it was twisted at a comical angle from the elbow.

'You shall love the Lord your God with all your heart–' he whispered, and with his right hand he tore loose the chin strap and let his helmet drop to the floor-boards. The Avtur soaked into the soft dark mop of his hair and ran down his neck behind his ears, and he thought about the flames of hell.

Painfully he dragged himself out through the opening in the canopy, and now not even prayer could hold off the dark hordes of terror that assaulted his soul.

'–For the anger of God will kindle against you–'

Laboriously he crawled across the slippery sleek metal of the wing root and fell to the ground. He fell face-down and lay for a moment, exhausted by fear and effort.

'–remember all the commands of God–'

He heard voices then as he lay with his face against the dusty earth, and he lifted his head and saw the women from the orchard running towards him across the open field. The voices were shrill but faint and the words were in Hebrew. He knew that he was home.

Steadying himself against the shattered body of the Mirage, he came to his feet with the broken arm dangling at his side, and he tried to shout to them.

'Go back! Beware!' but his voice was a throaty croak, and they ran on towards him. Their dresses and aprons were gay spots of colour against the dry brown earth.

He pushed himself away from the aircraft and staggered to meet the running women.

'Go back!' he croaked in his own terrible distress, with the grip of his G-suit strangling his movements and the evaporating fuel cold as ice in his hair and down his face.

Within the battered hull of the Mirage a puddle of Avtur had been heated by the white-hot shell of the jet compressor. Its low volatility at last was raised to flash point and a dying spark from the electronic equipment was enough to ignite it.

With a dull but awful roar, the Mirage bloomed with dark crimson flame and sooty black smoke, the wind ripped the flames outwards in great streamers and pennants that engulfed all around them, and David staggered onwards in the midst of the roaring furnace that seemed to consume the very air.

He held his breath–if he had not, the flame would have scorched his lungs. He closed his eyes tightly against the agony and ran on blindly. His body and his limbs were protected by the fireproof pressure suit and boots and gloves–but his head was bare and soaked with fuel.

As he ran his head burned like a torch. His hair frizzled off, in a stinking puff of flame and the skin of his scalp and neck and face was exposed. The flames burnt his ears off and most of his nose, they flayed off his skin in a blistering sheet and then they ate into the raw flesh, they burnt away his lips and exposed his teeth and part of the bone of his jaw. They ate through his eyelids and stripped the living meat from his cheeks.

David ran on through the burning air and smoke, and he did not believe that such pain was possible. It exceeded all his imaginings and swamped all the senses of his body and mind–but he knew he must not scream. The pain was a blackness and the vivid colours of flame in his tightly closed eyes, it was a roaring in his ears like all the winds of the world, and in his flesh it was the goads and whips and burning hooks of hell itself. But he knew he could not let this terrible fire enter his body and he ran on without screaming.

The women from the orchard were brought up short by the sudden forest of flame and black smoke that rose up in front of them, engulfing the squashed-insect body of the aircraft, and closing around the running figure of the pilot.

It was a solid impenetrable wall of heat and smoke that blotted out all ahead of them, and forced them to draw back, awed and horrified, before its raging hot breath. They stood in a small group, panting and wild-eyed.

Then abruptly a freak gust of wind opened the heavy oily curtains of smoke, and out of them stumbled a dreadful thing with a scorched and smoking body and a head of flame.

Blindly it came out of the smoke, one arm hanging and its feet dragging and staggering in the soft earth. They stared at this thing in horror, frozen in silence, and it came towards them.

Then a strapping girl, with a strong brown body and a mane of dark hair, uttered a cry of compassion–and raced to meet him.

As she ran, she stripped off her heavy voluminous skirt of thick wool, leaving her strong brown legs bare. She reached David and she swirled the skirt over his head, smothering the flames that still ate into his flesh. The other women followed her, using their clothing to wrap him as he fell and rolled on the earth.

Only then did David begin to scream, from that lipless mouth with the exposed teeth. It was a sound that none of them would ever forget. As he screamed the eyes were open, with the lashes and brow and most of the lids burned away. The eyes were dark indigo blue in the glistening mask of wet scorched meat, and the little blood vessels, sealed by the heat, popped open and dribbled and spurted. As he screamed, the blood and lymph bubbled from the nostril holes where his nose had been, and his body writhed and heaved and convulsed as spasm after spasm of unbearable agony hit him.

The women had to hold him down to control his struggles, and to prevent him tearing with clawed fingers at the ruins of his face.

He was still screaming when the doctor from the kibbutz slashed open the sleeve of his pressure suit with a scalpel and pressed the morphine needle into the twitching jumping muscles of his arm.

The Brig saw the last bright radar image fade from the plot and heard the young radar officer report formally. 'No further contact.' And a great silence fell on the command bunker.

They were all watching him. He stood hunched over the plot and his big bony fists were clasped at his sides. His face was stiff and expressionless, but his eyes were terrible.

It seemed that the frantic voices of his two pilots still echoed from the speakers above his head, as they called to each other in the extremes of mortal conflict.

They had all heard David's voice, hoarse with sorrow and fear.

'Joe! No, Joe! Oh God, no!' and they knew what that meant. They had lost them both, and the Brig was still stunned by the sudden incalculable turn that the sortie had taken.

At the moment he had lost control of his fighters he had known that disaster was unavoidable–and now his son was dead. He wanted to cry out aloud, to protest against the futility of it. He closed his eyes tightly for a few seconds, and when he opened them, he was in control again.

'General alert,' he snapped. 'All squadrons to "Red" standby–' he knew they faced an international crisis. 'I want air cover over the area they went down. They may have ejected. Put up two Phantom flights and keep an umbrella over them. I want helicopters sent in immediately, with paratrooper guards and medical teams–'

Command bunker moved swiftly into general alert procedure.

'Get me the Prime Minister,' he said, he was going to have to do a lot of explaining, and he spared a few vital seconds to damn David Morgan roundly and bitterly.

The airforce doctor took one look at David's charred and scorched head and he swore softly.

'We'll be lucky to save this one.'

Loosely he swathed the head in Vaseline bandages and they hurried with David's blanket-wrapped body on the stretcher to the Bell 205 helicopter waiting in the orchard.

The Bell touched down on the helipad at Hadassah Hospital and a medical team was ready for him. One hour and fifty-three minutes after the Mirage hit the irrigation canal David had passed through the sterile lock into the special burns unit on the third floor of the hospital—into a quiet and secluded little world where everybody wore masks and long green sterile robes and the only contact with the outside world was through the double-glazed windows and even the air he breathed was scrubbed and cleaned and filtered.

However, David was enfolded in the soft dark clouds of morphine and he did not hear the quiet voices of the masked figures as they worked over him.

'It's third degree over the entire area—'

'No attempt to clean it or touch it, sister, not until it stabilizes. I am going to spray with Epigard, and we'll go to intra-muscular Tetracycline four-hourly against infection—'

'It will be two weeks before we dare touch it.'

'Very well, doctor.'

'Oh, and sister, fifteen milligrams of morphine six-hourly. We are going to have a lot of pain with this one.'

Pain was infinity, an endless ocean across which the wave-patterns marched relentlessly to burst up the beaches of his soul. There were times when the surf of pain ran high and each burst of it threatened to shatter his reason. Again there were times when it was low, almost gentle in its throbbing rhythm and he drifted far out upon the ocean of pain to where the morphine mists enfolded him. Then the mists parted and a brazen sun beat down upon his head, and he squirmed and writhed and cried out. His skull seemed to bloat and swell until it must burst, and the open nerve-ends screamed for surcease.

Then suddenly there was the sharply beloved sting of the needle in his flesh, and the mists closed about him once more.

'I don't like the look of this at all. Have we taken a culture, sister?'

'Yes, doctor.'

'What are we growing?'

'I'm afraid it's strep.'

'Yes. I thought so. I think we'll have to change to Cloxacillin—see if we get a better response with that.'

With the pain, David became aware of a smell. It was the smell of carrion and things long dead, the smell of vermin in dirty blankets, of vomit and excreta, and the odour of wet garbage festering in dark alleys—and at last he came to know that the smell was the rotting of his own flesh as the bacteria of Streptococcus infection attacked the exposed tissue.

They fought it with the drugs, but now the pain was underlined with the fevers of infection and the terrible burning thirsts which no amount of liquids could slake.

With the fever came the nightmares and the fantasies to plague and goad him even further beyond the limits of his endurance.

'Joe—' he cried out in his agony,˙ try for the sun, Joe. Break left now—Go! Go!' And then he was sobbing from the ruined and broken mouth. 'Oh, Joe! Oh God, no! Joe.'

Until the night-sister could no longer bear it and she came hurrying with the syringe, and his screams turned to babbling and then into the low whimper and moan of the drug sleep.

'We'll start with the acriflavin dressings now, sister.'

When they changed the dressings every forty-eight hours it was under general anaesthetic for the entire head was of raw flesh, a bland expressionless head, a head like a child's drawing, crude lines and harsh colours, hairless, earless, streaked and mottled with yellow runs and patches of soft pus and corruption.

'We are getting a response from the Cloxacillin, it's looking a lot healthier, sister.'

The naked flesh of his eyelids had contracted, pulling back like the glistening petals of a pink rose, exposing the eyeballs to the air without respite. They had filled the eyes' sockets with a yellow ointment to soothe and moisten them, to keep out the loathsome infection that covered his head. The ointment prevented vision.

'I think we'll go for an abdominal pedicel now. Will you prep for afternoon theatre, please, sister?'

Now it was time for the knife, and David was to learn that the pain and the knife lived together in terrible sin. They lifted a long flap of skin and flesh from his belly, leaving it still attached at one end, and they rolled it into a fat sausage, then they strapped his good arm, the one without the plaster cast, to his side and they stitched the free end of the sausage to his forearm, training it to draw its blood supply from there. Then they brought him back from theatre and left him trussed and helpless and blind with the pedicel fastened to his arm, like a remora to the belly of a shark.

'Well, we have saved both eyes,' the voice was proud, fond almost, and David looked up and saw them for the first time. They were gathered around his cot, a circle of craning heads, mouths and noses covered by surgical masks, but his vision was still smeary with ointment and distorted by the drip irrigation that had replaced it.

'Now we will go for the eyelids.'

It was the knife again, the contracted and bunched-up eyelids split and re-shaped and stitched, the knife and pain and the familiar sickly tissue taste and stink of anaesthetic that saturated his body and seemed to exude from the very pores of his skin.

'Beautiful, really lovely—we have cleaned up the infection nicely. Now we can begin.'

The head was cleansed of its running rivers of pus, and now it was glistening and wet, bald and bright red, the colour of a cocktail cherry as granulation tissue formed. There were two gnarled and twisted flaps for ears, the double row of teeth startlingly white and perfect where the lips had been eaten away, a long white blade of exposed bone outlined the point of the jaw, the nose was a stump with the nostrils like the double muzzles of a shotgun, and only the eyes were still beautiful—dark indigo and flawlessly white between the lids of shocking crimson and neatly laid˙black stitches.

'We'll begin at the back of the neck. Will you prep for this afternoon's theatre, please, sister?'

It was a variation on the theme of the knife. They planed sheets of live skin from his thighs and meshed them to allow a wider spread, then they laid them over the exposed flesh, covering a little at each session, and evaluating each attempt while David lay in his cot and rode the long swells of pain.

'That one is no good. I'm afraid we will have to scrap it and try again.'

While his thighs grew a new crop of skin, they planed fresh sheets from his calves, so that each donor-site became a new source of pain.

'Lovely! An edge-to-edge take with that graft.'

Slowly the cap of skin extended up across the nape of his neck and over his scalp. The meshing of the skin grafts gave them a patterned effect, regular as the scales of a fish, and the new grafts were hard-looking and raised.

'We can move the pedicel up now.'

'This afternoon's theatre, doctor?'

'Yes, please, sister.'

David came to know that they operated every Thursday in the burns unit. He came to dread the Thursday morning rounds when the consultant and his staff crowded around his cot and touched and prodded and discussed the restructuring of his flesh with an impersonal candour that chilled him.

They freed the fat sausage of flesh from his belly and it dangled from his arm like some grotesque white leech, seeming to have a life of its own, drawing blood and sustenance from its grip upon his forearm.

They lifted his arm and strapped it across his chest, and the raw end of the pedicel they split and stitched to his jaw and to the stump of his nose.

'It's taken very nicely. We will begin shaping it this afternoon. We'll have him at the head of the theatre list. Will you see to that please, sister?'

With the living flesh that they had stolen from his belly they fashioned a crude lump of a nose, taut, narrow lips and a new covering for his jaw-bone.

'The oedema has settled. This afternoon I will go for the bone-graft on the jaw.'

They opened his chest and split his fourth rib laterally, robbing it of a long sliver of bone and they grafted this to the damaged jaw-bone, then they spread the flesh of the pedicel over it and stitched it all into place.

On Thursdays it was the knife and the stink of anaesthetic, and for the days between it was the ache and pain of abused and healing flesh.

They fined down the new nose, piercing it with nostrils, they finished the reconstruction of his eyelids. They laid the last grafts behind his ears, they cut a double zig-zag incision around the base of his jaw where the contracting scar tissue was trying to draw his chin down on to his chest. The new lips took firm hold on the existing muscles and David gained control of them so he could form his words again and speak clearly.

The last area of raw flesh was closed beneath the patchwork of skin grafts, flesh grafts and stitches. David was no longer a high-infection risk and he was moved from a sterile environment. Once again he saw human faces, not merely eyes peering over white surgical masks. The faces were friendly, cheerful faces. Men and women proud of their achievement in saving him from death and refleshing his ravaged head.

'You'll be allowed visitors now, I expect you'll welcome that,' said the consultant. He was a distinguished-looking young surgeon who had left a highly paid post at a Swiss Clinic to head this burns and plastic surgery unit.

'I don't think I will be having any visitors,' David had lost contact with the reality of the outside world during the nine months in the burns unit.

'Oh, yes, you will,' the surgeon told him. 'We've had regular inquiries on your progress from a number of people. Isn't that correct, sister?'

'That's right, doctor.'

'You can let them know that he is allowed visitors now.'

The consultant and his group began to move on.

'Doctor,' David called him back. 'I want a look at a mirror,' and they were silent, immediately embarrassed. This request of his had been denied many times over the last months.

'Damn it,' David became angry. 'You can't protect me from it for ever.'

The consultant gestured for the others to leave and they filed out of the ward, while he came back to David's bed.

'All right, David,' he agreed gently. 'We'll find you a mirror–though we don't have much use for them around here.' For the first time in the many months he had known him, David glimpsed the depths of his compassion, and he wondered at it. That a man who lived constantly amongst great pain and terrible disfigurement could still be moved by it.

'You must understand that how you are now is not how you will always be. All I have been able to do, so far, is heal your exposed flesh and make you functional again. You are once more a viable human being. You have not experienced the loss of any of your faculties–but I will not pretend that you are beautiful. However, there remains much that I can still do to change that. Your ears, for example, can be reconstructed with the material I have reserved for that purpose–' He indicated the stump of the pedicel that still hung from David's forearm '–There is much fine work still to be done about the nose and mouth and eyes.' He paced slowly the length of the ward and looked out into the sunlight for a moment before turning back again and coming forward to face David.

'But let me be truthful with you. There are limitations to what I can do. The muscles of expression, those delicate little muscles around the eyes and mouth have been destroyed. I cannot replace those. The hair follicles of your lashes and brows and scalp have been burned away. You will be able to wear a wig, but–'

David turned to his bedside locker and took from the drawer his wallet. He opened it and drew out a photograph. It was the one which Hannah had taken so long ago of Debra and David sitting at the rock-pool in the oasis of Ein Gedi and smiling at each other. He handed it to the surgeon.

'Is that what you looked like, David? I never knew.' The regret showed like a quick shadow in his eyes.

'Can you make me look like that again?'

The surgeon studied the photograph a moment longer, the young god's face with the dark mop of hair and the clean pure lines of the profile.

'No,' he said. 'I could not even come close.'

'That's all I wanted to know.' David took the photograph back from him. 'You say I'm functional now. Let's leave it at that, shall we?'

'You don't want further cosmetic surgery? We can still do a lot–'

'Doctor, I've lived under the knife for nine months. I've had the taste of antibiotics and anaesthetics in my mouth, and the stink of it in my nostrils for all that time. Now all I want is a little escape from pain–a little peace and the taste of clean air.'

'Very well,' the surgeon agreed readily. 'It is not important that we do it now. You could come back at any time in the future.' He walked to the door of the ward. 'Come on. Let's go find a mirror.'

There was one in the nurses' room beyond the double doors at the end of the passage. The room itself was empty and the mirror was set into the wall above the wash basin.

The surgeon stood in the doorway and leaned against the jamb. He lit a cigarette and watched as David crossed towards the mirror and then halted abruptly as he saw his own image.

He wore the blue hospital dressing-gown over his pyjamas. He was tall and finely proportioned. His shoulders were wide, his hips narrow, and he had the same lithe and beautiful man's body.

However, the head that topped it was something from a nightmare. Involuntarily he gasped out loud and the gash of a mouth parted in sympathy. It was a tight lipless mouth, like that of a cobra, white-rimmed and harsh.

Drawn by the awful fascination of horror, David drew closer to the mirror. The thick mane of his dark hair had concealed the peculiar elongation of his skull. He had never realized that it jutted out behind like that, for now the hair was gone and the bald curve was covered with meshed skin, thickened and raised.

The skin and flesh of his face was a patchwork, joined by seams of scar tissue drawn tightly over his cheekbones, giving him a vaguely Asiatic appearance, but the eyes were round and startled, with clumsy lids and puffed dead-looking flesh beneath.

His nose was a shapeless blob, out of balance with his other coarsened features and his ears were gnarled excrescences, seemingly fastened haphazardly to the sides of his head. The whole of it was bland and bald and boiled-looking.

The gash of a mouth twisted briefly in a horrid rictus, and then regained its frozen shape.

'I can't smile,' said David.

'No,' agreed the surgeon. 'You will have no control of your expressions.'

That was the truly horrifying aspect of it. It was not the twisted and tortured flesh, with the scarring and stitch marks still so evident–it was the expressionlessness of this mask. The frozen features seemed long dead, incapable of human warmth or feeling.

'Yeah! But you should have seen the other guy!' David said softly, and the surgeon chuckled without mirth.

'We'll have those last few stitches behind your ears out tomorrow–I shall remove what remains of the pedicel from your arm–and then you can be discharged. Come back to us when you are ready.'

David ran his hand gingerly over the bald patterned skull.

'I'm going to save a fortune in haircuts and razor blades,' he said, and the surgeon turned quickly away and walked down the passage, leaving David to get to know his new head.

The clothes that they had found for him were cheap and ill-fitting–slacks and open-neck shirt, a light jacket and sandals–and he asked for some head covering, anything to conceal the weird new shape of his scalp. One of the nurses found him a cloth cap, and then told him that a visitor was waiting for him in the hospital superintendent's department.

He was a major from the military provost marshal's office, a lean grey-haired man with cold grey eyes and a tight hard mouth. He introduced himself without offering to shake hands and then opened the file on the desk in front of him.

'I have been instructed by my office to ask for the formal resignation of your commission in the Israeli Air Force,' he started, and David stared at him. In the long pain-filled, fever-hot nights, the thought of flying once more had seemed like a prospect of paradise.

'I don't understand,' he mumbled, and reached for a cigarette, breaking the first match and then puffing quickly as the second flared. 'You want my resignation—and if I refuse?'

'Then we shall have no alternative other than to convene a court martial and to try for dereliction of duty, and refusing in the face of the enemy to obey the lawful orders of your superior officer.'

'I see,' David nodded heavily, and drew on the cigarette. The smoke stung his eyes.

'It doesn't seem I have any choice.'

'I have prepared the necessary documents. Please sign here, and here, and I shall sign as witness.'

David bowed over the papers and signed. The pen scratched loudly in the silent room.

'Thank you.' The major gathered his papers, and placed them in his briefcase. He nodded at David and started for the door.

'So now I am an outcast,' said David softly, and the man stopped. They stared at each other for a moment, and then the major's expression altered slightly, and the cold grey eyes became ferocious.

'You are responsible for the destruction of two warplanes that are irreplaceable and whose loss has caused us incalculable harm. You are responsible for the death of a brother officer, and for bringing our country to the very brink of open war which would have cost many thousands more of our young people's lives—and possibly our very existence. You have embarrassed our international friends—and given strength to our enemies.' He paused and drew a deep breath. 'The recommendation of my office was that you be brought to trial and that the prosecution be instructed to ask for the death penalty. It was only the personal intervention of the Prime Minister and of Major-General Mordecai that saved you from that. In my view, instead of bemoaning your fate, you should consider yourself highly fortunate.'

He turned away and his footsteps cracked on the stone floor as he strode from the room.

In the bleak impersonal lobby of the hospital, David was suddenly struck by a reluctance to walk on out into the spring sunshine through the glass swing doors. He had heard that long-term prisoners felt this way when the time came for their release.

Before he reached the doors he turned aside and went down to the hospital synagogue. In a corner of the quiet square hall he sat for a long time. The stained-glass windows, set high in the nave, filled the air with shafts of coloured light when the sun came through, and a little of the peace and beauty of that place stayed with him and gave him courage when at last he walked out into the square and boarded a bus for Jerusalem.

He found a seat at the rear, and beside a window. The bus pulled away and ground slowly up the hill towards the city.

He became aware that he was being watched, and he lifted his head to find that a woman with two young children had taken the seat in front of him. She was a poorly dressed, harassed-looking woman, prematurely aged and she held the grubby younger infant on her lap and fed it from a plastic bottle. However, the second child was an angelic little girl of four or five years. She had huge dark eyes and a head of thick curls. She stood on the seat facing backwards, with one thumb thrust deeply into her mouth. She was watching David steadily over the back of the seat, studying his face with that total absorption and candour of the child. David felt a sudden warmth of emotion for the child, a longing for the comfort of human contact, of which he had been deprived all these months.

He leaned forward in his seat, trying to smile, reaching out a gentle hand to touch the child's arm.

She removed her thumb from her mouth and shrank away from him, turning to her mother and clinging to her arm, hiding her face in the woman's blouse.

At the next stop David stepped down from the bus and left the road to climb the stony hillside.

The day was warm and drowsy, with the bee murmur and the smell of the blossoms from the peach orchards. He climbed the terraces and rested at the crest, for he found he was breathless and shaky. Months in hospital had left him unaccustomed to walking far, but it was not that alone. The episode with the child had distressed him terribly.

He looked longingly towards the sky. It was clear and brilliant blue, with high silver cloud in the north. he wished he could ascend beyond those clouds. He knew he would find peace up there.

A taxi dropped him off at the top of Malik Street. The front door was unlocked, swinging open before he could fit his key to the lock.

Puzzled and alarmed he stepped into the living-room. It was as he had left it so many months before, but somebody had cleaned and swept, and there were fresh flowers in a vase upon the olive-wood table—a huge bouquet of gaily coloured dahlias, yellow and scarlet.

David smelled food, hot and spicy and tantalizing after the bland hospital fare.

'Hello,' he called. 'Who is there?'

'Welcome home!' There was a familiar bellow from behind the closed bathroom door. 'I didn't expect you so soon—and you've caught me with my skirts up and pants down.'

There was a scuffling sound and then the toilet flushed thunderously and the door was flung open. Ella Kadesh appeared majestically through it. She wore one of her huge kaftans, it was a blaze of primary colours. Her hat was apple-green in colour, the brim pinned up at the side like an Australian bush hat by an enormous jade brooch and a bunch of ostrich feathers.

Her heavy arms were flung wide in a gesture of welcome, and the face was split in a huge grin of anticipation. She came towards him, and the grin persisted long after the horror had dawned in her bright little eyes. Her steps slowed.

'David?' Her voice was uncertain. 'It is you, David?'

'Hello, Ella.'

'Oh God. Oh, sweet holy name of God. What have they done to you, my beautiful young Mars—'

'Listen, you old bag,' he said harshly, 'if you start blubbering I'm going to throw you down the steps.'

She made a huge effort to control it, fighting back the tears that flooded into her eyes, but her jowls wobbled and her voice was thick and nasal as she enfolded him in her huge arms and hugged him to her bosom.

'I've got a case of cold beers in the refrigerator—and I made a pot of curry for us. You'll love my curry, it's the thing I do best—'

David ate with enormous appetite, washing down the fiery food with cold beer, and he listened to Ella talk. She spouted words like a fountain, using their flow to cover her pity and embarrassment.

'They would not let me visit you, but I telephoned every week and kept in touch that way. The sister and I got very friendly, she let me know you were coming today. So I drove up to make sure you had a welcome—'

She tried to avoid looking directly at his face, but when she did the shadows appeared in her eyes, even though she made a convincing effort at gaiety. When he finished eating at last, she asked, 'What will you do now, David?'

'I would have liked to go back and fly. It's the thing I like to do best—but they have forced me to resign my commission. I disobeyed orders, Joe and I followed them across the border, and they don't want me any more.'

'There was nearly open war, David. It was a crazy thing that you and Joe did.'

David nodded. 'I was mad. I wasn't thinking straight that day—after Debra—'

Ella interrupted quickly. 'Yes, I know. Share another beer?'

David nodded distractedly. 'How is she, Ella?' It was the question he had wanted to ask all along.

'She is just fine, Davey. She has begun the new book, and if anything it's better than the first. I think she will become a very important writer—'

'Her eyes? Is there any improvement?'

Ella shook her head. 'She has come to terms with that now. It doesn't seem to bother her any longer, just as you will come to accept what has happened—'

David was not listening. 'Ella, in all that time, when I was in hospital, every day I hoped—I knew it was useless, but I hoped to hear from her. A card, a word—'

'She didn't know, Davey.'

'Didn't know?' David demanded and leaned across the table to grip Ella's wrist. 'What do you mean?'

'After Joe—was killed, Debra's father was very angry. He believed that you were responsible.'

David nodded, the blank mask of his face concealing his guilt.

'Well, he told Debra that you had left Israel, and gone back to your home. We were all sworn to silence—and that's what Debra believes now.'

David released Ella's wrist, picked up his beer glass and sipped at the head of froth.

'You still haven't answered my question, David. What are you going to do now?'

'I don't know, Ella. I guess I'll have to think about that.'

A harsh warm wind came off the hills and ruffled the surface of the lake, darkening it to black and flecking it with white crests. The fishing boats along the curve of the shore tugged restlessly at their mooring ropes, and the fishing nets upon their drying racks billowed like bridal veils.

The wind caught Debra's hair and shook it out in a loose cloud. It pressed the silk dress she wore against her body, emphasizing the heavy roundness of her breasts and the length of her legs.

She stood on the battlements of the crusader castle, leaning both hands lightly on the head of her cane and she stared out across the water, almost as though she could see beyond it.

Ella sat near her, on a fallen block of masonry out of the wind, but she pinned her hat down with one hand as he spoke, watching Debra's face intently to judge her reactions.

'At the time it seemed the kindest thing to do. I agreed to keep the truth from you, because I did not want you to torture yourself–'

Debra spoke sharply. 'Don't ever do that again.'

Ella made a moue of resignation and went on. 'I had no way of knowing how bad he was, they would not let me see him, and so I suppose I was a coward and I let it drift.'

Debra shook her head angrily, but she remained silent. Ella wondered again that sightless eyes could contain so much expression, for Debra's emotions blazed clearly in the honey-coloured sparks as she turned her head towards Ella.

'It was not the time to distract you. Don't you see, my dear? You were adjusting so nicely–working so well on your book. I did not see that we could gain anything by telling you. I decided to co-operate with your father–and see how things turned out later.'

'Then why are you telling me all this now?' Debra demanded. 'What has happened to change your mind–what has happened to David'

'Yesterday at noon David was discharged from Hadassah Hospital.'

'Hospital?' Debra was puzzled. 'You don't mean he has been in hospital all this time, Ella. Nine months–it's impossible!'

'It's the truth.'

'He must have been terribly hurt,' Debra's anger had changed to concern. 'How is he, Ella? What happened? Is he healed now?'

Ella was silent a moment, and Debra took a pace towards her. 'Well?' she asked.

'David's plane flamed out and he was very badly burned above the head. He has recovered completely now. His burns have healed–but–'

Ella hesitated again, and Debra groped for her hand and found it. 'Go on, Ella! But–?'

'David is no longer the most beautiful man I have ever seen.'

'I don't understand?'

'He is no longer swift and vital and–any woman who sees him now will find it difficult to be near him, let alone love him.'

Debra was listening intently, her expression rapt and her eyes soft-focused.

'He is very conscious of the way he looks now. He is searching for some place to hide, I think. He talks of wanting to fly as though it is some form of escape. He knows he is alone now, cut off from the world by the mask he wears–'

Debra's eyes had misted, and Ella made her gravelly voice gentler and she went on.

'But there is somebody who will never see that mask.' Ella drew the girl closer to her. 'Somebody who remembers only the way he was before.' Debra's grip tightened on Ella's hand, and she began to smile–it was an expression that seemed to radiate from deep within her.

'He needs you now, Debra,' Ella said softly. 'That is all there is left for him.

Will you change your decision now?'

'Fetch him to me, Ella,' Debra's voice shook. 'Fetch him to me as soon as you can.'

David climbed the long line of steps towards Ella's studio. It was a day of bright sunlight and he wore open sandals and light silk slacks of a bronze colour and a short-sleeved shirt with a wide V-neck. His arms were pale from lack of sun, the dark hair of his chest contrasting strongly against the soft cream–and upon his head he wore a wide-brimmed white straw hat to guard the cicatrice from the sun and to soften his face with shadow.

He paused, and he could feel the break of sweat under the shirt and the pumping of his lungs. He despised the weakness of his body and the quivering of his legs as he came out on the terrace. It was deserted, and he crossed to the shuttered doors and went into the gloom.

Ella Kadesh sitting on a Samarkand carpet in the centre of the paved floor was an astonishing sight. For she was dressed in a brief bikini costume adorned with pink roses that almost disappeared under the rolls of ponderous flesh that hung over it from belly and breast. She was in the yoga position of Padmasana, the sitting lotus, and her massive legs were twisted and entwined like mating pythons. Her hands were held before her palm to palm and her eyes were closed in meditation; upon her head her ginger wig was set four square like that of a judge.

David leaned in the doorway and before he could recover his breath he began to laugh. It began as a wheezy little chuckle, and then suddenly he was really laughing, from deep down–great gusts of it that shook his helpless body, and flogged his lungs. It was not mirth but a catharsis of the last dregs of suffering, it was the moment of accepting life again, a taking up once more of the challenge of living.

Ella must have recognized it as such, for she did not move, squatting like some cheerful buddha on the brilliant carpet, and she opened one little eye. The effect was even more startlingly comic, and David reeled away from the door, and fell into one of the chairs.

'Your soul is a desert, David Morgan,' said Ella. 'You have no recognition of beauty, all loveliness would wither on the dung heap which–' But the rest of it was lost as she also began to giggle and the yoga pose broke down, melting like a jelly on a hot day, and she traded him hoot for hoot and bellow for bellow of laughter.

'I'm stuck,' she gasped at last. 'Help me, Davey, you oaf–' And he staggered to her, knelt and struggled to help her unlock her interwoven legs. They came apart with little creaking and popping sounds and Ella collapsed face down on the carpet groaning and giggling at the same time.

'Get out of here,' she moaned. 'Leave me to die in peace. Go and find your woman, she is down on the jetty.'

She watched him go quickly, and then she dragged herself up and went to the door. The laughter dried up and she whispered aloud, 'My two poor little crippled kittens–I wonder if I have done the right thing.' The shadows of doubt crossed her face, and then faded. 'Well, it's too damn late for worry now, Kadesh, you interfering old bag, you should have thought about that before.'

A gaudily coloured towel and beach jacket were spread upon the jetty and a transistor radio, with its volume turned high, blared out a heavy rock tune. Far out in the bay Debra was swimming alone, a steady powerful overarm crawl. Her brown arms flashed wetly in the sun at each stroke and the water churned to froth at the beat of her legs.

She stopped to tread water. Her bathing cap was plain white, and he could see that she was listening for the sound of the radio for she began to swim again, heading directly in towards the jetty.

She came out of the water, pulling off the cap and shaking out her hair. Her body was dark, sun-browned and bejewelled with drops, the muscles looked firm and hard and her tread was confident and sure as she came up the stone steps and picked up her towel.

As she dried herself David stood near and watched her avidly, seeming to devour her with his eyes, trying to make up in that first minute for all those many months. He had pictured her so clearly, and yet there was much he had forgotten. Her hair was softer, cloudier than he remembered. He had forgotten the plasticity and lustre of her skin, it was darker also than it had been before – almost the colour of her eyes – she must have spent many hours each day in the sun. Suddenly and unaffectedly she threw her towel down and adjusted the top of her brief costume, pulling open the thin fabric and cupping one fat breast in her hand to settle it more comfortably, David felt his need of her so strongly that it seemed he could not contain it all within the physical bounds of his chest. He moved slightly and the gravel crunched softly under his shoes.

Instantly the lovely head turned towards him and froze in the attitude of listening. The eyes were wide open, intelligent and expressive, they seemed to look slightly to one side of him – and David had a powerful impulse to turn and glance behind him, following their steady gaze.

'David?' she asked softly. 'Is that you, David?'

He tried to answer her, but his voice failed him and his reply was a small choking sound. She ran to him, swiftly and long-legged as a roused foal, with her arms reaching out and her face lighting with joy.

He caught her up, and she clung to him fiercely, almost angrily – as though she had been too long denied.

'I've missed you, David.' Her voice was fierce also. 'Oh, God, you'll never know how I have missed you,' and she pressed her mouth to the stark gash in his mask of flesh.

This was the first human being who had treated him without reserve – without pity or revulsion – in all those months, and David felt his heart swell harder and his embrace was as fierce as hers.

She broke at last, leaning back to press her hips unashamedly against his, exulting in the hard thrustingness of his arousal, proud to have evoked it – and quickly, questioningly she ran her hands over his face, feeling the new contours and the unexpected planes and angles.

She felt him begin to pull away, but she stopped him and continued her examination.

'My fingers tell me that you are still beautiful –'

'You have lying fingers,' he whispered, but she ignored his words, and pushed forward teasingly with her hips.

'And I'm getting another very powerful message from further south.' She gave a breathless little laugh. 'Come with me, please, sir.'

Holding his hand, she ran lightly up the steps, dragging him after her. He was amazed at the agility and confidence with which she negotiated the climb.

She drew him into the cottage and as he looked about him, quickly taking it all in, she closed and bolted the door. Immediately the room was cool and dim and intimate.

On the bed her body was still damp and cold from the lake, but her lips were hot as she strained against him urgently. The two beautiful young bodies meshed hungrily, almost as if they were attempting to find sanctuary within each other, desperately flesh sought haven within flesh, within each other's encircling arms and legs they searched for and found surcease from the loneliness and the darkness.

The physical act of love, no matter how often repeated, was insufficient for their needs; even in the intervals between they clung desperately to each other; sleeping pressed together, they groped drowsily but anxiously for each other if the movements of sleep separated them for even an instant. They talked holding hands, she reaching up to touch his face at intervals, he staring into her golden eyes. Even when she prepared their simple meals, he stood close beside or behind her so that she could sway against him and feel him there. It was as though they lived in momentary dread of being once more separated.

It was two days before they left the sanctuary of the cottage and walked together along the lake shore or swam from the jetty and lay in the warm sun. But even when Ella looked down at them from the terrace and waved, David asked, 'Shall we go up to her?'

'No,' Debra answered quickly. 'Not yet. I'm not ready to share you with anybody else yet. Just a little while more, please, David.'

And it was another three days before they climbed the path to the studio. Ella had laid on one of her gargantuan lunches, but she had invited no other guests and they were grateful to her for that.

'I thought I'd have to send down a party of stretcher-bearers to carry you up, Davey,' Ella greeted him, with a lecherous chuckle.

'Don't be crude, Ella,' Debra told her primly, flushing to a dark rose brown, and Ella let fly with one of her explosive bursts of mirth that was so contagious they must follow it.

They sat beneath the palm trees and drank wine from the earthenware jugs, and ate hugely, laughing and talking without restraint, David and Debra so involved with each other that they were not aware of Ella's shrewdly veiled appraisal.

The change in Debra was dramatic, all the coolness and reserve were gone now, the armour in which she had clad her emotions was stripped away. She was vital and eager and blooming with love.

She sat close beside David, laughing with delight at his sallies, and leaning to touch and caress him, as though to reassure herself of his presence.

Ella glanced again at David, trying to smile naturally at him, but guiltily aware of the sneaking sensation of repulsion she still felt—repulsion and aching pity—when she looked at that monstrous head. She knew that if she saw it every day for twenty years, it would still disturb her.

Debra laughed again at something David had said and turned her face to him, offering her mouth with a touching innocence.

'What a terrible thing to say,' she laughed. 'I think a gesture of contrition is called for,' and responded eagerly as the great ravaged head bent to her and the thin slit of a mouth touched hers.

It was disquieting to see the lovely dark face against that mask of ruined flesh, and yet it was also strangely moving.

'It was the right thing. For once I did the right thing,' Ella decided, watching them, and feeling a vague envy. These two were bound together completely, made strong by their separate afflictions. Before it had been a mutual itching of the flesh, a chance spark struck from two minds meeting, but now it was something that transcended that.

Ella recalled regretfully a long line of lovers stretching back to the shadowy edges of her memory, receding images which seemed unreal now. If only there had been something to bind her to one of those, if only she had been left something more valuable than half-remembered words and faded memories of brief mountings and furtive couplings. She sighed, and they looked to her questioningly.

'A sad sound, Ella, darling,' Debra said. 'We are selfish, please forgive us.'

'Not sad, my children,' Ella denied hotly, scattering the old phantoms of her memory. 'I am happy for you. You have something very wonderful–strong and bright and wonderful. Protect it as you would your life.'

She took up her wine glass. 'I give you a toast. I give you David and Debra–and a love made invincible by suffering.' And they were serious for a moment while they drank the toast together in golden yellow wine, sitting in golden yellow sunlight, then the mood resumed and they were gay once more.

Once the first desperate demands of their bodies had been met, once they had drawn as close together as physical limits would allow, then they began a coupling of the spirit. They had never really spoken before, even when they had shared the house on Malik Street, they had used only the superficial word symbols.

Now they began learning really to talk. Some nights they did not sleep but spent the fleeting hours of darkness in exploring each other's minds and bodies, and they delighted to realize that this exploration would never be completed–for the area of their minds were boundless.

During the day the blind girl taught David to see. He found that he had never truly used his eyes before, and now that he must see for both of them he had to learn to make the fullest use of his sight. He must learn to describe colour and shape and movement accurately and incisively, for Debra's demands were insatiable.

In turn, David, whose own confidence had been shattered by his disfigurement, taught confidence to the girl. She learned to trust him implicitly as he grew to anticipate her needs. She learned to step out boldly beside him, knowing that he would guide or caution her with a light touch or a word. Her world had shrunk to the small area about the cottage and jetty within which she could find her way surely. Now with David beside her, her frontiers fell back and she was free to move wherever she chose.

Yet they ventured out together only cautiously at first, wandering along the lakeside together or climbing the hills towards Nazareth, and each day they swam in the green lake waters and each night they made love in the curtained alcove.

David grew hard and lean and sun-tanned again, and it seemed they were complete for when Ella asked, 'Debra, when are you going to make a start on the new book?' she laughed and answered lightly.

'Sometime within the next hundred years.'

A week later she asked of David this time:

'Have you decided what you are going to do yet, Davey?'

'Just what I'm doing now,' he said, and Debra backed him up quickly. 'For ever!' she said. 'Just like this for ever.'

Then without thinking about it, without really steeling themselves to it, they went to where they would meet other people in the mass.

David borrowed the speedboat, picked up a shopping list from Ella, and they planed down along the lake shore to Tiberias, with the white wake churning out behind them and the wind and drops of spray in their faces.

They moored in the tiny harbour of the marina at Lido Beach and walked up into the town. David was so engrossed with Debra that the crowds about him were unreal, and although he noticed a few curious glances they meant very little to him.

Although it was early in the season, the town was filled with visitors, and the buses were parked in the square at the foot of the hill and along the lake front, for this was full on the tourist route.

David carried a plastic bag that grew steadily heavier until it was ready to overflow.

'Bread, and that's the lot,' Debra mentally ticked off the list.

They went down the hill under the eucalyptus trees and found a table on the harbour wall, beneath a gaily coloured umbrella.

They sat touching each other and drank cold beer and ate pistachio nuts, oblivious of everything and everybody about them even though the other tables were crowded with tourists. The lake sparkled and the softly rounded hills seemed very close in the bright light. Once a flight of Phantoms went booming down the valley, flying low on some mysterious errand, and David watched them dwindle southward without regrets.

When the sun was low they went to where the speedboat was moored, and David handed Debra down into it. On the wall above them sat a party of tourists, probably on some package-deal pilgrimage, and they were talking animately—their accents were Limehouse, Golders Green and Merseyside, although the subtleties of pronunciation were lost on David.

He started the motor and pushed off from the wall, steering for the harbour mouth with Debra sitting close beside him and the motor burbling softly.

A big red-faced tourist looked down from the wall and, supposing that the motor covered his voice, nudged his wife.

'Get a look at those two, Mavis. Beauty and the beast, isn't it?'

'Cork it, Bert. They might understand.'

'Go on, luv! They only talk Yiddish or whatever.'

Debra felt David's arm go rigid under her hand, felt him begin to pull away, sensing his outrage and anger—but she gripped his forearm tightly and restrained him.

'Let's go, Davey, darling. Leave them, please.'

Even when they were alone on the safety of the cottage, David was silent and she could feel the tension in his body and the air was charged with it.

They ate the evening meal of bread and cheese and fish and figs in the same strained silence. Debra could think of nothing to say to distract him for the careless words had wounded her as deeply. Afterwards she lay unsleeping beside him. He lay on his back, not touching her, with his arms at his sides and his fists clenched. When at last she could bear it no longer, she turned to him and stroked his face, still not knowing what to say. It was David who broke the silence at last.

'I want to go away from people. We don't need people—do we?'

'No,' she whispered. 'We don't need them.'

'There is a place called Jabulani. It is deep in the African bushveld, far from the nearest town. My father bought it as a hunting lodge thirty years ago–and now it belongs to me.'

'Tell me about it.' Debra laid her head on his chest, and he began stroking her hair, relaxing as he talked.

'There is a wide plain on which grow open forests of mopani and mohobahoba, with some big fat old baobabs and a few ivory palms. In the open glades the grass is yellow gold and the fronds of the ilala palms look like beggars' fingers. At the end of the plain is a line of hills, they turn blue at a distance and the peaks are shaped like the turrets of a fairy castle with tumbled blocks of granite. Between the hills rises a spring of water, a strong spring that has never dried and the water is very clear and sweet–'

'What does Jabulani mean?' Debra asked when he had described it to her.

'It means the "place of rejoicing",' David told her.

'I want to go there with you,' she said.

'What about Israel?' he asked. 'Will you not miss it?'

'No,' she shook her head. 'You see, I will take it with me–in my heart.'

Ella went up to Jerusalem with them, filling the back seat of the Mercedes. She would help Debra select the furniture they would take with them from the house and have it crated and shipped. The rest of it she would sell for them. Aaron Cohen would negotiate the sale of the house, and both David and Debra felt a chill of sadness at the thought of other people living in their home.

David left the women at it and he drove out to Ein Karem and parked the Mercedes beside the iron gate in the garden wall.

The Brig was waiting for him in that bleak and forbidding room above the courtyard. When David greeted him from the doorway he looked up coldly, and there was no relaxation of the iron features, no warmth or pity in the fierce warrior eyes.

'You come to me with the blood of my son upon your hands,' he said, and David froze at the words and held his gaze. After a few moments the Brig indicated the tall-backed chair against the far wall, and David crossed stiffly to it and sat down.

'If you had suffered less, I would have made you answer for more,' said the Brig. 'But vengeance and hatred are barren things–as you have discovered.'

David dropped his eyes to the floor.

'I will not pursue them further, despite the dictates of my heart, for that is what I am condemning in you. You are a violent young man, and violence is the pleasure of fools and only the last resort of wise men. The only excuse for it is to protect what is rightfully yours–any other display of violence is abuse. You abused the power I gave you–and in doing it you killed my son, and brought my country to the verge of war.'

The Brig stood up from his desk, and he crossed to the window and looked down into the garden. They were both silent while he stroked his moustache and remembered his son.

At last the Brig sighed heavily and turned back into the room.

'Why do you come to me?' he asked.

'I wish to marry your daughter, sir.'

'You are asking me–or telling me?' the Brig demanded, and then without waiting for an answer returned to his desk and sat down. 'If you abuse this also–if you bring her pain or unhappiness, I will seek you out. Depend upon it.'

David stood up and settled the cloth cap over his gross head, pulling the brim well down.

'We would like you to be at the wedding. Debra asked that particularly–for you and her mother.'

The Brig nodded. 'You may tell her that we will be there.'

The synagogue at Jerusalem University is a gleaming white structure, shaped like the tent of a desert wanderer, with the same billowing lines.

The red-bud trees were in full bloom and the wedding party was larger than they had planned, for apart from the immediate family there were Debra's colleagues from the university, Robert and some of the other boys from the squadron, Ella Kadesh, Doctor Edelman the baby-faced eye surgeon who had worked on Debra, Aaron Cohen and a dozen others.

After the simple ceremony, they walked through the university grounds to one of the reception rooms that David had hired. It was a quiet gathering with little laughter or joking. The young pilots from David's old squadron had to leave early to return to base, and with them went any pretence of jollity.

Debra's mother was still not yet fully recovered, and the prospect of Debra's departure reduced her to quiet grey weeping. Debra tried without success to comfort her.

Before he left, Dr Edelman drew David aside.

'Watch for any sign of atrophy in her eyes, any cloudiness, excessive redness–any complaints of pain, headaches–'

'I will watch for it.'

'Any indications, no matter how trivial–if you have any doubts, you must write to me.'

'Thank you, doctor.'

They shook hands. 'Good luck in your new life,' said Edelman.

Through it all Debra showed iron control, but even she at last succumbed and she, her mother, and Ella Kadesh all broke down simultaneously at the departure barrier of Lod Airport and hung round each other's necks, weeping bitterly.

The Brig and David stood by, stiff and awkward, trying to look as though they were not associated with the weeping trio, until the first warning broadcast gave them an excuse for a brief handshake and David took Debra's arm and drew her gently away.

They climbed the boarding ladder into the waiting Boeing without looking back. The giant aircraft took off and turned away southwards, and as always the sensation of flight soothed David; all the cares and tensions of these last few days left on the earth behind and below, he felt a new lightness of the spirit–excitement for what lay ahead.

He reached across and squeezed Debra's arm.

'Hello there, Morgan,' he said, and she turned towards him and smiled happily–blindly.

It was necessary to spend some time in Cape Town before they could escape to the sanctuary of Jabulani in the north.

David took a suite at the Mount Nelson Hotel, and from there he was able to settle the numerous issues that had piled up in his absence.

The accountants who managed his trust funds demanded ten days of his time and they spent it in the sitting-room of the suite, poring over trust documents and accounts.

In two years his income had grossly exceeded his spending, and the unused portion of his income had to be re-invested. In addition the third trust fund would soon pass to him and there were formalities to be completed.

Debra was hugely impressed by the extent of David's wealth.

'You must be almost a millionaire,' she said in a truly awed voice, for that was as rich as Debra could imagine.

'I'm not just a pretty face,' David agreed, and she was relieved that he could talk so lightly about his appearance.

Mitzi and her new husband came to visit them in their suite. However, the evening was not a success. Although Mitzi tried to act as though nothing had changed, and though she still called him 'warrior', yet it was apparent that she and her feelings had altered.

She was heavily pregnant and more shapeless than David would have thought possible. It was half-way through the evening before David realized the true reason for all the reserve. At first he thought that his disfigurement was worrying them, but after Mitzi had given a half-hour eulogy of the strides that Cecil was making at Morgan Group and the immense trust that Paul Morgan had placed in him, Cecil had asked innocently, 'Are you thinking of joining us at the Group? I'm sure we could find something useful for you to do—ha, ha!'

David could assure them quietly.

'No, thank you. You won't have to worrry about me, Cecil, old boy. You take over from Uncle Paul with my blessing.'

'Good Lord, I didn't mean that.' Cecil was shocked, but Mitzi was less devious.

'He really will be very good, warrior, and you never were interested, were you?'

After that evening they did not see the couple again, and Paul Morgan was in Europe, so David fulfilled his family obligations without much pain or suffering and he could concentrate on the preparations for the move to Jabulani.

Barney Venter spent a week with them in choosing a suitable aircraft to handle the bush airstrip and yet give David the type of performance he enjoyed. At last they decided on a twin-engined Piper Navajo, a six-seater with two big 300-h.p. Lycoming engines and a tricycle undercart, and Barney walked around it with his hands on his hips.

'Well, she's no Mirage.' He kicked the landing-wheel and then checked himself and glanced quickly at David's face.

'I've had enough of Mirages,' David told him. 'They bite!'

On the last day David drove out with Debra to a farm near Paarl. The owner's wife was a dog breeder and when they went down to the kennels one of her labrador pups walked directly to Debra and placed a cold nose on her leg as he inhaled her, scent. Debra squatted and groped for his head and after fondling for a few moments she in her turn leaned forward and sniffed the pup's fur.

'He smells like old leather,' she said. 'What colour is he?'

'Black,' said David. 'Black as a Zulu.'

'That's what we'll call him,' said Debra. 'Zulu.'

'You want to choose this one?' David asked.

'No,' Debra laughed. 'He chose us.'

When they flew northwards the next morning the pup was indignant at being placed in the back seat and with a flying scrambling leap he came over Debra's shoulder and took up position in her lap, which seemed to suit them both very well.

'It looks like I have competition,' David muttered ruefully.

From the brown plateau of the high veld, the land dropped away steeply down the escarpment to the bush veld of southern Africa.

David picked up his landmark on the little village of Bush Buck Ridge and the long slim snake of the Sabi River as it twisted through the open forests of the plain. He altered course slightly northwards and within ten minutes he saw the low line of blue hills which rose abruptly out of the flat land.

'There it is, ahead of us,' David told Debra and his tone was infectious. She hugged the dog closer to her and leaned towards David.

'What does it look like?'

The hills were forested with big timber, and turreted with grey rock. At their base the bush was thick and dark. The pools glinted softly through the dark foliage. He described them to her.

'My father named them "The String of Pearls", and that's what they look like. They rise out of the run-off of rain water from the sloping ground beyond the hills. They disappear just as suddenly again into the sandy earth of the plain,' David explained as he circled the hills, slowly losing height. 'They are what give Jabulani its special character, for they provide water for all the wild life of the plain. Birds and animals are drawn from hundreds of miles to the Pearls.' He levelled out and throttled back, letting the aircraft sink lower. 'There is the homestead, white walls and thatch to keep it cool in the hot weather, deep shaded verandas and high rooms—you will love it.'

The airstrip seemed clear and safe, although the windsock hung in dirty tatters from its pole. David circled it carefully before lining up for the landing, and they taxied towards the small brick hangar set amongst the trees. David kicked on the wheel brakes and cut the engines.

'This is it,' he said.

Jabulani was one of a block of estates that bounded the Kruger National Park—the most spectacular nature reserve on earth. These estates were not productive, in that they were unsuitable for the growth of crops and few of them were used for grazing of domestic animals; their immense value lay in the unspoiled bush veld and the wild life—in the peace and space upon which wealthy men placed such a premium that they would pay large fortunes for a piece of this *Lebensraum*.

When David's grandfather had purchased Jabulani he had paid a few shillings an acre, for in those days the wilderness was still intact.

It had been used as a family hunting estate down the years, and as Paul Morgan had never shown interest in the veld, it had passed to David's father and so to David.

Now the eighteen thousand acres of African bush and plain, held as freehold land, was a possession beyond price.

Yet the Morgan family had made little use of it these last fifteen years. David's father had been an enthusiastic huntsman, and with him most of David's school holidays had been spent here. However, after his father's death, the visits to Jabulani had become shorter and further apart.

It was seven years since the last visit, when he had brought up a party of brother officers from Cobra Squadron.

Then it had been immaculately run by Sam, the black overseer, butler and game ranger.

Under Sam's management there had always been fresh crisp linen on the beds, highly polished floors, the exterior walls of the buildings had been snowy white and the thatch neat and well-tended. The deep-freeze had been well stocked with steak and the liquor cupboard filled—with every bottle accounted for.

Sam ran a tight camp, with half a dozen willing and cheerful helpers.

'Where is Sam?' was the first question David asked of the two servants who hurried down from the homestead to meet the aircraft.

'Sam gone.'

'Where to?' And the answer was the eloquent shrug of Africa. Their uniforms were dirty and needed mending, and their manners disinterested.

'Where is the Land-Rover?'

'She is dead.'

They walked up to the homestead and there David had another series of unpleasant surprises.

The buildings were dilapidated, looking forlorn and neglected under their rotting black thatch. The walls were dingy, grey-brown with the plaster falling away in patches.

The interiors were filthy with dust, and sprinkled with the droppings of the birds and reptiles that made their homes in the thatch.

The mosquito gauze, that was intended to keep the wide verandas insect-free, was rusted through and breaking away in tatters.

The vegetable gardens were overgrown, the fences about them falling to pieces. The grounds of the homestead itself were thick with rank weed, and not only the Land-Rover had died. No single piece of machinery on the estate—water pump, toilet cistern, electricity generator, motor vehicle—was in working order.

'It's a mess, a frightful mess,' David told Debra as they sat on the front step and drank mugs of sweet tea. Fortunately David had thought to bring emergency supplies with them.

'Oh, Davey. I am so sorry, because I like it here. It's peaceful, so quiet. I can just feel my nerves untying themselves.'

'Don't be sorry. I'm not. Those old huts were built by Gramps back in the twenties—and they weren't very well built even then.' David's voice was full of a new purpose, a determination that she had not heard for so long. 'It's a fine excuse to tear the whole lot down, and build again.'

'A place of our own?' she asked.

'Yes,' said David delightedly. That's it. That's just it!'

They flew into Nelspruit, the nearest large town, the following day. In the week of bustle and planning that followed they forgot their greater problems. With an architect they planned the new homestead with care, taking into consideration all their special requirements—a large airy study for Debra, workshop and office for David, a kitchen laid out to make it safe and easy for a blind cook, rooms without dangerous split levels and with regular easily learned shapes, and finally a nursery section. When David described this addition Debra asked cautiously, 'You making some plans that I should know about?'

'You'll know about it, all right,' he assured her.

The guest house was to be separate and self-contained and well away from the main homestead, and the small hutment for the servants was a quarter of a mile beyond that, screened by trees and the shoulder of the rocky kopje that rose behind the homestead.

David bribed a building contractor from Nelspruit to postpone all his other work, load his workmen on four heavy trucks and bring them out to Jabulani.

They began on the main house, and while they worked David was busy resurfacing the airstrip, repairing the water pumps and such other machinery as still had life left in it. However, the Land-Rover and the electricity generator had to be replaced.

Within two months the new homestead was habitable, and they could move. Debra set up her tape recorders beneath the big windows overlooking the shaded front garden, where the afternoon breeze could cool the room and waft in the perfume of the frangipani and poinsettia blooms.

While David was completely absorbed in making Jabulani into a comfortable home, Debra made her own arrangements.

Swiftly she explored and mapped in her mind all her immediate surroundings. Within weeks she could move about the new house with all the confidence of a person with normal sight and she had trained the servants to replace each item of furniture in its exact position. Always Zulu, the labrador pup, moved like a glossy black shadow beside her. Early on he had decided that Debra needed his constant care, and had made her his life's work.

Quickly he learned that it was useless staring at her or wagging his tail, to attract her attention he must whine or pant. In other respects she was also slightly feeble-minded, the only way to prevent her doing stupid things like falling down the front steps or tripping over a bucket left in the passage by a careless servant was to bump her with his shoulder, or with his nose.

She had fallen readily into a pattern of work that kept her in her workroom until noon each day, with Zulu curled at her feet.

David set up a large bird bath under the trees outside her window, so the tapes she made had as a background the chatter and warble of half a dozen varieties of wild birds. She had discovered a typist in Nelspruit who could speak Hebrew, and David took the tapes in to her whenever he flew to town for supplies and to collect the mail, and he brought each batch of typing back with him for checking.

They worked together on this task, David reading each batch of writing or correspondence aloud to her and making the alterations she asked for. He made it a habit of reading almost everything, from newspapers to novels, aloud.

'Who needs braille with you around,' Debra remarked, but it was more than just the written word she needed to hear from him. It was each facet and dimension of her new surroundings. She had never seen any of the myriad birds that flocked to drink and bathe below her window, though she soon recognized each individual call and would pick out a stranger immediately.

'David, there's a new one, what is it? What does he look like?'

And he must describe not only its plumage, but its mannerisms and its habits. At other times he must describe to her exactly how the new buildings fitted into their surroundings, the antics of Zulu the labrador, and supply accurate descriptions of the servants, the view from the window of her workroom—and a hundred other aspects of her new life.

In time the building was completed and the strangers left Jabulani, but it was not until the crates from Israel containing their furniture and other possessions from Malik Street arrived that Jabulani started truly to become their home.

The olive-wood table was placed under the window in the workroom.

'I haven't been able to work properly, there was something missing—' Debra ran her fingers caressingly across the inlaid ivory and ebony top '—until now.'

Her books were in shelves on the wall beside the table, and the leather suite in the new lounge looked very well with the animal-skin rugs and woven wool carpets.

David hung the Ella Kadesh painting above the fireplace, Debra determining the precise position for him by sense of touch.

'Are you sure it shouldn't be a sixteenth of an inch higher?' David asked seriously.

'Let's have no more lip from you, Morgan, I have to know exactly where it is.'

Then the great brass bedstead was set up in the bedroom, and covered with the ivory-coloured bedspread. Debra bounced up and down on it happily.

'Now, there is only one thing more that is missing,' she declared.

'What's that?' he asked with mock anxiety. 'Is it something important?'

'Come here.' She crooked a finger in his general direction. 'And I'll show you just how important it is.'

During the months of preparation they had not left the immediate neighbourhood of the homestead, but now quite suddenly the rush and bustle was over.

'We have eighteen thousand acres and plenty of four-footed neighbours—let's go check it all out,' David suggested.

They packed a cold lunch and the three of them climbed into the new Land-Rover with Zulu relegated to the back seat. The road let naturally down to the String of Pearls for this was the focal point of all life upon the estate.

They left the Land-Rover amongst the fever trees and went down to the ruins of the thatched summer house on the bank of the main pool.

The water aroused all Zulu's instincts and he plunged into it, paddling out into the centre with obvious enjoyment. The water was clear as air, but shaded to black in the depths.

David scratched in the muddy bank and turned out a thick pink earthworm. He threw it into the shallows and a dark shape half as long as his arm rushed silently out of the depths and swirled the surface.

'Wow!' David laughed. 'There are still a few fat ones around. We will have to bring down the rods. I used to spend days down here when I was a kid.'

The forest was filled with memories and as they wandered along the edge of the reed banks he reminisced about his childhood, until gradually he fell into silence, and she asked:

'Is something wrong, David?' She had grown that sensitive to his moods.

'There are no animals.' His tone was puzzled. 'Birds, yes. But we haven't seen a single animal, not even a duiker, since we left the homestead.' He stopped at a place that was clear of reeds, where the bank shelved gently. 'This used to be a favourite drinking place. It was busy day and night—the herds virtually lining up for a chance to drink.' He left Debra and went down to the edge, stooping to examine the ground carefully. 'No spoor even, just a few kudu and a small troop of baboon. There has not been a herd here for months, or possibly years.'

When he came back to her she asked gently, 'You are upset?'

'Jabulani without its animals is nothing,' he muttered. 'Come on, let's go and see the rest of it. There is something very odd here.'

The leisurely outing became a desperate hunt, as David scoured the thickets and the open glades, followed the dried water courses and stopped the Land-Rover to examine the sand beds for signs of wild life.

'Not even an impala,' he was worried and anxious. 'There used to be thousands of them. I remember herds of them, silky brown and graceful as ballet dancers, under nearly every tree.'

He turned the Land-Rover northwards, following an overgrown track through the trees.

'There is grazing here that hasn't been touched. It's lush as a cultivated garden.'

A little before noon they reached the dusty, corrugated public road that ran along the north boundary of Jabulani. The fence that followed the edge of the road was ruinous, with sagging and broken wire and many of the uprights snapped off at ground level.

'Hell, it's a mess,' David told her, as he turned through a gap in the wire on to the road, and followed the boundary for two miles until they reached the turn-off to the Jabulani homestead.

Even the signboard hanging above the stone pillars of the gateway, which David's father had fashioned in bronze and of which he had been so proud, was now dilapidated and hung askew.

'Well, there's plenty of work to keep us going,' said David with a certain relish.

Half a mile beyond the gates the road turned sharply, hedged on each side by tall grass, and standing full in the sandy track was a magnificent kudu bull, ghostly grey and striped with pale chalky lines across the deep powerful body. His head was held high, armed with the long corkscrew black horns, and his huge ears were spread in an intent listening attitude.

For only part of a second he posed like that, then, although the Land-Rover was still two hundred yards off, he exploded into a smoky blur of frantic flight. His great horns laid along his back as he fled through the open bush in a series of long, lithe bounds, disappearing so swiftly it seemed he had been only a fantasy, and David described it to Debra.

'He took off the very instant he spotted us. I remember when they were so tame around here that we had to chase them out of the vegetable garden with sticks.'

Again he swung off the main track and on to another overgrown path, on which the new growth of saplings was already thick and tall. He drove straight over them in the tough little vehicle.

'What on earth are you doing?' Debra shouted above the crash and swish of branches.

'In this country when you run out of road, you just make your own.'

Four miles farther on, they emerged abruptly on to the fire-break track that marked the eastern boundary of Jabulani, the dividing line between them and the National Park which was larger than the entire land area of the state of Israel, five million acres of virgin wilderness, three hundred and eighty-five kilometres long and eighty wide, home of more than a million wild animals, the most important reservoir of wild life left in Africa.

David stopped the Land-Rover, cut the engine and jumped down. After a moment of shocked and angry silence he began to swear.

'What's made you so happy?' Debra demanded.

'Look at that—just look at that!' David ranted.

'I wish I could.'

'Sorry, Debs. It's a fence. A game fence!'

It stood eight feet high and the uprights were hardwood poles thick as a man's thigh, while the mesh of the fence was heavy gauge wire. 'They have fenced us off. The National Park's people have cut us off! No wonder there are no animals.'

As they drove back to the homestead David explained to her how there had always been an open boundary with the Kruger National Park. It had suited everybody well enough, for Jabulani's sweet grazing and the perennial water of the pools helped to carry the herds through times of drought and scarcity.

'It's becoming very important to you, this business of the wild animals.' Debra had listened silently, fondling the labrador's head, as David spoke.

'Yes, suddenly it's important. When they were here, I guess I just took them for granted—but now they are gone, well, now they are very important,' he laughed abruptly and bitterly. 'I wonder how often that's been said in Africa—now they are gone it's suddenly important.'

They drove on for a mile or two without speaking and then David said with determination, 'I'm going to get them to pull that fence out. They can't cut us off like that. I'm going to get hold of the head warden, now, right away.'

David remembered Conrad Berg from his childhood when he had been the warden in charge of the southern portion of the park, but not yet the chief. There was a body of legend about the man that had been built up over the years, and two of these stories showed clearly the type of man he was.

Caught out in a lonely area of the reserve after dark with a broken-down truck, he was walking home when he was attacked by a full-grown male lion. In the struggle he had been terribly mauled, half the flesh torn from his back and the bone of his shoulder and arm bitten through. Yet he had managed to kill the animal with a small sheath knife, stabbing it repeatedly in the throat until he hit the jugular. He had then stood up and walked five miles through the night with the hyena pack following him expectantly, waiting for him to drop.

On another occasion one of the estate owners bounding the park had poached one of Berg's lions, shooting it down half a mile inside the boundary. The poacher was a man high in government, wielding massive influence, and he had laughed at Conrad Berg.

'What are you going to do about it, my friend? Don't you like your job?'

Doggedly, ignoring the pressure from above, Berg had collected his evidence and issued a summons. The pressure had become less subtle as the court date approached, but he had never wavered. The important personage finally stood in the dock, and was convicted. He was sentenced to a thousand pounds' fine or six months at hard labour.

Afterwards he had shaken Berg's hand and said to him, 'Thank you for a lesson in courage,' and perhaps this was one of the reasons Berg was now chief warden.

He stood beside his game fence where he had arranged over the telephone to meet David. He was a big man, broad and tall and beefy, with thick heavily muscled arms still scarred from the lion attack, and a red sunburned face.

He wore the suntans and slouch hat of the Park's service, with the green cloth badges on his epaulets.

Behind him was parked his brown Chevy truck with the Park Board's emblem on the door, and two of his black game rangers seated in the back. One of them was holding a heavy rifle.

Berg stood with his clenced fists on his hips, his hat pushed back and a forbidding expression on his face. He so epitomized the truculent male animal guarding its territory that David muttered to Debra, 'Here comes trouble.'

He parked close beside the fence and he and Debra climbed down and went to the wire.

'Mr Berg. I am David Morgan. I remember you from when my father owned Jabulani. I'd like you to meet my wife.'

Berg's expression wavered. Naturally he had heard all the rumours about the new owner of Jabulani; it was a lonely isolated area and it was his job to know about these things. Yet he was unprepared for this dreadfully mutilated young man, and his blind but beautiful wife.

With an awkward gallantry Berg doffed his hat, then realized she would not see the gesture. He murmured a greeting and when David thrust his hand through the fence he shook it cautiously.

Debra and David were working as a team and they turned their combined charm upon Berg, who was a simple and direct man. Slowly his defences softened as they chatted. He admired Zulu, he also kept labradors and it served as a talking-point while Debra unpacked a Thermos of coffee and David filled mugs for all of them.

'Isn't that Sam?' David pointed to the game ranger in the truck who held Berg's rifle.

'Ja.' Berg was guarded.

'He used to work on Jabulani.'

'He came to me of his own accord,' Berg explained, turning aside any implied rebuke.

'He wouldn't remember me, of course, not the way I look now. But he was a fine ranger, and the place certainly went to the bad without him to look after it,' David admitted before he went into a frontal assault. 'The other thing which has ruined us is this fence of yours.' David kicked one of the uprights.

'You don't say?' Berg swished the grounds of his coffee around the mug and flicked it out.

'Why did you do it?'

'For good reason.'

'My father had a gentleman's agreement with the Board, the boundary was open at all times. We have got water and grazing that you need.'

'With all respects to the late Mr Morgan,' Conrad Berg spoke heavily, 'I was never in favour of the open boundary.'

'Why not?'

'Your daddy was a *sportsman*.' He spat the word out, as though it were a mouthful of rotten meat. 'When my lions got to know him and learned to stay this side of the line—then he used to bring down a couple of donkeys and parade them along the boundary—to tempt them out.'

David opened his mouth to protest, and then closed it slowly. He felt the seamed scars of his face mottling and staining with a flush of shame. It was true, he remembered the donkeys and the soft wet lion skins being pegged out to dry behind the homestead.

'He never poached,' David defended him. 'He had an owner's licence and they were all shot on our land.'

'No, he never poached,' Berg admitted. 'He was too damned clever for that. He knew I would have put a rocket up him that would have made him the first man on the moon.'

'So that's why you put up the fence.'

'No.'

'Why then?'

'Because for fourteen years Jabulani has been under the care of an absentee landlord who didn't give a good damn what happened to it. Old Sam here—' he motioned at the game ranger in the truck '—did his best, but still it became a poacher's paradise. As fast as the grazing and water you boast of pulled my game out of the Park, so they were cut down by every sportsman with an itchy trigger finger. When Sam tried to do something about it, he got badly beaten up, and when that didn't stop him somebody put fire into his hut at night. They burned two of his kids to death—'

Daved felt his very soul quail at the thought of the flames on flesh, his cheeks itched at the memory.

'I didn't know,' he said gruffly.

'No, you were too busy making money or whatever is your particular form of pleasure,' Berg was angry. 'So at last Sam came to me and I gave him a job. Then I strung this fence.'

'There is nothing left on Jabulani—a few kudu, and a duiker or two—but otherwise it's all gone.'

'You are so right. It didn't take them long to clean it out.'

'I want it back.'

'Why?' Berg scoffed. 'So you can be a sportsman like your daddy? So you can fly your pals down from Jo'burg for the weekend to shoot the shit out of my lions?' Berg glanced at Debra, and immediately his red face flushed a deep port-wine colour. 'I'm sorry, Mrs Morgan, I did not mean to say that.'

'That's perfectly all right, Mr Berg. I think it was very expressive.'

'Thank you, ma'm.' Then he turned furiously back to David. 'Morgan's Private Safari Service, is that what you are after?'

'I would not allow a shot fired on Jabulani,' said David.

'I bet—except for the pot. That's the usual story. Except for the pot, and you've got the battle of Waterloo being fought all over again.'

'No,' said David. 'Not even for the pot.'

'You'd eat butcher's beef?' Berg asked incredulously.

'Look here, Mr Berg. If you pull your fence out, I'll have Jabulani declared a private nature reserve—'

Berg had been about to say something, but David's declaration dried the words, and his mouth remained hanging open. He closed it slowly.

'You know what that means?' he asked at last. 'You place yourself under our jurisdiction, completely. We'd tie you up properly with a lawyer's paper and all that stuff: no owner's licence, no shooting lions because they are in cattle area.'

'Yes. I know. I've studied the act. But there is something more. I'd undertake to fence the other three boundaries to your satisfaction, and maintain a force of private game rangers that you considered adequate—all at my own expense.'

Conrad Berg lifted his hat and scratched pensively at the long sparse grey hairs that covered his pate.

'Man,' he said mournfully, 'how can I say no to that?' Then he began to smile, the first smile of the meeting. 'It looks like you are really serious about this then.'

'My wife and I are going to be living here permanently. We don't want to live in a desert.'

'Ja,' he nodded, understanding completely that a man should feel that way. The strong revulsion that he had originally felt for the fantastic face before him was fading.

'I think the first thing we should work on is these poachers you tell me about. Let's snatch a couple of those and make a few examples,' David went on.

Berg's big red face split into a happy grin.

'I think I'm going to enjoy having you as a neighbour,' he said, and again he thrust his hand through the fence. David winced as he felt his knuckles cracking in the huge fist.

'Won't you come to dinner with us tomorrow night? You and your wife?' Debra asked with relief.

'It will be a mighty great pleasure, ma'm.'

'I'll get out the whisky bottle,' said David.

'That's kind of you–' said Conrad Berg seriously, 'but the missus and I only drink Old Buck dry gin, with a little water.'

'I'll see to it,' said David just as seriously.

Jane Berg was a slim woman of about Conrad's age. She had a dried-out face, lined and browned by the sun. Her hair was sunbleached and streaked with grey, and, as Debra remarked, she was probably the only thing in the world that Conrad was afraid of.

'I'm talking, Connie,' was enough to halt any flow of eloquence from her huge spouse, or a significant glance at her empty glass sent him with elephantine haste for a refill. Conrad had a great deal of trouble finishing any story or statement, for Jane had to correct the details during the telling, while he waited patiently for an opportunity to resume.

Debra chose the main course with care so as not to give offence, beefsteaks from the deep freeze, and Conrad ate four of them with unreserved pleasure although he spurned the wine that David served.

'That stuff is poison. Killed one of my uncles,' and stayed with Old Buck gin, even through the dessert.

Afterwards they sat about the cavernous fireplace with its logs blazing cheerfully and Conrad explained, with Jane's assistance, the problems that David would face on Jabulani.

'You get a few of the blacks from the tribal areas coming in from the north–'

'Or across the river,' Jane added.

'Or across the river, but they are no big sweat. They set wire snares mostly, and they don't kill that much–'

'But it's a terribly cruel way, the poor animals linger on for days with the wire cutting down to the bone,' Jane elaborated.

'As I was saying, once we have a few rangers busy that will stop almost immediately. It's the white poachers with modern rifles and hunting lamps–'

'Killing lamps,' Jane corrected.

'–killing lamps, they do the real damage. They finished off all your game on Jabulani in a couple of seasons.'

'Where do they come from?' David asked, his anger was rising again, the same protective anger of the shepherd that he had felt as he flew the skies of Israel.

'There is a big copper mine fifty miles north of here at Phalabora, hundreds of bored miners with a taste for venison. They would come down here and blaze away at every living thing—but now it's not worth the trip for them. Anyway they were just the amateurs, the weekend poachers.'

'Who are the professionals?'

'Where the dirt road from Jabulani meets the big national highway, about thirty miles from here—'

'At a place called Bandolier Hill,' Jane supplied the name.

'—there is a general dealer's store. It's just one of those trading posts that gets a little of the passing trade from the main road, but relies on the natives from the tribal areas. The person who owns and runs it has been there eight years now, and I have been after him all that time, but he's the craftiest bastard—I'm sorry, Mrs Morgan—I have ever run into.'

'He's the one?' David asked.

'He's the one,' Conrad nodded. 'Catch him, and half your worries are over.'

'What's his name?'

'Akkers. Johan Akkers,' Jane gave her assistance, the Old Buck was making her slightly owl-eyed, and she was having a little difficulty with her enunciation.

'How are we going to get him?' David mused. 'There isn't anything left on Jabulani to tempt him—the few kudu we have got are so wild, it wouldn't be worth the effort.'

'No, you haven't got anything to tempt him right now, but about the middle of September—'

'More like the first week in September,' Jane said firmly with strings of hair starting to hang down her temples.

'—the first week in September the marula trees down by your pools will come into fruit, and my elephants are going to visit you. The one thing they just can't resist is marula berries, and they are going to flatten my fence to get at them. Before I can repair it a lot of other game are going to follow the jumbo over to your side. You can lay any type of odds you like that our friend Akkers is oiling his guns and drooling at the mouth right this minute. He will know within an hour when the fence goes.'

'This time he may get a surprise.'

'Let's hope so.'

'I think—' David said softly '—that we might run down to Bandolier Hill tomorrow to have a look at this gentleman.'

'One thing is for sure—' said Jane Berg indistinctly, '—a gentleman, he is not.'

The road down to Bandolier Hill was heavily corrugated and thick with white dust that rose in a banner behind the Land-Rover and hung in the air long after they had passed. The hill was rounded and thickly timbered and stood over the mean metalled highway.

The trading post was four or five hundred yards from the road junction, set back amidst a grove of mango trees with their deep green and glistening foliage. It was a type found all over Africa—an unlovely building of mud brick with a naked corrugated iron roof, the walls plastered thickly with posters advertising goods from tea to flashlight batteries.

David parked the Land-Rover in the dusty yard beneath the raised stoop. There was a faded sign above the front steps:

'Bandolier Hill General Dealers'.

At the side of the building was parked an old green Ford one-ton truck with local licence plates. In the shade of the stoop squatted a dozen or so potential customers, African women from the tribal area, dressed in long cotton print dresses, timeless in their patience and their expressions showing no curiosity about the occupants of the Land-Rover. One of the women was suckling her infant with an enormously elongated breast that allowed the child to stand beside her and watch the newcomers without removing the puckered black nipple from his mouth.

Set in the centre of the yard was a thick straight pole, fifteen feet tall, and on top of the pole was a wooden structure like a dog kennel. David exclaimed as from the kennel emerged a big brown furry animal. It descended the pole in one swift falling action, seemingly as lightly as a bird, and the chain that was fastened to the pole at one end was, at the other, buckled about the animal's waist by a thick leather strap.

'It's one of the biggest old bull baboons I've ever seen.' Quickly he described it to Debra, as the baboon moved out to the chain's limit, and knuckled the ground as he made a lesiurely circle about his pole, the chain clinking as it swung behind him. It was an arrogant display, and he ruffled out the thick mane of hair upon his shoulders. When he had completed the circle, he sat down facing the Land-Rover, in a repellently humanoid attitude, and thrust out his lower jaw as he regarded them through small brown, close-set eyes.

'A nasty beast,' David told Debra. He would weigh ninety pounds, with a long dog-like muzzle and a jaw full of yellow fangs. After the hyena, he was the most hated animal of the veld—cunning, cruel and avaricious, all the vices of man and none of his graces. His stare was unblinking and, every few seconds, he ducked his head in a quick aggressive gesture.

While all David's attention was on the baboon, a man had come out of the store and now leaned on one of the pillars of the veranda.

'What can I do for you, Mr Morgan?' he asked in a thick accent. He was tall and spare, dressed in slightly rumpled and not entirely clean khaki slacks and open-neck shirt, with heavy boots on his feet and braces hooked into his pants, crossing his shoulders.

'How did you know my name?' David looked up at him, and he was of middle age with close-cropped greying hair over a domed skull. His teeth were badly fitting with bright pink plastic gums and his skin was drawn over the bones of the cheeks, and his deep-set eyes gave him a skull-like look. He grinned at David's question.

'Could only be you, scarred face and blind wife—you the new owner of Jabulani. Heard you built a new house and all set to live there now.'

The man's hands were huge, out of proportion to the rest of his rangy body, they were clearly very powerful and the lean muscles of his forearms were as tough as rope.

He slouched easily against the pillar and took from his pocket a clasp knife and a stick of black wind-dried meat—the jerky of North America, boucan of the Caribbean, or the biltong of Africa—and he cut a slice as though it were a plug of tobacco, popping it into his mouth.

'Like I asked—what can we do for you?' he chewed noisily, his teeth squelching at each bite.

'I need nails and paint.' David climbed out of the Land-Rover.

'Heard you did all your buying in Nelspruit.' Akkers looked him over with a calculated insolence, studying David's ruined face with attention. David saw that his deep-set eyes were a muddy green in colour.

'I thought there was a law against caging or chaining wild animals.' Akkers had roused David's resentment almost immediately, and the needle showed in his tone. Akkers began to grin again easily, still chewing.

'You a lawyer—are you?'

'Just asking.'

'I got a permit—you want to see it?'

David shook his head, and turned to speak to Debra in Hebrew. Quickly he described the man.

'I think he can guess why we are here, and he's looking for trouble.'

'I'll stay by the car,' said Debra.

'Good.' David climbed the steps to the veranda.

'What about the nails and paint?' he asked Akkers.

'Go on in,' he was still grinning. 'I got a nigger helper behind the counter. He will look after you.'

David hesitated and then walked on into the building. It smelled of carbolic soap and kerosene and maize meal. The shelves were loaded with cheap groceries, patent medicines, blankets and bolts of printed cotton cloth. From the roof hung bunches of army surplus boots and greatcoats, axe-heads and storm lanterns. The floor was stacked with tin trunks, pick handles, bins of flour and maize meal and the hundreds of other items that traditionally make up the stock of the country dealer. David found the African assistant and began his purchase.

Outside in the sunlight Debra climbed from the Land-Rover and leaned lightly against the door. The labrador scrambled down after her and began sniffing the concrete pillars of the veranda with interest where other dogs before him had spurted jets of yellow urine against the white-washed plaster.

'Nice dog,' said Akkers.

'Thank you.' Debra nodded politely.

Akkers glanced quickly across at his pet baboon, and his expression was suddenly cunning. A flash of understanding passed between man and animal. The baboon ducked its head again in that nervous gesture, then it rose from its haunches and drifted back to the pole. With a leap and bound it shot up the pole and disappeared into the opening of its kennel.

Akkers grinned and carefully cut another slice of the black biltong.

'You like it out at Jabulani?' he asked Debra, and at the same time he offered the scrap of dried meat to the dog.

'We are very happy there,' Debra replied stiffly, not wanting to be drawn. Zulu sniffed the proffered titbit, and his tail beat like a metronome. No dog can resist the concentrated meat smell and taste of biltong. He gulped it eagerly. Twice more Akkers fed him the scraps, and Zulu's eyes glistened and his soft silky muzzle was damp with saliva.

The waiting women in the shade of the veranda were watching with lively interest now. They had seen this happen before with a dog, and they waited expectantly. David was in the building, out of sight. Debra stood blind and unsuspecting.

Akkers cut a larger piece of the dried meat and offered it to Zulu, but when he reached for it he pulled his hand away, teasing the dog. With his taste for biltong now firmly established, Zulu tried again for the meat as it was offered. Again it was pulled away at the last moment. Zulu's black wet nose quivered with anxiety, and the soft ears were cocked.

Akkers walked down the steps with Zulu following him eagerly, and at the bottom he showed the dog the biltong once more, letting him sniff it. Then he spoke softly but urgently, 'Get it, boy,' and threw the scrap of biltong at the base of the baboon's pole. Zulu bounded forward, still slightly clumsy on his big puppy paws, into the circle of the chain where the baboon's paws had beaten the earth hard. He ran on under the pole and grubbed hungrily for the biltong in the dust.

The bull baboon came out of his kennel like a tawny grey blur and dropped the fifteen feet through the air; his limbs were spread and his jaws were open in a snarl like a great red trap, and the fangs were vicious, long and yellow and spiked. He hit the ground silently, and his muscles bunched as they absorbed the shock and hurled the long lithe body feet first at the unsuspecting pup. The baboon crashed into him, taking him on the shoulder with all the weight of his ninety pounds.

Zulu went down and over, rolling on his back with a startled yelp, but before he could find his feet or his wits, the baboon was after him.

Debra heard the pup cry, and started forward, surprised but not yet alarmed.

As he lay on his back, Zulu's belly was unprotected, sparsely covered with the silken black hair, the immature penis protruding pathetically, and the baboon went on to him in a crouching leap, pinning him with powerful furry legs as he bowed his head and buried the long yellow fangs deep into the pup's belly.

Zulu screamed in dreadful agony, and Debra screamed in sympathy and ran forward.

Akkers shot out a foot as she passed him and tripped her, sending her sprawling on her hands and knees.

'Leave it, lady,' he warned her, still grinning. 'You'll get hurt if you interfere.'

The baboon locked its long curved eye teeth into the tender belly, and then hurled the pup away from it with all the fierce strength of its four limbs. The thin wall of the stomach was ripped through, and the purple ropes of the entrails came out, hanging festooned in the baboon's jaws.

Again the disembowelled pup screamed, and Debra rolled blindly to her feet.

'David!' she cried wildly. 'David—help me!'

David came out of the building running; pausing in the doorway he took in the scene at a glance and snatched up a pick handle from the pile by the door. He jumped off the veranda, and in three quick strides he had reached the pup.

The baboon saw him coming and released Zulu. With uncanny speed, he whirled and leapt for the pole, racing upwards to perch on the roof of the kennel, his jowls red with blood, as he shrieked and jabbered, bouncing up and down with excitement and triumph.

David dropped the pick and gently lifted the crawling crippled black body. He carried Zulu to the Land-Rover and ripped his bush jacket into strips as he tried to bind up the torn belly, pushing the hanging entrails back into the hole with his fist.

'David, what is it?' Debra pleaded with him, and as he worked he explained it in a few terse Hebrew sentences.

'Get in,' he told her and she clambered into the passenger seat of the Land-Rover. He laid the injured labrador in her lap, and ran around to the driver's seat.

Akkers was back at the doorway of his shop, standing with thumbs hooked into his braces, and he was laughing. The false teeth clucked in the open mouth as he laughed, rocking back and forth on his heels.

On its kennel the baboon shrieked and cavorted, sharing its master's mirth.

'Hey, Mr Morgan,' Akkers giggled, 'don't forget your nails!'

David swung round to face him, his face felt tight and hot, the cicatrice that covered his cheeks and forehead was inflamed and the dark blue eyes blazed with a terrible anger. He started up the steps. His mouth was a pale hard slit, and his fists were clenched at his sides.

Akkers stepped backwards swiftly and reached behind the shop counter. He lifted out an old double-barrelled shotgun, and cocked both hammers with a sweep of his thick bony thumb.

'Self defence, Mr Morgan, with witnesses,' he giggled with sadistic relish. 'Come one step closer and we will get a look at your guts also.'

David paused at the top of the steps, and the gun—held in one huge fist—pointed at his belly.

'David hurry—oh, please hurry,' Debra called anxiously from the Land-Rover, with the weakly squirming body of the pup in her lap.

'We'll meet again.' David's anger had thickened his tongue.

'That will be fun,' said Akkers, and David turned away and ran down the steps.

Akkers watched the Land-Rover pull away and swing into the road in a cloud of dust, before he set the shotgun aside. He went out into the sunlight, and the baboon scrambled down from its pole and rushed to meet him. It jumped up on to his hip and clung to him like a child.

Akkers took a boiled sweet from his pocket and placed it tenderly between the terrible yellow fangs.

'You lovely old thing,' he chuckled, scratching the high cranium with its thick cap of grey fur and the baboon squinted up at his face with narrow brown eyes, chattering softly.

Despite the rough road surface, David covered the thirty miles back to Jabulani in twenty-five minutes. He skidded the vehicle to a halt beside the hangar, and ran with the pup in his arms to the aircraft.

During the flight Debra nursed him gently in her lap, and her skirts were sodden with his dark blood. The pup had quieted, and except for an occasional whimper now lay still. Over the W/T David arranged for a car to meet them at Nelspruit airfield and forty-five minutes after take-off they had Zulu on the theatre table in the veterinary surgeon's clinic.

The veterinary surgeon worked with complete concentration for over two hours at repairing the torn entrails and suturing the layers of abdominal muscle.

The pup was so critically injured, and infection was such a real danger, that they dared not return to Jabulani until it had passed. Five days later when they flew home with Zulu still weak and heavily strapped but out of danger, David altered his flight path to bring them in over the trading store at Bandolier Hill.

The iron roof shone like a mirror in the sun, and David felt his anger very cold and hard and determined.

'The man is a threat to us,' he said aloud. 'A real threat to each of us, and to what we are trying to build at Jabulani.'

Debra nodded her agreement, stroking the pup's head and not trusting herself to speak. Her own anger was as fierce as David's.

'I'm going to get him,' he said softly, and he heard the Brig's voice in his memory.

'The only excuse for violence is to protect that which belongs to you.'

He banked steeply away and lined up for his approach to the the landing-strip at Jabulani.

Conrad Berg called again to sample the Old Buck gin, and to tell David that his application to have Jabulani declared a private nature reserve had been approved by the Board and that the necessary documentation would soon be ready for signature.

'Do you want me to pull the fence out now?'

'No,' David answered grimly. 'Let it stand. I don't want Akkers frightened off.'

'Ja,' Conrad agreed heavily. 'We have got to get him.' He called Zulu to him and examined the scar that was ridged and shaped like forked lightning across the pup's belly. 'The bastard,' he muttered, and then glanced guiltily at Debra. 'Sorry, Mrs Morgan.'

'I couldn't agree more, Mr Berg,' she said softly, and Zulu watched her lips attentively when she spoke—his head cocked to one side.

Like all young things, he had healed cleanly and quickly.

The marula grove that ran thickly along the base of the hills about the String of Pearls came into flower.

The boles were straight and sturdy, each crowned with a fully rounded, many-branched head of dense foliage, and the red flowers made a royal show.

Almost daily David and Debra would wander together through the groves, down the rude track to the pools, and Zulu regained his strength on these leisurely strolls which always culminated in a swim and a lusty shaking off of water droplets, usually on to the nearest bystander.

Then the green plum-shaped fruits that covered the female marulas thickly began to turn yellow as they ripened, and their yeasty smell was heavy on the warm evening breeze.

The herd came up from the Sabi, forsaking the lush reed beds for the promise of the marula harvest. They were led by two old bulls, who for forty years had made the annual pilgrimage to the String of Pearls, and there were fifteen breeding cows with calves running at heel and as many adolescents.

They moved up slowly from the south, feeding spread out, sailing like ghostly grey galleons through the open bush, overloaded bellies rumbling. Occasionally a tall tree would catch the attention of one of the bulls and he would place his forehead upon the thick trunk and, swaying rhythmically as he built up momentum, he would strain suddenly and bring it crackling and crashing down. A few mouthfuls of the tender tip leaves would satisfy him, or he might strip the bark and stuff it untidily into his mouth before moving on northwards.

When the reached Conrad Berg's fence the two bulls moved forward and examined it, standing shoulder to shoulder as though in consultation, fanning their great grey ears, and every few minutes picking up a large pinch of sand in their trunks to throw over their own backs against the worrisome attention of the stinging flies.

In forty years they had travelled, and knew exactly all the boundaries of their reserve. As they stood there contemplating the game fence, it was as though they were fully aware that its destruction would be a criminal act, and injurious to their reputations and good standing.

Conrad Berg was deadly serious when he discussed 'his' elephants sense of right and wrong with David. He spoke of them like schoolboys who had to be placed on good behaviour, and disciplined when they transgressed. Discipline might take the form of driving, darting with drugs, or formal execution with a heavy rifle. This ultimate punishment was reserved for the incorrigibles who raided cultivated crops, chased motor-cars or otherwise endangered human life.

Sorely tempted, the two old bulls left the fence and ambled back to the breeding herd that waited patiently for their decision amongst the thorn trees. For three days the herd drifted back and forth along the fence, feeding and resting and waiting—then suddenly the wind turned westerly and it came to them laden with the thick, cloyingly sweet smell of the marula berries.

David parked the Land-Rover on the firebreak road and laughed with delight.

'So much for Connie's fence!'

For reasons of pachyderm prestige, or perhaps merely for the mischievous delight of destruction, no adult elephant would accept the breach made by another.

Each of them had selected his own fence pole, hard wood uprights embedded in concrete, and had effortlessly snapped it off level with the ground. Over a length of a mile the fence was flattened, and the wire mesh lay across the firebreak.

Each elephant had used his broken pole like a tightrope, to avoid treading on the sharp points of the barbed wire. Then once across the fence they had streamed in a tight bunch down to the pools to spend a night in feasting, an elephantine gorge on the yellow berries, which ended at dawn when they had bunched up into closer order and dashed back across the ruined fence into the safety of the Park—perhaps pursued by guilt and remorse and hoping that Conrad Berg would lay the blame on some other herd.

However, the downed fence provided ready access for many others who had long hankered after the sweet untouched grazing and deep water holes.

Ugly little blue wildebeest with monstrous heads, absurdly warlike manes and curved horns in imitation of the mighty buffalo. Clowns of the bush, they capered with glee and chased each other in circles. Their companions the zebra were more dignified, ignoring their antics, and trotted in businesslike fashion down to the pools. Their rumps were striped and glossy and plump, their heads up and ears pricked.

Conrad Berg met David at the remains of his fence, climbing out of his own truck and picking his way carefully over the wire. Sam, the African ranger, followed him.

Conrad shook his head as he surveyed the destruction, chuckling ruefully.

'It's old Mahommed and his pal One-Eye, I'd know that spoor anywhere. They just couldn't help themselves—the bastards—' He glanced quickly at Debra in the Land-Rover.

'That's perfectly all right, Mr Berg,' she forestalled his apology.

Sam had been casting back and forth along the soft break road and now he came to where they stood.

'Hello, Sam,' David greeted him. It had taken a lot of persuasion to get Sam to accept that this terribly disfigured face belonged to the young *nkosi* David who he had taught to track, and shoot and rob a wild beehive without destroying the bees.

Sam saluted David with a flourish. He took his uniform very seriously and conducted himself like a guardsman now. It was difficult to tell his age, for he had the broad smooth moonface of the Nguni—the aristocratic warrior tribes of Africa—but there was a frosting of purest white on the close-curled hair of his temples under the slouch hat, and David knew he had worked at Jabulani for forty years before leaving. The man must be approaching sixty years of age.

Quickly he made his report to Conrad, describing the animals and the numbers which had crossed into Jabulani.

'There is also a herd of buffalo, forty-three of them,' Sam spoke in simple Zulu that David could still follow. 'They are the ones who drank before at Ripape Dam near Hlangulene.'

'That will bring Akkers running—the sirloin of a young buffalo makes the finest biltong there is,' Conrad observed dryly.

'How long will it be before he knows the fence is down?' David asked, and Conrad fell into a long rapid-fire discussion with Sam that lost David after the first few sentences. However, Conrad translated at the end.

'Sam says he knows already, all your servants and their wives buy at his store and he pays them for that sort of information. It turns out that there is bad blood between Sam and Akkers. Sam suspects him of arranging to have him beaten, on a lonely road on a dark night. Sam was in hospital three months—he also accused Akkers of having his hut fired to drive him off Jabulani.'

'It adds up, doesn't it?' David agreed.

'Old Sam is dead keen to help us grab Akkers—and he has a plan of action all worked out.'

'Let's hear it.'

'Well, as long as you are in residence at Jabulani Akkers is going to restrict his activities to night poaching with a killing lamp. He knows every trick there is and we will never get him.'

'So?'

'You must tell your servants that you are leaving for two weeks, going to Cape Town on business. Akkers will know as soon as you leave and he will believe he has the whole of Jabulani to himself—' For an hour more they discussed the details of the plan, then they shook hands and parted.

As they drove back to the homestead they emerged from the open forest into one of the glades of tall grass, and David saw the brilliant white egrets floating like snow flakes over the swaying tops of golden grass.

'Something in there,' he said and cut the engine. They waited quietly until David saw the movement in the grass, the opening and closing at the passage of heavy bodies. Then three egrets, sitting in a row, moved slowly towards him, borne on the back of a concealed beast as it grazed steadily forward.

'Ah, the buffalo!' David exclaimed as the first of them appeared, a great black bovine shape. It stopped as it saw the Land-Rover on the edge of the trees and it regarded them intently from beneath the wide spread of its horns, with its muzzle lifted high. It showed no alarm for these were Park animals, almost as tame as domestic cattle.

Gradually the rest of the herd emerged from the tall grass. Each in turn scrutinized the vehicle and then resumed feeding once more. There were forty-three of them, as Sam had predicted, and amongst them were some fine old bulls standing five and a half feet tall at the shoulder and weighing little less than 2000 lb. Their horns were massively bossed, meeting in the centre of the head and curving downwards and up to blunt points, with a rugged surface that became polished black at the tips.

Crawling over their heavy trunks and thick short legs were numbers of ox-peckers, dull-plumaged birds with scarlet beaks and bright beady eyes. Sometimes head down they scavenged for the ticks and other blood-sucking body vermin in the folds of skin between the limbs. Occasionally one of the huge beasts would snort and leap, shaking and swishing its tail, as a sharp beak pried into a delicate portion of its anatomy, under the tail or around the heavy dangling black scrotum. The birds fluttered up with hissing cries, waited for the buffalo to calm down and then settled again to their scurrying and searching.

David photographed the herd until the light failed, and they drove home in the dark.

Before dinner David opened a bottle of wine and they drank it together on the stoop, sitting close and listening to the night sounds of the bush—the cries of the night birds, the tap of flying insects against the wire screen and the other secret scurrying and rustling of small animals.

'Do you remember once I told you that you were spoiled, and not very good marriage material?' Debra asked softly, nestling her dark head against his shoulder.

'I'll never forget it.'

'I'd like to withdraw that remark formally,' she went on, and he moved her gently away so that he could study her face. Sensing his eyes upon her she smiled, that shy little smile of hers. 'I fell in love with a little boy, a spoiled little boy, who thought only of fast cars and the nearest skirt—' she said, '—but now I have a man, a grown man,' she smiled again, 'and I like it better this way.'

He drew her back to him and kissed her, their lips melded in a lingering embrace before she sighed happily and laid her head back upon his shoulder. They were silent for a while before Debra spoke again.

'These wild animals—that mean so much to you—'

'Yes?' he encouraged her.

'I am beginning to understand. Although I have never seen them, they are becoming important to me also.'

'I'm glad.'

'David, this place of ours—it's so peaceful, so perfect. It's a little Eden before the fall.'

'We will make it so,' he promised, but in the night the gunfire woke him. He rose quickly, leaving her lying warm and quietly sleeping, and he went out on the stoop.

It came again, faintly on the still night, distance muting it to a small unwarlike popping. He felt his anger stirring again, as he imagined the long white shaft of the killing lamp, questing relentlessly through the forest until it settled suddenly upon the puzzled animal, holding it mesmerized in the beam, the blinded eyes glowing like jewels, making a perfect aiming point in the field of the telescopic rifle sight.

Then suddenly the rifle blast, shocking in the silence, and the long licking flame of the muzzle flash. The beautiful head snapping back at the punch of the bullet and the soft thump of the falling body on the hard earth, the last spasmodic kicking of hooves and again the silence.

He knew it was useless to attempt pursuit now, the gunman would have an accomplice in the hills above them ready to flash a warning if any of the homestead lights came on, or if an auto engine whirred into life. Then the killing lamp would be doused and the poacher would creep away. David would search the midnight expanse of Jabulani in vain. His quarry was cunning and experienced in his craft of killing, and would only be taken by greater cunning.

David could not sleep again. He lay awake beside Debra, and listened to her soft breathing—and at intervals to the distant rifle fire. The game was tame and easily approached, innocent after the safety of the Park. It would run only a short distance after each shot, and then it would stand again staring without comprehension at the mysterious and dazzling light that floated towards it out of the darkness.

David's anger burned on through the night, and in the dawn the vultures were up. Black specks against the pink dawn sky, they appeared in ever-increasing numbers, sailing high on wide pinions, tracing wide swinging circles before beginning to drop towards the earth.

David telephoned Conrad Berg at Skukuza Camp, then he and Debra and the dog climbed into the Land-Rover, warmly dressed against the dawn chill. They followed the descent of the birds to where the poacher had come on the buffalo herd.

As they approached the first carcass, the animal scavengers scattered—slope-backed hyena cantering away into the trees, hideous and cowardly, looking back over their misshapen shoulders, grinning apologetically—little red jackal with silvery backs and alert ears, trotting to a respectful distance before standing and starting back anxiously.

The vultures were less timid, seething like fat brown maggots over the carcass as they squawled and squabbled, fouling everything with their stinking droppings and loose feathers, leaving the kill only when the Land-Rover was very close and then flapping heavily up into the trees to crouch there grotesquely with their bald scaly heads out-thrust.

There were sixteen dead buffalo, lying strung out along the line of the herd's flight. On each carcass the belly had been split open to let the vultures in, and the sirloin and fillet had been expertly removed.

'He killed them just for a few pounds of meat?' Debra asked incredulously.

'That's all,' David confirmed grimly. 'But that's not bad—sometimes they'll kill a wildebeest simply to make a fly whisk of its tail, or they'll shoot a giraffe for the marrow in its bones.'

'I don't understand.' Debra's voice was hopeless. 'What makes a man do it? He can't need the meat that badly.'

'No,' David agreed. 'It's deeper than that. This type of killing is a gut thing. This man kills for the thrill of it, he kills to see an animal fall, to hear the death cry, to smell the reek of fresh blood—' his voice choked off, 'this is one time you can be thankful you cannot see,' he said softly.'

Conrad Berg found them waiting beside the corpses, and he set his rangers to work butchering the carcasses.

'No point in wasting all that meat. Food there for a lot of people.'

Then he put Sam to the spoor. There had been four men in the poaching party, one wearing light rubber-soled shoes and the others bare-footed.

'One white man, big man, long legs. Three black men, carry meat, blood drip here and here.'

They followed Sam slowly through the open forest as he parted the grass with his long thin tracking staff, and moved towards the unsurfaced public road.

'Here they walk backwards,' Sam observed, and Conrad explained grimly.

'Old poacher's trick. They walk backwards when they cross a boundary. If you cut the spoor while patrolling the fence you think they have gone the other way—leaving instead of entering—and you don't bother following them.'

The spoor went through the gap in the fence, crossed the road and entered the tribal land beyond. It ended where a motor vehicle had been parked amongst a screening thicket of wild ebony. The tracks bumped away across the sandy earth and rejoined the public road.

'Plaster casts of the tyre tracks?' David asked.

'Waste of time.' Conrad shook his head. 'You can be sure they are changed before each expedition, he keeps this set especially and hides it when it's not in use.'

'What about spent cartridge shells?' David persisted.

Conrad laughed briefly. 'They are in his pocket, this is a fly bird. He's not going to scatter evidence all over the country. He picks up as he goes along. No—we'll have to sucker him into it.' And his manner became businesslike. 'Right, have you selected a place to stake old Sam out?'

'I thought we would put him up on one of the kopjes, near the String of Pearls. He'll be able to cover the whole estate from there, spot any dust on the road, and the height will give the two-way radio sufficient range.'

After lunch David loaded their bags into the luggage compartment of the Navajo. He paid the servants two weeks' wages in advance.

'Take good care.' He told them. 'I shall return before the end of the month.'

He parked the Land-Rover in the open hangar with the key in the ignition facing the open doorway, ready for a quick start. He took off and kept on a westerly heading, passing directly over Bandolier Hill and the buildings amongst the mango trees. They saw no sign of life, but David held his course until the hill sank from view below the horizon, then he came around on a wide circle to the south and lined up for Skukuza, the main camp of the Kruger National Park.

Conrad Berg was at the airstrip in his truck to meet the Cessna, and Jane had placed fresh flowers in the guest room. Jabulani lay fifty miles away to the north-west.

It was like squadron 'Red' standby again, with the Navajo parked under one of the big shade trees at the end of the Skukuza airstrip, and the radio set switched on, crackling faintly on the frequency tuned to that of Sam's transmitter, as he waited patiently on the hill-top above the pools.

The day was oppressively hot, with the threat of a rainstorm looming up out of the east, great cumulus thunderheads striding like giants across the bushveld.

Debra and David and Conrad Berg sat in the shade of the aircraft's wing, for it was too hot in the cockpit. They chatted in desultory fashion, but always listening to the radio crackle, and they were tense and distracted.

'He is not going to come,' said Debra a little before noon.

'He'll come,' Conrad contradicted her. 'Those buffalo are too much temptation. Perhaps not today—but tomorrow or the next day he'll come.'

David stood up and climbed in through the open door of the cabin. He went forward to the cockpit.

'Sam,' he spoke into the microphone. 'Can you hear me?'

There was a long pause, presumably while Sam struggled with radio procedure, then his voice, faint but clear: 'I hear you, *Nkosi*.'

'Have you seen anything?'

'There is nothing.'

'Keep good watch.'

'*Yebho, Nkosi*.'

Jane brought a cold picnic lunch down to the airstrip, they ate heartily despite the tension, and they were about to start on the milk tart, when suddenly the radio set throbbed and hummed. Sam's voice carried clearly to where they sat.

'He has come!'

'Red standby—Go! Go!' shouted David, and they rushed for the cabin door, Debra treading squarely in the centre of Jane's milk tart before David grabbed her arm and guided her to her seat.

'Bright Lance, airborne and climbing,' David laughed with excitement and then memory stabbed him with a sharp blade. He remembered Joe hanging out there at six o'clock but he shut his mind to it and he banked steeply on to his heading, not wasting time in grabbing for altitude but staying right down at tree-top level.

Conrad Berg was hunched in the seat behind them, and his face was redder than usual—seeming about to burst like an over-ripe tomato.

'Where is the Land-Rover key?' he demanded anxiously.

'It's in the ignition—and the tank is full.'

'Can't you go faster?' Conrad growled.

'Have you got your walkie-talkie?' David checked him.

'Here!' It was gripped in one of his huge paws, and his double-barrelled ·450 magnum was in the other.

David was hopping the taller trees, and sliding over the crests of higher ground with feet to spare. They flashed over the boundary fence and ahead of them lay the hills of Jabulani.

'Get ready,' he told Conrad, and flew the Navajo into the airstrip, taxiing up to the hangar where the Land-Rover waited.

Conrad jumped down at the instant that David braked to a halt, then he slammed the cabin door behind him and raced to the Land-Rover. Immediately David opened the throttle and swung the aircraft around, lining up for his take-off before the Navajo had gathered full momentum.

As he climbed, he saw the Land-Rover racing across the airstrip, dragging a cloak of dust behind it.

'Do you read me, Connie?'

'Loud and clear,' Conrad's voice boomed out of the speaker, and David turned for the grey ribbon of the public road that showed through the trees, beyond the hills.

He followed it, flying five hundred feet above it, and he searched the open parkland.

The green Ford truck had been concealed from observation at ground level, again in a thicket of wild ebony, but it was open from the sky. For Akkers had never thought of discovery coming from there.

'Connie, I've got the truck. He's stashed it in a clump of ebony about half a mile down the bank of the Luzane stream. Your best route is to follow the road to the bridge, then go down into the dry river bed and try and cut him off before he gets to the truck.'

'Okay, David.'

'Move it, man.'

'I'm moving.' David saw the Land-Rover's dust above the trees, Conrad must have his foot down hard.

'I'm going to try and spot the man himself—chase him into your arms.'

'You do that!'

David started a long climbing turn towards the hills, sweeping and searching, up and around. Below him the pools glinted and he opened the throttles slightly, seeking altitude to clear the crests.

From the highest peak, a tiny figure waved frantically.

'Sam,' he grunted. 'Doing a war dance.' He altered course slightly to pass him closely, and Sam stopped his imitation of a windmill and stabbed with an extended arm towards the west. David acknowledged with a wave, and turned again, dropping down the western slopes.

Ahead of him the plain spread, dappled like a leopard's back with dark bush and golden glades of grass. He flew for a minute before he saw a black mass, moving slowly ahead of him, dark and amorphous against the pale grass. The remains of the buffalo herd had bunched up and were running without direction, desperate from the harrying they had received.

'Buffalo,' he told Debra. 'On the run. Something has alarmed them.' She sat still and intent beside him, hands in her lap, staring unseeingly ahead.

'Ah!' David shouted. 'Got him—with blood on his hands!'

In the centre of one of the larger clearings lay the black beetle-body of a dead buffalo, its belly swollen and its legs sticking out stiffly as it lay on its side.

Four men stood around it in a circle, obviously just about to begin butchering the carcass. Three of them were Africans, one with a knife in his hand.

The fourth man was Johan Akkers. There was no mistaking the tall gaunt frame. He wore an old black Fedora hat on his head, strangely formal attire for the work in which he was engaged, and his braces criss-crossed his tan-coloured shirt. He carried a rifle at the trail in his right hand, and at the sound of the aircraft engines he swung round and stared into the sky, frozen with the shock of discovery.

'You swine. Oh, you bloody swine,' whispered David, and his anger was strong and bright against the despoilers.

'Hold on!' he warned Debra, and flew straight at the man, dropping steeply on to him.

The group around the dead buffalo scattered, as the aircraft bore down on them, each man picking his own course and racing away on it, but David selected the lanky galloping frame with the black hat jammed down over the ears and sank down behind him. The tips of his propellers clipped the dry grass, as he swiftly overtook the running Akkers.

He was set to fly into him, driven by the unreasoning anger of the male animal protecting his own, and he lined up to cut him down with the spinning propeller blades.

As David braced himself for the impact Akkers glanced back over his shoulder, and his face was muddy grey with fright, the skull eyes dark and deeply set. He saw the murderous blades merely feet from him, and he threw himself flat into the grass.

The Navajo roared inches over his prone body, and David pulled it round in a steep turn, with the wing-tip brushing the grass. As he came round he saw that Akkers was up and running, and that he was only fifty paces from the edge of the trees.

David levelled out, aimed for the fugitive again but realized that he could not reach him before he was into the trees. Swiftly he sped across the clearing, but the lumbering figure drew slowly closer to the timber line and as he reached the sanctuary of a big leadwood trunk, Akkers whirled and raised the rifle to his shoulder. He aimed at the approaching aircraft; although the rifle was unsteady in his hands the range was short.

'Down,' shouted David, pushing Debra's head below the level of the windshield, and he pulled open the throttles and climbed very steeply away.

Even above the bellow of the engines David heard the heavy bullet clang into the fuselage of the aircraft.

'What's happening, David?' Debra pleaded.

'He fired at us, but we've got him on the run. He'll head back for his truck now, and Conrad should be there waiting for him.'

Akkers kept under cover of the trees, and circling above him David caught glimpses of the tall figure trotting purposefully along his escape route.

'David, can you hear me?' Conrad's voice boomed suddenly in the tense cockpit.

'What is it, Connie?'

'We've got trouble. I've hit a rock in your Land-Rover and knocked out the sump. She's had it, pouring oil all over the place.'

'How the hell did you do that?' David demanded.

'I was trying a short cut.' Conrad's chagrin carried clearly over the ether.

'How far are you from the Luzane stream?'

'About three miles.'

'God, he'll beat you to it,' David swore. 'He's two miles from the truck and going like he's got a tax collector after him.'

'You have not seen old Connie move yet. I'll be there waiting for him,' Berg promised.

'Good luck,' David called, and the transmission went dead.

Below them Akkers was skirting the base of the hills, his black hat bobbing along steadily amongst the trees. David kept his starboard wing pointed at him and the Navajo turned steadily, holding station above him.

Other movement caught David's eye on the open slope of the hill above Akkers. For a moment he thought it was an animal, then with an intake of breath he realized that he was mistaken.

'What is it?' Debra demanded, sensing his concern.

'It's Sam, the damned fool. Connie told him not to leave his post—he's unarmed—but he's haring down the slope to try and cut Akkers off.'

'Can't you stop him?' Debra asked anxiously, and David didn't bother to answer.

He called Conrad four times before there was a reply. Conrad's voice was thick and wheezing with the effort of running.

'Sam is on to Akkers. I think he's going to confront him.'

'Oh God damn him,' groaned Conrad. 'I'll kick his black ass for him.'

'Hold on,' David told him, 'I'm going around for a closer look.'

David saw it all quite plainly, he was only three hundred feet above them when Akkers became aware of the running figure on the slope above him. He stopped dead, and half-lifted the rifle; perhaps he shouted a warning but Sam kept on down, bounding over the rocky ground towards the man who had burned his children to death.

Akkers lifted the rifle to his shoulder and aimed deliberately, the rifle jumped sharply, the barrel kicking upwards at the recoil and Sam's legs kept on running while his upper torso was flung violently backwards by the strike of the heavy soft-nosed bullet.

The tiny brown-clad body bounced and rolled down the slope, before coming to a sprawling halt in a clump of scrub.

David watched Akkers reload the rifle, stooping to pick up the empty cartridge shell. Then he looked up at the circling aircraft above him, David may have been mistaken but it seemed the man was laughing–that obscene tooth-clucking giggle of his–then he started off again at a trot towards the truck.

'Connie,' David spoke hoarsely into his handset, 'he just killed Sam.'

Conrad Berg ran heavily over the broken sandy ground. He had lost his hat and sweat poured down his big red face, stinging his eyes and plastering the lank grey hair down his forehead. The walkie-talkie set bounced on his back, and the butt of the rifle thumped rhythmically against his hip.

He ran with grim concentration, trying to ignore the swollen pounding of his heart and the torture of breath that scalded his lungs. A thorn branch clawed at his upper arms, raking thin bloody lines through his skin, but he did not break the pattern of his run.

He turned his red and streaming face to the sky and saw David's aircraft, circling ahead of him and slightly to his left. That marked for him Akkers' position–and it was clear that Conrad was losing ground in his desperate race to head off the escape.

The radio set on his back buzzed, but he ignored the call, he could not halt now. To break his run would mean he would only slump down exhausted. He was a big heavy man, the air was hot and enervating, and he had run three miles through loose and difficult going–he was almost finished. He was burning the last of his reserves now.

Suddenly the earth seemed to fall away under him, and he pitched forward and half-slid–half-rolled–down the steep bank of the Luzane stream, to finish lying on his back in the white river sand, clean and grainy as sugar. The radio was digging painfully into his flesh and he dragged it out from under him.

Still lying in the sand he panted like a dog, blinded by sweat and he fumbled the transmit button of the set.

'David–' he croaked thickly, 'I am in the bed of the stream–can you see me?'

The aircraft was arcing directly overhead now, and David's answer came back immediately.

'I see you, Connie, you are a hundred yards down-stream from the truck. Akkers is there, Connie, has just reached the truck, he'll be coming back down the river bed at any moment.'

Painfully, gasping, choking for breath, Conrad Berg dragged himself to his knees–and at that moment he heard the whirr and catch and purr of an engine. He unstrapped the heavy radio and laid it aside, then he unslung his rifle, snapped open the breech to check the load, and pulled himself to his feet.

Surprised at the weakness of his own massive body, he staggered into the centre of the river bed.

The dry river bed was eight feet deep with banks cut sheer by flood water, and it was fifteen feet wide at this point, and the floor was of smooth white sand, scattered with small water-rounded stones no bigger than a baseball. It made a good illegal access road into Jabulani, and the tracks of Akkers' truck were clearly etched in the soft sand.

Around a bend in the stream Conrad heard the truck revving and roaring as it came down a low place in the bank into the smooth bed.

Conrad stood squarely in the middle of the river bed with the rifle held across his hip, and he fought to control his breathing. The approaching roar of the truck reached a crescendo as it came skidding wildly around the bend in the stream, and raced down towards him. Showers of loose sand were thrown out from under the spinning rear wheels.

Johan Akkers crouched over the steering wheel, with the black hat pulled down to his eyebrows, and his face was grey and glistening with sweat, and he saw Conrad blocking the river bed.

'Stop!' Conrad shouted, hefting the rifle. 'Stop or I shoot!'

The truck was swaying and sliding, the engine screamed in tortured protest. Akkers began to laugh, Conrad could see the open mouth and the shaking shoulders. There was no slackening in the truck's roaring, rocking charge.

Conrad lifted the rifle and sighted down the stubby double barrels. At that range he could have put a bullet through each of Johan Akkers' deep-set eyes, and the man made no effort to duck or otherwise avoid the menace of the levelled rifle. He was still laughing, and Conrad could clearly see the teeth lying loosely on his gums. He steeled himself with the truck fifty feet away, and racing down upon him.

It takes a peculiar state of mind before one man can deliberately and cold-bloodedly shoot down another. It must either be the conditioned reflex of the soldier or law-enforcement officer, or it must be the terror of the hunted, or again it must be the unbalanced frenzy of the criminal lunatic.

None of these was Conrad Berg. Like most big strong men, he was essentially a gentle person. His whole thinking was centred on protecting and cherishing life—he could not pull the trigger.

With the truck fifteen feet away, he threw himself aside, and Johan Akkers swung the wheel wildly, deliberately driving for him.

He caught Berg a glancing blow with the side of the truck, hurling him into the earthen bank of the stream. The truck went past him, slewing out of control. It hit the bank farther down the stream in a burst of earth and loose pebbles, swaying wildly as Akkers fought the bucking wheel. He got it under control again, jammed his foot down on the accelerator and went roaring on down the river bed, leaving Conrad lying in the soft sand below the bank.

As the truck hit him, Conrad felt the bone in his hip shatter like glass, and the breath driven from his lungs by the heavy blow of metal against his rib cage.

He lay in the sand on his side and felt the blood well slowly into his mouth. It had a bitter salt taste, and he knew that one of the broken ribs had pierced his lung like a lance and that the blood sprang from deep within his body.

He turned his head and saw the radio set lying ten paces away across the river bed. He began to drag himself towards it and his shattered leg slithered after him, twisted at a grotesque angle.

'David,' he whispered into the microphone, 'I couldn't stop him. He got away,' and he spat a mouthful of blood into the white sand.

David picked the truck up as it came charging up the river bank below the concrete bridge of the Luzane, bounced and bumped over the drainage ditch and swung on to the road. It gathered speed swiftly and raced westwards towards Bandolier Hill and the highway. Dust boiled out from behind the green chassis, marking its position clearly for David as he turned two miles ahead of it.

After crossing the Luzane the road turned sharply to avoid a rocky outcrop, and then ran arrow-straight for two miles, hedged in with thick timber and undulating like a switchback, striking across the water shed and the grain of the land.

As David completed his turn he lowered his landing gear, and throttled back. The Navajo sank down, lined up on the dusty road as though it was a landing-strip.

Directly ahead was the dust column of the speeding truck. They were on a head-on course, but David concentrated coldly on bringing the Navajo down into the narrow lane between the high walls of timber. He was speaking quietly to Debra, reassuring her and explaining what he was going to attempt.

He touched down lightly on the narrow road, letting her float in easily, and when she was down he opened the throttles again, taking her along the centre of the road under power but holding her down. He had speed enough to lift the Navajo off, if Akkers chose a collision rather than surrender.

Ahead of them was another hump in the road, and as they rolled swiftly towards it the green truck suddenly burst over the crest, not more than a hundred yards ahead.

Both vehicles were moving fast, coming together at a combined speed of almost two hundred miles an hour, and the shock of it was too much for Johan Akkers.

The appearance of the aircraft dead in the centre of the road, bearing down on him with the terrible spinning discs of the propellers was too much for nerves already run raw and ragged.

He wrenched the wheel hard over, and the truck went into a broadside dry skid. It missed the port wing-tip of the Navajo as it went rocketing off the narrow road.

The front wheels caught the drainage ditch and the truck went over, cartwheeling twice in vicious slamming revolutions that smashed the glass from her windows and burst the doors open. The truck ended on its side against one of the trees.

David shut the throttles and thrust his feet hard down on the wheel brakes, bringing the Navajo up short.

'Wait here,' he shouted at Debra, and jumped down into the road. His face was a frozen mask of scar tissue, but his eyes were ablaze as he sprinted back along the road towards the wreckage of the green truck.

Akkers saw him coming, and he dragged himself shakily to his feet. He had been thrown clear and now he staggered to the truck. He could see his rifle lying in the cab, and he tried to scramble up on to the body to reach down through the open door. Blood from a deep scratch in his forehead was running into his eyes blinding him, he wiped it away with the back of his hand and glanced around.

David was close, hurdling the irrigation ditch and running towards him. Akkers scrambled down from the battered green body, and groped for the hunting knife on his belt. It was eight inches of Sheffield steel with a bone handle, and it had been honed to a razor edge.

He hefted it under-handed, in the classical grip of the knife-fighter and wiped the blood from his face with the palm of his free hand.

He was crouching slightly, facing David, and the haft of the knife was completely covered by the huge bony fist.

David stopped short of him, his eyes fastened on the knife, and Akkers began to laugh again. It was a cracked falsetto giggle, the hysterical laughter of a man driven to the very frontiers of sanity.

The point of the knife weaved in the slow mesmeric movement of an erect cobra, and it caught the sunlight in bright points of light. David watched it, circling and crouching, steeling himself, summoning all the training of paratrooper school, screwing up his nerve to go in against the naked steel.

Akkers feinted swiftly, leaping in, and when David broke away, he let out a fresh burst of high laughter.

Again they circled, Akkers mouthing his teeth loosely, sucking at them, giggling, watching with those muddy green eyes from their deep, close-set sockets. David moved back slowly ahead of him, and Akkers drove him back against the body of the truck, cornering him there.

He came then, flashing like the charge of a wounded leopard. His speed and strength were shocking, and the knife hissed upwards for David's belly.

David caught the knife hand at the wrist, blocking the thrust and trapping the knife low down. They were chest to chest now, face to face, like lovers, and Akkers' breath stank of unwashed teeth.

They strained silently, shifting like dancers to balance each other's heaves and thrusts.

David felt the knife hand twisting in his grip. The man had hands and arms like steel, he could not hold him much longer. In seconds it would be free, and the steel would be probing into his belly.

David braced his legs and twisted sideways. The move caught Akkers off-balance and he could not resist it. David was able to get his other hand on to the knife arm, but even with both hands he was hard put to hold on.

They swayed and shuffled together, panting, grunting, straining, until they fell, still locked together, against the bonnet of the truck. The metal was hot and smelled of oil.

David was concentrating all his strength on the knife, but he felt Akkers' free hand groping for his throat. He ducked his head down on his shoulders, pressing his chin against his chest but the fingers were steel hard and powerful as machinery. They probed mercilessly into his flesh, forcing his chin up, and settling on his throat, beginning to squeeze the life out of him.

Desperately David hauled at the knife arm, and found it more manageable now that Akkers was concentrating his strength on strangling him.

The open windscreen of the truck was beside David's shoulder, the glass had been smashed out of it, but jagged shards of it still stood in the metal rim, forming a crude but ferocious line of saw-teeth.

David felt the fingers digging deep into his throat, crushing the gristle of his larynx and blocking off the arteries that fed his brain. His vision starred and then began to fade darkly, as though he were pulling eight G's in a dogfight.

With one last explosive effort David pulled the knife arm around on to the line of broken glass, and he dragged it down, sawing it desperately across the edge.

Akkers screamed and his strangling grip relaxed, back and forth David sawed the arm, slashing and ripping through skin and fat and flesh, opening a wound like a ragged-petalled rose, hacking down into the nerves and arteries and sinews so that the knife dropped from the lifeless fingers and Akkers screamed like a woman.

David broke from him and shoved him away. Akkers fell to his knees still screaming and David clutched at his own throat massaging the bruised flesh, gasping for breath and feeling the flow of fresh blood to his brain.

'God Jesus, I'm dying. I'm bleeding to death. Oh sweet Jesus, help me!' screamed Akkers, holding the mutilated arm to his belly. 'Help me, oh God, don't let me die. Save me, Jesus, save me!'

Blood was streaming and spurting from the arm, flooding the front of his trousers. As he screamed his teeth fell from his mouth, leaving it a dark and empty cave in the palely glistening face.

'You've killed me. I'll bleed to death!' he screamed at David, thrusting his face towards David. 'You've got to save me—don't let me die.'

David pushed himself away from the truck and took two running steps towards the kneeling man, then he swung his right leg and his whole body into a flying kick that took Akkers cleanly under the chin and snapped his head back.

He went over backwards and lay still and quiet, and David stood over him, sobbing and gasping for breath.

For purposes of sentence Mr Justice Barnard of the Transvaal division of the Supreme Court took into consideration four previous convictions—two under the wildlife conservation act, one for aggravated assault, and the fourth for assault with intent to do grievous bodily harm.

He found Johan Akkers guilty of twelve counts under the Wildlife Conservation Act, but considered these as one when sentencing him to three years at hard labour without option of a fine, and confiscation of firearms and motor vehicles used in commission of these offences.

He found him guilty of one count of aggravated assault, and sentenced him to three years at hard labour without option.

The prosecutor altered one charge from attempted murder to assault with intent to do grievous bodily harm. He was found guilty as charged on this count, and the sentence was five years' imprisonment without option.

On the final charge of murder he was found guilty and Justice Barnard said in open court:

'In considering sentence of death on this charge, I was obliged to take into account the fact that the accused was acting like an animal in a trap, and I am satisfied that there was no element of premeditation—'

The sentence was eighteen years' imprisonment, and all sentences were to run consecutively. They were all confirmed on appeal.

As Conrad Berg said from his hospital bed with one heavily plastered leg in traction, and a glass of Old Buck gin in his hand, 'Well, for the next twenty-eight years we don't have to worry about that bastard—I beg your pardon, Mrs Morgan.'

'Twenty-nine years, dear,' Jane Berg corrected him firmly.

In July the American edition of *A Place of Our Own* was published, and it dropped immediately into that hungry and bottomless pool of indifference wherein so many good books drown. It left not a sign, not a ripple of its passing.

Bobby Dugan, Debra's new literary agent in America, wrote to say how sorry he was—and how disappointed. He had expected at least some sort of critical notice to be taken of the publication.

David took it as a personal and direct insult. He ranted and stormed about the estate for a week, and it seemed that at one stage he might actually journey to America to commit a physical violence upon that country—a sort of one-man Vietnam in reverse.

'They must be stupid,' he protested. 'It's the finest book ever written.'

'Oh, David!' Debra protested modestly.

'It is! And I'd love to go over there and rub their noses in it,' and Debra imagined the doors of editorial offices all over New York being kicked open, and literary reviewers fleeing panic-stricken, jumping out of skyscraper-windows or locking themselves in the women's toilets to evade David's wrath.

'David my darling, you are wonderful for me,' she giggled with delight, but it had hurt. It had hurt very badly. She felt the flame of her urge to write wane and flutter in the chill winds of rejection.

Now when she sat at her desk with the microphone at her lips, the words no longer tumbled and fought to escape, and the ideas no longer jostled each other. Where before she had seen things happening as though she were watching a play, seen her characters laugh and cry and sing, now there was only the dark cloud banks rolling across her eyes—unrelieved by colour or form.

For hours at a time she might sit at her desk and listen to the birds in the garden below the window.

David sensed her despair, and he tried to help her through it. When the hours at the desk proved fruitless he would insist she leave it and come with him along the new fence lines, or to fish the big blue Mozambique bream in the deep water of the pools.

Now that she had completely learned the layout of the house and its immediate environs, David began to teach her to find her way at large. Each day they would walk down to the pools and Debra learned her landmarks along the track; she would grope for them with the carved walking-stick David had given her. Zulu soon realized his role in these expeditions, and it was David's idea to clip a tiny silver bell on to his collar so that Debra could follow him more readily. Soon she could venture out without David, merely calling her destination to Zulu and checking him against her own landmarks.

David was busy at this time with the removal of Conrad's game fence, as he was still laid up with the leg, and with building his own fences to enclose the three vulnerable boundaries of Jabulani. In addition there was a force of African rangers to recruit and train in their duties. David designed uniforms for them, and built outposts for them at all the main access points to the estate. He flew into Nelspruit at regular intervals to consult Conrad Berg on these arrangements, and it was at his suggestion that David began a water survey of the estate. He wanted surface water on the areas of Jabulani that were remote from the pools, and he began studying the feasibility of building catchment dams or sinking boreholes. His days were full and active, and he became hard and lean and sunbrowned. Yet always there were many hours spent in Debra's company.

The 35-mm. colour slides that David had taken of the buffalo herd before Johan Akkers had decimated it, were returned by the processing laboratory and they were hopelessly inadequate. The huge animals seemed to be standing on the horizon, and the ox-peckers on their bodies were tiny grey specks. This failure spurred David, and he returned from one trip to Nelspruit with a 600-mm. telescopic lens.

While Debra was meant to be working, David set up his camera beside her and photographed the birds through her open window. The results were mixed. Out of thirty-six exposures, thirty-five could be thrown away, but one was beautiful, a grey-headed bush shrike at the moment of flight, poised on spread wings with the sunlight catching his vivid plumage and his sparkling eye.

David was hooked by the photography bug, and there were more lenses and cameras and tripods, until Debra protested that it was a hobby which was completely visual, and from which she was excluded.

David had one of his inspirations of genius. He sent away for pressings of June Stannard's bird song recordings—and Debra was enchanted. She listened to them intently, her whole face lighting with pleasure when she recognized a familiar call.

From there it was a natural step for her to attempt to make her own bird recordings, which included the tinkle of Zulu's silver bell, the buzz of David's Land-Rover, the voices of the servants arguing in the kitchen yard—and faintly, very faintly, the chatter of a glossy starling.

'It's no damned good,' Debra complained bitterly. 'I wonder how she got hers so clear and close.'

David did some reading, and built a parabolic reflector for her. It did not look particularly lovely, but it worked. Aimed at a sound source it gathered and directed the sound waves into the microphone.

From the window of Debra's study they became more adventurous and moved out. He built permanent and comfortable hides beside the drinking places at the pools, and when his rangers reported a nesting site of an interesting bird species, they would built temporary blinds of thatch and canvas—sometimes on tall stilts—where David and Debra spent many silent and enjoyable hours together, shooting film and catching sound. Even Zulu learned to lie still and silent with his bell removed on these occasions.

Slowly they had begun to build up a library of photographs and recordings of a professional standard—until at last David plucked up sufficient courage to send to *African Wild Life Magazine* a selection of a dozen of his best slides. Two weeks later, he received a letter of acceptance, with a cheque for a hundred dollars. This payment represented a return of approximately one-twentieth of one per cent of his capital outlay on equipment. David was ecstatic, and Debra's pleasure almost as great as his. They drank two bottles of Veuve Clicquot for dinner, and under the spell of excitement and champagne their love-making that night was particularly inventive.

When David's photographs were published in *Wild Life* accompanied by Debra's text, they reaped an unexpected harvest of letters from persons of similar interest all over the world, and a request from the editors for a full-length, illustrated article on Jabulani, and the Morgans' plans for turning it into a game sanctuary.

Debra made a lovely model for David's photographs that he compiled for the article, and she also worked with care on the text—while David fed her ideas and criticism.

Debra's new book lay abandoned, but her disappointment was forgotten in the pleasure of working together.

Their correspondence with other conservationists provided them with sufficient intellectual stimulus, and the occasional company of Conrad Berg and Jane satisfied their need for human contact. They were still both sensitive about being with other people, and this way they could avoid it.

The *Wild Life* article was almost complete and ready for posting, when a letter arrived from Bobby Dugan in New York. The editor of *Cosmopolitan* magazine had chanced upon one of the few copies of *A Place of Our Own* in circulation. She had liked it, and the magazine was considering serialization of the book—possibly linked with a feature article on Debra. Bobby wanted Debra to let him have a selection of photographs of herself, and four thousand words of autobiographical notes.

The photographs were there, ready to go to *Wild Life,* and Debra ran through the four thousand words in three hours with David making suggestions, some helpful and some bawdy.

They sent off the tape and pictures in the same post as the article to *Wild Life.* For nearly a month they heard nothing more about it and then something happened to drive it from their minds.

They were in the small thatch and daub hide beside the main pool, sitting quietly and companionably during a lull in the evening activity. David had his camera tripod set up in one of the viewing windows and Debra's reflector was raised above the roof of the hide, daubed with camouflage paint and operated by a handle over her head.

The water was still and black, except where a surface-feeding bream was rising near the far reed banks. A flock of laughing doves was lining up with a chittering troop of spotted guinea fowl at the water's edge, sipping water and then pointing their beaks to the sky as they let it run down their throats.

Suddenly David took her wrist as a cautionary signal, and by the intensity of his grip she knew that he had seen something unusual and she leaned close against him so that she could hear his whispered descriptions, and with her right hand she switched on the recorder and then reached up to aim the reflector.

A herd of the rare and shy nyala antelope were approaching the drinking place timidly, clinging until the last possible moment to the security of the forest. Their ears were spread, and their nostrils quivered and sucked at the air, huge dark eyes glowing like lamps in the gloom.

There were nine hornless females, delicate chestnut in colour, striped with white, dainty-stepping and suspicious, as they followed the two herd bulls. These were so dissimilar from their females as though to belong to a different species. Purplish black, and shaggy with a rough mane extending from between the ears to the crupper. Their horns were thick and corkscrewed, tipped with cream, and between their eyes was a vivid white chevron marking.

Advancing only a step at a time, and then pausing to stare with the limitless patience of the wild, searching for a hint of danger, they came slowly down the bank.

They passed the hide so closely that David was afraid to press the trigger of his camera lest the click of the shutter frighten them away.

He and Debra sat frozen as they reached the water; Debra smiled happily as she picked up the soft snort with which the lead bull blew the surface before drinking, and the liquid slurping with which he drew his first mouthful.

Once they were all drinking David aimed and focused with care, but at the click of the shutter the bull nearest him leapt about and uttered a hoarse, throbbing alarm bark. Instantly the entire herd whirled and raced away like pale ghosts through the dark trees.

'I got it! I got it!' exulted Debra. 'Wow! He was so close, he nearly burst my eardrums.'

The excitement on Jabulani was feverish. Nyala antelope had never been seen on the estate before, not even in David's father's time, and all steps were taken to encourage them to remain. The pools were immediately placed out of bounds to all the rangers and servants, lest the human presence frighten the herd off before they had a chance to settle down and stabilize their territory.

Conrad Berg arrived, still using a stick and limping heavily as he would for the rest of his life. From the hide he watched the herd with David and Debra, and then back at the homestead he sat before the log fire, eating prime beef steak and drinking Old Buck while he gave his opinion.

'They aren't from the Park, I shouldn't think. I would have recognized a big old bull like that if I'd ever seen him before—they have probably sneaked in from one of the other estates—you haven't got the south fence up yet, have you?'

'Not yet.'

'Well, that's where they have moved from—probably sick of being stared at by all the tourists. Come up here for a bit of peace.' He took a swallow of his gin. 'You're getting a nice bit of stuff together here, Davey—another few years and it will be a real show-place. Have you got any plans for visitors—you could make a good thing out of this place, like they have at Mala-Mala. Five-star safaris at economy prices—'

'Connie, I'm just too damn selfish to want to share this with anybody else.'

The distractions and the time had given Debra an opportunity to recover from the American failure of *A Place of Our Own*, and one morning she sat down at her desk and began working again on her second novel. That evening she told David:

'One of the blocks I have had is that I hadn't a name for it. It's like a baby—you have to give it a name or it's not really a person.'

'You have got a name for it?' he asked.

'Yes.'

'Would you like to tell me?'

She hesitated, shy at saying it to some other person for the first time. 'I thought I'd call it—*A Bright and Holy Thing*,' she said, and he thought about it for a few moments, repeating it softly.

'You like it?' she asked anxiously.

'It's great,' he said. 'I like it. I really do.'

With Debra once more busy on her novel it seemed each day was too short for the love and laughter and industry which filled it.

The call came through while David and Debra were sitting around the barbecue in the front garden. David ran up to the house when the telephone bell insisted.

'Miss Mordecai?' David was puzzled, the name was vaguely familiar.

'Yes. I have a person-to-person call from New York for Miss Debra Mordecai,' the operator repeated impatiently, and David realized who she was talking about.

'She'll take it,' he said, and yelled for Debra. It was Bobby Dugan, and the first time she had heard his voice.

'Wonder girl,' he shouted over the line. 'Sit down, so you don't fall down. Big Daddy has got news for you that will blow your mind! *Cosmopolitan* ran the article on you two weeks ago. They did you real proud, darling, full-page photograph—God, you looked good enough to eat—'

Debra laughed nervously and signalled David to put his ear against hers to listen.

'—the mag hit the stands Saturday, and Monday morning was a riot at the book stores. They were beating the doors down. You've caught the imagination of everybody here, darling. They sold seventeen thousand hardback in five days, you jumped straight into the number five slot on the *New York Times* bestseller list—it's a freak, a phenomenon, a mad crazy runner—darling, we are going to sell half a million copies of this book standing on our heads. All the big papers and mags are screaming for review copies—they've lost the ones we sent them three months ago. Doubleday are reprinting fifty thousand—and I told them they were crazy—it should have been a hundred thousand—it's only just starting—next week will see the west coast catch fire and they'll be screaming for copies across the whole country—' There was much more, Bobby Dugan riding high, shouting his plans and his hopes, while Debra laughed weakly and kept saying, 'No! I can't believe it!' and 'It's not true!'

They drank three bottles of Veuve Clicquot that night, and a little before midnight Debra fell pregnant to David Morgan.

'Miss Mordecai combines superb use of language and a sure literary touch with the readability of a popular bestseller,' said the *New York Times*.

'Who says good literature has to be dull?' asked *Time*, 'Debra Mordecai's talent burns like a clean white flame.'

'Miss Mordecai takes you by the throat, slams you against the wall, throws you on the floor and kicks you in the guts. She leaves you as shaken and weak as if you had been in a car smash,' added the *Free Press*.

Proudly David presented Conrad Berg with a signed copy of *A Place of Our Own*. Conrad had finally been prevailed upon to drop the 'Mrs Morgan' and call Debra by her given name. He was so impressed with the book that he had an immediate relapse.

'How do you think of those things, Mrs Morgan?' he asked with awe.

'Debra,' Debra prompted him.

'She doesn't think of them,' Jane Berg explained helpfully. 'It just comes to her—it's called *inspiration*.'

Bobby Dugan was correct, they had to reprint another fifty thousand copies.

It seemed as though the fates, ashamed of the cruel pranks they had played upon them, were determined to shower Debra and David with gifts.

As Debra sat at her olive-wood table, growing daily bigger with her child, once again the words flowed as strongly and as crystal clear as the spring waters of the String of Pearls. However, there was still time to help David with the illustrated publication he was compiling on the birds of prey of the bushveld, and to accompany him on the daily expeditions to different areas of Jabulani, and to plan the furnishings and the layout of the empty nursery.

Conrad Berg came to her secretly to enlist her aid in his plan to have David nominated to the Board of the National Parks Committee. They discussed it in length and great detail. A seat on the Board carried prestige and was usually reserved for men of greater age and influence than David. However, Conrad was confident that the dignity of the Morgan name combined with David's wealth, ownership of Jabulani, demonstrated interest in conservation and his ability to devote much time to the affairs of the Board would prevail.

'Yes,' Debra decided. 'It will be good for him to meet people and get out a little more. We are in danger of becoming recluses here.'

'Will he do it?'

'Don't worry,' Debra assured him, 'I'll see to it.'

Debra was right. After the initial uneasiness of the first meeting of the Board, and once the other members became accustomed to that dreadful face and realized that behind it was a warm and forceful person, David gathered increasing confidence with each subsequent journey to Pretoria where the Board met. Debra would fly up with him and while they were at their deliberations she and Jane Berg shopped for the baby and the other items of luxury and necessity that were not readily come by in Nelspruit.

However, by November Debra was carrying low and she felt too big and uncomfortable to make the long flight in the cockpit of the Navajo, especially as the rains were about to break and the air was turbulent with storm cloud and static and heavy thermals. It would be a bumpy trip, and she was deeply involved in the last chapters of the new book.

'I'll be perfectly all right here,' she insisted. 'I've got a telephone and I have also got six game rangers, four servants and a fierce hound to guard me.'

David argued and protested for five days before the meeting and agreed only after he had worked out a timetable.

'If I leave here before dawn I'll be at the meeting by nine, we'll be finished by three and I can be back here by six-thirty at the latest,' he muttered. 'If it wasn't the budget and financial affairs vote, I would cut it—tell them I was sick.'

'It's important, darling. You go.'

'You sure now?'

'I won't even notice you're not here.'

'Don't get too carried away by it,' he told her ruefully. 'I might stay just to punish you.'

In the dawn the thunderheads were the colour of wine and flame and ripe fruit, fuming and magnificent, towering high above the tiny aircraft, high above the utmost ceiling of which it was capable.

David flew the corridors of open sky alone and at peace, wrapped in the euphoria of flight which never failed for him. He altered course at intervals to avoid the mountainous upsurges of cloud; within them lurked death and disaster, great winds that would tear the wings from his machine and send the pieces whirling on high, up into the heights where a man would perish from lack of oxygen.

He landed at Grand Central where a hire car was waiting for him, and spent the journey into Pretoria reading through the morning papers. It was only when he saw the meteorological prediction of a storm front moving in steadily from the Mozambique channel that he felt a little uneasy.

Before he entered the conference-room he asked the receptionist to take a telephone call to Jabulani.

'Two-hour delay, Mr Morgan.'

'Okay, call me when it comes through.'

When they broke for lunch he asked her again.

'What happened to my call?'

'I'm sorry, Mr Morgan. I was going to tell you. The lines are down. They are having very heavy rainfall in the low veld.'

His vague uneasiness became mild alarm.

'Would you call the meteorological office for me, please?'

The weather was down solid. From Barberton to Mpunda Milia and from Lourenço Marques to Machadodorp, the rain was heavy and unrelenting. The cloud ceiling was above twenty thousand feet and it was right down on the ground. The Navajo had no oxygen or electronic navigational equipment.

'How long?' David demanded of the meteorological officer. 'How long until it clears?'

'Hard to tell, sir. Two or three days.'

'Damn! Damn!' said David bitterly, and went down to the canteen on the ground floor of the government building. Conrad Berg was at a corner table with two other members of the Board, but when he saw David he jumped up and limped heavily but urgently across the room.

'David,' he took his arm, and his round red face was deadly serious. 'I've just heard–Johan Akkers broke jail last night. He killed a guard and got clean away. He's been loose for seventeen hours.'

David stared at him, unable to speak with the shock of it.

'Is Debra alone?'

David nodded, his face stiff with scar tissue, but his eyes dark and afraid.

'You'd better fly down right away to be with her.'

'The weather–they've grounded all aircraft in the area.'

'Use my truck!' said Conrad urgently.

'I need something faster than that.'

'Do you want me to come with you?'

'No,' said David. 'If you aren't there this afternoon, they won't approve the new fencing allocations. I'll go on my own.'

Debra was working at her desk when she heard the wind coming. She switched off her tape recorder and went out on to the veranda with the dog following her closely.

She stood listening, not sure of what she was hearing. It was a soughing and sighing, a far-off rushing like that of a wave upon a pebble beach.

The dog pressed against her leg and she squatted beside him, placing one arm around his neck, listening to the gathering rush of the wind, hearing the roar of it building up swiftly, the branches of the marula forest beginning to thrash and rattle.

Zulu whimpered, and she hugged him a little closer.

'There, boy. Gently. Gently,' she whispered and the wind struck in a mighty squalling blast, crashing through the tree-tops, tearing and cracking the upper branches.

It banged into the insect screen of the veranda with a snap like a mainsail filling, and unsecured windows and doors slammed like cannon shots.

Debra sprang up and ran back into her workroom, the window was swinging and slamming, dust and debris boiling in through it. She put her shoulder to it, closing it and securing the latch, then she ran to do the same to the other windows and bumped into one of the house servants.

Between them they battened down all the doors and windows.

'Madam, the rain will come now. Very much rain.'

'Go to your families now,' Debra told them.

'The dinner, madam?'

'Don't worry, I'll make that,' and thankfully they streamed away through the swirling dust to their hutments beyond the kopje.

The wind blew for fifteen minutes, and Debra stood by the wire screen and felt it tugging and whipping her body. Its wildness was infectious, and she laughed aloud, elated and excited.

Then suddenly the wind was passed, as swiftly as it had come, and she heard it tearing and clawing its way over the hills above the pools.

In the utter silence that followed the whole world waited, tensed for the next onslaught of the elements. Debra felt the cold, the sudden fall in temperature as though the door to a great ice-box had opened and she hugged her arms and shivered; she could not see the dense dark cloud banks that rolled across Jabulani, but somehow she sensed their menace and their majesty in the coldness that swamped her.

The first lightning bolt struck with a crackling electric explosion that seemed to singe the air about her, and Debra was taken so unawares that she cried out aloud. The thunder broke, and seemed to shake the sky and rock the earth's very foundations.

Debra turned and groped her way back into the house, locking herself into her room, but walls could not diminish the fury of the rain when it came. It drummed and roared and deafened, battering the window panes, and striking the walls and doors, pouring through the screen to flood the veranda.

As overpowering as was the rainstorm, yet it was the lightning and the thunder that racked Debra's nerves. She could not steel herself for each mighty crack and roar. Each one caught her off balance, and it seemed that they were aimed directly at her.

She crouched on her day bed, clinging to the soft warm body of the dog for a little comfort. She wished she had not allowed the servants to leave, and she thought that her nerve might crack altogether under the bombardment.

Finally she could stand it no longer. She groped her way into the living-room. In her distress she had almost lost her way about her own home, but she found the telephone and lifted it to her ear.

Immediately she knew that it was dead, there was no tone to it but she cranked the handle wildly, calling desperately into the mouthpiece, until finally she let it fall and dangle on its cord.

She began to sob as she stumbled back to her workroom, hugging the child in her big belly, and she fell upon the day bed and covered her ears with both hands.

'Stop it,' she screamed. 'Stop it, oh please God, make it stop.'

The new national highway as far as the coal-mining town of Witbank was broad and smooth, six lanes of traffic, and David eased the hired Pontiac into the fast lane and went flat, keeping his foot pressed down hard. She peaked out at a hundred and thirty miles an hour, and she sat so solid upon the road that he hardly needed to drive her. His mind was free to play with horror stories, and to remember Johan Akkers' face as he stood in the dock glaring across the Court Room at them. The deep-set muddy eyes, and the mouth working as though he were about to spit. As the warders had led him to the stairs down to the cells he had pulled free and shouted back.

'I'm going to get you, Scarface,' he giggled. 'If I have to wait twenty-nine years—I'm going to get you,' and they took him away.

After Witbank the road narrowed. There was heavy traffic and the bends had dangerous camber and deceptive gradients. David was able to concentrate on keeping the big car on the road, and to drive the phantoms from his mind.

He took the Lydenburg turn off, cutting the corner of the triangle, and the traffic thinned out to an occasional truck. He was able to go flat out again, and race along the edge of the high escarpment. Then suddenly the road turned and began its plunge down into the low veld.

When he emerged from the Erasmus tunnel David ran into the rain. It was a solid grey bank of water that filled the air and buffeted the body of the Pontiac. It flooded the road, so David had difficulty following its verge beneath the standing sheets of water, and it swamped the windshield, so that the efforts of the wipers to clear it were defeated.

David switched on his headlights and drove as fast as he dared, craning forward in his seat to peer into the impenetrable blue-grey curtains of rain.

Darkness came early in the rain, beneath the lowering black clouds, and the wet road dazzled him with the reflections of his own headlights, while the fat falling drops seemed as big as hail stones. He was forced to moderate his speed a little more, creeping down the highway towards Bandolier Hill.

In the darkness he almost missed the turning, and he reversed back to it, swinging on to the unmade surface.

It was slushy with mud, puddled and swampy, slippery as grease. Again he was forced to lower his speed. Once he lost it, and slid broadside into the drainage ditch. By packing loose stones under the wheels and racing the engine he pulled the Pontiac out and drove on.

By the time he reached the bridge over the Luzane stream, he had been six hours at the wheel of the Pontiac, and it was a few minutes after eight o'clock in the evening.

As he reached the bridge the rain stopped abruptly, a freak hole in the weather. Directly overhead the stars showed mistily, while around them the cloud banks swirled, turning slowly, as though upon the axis of a great wheel.

David's headlights cut through the darkness, out across the mad brown waters to the far bank a hundred yards away. The bridge was submerged under fifteen feet of flood water, and the water was moving so swiftly that its waves and whirlpools seemed sculptured in polished brown marble, and the trunks of uprooted trees dashed downstream upon the flood.

It seemed impossible that the bed of this raging torrent had been the narrow sandy bed in which Johan Akkers had run down Conrad with the green Ford truck.

David climbed out of the Pontiac and walked down to the edge of the water. As he stood there he saw the level creeping up perceptibly towards his feet. It was still rising.

He looked up at the sky, and judged that the respite in the weather would not last much longer.   .

He reached his decision and ran back to the Pontiac. He reversed well back on to the highest ground and parked it off the verge with the headlights still directed at the river edge. Then, standing beside the door, he stripped down to his shirt and underpants. He pulled his belt from the loops of his trousers and buckled it about his waist, then he tied his shoes to the belt by their laces.

Barefooted he ran to the edge of the water, and began to feel his way slowly down the bank. It shelved quickly and within a few paces he was knee-deep and the current plucked at him, viciously trying to drag him off-balance.

He poised like that, braced against the current, and waited, staring upstream. He saw the tree trunk coming down fast on the flood, with its roots sticking up like beseeching arms. It was swinging across the current and would pass him closely.

He judged his moment and lunged for it. Half a dozen strong strokes carried him to it and he grasped one of the roots. Instantly he was whisked out of the beams of the headlight into the roaring fury of the river. The tree rolled and bucked, carrying him under and bringing him up coughing and gasping.

Something struck him a glancing blow and he felt his shirt tear and the skin beneath it rip. Then he was under water again, swirling end over end and clinging desperately to his log.

All about him the darkness was filled with the rush and threat of crazy water, and he was buffeted and flogged by its raw strength, grazed and bruised by rocks and driftwood.

Suddenly he felt the log check and bump against an obstruction, turning and swinging out into the current again.

David was blinded with muddy water and he knew there was a limit to how much more of this treatment he could survive. Already he was weakening quickly. He could feel his mind and his movements slowing, like a battered prize fighter in the tenth round.

He gambled it all on the obstruction which the log had encountered being the far bank, and he released his death-grip on the root and struck out sideways across the current with desperate strength.

His overarm stroke ended in the trailing branches of a thorn tree hanging over the storm waters. Thorns tore the flesh of his palm as his grip closed over them, and he cried out at the pain but held on.

Slowly he dragged himself out of the flood and crawled up the bank, hacking and coughing at the water in his lungs. Clear of the river, he fell on his face in the mud and vomited a gush of swallowed water that shot out of his nose and mouth.

He lay exhausted for a long while, until his coughing slowed and he could breathe again. His shoes had been torn from his belt by the current. He dragged himself to his feet and staggered forward into the darkness. As he ran, he held his hand to his face, pulling the broken thorns from the flesh of his palm with his teeth.

Stars were still showing overhead and by their feeble light he made out the road, and he began to run along it, gathering strength with each pace. It was very still now, with only the dripping of the trees and the occasional far-out mutter of thunder to break the silence.

Two miles from the homestead, David made out the dark bulk of something on the side of the road, and it was only when he was a few paces from it that he realized it was an automobile—a late model Chevy. It had been abandoned, bogged down in one of the greasy mudholes that the rains had opened.

The doors were unlocked and David switched on the interior and parking lights. There was dried blood on the seat, a dark smear of it, and on the back seat was a bundle of clothing. David untied it quickly and recognized immediately the coarse canvas suiting as regulation prison garb. He stared at it stupidly for a moment, until the impact of it struck him.

The car was stolen, the blood probably belonging to the unfortunate owner. The prison garb had been exchanged for other clothing, probably taken from the body of the owner of the Chevy.

David knew then beyond all possible doubt that Johan Akkers was at Jabulani, and that he had arrived before the bridge over the Luzane stream had become impassable—probably three or four hours previously.

David threw the prison suiting back into the car, and he began to run.

Johan Akkers drove the Chevy across the Luzane bridge with the rising waters swirling over the guard rail, and with the rain teeming down in blinding white sheets.

The muddy water shoved at the body of the car, making steering difficult, and it seeped in under the doors, flooding the floorboards and swirling about Akkers' feet; but he reached the safety of the far bank and raced the engine as he shot up it. The wheels spun on the soft mud, and the Chevy skidded and swayed drunkenly in the loose footing.

The closer he drew to Jabulani the more reckless he became in his haste.

Before his conviction and imprisonment, Akkers had been a twisted and blighted creature, a man of deep moods and passionate temper. Feeling himself rejected and spurned by his fellow men he had lived in a world of swift defensive violence, but always he had kept within the bounds of reason.

However, during the two years that he had laboured and languished within prison walls, his anger and his lust for vengeance had driven him over that narrow boundary.

Vengeance had become the sole reason for his existence, and he had rehearsed it a hundred times each day. He had planned his prison break to give himself three days of freedom—after that it did not matter. Three days would be enough.

He had infected his own jaw, running a needle poisoned with his excreta deeply into the gum. They had taken him to the dental clinic as he had planned. The guard had been easily handled, and the dentist had co-operated with a scalpel held to his throat.

Once clear of the prison, Akkers had used the scalpel, vaguely surprised by the volume of blood that could issue from a human throat. He had left the dentist slumped over his steering-wheel on a plot of waste ground and, with his white laboratory gown over his prison suit, he had waited at a set of traffic lights.

The shiny new Chevy had pulled up for a red light and Akkers had opened the passenger door and slid in beside the driver.

He had been a smaller man than Akkers, plump and prosperous-looking, with a smooth pale face and soft little hairless hands on the steering-wheel. He had obeyed meekly Akkers' instruction to drive on.

Akkers had rolled his soft white body, clad only in vest and shorts, into a clump of thick grass beside a disused secondary road and pulled the grass closed over him, then he had beaten the first road block out of the city area by forty minutes.

He stayed on the side roads, picking his way slowly eastwards. The infection in his jaw had ached intolerably despite the shot of antibiotics the dentist had given him, and his crippled claw of a hand had been awkward and clumsy on the gear lever—for the severed nerves and sinews had never knitted again. The hand was a dead and insensate thing.

Using the caution of a natural predator and helped by the news flashes on the radio, he had groped his way carefully through the net that was spread for him, and now he was on Jabulani and he could restrain himself no longer.

He hit the mud hole at forty and the Chevy whipped and spun, slewing her back end deep into the mud and high-centring her belly on the soft ooze.

He left her there and went on swiftly through the rain, loping on long legs. Once he giggled and sucked at his teeth, but then he was silent again.

It was dark by the time he climbed the kopje behind Jabulani homestead. He lay there for two hours peering down into the driving rain, waiting for the darkness. Once night fell, he could see no lights, and he began to worry, there should have been lights burning.

He left the kopje and moved cautiously through the darkness down the hill. He avoided the servants' quarters, and went through the trees to the landing-strip.

He ran into the side of the hangar in the dark and followed the wall to the side doorway.

Frantically he spread his arms and felt for the aircraft that should be here—and when he realized that it was not he let out a groan of frustration.

They were gone. He had planned and schemed in vain, all his desperate striving was in vain.

Growling like an animal, he smashed the fist of his good hand against the wall, enjoying the pain of it in his frustration, and his anger and his hatred was so strong that it shook his body like a fever, and he cried out aloud, a formless animal cry without coherence or sense.

Suddenly the rain stopped. The heavy drum of it upon the iron roof of the hangar ceased so abruptly that Akkers was distracted. He went to the opening and looked out.

The stars were swimming mistily above him, and the only sound was the gurgle and chuckle of running water and the dripping of the trees.

There was the glimmering of light now, and he saw the white walls of the homestead shine amongst the trees. He could do damage there, Akkers realized. He could find there some outlet for his terrible frustration. There was furniture to smash, and the thatch would burn—if lit from inside, the thatch would burn even in this weather.

He started towards the homestead through the dark sodden trees.

Debra woke in the silence. She had fallen asleep in the midst of the storm, perhaps as a form of escape.

Now she groped for the warm comforting body of the dog but he was gone. There was a patch of warmth on the bed beside her where he had lain.

She listened intently and there was nothing but the soft sounds of water in the guttering and far-off the growl of thunder. She remembered her earlier panic and she was ashamed.

She stood up from the bed and she was shivering with the cold in her loose, free-flowing dark blue maternity blouse, and the elastic-fronted slacks that were adjustable to her expanding waistline. She felt with her toes and found the light ballet pumps on the stone floor and pushed her feet into them.

She started towards her dressing-room for a sweater, then she would make herself a cup of hot soup, she decided.

Zulu started barking. He was outside in the front garden. Clearly he had left the house through the small hinged doorway that David had built especially for him in the veranda wall.

The dog had many barks, each with a different meaning which Debra understood.

A self-effacing woof, that was the equivalent of the watchman's 'Ten o'clock on a June night—and all's well.'

Or a longer-drawn-out yowl, that meant, 'There is a full moon out tonight, and the wolf's blood in my veins will not allow me to sleep.'

A sharper, meaningful bark, 'Something is moving down near the pumphouse. It may be a lion.'

And then there was an urgent clamouring chorus, 'There is dire danger threatening. Beware! Beware!'

It was the danger bark now, and then growling through closed jaws as though he were worrying something.

Debra went out on to the veranda and she felt the puddled rainwater soaking through her light shoes. Zulu was harrying something in the front garden, she could hear the growling and scuffling, the movement of bodies locked in a struggle. She stood silently, uncertain of what to do, knowing only that she could not go out to Zulu. She was blind and helpless against the unknown adversary. As she hesitated she heard clearly the sound of a heavy blow. It cracked on bone, and she heard the thump of a body falling. Zulu's growls were cut off abruptly, and there was silence. Something had happened to the dog. Now she was completely alone in the silence.

No, not silence. There was the sound of breathing—a heavy panting breath. Debra shrank back against the veranda wall, listening and waiting.

She heard footsteps, human footsteps coming through the garden towards the front door. The footsteps squelched and splashed in the rain puddles.

She wanted to call out a challenge, but her voice was locked in her constricted throat. She wanted to run, but her legs were paralysed by the sound of the intruder climbing the front steps.

A hand brushed against the wire screening, and then settled on the handle, rattling it softly.

At last Debra found her voice. 'Who is that?' she called, a high panicky cry that ran out into the night silence.

Instantly the soft sounds ceased. The intruder was frozen by her challenge. She could imagine whoever it was standing on the top step, peering through the screening into the darkness of the veranda, trying to make her out in the gloom. Suddenly she was thankful for the dark blouse and black slacks.

She waited motionlessly, listening, and she heard a little wind shake the tree-tops, bringing down a sudden quick patter of droplets. A hunting owl called down near the dam. She heard the thunder murmur bad-temperedly along the hills, and a nightjar screeched harshly from amongst the poinsettia bushes.

The silence went on for a long time, and she knew she could not stand it much longer. She could feel her lips beginning to quiver and the cold and fear and the weight of the child were heavy upon her bladder, she wanted to run—but there was nowhere to run to.

Then suddenly the silence was broken. In the darkness there was the sound of a man giggling. It was shockingly close and clear, and it was a crazy sound. The shock of it seemed to clutch at her heart and crush the air from her lungs.

Her legs went weak under her, beginning to shake, and the pressure on her bladder was intolerable—for she recognized the sound of that laughter, the sick insane sound of it was graven upon her mind.

A hand shook the door handle, jerking and straining at it. Then a shoulder crashed into the narrow frame. It was a screen door—not built to withstand rough treatment. Debra knew it would yield quickly.

She screamed then, a high ringing scream of terror, and it seemed to break the spell which held her. Her legs would move again, and her brain would work.

She whirled and ran back into her workroom, slamming the door and locking it swiftly.

She crouched beside the door, thinking desperately. She knew that as soon as he broke into the house Akkers need only switch on a light. The electricity generator would automatically kick in on demand, and in the light he would have her at his mercy. Her only protection was darkness. In the darkness she would have the advantage, for she was accustomed to it.

She had heard the nightjar and the owl calling so she knew that night had fallen, and it was probable that the rain cloud still blanketed moon and stars. Darkness was out there in the forest. She must get out of the house, and try to reach the servants' quarters.

She hurried through the rooms towards the rear of the house, and as she went she thought of a weapon. The firearms were locked in the steel cabinet in David's office—and the key was with him. She ran through to the kitchen and her heavy walking-stick was in its place by the door. She grasped it thankfully and slipped open the door catch.

At that moment she heard the front door crash open, with the lock kicked in, and she heard Akkers charge heavily into the living-room. She closed the kitchen door behind her and started across the yard. She tried not to run, she counted her steps. She must not lose her way. She must find the track around the kopje to the servants' hutments.

Her first landmark was the gate in the fence that ringed the homestead. Before she reached it she heard the electricity generator throb to life in the power house beyond the garages. Akkers had found a light switch.

She was slightly off in her direction and she ran into the barbed-wire fence. Frantically she began to feel her way along it, trying for the gate. Above her head she heard the buzz and crackle of the element in one of the arc lamps that lined the fence and could flood the gardens with light.

Akkers must have found the switch beside the kitchen door, and Debra realized that she must be bathed in the light of the arcs.

She heard him shout behind her, and knew that he had seen her. At that moment she found the gate, and with a sob of relief she tore it open and began to run.

She must get out of the light of the arcs, she must find the darkness. Light was mortal danger, darkness was sanctuary.

The track forked, left to the pools, right to the hutments. She took the right-hand path and ran along it. Behind her she heard the gate clank shut. He was after her.

She counted as she ran, five hundred paces to the rock on the left side of the path that marked the next fork. She tripped over it, falling heavily and barking her shins.

She rolled to her knees, and she had lost the walking-stick. She could not waste precious seconds in searching for it. She groped for the path and ran on.

Fifty paces and she knew she was on the wrong fork. This path led down to the pumphouse—and she was not familiar with it. It was not one of her regular routes.

She missed a turn and ran into broken ground. She stumbled on until rank grass wrapped about her ankles and brought her down again, falling heavily on her side so that she was winded.

She was completely lost, but she knew she was out of the arc lights now. With luck she was shielded by complete darkness—but her heart was racing and she felt nauseous with terror.

She tried to control her gulping, sobbing breath, and to listen.

She heard him coming then, pounding footsteps that rang clearly, even on the rain-soaked earth. He seemed to be coming directly to where she lay, and she shrank down against the wet earth and she pressed her face into her arms to hide her face and muffle her breathing.

At the last moment his blundering footsteps passed her closely, and ran on. She felt sick with relief, but it was premature for abruptly the footsteps ceased and he was so close she could hear him panting.

He was listening for her, standing close beside where she lay in the grass. They stayed like that during the long slow passage of minutes. For Debra it seemed an eternity of waiting—broken at last by his voice.

'Ah! There you are,' he giggled, 'there you are. I can see you.'

Her heart jumped with shock, he was closer than she had thought. Almost she jumped up and began to run again—but some deeper sense restrained her.

'I can see you hiding there,' he repeated, giggling and snickering. 'I've got a big knife here, I'm going to hold you down and cut–'.

She quailed in the grass, listening to the awful obscenities that poured from his mouth. Then suddenly she realized that she was safe here. She was covered by the night and the thick grass, and he had lost her. He was trying to panic her, make her run again and betray her position. She concentrated all her attention on remaining absolutely still and silent.

Akkers' threats and sadistic droolings ended in silence again. He listened for her with the patience of the hunter, and the long minutes dragged by.

The ache in her bladder was like a red-hot iron, and she wanted to sob out loud. Something loathsome crawled out of the wet grass over her arm. Her skin prickled with fresh horror at the feel of multiple insect feet on her skin, but she steeled herself not to move.

The thing, scorpion or spider, crawled across her neck and she knew her nerves would crack within seconds.

Suddenly Akkers spoke again. 'All right!' he said, 'I'm going back to fetch a flashlight. We'll see how far you get then. I'll be back soon—don't think you'll beat old Akkers. He's forgotten more tricks than you'll ever learn.'

He moved away heavily, noisily, and she wanted to strike the insect from her cheek and run again, but some instinct warned her. She waited five minutes, and then ten. The insect moved up into her hair.

Akkers spoke again out of the darkness near her. 'All right, you clever bitch. We'll get you yet,' and she heard him move away. This time she knew he had gone.

She brushed the insect from her hair, shuddering with horror. Then she stood up and moved quietly into the forest. Her fingers were stiff with cold on the fastenings of her slacks, but she loosened them and squatted to relieve the burning ache in her lower belly.

She stood up again and felt the child move within her body. The feel of it evoked all her maternal instincts of protection. She must find a safe place for her child. She thought of the hide by the pools.

How to reach them? For she was now completely lost. Then she remembered David telling her about the wind, the rain wind out of the west, now reduced to an occasional light air, and she waited for the next breath of it on her cheek. It gave her direction. She turned her back to the next gust and set off steadily through the forest with hands held out ahead to prevent herself running into one of the trunks. If only she could reach the pools, she could follow the bank to the hide.

As the cyclonic winds at the centre of the storm turned upon their axis, so they swung, changing direction constantly and Debra followed them faithfully, beginning a wide aimless circle through the forest.

Akkers raged through the brightly lit homestead of Jabulani, jerking open drawers and kicking in locked cupboard doors.

He found the gun cabinet in David's office, and ransacked the desk drawers for keys. He found none, and giggled and swore with frustration.

He crossed the room to the built-in cupboard unit. There was a sealed-cell electric lantern on the shelf with a dozen packets of shotgun shells. he took down the lantern eagerly and thumbed the switch. The beam was bright white, even in the overhead lights—and he sucked his teeth and chuckled happily.

Once more he ran into the kitchen, pausing to select a long stainless-steel carving knife from the cutlery drawer before hurrying across the yard to the gate and along the path.

In the lantern beam, Debra's footprints showed clearly in the soft earth with his own overlaying them. He followed them to where she had blundered off the path, and found the mark of her body where she had lain.

'Clever bitch, he chuckled again and followed her tracks through the forest. She had laid an easy trail to follow, dragging a passage through the rain-heavy grass and wiping the droplets from the stems. To the hunter's eye it was a clearly blazed trail.

Every few minutes he paused to throw the beam of the lantern ahead of him amongst the trees. He was thrilling now to the hunter's lust, the primeval force which was the mainspring of his existence. His earlier set-back made the chase sweeter for him.

He went on carefully, following the wandering trail, the aimless footprints turning haphazardly in a wide circle.

He stopped again and panned the lantern beam across the rain-laden grass tops, and he saw something move at the extreme range of the lamp, something pale and round.

He held it in the lantern beam, and saw the woman's pale strained face as she moved forward slowly and hesitantly. She went like a sleep-walker, with arms extended ahead of her, and with shuffling uncertain gait.

She was coming directly towards him, oblivious of the light which held her captive in its beam. Once she paused to hug her swollen belly and sob with weariness and fear.

The legs of her trousers were sodden with rain water and her flimsy shoes were already torn, and as she hobbled closer he saw that her arms and her lips were blue and shivering with the cold.

Akkers stood quietly watching her coming towards him, like a chicken drawn to the swaying cobra.

Her long dark hair hung in damp ropes down her shoulders, and dangled in her face. Her thin blouse was wet also with drops fallen from the trees, and it was plastered over the thrusting mound of her belly.

He let her come closer, enjoying the fierce thrill of having her in his power. Drawing out the final consummation of his vengeance—hoarding each moment of it like a miser.

When she was five paces from him he played the beam full in her face, and he giggled.

She screamed, her whole face convulsing, and she whirled like a wild animal and ran blindly. Twenty paces before she ran headlong into the stem of a marula tree.

She fell back, collapsing to her knees and sobbed aloud, clutching at her bruised cheek.

Then she scrambled to her feet and stood shivering, turning her head and cocking it for the next sound.

Silently he moved around her, drawing close and he giggled again, close behind her.

She screamed again and ran blindly, panic-stricken, witless with terror until an ant-bear hold caught her foot and flung her down heavily to the ground, and she lay there sobbing.

Akkers moved leisurely and silently after her, he was enjoying himself for the first time in two years. Like a cat he did not want to end it, he wanted it to last a long time.

He stooped over her and whispered a filthy word, and instantly she rolled to her feet and was up and running again—wildly, sightlessly, through the trees. He followed her, and in his crazed mind she became a symbol of all the thousand animals he had hunted and killed.

David ran barefooted in the soft earth of the road. He ran without feeling his bruised and torn skin, without feeling the pounding of his heart nor the protest of his lungs.

As the road rounded the shoulder of the hill and dipped towards the homestead he stopped abruptly, and stared panting at the lurid glow of the arc lights that floodlit the grounds and garden of Jabulani. It made no sense that the floodlights should be burning, and David felt a fresh flood of alarm. He sprinted on down the hill.

He ran through the empty, ransacked rooms shouting her name—but the echoes mocked him.

When he reached the front veranda he saw something moving in the darkness, beyond the broken screen door.

'Zulu!' He ran forward. 'Here, boy! Here, boy! Where is she?'

The dog staggered up the steps towards him, his tail wagged a perfunctory greeting, but he was obviously hurt. A heavy blow along the side of his head had broken the jaw, or dislocated it, so that it hung lopsided and grotesque. He was still stunned, and David knelt beside him.

'Where is she, Zulu? Where is she?' The dog seemed to make an effort to gather its scattered wits. 'Where is she, boy? She's not in the house. Where is she? Find her, boy, find her.'

He led the labrador out into the yard, and he followed gamely as David circled the house. At the back door Zulu picked up the scent on the fresh damp earth. He started resolutely towards the gate, and David saw the footprints in the floodlights, Debra's and the big masculine prints which ran after them.

As Zulu crossed the yard, David turned back into his office. The lantern was missing from its shelf, but there was a five-cell flashlight near the back. He shoved it into his pocket and grabbed a handful of shotgun shells. Then he went quickly to the gun cabinet and unlocked it. He snatched the Purdey shotgun from the rack and loaded it as he ran.

Zulu was staggering along the path beyond the gates, and David hurried after him.

Johan Akkers was no longer a human being, he had become an animal. The spectacle of the running quarry had roused the predator's single-minded passion to chase and drag down and kill—yet it was seasoned .with a feline delight in torment. He was playing with his wounded dragging prey, running it when he could have ended it, drawing it out, postponing the climax, the final consuming thrill of the kill.

The moment came at last, some deep atavistic sense of the ritual of the hunt—for all sport killing has its correct ceremony—and Akkers knew it must end now.

He came up behind the running figure and reached out to take a twist of the thick dark hair in the crippled claw of his hand, wrapping it with a quick movement about his wrist and jerking back her head, laying open the long pale throat for the knife.

She turned upon him with a strength and ferocity he had not anticipated. Her body was hard and strong and supple, and now that she could place him she drove at him with the wild terror of a hunted thing.

He was unprepared, her attack took him off-balance, and he went over backwards with her on top of him, and he dropped the knife and the lantern into the grass to protect his eyes, for she was tearing at them with long sharp nails. He felt them rip into his nose and cheek, and she screeched like a cat—for she was also an animal in this moment.

He freed the stiff claw from the tangle of her hair, and he drew it back, holding her off with his right hand—and he struck her. It was like a wooden club, stiff and hard and without feeling. A single blow with it had stunned the labrador and broken his jaw. It hit her across the temple, a sound like an axe swung at a tree trunk. It knocked all the fight out of her, and he came up on his knees, holding her with his good hand and with the other he clubbed her mercilessly, beat her head back and across with a steady rhythm. In the light of the fallen lantern, the black blood spurted from her nose, and the blows cracked against her skull, steady and unrelenting. Long after she was still and senseless he continued to beat her. Then at last he let her drop, and he stood up. He went to the lantern and played the beam in the grass. The knife glinted up at him.

There is an ancient ceremony with which a hunt should end. The culminating ceremony of the gralloch, when the triumphant huntsman slits open the paunch of his game, and thrusts his hand into the opening to draw out the still-warm viscera.

Johan Akkers picked the knife out of the grass and set down the lantern so the beam fell upon Debra's supine figure.

He went to her and, with his foot, rolled her on to her back. The dark black mane of sodden hair smothered her face.

He knelt beside her and hooked one iron-hard finger into the front of her blouse. With a single jerk he ripped it cleanly open, and her big round belly bulged into the lantern light. It was white and full and ripe with the dark pit of the navel in its centre.

Akkers giggled and wiped the rain and sweat from his face with his arm. Then he changed his grip on the knife, reversing it so the blade would go shallow, opening the paunch neatly from crotch to rib cage without cutting into the intestines, a stroke as skilful as a surgeon's that he had performed ten thousand times before.

Movement in the shadows at the edge of the light caused him to glance up. He saw the black dog rush silently at him, saw its eyes glow in the lantern light.

He threw up his arm to guard his throat and the furry body crashed into him. They rolled together, with Zulu mouthing him, unable to take a grip with his injured jaws.

Akkers changed his grip on the hilt of the carving knife and stabbed up into the dog's rib cage, finding the faithful heart with his first thrust. Zulu yelped once, and collapsed. Akkers pushed the glossy black body aside, pulling out the knife and he crawled back to where Debra lay.

The distraction that Zulu had provided gave David a chance to come up.

David ran to Akkers, and the man looked up with the muddy green eyes glaring in the lantern light. He growled at David with the long blade in his hand dulled by the dog's blood. He started to come to his feet, ducking his head in exactly the same aggressive gesture as the bull baboon.

David thrust the barrels of the shotgun into his face and he pulled both triggers. The shot hit solidly, without spreading, tearing into him in the bright yellow flash and thunder of the muzzle blast, and it took away the whole of Akkers' head above the mouth, blowing it to nothingness. He dropped into the grass with his legs kicking convulsively, and David hurled the shotgun aside and ran to Debra.

He knelt over her and he whispered, 'My darling, oh my darling. Forgive me, please forgive me. I should never have left you.' Gently he picked her up and holding her to his chest, he carried her up to the homestead.

Debra's child was born in the dawn. It was a girl, tiny and wizened and too early for her term. If there had been skilled medical attention available she might have lived, for she fought valiantly. But David was clumsy and ignorant of the succour she needed. He was cut off by the raging river and the telephone was still dead, and Debra was still unconscious.

When it was over he wrapped the tiny little blue body in a clean sheet and laid it tenderly in the cradle that had been prepared for her. He felt overwhelmed by a sense of guilt at having failed the two persons who needed him.

At three o'clock that afternoon, Conrad Berg forced a passage of the Luzane stream with the water boiling above the level of the big wheels of his truck, and three hours later they had Debra in a private ward of the Nelspruit hospital. Two days later she became conscious once more, but her face was grotesquely swollen and purple with bruises.

Near the crest of the kopje that stood above the homestead of Jabulani there was a natural terrace, a platform which overlooked the whole estate. It was a remote and peaceful place and they buried the child there. Out of the rock of the kopje David built a tomb for her with his own hands.

It was best that Debra had never felt the child in her arms, or at her breast. That she had never heard her cry or smelled the puppy smell of her.

Her mourning was therefore not crippling and corrosive, and she and David visited the grave regularly. One Sunday morning as they sat upon the stone bench beside it, Debra talked for the first time about another baby.

'You took so long with the first one, Morgan,' she complained. 'I hope you've mastered the technique.'

They walked down the hill again, put the rods and a picnic basket into the Land-Rover and drove down to the pools.

The Mozambique bream came on the bite for an hour just before noon and they fought over the fat yellow wood grubs that David was baiting. Debra hung five, all around three pounds in weight, and David had a dozen of the big blue fish before it went quiet and they propped the rods and opened the cold box.

They lay together on the rug beneath the outspread branches of the fever trees, and drank white wine cold from the icebox.

The African spring was giving way to full summer, filling the bush with bustle and secret activity. The weaver birds were busy upon their basket nests, tying them to the bending tips of the reeds, fluttering brilliant yellow wings as they worked with black heads bobbing. On the far bank of the pool a tiny bejewelled kingfisher sat his perch on a dead branch above the still water, plunging suddenly, a speck of flashing blue to shatter the surface and emerge with a silver sliver wriggling in his outsize beak. Hosts of yellow and bronze and white butterflies lined the water's edge below where they lay, and the bees flew like golden motes of light to their hive in the cliff, high above the quiet pools.

The water drew all life to it, and a little after noonday David touched Debra's arm.

'The nyala are here–' he whispered.

They came through the grove on the far side of the pool. Timid and easily spooked, they approached a few cautious steps at a time before pausing to stare about them with huge dark eyes, questing muzzles and widespread ears; striped and dainty and beautiful they blended with the shadows of the grove.

'The does are all belly now,' David told her. 'They'll be dropping their lambs within the next few weeks. Everything is fruitful.' He half-turned towards her and she sensed it and moved to meet him. When the nyala had drank and gone, and a white-headed fish eagle circled high above them on dark chestnut wings, chanting its weird and haunting cry, they made love in the shade beside the quiet water.

David studied her face as he loved her. She lay beneath him with her eyes closed, and her dark hair spread in a shiny black sheet upon the rug. The bruise on her temple had faded to soft yellow and palest blue, for it was two months since she had left hospital. The white fleck of the grenade scar stood out clearly against the pale bruising. The colour rose in Debra's cheeks, and the light dew of perspiration bloomed across her forehead and upper lip and she made little cooing sounds, and them whimpered softly like a suckling puppy.

David watched her, his whole being engorged and heavy with the weight of his love. From above them an errant beam of sunlight broke through the canopy of leaves and fell full upon her upturned face, lighting it with a warm golden radiance so that it seemed to be the face of a madonna from some medieval church window. It was too much for David and his love broke like a wave, and she felt it and cried out. Her eyes flew wide, and he looked down into their gold-flecked depths. The pupils were huge black pools but as the sunlight struck full into them they shrank rapidly to black pinpoints.

Even in the extremity of his love, David was startled by the phenomenon, and long afterwards when they lay quietly together she asked, 'What is it, David? Is something wrong?'

'No, my darling. What could possibly be wrong?'

'I feel it, Davey. You send out the strongest signals—I am sure I could pick them up from half-way around the world.'

He laughed, and drew away from her almost guiltily. He had imagined it perhaps, a trick of the light, and he tried to dismiss it from his mind.

In the cool of the evening he packed up the rods and the rug and they strolled back to where he had parked and they took the firebreak road home, for David wanted to check the southern fence line. They had driven for twenty minutes in silence before Debra touched his arm.

'When you are ready to tell me about whatever is bugging you—I'm ready to listen,' and he began talking again to distract both her and himself, but a little too glibly.

In the night he rose and went to the bathroom. When he returned he stood for many seconds beside their bed looking down at her dark sleeping shape. He would have left it then, but at that moment a lion began roaring down near the pools. The sound carried clearly through the still night across the two miles that separated them.

It was the excuse that David needed. He took the five-cell flashlight from his bedside table and shone it into Debra's face. It was serene and lovely, and he felt the urge to stoop and kiss her, but instead he called.

'Debra! Wake up, darling!' and she stirred and opened her eyes. He shone the beam of the flashlight full into them and again, unmistakably, the wide black circles of the pupils contracted.

'What is it, David?' she murmured sleepily, and his voice was husky as he replied.

'There is a lion holding a concert down near the pools. Thought you might want to listen.' She moved her head, averting her face slightly, almost as though the powerful beam of the flashlight was causing discomfort, but her voice was pleased.

'Oh yes. I love that big growly sound. Where do you suppose this one is from?'

David switched out the flashlight and slipped back into bed beside her.

'Probably coming up from the south. I bet he has dug a hole under the fence you could drive a truck through.' He tried to speak naturally as they reached for each other beneath the bedclothes and lay close and warm, listening to the far-away roaring until it faded with distance as the lion moved back towards the reserve. They made love then, but afterwards David could not sleep and he lay with Debra in his arms until the dawn.

Still it was a week before David could bring himself to write the letter:

Dear Dr Edelman,

    We agreed that I should write to you if any change occurred in the condition of Debra's eyes, or her health.

    Recently Debra was involved in unfortunate circumstances, in which she was struck repeated heavy blows about the head and was rendered unconscious for a period of two and a half days.

She was hospitalized for suspected fracture of the skull, and concussion, but was discharged after ten days.

This occurred about two months ago. However, I have since noticed that her eyes have become sensitive to light. As you are well aware, this was not previously the case, and she has showed no reaction whatsoever until this time. She has also complained of severe headaches.

I have repeatedly tested my observations with sunlight and artificial light, and there can be no doubt that under the stimulus of a strong light source, the pupils of her eyes contract instantly and to the same degree as one would expect in a normal eye.

It now seems possible that your original diagnosis might have to be revised, but—and I would emphasize this most strongly—I feel that we should approach this very carefully. I do not wish to awaken any false or ill-founded hope.

For your advice in this matter I would be most grateful, and I wait to hear from you.

Cordially yours,
David Morgan

David sealed and addressed the letter, but when he returned from the shopping flight to Nelspuit the following week, the envelope was still buttoned in the top pocket of his leather jacket.

The days settled into their calmly contented routine. Debra completed the first draft of her new novel, and received a request from Bobby Dugan to carry out a lecture tour of five major cities in the United States. *A Place of Our Own* had just completed its thirty-second week on the *New York Times* bestseller list—and her agent informed her that she was 'hotter than a pistol'.

David said that as far as he was concerned she was probably a lot hotter than that. Debra told him he was a lecher, and she was not certain what a nice girl like herself was doing shacked up with him. Then she wrote to her agent, and refused the lecture tour.

'Who needs people?' David agreed with her, knowing that she had made the decision for him. He knew also that Debra as a lovely, blind, bestselling authoress would have been a sensation, and a tour would have launched her into the superstar category.

This made his own procrastination even more corrosive. He tried to re-think and rationalize his delay in posting the letter to Dr Edelman. He told himself that the light-sensitivity did not mean that Debra could ever regain her vision; that she was happy now, had adjusted and found her place and that it would be cruel to disrupt all this and offer her false hope and probably brutal surgery.

In all his theorizing he tried to make Debra's need take priority, but it was deception and he knew it. It was special pleading, by David Morgan, for David Morgan—for if Debra ever regained her sight, the delicately balanced structure of his own happiness would collapse in ruin.

One morning he drove the Land-Rover alone to the farthest limits of Jabulani and parked in a hidden place amongst camel thorn trees. He switched off the engine and, still sitting in the driving-seat, he adjusted the driving-mirror and stared at his own face. For nearly an hour he studied the ravaged expanse of inhuman flesh, trying to find some redeeming feature in it—apart from the eyes—and at the end he knew that no sighted woman would ever be able to live close to that, would ever be able to smile at it, kiss and touch it, to reach up and caress it in the critical moments of love.

He drove home slowly, and Debra was waiting for him on the shady cool stoop and she laughed and ran down the steps into the sunlight when she heard the Land-Rover. She wore faded denims and a bright pink blouse, and when he came to her she lifted her face and groped blindly but joyously with her lips for his.

Debra had arranged a barbecue for that evening, and although they sat close about the open fire under the trees and listened to the night sounds, the night was cool. Debra wore a cashmere sweater over her shoulders, and David had thrown on his flying jacket.

The letter lay against his heart, and it seemed to burn into his flesh. He unbottoned the leather flap and took it out. While Debra chatted happily beside him, spreading her hands to the crackling leaping flames, David examined the envelope turning it slowly over and over in his hands.

Then suddenly, as though it were a live scorpion, he threw it from him and watched it blacken and curl and crumple to ash in the flames of the fire.

It was not so easily done, however, and that night as he lay awake, the words of the letter marched in solemn procession through his brain, meticulously preserved and perfectly remembered. They gave him no respite, and though his eyes were gravelly and his head ached with fatigue, he could not sleep.

During the days that followed he was silent and edgy. Debra sensed it, despite all his efforts to conceal it—and she was seriously alarmed, believing that he was angry with her. She was anxiously loving, distracted from all else but the need to find and cure the cause of David's ills.

Her concern only served to make David's guilt deeper.

Almost in an act of desperation they drove one evening down to the String of Pearls, leaving the Land-Rover they walked hand in hand to the water's edge. They found a fallen log screened by reeds and sat quietly together. For once neither of them had anything to say to each other.

As the big red sun sank to the tree-tops and the gloom thickened amongst the trees of the grove, the nyala herd came stepping lightly and fearfully through the shadows.

David nudged Debra, and she turned her head into a listening attitude and moved a little closer to him as he whispered.

'They are really spooky this evening, they look as though they are standing on springs and I can see their muscles trembling from here. The old bulls seem to be on the verge of a nervous breakdown, they are listening so hard their ears have stretched to twice their usual length, I swear. There must be a leopard lurking along the edge of the reed bed—' he broke off, and exclaimed softly, 'oh, so that's it!'

'What is it, David?' Debra tugged at his arm insistently, her curiosity spurring her.

'A new fawn!' David's delight was in his voice. 'One of the does has lambed. Oh God, Debra! His legs are still wobbly and he is the palest creamy beige—' He described the fawn to her as it followed the mother unsteadily into the open. Debra was listening with such intensity, that it was clear the act of birth and the state of maternity had touched some deep chord within her. Perhaps she was remembering her own dead infant. Her grip on his arm tightened, and her blind eyes seemed to glow in the gathering dusk—and suddenly she spoke. Her voice low, but achingly clear, filled with all the longing and sadness which she had suppressed.

'I wish I could see it,' she said. 'Oh God! God! Let me see. Please, let me see!' and suddenly she was weeping; great racking sobs that shook her whole body.

Across the pool the nyala herd took fright, and dashed away among the trees. David took Debra and held her fiercely to his chest, cradling her head, so her tears were wet and cold through the fabric of his shirt—and he felt the icy winds of despair blow across his soul.

He re-wrote the letter that night by the light of a gas lamp while Debra sat across the room knitting a jersey she had promised him for the winter and believing that he was busy with the estate accounts. David found that he could repeat the words of the original letter perfectly and it took him only a few minutes to complete and seal it.

'Are you working on the book tomorrow evening?' he asked casually, and when she told him she was, he went on. 'I have to nip into Nelspruit for an hour or two.'

David flew high as though to divorce himself from the earth. He could not really believe he was going to do it. He could not believe that he was capable of such sacrifice. He wondered whether it was really possible to love somebody so deeply that he would chance destroying that love for the good of the other–and he knew that it was, and as he flew on southwards he found that he could face it at last.

Of all persons, Debra needed her vision, for without it the great wings of her talent were clipped. Unless she could see it, she could not describe it. She had been granted the gift of the writer, and then half of it had been taken from her. He understood her cry, 'Oh God! God! Let me see. Please, let me see,' and he found himself wishing it for her also. Beside her need his seemed trivial and petty, and silently he prayed.

'Please God, let her see again.'

He landed the Navajo at the airstrip and called the taxi and had it drive him directly to the Post Office, and wait while he posted the letter and collected the incoming mail from the box.

'Where now?' the driver asked as he came out of the building, and he was about to tell him to drive back to the airfield when he had inspiration.

'Take me down to the bottle store, please,' he told the driver and he bought a case of Veuve Clicquot champagne.

He flew homewards with a soaring lightness of the spirit. The wheel was spinning and the ball clicking, nothing he could do now would dictate its fall. He was free of doubt, free of guilt–whatever the outcome, he knew he could meet it.

Debra sensed it almost immediately, and she laughed aloud with relief, and hugged him about the neck.

'But what *happened?*' she kept demanding. 'For weeks you were miserable. I was worrying myself sick–and then you go off for an hour or two and you come back humming like a dynamo. What on earth is going on, Morgan?'

'I have just found out how much I love you,' he told her, returning her hug.

'Plenty?' she demanded.

'Plenty!' he agreed.

'That's my baby!' she applauded him.

The Veuve Clicquot came in useful. In the batch of mail that David brought back with him from Nelspruit was a letter from Bobby Dugan. He was very high on the first chapters of the new novel that Debra had airmailed to him, and so were the publishers; he had managed to hit them for an advance of $100,000 dollars.

'You're rich!' David laughed, looking up from the letter.

'The only reason you married me,' agreed Debra. 'Fortune hunter!' but she was laughing with excitement, and David was proud and happy for her.

'They like it, David.' Debra was serious then. 'They *really* like it. I was so worried.' The money was meaningless, except as a measure of the book's value. Big money is the sincerest type of praise.

'They would have to be feeble-minded not to like it,' David told her, and then went on. 'It just so happens that I have a case of French champagne with me, shall I put a bottle or ten on the ice?'

'Morgan, man of vision,' Debra said. 'At times like this, I know why I love you.'

The weeks that followed were as good then as they had ever been. David's appreciation was sharper, edged by the storm shadows on the horizon, the time of plenty made more poignant by the possibility of the drought years coming. He tried to draw it out beyond its natural time. It was five weeks more before he flew to Nelspruit again, and then only because Debra was anxious to learn of any further news from her publishers and agent, and to pick up her typing.

'I would like to have my hair set, and although I know we don't really need them, David, my darling, we should keep in touch with people—like once a month—don't you think?'

'Has it been that long?' David asked innocently, although each day had been carefully weighed and tallied, the actuality savoured and the memory stored for the lean times ahead.

David left Debra at the beauty salon, and as he went out he could hear her pleading with the girl not to 'put it up into those tight little curls and plaster it with lacquer' and even in the anxiety of the moment, David grinned for he had always thought of the hairstyle she was describing as 'Modern Cape Dutch' or 'Randburg Renaissance'.

The postbox was crammed full and David sorted quickly through the junk mail and picked out three letters from Debra's American agent, and two enveloped with Israeli stamps. Of these one was addressed in a doctor's prescription scrawl, and David was surprised that it had found its destination. The writing on the second envelope was unmistakable, it marched in martial ranks, each letter in step with the next, and the high strokes were like the weapons of a company of pike men, spiky and abrupt.

David found a bench in the park under the purple jacaranda trees, and he opened Edelman's letter first. It was in Hebrew, which made deciphering even more difficult.

Dear David,
   Your letter came as a surprise, and I have since studied the X-ray plates once more. They seem unequivocal, and upon an interpretation of them I would not hesitate to confirm my original prognosis—

Despite himself, David felt the small stirrings of relief.

—However, if I have learned anything in twenty-five years of practice, it is humility. I can only accept that your observations of light-sensitivity are correct. Having done so, then I must also accept that there is at least partial function of the optic nerves. This presupposes that the nerve was not completely divided, and it seems reasonable to believe now that it was only partially severed, and that now—possibly due to the head blows that Debra received—it has regained some function.
   The crucial question is just how great that recovery is, and again I must warn you that it may be as minimal as it is at the present time, when it amounts to nothing more than light sensitivity without any increase to the amount of vision. It may, however, be greater, and it is within the realms of possibility that with treatment some portion of sight may be regained. I do not expect, however, that this will amount to more than a vague definition of light or shape, and a decision would have to be made as to whether any possible benefit might not be outweighed by the undesirability of surgery within such a vulnerable area.
   I would, of course, be all too willing to examine Debra myself. However, it will probably be

inconvenient for you to journey to Jerusalem, and I have therefore taken the liberty of writing to a colleague of mine in Cape Town who is one of the leading world authorities on optical trauma. He is Dr Reuben Friedman and I enclose a copy of my letter to him. You will see that I have also despatched to him Debra's original X-ray plates and a clinical history of her case.

I would recommend most strongly that you take the first opportunity of presenting Debra to Dr Friedman, and that you place in him your complete confidence. I might add that the optical unit of Groote Schuur Hospital is rightly world-renowned and fully equipped to provide any treatment necessary–they do not restrict their activities to heart transplants!

I have taken the liberty of showing your letter to General Mordecai, and of discussing the case with him–

David folded the letter carefully. 'Why the hell did he have to bring the Brig into it, talk about a war horse in a rose garden–' and he opened the Brig's letter.

Dear David,
Dr Edelman has spoken with me. I have telephoned Friedman in Cape Town, and he has agreed to see Debra.

For some years I have been postponing a lecture tour to South Africa which the S.A. Zionist Council has been urging upon me. I have today written to them and asked them to make the arrangements.

This will give us the excuse to bring Debra to Cape Town. Tell her I have insufficient time to visit you on your farm, but insist upon seeing her.

I will give you my dates later, and expect to see you then–

It was in typical style, brusque and commanding, presupposing acquiescence. It was out of David's hands now. There was no turning back, but there was still the chance that it would not work. He found himself hoping for that–and his own selfishness sickened him a little. He turned over the letter and on the reverse he drafted a dummy letter from the Brig setting out his plans for the forthcoming tour. This was for Debra, and he found faint amusement in aping the Brig's style, so that he might read it aloud to Debra convincingly.

Debra was ecstatic when he read it to her and he experienced a twinge of conscience at this deceit.

'It will be wonderful seeing him again, I wonder if Mother will be coming out with him–?'

'He didn't say, but I doubt it.' David sorted the American mail into chronological order from the post marks, and read them to her. The first two were editorial comment on *Burning Bright* and were set aside for detailed reply–but the third letter was another with hard news.

United Artists want to film *A Place of Our Own* and were talking impressively heavy figures for the twelve-month option against an outright purchase of the property and a small percentage of the profits. However, if Debra would go to California and write the screenplay, Bobby Dugan felt sure he could roll it all into a quarter-million-dollar package. He wanted her to weigh the fact that even established novelists were seldom asked to write their own screenplays–this was an offer not to be lightly spurned, and he urged Debra to accept.

'Who needs people?' Debra laughed it away quickly, too quickly–and David caught the wistful expression before she turned her head away and asked brightly, 'Have you got any of that champagne left, Morgan? I think we can celebrate–don't you?'

'The way you're going, Morgan, I'd best lay in a store of the stuff,' he replied, and went to the gas refrigerator. It foamed to the rim of the glass as he poured the wine, and before it subsided and he had carried the glass to her, he had made his decision.

'Let's take his advice seriously, and think about you going to Hollywood,' he said, and put the glass in her hand.

'What's to think about?' she asked. 'This is where we belong.'

'No, let's wait a while before replying—'

'What do you mean?' She lowered the glass without tasting the wine.

'We will wait until—let's say, until after we have seen the Brig in Cape Town.'

'Why?' She looked puzzled. 'Why should it be different then?'

'No reason. It's just that it is an important decision—the choice of time is arbitrary, however.'

'Beseder!' she agreed readily, and raised the glass to toast him. 'I love you.'

'I love you,' he said, and as he drank he was glad that she had so many roads to choose from.

The Brig's arrangements allowed them three more weeks before the rendezvous in Cape Town, and David drew upon each hour to the full, anticipating his chances of expulsion from their private Eden.

They were happy days and it seemed that nature had conspired to give them of her best. The good rains fell steadily, always beginning in the afternoon after a morning of tall clouds and heavy air filled with static and the feel of thunder. In the sunset the lightning played and flickered across the gilt cloud banks, turned by the angry sun to the colour of burnished bronze and virgins' blushes. Then in the darkness as they lay entwined, the thunder struck like a hammer blow and the lightning etched the window beyond the bed to a square of blinding white light, and the rain came teeming down with the sound of wild fire and running hooves. With David beside her, Debra was unafraid.

In the morning it was bright and cool, the trees washed sparkling clean so that the leaves glinted in the early sun and the earth was dark with water and spangled with standing pools.

The rains brought life and excitement to the wild things, and each day held its small discoveries—unexpected visitations, and strange occurrences.

The fish eagles moved their two chicks from the great shaggy nest in the mhobahoba at the head of the pools and taught them to perch out on the bare limb that supported it. They sat there day after day, seeming to gather their courage. The parent birds were frenetic in their ministrations, grooming their offspring for the great moment of flight.

Then one morning, as he and Debra ate breakfast on the stoop, David heard the swollen chorus of their chanting cries, harsh with triumph, and he took Debra's hand and they went down the steps into the open. David looked up and saw the four dark shapes spread on wide wings against the clear blue of the sky—and his spirit soared with them in their moment of achievement. They flew upwards in great sweeping circles, until they dwindled to specks and vanished, gone to their autumn grounds upon the Zambezi River, two thousand miles to the north.

There was, however, one incident during those last days that saddened and subdued them both. One morning, they walked four miles northwards beyond the line of hills to a narrow wedge-shaped plain on which stood a group of towering leadwood trees.

A pair of martial eagles had chosen the tallest leadwood as their mating ground. The female was a beautiful young bird but the male was past his prime. They had begun constructing their nest on a high fork, but the work was interrupted by the intrusion of a lone male eagle, a big young bird, fierce and proud and acquisitive. David had noticed him lurking about the borders of the territory, carefully avoiding overflying the airspace claimed by the breeding pair, choosing a perch on the hills overlooking the plain and gathering his confidence for the confrontation he was so clearly planning. The impending conflict had its particular fascination for David and his sympathy was with the older bird as he made his warlike show, screeching defiance from his perch upon the high branches of the leadwood or weaving his patrols along his borders, turning on his great wings always within the limits of that which he claimed as his own.

David had decided to walk up to the plain that day, in order to choose a site for the photographic blind he planned to erect overlooking the nest site, and also in curiosity as to the outcome of this primeval clash between the two males.

It seemed more than chance that he had chosen the day when the crisis was reached.

David and Debra came up through the gap in the hills and paused to sit on an outcrop of rock overlooking the plain, while they regained their breath. The battlefield was spread below them.

The old bird was at the nest, a dark hunched shape with white breast and head set low on the powerful shoulders. David looked for the invader, sweeping the crests of the hills with his binoculars, but there was no sign of him. He dropped the binoculars to his chest and he and Debra talked quietly for a while.

Then suddenly David's attention was attracted by the behaviour of the old eagle. He launched suddenly into flight, striking upwards on his great black pinions, and there was an urgency in the way he bored for height.

His climb brought him close over their heads, so that David could clearly see the cruel curve of the beak and the ermine black splashes that decorated the imperial snow of his breast.

He opened the yellow beak and shrieked a harsh challenge, and David turned quickly in the old fighter pilot's sweep of sky and cloud. He saw the cunning of it immediately. The younger bird had chosen his moment and his attack vector with skill beyond his years. He was towering in the sun, high and clear, a flagrant trespasser, daring the old eagle to come up at him and David felt his skin crawl in sympathy as he watched the defender climb slowly on flogging wings.

Quickly, and a little breathlessly, he described it to Debra and she reached for his hand, her sympathy with the old bird also.

'Tell me!' she commanded.

The young bird sailed calmly in waiting circles, cocking his head to watch his adversary's approach.

'There he goes!' David's voice was taut, as the attacker went wing over and began his stoop.

'I can hear him,' Debra whispered, and the sound of his wings carried clearly to them, rustling like a bush fire in dry grass as he dived on the old bird.

'Break left! Go! Go! Go!' David found he was calling to the old eagle as though he were flying wingman for him, and he gripped Debra's hand until she winced. The old eagle seemed almost to hear him, for he closed his wings and flicked out of the path of the strike, tumbling for a single turn so that the attacker hissed by him with talons reaching uselessly through air, his speed plummeting him down into the basin of the plain.

The old bird caught and broke out of his roll with wings half-cocked, and streaked down after the other. In one veteran stroke of skill he had wrested the advantage.

'Get him!' screamed David. 'Get him when he turns! Now!'

The young bird was streaking towards the tree-tops and swift death, he flared his wings to break his fall, turning desperately to avoid the lethal stoop of his enemy. In that moment he was vulnerable and the old eagle reached forward with his terrible spiked talons and without slackening the searing speed of his dive he hit the other bird in the critical moment of his turn.

The thud of the impact carried clearly to the watchers on the hill and there was a puff of feathers like the burst of explosives, black from the wings and white from the breast.

Locked together by the old bird's honed killing claws, they tumbled, wing over tangled wing, feathers streaming from their straining bodies and then drifting away like thistledown on the light breeze.

Still joined in mortal combat, they struck the top branches of one of the leadwood trees, and fell through them to come to rest at last in a high fork as an untidy bundle of ruffled feathers and trailing wings.

Leading Debra over the rough ground David hurried down the hill and through the coarse stands of arrow grass to the tree.

'Can you see them?' Debra asked anxiously, as David focused his binoculars on the struggling pair.

'They are trapped,' David told her. 'The old fellow has his claws buried to the hilt in the other's back. He will never be able to free them and they have fallen across the fork, one on either side of the tree.'

The screams of rage and agony rang from the hills about them, and the female eagle sailed anxiously above the leadwood. She added her querulous screeching to the sound of conflict.

'The young bird is dying.' David studied him through the lens, watching the carmine drops ooze from the gaping yellow beak to fall and glisten upon the snowy breast, like a dying king's rubies.

'And the old bird–' Debra listened to the clamour with face upturned, her eyes dark with concern.

'He will never get those claws loose, they lock automatically as soon as pressure is applied and he will not be able to lift himself. He will die also.'

'Can't you do something?' Debra was tugging at his arm. 'Can't you help him?'

Gently he tried to explain to her that the birds were locked together seventy feet above the earth. The bole of the leadwood was smooth and without branches for the first fifty feet of its height. It would take days of effort to reach the birds, and by then it would be too late.

'Even if one could reach them, darling, they are two wild creatures, fierce and dangerous, those beaks and talons could tear the eyes out of your head or rip you to the bone–nature does not like interference in her designs.'

'Isn't there anything we can do?' she pleaded.

'Yes,' he answered quietly. 'We can come back in the morning to see if he has been able to free himself. But we will bring a gun with us, in case he has not.'

In the dawn they came together to the leadwood tree. The young bird was dead, hanging limp and graceless, but the old bird was still alive, linked by his claws to the carcass of the other, weak and dying but with the furious yellow flames still burning in his eyes. He heard their voices and twisted the shaggy old head and opened his beak in a last defiant cry.

David loaded the shotgun, snapping the barrels closed and staring up at the old eagle. 'Not you alone, old friend,' he thought, and he lifted the gun to his shoulder and hit him with two charges of buckshot. They left him hanging in tatters with trailing wings and the quick patter of blood slowing to a dark steady drip. David felt as though he had destroyed a part of himself in that blast of gunfire, and the shadow of it was cast over the bright days that followed.

These few days sped past too swiftly for David, and when they were almost gone he and Debra spent the last of them wandering together across Jabulani, visiting each of their special places and seeking out the various herds or individual animals almost as if they were taking farewell of old friends. In the evening they came to the place amongst the fever trees beside the pools, and they sat there until the sun had fallen below the earth in a splendour of purples and muted pinks. Then the mosquitoes began whining about their heads, and they strolled back hand in hand and came to the homestead in the dark.

They packed their bags that night and left them on the stoop, ready for an early start. Then they drank champagne beside the barbecue fire. The wine lifted their mood and they laughed together in their little island of firelight in the vast ocean of the African night—but for David there were echoes from the laughter, and he was aware of a sense of finality, of an ending of something and a new beginning.

When they took off from the landing-strip in the early morning, David circled twice over the estate, climbing slowly, and the pools glinted like gunmetal amongst the hills as the low sun touched them. The land was lush with the severe unpromising shade of green, so different from that of the lands of the northern hemisphere, and the servants stood in the yard of the homestead, shading their eyes and waving up at them, their shadows lying long and narrow against the ruddy earth.

David came around and steadied on course.

'Cape Town, here we come,' he said, and Debra smiled and reached across to lay her hand upon his leg in warm and companionable silence.

They had the suite at the Mount Nelson Hotel, preferring its ancient elegance and spacious palmy gardens to the modern slabs of glass and concrete upon the foreshore and the rocks of Sea Point. They stayed in the suite for two days, awaiting the Brig's arrival, for David had grown unaccustomed to humanity in its massed and unlovely multitudes, and found the quick inquisitive glances and murmurs of pity that followed him hard to stomach.

On the second day the Brig arrived. He knocked on the door of the suite and then entered with his aggressive and determined stride. He was lean and hard and brown, as David remembered, and when he and Debra had embraced, he turned to David and his hand was dry and leathery—but it seemed that he looked at David with a new calculation in the fierce warrior eyes.

While Debra bathed and dressed for the evening, he took David to his own suite and poured whisky for him without asking his preference. He gave David the glass and began immediately to discuss the arrangements he had made.

'Friedman will be at the reception. I will introduce him to Debra and let them talk for a while, then he will be seated next to her at the dinner-table. This will give us the opportunity to persuade Debra to undergo an examination later—'

'Before we go any further, sir,' David interrupted, 'I want your assurance that at no time will it ever be suggested to her that there is a possibility of Debra regaining her sight.'

'Very well.'

'I mean, at no time whatsoever. Even if Friedman determines that surgery is necessary, it must be for some other reason than to restore sight—'

'I don't think that is possible,' the Brig snapped angrily. 'If matters go that far, then Debra must be told. It would not be fair—'

It was David's turn for anger, although the frozen mask of his features remained immobile, the lipless slit of mouth turned pale and blue eyes glared.

'Let me determine what is fair. I know her as you never can, I know what she feels and what she is thinking. If you offer her a chance of sight, you will create for her the same dilemma in which I have been trapped since the possibility first arose. I would spare her that.'

'I do not understand you,' the Brig said stiffly. The hostility between them was a tangible essence that seemed to fill the room with the feel of thunder on a summer's day.

'Then let me explain,' David held his eyes, refusing to be brow-beaten by this fierce and thrusting old warrior. 'Your daughter and I have achieved an extraordinary state of happiness.'

The Brig inclined his head, acknowledging. 'Yes, I will accept your word for that—but it is an artificial state. It's a hot-house thing, reared in isolation—it has no relation to the real world. It's a dream state.'

David felt his anger begin to shake the foundations of his reason. He found it offensive that anybody should speak of Debra and his life in those terms—but at the same time he could see the justification.

'You may say so, sir. But for Debra and me, it is very real. It is something of tremendous value.'

The Brig was silent now.

'I will tell you truly that I thought long and hard before I admitted that there was a chance for Debra, and even then I would have hidden it for my own selfish happiness—'

'You still do not make sense. How can Debra regaining her sight affect you?'

'Look at me,' said David softly, and the Brig glared at him ferociously, expecting more, but when nothing further came his expression eased and he did look at David—for the first time truly seeing the terribly ravaged head, the obscene travesty of human shape—and suddenly he thought on it from David's side, whereas before he had considered it only as a father.

His eyes dropped and he turned to replenish his whisky glass.

'If I can give her sight, I will do it. Even though it will be an expensive gift for me, she must take it.' David felt his voice trembling. 'But I believe that she loves me enough to spurn it, if she were ever given the choice. I do not want her ever to be tortured by that choice.'

The Brig lifted his glass and took a deep swallow, half the contents at a gulp.

'As you wish,' he acquiesced, and it may have been the whisky, but his voice sounded husky with an emotion David had never suspected before.

'Thank you, sir.' David set down his own glass, still untasted. 'If you'll excuse me, I think I should go and change now.' He moved to the door.

'David!' the Brig called to him and he turned back. The gold tooth gleamed in the dark bristly patch of moustache, as the Brig smiled a strangely embarrassed but gentle smile.

'You'll do,' he said.

The reception was in the banquet-room at the Heerengracht Hotel, and as David and Debra rode up together in the elevator she seemed to sense his dread, for she squeezed his arm.

'Stay close to me tonight,' she murmured. 'I'll need you,' and he knew it was said to distract him and he was grateful to her. They would be a freak show, and even though he was sure most of the guests had been prepared, yet he knew it would be an ordeal. He leaned to brush her cheek with his.

Her hair was loose and soft, very dark and glossy—and the sun had gilded her face to gold. She wore a plain green sheath that fell in simple lines to the floor, but left her arms and shoulders bare. They were amongst and smooth, with the special lustre of the skin highlighting the smooth flow of her flesh.

She wore little make-up, a light touch on the lips only, and the serene expression of her eyes enhanced the simple grace of her carriage as she moved on his arm, giving David just that courage he needed to face the crowded room.

It was an elegant gathering, women in rich silks and jewellery, the men dark-suited, with the heaviness of body and poise which advertises power and wealth—but the Brig stood out amongst them, even in a civilian suit, lean and hard where they were plump and complacent—like a falcon amongst a flock of pheasants.

He brought Reuben Friedman to them and introduced them casually. He was a short heavily built man, with a big alert head seeming out of proportion to his body. His hair was cropped short and grizzled to the round skull, but David found himself liking the bright bird eyes and the readiness of his smile. His hand was warm, but dry and firm. Debra was drawn to him also, and smiled when she picked up the timbre of his voice and the essential warmth of his personality.

As they went in to dinner, she asked David what he looked like, and laughed with delight when he replied.

'Like a koala bear,' and they were talking easily together before the fish course was served. Friedman's wife, a slim girl with horn-rimmed spectacles, neither beautiful nor plain, but with her husband's forthright friendly manner, leaned across him to join the conversation and David heard her say,

'Won't you come to lunch tomorrow? If you can stand a brood of squalling kids.'

'We don't usually—' Debra replied, but David could hear her wavering, and she turned to him.

'May we—?' and he agreed and then they were laughing like old friends, but David was silent and withdrawn, knowing it was all subterfuge and suddenly oppressed by the surging chorus of human voices and the clatter of cutlery. He found himself longing for the night silence of the bushveld, and the solitude which was not solitude with Debra to share it.

When the master of ceremonies rose to introduce the speaker, David found it an intense relief to know the ordeal was drawing to a close and he could soon hurry away with Debra to hide from the prying, knowing eyes.

The introductory speech was smooth and professional, the jokes raised a chuckle—but it lacked substance, five minutes after you would not remember what had been said.

Then the Brig rose and looked about him with a kind of Olympian scorn, the warrior's contempt for the soft men, and though these rich and powerful men seemed to quail beneath the stare, yet David sensed that they enjoyed it. They derived some strange vicarious pleasure from this man. He was a figure-head—he gave to them a deep confidence, a point on which their spirits could rally. He was one of them, and yet apart. It seemed that he was a storehouse of the race's pride and strength.

Even David was surprised by the power that flowed from the lean old warrior, the compelling presence with which he filled the huge room and dominated his audience. He seemed immortal and invincible, and David's own emotions stirred, his own pulse quickened and he found himself carried along on the flood.

'—but for all of this there is a price to pay. Part of this price is constant vigil, constant readiness. Each of us is ready at any moment to answer the call to the defence of what is ours—and each of us must be ready to make without question whatever sacrifice is demanded. This can be life itself, or something every bit as dear—'

Suddenly David realized that the Brig had singled him out, and that they were staring at each other across the room. The Brig was sending him a message of strength, of courage—but it was misinterpreted by others in the gathering.

They saw the silent exchange between the two men, and many of them knew that David's terrible disfigurement and Debra's blindness were wounds of war. They misunderstood the Brig's reference to sacrifice, and one of them began to applaud.

Immediately it was taken up, a smattering here and there amongst the tables, but quickly the sound rose—became thunder. People were staring at David and Debra as they clapped, other heads turned towards them. Chairs began to scrape as they were pushed back and men and women came to their feet, their faces smiling and their applause pounding, until it filled the hall with sound and they were all standing.

Debra was not sure what it was all about, until she felt David's desperate hand in hers and heard his voice.

'Let's get out of here—quickly. They are all staring. They are staring at us—'

She could feel his hand shaking and the strength of his distress at being the subject of their ghoulish curiosity.

'Come, let's get away.' And she rose at his urging with her heart crying out in pain for him, and followed him while the thunder of applause burst upon his defenceless head like the blows of an enemy and their eyes wantonly raked his ravaged flesh.

Even when they reached the sanctuary of their own suite, he was still shaking like a man in fever.

'The bastard,' he whispered, as he poured whisky in a glass and the neck of the bottle clattered against the crystal rim. 'The cruel bastard—why did he do that to us?'

'David.' She came to him groping for his hand. 'He didn't mean it to hurt. I know he meant it well, I think he was trying to say he was proud of you.'

David felt the urge to flee, to find relief from it all within the sanctuary of Jabulani. The temptation to say to her 'Come' and lead her there, knowing that she would do so instantly, was so strong that he had to wrestle with it, as though it were a physical adversary.

The whisky tasted rank and smoky. It offered no avenue of escape and he left the glass standing upon the counter of the private bar and turned instead to Debra.

'Yes,' she whispered into his mouth. 'Yes, my darling,' and there was a woman's pride, a woman's joy in being the vessel of his ease. As always she was able to fly with him above the storm, using the wild winds of love to drive them both aloft, until they broke through together into the brightness and peace and safety.

David woke in the night while she lay sleeping. There was a silver moon reflecting from the french windows and he could study her sleeping face, but after a while it was not sufficient for his need and he reached across gently and switched on the bedside lamp.

She stirred in her sleep, coming softly awake with small sighs and tumbling black hair brushed from her eyes with a sleep-clumsy hand, and David felt the first chill of impending loss. He knew he had not moved the bed when he lit the lamp, what had disturbed her he knew beyond doubt was the light itself—and this time not even their loving could distract him.

Reuben Friedman's dwelling proclaimed his station in the world. It was built above the sea with lawns that ran down to the beach and big dark green melkhout trees surrounding the swimming-pool, with an elaborate Cabana and barbecue area. Marion Friedman's horde of kids were especially thinned out for the occasion, probably farmed out with friends, but she retained her two youngest. These came to peer in awe at David for a few minutes, but at a sharp word from their mother they went off to the pool and became immersed in water and their own games.

The Brig had another speaking engagement, so the four adults were left alone, and after a while they relaxed. Somehow the fact that Reuben was a doctor seemed to set both David and Debra at their ease. Debra remarked on it, when the conversation turned to their injuries and Reuben asked solicitously,

'You don't mind talking about it?'

'No, not with you. Somehow it's all right to bare yourself in front of a doctor.'

'Don't do it, my dear,' Marion cautioned her. 'Not in front of Ruby anyway—look at me, six kids, already!' And they laughed.

Ruby had been out early that morning and taken half a dozen big crayfish out of the crystal water, from a kelp-filled pool in the rocks which he boasted was his private fishing-ground.

He wrapped them in fresh kelp leaves and steamed them over the coals until they turned bright scarlet and the flesh was milk white and succulent as he broke open the carapaces.

'Now, if that isn't the finest spring chicken you have ever seen—' he crowed as he held up the dismembered shellfish, '—you all bear witness that it's got two legs and feathers.'

David admitted that he had never tasted poultry like it and as he washed it down with a dry Cape Riesling he found it was no terrible hardship to reach for another. Both he and Debra were enjoying themselves, so that it came as a jolt when Reuben at last began on the real purpose of their meeting.

He was leaning across Debra to refill her wine glass, when he paused and asked her.

'How long is it since your eyes were last checked out, my dear?' and gently he placed his hand under her chin and tilted her face to look into her eyes. David's nerves snapped taut, and he moved quickly in his chair, watching intently.

'Not since I left Israel—though they took some X-rays when I was in hospital.'

'Any headaches?' Ruby asked, and she nodded. Ruby grunted and released her chin.

'I suppose they could strike me off, drumming up business, but I do think that you should have periodic checks. Two years is a long time, and you have foreign matter lodged inside your skull.'

'I hadn't even thought about it.' Debra frowned slightly and reached up to touch the scar on her temple. David felt his conscience twinge as he joined actively in the conspiracy.

'It can't do any harm, darling. Why not let Ruby give you a going over while we are here? Heaven knows when we will have another opportunity.'

'Oh, David—' Debra disparaged the idea. 'I know you are itching to head for home—and so am I.'

'Another day or two won't matter, and now that we have thought about it, it's going to worry us.'

Debra turned her head in Ruby's direction. 'How long will it take?'

'A day. I'll give you an examination in the morning, and then we'll shoot some X-ray plates in the afternoon.'

'How soon could you see her?' David asked, his voice unnatural for he knew that the appointment had been arranged five weeks previously.

'Oh, I'm sure we could fit her in right away—tomorrow—even if we have to do a little juggling. Yours is a rather special case.'

David reached across and took Debra's hand. 'Okay, darling?' he asked.

'Okay, David,' she agreed readily.

Ruby's consulting-rooms were in the Medical Centre that towered above the harbour and looked out across Table Bay to where the black south-easter was hacking the tops from the waves in bursts of white, and shrouding the far shores of the bay in banks of cloud as grey as wood smoke.

The rooms were decorated with care and taste: two original landscapes by Pierneef and some good carpets, Samarkand and a gold-washed Abedah—even Ruby's receptionist looked like a hostess from a Playboy Club, without the bunny ears and tail. It was clear that Dr Friedman enjoyed the good things of life.

The receptionist was expecting them, but still could not control the widening of her eyes and the shocked flight of colour from her cheeks as she looked at David's face.

'Dr Friedman is waiting for you, Mr and Mrs Morgan. He wants you both to go through, please.'

Ruby looked different without his prosperous paunch bulging over the waistband of a bathing costume, but his greeting was warm as he took Debra's arm.

'Shall we let David stay with us?' he asked Debra in mock conspiracy.

'Let's,' she answered.

After the usual clinical history which Ruby pursued relentlessly, he seemed satisfied and they went through into his examination-room. The chair looked to David to be identical to a dentist's, and Ruby adjusted it for Debra to lie back comfortably while he made a physical examination, directing light through the pupils deep into the body of each eye.

'Nice healthy eyes,' he gave his opinion at last, 'and very pretty also, what do you say, David?'

'Smashing,' David agreed, and Ruby sat Debra upright while he attached electrodes to her arm and swung forward a complicated-looking piece of electronic equipment.

'ECG,' David guessed, and Ruby chuckled and shook his head.

'No–it's a little invention of my own. I'm quite proud of it, but in reality it's only a variation on the old-fashioned lie-detector.'

'Question time again?' Debra asked.

'No. We are going to flash lights at you, and see just what sort of subconscious reaction you have to them.'

'We know that already,' Debra told him, and they both heard the edge in her voice now.

'Perhaps. It's just an established routine we work to.' Ruby soothed her, and then to David. 'Stand back here, please. The lights are pretty fierce, and you don't want to be looking into them.'

David moved back and Ruby adjusted the machine. A roll of graph paper began running slowly under a moving stylus which settled almost immediately into a steady rhythmic pattern. On a separate glass screen a moving green dot of light began to repeat the same rhythm, leaving a fading trail across the screen like the tail of a comet. It reminded David of the interceptor radar screen on the instrument panel of a Mirage jet. Ruby switched out the top lights, plunging the room into utter darkness, except for the pulsing green dot on the screen.

'Are we ready now, Debra? Look straight ahead, please. Eyes open.'

Soundlessly a brilliant burst of blue light filled the room, and distinctly David saw the green dot on the screen jump out of its established pattern, and for a beat or two it went haywire, then settled again into the old rhythm. Debra had seen the light flash, even though she was unaware of it; the pulse of light had registered on her brain and the machine had recorded her instinctive reaction.

The play with light went on for another twenty minutes while Ruby adjusted the intensity of the light source and varied the transmissions. At last he was satisfied, and turned the top lights up.

'Well?' Debra demanded brightly. 'Do I pass?'

'There's nothing more I want from you,' Ruby told her. 'You did just great, and everything is the way we want it.'

'Can I go now?'

'David can take you to lunch, but this afternoon I want you at the radiologist's. My receptionist arranged it for 2.30, I believe, but you had best check with her.' Neatly Ruby countered any attempt of David's to get him alone.

'I shall let you know as soon as I have the X-ray results. Here, I'll write down the radiologist's address.' Ruby scribbled on his prescription pad and handed it to David.

'See me *alone* tomorrow 10 a.m.'

David nodded and took Debra's arm. He stared at Ruby a moment trying to draw some reaction from him, but he merely shrugged his shoulders and rolled his eyes in a music-hall comedian's gesture of uncertainty.

The Brig joined them for lunch in their suite at the Mount Nelson, for David still could not endure the discomfort of the public rooms. The Brig drew upon some hidden spring of charm, as though sensing that his help was needed, and he had both of them laughing naturally with stories of Debra's childhood and the family's early days after leaving America. David was grateful to him, for the time passed so quickly that he had to hurry Debra to her appointment.

'I am going to use two different techniques on you, my dear—' David wondered what it was about her that made all males over forty refer to Debra as though she were twelve years old. 'First of all we will do five of what we call police mug shots, front, back, sides and top—' The radiologist was a red-faced, grey-haired man with big hands and heavy shoulders like a professional wrestler. 'We aren't even going to make you take your clothes off—' he chuckled, but David thought he detected a faint note of regret. 'Then after that, we are going to be terribly clever and take a continuous moving shot of the inside of your head. It's called tomography. We are going to clamp your head to keep it still and the camera is going to describe a circle around you, focused on the spot where all the trouble is. We are going to find out everything that's going on in that pretty head of yours—'

'I hope it doesn't shock you too much, doctor,' Debra told him, and he looked stunned for a moment, then let out a delighted guffaw, and later David heard him repeating it to the sister with gusto.

It was a long tedious business, and afterwards when they drove back to the hotel, Debra leaned close to him and said, 'Let's go home, David. Soon as we can?'

'Soon as we can,' he agreed.

David did not want it that way, but the Brig insisted on accompanying David on his visit to Ruby Friedman the following morning. For one of the very few times in his life David had lied to Debra, telling her he was meeting with the Morgan Trust accountants, and he had left her in a lime-green bikini lying beside the hotel swimming pool, brown and slim and lovely in the sunlight.

Ruby Friedman was brusque and businesslike. He seated them opposite his desk and came swiftly to the core of the business.

'Gentlemen,' he said. 'We have a problem, a hell of a problem. I am going to show you the X-ray plates first to illustrate what I have to tell you—' Ruby swivelled his chair to the scanner and switched on the book-light to bring the prints into high relief. 'On this side are the plates that Edelman sent me from Jerusalem. You can see the grenade fragment.' It was stark and hard edged, a small triangular shard of steel lying in the cloudy bone structure. 'And here you can see the track though the optic chiasma, the disruption and shattering of the bone is quite evident. Edelman's original diagnosis—based on these plates, and on the complete inability to define light or shape—seems to be confirmed. The optic nerve is severed, and that's the end of it.' Quickly he unclipped the plates, and fitted others to the scanner. 'All right. Now here are the second set of plates, taken yesterday. Immediately notice how the grenade fragment has been consolidated and encysted.' The stark outline was softened by the new growth of bone around it. 'That is good, and expected. But here in the channel of the chiasma we find the growth of some sort that leaves itself open to a number of interpretations. It could be scarring, the growth of bone chips, or some other type of growth either benign or malignant.' Ruby arranged another set of plates upon the scanner. 'Finally, this is the plate exposed by the technique of tomography, to establish the contours of this excrescence. It seems to conform to the shape of the bony channel of the chiasma, except here–' Ruby touched a small half-round notch which was cut into the upper edge of the growth, '–this little spot runs through the main axis of the skull, but is bent upwards in the shape of an inverted U. It is just possible that this may be the most significant discovery of our whole examination.' Ruby switched off the light of the scanner.

'I don't understand any of this,' the Brig's voice was sharp. He did not like being bludgeoned by another man's special knowledge.

'No, of course.' Ruby was smooth. 'I am merely setting the background for the explanations that will follow.' He turned back to the desk, and his manner changed. He was no longer lecturing, but leading with authority.

'Now as to my own conclusions. There can be absolutely no doubt that certain function of the optic nerve remains. It is still conveying impulses to the brain. At least a part of it is still intact. The question arises as to just how much that is, and to what extent that function can be improved. It is possible that the grenade fragment cut through part of the nerve–severing five strands of a six-strand rope, or four or three. We do not know the extent, but what we do know is that damage of that nature is irreversible. What Debra may be left with is what she has now–almost nothing.'

Ruby paused and was silent. The two men opposite him watched his face intently, leaning forward in their seats.

'That is the dark side–if it is true, then Debra is for all practical purposes blind and will remain that way. However, there is another side to the question. It is possible that the optic nerve has suffered little damage, or none at all, please God–'

'Then why is she blind?' David asked angrily. He felt baited, driven by words, goaded like the bull from so long ago. 'You can't have it both ways.'

Ruby looked at him, and for the first time saw beyond that blank mask of scarred flesh and realized the pain he was inflicting, saw the hurt in the dark eyes, blue as rifle steel.

'Forgive me, David. I have been carried away by the intriguing facts of this case, seeing it from my own academic point of view rather than yours, I'm afraid. I will come to it now without further hedging.' He leaned back in his chair and went on speaking. 'You recall the notch in the outline of the chiasma. Well, I believe that is the nerve itself, twisted out of position, kinked and pinched like a garden hose by bone fragments and the pressure of the metal fragment so that it is no longer capable of carrying impulses to the brain.'

'The blows on her temple–?' David asked.

'Yes. Those blows may have been just sufficient to alter the position of the bone fragments, or of the nerve itself, so as to enable the passage of a minimal amount of impulse to the brain–like the garden hose, movement could allow a little water to pass through but still hold back any significant flow, but once the twist is straightened the full volume of flow would be regained.'

They were all silent then, each of them considering the enormity of what they had heard.

'The eyes,' the Brig said at last. 'They are healthy?'

'Perfectly,' Ruby nodded.

'How could you find out—I mean, what steps would you take next?' David asked quietly.

'There is only one way. We would have to go to the site of the trauma.'

'Operate?' David asked again.

'Yes.'

'Open Debra's skull?' The horror of it showed only in his eyes.

'Yes,' Ruby nodded.

'Her head—' David's own flesh quailed in memory of the ruthless knife. He saw the lovely face mutilated and the pain in those blind eyes. 'Her face—' His voice shook now. 'No, I won't let you cut her. I won't let you ruin her, like they have me—'

'David!' The Brig's voice cracked like breaking ice, and David sank back in his chair.

'I understand how you feel,' Ruby spoke gently, his voice in contrast to the Brig's. 'But we will go in from behind the hairline, there will be no disfigurement. The scar will be covered by her hair when it grows out, and the incision will not be very large anyway—'

'I won't have her suffer more.' David was trying to control his voice, but the catch and break were still in it. 'She has suffered enough, can't you see that—'

'We are talking about giving her back her sight,' the Brig broke in again. His voice was hard and cold. 'A little pain is a small price to pay for that.'

'There will be very little pain, David. Less than an appendectomy.' Again they were silent, the two older men watching the younger in the agony of his decision.

'What are the chances?' David looked for help, wanting the decision made for him, wanting it taken out of his hands.

'That is impossible to say.' Ruby shook his head.

'Oh God, how can I judge if I don't know the odds?' David cried out.

'All right. Let me put it this way—there is a possibility, not probability, that she may regain a useful part of her sight.' Ruby chose his words with care. 'And there is a remote possibility that she may regain full vision or almost full vision.'

'That is the best that can happen.' David agreed. 'But what is the worst?'

'The worst that can happen is there will be no change. She will have undergone a deal of discomfort and pain to no avail.'

David jumped out of his chair and crossed to the windows. He stared out at the great sweep of bay where the tankers lay moored and the far hills of the Tygerberg rose smoky blue to the brilliant sky.

'You know what the choice must be, David.' The Brig was ruthless, allowing him no quarter, driving him on to meet his fate.

'All right,' David surrendered at last, and turned back to face them. 'But on one condition. One on which I insist. Debra must not be told that there is a chance of her regaining her sight—'

Ruby Friedman shook his head. 'She must be told.'

The Brig's moustache bristled fiercely. 'Why not? Why don't you want her to know?'

'You know why.' David answered without looking at him.

'How will you get her there—if you don't explain it to her?' Ruby asked.

'She has been having headaches—we'll tell her there is a growth—that you've discovered a growth—that it has to be removed. That's true, isn't it?'

'No.' Ruby shook his head. 'I couldn't tell her that. I can't deceive her.'

'Then I will tell her,' said David, his voice firm and steady now. 'And I will tell her when we discover the result after the operation. Good or bad. I will be the one who tells her—is that understood? Do we agree on that?'

And after a moment the two others nodded and murmured their agreement to the terms David had set.

David had the hotel chef prepare a picnic basket, and the service bar provided a cool bag with two bottles of champagne.

David craved for the feeling of height and space, but he needed also to be able to concentrate all his attention on Debra, so he reluctantly rejected the impulse to fly with her—and instead they took the cableway up the precipitous cliffs of Table Mountain, and from the top station they found a path along the plateau and followed it, hand in hand, to a lonely place upon the cliff's edge where they could sit together high above the city and the measureless spread of ocean.

The sounds of the city came up two thousand feet to them, tiny and disjointed, on freak gusts of the wind or bouncing from the soaring canyons of grey rock—the horn of an automobile, the clang of a locomotive shunting in the train yards, the cry of a muezzin calling the faithful of Islam to pray, and the distant shrilling of children released from the classroom—yet all these faint echoes of humanity seemed to enhance their aloneness and the breeze out of the south-east was sweet and clean after the filthy city air.

They drank the wine together, sitting close while David gathered his resolve. He was about to speak when Debra forestalled him.

'It's good to be alive and in love, my darling,' she said. 'We are very lucky, you and I. Do you know that, David?'

He made a sound in his throat that could have been agreement, and his courage failed him.

'If you could, would you change anything?' he asked at last, and she laughed.

'Oh, sure. One is never absolutely content until and unless one is dead. I'd change many small things—but not the one big thing. You and I.'

'What would you change?'

'I would like to write better than I do, for one thing.'

They were silent again, sipping the wine.

'Sun is going down fast now,' he told her.

'Tell me,' she demanded, and he tried to find words for the colours, that flickered over the cloud banks and the way the ocean shimmered and dazzled with the last rays of gold and blood—and he knew he could never tell it to her. He stopped in the middle of a sentence.

'I saw Ruby Friedman today,' he said abruptly, unable to find a gentle approach, and she went still beside him in that special way of hers, frozen like a timid wild thing at the scent of some fearful predator.

'It's bad!' she said at last.

'Why do you say that?' he demanded quickly.

'Because you brought me here to tell me—and because you are afraid.'

'No,' David denied it.

'Yes. I can feel it now, very clearly. You are afraid for me.'

'It's not true,' David tried to reassure her. 'I'm a little worried, that's all.'

'Tell me,' she said.

'There is a small growth. It's not dangerous—yet. But they feel something should be done about it—' He stumbled through the explanation he had so carefully prepared, and when he ended she was silent for a moment.

'It is necessary, absolutely necessary?' she asked.

'Yes,' he told her, and she nodded, trusting him completely—then she smiled and squeezed his arm.

'Don't fret yourself, David, my darling. It will be all right. You'll see, they can't touch us. We live in a private place where they can't touch us.' Now it was she who was striving to comfort him.

'Of course it will be all right.' He hugged her to him roughly, slopping a little wine over the rim of his glass.

'When?' she asked.

'Tomorrow you will go in, and they'll do it the following morning.'

'So soon?'

'I thought it best to have it over with.'

'Yes. You are right.'

She sipped her wine, withdrawn, fearful, despite her brave show.

'They are going to cut my head open?'

'Yes,' he said, and she shuddered against him.

'There is no risk,' he said.

'No. I'm sure there isn't,' she agreed quickly.

He woke in the night with the instant knowledge that he was alone, that she was not curled warm and sleeping beside him.

Quickly he slipped from the bed and crossed to the bathroom. It was empty and he padded to the sitting-room of the suite and switched on the lights.

She heard the click of the switch and turned her head away, but not before he had seen the tears glowing on her cheeks like soft grey pearls. He went to her quickly.

'Darling,' he said.

'I couldn't sleep,' she said.

'That's all right.' He knelt before the couch on which she sat, but he did not touch her.

'I had a dream,' she said. 'There was a pool of clear water and you were swimming in it, looking up at me and calling to me. I saw your dear face clearly, beautiful and laughing—' David realized with a jolt in his guts that she had seen him in her dream as he had been, she had seen the beautiful dream-David, not the monstrous ravaged thing he was now. 'Then suddenly you began to sink, down, down, through the water, your face fading and receding—' Her voice caught and broke, and she was silent for a moment. 'It was a terrible dream, I cried out and tried to follow you, but I could not move and then you were gone down into the depths. The water turned dark and I woke with only the blackness in my head. Nothing but swirling mists of blackness.'

'It was only a dream,' he said.

'David,' she whispered. 'Tomorrow, if anything happens tomorrow—'

'Nothing will happen,' he almost snarled the denial, but she put out a hand to his face, finding his lips and touching them lightly to silence them.

'Whatever happens,' she said, 'remember how it was when we were happy. Remember that I loved you.'

The hospital of Groote Schuur sits on the lower slopes of Devil's Peak, a tall conical peak divided from the massif of Table Mountain by a deep saddle. Its summit is of grey rock and below it lie the dark pine forests and open grassy slopes of the great estate that Cecil John Rhodes left to the nation. Herds of deer and indigenous antelope feed quietly in the open places and the south-east wind feathers the crest with a flying pennant of cloud.

The hospital is a massive complex of brilliant white buildings, substantial and solid-looking blocks, all roofed in burnt red tiles.

Ruby Friedman had used all his pull to secure a private ward for Debra, and the sister in charge of the floor was expecting her. They took her from David and led her away, leaving him feeling bereft and lonely, but when he returned to visit her that evening she was sitting up in the bed in the soft cashmere bedjacket that David had given her and surrounded by banks of flowers which he had ordered.

'They smell wonderful,' she thanked him. 'It's like being in a garden.'

She wore a turban around her head and, with the serene golden eyes seeming focused on a distant vision, it gave her an exotic and mysterious air.

'They have shaved your head.' David felt a slide of dismay, he had not expected that she must also sacrifice that lustrous mane of black silk. It was the ultimate indignity, and she seemed to feel it also, for she did not answer him and instead told him brightly how well they were treating her, and what pains they were taking for her comfort. 'You'd think I was some sort of queen,' she laughed.

The Brig was with David, gruff and reserved and patently out of place in these surroundings. His presence cast restraint upon them and it was a relief when Ruby Friedman arrived. Bustling and charming, he complimented Debra on the preparations she had undergone.

'Sister says that you are just fine, all nicely shaved and ready. Sorry, but you aren't allowed anything to eat or drink except the sleeping pill I've prescribed.'

'When do I go to theatre?'

'We've got you down bright and early. Eight o'clock tomorrow. I am tremendously pleased that Billy Cooper is the surgeon, we were very lucky to get him, but he owes me a favour or two. I will be assisting him, of course, and he'll have one of the best surgical teams in the world backing him up.'

'Ruby, you know how some women have their husbands with them when they are confined—'

'Yes.' Ruby looked uncertain, taken aback by the question.

'Well, couldn't David be there with me tomorrow? Couldn't we be together, for both our sakes, while it happens?'

'With all due respects, my dear, but you are not having a baby.'

'Couldn't you arrange for him to be there?' Debra pleaded, with eloquent eyes and an expression to break the hardest heart.

'I'm sorry,' Ruby shook his head. 'It's completely impossible—' then he brightened. 'But I tell you what. I could get him into the students' room. It will be the next best thing, in fact he would have a better view of the proceedings than if he were in theatre. We have closed-circuit television relayed to the students' room and David could watch from there.'

'Oh, please!' Debra accepted immediately. 'I'd like to know he was close, and that we were in contact. We don't like being parted from each other, do we, my darling?' She smiled at where she thought he was, but he had moved aside and the smile missed him. It was a gesture that wrenched something within him.

'You will be there, David, won't you?' she asked, and though the idea of watching the knife at work was repellent to him, he forced himself to reply lightly.

'I'll be there,' and he almost added, 'always', but he cut off the word.

This early in the morning there were only two others in the small lecture-room with its double semi-circular rows of padded chairs about the small television screen, a plump woman student with a pretty face and shaggy-dog hairstyle and a tall young man with a pale complexion and bad teeth. They both wore their stethoscopes dangling with calculated nonchalance from the pockets of their white linen jackets. After the first startled glance they ignored David, and they spoke together in knowing medical jargon.

'The Coop's doing an exploratory through the parietal.'

'That's the one I want to watch—'

The girl affected blue Gauloises cigarettes, rank and stinking in the confined room. David's eyes felt raw and gravelly for he slept little during the night, and the smoke irritated them. He kept looking at his watch, and imagining what was happening to Debra during these last minutes—the undignified purging and cleansing of her body, the robing, and the needles of sedation and anti-sepsis.

The slow drag of minutes ended at last when the screen began to glow and hum, the image shimmered and strobed then settled down into a high view of the theatre. The set was in colour, and the green theatre gowns of the figures moving around the operating-table blended with the subdued theatre green walls. Height had foreshortened the robed members of the operating team and the muttered and disjointed conversation between the surgeon and his anaesthetist was picked up by the microphones.

'Are we ready there yet, Mike?'

David felt the sick sensation in the pit of his stomach, and he wished he had eaten breakfast. It might have filled the hollow place below his ribs.

'Right,' the surgeon's voice sharpened as he turned towards the microphone. 'Are we on telly?'

'Yes, doctor,' the theatre sister answered him, and there was a note of resignation in the surgeon's voice as he spoke for the unseen audience.

'Very well, then. The patient is a twenty-six-year-old female. The symptoms are total loss of sight in both eyes, and the cause is suspected damage or constriction of the optic nerve in or near the optic chiasma. This is a surgical investigation of the site. The surgeon is Dr William Cooper, assisted by Dr Reuben Friedman.'

As he spoke, the camera moved in on the table and with a start of surprise David realized that he had been looking at Debra without knowing it. Her face and the lower part of her head were obscured by the sterile drapes that covered all but the shaven round ball of her skull. It was inhuman-looking, egglike, painted with Savlon antiseptic that glistened in the bright, overhead lights.

'Scalpel please, sister.'

David leaned forward tensely in his seat, and his hands tightened on the armrests, so the knuckles turned white, as Cooper made the first incision drawing the blade across the smooth skin. The flesh opened and immediately the tiny blood vessels began to dribble and spurt. Hands moved in the screen on the television, clad in rubber so that they were yellow and impersonal, but quick and sure.

An oval flap of skin and flesh was dissected free and was drawn back, exposing the gleaming bone beneath, and again David's flesh crawled as though with living things, as the surgeon took up a drill that resembled exactly a carpenter's brace and bit. His voice continued its impersonal commentary, as he began to drill through the skull, cranking away at the handle as the gleaming steel bit swiftly through the bone. He pierced the skull with four round drill holes, each set at the corners of a square.

'Peri-osteal elevator, please, sister.'

Again David's stomach clenched as the surgeon slid the gleaming steel introducer into one of the drill holes and manoeuvred it gently until its tip reappeared through the next hole in line. Using the introducer, a length of sharp steel wire saw was threaded through the two holes and lay along the inside of the skull. Cooper sawed this back and forth and it cut cleanly through the bone. Four times he repeated the procedure, cutting out the sides of the square, and when he at last lifted out the detached piece of bone he had opened a trapdoor into Debra's skull.

As he worked David's gorge had risen until it pressed in his throat, and he had felt the cold glistening sheen of nauseous sweat across his forehead, but now as the camera's eye peered through the opening he felt his wonder surmount his horror, for he could see the pale amorphous mass of matter, enclosed in its tough covering membrane of the dura mater that was Debra's brain. Deftly Cooper incised a flap in the dura.

'We have exposed now the frontal lobe, and it will be necessary to displace this to explore the base of the skull.'

Working swiftly, but with obvious care and skill, Cooper used a stainless steel retractor, shaped like a shoe horn, to slide under the mass of brain and to lift it aside. Debra's brain–staring at it, David seemed to be looking into the core of her being, it was vulnerable and exposed, everything that made her what she was. What part of that soft pale mass contained her writer's genius, he wondered, from which of its many soft folds and coils sprang the fruitful fountain of her imagination, where was her love for him buried, what soft and secret place triggered her laughter and where was the vale of her tears? Its fathomless mystery held him intent as he watched the retractor probe deeper and deeper through the opening, and slowly the camera moved in to peer into the gaping depths of Debra's skull.

Cooper opened the far end of the dura mater and commented on his progress.

'We have here the anterior ridge of the sphenoid sinus, note this as our point for access to the chiasma–'

David was aware of the changed tone of the surgeon's voice, the charging of tension as the disembodied hands moved slowly and expertly towards their goal.

'Now this is interesting, can we see this on the screen, please? Yes! There is very clearly a bone deformation here–'

The voice was pleased, and the two students beside David exclaimed and leaned closer. David could see soft wet tissue and hard bright surfaces deep in the bottom of the wound, and the necks of steel instruments crowding into it, like metallic bees into the stamen of a pink and yellow bloom. Cooper scratched through to the metal of the grenade fragment.

'Now here we have the foreign body, can we have a look at those X-ray plates again, sister–'

The image cut quickly to the X-ray scanner, and again the students exclaimed. The girl puffed busily on her stinking Gauloise.

'Thank you.'

The image cut back to the operating field, and now David saw the dark speck of the grenade fragment lodged in the white bone.

'We will go for this, I think. Do you agree, Dr Friedman?'

'Yes, I think you should take it.'

Delicately the long slender steel insects worried the dark fragment, and at last with a grunt of satisfaction it came free of its niche, and Cooper drew it out carefully. David heard the metallic ping as it was dropped into a waiting dish.

'Good! Good!' Cooper gave himself a little encouragement as he plugged the hole left by the fragment with beeswax to prevent haemorrhage. 'Now we will trace out the optic nerves.'

They were two white worms, David saw them clearly, converging on their separate trails to meet and blend at the opening of the bony canal into which they disappeared.

'We have got extraneous bone-growth here, clearly associated with the foreign body we have just removed. It seems to have blocked off the canal and to have squeezed or severed the nerve. Suggestions, Dr Friedman?'

'I think we should excise that growth and try and ascertain just what damage we have to the nerve in that area.'

'Good. Yes, I agree. Sister, I will use a fine bone-nibbler to get in there.'

The swift selection and handling of the bright steel instruments again, and then Cooper was working on the white bone growth which grew in the shape of coral from a tropical sea. He nibbled at it with the keen steel, and carefully removed each piece from the field as it came away.

'What we have here is a bone splinter that was driven by the steel fragment into the canal. It is a large piece, and it must have been under considerable pressure, and it has consolidated itself here–'

He worked on carefully, and gradually the white worm of the nerve appeared from beneath the growth.

'Now, this is interesting.' Cooper's tone altered. 'Yes, look at this. Can we get a better view here, please?' The camera zoomed in a little closer, and the focus realigned. 'The nerve has been forced upwards, and flattened by pressure. The constriction is quite obvious, it has been pinched off–but it seems to be intact.'

Cooper lifted another large piece of bone aside, and now the nerve lay exposed over its full length.

'This is really remarkable. I expect that it is a one in a thousand chance, or one in a million. There appears to be no damage to the actual nerve, and yet the steel fragment passed so close to it that it must have touched it.'

Delicately, Cooper lifted the nerve with the blunt tip of a probe.

'Completely intact, but flattened with pressure. Yet I don't suspect any degree of atrophy, Dr Friedman?'

'I think we can confidently expect good recovery of function.' Despite the masked features, the triumphant attitude of the two men was easily recognized, and watching them, David felt his own emotions at war. With a weight upon his spirits he watched Cooper close up, replacing the portion of Debra's skull that he had removed, and once the flap of scalp was stitched back into place there was little external evidence of the extent and depth of their penetration. The image on the screen changed to another theatre where a small girl was to receive surgery for a massive hernia, and the fickle interest of the watching students changed with it.

David stood up and left the room. He rode up in the elevator and waited in the visitors' room on Debra's floor until the elevator doors opened again and two white uniformed male nurses trundled Debra's stretcher down the corridor to her room. She was deadly pale, with dark bruised-looking eyes and lips, her head swathed in a turban of white bandages. There was a dull brown smear of blood on the sheets that covered her and a whiff of anaesthetic hung in the corridor after she was gone.

Ruby Friedman came then, changed from theatre garb into an expensive light-weight grey mohair suit and a twenty-guinea Dior silk tie. He looked tanned and healthy, and mightily delighted with his achievement.

'You watched?' he demanded, and when David nodded he went on exuberantly, 'It was extraordinary.' He chuckled, and rubbed his hands together with glee.

'My God, something like this makes you feel good. Makes you feel that if you never do another thing in your life, it was still worthwhile.' He was unable to restrain himself any longer and he threw a playful punch at David's shoulder. 'Extraordinary,' he repeated, drawing it out into two words with relish, rolling the word around his tongue.

'When will you know?' David asked quietly.

'I know already, I'll stake my reputation on it!'

'She will be able to see as soon as she comes around from the anaesthetic?' David asked.

'Good Lord, no!' Ruby chuckled. 'That nerve has been pinched off for years, it's going to take time to recover.'

'How long?'

'It's like a leg that has gone to sleep when you sit wrongly. When the blood flows back in, it's still numb and tingling until the circulation is restored.'

'How long?' David repeated.

'Immediately she wakes, that nerve is going to start going crazy, sending all sorts of wild messages to the brain. She's going to see colours and shapes as though she is on a drug binge, and it's going to take time to settle down—two weeks to a month, I would guess—then it will clear, the nerve will have recovered its full and normal function and she will begin having real effective vision.'

'Two weeks,' David said, and he felt the relief of a condemned man hearing of his reprieve.

'You will tell her the good news, of course.' Ruby gave another buoyant chuckle, shaped up to punch David again and then controlled himself. 'What a wonderful gift you have been able to give her.'

'No,' David answered him. 'I won't tell her yet, I will find the right time later.'

'You will have to explain the initial vision she will experience, the colour and shape hallucinations, they will alarm her.'

'We will just tell her that it's the normal after-effect of the operation. Let her adjust to that before telling her.'

'David, I—' Ruby began seriously, but he was cut off by the savage blaze of blue in the eyes that watched him from the mask of scarred flesh.

'I will tell her!' The voice shook with such fury, that Ruby took a step backwards. 'That was the condition, I will tell her when I judge the time is ripe.'

Out of the darkness a tiny amber light glowed, pale and far off, but she watched it split like a breeding amœba and become two, and each of those split and split again until they filled the universe in a great shimmering field of stars. The light throbbed and pulsed, vibrant and triumphant, and it changed from amber to brightest purest white like the sparkle from a paragon diamond, then it turned to the blue of sunlight on a tropical ocean, to soft forest greens and desert golds—an endless cavalcade of colours, changing, blending, fading, flaring in splendour that held her captive.

Then the colours took shape, they spun like mighty Catherine wheels, and soared and exploded, showered down in rivers of flame that burst again into fresh cascades of light.

She was appalled by the dimensions of shape and colour that engulfed her, bewildered by the beauty of it and at last she could bear it no longer in silence and she cried out.

Instantly there was a hand in hers, a strong hard familiar hand, and his voice, dearly beloved, reassuring and firm.

'David,' she cried with relief.

'Quietly, my darling. You must rest.'

'David. David.' She heard the sob in her own voice as new torrents of colour poured over her, insupportable in their richness and variety, overwhelming in their depth and range.

'I'm here, my darling. I'm here.'

'What's happening to me, David? What's happening?'

'You are all right. The operation was a success. You are just fine.'

'Colours,' she cried. 'Filling my whole head. I've never known it like this.'

'It's the result of the operation. It shows that it was a success. They removed the growth.'

'I'm frightened, David.'

'No, my darling. There is nothing to be afraid of.'

'Hold me, David. Hold me safe.' And in the circle of his arms the fear abated, and slowly she learned to ride the oceanic waves and washes of colour, came gradually to accept and then at last to look upon them with wonder and with intense pleasure.

'It's beautiful, David. I'm not frightened any more, not with you holding me. It's wonderful.'

'Tell me what you see,' he said.

'I couldn't. It's impossible. I couldn't find the words.'

'Try!' he said.

David was alone in the suite, and it was after midnight when the call that he had placed to New York came through.

'This is Robert Dugan, to whom am I speaking?' Bobby's voice was crisp and businesslike.

'It's David Morgan.'

'Who?'

'Debra Mordecai's husband.'

'Well, hello there, David.' The agent's voice changed, becoming expansive. 'It's sure nice to talk to you. How is Debra?' It was obvious that Dugan's interest in David began and ended with his wife.

'That's why I am calling. She's had an operation and she's in hospital at the moment.'

'God! Not serious, is it?'

'She's going to be fine. She'll be up in a few days and ready for work in a couple of weeks.'

'Glad to hear it, David. That's great.'

'Look here, I want you to go ahead and set up that script-writing contract for *A Place of Our Own*.'

'She's going to do it?' Dugan's pleasure carried six thousand miles with no diminution.

'She'll do it now.'

'That's wonderful news, David.'

'Write her a good contract.'

'Depend on it, boyo. That little girl of yours is hot property. Playing hard to get hasn't done her any harm, I tell you!'

'How long will the script job last?'

'They'll want her for six months,' Dugan guessed. 'The producer who will do it is making a movie in Rome right now. He'll probably want Debra to work with him there.'

'Good,' said David. 'She'll like Rome.'

'You coming with her, David?'

'No,' David answered carefully. 'No, she'll be coming on her own.'

'Will she be able to get by on her own?' Dugan sounded worried.

'From now on she'll be able to do everything on her own.'

'Hope you are right,' Dugan was dubious.

'I'm right.' David told him abruptly. 'One other thing. That lecture tour, is it still on?'

'They are beating the door down. Like I said, she's hotter than a pistol.'

'Set it up for after the script job.'

'Hey, David boy. This is the business. Now we are really cooking with gas. We are going to make your little girl into one very big piece of property.'

'Do that,' said David. 'Make her big. Keep her busy, you hear. Don't give her time to think.'

'I'll keep her busy.' Then as though he had detected something in David's voice. 'Is something bugging you, David? You got some little domestic problem going there, boy? You want to talk about it?'

'No, I don't want to talk about it. You just look after her. Look after her well.'

'I'll look after her,' Dugan's tone had sobered. 'And David—'

'What is it?'

'I'm sorry. Whatever it is, I'm sorry.'

'That's okay.' David had to end the conversation then, immediately. His hand was shaking so that he knocked the telephone from the table and the plastic cracked through. He left it lying and went out into the night. He walked alone through the sleeping city, until just before the morning he was weary enough to sleep.

The streams of colour settled to steady runs and calmly moving patterns, no longer the explosive bursts of brightness that had so alarmed her. After the grey shifting banks of blindness that had filled her head like dirty cotton wool for those long years, the new brightness and beauty served to buoy her spirits, and after the main discomfort of her head surgery had passed in the first few days, she was filled with a wondrous sense of well-being, a formless optimistic expectation, such as she had not experienced since she was a child anticipating the approach of a long-awaited holiday.

It was as though in some deep recess of her subconscious she was vaguely aware of the imminent return of her sight. However, the knowledge seemed not to have reached her conscious mind. She knew there was change, she welcomed her release from the dark and sombre dungeons of nothingness into the new brightness, but she did not realize that there was more to come, that after colour and fantasy would follow shape and reality.

Each day David waited for her to say something that might show that she had realized that her sight was on the way back; he hoped for and at the same time dreaded this awareness–but it did not come.

He spent as much of each day with her as hospital routine would allow, and he hoarded each minute of it, doling out time like a miser paying coins for a diminishing hoard. Yet Debra's ebullient mood was infectious, and he could not help but laugh with her and share the warm excitement as she anticipated her release from the hospital and their return together to the sanctuary of Jabulani.

There were no doubts in her mind, no shadows across her happiness, and gradually David began to believe that it would last. That their happiness was immortal and that their love could survive any pressure placed upon it. It was so strong and fine when they were together now, carried along by Debra's bubbling enthusiasm, that surely she could regain her sight and weather the first shock of seeing him.

Yet he was not sure enough to tell her yet, there was plenty of time. Two weeks, Ruby Friedman had told him, two weeks before she would be able to see him and it was vitally important to David that he should extract every grain of happiness that was left to him in that time.

In the lonely nights he lay with the frantic scurryings of his brain keeping him from sleep. He remembered that the plastic surgeon had told him there was more they could do to make him less hideous. He could go back and submit to the knife once more, although his body cringed at the thought. Perhaps they could give Debra something less horrifying to look at.

The following day he braved the massed stares of hundreds of shoppers to visit Stuttafords Departmental Store in Adderley Street. The girl in the wig department, once she had recovered her poise, took him into a curtained-off cubicle and entered into the spirit of finding a wig to cover the domed cicatrice of his scalp.

David regarded the fine curly head of hair over the frozen ruins of his face, and for the first time ever he found himself laughing at it, although the effect of laughter was even more horrifying as the tight lipless mouth writhed like an animal in a trap.

'God!' he laughed. 'Frankenstein in drag!' and for the sales girl who had been fighting to control her emotions this was too much. She broke into hysterical giggles of embarrassment.

He wanted to tell Debra about it, making a joke of it and at the same time prepare her for her first sight of his face, but somehow he could not find the words. Another day passed with nothing accomplished, except a few last hours of warmth and happiness shared.

The following day Debra began to show the first signs of restlessness. 'When are they going to let me out, darling? I feel absolutely wonderful. It's ridiculous to lie in bed here. I want to get back to Jabulani–there is so much to do.' Then she giggled. 'And they've had me locked up here ten days now. I'm not used to convent life, and to be completely honest with you, my big lusty lover, I am climbing the wall—'

'We could lock the door,' David suggested.

'God, I married a genius,' Debra cried out delightedly, and then later. 'That's the first time it ever happened for me in Technicolor. I think I could get hooked on that.'

That evening Ruby Friedman and the Brig were waiting for him when he returned to his suite, and they came swiftly to the reason for their visit.

'You have already left it too long. Debra should have been told days ago,' the Brig told him sternly.

'He is right, David. You are being unfair to her. She must have time to come to terms, latitude for adjustment.'

'I'll tell her when I get the opportunity,' David muttered doggedly.

'When will that be?' the Brig demanded, the gold tooth glowing angrily in its furry nest.

'Soon.'

'David,' Ruby was placatory, 'it could happen at any time now. She has made strong and vigorous progress, it could happen much sooner than I expected.'

'I'll do it,' said David. 'Can't you stop pushing me? I said I'll do it—and I will. Just get off my back, won't you.'

'Right.' The Brig was brisk now. 'You've got until noon tomorrow. If you haven't told her by then, I'm going to do it.'

'You're a hard old bastard, aren't you,' David said bitterly, and anger paled the Brig's lips and they could see the effort he made to force it down.

'I understand your reluctance,' he spoke carefully. 'I sympathize. However, my first and only concern is for Debra. You are indulging yourself, David. You are wallowing in self-pity, but I am not going to allow that to hurt her more. She has had enough. No more delay. Tell her, and have done.'

'Yes,' David nodded, all the fight gone out of him. 'I will tell her.'

'When?' the Brig persisted.

'Tomorrow,' said David. 'I will tell her tomorrow morning.'

It was a bright warm morning, and the garden below his room was gay with colour. David lingered over breakfast in his suite, and he read all of the morning papers from end to end, drawing out the moment to its utmost. He dressed with care afterwards, in a dark suit and a soft lilac shirt, then, when he was ready to leave, he surveyed his image in the full-length mirror of the dressing-room.

'It's been a long time—and I'm still not at ease with you,' he told the figure in the mirror. 'Let's pray that somebody loves you more than I do.'

The doorman had a cab ready for him under the portico, and he settled in the back seat with the leaden feeling in his stomach. The drive seemed much shorter this morning, and when he paid off the cab and climbed the steps to the main entrance of Groote Schuur, he glanced at his wrist-watch. It was a few minutes after eleven o'clock. He was hardly aware of the curious glances as he crossed the lobby to the elevators.

The Brig was waiting for him in the visitors' room on Debra's floor. He came out into the corridor, tall and grim, and unfamiliar in his civilian clothes.

'What are you doing here?' David demanded, it was the ultimate intrusion and he resented it fiercely.

'I thought I might be of help.'

'Good on you!' said David sardonically, making no effort to hide his anger.

The Brig let the anger slide past him, not acknowledging it with either word or expression as he asked mildly, 'Would you like me to be with you?'

'No.' David turned away from him as he spoke. 'I can manage, thank you,' and he set off along the corridor.

'David!' the Brig called softly, and David hesitated and then turned back. 'What is it?' he asked.

For a long moment they stared at each other, then abruptly the Brig shook his head. 'No,' he said. 'It's nothing,' and watched the tall young man with the monstrous head turn and walk swiftly towards Debra's room. His footsteps echoed hollowly along the empty corridor, like the tread of a man upon the gallows steps.

The morning was warm with a light breeze off the sea. Debra sat in her chair by the open window, and the warm air wafted the scent of the pine forests to her. Resinous and clean-smelling, it mingled with the faint whiff of the sea and the kelp beds. She felt quiet and deeply contented, even though David was late this morning. She had spoken to Ruby Friedman when he made his rounds earlier, and he had teased her and hinted that she would be able to leave in a week or so, and the knowledge rounded out her happiness.

The warmth of the morning was drowsy, and she closed her eyes subduing the strong rich flow of colour into a lulling cocoon of soft shades which enfolded her, and she lay on the downy edges of sleep.

David found her like that, sitting in the deep chair with her legs curled sideways under her and her face side-lit by the reflected sunlight from the window. The turban of white bandages that swathed her head was crisp and fresh and her gown was white as a bride's, with cascades of filmy lace.

He stood before her chair studying her with care, her face was pale, but the dark bruises below her eyes had cleared and the set of her full lips were serene and peaceful.

With infinite tenderness he leaned forward and laid his open hand against her cheek. She stirred drowsily, and opened eyes that were honey brown and flecked with bright flakes of gold. They were beautiful, and vague, misty and sightless—then suddenly he saw them change, the look of them was sharp and aware. Her gaze focused, and steadied. She was looking at him—and seeing him.

Debra was roused from the warm edge of sleep by the touch upon her cheek, as light as the fall of an autumn leaf. She opened her eyes to soft golden clouds, then suddenly like the morning wind slashing away the sea mist, the clouds rolled open and she looked beyond to the monster's head that swam towards her, a colossal disembodied head that seemed must arise from the halls of hell itself, a head so riven with livid lines and set with the bestial, crudely worked features of one of the dark hosts, that she flung herself back in her chair, cringing away from the terror of it, and she lifted her hands to her face and she screamed.

David turned and ran from the room, slamming the door behind him, his feet pounded down the passage and the Brig heard him coming and stepped into the corridor.

'David!' He reached out a hand to him, to hold him back, but David struck out at him wildly, a blow that caught him in the chest throwing him back heavily against the wall. When he regained his balance, and staggered from the wall clutching his chest, David was gone. His frantic footsteps clattered up from the well of the stairs.

'David!' he called, his voice croaking. 'Wait!' But he was gone, his footsteps fading, and the Brig let him go. Instead he turned and hurried painfully down the corridor to where the hysterical sobs of his daughter rang from behind the closed door.

She looked up from her cupped hands when she heard the door open, and wonder dawned through the terror in her eyes.

'I can see you,' she whispered, 'I can see.'

He went to her quickly and took her in the protective circle of his arms.

'It's all right,' he told her awkwardly, 'it's going to be all right.'

She clung to him, stifling the last of her sobs.

'I had a dream,' she murmured, 'a terrible dream,' and she shuddered against him. Then suddenly she pulled away.

'David,' she cried, 'where is David? I must see him.'

The Brig stiffened, realizing that she had not recognized reality.

'I must see him,' she repeated, and he replied heavily, 'You have already seen him, my child.'

For many seconds she did not understand, and then slowly it came to her.

'David?' she whispered, her voice catching and breaking. 'That was David?'

The Brig nodded, watching her face for the revulsion and the horror.

'Oh dear God,' Debra's voice was fierce. 'What have I done? I screamed when I saw him. What have I done to him? I've driven him away.'

'So you still want to see him again?' the Brig asked.

'How can you say that?' Debra blazed at him. 'More than anything on this earth. You must know that!'

'Even the way he is now?'

'If you think that would make any difference to me—then you don't know me very well.' Her expression changed again, becoming concerned. 'Find him for me,' she ordered. 'Quickly, before he has a chance to do something stupid.'

'I don't know where he has gone,' the Brig answered, his own concern aroused by the possibility which Debra had hinted at.

'There is only one place he would go when he is hurt like this,' Debra told him. 'He will be in the sky.'

'Yes,' the Brig agreed readily.

'Get down to Air Traffic Control, they'll let you speak to him.' The Brig turned for the door and Debra's voice urged him on.

'Find him for me, Daddy. Please find him for me.'

The Navajo seemed to come around on to a southerly heading under its own volition. It was only when the sleek, rounded nose settled on course, climbing steadily upwards towards the incredibly tall and unsullied blue of the heavens that David knew where he was going.

Behind him, the solid flat-topped mountain with its glistening wreaths of cloud fell away. This was the last of the land, and ahead lay only the great barren wastes of ice and cruel water.

David glanced at his fuel gauges. His vision was still blurred but he saw the needles registering a little over the half-way mark on the dials.

Three hours' flying perhaps, and David felt a chill relief that there was to be a term to his suffering. He saw clearly then how it would end down there in the wilderness below the shipping lanes. He would continue to bore for height, climbing steadily until at last his engines starved and failed. Then he would push the nose down into a vertical dive and go in hard and fast, like the final suicide stoop of a maimed and moribund eagle. It would be over swiftly, and the metal fuselage would carry him down to a grave that could not be as lonely as the desolation in which he now existed.

The radio crackled and hummed into life. He heard Air Traffic snarl his call sign through the static crackle, and he reached for the switch to kill the set—when the well-remembered voice stayed his hand.

'David, this is the Brig.' The words and the tone in which they were spoken transported him back to another cockpit in another land.

'You disobeyed me once before. Don't do it again.'

David's mouth tightened into a thin colourless line and again he reached for the switch. He knew they were watching him on the radar plot, that they knew his course, and that the Brig had guessed what he intended. Well, there was nothing they could do about it.

'David,' the Brig's voice softened, and some sure instinct made him choose the only words to which David would listen. 'I have just spoken to Debra. She wants you. She wants you desperately.'

David's hand hovered over the switch.

'Listen to me, David. She needs you—she will always need you.'

David blinked, for he felt tears scalding his eyes once more. His determination wavered.

'Come back, David. For her sake, come back.'

Out of the darkness of his soul, a light shone, a small light which grew and spread until it seemed to fill him with its shimmering brightness.

'David, this is the Brig.' Again it was the voice of the old warrior, hard and uncompromising. 'Return to base immediately.'

David grinned, and lifted the microphone to his mouth. He thumbed the transmit button, and spoke the old acknowledgement in Hebrew.

'Beseder! This is Bright Lance leader, homeward bound,' and he brought the Navajo around steeply.

The mountain was blue and low on the horizon, and he let the nose sink gradually towards it. He knew that it would not be easy—that it would require all his courage and patience, but he knew that in the end it would be worth it all. Suddenly he needed desperately to be alone with Debra, in the peace of Jabulani.

Wilbur Smith

Shout at
the Devil

FOREWORD

I will not deny that this story was suggested to me by the action in World War I, when the German mercantile raider *Königsberg* was sunk in the Kikunya channel of the Rufiji delta by ships of the Royal Navy.

However, I will most emphatically deny that the rogues and scoundrels depicted in my tale bear the slightest resemblance to any members of the company of men that operated to the destruction of *Königsberg*. In particular, I would strongly resist the suggestion that Flynn Patrick O'Flynn is based on the character of the gallant Colonel 'Jungle Man' Pretorius, who actually went aboard *Königsberg*, disguised as a native bearer, and paced out the ranges for the guns of His Majesty's warships *Severn* and *Mersey*.

I would like to express my thanks to Lieutenant-Commander Mathers (R.N. retired) for his assistance in my researches.

PART I

I

Flynn Patrick O'Flynn was an ivory poacher by profession, and modestly he admitted that he was the best on the east coast of Africa.

Rachid El Keb was an exporter of precious stones, of women for the harems and great houses of Arabia and India, and of illicit ivory. This he admitted only to his trusted clients; to the rest he was a rich and respectable owner of coastal shipping.

In an afternoon during the monsoon of 1912, drawn together by their mutual interest in pachyderms, Flynn and Rachid sat in the back room of El Keb's shop in the Arab quarter of Zanzibar, and drank tea from tiny brass thimbles. The hot tea made Flynn O'Flynn perspire even more than usual. It was so humid hot in the room that the flies sat in languid stupor upon the low ceiling.

'Listen, Kebby, you lend me just one of those stinking little ships of yours and I'll fill her so high with tusks, she'll damn nigh sink.'

'Ah!' replied El Keb carefully, and went on waving the palm-leaf fan in his own face—a face that resembled that of a suspicious parrot with a straggly, goatee beard.

'Have I ever let you down yet?' Flynn demanded aggressively, and a drop of sweat fell from the tip of his nose on to his already damp shirt.

'Ah!' El Keb repeated.

'This scheme has a flair. It has the touch of greatness to it. This scheme . . .' Flynn paused to find a suitable adjective, '. . . this scheme is Napoleonic. It is Caesarian!'

'Ah!' El Keb said again, and refilled his tea cup. Lifting it delicately between thumb and forefinger, he sipped before speaking. 'It is necessary only that I should risk the total destruction of a sixty-foot dhow worth . . .' prudently he inflated the figure, '. . . two thousand English pounds?'

'Against an almost certain recovery of twenty thousand,' Flynn cut in quickly, and El Keb smiled a little, almost dreamily.

'You'd put the profits so high?' he asked.

'That's the lowest figure. Good God, Kebby! There hasn't been a shot fired in the Rufiji basin for twenty years. You know damn well it's the Kaiser's private hunting reserve. The Jumbo are so thick in there I could round them up and drive them in like sheep.' Involuntarily Flynn's right forefinger crooked and twitched as though it were already curled around a trigger.

'Madness,' whispered El Keb, with the gold gloat softening the shape of his lips. 'You'd sail into the Rufiji river from the sea, hoist the Union Jack on one of the islands in the delta, and fill the dhow with German ivory. Madness.'

'The Germans have formally annexed none of those islands. I'd be in and out again before Berlin had sent their first cable to London. With ten of my gun-boys hunting, we'd fill the dhow in two weeks.'

'The Germans would have a gunboat there in a week. They've got the *Blücher* lying at Dar es Salaam under steam, heavy cruiser with nine-inch guns.'

'We'd be under protection of the British flag. They couldn't dare touch us—not on the high seas—not with things the way they are now between England and Germany.'

'Mr O'Flynn, I was led to believe you were a citizen of the United States of America.'

'You damn right I am.' Flynn sat up a little straighter, a little more proudly.

'You'd need a British captain for the dhow,' El Keb mused, and stroked his beard thoughtfully.

'Jesus, Kebby, you didn't think I was fool enough to sail that cow in myself?' Flynn looked pained. 'I'll find someone else to do that, and to sail her out again through the Imperial German Navy. Me, I'm going to walk in from my base camp in Portuguese Mozambique and go out the same way.'

'Forgive me.' El Keb smiled again. 'I underestimated you.' He stood up quickly. The splendour of the great jewelled dagger at his waist was somewhat spoiled by the unwashed white of his ankle-length robe. 'Mr O'Flynn, I think I have just the man to captain your dhow for you. But first it is necessary to alter his financial circumstances so that he might be willing to accept employment.'

2

The leather purse of gold sovereigns had been the pivot on which the gentle confusion of Sebastian Oldsmith's life turned. It had been presented to him by his father when Sebastian had announced to the family his intention of sailing to Australia to make his fortune in the wool trade. It had comforted him during the voyage from Liverpool to the Cape of Good Hope, where the captain had unceremoniously deposited him after Sebastian's misalliance with the daughter of the gentleman who was proceeding to Sydney to take up his appointment as Governor of New South Wales.

In gradually dwindling quantity the sovereigns had remained with him through the series of misfortunes that ended in Zanzibar, when he awoke from heat-drugged sleep in a shoddy room to find that the leather purse and its contents were gone, and with them were gone the letters of introduction from his father to certain prominent wool-brokers of Sydney.

It occurred to Sebastian as he sat on the edge of his bed that the letters had little real value in Zanzibar, and with increasing bewilderment, he reviewed the events that had blown him so far off his intended course. Slowly his forehead creased in the effort of thought. It was the high, intelligent forehead of a philosopher crowned by a splendid mass of shiny black curls; his eyes were dark brown, his nose long and straight, his jaw firm, and his mouth sensitive. In his twenty-second year, Sebastian had the face of a young Oxford don;

which proves, perhaps, how misleading looks can be. Those who knew him well would have been surprised that Sebastian, in setting out for Australia, had come as close to it as Zanzibar.

Abandoning the mental exercise that was already giving him a slight headache, Sebastian stood up from the bed and, with the skirt of his nightshirt flapping around his calves, began his third minute search of the hotel room. Although the purse had been under his mattress when he went to sleep the preceding evening, this time Sebastian emptied the water jug and peered into it hopefully. He unpacked his valise and shook out each shirt. He crawled under the bed, lifted the coconut matting, and probed every hole in the rotten flooring before giving way to despair.

Shaved, the bedbug bites on his person anointed with saliva, and dressed in the grey three-piece suit which was showing signs of travel fatigue, he brushed his derby hat and placed it carefully over his curls, picked up his cane in one hand, and lugging his valise in the other, he went down the stairs into the hot noisy lobby of the Hotel Royal.

'I say,' he greeted the little Arab at the desk with the most cheerful smile he could muster. 'I say, I seem to have lost my money.'

A silence fell upon the room. The waiters carrying trays out to the hotel veranda slowed and stopped, heads turned towards Sebastian with the same hostile curiosity as if he had announced that he was suffering from a mild attack of leprosy.

'Stolen, I should imagine,' Sebastian went on, grinning. 'Nasty bit of luck, really.'

The silence exploded as the bead curtains from the office were thrown open and the Hindu proprietor erupted into the room with a loud cry of, 'Mr Oldsmith, what about your bill?'

'Oh, the bill. Yes, well, let's not get excited. I mean, it won't help, now, will it?'

And the proprietor proceeded to become very excited indeed. His cries of anguish and indignation carried to the veranda, where a dozen persons were already beginning the daily fight against heat and thirst. They crowded into the lobby to watch with interest.

'Ten days you owe. Nearly one hundred rupees.'

'Yes, it's jolly unfortunate, I know.' Sebastian was grinning desperately, when a new voice added itself to the uproar.

'Now just hold on a shake.' Together Sebastian and the Hindu turned to the big red-faced, middle-aged man with the pleasantly mixed American and Irish accent. 'Did I hear you called Mr Oldsmith?'

'That is correct, sir.' Sebastian knew instinctively that here was an ally.

'An unusual name. You wouldn't be related to Mister Francis Oldsmith, wool merchant of Liverpool, England?' Flynn O'Flynn inquired politely. He had perused Sebastian's letters of introduction passed on to him by Rachid El Keb.

'Good Lord!' Sebastian cried with joy. 'Do you know my pater?'

'Do I know Francis Oldsmith?' Flynn laughed easily, and then checked himself. His acquaintance was limited to the letterheads. 'Well, I don't exactly know him person to person, you understand, but I think I can say I know *of* him. Used to be in the wool business myself once.' Flynn turned genially to the hotel proprietor and breathed on him a mixture of gin fumes and good-fellowship. 'One hundred rupees was the sum you mentioned.'

'That's the sum, Mr O'Flynn.' The proprietor was easily soothed.

'Mr Oldsmith and I will be having a drink on the veranda. You can bring the receipt to us there.' Flynn placed two sovereigns on the counter; sovereigns that had so recently reposed beneath Sebastian's mattress.

With his boots propped on the low veranda wall, Sebastian regarded the harbour over the rim of his glass. Sebastian was not a drinking man, but in view of Flynn O'Flynn's guardianship he could not be churlish and refuse hospitality. The number of craft in the bay suddenly multiplied miraculously before his eyes. Where a moment before one stubby little dhow had been tacking in through the entrance, there were now three identical boats sailing in formation. Sebastian closed one eye and by focusing determinedly, he reduced the three back to one. Mildly elated with his success, he turned his attention to his new friend and business partner who had pressed such large quantities of gin upon him.

'Mr O'Flynn,' he said with deliberation, slurring the words slightly.

'Forget that mister, Bassie, call me Flynn. Just plain Flynn, the same as in gin.'

'Flynn,' said Sebastian. 'There isn't anything—well, there isn't anything funny about this?'

'How do you mean *funny*, boy?'

'I mean'—and Sebastian blushed slightly. 'There isn't anything illegal, is there?'

'Bassie.' Flynn shook his head sorrowfully. 'What do you take me for, Bassie? You think I'm a crook or something, boy?'

'Oh, no, of course not, Flynn,' and Sebastian blushed a shade deeper. 'I just thought—well, all these elephants we're going to shoot. They must belong to somebody. Aren't they German elephants?'

'Bassie, I want to show you something.' Flynn set down his glass and groping in the inside pocket of his wilted tropical suit, he produced an envelope. 'Read that, boy!'

The address at the head of the sheet of cheap notepaper was 'The Kaiserhof. Berlin. Dated June 10th, 1912', and the body of the letter read:

Dear Mr Flynn O'Flynn,
   I am worried about all those elephants down in the Rufiji basin eating up all the grass and smashing up all the trees and things, so if you've got time, would you go down there and shoot some of them as they're eating up all the grass and smashing up all the trees and things.
              Yours sincerely,
                   Kaiser Willem III,
                   Emperor of Germany

A vague uneasiness formed through the clouds of gin in Sebastian's skull. 'Why did he write to you?'

'Because he knows I'm the best goddamned elephant hunter in the world.'

'You'd expect him to use better English, wouldn't you?' Sebastian murmured.

'What's wrong with his English?' Flynn demanded truculently. He had spent some time in composing the letter.

'Well, I mean that bit about eating up all the grass—he said that twice.'

'Well, you've got to remember he's a German. They don't write English too good.'

'Of course! I hadn't thought of that.' Sebastian looked relieved and lifted his glass. 'Well, good hunting!'

'I'll drink to that,' and Flynn emptied his glass.

3

Sebastian stood with both hands gripping the wooden rail of the dhow and stared out across a dozen miles of water at the loom of the African mainland. The monsoon wind had ruffled the sea to a dark indigo and it flipped spray from the white-caps into Sebastian's face. Overlaying the clean salt of the ocean was the taint of the mangrove swamps, an evil smell as though an animal had died in its own cage. Sebastian sniffed it with distaste as he searched the low green line of the coast for the entrance to the maze of the Rufiji delta.

Frowning, he tried to reconstruct the admiralty chart in his mind. The Rufiji river came to the sea through a dozen channels spread over forty miles, and in doing so, it carved fifty, maybe a hundred, islands out of the mainland.

Tidal water washed fifteen miles upstream, past the mangroves to where the vast grass swampland began. It was there in the swampland that the elephant herds had taken shelter from the guns and arrows of the ivory hunters, protected by Imperial decree and by a formidable terrain.

The murderous-looking ruffian who captained the dhow uttered a string of singsong orders, and Sebastian turned to watch the complicated manoeuvre of tacking the ungainly craft. Half-naked seamen dropped out of the rigging like over-ripe brown fruit and swarmed around the sixty-foot teak boom. Bare feet padding on the filthy deck, they ran the boom back and forward again. The dhow creaked like an old man with arthritis, came round wearily on to the wind, and butted its nose in towards the land. The new motion, combined with the swamp smell and the smell of freshly stirred bilges, moved something deep within Sebastian. His grip upon the rail increased, and new sweat popped out like little blisters on his brow. He leaned forward, and, to shouts of encouragement from the crew, made another sacrifice to the sea gods. He was still draped worshipfully across the rail as the dhow wallowed and slid in the turbulent waters of the entrance, and then passed into the calm of the southernmost channel of the Rufiji basin.

Four days later, Sebastian sat cross-legged with the dhow captain on a thick Bokhara carpet spread upon the deck, and they explained to each other in sign language that neither of them had the vaguest idea where they were. The dhow was anchored in a narrow waterway hemmed in by the twisted and deformed trunks of the mangroves. The sensation of being lost was not new to Sebastian, and he accepted it with resignation, but the dhow captain, who could run from Aden to Calcutta and back to Zanzibar with the certainty of a man visiting his own outhouse, was not so stoical. He lifted his eyes to the heavens and called upon Allah to intercede with the djinn who guarded this stinking labyrinth, who made the waters flow in strange, unnatural ways, who changed the shape of each island, and thrust mud banks in their path. Driven on by his own eloquence, he leapt to the rail and screamed defiance into the brooding mangroves until flocks of ibis rose and milled in the heat mists above the dhow. Then he flung himself down on the carpet and fixed Sebastian with a stare of sullen malevolence.

'It's not really my fault, you know.' Sebastian wriggled with embarrassment under the stare. Then once again he produced his admiralty chart, spread it on the deck, and placed his finger on the island which Flynn O'Flynn had ringed in blue pencil as the rendezvous. 'I mean, it *is* rather your cup of tea, finding the place. After all, you *are* the navigator, aren't you?'

The captain spat fiercely on his deck, and Sebastian flushed.

'Now that sort of thing isn't going to get us anywhere. Let's try and behave like gentlemen.'

This time the captain hawked it up from deep down in his throat and spat a lump of yellow phlegm into the blue pencil circle on Sebastian's map, then he rose to his feet and stalked away to where his crewmen squatted in a group under the poop.

In the short dusk, while the mosquitoes whined in a thin mist about Sebastian's head, he listened to the Arabic muttering and saw the glances that were directed at him down the length of the dhow. So when the night closed over the ship like a bank of black steam, he took up a defensive position on the foredeck and waited for them to come. As a weapon he had his cane of solid ebony. He laid it across his lap and sat against the rail until the darkness was complete, then, silently, he changed his position and crouched beside one of the water barrels that was lashed to the base of the mast.

They were a long time coming. Half the night had wasted away before he heard the stealthy scuff of bare feet on the planking. The absolute blackness of the night was filled with the din of the swamp; the boom and tonk of frogs, the muted buzz of insects, and the occasional snort and splash of a hippo, so that Sebastian had difficulty in deciding how many they had sent against him. Crouching by the water barrel he strained his eyes unavailingly into the utter blackness and tuned his hearing to filter out the swamp noises and catch only those soft little sounds that death made as it came down the deck towards him.

Although Sebastian had never scaled any academic heights, he had boxed light heavyweight for Rugby, and fast-bowled for Sussex the previous cricket season when he had led the county bowling averages. So, although he was afraid now, Sebastian had a sublime confidence in his own physical prowess and it was not the kind of fear that filled his belly with oily warmth, nor turned his ego to jelly, but rather, it keyed him to a point where every muscle in his body quivered on the edge of exploding. Crouching in the night he groped for the cane that he had laid on the deck beside him. His hand fell on the bulky sackful of green coconuts that made up part of the dhow's deck cargo. They were carried to supplement, with their milk, the meagre supply of fresh water on board. Quickly Sebastian tore open the fastenings of the sack and hefted one of the hard round fruits.

'Not quite as handy as a cricket ball, but—' murmured Sebastian and came to his feet. Using the short run up, he delivered the fast ball with which he had shattered the Yorkshire first innings the previous year. It had the same effect on the Arab first innings. The coconut whirred and cracked against the skull of one of the approaching assassins and the rest retired in confusion.

'Now send the men,' roared Sebastian and bowled a short lifter that hastened the retreat.

He selected another coconut and was about to deliver that also when there was a flash and a report from aft, and something howled over Sebastian's head. Hastily he ducked behind the sack of coconuts.

'My God, they've got a gun up there!' Sebastian remembered then the ancient muzzle-loading Jezail he had seen the captain polishing lovingly on their first day out from Zanzibar, and he felt his anger rising in earnest.

He jumped to his feet and hurled his next coconut with fury.

'Fight fair, you dirty swine!' he yelled.

There was a delay while the dhow captain went through the complicated process of loading his piece. Then a cannon report, a burst of flame, and another potleg howled over Sebastian's head.

Through the dark hours before dawn the lively exchange of jeers and curses, of coconuts and potlegs continued. Sebastian more than held his own, for he scored four howls of pain and a yelp, while the dhow captain succeeded only in shooting a great deal of his own standing rigging. But as the light of the new day increased, so Sebastian's advantage waned. The Arab captain's shooting improved to such an extent that Sebastian spent most of his time crouching behind the sack of coconuts. Sebastian was nearly exhausted. His right arm and shoulder ached unmercifully, and he could hear the first stealthy advance of the Arab crew as they crept down the deck towards his hide. In daylight they could surround him and use their numbers to drag him down.

While he rested for the final effort, Sebastian looked out at the morning. It was a red dawn, angry and beautiful through the swamp mists so the water glowed with a pink sheen and the mangroves stood very dark around the ship.

Something splashed farther up the channel, a water bird perhaps. Sebastian looked for it without interest, and heard it splash again and then again. He stirred and sat up a little straighter. The sound was too regular for that of a bird or a fish.

Then around the bend in the channel, from behind the wall of mangroves, driven on by urgent paddles, shot a dug-out canoe. Standing in the bow with a double-barrelled elephant gun under his arm and a clay pipe sticking out of his red face, was Flynn O'Flynn.

'What the hell's going on here?' he roared. 'Are you fighting a goddamned war? I've been waiting a week for you lot!'

'Look out, Flynn!' Sebastian yelled a warning. 'That swine has got a gun!'

The Arab captain had jumped to his feet and was looking around uncertainly. Long ago he had regretted his impulse to rid himself of the Englishman and escape from this evil swamp, and now his misgivings were truly justified. Having committed himself, however, there was only one course open to him. He lifted the Jezail to his shoulder and aimed at O'Flynn in the canoe. The discharge blew a long grey spurt of powder smoke from the muzzle, and the potleg lifted a burst of spray from the surface of the water beyond the canoe. The echoes of the shot were drowned by the bellow of O'Flynn's rifle. He fired without removing the pipe from his mouth and the narrow dug-out rocked dangerously with the recoil.

The heavy bullet picked up the Arab captain's scrawny body, his robe fluttered like a piece of old paper, and his turban flew from his head and unwound in mid-air as he was flung clear of the rail to drop with a tall splash alongside. He floated face down, trapped air ballooning his robe about him, and then he drifted away slowly on the sluggish current. His crew, stunned and silent, stood by the rail and watched him depart.

Dismissing the neat execution as though it had never happened, O'Flynn glared up at Sebastian and roared, 'You're a week late. I haven't been able to do a goddamned thing until you got here. Now let's get the flag up and start doing some work!'

4

The formal annexation of Flynn O'Flynn's island took place in the relative cool of the following morning. It had taken some hours for Flynn to convince Sebastian of the necessity of occupying the island for the British Crown, and he succeeded only by casting Sebastian in the role of empire builder. He made some flattering comparisons between Clive of India and Sebastian Oldsmith of Liverpool.

The next problem was the choice of a name. This stirred up a little Anglo-American enmity, with Flynn O'Flynn campaigning aggressively for 'New Boston'. Sebastian was horrified, his patriotic ardour burned brightly.

'Now hold on a jiffy, old chap,' he protested.

'What's wrong with it? You just tell me what's wrong with it!'

'Well, first of all this is going to be one of His Britannic Majesty's possessions, you know.'

'New Boston,' O'Flynn repeated. 'That sounds good. That sounds real good.'

Sebastian shuddered. 'I think it would be—well, not quite suitable. I mean, Boston was the place where they had that tea thing, you know.'

The argument raged more savagely as Flynn lowered the level in the gin bottle, until finally Sebastian stood up from the carpet on the floor of the dhow cabin, his eyes blazing with patriotic outrage. 'If you would care to step outside, sir,' he enunciated with care as he stood over the older man, 'we can settle this matter.' The dignity of the challenge was spoiled by the low roof of the cabin which made it necessary for Sebastian to stoop.

'Man, I'd eat you without spitting the bones.'

'That, sir, is your opinion. But I must warn you I was highly thought of in the light heavyweight division.'

'Oh, goddamn it,' Flynn shook his head wearily and capitulated. 'What difference does it make what we call the mother-loving place. Sit down, for God's sake. Here! Let's drink to whatever you want to call it.'

Sebastian sat on the carpet, and accepted the mug that Flynn handed him. 'We shall call it—' he paused dramatically, 'we shall call it New Liverpool,' and he lifted the mug.

'You know,' said Flynn, 'for a limey, you aren't a bad guy,' and the rest of that night was devoted to celebrating the birth of the new colony.

In the dawn the empire builders were paddled ashore in the dug-out by two of Flynn's gun-bearers.

The canoe ran aground on the narrow muddy beach of New Liverpool, and the sudden halt threw both of them off-balance. They collapsed gently together on to the floor of the dug-out, and had to be assisted ashore by the paddlers.

Sebastian was formally dressed for the occasion, but had buttoned his waistcoat awry and he kept tugging at it as he peered about him.

Now at high tide New Liverpool was about a thousand yards long and half as broad. At the highest point it rose not more than ten feet above the level of the Rufiji river. Fifteen miles from the mouth the water was only slightly tainted with salt and the mangrove trees had thinned out and given way to tall matted elephant grass and slender bottle palms.

Flynn's gun-bearers and porters had cleared a small opening above the beach, and had erected a dozen grass huts around one of the palm trees. It was a dead palm, its crown leaves long gone, and Flynn pointed an unsteady finger at it.

'Flag pole,' he said indistinctly, took Sebastian's elbow, and led him towards it.

Tugging at his waistcoat with one hand and clutching the bundled Union Jack that Flynn had provided in the other, Sebastian felt a surge of emotion within him as he looked up at the slender column of the palm tree.

'Leave me,' he mumbled and shook off Flynn's guiding hand. 'We got to do this right. Solemn occasion—very solemn.'

'Have a drink.' Flynn offered him the gin bottle, and when Sebastian waved it away, he lifted it to his own lips.

'Shouldn't drink on parade.' Sebastian frowned at him. 'Bad form.'

Flynn coughed at the vicious sting of the liquor and smote himself on the chest with his free hand.

'Should draw the men up in a hollow square,' Sebastian went on. 'Ready to salute the flag.'

'Jesus, man, get on with it,' grumbled Flynn.

'Got to do it right.'

'Oh, hell,' Flynn shrugged with resignation, then issued a string of orders in Swahili.

Puzzled and amused, Flynn's fifteen retainers gathered in a ragged circle about the flag pole. They were a curious band, gathered from half a dozen tribes, dressed in an assortment of cast-off western clothing, half of them armed with ancient double-barrelled elephant rifles from which Flynn had carefully filed the serial numbers so they could never be traced back to him.

'Fine body of men.' Sebastian beamed at them in alcoholic goodwill, unconsciously using the words of a Brigadier who had inspected Sebastian's cadet parade at Rugby.

'Let's get this show on the road,' Flynn suggested.

'My friends,' Sebastian obliged, 'we are gathered here today . . .' It was a longish speech, but Flynn weathered it by nipping away quietly at the gin bottle, and at last Sebastian ended with his voice ringing and tears of great emotion pricking his eyelids, '. . . In the sight of God and man, I hereby declare this island part of the glorious Empire of His Majesty, George V, King of England, Emperor of India, Protector of the Faith . . .' His voice wavered as he tried to remember the correct form, and he ended lamely, '. . . and all that sort of thing.'

A silence fell on the assembly and Sebastian fidgeted with embarrassment. 'What do I do now?' he inquired of Flynn O'Flynn in a stage whisper.

'Get that goddamn flag up.'

'Ah, the flag!' Sebastian exclaimed with relief, and then uncertainly, 'How?'

Flynn considered this at length. 'I guess you have to climb up the palm tree.'

With shrill cries of encouragement from the gun-bearers, and with Flynn shoving and cursing from below, the Governor of New Liverpool managed to scale the flag pole to a height of about fifteen feet. There he secured the flag and descended again so swiftly he tore the buttons off the front of his waistcoast, and twisted his ankle. He was borne away to one of the grass huts singing 'God save our Gracious King' in a voice broken with gin, pain, and patriotism.

For the rest of their stay on the island the Union Jack flew at half mast above the encampment.

Carried initially by two Wakamba fishermen, it took fully ten days for the word of the annexation to reach the outpost of the German Empire one hundred miles away at Mahenge.

5

Mahenge was in the bush country above the coastal lowlands. It consisted, in its entirety, of four trading posts owned by Indian shopkeepers—and the German boma.

The German boma was a large stone building, thatched, set about with wide verandas over which purple bougainvillaea climbed in profusion. Behind it stood the barracks and parade ground of the African Askari, and before it a lonely flag pole from which streamed the black, red, and yellow of the empire. A speck in the vastness of the African bush, seat of government for an area the size of France. An area that spread south to the Rovuma river and the border of Portuguese Mozambique, east to the Indian Ocean, and west to the uplands of Sao Hill and Mbeya.

From this stronghold the German Commissioner (Southern Province) wielded the limitless powers of a medieval robber baron. One of the Kaiser's arms, or, more realistically, one of his little fingers, he was answerable only to Governor Schee in Dar es Salaam. But Dar es Salaam was many tortuous miles away, and Governor Schee was a busy man not to be troubled with trivialities. Just as long as the Herr Commissioner Herman Fleischer collected the taxes, he was free to collect them in his own sweet way; though very few of the indigenous inhabitants of the southern province would have described Herman Fleischer's ways as sweet.

At the time that the messenger, carrying the news of the British annexation of New Liverpool, trotted up over the last skyline and saw through the acacia thorn trees ahead of him the tiny clustered buildings of Mahenge, Herr Fleischer was finishing his midday meal.

A man of large appetite, his luncheon consisted of approximately two pounds of *Eisbein,* as much pickled cabbage, and a dozen potatoes, all swimming in thick gravy. Having aroused his taste-buds, he then went on to the sausage. The sausage came by weekly fast-runner from Dodoma in the north, and was manufactured by a man of genius, a Westphalian immigrant who made sausage with the taste of the Black Forest in them. The sausage, and the Hansa beer cooling in its earthenware jug, aroused in Herr Fleischer a delicious nostalgia. He ate not quietly but steadily, and, these quantities of food confined within the thick grey corduroy of his tunic and breeches, built up a pressure that squeezed the perspiration from his face and neck, forcing him to pause and mop up at regular intervals.

When he sighed at last and sagged back in his chair, the leather thongs squeaked a little under him. A bubble of trapped gas found its way up through the sausage and passed in genteel eruption between his lips. Tasting it, he sighed again in happiness, and squinted out from the deep shade of the veranda into the flat shimmering glare of the sunlight.

Then he saw the messenger coming. The man reached the steps of the veranda and squatted down in the sun with his loincloth drawn up modestly between his legs. His body was washed shiny black with sweat, but his legs were powdered with fine dust to the knees, and his chest swelled and subsided as he drank the thin hot air. His eyes were downcast, he could not look directly at the Bwana Mkuba until his presence was formally acknowledged.

Herman Fleischer watched him broodingly, his mood evaporating, for he had been looking forward to his afternoon siesta–and the messenger had spoiled that. He looked away at the low cloud above the hills in the south and sipped his beer. Then he selected a cheroot from the box before him and lit it. The cheroot burned slowly and evenly, restoring a little of his good humour. He smoked it short before flicking the stub over the veranda wall.

'Speak,' he grunted, and the messenger lifted his eyes, and gasped with wonder and awe at the beauty and dignity of the Commissioner's person. Although this was ritual admiration, it never failed to stir a faint pleasure in Herr Fleischer.

'I see you, Bwana Mkuba–Great Lord,' and Fleischer inclined his head slightly. 'I bring you greetings from Kalani, headman of Batja, on the Rufiji. You are his father, and he crawls on his belly before you. Your hair of yellow, and the great fatness of your body, blind him with beauty.'

Herr Fleischer stirred restlessly in his chair. References to his corpulence, however well-intentioned, always annoyed him. 'Speak' he repeated.

'Kalani says thus: "Ten suns ago, a ship came into the delta of the Rufiji, and stopped by the Island of the Dogs, Inja. On the island, the men of this ship have built houses, and above the houses, they have placed on a dead palm tree the cloth of the Insingeese which is of blue and white and red, having many crosses within crosses." '

Herr Fleischer struggled upright in his chair and stared at the messenger. The pink of his complexion slowly became cross-veined with red and purple.

'Kalani also says: "Since their coming the voices of their guns have never ceased to speak along the Rufiji river, and there has been a great killing of elephants, so that in the noon-day the sky is dark with the birds that come for the meat." '

Herr Fleischer was thrashing around in his chair, speech was locked in his throat, and his face had swollen so it threatened to burst like an over-ripe fruit.

'Kalani says further: "Two white men are on the island. One is a man who is very thin and young and is therefore of no account. The other white man Kalani has seen only at a great distance, but by the redness of this man's face, and by his bulk, he knows in his heart it is Fini." '

At the name Herr Fleischer became articulate, if not coherent–he bellowed like a bull in rut. The messenger winced, such a bellow from the Bwana Mkuba usually preceded a multiple hanging.

'Sergeant!' The next bellow had form, and Herr Fleischer was on his feet, struggling to clinch the buckle of his belt.

'Rasch!' he roared again. O'Flynn was in German territory again; O'Flynn was stealing German ivory once more–and compounding the insult by flying the Union Jack over the Kaiser's domain.

'Sergeant, where the thunder of God are you?' With incredible speed for a fat man Herr Fleischer raced down the long length of the veranda. For three years now, ever since his arrival in Mahenge, the name of Flynn O'Flynn had been enough to ruin his appetite, and produce in him a condition very close to epilepsy.

Around the corner of the veranda appeared the sergeant of the Askari, and Herr Fleischer braked just in time to avert collision.

'A storm patrol,' bellowed the Commissioner, blowing a cloud of spittle in his agitation. 'Twenty men. Full field packs, and one hundred pounds of ammunition. We leave in an hour.'

The sergeant saluted and doubled away across the parade ground. A minute later a bugle began singing with desperate urgency.

Slowly, through the black mists of rage, reason returned to Herman Fleischer. He stood with shoulders hunched, breathing heavily through his mouth, and mentally digested the full import of Kalani's message.

This was not just another of O'Flynn's will-o'-the-wisp forays across the Rovuma from Mozambique. This time he had sailed brazenly into the Rufiji delta, with a full-scale expedition, and hoisted the British flag. A queasy sensation, not attributable to the pickled pork, settled on Herr Fleischer's stomach. He knew the makings of an international incident when he saw one.

This, perhaps, was the goad that would launch the fatherland on the road of its true destiny. He gulped with excitement. They had flapped that hated flag in the Kaiser's face just once too often. This was history being made, and Herman Fleischer stood in the centre of it.

Trembling a little, he hurried into his office, and began drafting the report to Governor Schee that might plunge the world into a holocaust from which the German people would rise as the rulers of creation.

An hour later, he rode out of the boma on a white donkey with his slouch uniform hat set well forward on his head to shield his eyes from the glare. Behind him his black Askari marched with their rifles at the slope. Smart in their pillbox kepis with the backflaps hanging to the shoulder, khaki uniforms freshly pressed, and putteed legs rising and falling in unison, they made as gallant a show as any commander could wish.

A day and a half march would bring them to the confluence of the Kilombero and Rufiji rivers where the Commissioner's steam launch was moored.

As the buildings of Mahenge vanished behind him, Herr Fleischer relaxed and let his ample backside conform to the shape of the saddle.

6

'Now, have you got it straight?' Flynn asked without conviction. The past eight days of hunting together had given him no confidence in Sebastian's ability to carry out a simple set of instructions without introducing some remarkable variation of his own. 'You go down the river to the island, and you load the ivory on to the dhow. Then you come back here with all the canoes to pick up the next batch.' Flynn paused to allow his words to absorb into the spongy tissue of Sebastian's head before he went on. 'And for Chrissake don't forget the gin.'

'Right you are, old chap.' With eight days' growth of black beard, and the skin peeling from the tip of his sunburned nose, Sebastian was beginning to fit the role of ivory poacher. The wide-brimmed terai hat that Flynn had loaned him came down to his ears, and the razor edges of the elephant grass had shredded his trouser legs and stripped the polish from his boots. His wrists and the soft skin behind his ears were puffy and speckled with spots of angry red where the mosquitoes had drunk deep, but he had lost a little weight in the heat and the ceaseless walking, so now he was lean and hard-looking.

They stood together under a monkey-bean tree on the bank of the Rufiji, while at the water's edge the bearers were loading the last tusks into the canoes. There was a purple-greenish smell hanging over them in the steamy heat, a smell which Sebastian hardly noticed now—for the last eight days had seen a great killing of elephant, and the stink of green ivory was as familiar to him as the smell of the sea to a mariner.

'By the time you get back tomorrow morning the boys will have brought in the last of the ivory. We'll have a full dhow-load and you can set off for Zanzibar.'

'What about you? Are you staying on here?'

'Not bloody likely. I'll light out for my base camp in Mozambique.'

'Wouldn't it be easier for you to come along on the dhow? It's nearly two hundred miles to walk.' Sebastian was solicitous; in these last days he had conceived a burning admiration for Flynn.

'Well, you see, it's like this . . .' Flynn hesitated. This was no time to trouble Sebastian with talk of German gunboats waiting off the mouth of the Rufiji. 'I have to get back to my camp, because . . .' Suddenly inspiration came to Flynn O'Flynn. 'Because my poor little daughter is there all alone.'

'You've got a daughter?' Sebastian was taken by surprise.

'You damn right I have.' Flynn experienced a sudden rush of paternal affection and duty. 'And the poor little thing is there all alone.'

'Well, when will I see you again?' The thought of parting from Flynn, of being left to try and find his own way to Australia, saddened Sebastian.

'Well,' Flynn was tactful. 'I hadn't really given that much thought.' This was a lie. Flynn had thought about it ceaselessly for the last eight days. He was eagerly anticipating waving farewell to Sebastian Oldsmith for all time.

'Couldn't we . . .' Sebastian blushed a little under his sun-reddened cheeks. 'Couldn't we sort of team up together. I could work for you, sort of as an apprentice?'

The idea made Flynn wince. He almost panicked at the thought of Sebastian permanently trailing along behind him and discharging his rifle at random intervals. 'Well now, Bassie boy,' he clasped a thick arm around Sebastian's shoulders, 'first you sail that old dhow back to Zanzibar and old Kebby El Keb will pay you out your share. Then you write to me, hey? How about that? You write me, and we'll work something out.'

Sebastian grinned happily. 'I'd like that, Flynn. I'd truly like that.'

'All right, then, off you go. And don't forget the gin.'

With Sebastian standing in the bows of the lead canoe, the double-barrelled rifle clutched in his hands, and the terai hat pulled down firmly over his ears, the little flotilla of heavily laden canoes pulled out from the bank and caught the current. Paddles dipped and gleamed in the evening sunlight as they arrowed away towards the first bend downstream.

Still standing unsteadily in the frail craft, Sebastian looked back and waved his rifle at Flynn on the bank.

'For Chrissake, be careful with that goddamn piece,' Flynn bellowed too late. The rifle fired, and the recoil toppled Sebastian sprawling on to the pile of ivory behind him. The canoe rocked dangerously while the paddlers struggled to keep it from capsizing, and then disappeared around the bend.

Twelve hours later, the canoes reappeared around the same bend, and headed towards the lone monkey-bean tree on the bank. The canoes rode lightly, empty of ivory, and the paddlers were singing one of the old river chants.

Freshly shaved, wearing a clean shirt, and his other pair of boots, a case of Flynn's liquor between his knees, Sebastian peered eagerly ahead for the first glimpse of the big American.

A fine blue tendril of camp-fire smoke smeared out across the river, but there were no figures waving a welcome from the bank. Suddenly Sebastian frowned as he realized that the silhouette of the monkey-bean tree had altered. He wrinkled his eyes, peering ahead uncertainly.

Behind him rang the first cry of alarm from his boatmen. 'Allemand!' And the canoe swerved under him.

He glanced back and saw the other canoes wheel away in tight circles aimed downstream, the boatmen jabbering in terror as they leaned forward to thrust against the paddles.

His own canoe was in swift pursuit of the others as they darted beyond the bend.

'Hey!' Sebastian shouted at the sweat-shiny backs of his paddlers. 'What do you think you're doing?'

They gave him no answer, but the muscles beneath their black skins bunched and rippled in their frantic efforts to drive the canoe faster.

'Stop that immediately!' Sebastian yelled at them. 'Take me back, dash it all. Take me to the camp.'

In desperation Sebastian lifted the rifle and aimed at the nearest man. 'I'm not joking,' he yelled again. The native glanced over his shoulder into the gaping twin muzzles and his face, already twisted with fear, now convulsed into a mask of terror. They had all developed a healthy reverence for the way Sebastian handled that rifle.

The man stopped paddling, and one by one the others followed his example. Sitting frozen under the hypnotic eyes of Sebastian's rifle.

'Back!' said Sebastian and gestured eloquently upstream. Reluctantly the man nearest him dipped his paddle and the canoe turned broadside across the current. 'Back!' Sebastian repeated and the men dipped again.

Slowly, warily, the single canoe crept upstream towards the monkey-bean tree and the grotesque new fruit that hung from its branches.

The hull slid in on to the firm mud and Sebastian stepped ashore.

'Out!' he ordered the boatmen and gestured again. He wanted them well away from the canoe, for he knew that, otherwise, the moment his back was turned they would set off downstream again with renewed enthusiasm. 'Out!' and he herded them up the steep bank into Flynn O'Flynn's camp.

The two bearers who had died of gunshot wounds lay beside the smouldering fire. But the four men in the monkey-bean tree had been less fortunate. The ropes had cut deeply into the flesh of their necks and their faces were swollen, mouths wide in the last breath that had never been taken. On the lolling tongues the flies crawled like metallic green bees.

'Cut them down!' Sebastian roused himself from the nausea that was bubbling queasily up from his stomach. The boatmen stood paralysed and Sebastian felt anger now mixed with his revulsion. Roughly he shoved one of the men towards the tree. 'Cut them down,' he repeated, and thrust the handle of his hunting knife into the man's hand. Sebastian turned away as the native shinned up into the fork of the tree with the knife blade clamped between his teeth. Behind him he heard the heavy meaty thuds as the dead men dropped from the tree. Again his stomach heaved, and he concentrated on his search of the trampled grass around the camp.

'Flynn!' he called softly. 'Flynn. I say, Flynn! Where are you?' There were the prints of hobnailed boots in the soft earth, and at one place he stooped and picked up the shiny brass cylinder of an empty cartridge case. Stamped into the metal of the base around the detonator cap were the words *Mauser Fabriken. 7 mm.*

'Flynn!' more urgently now as the horror of it came home to him. 'Flynn!' and he heard the grass rustle near him. He swung towards it, half raising the rifle.

'Master!' and Sebastian felt disappointment swoop in his chest.

'Mohammed. Is that you, Mohammed?' and he recognized the wizened little figure with the eternal fez perched on the woolly head as it emerged. Flynn's chief gun-boy, the only one with a little English.

'Mohammed,' with relief, and then quickly, 'Fini? Where is Fini?'

'They shot him, master. The Askari came in the early morning before the sun. Fini was washing. They shot him and he fell into the water.'

'Where? Show me where.'

Below the camp, a few yards from where the canoe was drawn up, they found the pathetic little bundle of Flynn's clothing. Beside it was a half-consumed cake of cheap soap and a metal hand-mirror. There were the deep imprints of naked feet in the mud, and Mohammed stooped and broke off one of the green reeds at the water's edge. Wordlessly he handed it to Sebastian. A drop of blood had dried black on the leaf, and it crumbled as Sebastian touched it with his thumbnail.

'We must find him. He might still be alive. Call the others. We'll search the banks downstream.'

In an agony of loss Sebastian picked up Flynn's soiled shirt and crumpled it in his fist.

7

Flynn shucked off his pants and the filthy bush-shirt. Shivering briefly in the chill of dawn, he hugged himself and massaged his upper arms while he peered into the shallow water, searching the bottom for the telltale chicken-wire pattern that would mean a crocodile was buried in the mud waiting for him.

His body was porcelain-white where clothing had protected it from the sun, but his arms were chocolate-brown, and a deep vee of the same brown dipped down from his throat on to his chest. Above it the battered red face was creased and puffy with sleep, and his long, greying hair was tangled and matted. He belched thunderously, and grimaced at the taste of old gin and pipe tobacco, then, satisfied that no reptile lay in ambush, he stepped into the water and lowered his massive hams to sit waist-deep. Snorting, he scooped water with his cupped hands over his head, then lumbered out on to the bank again. Sixty seconds is a long time to stay in a river like the Rufiji, for the crocodiles come quickly to the sound of splashing.

Naked, dripping, hair plastered down across his face, Flynn began to soap himself, working up a thick lather at his crotch and tenderly massaging his abundant genitalia, he washed away the sloth of sleep and his appetite stirred. He called up at the camp, 'Mohammed, beloved of Allah and son of his prophet, shake your black arse out of the sack and get the coffee brewing.' Then as an afterthought, he added, 'And put a little gin in it.'

Soapsuds filled Flynn's armpits, and coated the melancholy sag of his belly when Mohammed came down the bank to him. Mohammed was balancing a large enamel mug from which curled little wisps of aromatic steam, and Flynn grinned at him, and spoke in Swahili. 'Thou art kind and merciful; this charity will be writ against your name in the Book of Paradise.'

He reached for the mug, but before his fingers touched it, there was a fusillade of gunfire above them and a bullet hit Flynn high up in the thigh. It spun him sideways so he sprawled half in mud and half in water.

Lying stunned with the shock, he heard the rush of Askari into the camp, heard their shouted triumph as they clubbed with the gun-butt those who had survived the first volley. Flynn wriggled into a sitting position.

Mohammed was coming to him anxiously.

'Run,' grunted Flynn. 'Run, damn you.'

'Lord . . .'

'Get out of here,' savagely Flynn lashed out at him, and Mohammed recoiled. 'The rope, you fool. They'll give you the rope and wrap you in a pigskin.'

A second longer Mohammed hesitated, then he ducked and scampered into the reeds.

'Find Fini,' roared a bull voice in German. 'Find the white man.'

Flynn realized then that it was a stray bullet that had hit him—perhaps even a ricochet. His leg was numb from the hip down, but he dragged himself into the water. He could not run, so he must swim.

'Where is he? Find him!' raged the voice, and suddenly the grass on the bank burst open and Flynn looked up.

For the first time they confronted each other. These two who had played murderous hide-and-seek for three long years across ten thousand square miles of bush.

'Ja!' Fleischer's jubilant bellow as he swung and sighted the pistol at the man in the water below him. 'This time!' aiming carefully, steadying the Luger with both hands.

The brittle snapping sound of the shot, and the slap of the bullet into the water a foot from Flynn's head was followed by Fleischer's snarl of disappointment.

Filling his lungs, Flynn ducked below the surface. Frog-kicking with his good leg, trailing the wounded one, he turned with the current and swam. He swam until his trapped breath threatened to explode in his chest, and coloured lights flashed and twinkled behind his clenched eyelids. Then he clawed to the surface. On the bank Fleischer was waiting for him with half a dozen of his Askari. 'There he is!' as Flynn blew like a whale thirty yards downstream. Gunfire crackled and the water whipped and leaped and creamed around Flynn's head.

'Shoot straight!' Howling in frustration and blazing wildly with the Luger, Fleischer watched the head disappear and Flynn's fat white buttocks break the surface for an instant as he dived. Sobbing with anger and exertion, Fleischer turned his fury on the Askari around him. 'Pigs! Stupid black pig dogs!' And he swung the empty pistol against the nearest head, knocking the man to his knees. Intent on avoiding the flailing pistol, none of them were ready when Flynn surfaced for the second time. A desultory volley kicked fountains no closer than ten feet to Flynn's bobbing head, and he dived again.

'Come on! Chase him!' Herding his Askari ahead of him, Fleischer trotted along the bank in pursuit. Twenty yards of good going, then they came to the first swamp hole and waded through it to be confronted by a solid barrier of elephant grass. They plunged into it and were swallowed so they no longer had sight of the river.

'Schnell! Schnell! He'll get away,' gasped Fleischer and the thick stems wrapped his ankles so that he fell headlong in the mud. Two of his Askari dragged him up and they staggered on until the thicket of tall grass ended, and they stood on the elbow of the river bend with a clear view a thousand yards downstream.

Disturbed by the gunfire, the birds were up, milling in confused flight above the reed-beds. Their alarm cries blended into a harsh chorus that spoiled the peace of the brooding dawn. They were the only living things in sight. From bank to far bank, the curved expanse of water was broken only by a few floating islands of papyrus grass; rafts of matted vegetation cut loose by the current and floating unhurriedly down towards the sea.

Panting, Herman Fleischer shook off the supporting hands of his two Askari and searched desperately for a glimpse of Flynn's bobbing head. 'Where did he go?' His fingers trembled as he fitted a new clip of ammunition into the Luger. 'Where did he go?' he demanded again, but none of his Askari drew attention to himself by venturing a reply.

'He must be on this side!' The Rufiji was half a mile wide here, Flynn could not have crossed it in the few minutes since they had last seen him. 'Search the bank!' Fleischer ordered. 'Find him!'

With relief the sergeant of his Askari turned on his men, quickly splitting them into two parties and sending them up and downstream to scour the water's edge.

Slowly Fleischer returned the pistol to its holster and fastened the flap, then he took a handkerchief from his pocket and mopped at his face and neck.

'Come on!' he snapped at his sergeant, and set off back towards the camp.

When he reached it his men had already set out the folding table and chair. New life had been stirred into Flynn's camp-fire, and the Askari cook was preparing breakfast.

Sitting at the table with the front of his tunic open, spooning up oatmeal porridge and wild honey, Fleischer was soothed into a better humour by the food, and by the thorough manner in which the execution of the four captives was conducted.

When the last of them had stopped twitching and kicking and hung quietly with his comrades in the monkey-bean tree, Herman wiped up the bacon grease in his plate with a hunk of black bread and popped it into his mouth. The cook removed the plate and replaced it with a mug of steaming coffee at the exact moment when the two parties of searchers straggled into the clearing to report that a few drops of blood at the water's edge was the only sign they had found of Flynn O'Flynn.

'Ja,' Herman nodded, 'the crocodiles have eaten him.' He sipped appreciatively at his coffee mug before he gave his next orders. 'Sergeant, take this up to the launch.' He pointed at the stack of ivory on the edge of the clearing. 'Then we will go down to the Island of the Dogs and find this other white man with his English flag.'

8

There was only the entry wound, a dark red hole from which watery blood still oozed slowly. Flynn could have thrust his thumb into it, but instead he groped gently around the back of his leg and located the lump in his flesh where the spent slug had come to rest just below the skin.

'God damn it, God damn it to hell,' he whispered in pain, and in anger, at the unlikely chance which had deflected the ricochet downwards to where he had stood below the bank, deflecting it with just sufficient velocity to lodge the bullet in his thigh instead of delivering a clean in-and-out wound.

Slowly he straightened the leg, testing it for broken bone. At the movement, the matt of drifting papyrus on which he lay rocked slightly.

'Might have touched the bone, but it's still in one piece,' he grunted with relief, and felt the first giddy swing of weakness in his head. In his ears was the faint rushing sound of a waterfall heard far off. 'Lost a bit of the old juice,' and from the wound a fresh trickle of bright blood broke and mingled with the water-drops to snake down his leg and drip into the dry matted papyrus. 'Got to stop that,' he whispered.

He was naked, his body still wet from the river. No belt or cloth to use as a tourniquet, but he must staunch the bleeding. His fingers clumsy with the weakness of the wound, he tore a bunch of the long sword-blade leaves from the reeds around him and began twisting them into a rope. Binding it around his leg above the wound, he pulled it tight, and knotted it. The dribble of blood slowed and almost stopped before Flynn sank back and closed his eyes.

Beneath him the island swung and undulated with the eddy of the current and the wavelets pushed up by the rising morning wind. It was a soothing motion, and he was tired—terribly, achingly, tired. He slept.

The pain and the cessation of motion woke him at last. The pain was a dull persistent throb, a pulse that beat through his leg and groin and his lower belly. Groggily he pulled himself on to his elbows and looked down on his own body. The leg was swollen, bluish-looking from the constriction of the grass rope. He stared at it dully, without comprehension, for a full minute before memory flooded back.

'Gangrene!' he spoke aloud, and tore at the knot. The rope fell away and he gasped at the agony of new blood flowing into the leg, clenching his fists and grinding his teeth against it. The pain slowed and settled into a steady beat, and he breathed again, wheezy as a man with asthma.

Then the change of his circumstances came through to the conscious level of his mind and he peered around shortsightedly. The river had carried him down into the mangrove swamps again, down into the maze of little islands and water-ways of the delta. His raft of papyrus had been washed in and stranded against a mud bank by the falling tide. The mud stank of rotting vegetation and sulphur. Near him a gathering of big green river crabs were clicking and bubbling over the body of a dead fish, their little eye-stalks raised in perpetual surprise. At Flynn's movement they sidled away towards the water with their red-tipped claws raised defensively.

Water! Instantly Flynn was aware of the gummy saliva that glued his tongue to the roof of his mouth. Reddened by the harsh sunlight, heated by the first fever of his wound, his body was a furnace that craved moisture.

Flynn moved and instantly cried out in pain. His leg had stiffened while he slept. It was now a heavy anchor, shackling him helplessly to the papyrus raft. He tried again, easing himself backwards on his hands and his buttocks, dragging the leg after him. Each breath was a sob in his dry throat, each movement a white-hot lance into his thigh. But he must drink, he had to drink. Inch by inch, he worked his way to the edge of the raft and slid from it on to the mud bank.

The water had receded with the tide, and he was still fifty paces from the edge. With the motion of a man swimming on his back, he moved across the slimy evil-smelling mud, and his leg slithered after him. It was beginning to bleed again, not copiously but a bright wine-drop at a time.

He reached the water at last, and rolled on to his side with the bad leg uppermost in an attempt to keep the wound out of the mud. On one elbow he buried his face in the water, drinking greedily. The water was warm, tainted with sea salt, and musky with rotted mangroves so it tasted like animal urine. But he gulped it noisily with his mouth and his nostrils and his eyes below the surface. At last he must breathe, and he lifted his head, panting for breath, coughing so the water shot up his throat, out through his nose, and dimmed his vision with tears. Gradually his breathing steadied and his eyes cleared. Before he bowed his head to drink again, he glanced out across the channel and saw it coming.

It was on the surface, still a hundred yards away but swimming fast, driving towards him with the great tail churning the water. A big one–at least fifteen feet of it–showing like the rough bark of a pine log, leaving a wide wake across the surface as it came.

And Flynn screamed, just once, but shrill and high and achingly clear. Forgetting the wound in his panic, he tried to get to his feet, pushing himself up with his hands–but the leg pinned him. He screamed again, in panic and in fear.

Belly down, he wriggled in frantic haste from the shallow water back on to the mud bank, dragging himself across the glutinous slime, clawing and threshing towards the papyrus raft where it lay stranded among the mangrove roots fifty yards away. Expecting each moment to hear the slithering rush of the huge reptile across the mud behind him, he reached the first of the mangroves and rolled on his side, looking back, coated with black mud, his face working in his terror and the sound of it spilling in an incoherent babble through his lips.

The crocodile was at the edge of the mud bank, still in the river. Only its head showed above the surface and the little piggy bright eyes watched him unwinkingly, each set on its knot of horny scale.

Desperately Flynn looked about him. The mud bank was a tiny island with this grove of a dozen mangroves set in the centre of it. The trunks of the mangroves were twice as thick as a man's chest, but without branches for the first ten feet of their height; smooth bark slimy with mud and encrusted with little colonies of freshwater mussels. Unwounded, Flynn would not have been able to climb any of them–with his leg those branches above him were doubly inaccessible.

Wildly now he searched for a weapon–anything, no matter how puny–to defend himself. But there was nothing. Not a branch of driftwood, not a rock—only the slick black sheet of mud around him.

He looked back at the crocodile. It had not moved. His first feeble hope that it might not come out on to the mud bank withered almost before it was born. It would come. Cowardly, loathsome creature it was—but in time it would gather its courage. It had smelled his blood; it knew him to be wounded, helpless. It would come.

Painfully Flynn leaned his back against the roots of the mangrove, and his terror settled down to a steady, pulsing fear—as steady as the pain in his leg. During the frantic flight across the bank, stiff mud had plugged the bullet hole and stopped the bleeding. But it does not matter now, Flynn thought, nothing matters. Only the creature out there, waiting while its appetite overcomes its timidity, swamps its reluctance to leave its natural element. It might take five minutes, or half a day—but, inevitably, it will come.

There was a tiny ripple around its snout, the first sign of its movement, and the long scaly head inched in towards the edge. Flynn stiffened.

The back showed, its scales like the patterned teeth of a file, and beyond it, the tail with the coxcomb double crest. Cautiously, on its short bowed legs, it waddled through the shallows. Wet and shiny, as broad across the back as a percheron stallion, more than a ton of cold, armoured flesh, it emerged from the water. Sinking elbow-deep into the soft mud, so its belly left a slide mark behind it. Grinning savagely, but with the jagged, irregular teeth lying yellow and long on its lips, and the small eyes watching him.

It came so slowly that Flynn lay passively against the tree, mesmerized by the deliberate waddling approach.

When it was half-way across the bank, it stopped—crouching, grinning—and he smelled it. The heavy odour of stale fish and musk on the warm air.

'Get away!' Flynn yelled at it, and it stood unmoving, unblinking. 'Get away!' He snatched up a handful of mud and hurled it. It crouched a little lower on its stubby legs and the fat crested tail stiffened, arching slightly.

Sobbing now, Flynn threw another handful of mud. The long grinning jaws opened an inch, then shut again. He heard the click as its teeth met, and it charged. Incredibly fast through the mud, grinning still, it slithered towards him.

This time Flynn's voice was a lunatic babble of horror and he writhed helplessly against the mangrove roots.

The deep booming note of the gun seemed not part of reality, but the crocodile reared up on its tail, drowning the echoes of the shot with its own hissing bellow, and above the next boom of the gun, Flynn heard the bullet strike the scaly body with a thump.

Mud sprayed as the reptile rolled in convulsions, and then, lifting itself high on its legs, it lumbered in ungainly flight towards the water. Again and again the heavy rifle fired, but the crocodile never faltered in its rush, and the surface of the water exploded like blown glass, as it launched itself from the bank and was gone in the spreading ripples.

Standing in the bows of the canoe with the smoking rifle in his hands, while the paddlers drove in towards the bank, Sebastian Oldsmith shouted anxiously, 'Flynn, Flynn—did it get you? Are you all right?'

Flynn's reply was a croak. 'Bassie. Oh, Bassie boy, for the first time in my life I'm real pleased to see you,' and he sagged only half conscious against the mangrove roots.

9

The sun burned down on the dhow where it lay at anchor off the Island of the Dogs, yet a steady breeze came down the narrow waterway between the mangroves and plucked at the furled sail on the boom.

With a rope sling under his armpits, they lifted Flynn from the canoe and swung him, legs dangling, over the bulwark. Sebastian was ready to receive him and lower him gently to the deck.

'Get that goddamn sail up, and let's get the hell out of the river,' gasped Flynn.

'I must tend to your leg.'

'That can wait. We've got to get out into the open sea. The Germans have got a steam launch. They'll be looking for us. We can expect them to drop in on us at any minute.'

'They can't touch us—we're under the protection of the flag,' Sebastian protested.

'Listen, you stupid, bloody limey,' Flynn's voice was a squawk of pain and impatience. 'That murdering Hun will give us a rope dance with or without the flag. Don't argue, get that sail up!'

They laid him on a blanket in the shadow of the high poop before Sebastian hurried forward to release the Arab crew from the hold. They came up shiny with sweat and blinking in the dazzle of the sun. It took perhaps fifteen seconds for Mohammed to explain to them the urgency of the situation, and this invoked a few seconds of paralysed horror before they scattered to their stations. Four of them were hauling ineffectively at the anchor rope, but the great lump of coral was buried in the gluey mud of the bottom. Sebastian pushed them aside impatiently and with one knife stroke, severed the rope.

The crew, with the enthusiastic assistance of Flynn's bearers and gun-boys, ran up the faded and patched old sail. The wind caught it and bellied it. The deck canted slightly and two Arabs ran back to the tiller. From under the bows came the faint giggle of water, and from the stern spread a wide oily wake. With a cluster of the Arabs and bearers calling directions in the bows to the steersmen at the rudder, the ancient dhow pointed downstream and ambled towards the sea.

When Sebastian went back to Flynn, he found old Mohammed squatting anxiously beside him and watching, as Flynn drank from the square bottle. Already a quarter of its contents had disappeared.

Flynn lowered the gin bottle, and breathed heavily through his mouth. 'Tastes like honey,' he gasped.

'Let's look at that leg.' Sebastian stooped over Flynn's naked, mud-besmeared body. 'My God, what a mess! Mohammed, get a basin of water and try and find some clean cloth.'

10

With the coming of evening, the breeze gathered strength, kicking up a chop on the widening waterways of the delta. All afternoon the little dhow had butted against the run of the tide, but now began the ebb and it helped push her down towards the sea.

'With any luck we'll reach the mouth before sunset.' Sebastian was sitting beside Flynn's blanket-wrapped form under the poop. Flynn grunted. He was weak with pain, and groggy with gin. 'If we don't, we'll have to moor somewhere for the night. Can't risk the channel in the dark.' He received no reply from Flynn and himself fell silent.

Except for the gurgle of the bow-wave and the singsong chant of the pilot, a lazy silence blanketed the dhow. Most of the crew and the bearers were strewn in sleep about the deck, although two of them worked quietly over the open galley as they prepared the evening meal.

The heavy miasma of the swamps blended poorly with the stench of the bilges and the cargo of green ivory in the holds. It seemed to act as a drug, increasing Sebastian's fatigue. His head sagged forward on his chest and his hands slipped from the rifle in his lap. He slept.

The magpie chatter of the crew, and Mohammed's urgent hands on his shoulder, shook him awake. He came to his feet and gazed blearily around him. 'What is it? What is the trouble, Mohammed?'

For answer, Mohammed shouted the crew into silence, and turned back to Sebastian. 'Listen, master.'

Sebastian shook the remnants of sleep from his head, then cocked it slightly. 'I can't hear . . .' He stopped, an expression of uncertainty on his face.

Very faintly in the still of the evening he heard it, a faint huffing rhythm, as though a train passed in the distance. 'Yes,' he said, still uncertain. 'What is it?'

'The toot-toot boat, she comes.'

Sebastian stared at him without comprehension.

'The Allemand. The Germans.' Mohammed's hands fluttered with agitation. 'They follow us. They chase. They catch. They . . .' He clutched his own throat with both hands and rolled his eyes. His tongue protruded from the corner of his mouth.

Flynn's entire retinue was gathered in a mob around Sebastian, and at Mohammed's graphic little charade, they burst once more into a frightened chorus. Every eye was on Sebastian, waiting for his lead, and he felt confused, uncertain. Instinctively he turned to Flynn. Flynn lay on his back, his mouth open, snoring. Quickly Sebastian knelt beside him. 'Flynn! Flynn!' Flynn opened his eyes but they were focused beyond Sebastian's face. 'The Germans are coming.'

'The Campbells are coming. Hurrah! Hurrah!' muttered Flynn and closed his eyes again. His usually red face was flushed hot-scarlet with fever.

'What must I do?' pleaded Sebastian.

'Drink it!' advised Flynn. 'Never hesitate. Drink it!' his eyes still closed, his voice slurred.

'Please, Flynn. Please tell me.'

'Tell you?' muttered Flynn in delirium. 'Sure! Have you heard the one about the camel and the missionary?'

Sebastian jumped to his feet and looked wildly about him. The sun was low, perhaps another two hours to nightfall. *If only we can hold them off until then.* 'Mohammed. Get the gun-boys up into the stern,' he snapped, and Mohammed, recognizing the new crispness in his voice, turned on the mob about him to relay the order.

The ten gun-boys scattered to gather their weapons and then crowded up on to the poop. Sebastian followed them, gazing anxiously back along the channel. He could see two thousand yards to the bend behind them and the channel was empty, but he was sure the sound of the steam engine was louder.

'Spread them along the rail,' he ordered Mohammed. He was thinking hard now; always a difficult task for Sebastian. Stubborn as a mule, his mind began to sulk as soon as he flogged it. He wrinkled his high scholar's forehead and his next thought emerged slowly. 'A barricade,' he said. The thin planking of the bulwark would offer little protection against the high-powered Mausers. 'Mohammed, get the others to carry up everything they can find, and pile it here to shield the steersmen and the gun-boys. Bring everything—water barrels, the sacks of coconuts, those old fishing-nets.'

While they hurried to obey the order, Sebastian stood in frowning concentration, prodding the mass within his skull and finding it as responsive as a lump of freshly kneaded dough. He tried to estimate the relative speeds of the dhow and a modern steam launch. Perhaps they were moving at half the speed of their pursuers. With a sliding sensation, he decided that even in this wind, sail could not hope to out-run a propeller-driven craft.

The word *propeller*, and the chance that at that moment he was forced to move aside to allow four of the men to drag an untidy bundle of old fishing-nets past, eased the next idea to the surface of his mind.

Humbled by the brilliance of his idea, he clung to it desperately, lest it somehow sink once more below the surface to be lost. 'Mohammed . . .' he stammered in his excitement. 'Mohammed. Those nets . . .' He looked back again along the wide channel, and saw it still empty. He looked ahead and saw the next bend coming towards them; already the helmsman was chanting the orders preparatory to tacking the dhow. 'Those nets. I want to lay them across the channel.'

Mohammed stared at him aghast, his wizened face crinkling deeper in disbelief.

'Cut off the corks. Leave every fourth one.' Sebastian grabbed his shoulders and shook him in agitation. 'I want the net to sag. I don't want them to spot it too soon.'

They were almost up to the bend now, and Sebastian pointed ahead. 'We'll lay it just around the corner.'

'Why, master?' pleaded Mohammed. 'We must run. They are close now.'

'The propeller,' Sebastian shouted in his face. He made a churning motion with his hands. 'I want to snag the propeller.'

A moment longer Mohammed stared at him, then he began to grin, exposing his bald gums.

While they worked in frantic haste the muffled engine beat from upstream grew steadily louder, more insistent.

The dhow wallowed and balked at the efforts of the helmsman to work her across the channel. Her head kept falling away before the wind, threatening to snarl the net in her own rudder, but slowly the line of bobbing corks spread from the mangroves on one side towards the far bank, while in grim concentration Sebastian and a group led by Mohammed paid the net out over the stern. Every few minutes they lifted their faces to glance at the bend upstream, expecting to see the German launch appear and hear the crackle of Mauser fire.

Gradually the dhow edged in towards the north bank, sowing the row of corks behind her, and abruptly Sebastian realized that the net was too short—too short by fifty yards. There would be a gap in their defence. If the launch cut the bend fine, hugging the bank as it came, then they were lost. Already the note of its engine was so close that he could hear the metallic whine of the drive shaft.

Now also there was a new problem. How to anchor the loose end of the net? To let it float free would allow the current to wash it away, and open the gap still further.

'Mohammed. Fetch one of the tusks. The biggest one you can find. Quickly. Go quickly.'

Mohammed scampered away and returned immediately, the two bearers with him staggering under the weight of the long curved shaft of ivory.

His hands clumsy with haste, Sebastian lashed the end rope of the net to the tusk. Then grunting with the effort, he and Mohammed hoisted it to the side rail, and pushed it overboard. As it splashed, Sebastian shouted to the helmsman, 'Go!' and pointed downstream. Thankfully the Arab wrenched the tiller across. The dhow spun on her heel and pointed once again towards the sea.

Silently, anxiously, Sebastian and his gun-boys lined the stern and gazed back at the bend of the channel. In the fists of each of them were clutched the short-barrelled elephant rifles, and their faces were set intently.

The chug of the steam engine rose louder and still louder.

'Shoot as soon as it shows,' Sebastian ordered. 'Shoot as fast as you can. Keep them looking at us, so they don't see the net.'

And the launch came around the bend; flying a ribbon of grey smoke from its single stack and the bold red, yellow, and black flag of the Empire at its bows. A neat little craft, forty-footer, low in the waist, small deck-house aft, gleaming white in the sunlight, and the white moustache of the bow wave curled about her bows.

'Shoot!' bellowed Sebastian as he saw the Askari clustered on the foredeck. 'Shoot!' and his voice was lost in the concerted blast of the heavy calibre rifles around him. One of the Askari was flung backwards against the deck-house, his arms spread wide as he hung there a moment in the attitude of crucifixion before subsiding gently on to the deck. His comrades scattered and dropped into cover behind the steel bulwark. A single figure was left alone on the deck; a massive figure in the light grey uniform of the German colonial service, with his wide-brimmed slouch hat, and gold gleaming at the shoulders of his tunic.

Sebastian took him in the notch of his rear sight, held the bead on his chest, and jerked the trigger. The rifle jumped joyously against his shoulder, and he saw a fountain of spray leap from the surface of the river a hundred yards beyond the launch. Sebastian fired again, closing his eyes in anticipation of the savage recoil of the rifle. When he opened them, the German officer was still on his feet, shooting back at Sebastian with a pistol in his outstretched right hand. He was making better practice than Sebastian. The fluting hum of his fire whipped about Sebastian's head, or smacked into the planking of the dhow.

Hastily Sebastian ducked behind the water barrel and clawed a pair of cartridges from his belt. Sharper, higher than the dull booming of the elephant rifles, climbed the brittle crackle of the Mauser fire as the Askari joined in.

Cautiously Sebastian lifted his eyes above the water barrel. The launch was cutting the bend fine, and with a sudden swoop of dismay, he knew it was going to clear the fish-net by twenty feet. He dropped his rifle on to the deck and jumped to his feet. A Mauser bullet missed his ear by so little that it nearly burst his eardrum. Instinctively he ducked, then checked the movement and instead ran to the helmsman. 'Get out of the way!' he yelled in his excitement and his fear. Roughly he shoved the man aside and, grasping the tiller, pushed it across. Perilously close the jibe, the dhow veered across the channel, opening the angle between it and the launch. Looking back Sebastian saw the fat German officer turn and shout an order towards the wheel-house. Almost immediately the bows of the launch swung, following the dhow's manœuvre, and Sebastian felt triumph flare in his chest. Now directly in the path of the launch lay the line of tiny black dots that marked the net.

His deep-drawn breath trapped in his lungs, Sebastian watched the launch sweep over the net. His grip on the tiller tightened until his knuckles threatened to push out through the skin, and then he expelled his breath in a howl of joy and relief.

For the line of corks was suddenly plucked below the surface, leaving the small disturbance of ripples where each had stood. For ten seconds the launch sped on, then abruptly the even sound of her passage altered, a harsh clattering intruded, and her bows swung suddenly as she slowed.

The gap between the two craft widened. Sebastian saw the German officer drag a frightened Askari from the wheel-house and club him unmercifully about the head, but the squeals of Teutonic fury were muted by the swiftly increasing distance, and then drowned by the tumultuous clamour of his own crew, as they pranced and danced about the deck.

The Arab helmsman hopped up on to the water barrel and hoisted the skirts of his dirty grey robe to expose his naked posterior at the launch in calculated mockery.

I I

Long after the dhow had sailed sedately first out of rifle range, and then out of sight, Herman Fleischer gave himself over completely to the epilepsy of frustrated anger. He raved about the tiny deck, lashing out with ham-sized fists while his Askari skittled around him trying to keep out of range. Repeatedly he returned to the unconscious form of his helmsman to kick him as he lay. At last his fury burned itself down to the level where it allowed him to trundle aft and hang over the stern rail peering down at the sodden bundle of netting which was wrapped around the propeller.

'Sergeant!' His voice was hoarse with strain. 'Get two men with knives over the side to cut that away!'

And a stillness fell upon them all. Every man tried to shrink himself down into insignificance, so that the choice might not fall on him. Two volunteers were selected, divested of their uniforms, and hustled to the stern, despite their terrified entreaties.

'Tell them to hurry,' grunted Herman, and went to his folding chair. His personal boy placed the evening meal with its attendant pitcher of beer on the table before him and Herman fell to.

Once from the stern there was a squeak and a splash, followed by a furious burst of rifle fire. Herman frowned and looked up from his plate.

'A crocodile has taken one of the men,' his sergeant reported in agitation.

'Well, put another one over,' said Herman and returned with unabated relish to his meal. This last batch of sausage was particularly tasty.

The netting had wound so tightly about the blades and shaft of the propeller, that it was an hour after midnight when the last of it was hacked away by lantern light.

The drive shaft had twisted slightly and run one of its bearings, so even at quarter speed there was a fearsome clattering and threshing sound from the stern as the launch limped slowly down the channel towards the sea.

In the grey and pallid pink of dawn they crept past the last island of mangroves and the launch lifted her head to the sluggish thrust of the Indian Ocean. It was a windless morning of flat calm, and Herman peered without hope into the misty half light that obscured the ocean's far horizon. He had come this far only on the slight chance that the dhow might have gone aground on a mud bank during her night run down the river.

'Stop!' he shouted at his battered helmsman. Immediately the agonized clatter of the propeller ceased, and the launch rose and fell uneasily on the long oil swells.

So they had got clear away then. He could not risk his damaged launch on the open sea. He must go back, and leave the dhow and its ivory and its many candidates for the rope, to head unmolested for that pest-hole of rogues and pirates of Zanzibar island.

Moodily he looked out across the sea and mourned that cargo of ivory. There had been perhaps a million Reichsmarks of it aboard, of which his unofficial handling fee would have been considerable.

Also he mourned the departure of the Englishman. He had never hanged one before.

He sighed and tried to comfort himself with the thought of that damned American, now well digested in the maw of a crocodile, but truly it would have been more satisfying to see him kick and spin on the rope.

He sighed again. Ah, well! At least he would no longer have the perpetual worry of Flynn O'Flynn's presence on his border, nor would he have to suffer the nagging of Governor Schee and his endless demands for O'Flynn's head.

Now it was breakfast time. He was about to turn away when something out there in the lightening dawn caught his attention.

A long low shape, its outline becoming crisper as he watched. There were cries from his Askari as they saw it also, huge in the dawn. The stark square turrets with their slim gun-barrels, the tall triple stacks and neat geometrical patterns of its rigging.

'The *Blücher*!' roared Herman in savage elation. 'The *Blücher*, by God!' He recognized the cruiser, for he had seen her not six months before, lying in Dar es Salaam harbour. 'Sergeant, bring the signal pistol!' He was capering with excitement. In reply to Herman's hasty message, Governor Schee must have sent the *Blücher* racing southwards to blockade the Rufiji mouth. 'Start the engine. Schnell! Run out to her,' he shouted at the helmsman as he slid one of the fat Very cartridges into the gaping breech of the pistol, snapped it closed, and pointed the muzzle to the sky.

Beside the tall bulk of the cruiser the launch was as tiny as a floating leaf, and Herman looked up with apprehension at the frail rope ladder he was expected to climb. His Askari assisted him across the narrow strip of water between the two vessels and he hung for a desperate minute until his feet found the rungs and he began his ponderous ascent. Sweating profusely he was helped on to the deck by two seamen and faced an honour guard of a dozen or more. Heading them was a young lieutenant in crisp, smart tropical whites.

Herman shrugged off the helping hands, drew himself to attention with a click of heels. 'Commissioner Fleischer.' His voice shaky with exertion.

'Lieutenant Kyller.' The officer clicked and saluted.

'I must see your captain immediately. A matter of extreme urgency.'

12

Kapitän zur See Count Otto von Kleine inclined his head gravely as he greeted Herman. He was a tall, thin man, who wore a neat, pointed blond beard with just a few threads of grey to give it dignity. 'The English have landed a full-scale expeditionary force in the Rufiji delta, supported by capital ships? This is correct?' he asked immediately.

'The report was exaggerated.' Herman regretted bitterly the impetuous wording of his message to the Governor; he had been fired with patriotic ardour at the time. 'In fact, it was only . . . ah,' he hesitated, 'one vessel.'

'Of what strength? What is her armament?' demanded von Kleine.

'Well, it was an unarmed vessel.'

And von Kleine frowned. 'Of what type?'

Herman flushed with embarrassment. 'An Arab dhow. Of about twenty-two metres.'

'But this is impossible. Ridiculous. The Kaiser has delivered an ultimatum to the British Consul in Berlin. He has issued mobilization orders to five divisions.' The captain spun on his heel and began to pace restlessly about his bridge, clapping his hands together in agitation. 'What was the purpose of this British invasion? Where is this . . . this dhow? What explanation must I send to Berlin?'

'I have since learned that the expedition was led by a notorious ivory poacher named O'Flynn. He was shot resisting arrest by my Askari, but his accessory, an unknown Englishman, escaped down the river last night in the dhow.'

'Where will they be headed?' The Captain stopped pacing and glared at Herman.

'Zanzibar.'

'This is stupidity, utter stupidity. We will be a laughing stock! A battle cruiser to catch a pair of common criminals!'

'But, Captain, you must pursue them.'

'To what purpose?'

'If they escape to tell their story, the dignity of the Emperor will be lowered throughout the length of Africa. Think if the British Press were to hear of this! Also, these men are dangerous criminals.'

'But I cannot board a foreign ship on the high seas. Especially if she flies the Union Jack. It would be an act of war—an act of piracy.'

'But, Captain, if she were to sink with all hands, sink without a trace?'

And Captain von Kleine nodded thoughtfully. Then abruptly he snapped his fingers and turned to his pilot. 'Plot me a course for Zanzibar Island.'

13

They lay becalmed below a sky of brazen cobalt, and every hour of the calm allowed the Mozambique current to push the little dhow another three miles off its course. Aimlessly she swung her head to meet each of the long swells, and then let it fall away into the troughs.

For the twentieth time since dawn, Sebastian climbed up on to the poop-deck and surveyed the endless waters, searching for a ruffle on the glassy surface that would herald the wind. But there was never any sign of it. He looked towards the west, but the blue line of the coast had long since sunk below the horizon.

'I'm an old dog, *Fisi*,' bellowed Flynn from the lower deck. 'Hear me laugh,' and he imitated faithfully the yammering cry of an hyena. All day Flynn had regaled the company with snatches of song and animal imitations. Yet his delirium was interspaced with periods of lucidity. 'I reckon this time old Fleischer got me good, Bassie. There's a sack of poison forming round that bullet. I can feel it there. A fat, hot sack of it. Reckon we've got to dig for it pretty soon. Reckon if we can't make it back to Zanzibar pretty soon, we're going to have to dig for it.' Then his mind escaped once more into the hot land of delirium.

'My little girl, I'll bring you a pretty ribbon. There, don't cry. A pretty ribbon for a pretty girl.' His voice syrupy, then suddenly harsh. 'You cheeky little bitch. You're just like that goddamned mother of yours. Don't know why I don't chase you out,' this last followed immediately by the hyena imitation again.

Now Sebastian turned away from the poop rail and looked down on Flynn. Beside him the faithful Mohammed was dipping strips of cloth in a bucket of seawater, wringing them out and then laying them on Flynn's flushed forehead in a futile attempt to reduce the fever.

Sebastian sighed. His responsibilities lay heavily. The command of the expedition had devolved squarely upon him. And yet, there was a sneaky sensation of pleasure, of pride in his execution of that command to be present. He went back and replayed in his mind the episode of the fish-net, remembering the quick decision that had altered the launch's course and lured it into the trap. He smiled at the memory, and the smile was not his usual self-effacing grin, but something harder. When he turned away to pace the narrow deck there was more spring in his step, and he set his shoulders square.

Again he stopped by the rail and looked towards the west. There was a cloud on the horizon, a tiny dark finger of it. And he watched it with hope that it might herald the start of the afternoon sea breeze. Yet it seemed unnatural. As he watched, it moved. He could swear it moved. Now his whole attention was fastened upon it. Realization began to flicker in him, building up until it was certainty.

A ship. By God, a ship!

He ran to the poop ladder, and slid down into the waist, across it to the mast. The crew and the bearers watched him with awakening interest. Some of them got to their feet.

Sebastian jumped on to the boom, balancing there a moment before he started to shin up the mast. Using the mainsail hoops like the rungs of a ladder, he reached the masthead and clung there, peering eagerly into the west.

There she was—no doubt about it. He could see the tips of the triple stacks, each with its feather of dark smoke, and he began to cheer.

Below him the rail was lined with his men, all peering out in the direction they took from him. Sebastian slid down the mast, the friction burning his hands in his haste. His feet hit the deck and he ran to Flynn. 'A ship. A big ship coming up fast.' Flynn rolled his head and looked at him vaguely. 'Listen to me, Flynn. There'll be a doctor aboard. We'll get you to a port in no time.'

'That's good, Bassie.' Flynn's brain clicked back into focus. 'You've done real good.'

She came up over the horizon with astonishing rapidity, and her silhouette changed as she altered course towards them. But not before Sebastian had seen the gun turrets.

'A warship!' he shouted. To his mind this proved her British—only one nation ruled the waves. 'They've seen us!' He waved his hands above his head.

Bows on, each second growing in size, grey and big, she bore down upon the little dhow.

Gradually the cheering of the crew faltered and subsided into an uneasy silence. Magnified by the still, hot air, huge on the velvety gloss of the ocean, lifting a bow wave of pearling white, the warship came on. No check in her speed, the ensign of her masthead streaming away from them so they could not see the colours.

'What are they going to do?' Sebastian asked aloud, and was answered by Flynn's voice. Sebastian glanced around. Balancing on his good leg with one arm draped around Mohammed's neck, Flynn was hopping across the deck towards him.

'I'll tell you what they're going to do! They're going to hit us smack-bang up the arse!' Flynn roared. 'That's the *Blücher*! That's a German cruiser!'

'They can't do that!' Sebastian protested.

'You'd like to bet? She's coming straight from the Rufiji delta—and my guess is she's had a chat with Fleischer. He's probably aboard her.' Flynn swayed against Mohammed, gasping with the pain of his leg before he went on. 'They're going to ram us, and then machine-gun anyone still floating.'

'We've got to make a life raft.'

'No time, Bassie. Look at her come!'

Less than five miles away, but swiftly narrowing the distance, the *Blücher*'s tall bows knifed towards them. Wildly Sebastian looked around the crowded deck, and he saw the pile of cork floats they had cut from the fish-nets.

Drawing his knife, he ran to one of the sacks of coconuts and cut the twine that closed the mouth. He slipped the knife back into its sheath, stooped, and up-ended the sack, spilling coconuts on to the deck. Then with the empty sack in his hand he ran to the pile of floats and dropped on his knees. In frantic haste he shovelled them into the sack, half filling it before he looked up again. The *Blücher* was two miles away, a tall tower of murderous grey steel.

With a length of rope Sebastian tied the sack closed and dragged it to where

Flynn stood supported by Mohammed.

'What are you doing?' Flynn demanded.

'Fixing you up! Lift your arms!' Flynn obeyed and Sebastian tied the free end of the rope around his chest at the level of his armpits. He paused to unlace and kick off his boots before speaking again. 'Mohammed, you stay with him. Hang on to the sack and don't let go.' He left them, trotting on bare feet to find his rifle propped against the poop. Buckling on his cartridge belt, he hurried back to the rail.

Sebastian Oldsmith was about to engage a nine-inch battle cruiser with a double-barrelled Gibbs ·500.

She was close now, hanging over them like a high cliff of steel. Even Sebastian could not miss a battle cruiser at two hundred yards, and the heavy bullets clanged against the armoured hull, ringing loudly above the hissing rush of the bow wave.

While he reloaded, Sebastian looked up at the line of heads in the bows of the *Blücher*; grinning faces below the white caps with their little swallow-tailed black ribbons. 'You bloody swines,' he shouted at them. Hatred stronger than he had ever dreamed possible, choked his voice. 'You filthy, bloody swine.' He lifted the rifle and fired without effect, and the *Blücher* hit the dhow.

It struck with a crash and the crackling roar of rending timber. It crushed her side and cut through in the screaming of dying men and the squeal of planking against steel.

It trod the dhow under, breaking her back, forcing her far below the surface. At the initial shock, Sebastian was hurled overboard, the rifle thrown from his hands. He struck the armoured plate of the cruiser a glancing blow and then dropped into the sea beside her. The thrust of the bow wave tumbled him aside, else he would have been dragged along the hull and his body shredded against the steel plate.

He surfaced just in time to suck a lungful of air before the turbulence of the great screws caught him and plucked him under again, driving him deep so the pressure stabbed like red-hot needles in his eardrums. He felt himself swirled end over end, buffeted, shaken vigorously as the water tore at his body.

Colour flashed and zigzagged behind his closed eyelids. There was a suffocating pain in his chest and his lungs pumped, urgently craving air, but he sealed his lips and kicked out with his legs, clawing at the water with his hands.

The churning wake of the cruiser released its grip upon him, and he was shot to the surface with such force that he broke clear to the waist before dropping back to drink air greedily. He unbuckled the heavy cartridge belt and let it sink before he looked about him.

The surface of the sea was scattered with floating debris, and a few bobbing wooden heads. Near him a section of torn planking rose in a burst of trapped air bubbles. Sebastian struck out for it and clung there, his legs hanging in the clear green water.

'Flynn,' he gasped. 'Flynn, where are you?'

A quarter of a mile away, the *Blücher* was circling slowly, long and menacing and shark-like, and he stared at it in hatred and in fear.

'Master!' Mohammed's voice behind him.

Sebastian turned quickly and saw the black face and the red face beside the floating sack of corks a hundred yards away. 'Flynn!'

'Goodbye, Bassie,' Flynn called. 'The old Hun is coming back to finish us off. Look! They've got machine guns set up on the bridge. See you on the other side, boy.'

Quickly Sebastian looked back at the cruiser and saw the clusters of white uniforms on the angle of her bridge.

'Ja, there are still some of them alive.' Through borrowed binoculars, Fleischer scanned the littered area of the wreck. 'You will use the Maxims, of course, Captain? It will be quicker than picking them off with rifles.'

Captain von Kleine did not answer. He stood tall on his bridge, slightly round-shouldered, staring out at the wreckage with his hands clasped behind him. 'There is something sad in the death of a ship,' he murmured. 'Even such a dirty little one as this.' Suddenly he straightened his shoulders and turned to Fleischer. 'Your launch is waiting for you at the mouth of the Rufiji. I will take you there, Commissioner.'

'But first the business of the survivors.'

Von Kleine's expression hardened. 'Commissioner, I sank that dhow in what I believed to be my duty. But now I am not sure that my judgement was not clouded by anger. I will not trespass further on my conscience by machine-gunning swimming civilians.'

'You will then pick them up. I must arrest them and give them trial.'

'I am not a policeman,' he paused and his expression softened a little. 'That one who fired the rifle at us. I think he must be a brave man. He is a criminal, perhaps, but I am not so old in the ways of the world that I do not love courage merely for its own sake. I would not like to know I have saved this man from the noose. Let the sea be the judge and the executioner.' He turned to his lieutenant. 'Kyller, prepare to drop one of the life rafts.' The lieutenant stared at him in disbelief. 'You heard me?'

'Yes, my Captain.'

'Then do it.' Ignoring Fleischer's squawks of protest, von Kleine crossed to the pilot. 'Alter course to pass the survivors at a distance of fifty metres.'

'Here she comes,' Flynn grinned tightly, without humour, and watched the cruiser swing ponderously towards them.

The cries of the swimmers around them, pleading mercy, were plaintive as the voices of sea birds—tiny on the immensity of the ocean.

'Flynn. Look at the bridge!' Sebastian's voice floated across to him. 'See him there. The grey uniform.'

Tears from the sting of sea salt in his wound, and the distortion of fever had blurred Flynn's vision, yet he could make out the spot of grey among the speckling of white uniforms on the bridge of the cruiser.

'Who is it?'

'You were right. It's Fleischer,' Sebastian shouted back, and Flynn began to curse.

'Hey, you filthy, fat butcher,' he bellowed, trying to drag himself up on to the floating sack of corks. 'Hey, you whore's chamber pot.' His voice carried above the murmur of the cruiser's engines running at dead-slow. 'Come on, you blood-smeared little pig.'

The tall hull of the cruiser was close now, so close he could see the bulky figure in grey turn to the tall white-uniformed officer beside him, gesticulating in what was clearly entreaty.

The officer turned away and moved to the rail of the bridge. He leaned out and waved to a group of seamen on the deck below him.

'That's right. Tell them to shoot. Let's get it over with. Tell them . . .'

A large square object was lifted over the rail by the gang below the bridge. It dropped and fell with a splash alongside.

Flynn's voice dried up, and he watched in disbelief as the white-clad officer lifted his right arm in a gesture that might have been a salute. The beat of the cruiser's engines mounted as it increased speed, and she swung away towards the west.

Flynn O'Flynn began to laugh, the cackling hysteria of relief and delirium. He rolled off the sack of corks and his head dropped forward, so the warm green water smothered his laughter. Mohammed took a handful of the grey hair and lifted his face to prevent him drowning.

14

Sebastian reached the raft, and grasped the rope that hung in loops around its sides. He paused to regain his breath before hauling himself up to lie gasping, the blood-warm seawater streaming from his sodden clothing, and watched the shape of the battle cruiser recede into the west.

'Master! Help me!'

The voice roused him and he sat up. Mohammed was struggling, dragging Flynn and the sack through the water. Among the floating wreckage a dozen others of the crew and the bearers were flapping their way towards the raft; the weaker swimmers were already failing, their cries becoming more pitiful, and their splashing more frenzied.

There were oars roped to the slatted deck of the raft. Quickly Sebastian cut one loose with his hunting knife and began rowing towards the pair. His progress was slow, for the raft was an ungainly bitch that balked and swung away from the thrust of the oar.

An Arab crewman reached the raft and scrambled aboard, then another, and another. Each of them freed an oar and helped with the rowing. They passed the body of one of the bearers floating just below the surface, both its legs cut off above the knees and the bone sticking out of the ragged meat of the stumps. This was not the only one—there was other human flotsam among the scattered wreckage, and the pinky-brown stains that drifted away on the current attracted the sharks.

The Arab beside Sebastian saw the first one and called out, pointing with the oar.

It came hunting, its fin waggling from side to side as it tacked up against the current, so that they could sense its excitement, the cold, unthinking excitement of Euselachii hunger. Below the surface, distorted and dark, showed the tapering length of its body. Not a big one. Perhaps nine feet in length and four hundred pound in weight, but big enough to chop a leg with one bite. No longer guided by the drift of blood-taste, picking up the vibrations of the swimmers, it straightened and came in on its first run.

'Shark!' Sebastian yelled at Flynn and Mohammed where they floundered ten yards away. And both of them panicked; no longer making for the raft, they tried to clamber on to the sack of corks. Terror has no logic. Their only concern was to lift their dangling legs from the water, but the sack was too small, too unstable and their panic attracted the shark's attention. It veered towards them, showing the full height of its curved triangular fin, each sweep of its tail breaking the surface as it drove in.

'This way,' shouted Sebastian. 'Come to the raft!' He was hacking at the water with the oar, while beside him the Arabs worked in equal dedication. 'This way, Flynn. For God's sake, this way.'

His voice penetrated their panic, and once more they struck out for the raft. But the shark was closing fast, long and dappled by sunlight through the surface ripple.

The sack was still tied to Flynn's body, and its resistance to the water slowed them as it dragged behind. The shark swerved and made its first pass; it seemed to hump up out of the water, and its mouth opened. The upper jaw bulged out, the lower jaw gaped, and the multiple rows of teeth came erect like the quills of a porcupine, *and it hit the sack.* Locking its jaws into the coarse jute material, worrying it, still humped out of the water, shaking its blunt head clumsily, scattering a spray of water drops that flew like shattered glass in the sun.

'Grab here!' commanded Sebastian, leaning out to offer the blade of the oar to the pair in the water. They clutched at it with the strength of fear, and Sebastian drew them in.

But the sack and the shark were still attached to Flynn, its threshing threatening to break Flynn's hold on the life-line around the raft.

Dropping to his knees, Sebastian fumbled the knife from its sheath and sawed at the rope. It parted. The shark, still worrying the sack, worked away from the raft and Sebastian helped the Arabs to drag first Flynn, and then Mohammed, over the side.

They were not finished yet. There were still half a dozen men in the water.

Realizing its error at last, the shark relinquished its hold on the sacking. It backed away. For a moment it hung motionless, puzzled, then it circled out towards the nearest sounds of splashing. One of the gun-boys, clawing at the water in exhausted dog-paddle. The shark hit him in the side, and pulled him under. Moments later he reappeared, his mouth an open pink cave as he screamed, the water about him clouded dark red-brown by his own blood. Again he was pulled under as the shark hit his legs, but again he floated. This time face down, wriggling feebly, and the shark circled him, dashing in to chop off a mouthful of his flesh, backing away to gulp it down before coming in again.

Then there was another shark, two more, ten, so many that Sebastian could not count them, as they circled and wove in ecstatic greed, until the sea around the raft trembled and swirled in agitation.

Sebastian and his Arabs managed to drag two more of the crew into the raft and they had a third half out of the water when a six-foot white-pointer shot up from the depths, and fastened on his thigh with such violence that it almost jerked all of them overboard. But they steadied themselves and held on to the man's arms, frozen in this gruesome tug-of-war, while the shark worried the leg, so dog-like in its determination that Sebastian expected it to growl.

Little Mohammed staggered to his feet, snatched up an oar and swung it against the pointed snout with all his strength. They had dragged the shark's head from the water, and the oar fell on it with a series of rubbery thumps, but the shark held on. Fresh, bright blood squirted and trickled from the leg in its jaws, running down the shark's glistening snake-like head into the open slits of its gill covers.

'Hold him!' gasped Sebastian, and drew his knife. The raft rocking crazily under him, he leaned over the man's outstretched body and drove the knife blade into the shark's expressionless little eye. It popped in a burst of clear fluid, and the shark stiffened and trembled. Sebastian withdrew the blade, and stabbed into the other eye. With a convulsive gulp the shark opened its jaws and slid back into the sea to meander blindly away.

There were no more swimmers. The little group on the raft huddled together and watched the shark pack milling hungrily, seeming to sniff at the tainted water as they gathered the last morsels of meat.

The shark victim hosed the deck with his severed femoral artery and died before any of them could arouse themselves to apply a tourniquet.

'Push him over,' grunted Flynn.

'No,' Sebastian shook his head.

'Chrissake, we're crowded enough as it is. Chuck the poor bastard over.'

'Later on, not now.' Sebastian could not stand to watch the sharks squabble over the corpse.

'Mohammed, get a couple of your lads on the oars. I want to pick up as many of those coconuts as we can.'

By the time darkness stopped them, they had retrieved fifty-two of the floating coconuts, sufficient to keep the seven of them thirst-free for a week.

It was cold that night. They crowded together for warmth and watched the underwater pyrotechnics, as the shark pack circled the raft in phosphorescent splendour.

15

'You've got to cut for it,' Flynn whispered, and he shivered with cold in the burning heat of the midday sun.

'I don't know anything about it,' Sebastian protested, yet he could see that Flynn was dying.

'No more do I. But this is certain—you've got to do it soon . . .' Flynn's eyes had sunk into plum-coloured cavities and the smell of his breath was that of something long dead.

Staring at the leg, Sebastian had difficulty controlling his nausea. It was swollen fat and purple. The bullet hole was covered with crusty black scab, but Sebastian caught a whiff of the putrefaction under it—and this time his nausea came up acid-sweet into the back of his throat. He swallowed it.

'You've got to do it, Bassie boy.'

Sebastian nodded, and tentatively laid his hand on the leg. Immediately he jerked his fingers away, surprised by the heat of the skin.

'You've got to do it,' urged Flynn. 'Feel for the slug. It's not deep. Just under the skin.'

He felt the lump. It moved under his fingers, the size of a green acorn in the taut hot flesh.

'It's going to hurt like Billy-o.' Sebastian's voice was hoarse.

The rowers were resting on their oars, watching with frank curiosity, while the raft eddied and swung in the drift of the Mozambique current. Above them the sail that Sebastian had rigged from salvaged planking and canvas, flapped wearily, throwing a shadow across the leg.

'Mohammed, you and one other to hold the master's shoulders. Two others to keep his legs still.'

Flynn lay quiescent, pinioned beneath them on the slats of the deck.

Sebastian knelt over him, gathering his resolve. The knife he had sharpened against the metal edge of the raft, and then scrubbed clean with coconut fibre and seawater. He had sluiced the leg also, and washed his hands until the skin tingled. Beside him on the deck stood half a coconut shell containing perhaps an ounce of evaporated salt scraped from the deck and the sail, ready to pack into the open wound. 'Ready?' he whispered.

'Ready,' grunted Flynn, and Sebastian located the lump of the bullet and drew the edge of the blade across it timidly. Flynn gasped, but human skin was tougher than Sebastian allowed. It did not part.

'Goddamn you!' Flynn was sweating already. 'Don't play with it. Cut, man, cut!'

This time Sebastian slashed, and the flesh split open under the blade. He dropped the knife and drew back in horror as the infection bubbled up through the lips of the knife wound. It looked like yellow custard mixed with prune juice–and the smell of it filled his nostrils and his throat.

'Go for the slug. Go for it with your fingers.' Flynn writhed beneath the men who held him. 'Hurry. Hurry. I can't take much more.'

Steeling himself, closing his throat against the vomit that threatened to vent at any moment, Sebastian slipped his little finger into the slit. Hooking with it for the bullet, finding it, easing it up although tissue clung to it reluctantly, until it popped from the wound and dropped on to the deck. A fresh gush of warm poison followed it out, flowing over Sebastian's hand, and he crawled to the edge of the raft, choking and gagging.

16

'If only we had some red cloth.' Flynn sat against the rickety mast. He was still very weak but four days ago the fever had broken with the release of the poison.

'What would you do with it?' Sebastian asked.

'Catch me one of those dolphins. Man, I'm so goddamned hungry I'd eat it raw.'

A four-day diet of coconut pulp and milk had left all their bellies grumbling.

'Why red?'

'They go for red. Make a lure.'

'You haven't any hooks or line.'

'Tie it to a bit of twine from the sack and tease them up to the surface–then harpoon one with your knife tied to an oar.'

Sebastian was silent, peering thoughtfully over the side at the deep flashes of gold where the shoal of dolphin played under the raft. 'It's got to be red, hey?' he asked, and Flynn looked at him sharply.

'Yeah. It's got to be red.'

'Well . . .' Sebastian hesitated, and then flushed with embarrassment under his tropical sunburn.

'What's wrong with you?'

Still blushing, Sebastian stood up and loosened his belt–then, shyly as a bride on her wedding night, he drew down his pants.

'My God,' breathed Flynn in shock, as he held up his hand to shield his eyes.

'Hau! Hau!' was the chorus of admiration from the crew.

'Got them at Harrods,' said Sebastian with becoming modesty.

Red, Flynn had asked for—but Sebastian's underpants were the brightest, most beautiful red; the most vivid sunset and roses red, he could have imagined. They hung in oriental splendour to Sebastian's knees.

'Pure silk,' said Sebastian, fingering the cloth. 'Ten shillings a pair.'

'Whoa now! Come on, little fishy. Come on here,' Flynn whispered as he lay on his belly, head and shoulders over the edge of the raft. On its thread of twine, the scrap of red danced deep in the green water. A long, slithering flash of gold shot towards it, and Flynn jerked the twine away at the last instant. The dolphin swirled and darted back. Again Flynn jerked the twine. Chameleon lines and dots of excitement showed against the gold of the dolphin's body. 'That's it, fishy. Chase it.' The other fish of the shoal joined hunt, forming a sparkling planetary system of movement around the lure. 'Get ready!'

'I'm ready.' Sebastian stood over him, poised like a javelin thrower. In the excitement he had forgotten to don his pants and his shirt-tails flapped around his thighs in a most undignified manner. But his legs were long and finely muscled, the legs of an athlete. 'Get back!' he snapped at the crew who were crowded around him so that the raft was listing dangerously. 'Get back—give me room,' and he hefted the oar with the long hunting knife lashed to the tip.

'Here they come.' Flynn's voice trembled with excitement as he worked the scrap of red cloth upwards, and the shoal followed it. 'Now!' he shouted as a single fish broke the surface—four feet of flashing gold, and Sebastian lunged. The steady hand and eye that had once clean-bowled the great Frank Woolley directed the oar. Sebastian hit the dolphin an inch behind the eye, and the blade slipped through to lacerate the gills.

For a few seconds the oar came alive in his hands as the dolphin twitched and fought on the blade, but there were no barbs to hold in the flesh, and the fish slipped from the knife.

'God damn it to hell!' bellowed Flynn.

'Dash it all!' echoed Sebastian.

But ten feet down the dolphin was mortally wounded; it jigged and whipped like a golden kite in a high wind while the rest of the shoal scattered.

Sebastian dropped the oar and began stripping his shirt.

'What are you doing?' demanded Flynn.

'Going after it.'

'You're mad. Sharks!'

'I'm so hungry, I'll eat a shark also,' and he dived over the side. Thirty seconds later he surfaced, blowing like a grampus but grinning triumphantly, with the dead dolphin clasped lovingly to his bosom.

They ate strips of raw fish seasoned with evaporated salt, squatting around the mutilated carcass of the dolphin.

'Well, I've paid a guinea for worse meals than this,' said Sebastian, and belched softly. 'Oh, I beg your pardon.'

'Granted,' Flynn grunted with his mouth full of fish; and they eyeing Sebastian's nudity with a world-weary eye, 'Stop boasting and put your pants on before you trip over it.'

Flynn O'Flynn was slowly, very slowly, revising his estimate of Sebastian Oldsmith.

17

The rowers had long since lost any enthusiasm they might have had for the task. They kept at it only in response to offers of bodily violence by Flynn–and the example set by Sebastian, who worked tirelessly. The thin layer of fat that had sheathed Sebastian's muscles was long since consumed, and his sun-baked body was a Michelangelo sculpture, as he leaned and dug and pulled the oar.

Six days they had dragged the raft across the southward push of the current. Six days of sun-blazing calm, with the sea flattening, until now in the late afternoon, it looked like an endless sheet of smooth green velvet.

'No,' said Mohammed. 'That means, *The two porcupines make love under the blanket.*'

'Oh!' Sebastian repeated the phrase without interrupting the rhythm of his rowing. Sebastian was a dogged pupil of Swahili, making up in determination what he lacked in brilliance. Mohammed was proud of him, and opposed any attempt by the other members of the crew to usurp his position as chief tutor.

'That's all right about the porcupines shagging themselves to a standstill,' grunted Flynn. 'But what does this mean . . .?' and he spoke in Swahili.

'It means, *Big winds will blow across the sea*,' interpreted Sebastian, and glowed with achievement.

'And I'm not joking either.' Flynn stood up, crouching to favour his bad leg, and shaded his eyes to peer into the east. 'You see that line of cloud?'

Laying aside the oar, Sebastian stood beside him and flexed the aching muscles of his back and shoulders. Immediately all activity ceased among the other rowers.

'Keep going, me beauties!' growled Flynn, and reluctantly they obeyed. Flynn turned back to Sebastian. 'You see it?'

'Yes.' It was drawn like a kohl line across the eyelid of a Hindu woman, smeared black along the horizon.

'Well, Bassie, there's the wind you've been griping about. But, my friend, I think it's a little more than you bargained for.'

In the darkness they heard it coming from far away, a muted sibilance in the night. One by one, the fat stars were blotted out in the east as dark cloud spread out to fill half the midnight sky.

A single gust hit the raft, and flogged the makeshift sail with a clap like a shotgun, and the sleepers woke and sat up.

'Hang on to those fancy underpants,' muttered Flynn, 'or you'll get them blown right up your backside.'

Another gust, another lull, but already there was the boisterous slapping of small waves against the sides of the raft.

'I'd better get that sail down.'

'You had, and all,' agreed Flynn, 'and while you're at it, use the rope to fix life-lines for us.' In haste, spurred on by the rising hiss of the wind, they lashed themselves to the slats of the deck.

The main force of the wind spun the raft like a top, splattering them with spray; the spray was icy cold in the warm rush of the wind. The wind was steady now and the raft moved uneasily—the jerky motion of an animal restless at the prick of spurs.

'At least it will push us towards the land,' Sebastian shouted across at Flynn.

'Bassie, boy, you think of the cutest things,' and the first wave came aboard, smothering Flynn's voice, breaking over their prostrate bodies, and then streaming out through the slatted deck. The raft wallowed in dismay, then gathered itself to meet the next rush of the sea.

Under the steady fury of the wind, the sea came up more swiftly than Sebastian believed was possible. Within minutes the waves were breaking over the raft with such weight as to squeeze the breath from their lungs, submerging them completely, driving the raft under before its buoyancy reasserted itself and lifted it, canting crazily, and they could gasp for air in the smother of spray.

Waiting for the lulls, Sebastian inched his way across the deck until he reached Flynn. 'How are you bearing up?' he bellowed.

'Great, just great,' and another wave drove them under.

'Your leg?' spluttered Sebastian as they came up.

'For Chrissake, stop yapping,' and they went under again.

It was completely dark, no star, no silver of moon, but each line of breaking water glowed in dull, phosphorescent malevolence as it dashed down upon them, warning them to suck air and cling with cramped fingers hooked into the slats.

For all eternity Sebastian lived in darkness, battered by the wind and the wild, flying water. The aching chill of his body dulled out into numbness. Slowly his mind emptied of conscious thought, so when a bigger wave scoured them, he heard the tearing sound of deck slats pulling loose, and the lost wail as one of the Arabs was washed away into the night sea—but the sound had no meaning to him.

Twice he vomited seawater that he had swallowed, but it had no taste in his mouth, and he let it run heedlessly down his chin and warm on to his chest, to be washed away by the next torrential wave.

His eyes burned without pain from the harsh rake of wind-flung spray, and he blinked them owlishly at each advancing wave. It seemed, in time, that he could see more clearly, and he turned his head slowly. Beside him, Flynn's face was a leprous blotch in the darkness. This puzzled him, and he lay and thought about it but no solution came, until he looked beyond the next wave, and saw the faint promise of a new day show pale through the black massed cloud-banks.

He tried to speak, but no sound came for his throat was swollen closed with the salt, and his tongue was tingling numb. Again he tried. 'Dawn coming,' he croaked, but beside him Flynn lay like a corpse frozen in rigor mortis.

Slowly the light grew over that mad, grey sea but the scudding black cloud-banks tried desperately to oppose its coming.

Now the seas were more awesome in their raging insanity. Each mountain of glassy grey rose high above the raft, shielding it for a few seconds from the whip of the wind, its crest blowing off like the plume of an Etruscan helmet, before it slid down, collapsing upon itself in the tumbling roar of breaking water.

Each time, the men on the raft shrank flat on the deck, and waited in bovine acceptance to be smothered again beneath the white deluge.

Once, the raft rode high and clear in a freak flat of the storm, and Sebastian looked about him. The canvas and rope, the coconuts and the other pathetic accumulation of their possessions were all gone. The sea had ripped away many of the deck slats so that the metal floats of the raft were exposed; it had torn the very clothing from them so they were clad in sodden tatters. Of the seven men who had ridden the raft the previous day, only he and Flynn, Mohammed and one more, were left–the other three were gone, gobbled up by the hungry sea.

Then the storm struck again, so that the raft reeled and reared to the point of capsizing.

Sebastian sensed it first in the altered action of the waves; they were steeper, marching closer together. Then, through the clamour of the storm, a new sound, like that of a cannon fired at irregular intervals with varying charges of gunpowder. He realized suddenly that he had been hearing this sound for some time, but only now had it penetrated the stupor of his fatigue.

He lifted his head, and every nerve of his being shrieked in protest at the effort. He looked about, but the sea stood up around him like a series of grey walls that limited his vision to a circle of fifty yards. Yet that discordant boom, boom, boom, was louder now and more insistent.

In the short, choppy waves, a side-break caught the raft and tossed it high–lifting him so he could see the land; so close that the palm trees showed sharply, bending their stems to the wind and threshing their long fronds in panic. He saw the beach, grey-white in the gloom and, beyond it, far beyond it, rose the watery blue of the high ground.

These things had small comfort for him when he saw the reef. It bared its black teeth at him, snarling through the white water that burst like cannon-fire upon it before cascading on into the comparative quiet of the lagoon. The raft was riding down towards it.

'Flynn,' he croaked. 'Flynn, listen to me!' but the older man did not move. His eyes were fixed open and only the movement of his chest, as he breathed, proved him still alive. 'Flynn.' Sebastian released one of his clawed hands from its grip on the wooden slatting. 'Flynn!' he said, and struck him across the cheek.

'Flynn!' The head turned towards Sebastian, the eyes blinked, the mouth opened, but no voice spoke.

Another wave broke over the raft. This time the cold, malicious rush of it stirred Sebastian, roused a little of his failing strength. He shook the water from his head. 'Land,' he whispered. 'Land,' and Flynn stared at him dully.

Two lines of surf away, the reef showed its ragged back again. Clinging with only one hand to the slatting, Sebastian fumbled the knife from its sheath and hacked clumsily at the life-line that bound him to the deck. It parted. He reached over and cut Flynn's line, sawing frantically at the wet hemp. That done, he slid back on his belly until he reached Mohammed and freed him also. The little African stared at him with bloodshot eyes from his wrinkled monkey face.

'Swim,' whispered Sebastian. 'Must swim,' and re-sheathing the knife, he tried to crawl over Mohammed to reach the Arab but the next wave caught the raft, rearing up under it as it felt the push of the land, rearing so steeply that this time the raft was overturned and they were thrown from it into the seething turmoil of the reef.

Sebastian hit the water flat, and was hardly under, before he had surfaced again. Beside him, close enough to touch, Flynn emerged. In the strength born of the fear of death, Flynn caught at Sebastian, locking both arms around his chest. The same wave that had capsized them, had poured over the reef and covered it completely, so that where the coral fangs had been was now only a frothy area of disturbed water. In it bobbed the debris of the raft, shattered into pieces against the reef. The mutilated corpse of the Arab was still roped to a piece of the wreckage. Flynn and Sebastian were locked like lovers in each other's arms and the next wave, following close upon the first, lifted them, and shot them forward over the submerged reef.

In one great swoop that left their guts behind them, they were carried over the coral which could have minced them into jelly, and tumbled into the quiet lagoon. With them went little Mohammed, and what remained of the raft.

The lagoon was covered by a thick scum of wind spume, creamy as the head of a good beer. So when the three of them staggered waist-deep towards the beach, supporting each other with arms around shoulders, they were coated with white froth. It made them look like a party of drunken snowmen returning home after a long night out.

18

Mohammed squatted with a pile of madafu, the shiny green coconuts, beside him. The beach was littered with them, for the storm had stripped the trees. He worked in feverish haste with Sebastian's hunting knife, his face frosted with dried salt, mumbling to himself through cracked and swollen lips, shaving down through the white, fibrous material of the shell, until he exposed the hollow centre filled with its white custard and effervescent milk. At this point the madafu was snatched from his hands by either Flynn or Sebastian. His despair growing deeper, he watched for a second the two white men drinking with heads thrown back, throats pulsing as they swallowed, spilled milk trickling from the corners of their mouths, eyes closed tight in their intense pleasure; then he picked up another nut and got to work on it. He opened a dozen before he was able to satiate the other two, and he held the next nut to his own mouth and whimpered with eagerness.

Then they slept. Bellies filled with the sweet, rich milk, they sagged backwards on the sand and slept the rest of that day and that night, and when they woke, the wind had dropped, although the sea still burst like an artillery bombardment on the reef.

'Now,' said Flynn, 'where, in the name of the devil and all his angels, are we?' Neither Sebastian nor Mohammed answered him. 'We were six days on the raft. We could have drifted hundreds of miles south before the storm pushed us in.' He frowned as he considered the problem. 'We might even have reached Portuguese Mozambique. We could be as far as the Zambesi river.'

Flynn focused his attention on Mohammed. 'Go!' he said. 'Search for a river, or a mountain that you know. Better still, find a village where we can get food—and bearers.'

'I'll go also,' Sebastian volunteered.

'You wouldn't know the difference between the Zambesi and the

Mississippi,' Flynn grunted impatiently. 'You'd be lost after the first hundred yards.'

Mohammed was gone for two days and a half, but Sebastian and Flynn ate well in his absence.

Under a sun shelter of palm fronds they feasted three times a day on crab and sand-clams, and big green rock-lobster which Sebastian fished from the lagoon, baking them in their shells over the fire that Flynn coaxed from two dry sticks.

On the first night the entertainment was provided by Flynn. For some years now, Flynn's intake of gin had averaged a daily two bottles. The abrupt cessation of supply resulted in a delayed but classic visitation of *delirium tremens*. He spent half the night hobbling up and down the beach brandishing a branch of driftwood, and hurling obscenities at the phantoms that had come to plague him. There was one purple cobra in particular which pursued him doggedly, and it was only after Flynn had beaten it noisily to death behind a palm tree, that he allowed Sebastian to lead him back to the shelter and seat him beside the camp-fire. Then he got the shakes. He shook like a man on a jack-hammer. His teeth rattled together with such violence that Sebastian was sure they must shatter. Gradually, however, the shakes subsided and by the following noon he was able to eat three large rock-lobsters and then collapse into a death-like sleep.

He woke in the late evening, looking as well as Sebastian had ever seen him, to greet the returning Mohammed and the dozen tall Angoni tribesmen who accompanied him. They returned Flynn's greeting with respect. From Beira to Dar es Salaam, the name 'Fini' was held in universal awe by the indigenous peoples. Legend credited him with the powers far above the natural order. His exploits, his skill with the rifle, his volcanic temper, and his seeming immunity from death and retribution, had formed the foundation of a belief that Flynn had carefully fostered. They said in whispers around the night fires when the women and the children were not listening that 'Fini' was in truth a reincarnation of the Monomatapa. They said further that in the intervening period between his death as the Great King and his latest birth as 'Fini', he had been first a monstrous crocodile, and then *Mowana Lisa*, the most notorious man-eating lion in the history of East Africa, a predator responsible for at least three hundred human killings. The day, twenty-five years previously, that Flynn had stepped ashore at Port Amelia was the exact day that *Mowana Lisa* had been shot dead by the Portuguese Chef D'Post at Sofala. All men knew these things—and only an idiot would take chances with 'Fini'—hence the respect with which they greeted him now.

Flynn recognized one of the men. 'Luti,' he roared, 'you scab on an hyena's backside!'

Luti smiled broadly, and bobbed his head in pleasure at being singled out by Flynn.

'Mohammed,' Flynn turned to his man. 'Where did you find him? Are we near his village?'

'We are a day's march away.'

'In which direction?'

'North.'

'Then we are in Portuguese territory!' exalted Flynn. 'We must have drifted down past the Rovuma river.'

The Rovuma river was the frontier between Portuguese Mozambique and

German East Africa. Once in Portuguese territory, Flynn was immune from the wrath of the Germans. All their efforts at extraditing him from the Portuguese had proved unsuccessful, for Flynn had a working agreement with the Chef D'Post, Mozambique, and through him with the Governor in Lourenço Marques. In a manner of speaking, these two officials were sleeping partners in Flynn's business, and were entitled to a quarterly financial statement of Flynn's activities, and an agreed percentage of the profits.

'You can relax, Bassie boy. Old Fleischer can't touch us now. And in three or four days we'll be home.'

The first leg of the journey took them to Luti's village. Lolling in their maschilles, hammock-like litters slung beneath a long pole and carried by four of Luti's men at a synchronized jog trot, Flynn and Sebastian were borne smoothly out of the coastal lowland into the hills and bush country.

The litter-bearers sang as they ran, and their deep melodious voices, coupled with the swinging motion of the maschille, lulled Sebastian into a mood of deep contentment. Occasionally he dozed. Where the path was wide enough to allow the maschilles to travel side by side, he lay and chatted with Flynn, at other times he watched the changing country with the animal life along the way. It was better than London Zoo.

Each time Sebastian saw something new, he called across for Flynn to identify it.

In every glade and clearing were herds of the golden brown impala; delicate little creatures that watched them in wide-eyed curiosity as they passed.

Troops of guinea-fowl, like a dark cloud shadow on the earth, scratched and chittered on the banks of every stream.

Heavy, yellow eland, with their stubby horns and swinging dewlaps, trotting in Indian file, formed a regal frieze along the edge of the bush.

Sable and roan antelope; purple-brown waterbuck, with a perfect circle of white branded on their rumps; buffalo, big and black and ugly; giraffe; dainty little klipspringer, standing like chamois on the tumbled granite boulders of a kopje. The whole land seethed and skittered with life.

There were trees so strange in shape and size and foliage that Sebastian could hardly credit them as existing. Swollen baobabs, fifty feet in circumference, standing awkwardly as prehistoric monsters, fat pods filled with cream of tartar hanging from their deformed branches. There were forests of msasa trees, leaves not green as leaves should be, but rose and chocolate and red. Fever trees sixty feet high, with bright yellow trunks, shedding their bark like the brittle parchment of a snake's skin. Groves of mopani, whose massed foliage glittered a shiny, metallic green in the sun; and in the jungle growth along the river banks, the lianas climbed up like long, grey worms and hung in loops and festoons among the wild fig and the buffalo-bean vines and the tree ferns.

'Why haven't we seen any sign of elephant?' Sebastian asked.

'Me and my boys worked this territory over about six months ago,' Flynn explained. 'I guess they just moved on a little—probably up north across the Rovuma.'

In the late afternoon they descended a stony path into a valley, and for the first time Sebastian saw the permanent habitations of man. In irregular shaped plots, the bottom land of the valley was cultivated, and the rich black soil threw up lush green stands of millet, while on the banks of the little stream stood Luti's village; shaggy grass huts, shaped like beehives, each with a circular mud-walled granary standing on stilts beside it. The huts were arranged in a rough circle around an open space where the earth was packed hard by the passage of bare feet.

The entire population turned out to welcome Flynn: three hundred souls, from hobbling old white heads with grinning toothless gums, down to infants held on mothers' naked hip, who did not interrupt their feeding but clung like fat black limpets with hands and mouth to the breast.

Through the crowd that ululated and clapped hands in welcome, Flynn and Sebastian were carried to the chief's hut and there they descended from the maschilles.

Flynn and the old chief greeted each other affectionately; Flynn because of favours received and because of future favours yet to be asked for, and the chief because of Flynn's reputation and the fact that wherever Flynn travelled, he usually left behind him large quantities of good, red meat.

'You come to hunt elephants?' the chief asked, looking hopefully for Flynn's rifle.

'No.' Flynn shook his head. 'I return from a journey to a far place.'

'From where?'

In answer, Flynn looked significantly at the sky and repeated, 'From a far place.'

There was an awed murmur from the crowd and the chief nodded sagely. It was clear to all of them that 'Fini' must have been to visit and commune with his *alter ego*, Monomatapa.

'Will you stay long at our village?' again hopefully.

'I will stay tonight only. I leave again in the dawn.'

'Ah!' Disappointment. 'We had hoped to welcome you with a dance. Since we heard of your coming, we have prepared.'

'No,' Flynn repeated. He knew a dance could last three or four days.

'There is a great brewing of palm wine which is only now ready for drinking,' the chief tried again, and this time his argument hit Flynn like a charging rhinoceros. Flynn had been many days without liquor.

'My friend,' said Flynn, and he could feel the saliva spurting out from under his tongue in anticipation. 'I cannot stay to dance with you but I will drink a small gourd of palm wine to show my love for you and your village.' Then turning to Sebastian he warned, 'I wouldn't touch this stuff, Bassie, if I were you—it's real poison.'

'Right,' agreed Sebastian. 'I'm going down to the river to wash.'

'You do that,' and Flynn lifted the first gourd of palm wine lovingly to his lips.

Sebastian's progress to the river resembled a Roman triumph. The entire village lined the bank to watch his necessarily limited ablutions with avid interest, and a buzz of awe went up when he disrobed to his underpants.

'Bwana Manali,' they chorused. 'Lord of the Red Cloth,' and the name stuck.

As a farewell gift the headman presented Flynn with four gourds of palm wine, and begged him to return soon—bringing his rifle with him.

They marched hard all that day and when they camped at nightfall, Flynn was semi-paralysed with palm wine, while Sebastian shivered and his teeth chattered uncontrollably.

From the swamps of the Rufiji delta, Sebastian had brought with him a souvenir of his visit—his first full go of malaria.

They reached Lalapanzi the following day, a few hours before the crisis of Sebastian's fever. Lalapanzi was Flynn's base camp and the name meant 'Lie Down', or more accurately, 'The Place of Rest'.

It was in the hills of a tiny tributary of the great Rovuma river, a hundred miles from the Indian Ocean, but only ten miles from German territory across the river. Flynn believed in living close to his principal place of business.

Had Sebastian been in full possession of his senses, and not wandering in the hot shadow land of malaria, he would have been surprised by the camp at Lalapanzi. It was not what anybody who knew Flynn O'Flynn would have expected.

Behind a palisade of split bamboo to protect the lawns and gardens from the attentions of the duiker and steenbok and kudu, it glowed like a green jewel in the sombre brown of the hills. Much hard work and patience must have gone into damming the stream, and digging the irrigation furrows, which suckled the lawns and flower-beds and the vegetable garden. Three indigenous fig trees dwarfed the buildings, crimson frangipani burst like fireworks against the green kikuyu grass, beds of bright barberton daisies ringed the gentle terraces that fell away to the stream, and a bougainvillaea creeper smothered the main building in a profusion of dark green and purple.

Behind the long bungalow, with its wide, open veranda, stood half a dozen circular rondavels, all neatly capped with golden thatch and gleaming painfully white, with burned limestone paint, in the sunlight.

The whole had about it an air of feminine order and neatness. Only a woman, and a determined one at that, could have devoted so much time and pain to building up such a speck of prettiness in the midst of brown rock and harsh thorn veld.

She stood on the veranda in the shade like a valkyrie, tall and sun-browned and angry. The full-length dress of faded blue was crisp with new ironing, and the neat mends in the fabric invisible except at close range. Gathered close about her waist, her skirt ballooned out over her woman's hips and fell to her ankles, slyly concealing the long straight legs beneath. Folded across her stomach, her arms were an amber brown frame for the proud double bulge of her bosom, and the thick braid of black hair that hung to her waist twitched like the tail of an angry lioness. A face too young for the marks of hardship and loneliness that were chiselled into it, was harder now by the expression of distaste it wore as she watched Flynn and Sebastian arriving.

They lolled in their maschilles, unshaven, dressed in filthy rags, hair matted with sweat and dust; Flynn full of palm wine, and Sebastian full of fever—although it was impossible to distinguish the symptoms of their separate disorders.

'May I ask where you've been these last two months, Flynn Patrick O'Flynn?' Although she tried to speak like a man, yet her voice had a lift and a ring to it.

'You may not ask, daughter!' Flynn shouted back defiantly.

'You're drunk again!'

'And if I am?' roared Flynn. 'You're as bad as that mother of yours (may her soul rest in peace), always going on and on. Never a civil word of welcome for your old Daddy, who's been away trying to earn an honest crust.'

The girl's eyes switched to the maschille that carried Sebastian, and narrowed in mounting outrage. 'Sweet merciful heavens, and what's this you've brought home with you now?'

Sebastian grinned inanely, and tried valiantly to sit up as Flynn introduced him. 'That is Sebastian Oldsmith. My very dear friend, Sebastian Oldsmith.'

'He's also drunk!'

'Listen, Rosa. You show some respect.' Flynn struggled to climb from his maschille.

'He's drunk,' Rosa repeated grimly. 'Drunk as a pig. You can take him straight back and leave him where you found him. He's not coming in this house.' She turned away, pausing only a moment at the front door to add, 'That goes for you also, Flynn O'Flynn. I'll be waiting with the shotgun. You just put one foot on the veranda before you're sober—and I'll blow it clean off.'

'Rosa—wait—he isn't drunk, please,' wailed Flynn, but the fly-screen door had slammed closed behind her.

Flynn teetered uncertainly at the foot of the veranda stairs, for a moment it looked as though he might be foolhardy enough to put his daughter's threat to the test, but he was not that drunk.

'Women,' he mourned. 'The good Lord protect us,' and he led his little caravan around the back of the bungalow to the farthest of the rondavel huts. This room was sparsely furnished in anticipation of Flynn's regular periods of exile from the main building.

19

Rosa O'Flynn closed the front door behind her and leaned back against it wearily. Slowly her chin sagged down to her chest, and she closed her eyes to imprison the itchy tears beneath the lids, but one of them squeezed through and quivered like a fat, glistening grape on her lashes, before falling to splash on the stone floor.

'Oh, Daddy, Daddy,' she whispered. It was an expression of those months of aching loneliness. The long, slow slide of days when she had searched desperately for work to fill her hands and her mind. The nights when, locked alone in her room with a loaded shotgun beside her bed, she had lain and listened to the sounds of the African bush beyond the window, afraid then of everything, even the four devoted African servants sleeping soundly with their families in their little compound behind the bungalow.

Waiting, waiting for Flynn to return. Lifting her head in the noonday and standing listening, hoping to hear the singing of his bearers as they came down the valley. And each hour the fear and the resentment building up within her. Fear that he might not come, and resentment that he left her for so long.

Now he had come. He had come drunk and filthy, with some oafish ruffian as a companion, and all her loneliness and fear had vented itself in that shrewish outburst. She straightened and pushed herself away from the door. Listlessly she walked through the shady cool rooms of the bungalow, spread with a rich profusion of animal skins and rough native-made furniture, until she reached her own room and sank down on the bed.

Beneath her unhappiness was a restlessness, a formless, undirected longing for something she did not understand. It was a new thing; only in these last few years had she become aware of it. Before she had gloried in the companionship of her father, never having experienced and, therefore, never missing the society of others. She had taken it as the natural order of things that much of

her time must be spent completely alone with only the wife of old Mohammed
to replace her natural mother—the young Portuguese girl who had died in the
struggle to give life to Rosa.

She knew the land as a slum child knows the city. It was her land and she
loved it.

Now all of it was changing, she was uncertain, without bearings in this sea of
new emotion. Lonely, irritable—and afraid.

A timid knocking on the back door of the bungalow roused her, and she felt a
leap of hope within her. Her anger at Flynn had long ago abated—now he had
made the first overture she could welcome him to the bungalow without
sacrifice of pride.

Quickly she bathed her face in the china wash-basin beside her bed, and
patted her hair into order before the mirror, before going through to answer
the knock.

Old Mohammed stood outside, shuffling his feet and grinning ingratiat-
ingly. He stood in almost as great an awe of Rosa's temper as that of Flynn
himself. It was with relief, therefore, that he saw her smile.

'Mohammed, you old rascal,' and he bobbed his head with pleasure.

'You are well, Little Long Hair?'

'I am well, Mohammed—and I can see you are also.'

'The Lord Fini asks that you send blankets and quinine.'

'Why?' Rosa frowned quickly. 'Is the fever on him?'

'Not on him, but on Manali, his friend.'

'Is he bad?'

'He is very bad.'

The rich hostility that her first glimpse of Sebastian had invoked in Rosa,
wavered a little. She felt the woman in her irresistibly drawn towards anything
wounded or sick, even such an uncouth and filthy specimen as she had seen
Sebastian to be.

'I will come,' she decided aloud, while silently qualifying her surrender by
deciding that under no circumstances would she let him in the house. Sick or
healthy, he would stay out there in the rondavel.

Armed with a pitcher of boiled drinking water, and a bottle of quinine
tablets, closely attended by Mohammed carrying an armful of cheap trade
blankets, she crossed to the rondavel and entered.

She entered it at an unpropitious moment. For Flynn had spent the last ten
minutes exhuming the bottle he had so carefully buried some months before
beneath the earthen floor of the rondavel. Being a man of foresight, he had
caches of gin scattered in unlikely places around the camp, and now, in
delicious anticipation, he was carefully wiping damp earth from the neck of the
bottle with the tail of his shirt. So engrossed with this labour he was not aware
of Rosa's presence until the bottle was snatched from his hands, and thrown
through the open side window to pop and tinkle as it burst.

'Now what did you do that for?' Flynn was hurt as deeply as a mother
deprived of her infant.

'For the good of your soul.' Icily Rosa turned from him to the inert figure on
the bed, and her nose wrinkled as she caught a whiff of unwashed body and
fever. 'Where did you find this one?' she asked without expecting an answer.

20

Five grains of quinine washed down Sebastian's throat with scalding tea, heated stones were packed around his body, and half a dozen blankets swaddled him to begin the sweat.

The malarial parasite has a thirty-six-hour life cycle, and now at the crisis, Rosa was attempting to raise his body temperature sufficiently to interrupt the cycle and break the fever. Heat radiated from the bed, filling the single room of the rondavel as though it were a kitchen. Only Sebastian's head showed from the pile of blankets, and his face was flushed a dusky brick colour. Although sweat spurted from every pore of his skin and ran back in heavy drops to soak his hair and his pillow, yet his teeth rattled together and he shivered so that the camp-bed shook.

Rosa sat beside his bed and watched him. Occasionally she leaned forward with a cloth in her hand and wiped the perspiration from his eyes and upper lip. Her expression had softened and become almost broody. One of Sebastian's curls had plastered itself wetly across his forehead, and, with her finger-tips, Rosa combed it back. She repeated the gesture, and then did it again, stroking her fingers through his damp hair, instinctively gentling and soothing him.

He opened his eyes, and Rosa snatched her hand away guiltily. His eyes were misty grey, unfocused as a new-born puppy's, and Rosa felt something squirm in her stomach.

'Please don't stop.' His voice was slurred with the fever, but even so Rosa was surprised at the timbre and inflection. it was the first time she had heard him speak and it was not the voice of a ruffian. Hesitating a moment, she glanced at the door of the hut to make sure they were alone before she reached forward to touch his face.

'You are kind—good and kind.'

'Sshh!' she admonished him.

'Thank you.'

'Sshh! Close your eyes.'

His eyes flickered down and he sighed, a gusty, broken sound.

The crisis came like a big wind and shook him as though he were a tree in its path. His body temperature rocketed, and he tossed and writhed in the camp-bed, trying to throw off the weight of blankets upon him, so that Rosa called for Mohammed's wife to help her restrain him. His perspiration soaked through the thin mattress and dripped to form a puddle on the earth floor beneath the bed, and he cried out in the fantasy of his fever.

Then, miraculously, the crisis was past, and he slumped into relaxation. He lay still and exhausted so that only the shallow flutter of his breathing showed there was life in him. Rosa could feel his skin cooling under her hand, and she saw the yellowish tinge with which the fever had coloured it.

'The first time it is always bad.' Mohammed's wife released her grip on the blanket-wrapped legs.

'Yes,' said Rosa. 'Now bring the basin. We must wash him and change his blankets, Nanny.'

She had worked many times with men who were sick or badly hurt; the servants and the bearers and the gun-boys, and, of course, with her father. But now, as Nanny peeled back the blankets and Rosa swabbed Sebastian's unconscious body with the moist cloth, she felt an inexplicable tension within her—a sense of dread mingled with tight excitement. She could feel new blood warming her cheeks, and she leaned forward, so that Nanny could not see her face as she worked.

The skin of his chest and upper arms was creamy-smooth as polished alabaster, where the sun had not stained it. Beneath her fingers it had an elastic hardness, a rubbery sensuality and warmth that disturbed her. When she realized suddenly that she was no longer wiping with the flannel but using it to caress the shape of hard muscle beneath the pale skin, she checked herself and made her actions brusque and businesslike.

They dried his upper body, and Nanny reached to jerk the blankets down below Sebastian's waist.

'Wait!' It came out of Rosa as a cry, and Nanny paused with her hand on the bedclothes and her head held at an angle, quizzical, birdlike. Her wizened old features crinkling in sly amusement.

'Wait,' Rosa repeated in confusion. 'First help me get the night-shirt on him,' and she snatched up one of Flynn's freshly ironed buι threadbare old night-shirts from the chair beside the bed.

'It cannot bite you, Little Long Hair,' the old woman teased her gently. 'It has no teeth.'

'You just stop that kind of talk,' snapped Rosa with unnecessary violence. 'Help me sit him up.'

Between them they lifted Sebastian and slipped the night-shirt down over his head, before lowering him to the pillow again.

'And now?' Nanny asked innocently. For answer, Rosa handed her the flannel, and turned to stare fixedly out of the rondavel window. Behind her she heard the rustle of blankets and then Nanny's voice.

'Hau! Hau!' The age-old expression of deep admiration, followed by a cackle of delighted laughter, as Nanny saw the back of Rosa's neck turning bright pink with embarrassment.

Nanny had smuggled Flynn's cut-throat razor out of the bungalow, and was supervising critically as Rosa stroked it gingerly over Sebastian's soapy cheeks. There was no sound medical reason why a malaria patient should be shaved immediately after emerging from the crisis, but Rosa had advanced the theory that it would make him feel more comfortable and Nanny had agreed enthusiastically. Both of them were enjoying themselves with all the sober delight of two small girls playing with a doll.

Despite Nanny's cautionary clucks and sharp hisses of indrawn breath, Rosa succeeded in removing the hair that covered Sebastian's face like the black pelt of an otter without inflicting any serious wounds. There was a nick on the chin and another below the left nostril, but neither of these bled more than a drop or two.

Rose rinsed the razor and then narrowed her eyes thoughtfully as she surveyed her handiwork, and that thing squirmed in her stomach again. 'I think,' she muttered, 'we should move him into the main bungalow. It will be more comfortable.'

'I will call the servants to carry him,' said Nanny.

21

Flynn O'Flynn was a busy man during the period of Sebastian's con-
valescence. His band of followers had been seriously depleted during the
recent exchange with Herman Fleischer on the Rufiji, so to replace his losses,
he press-ganged all the maschille-bearers who had carried them home from
Luti's village. These he put through a preliminary course of training and at the
end of four days selected a dozen of the most promising, to become gun-boys.
The remainder he dispatched .homeward despite their protests; they would
dearly have loved to stay for the glamour and reward that they were certain
would be heaped upon their more fortunate fellows.

Thereafter the chosen few were entered upon the second part of their
training. Securely locked in one of the rondavels behind the bungalow, Flynn
kept the tools of his trade. It was an impressive arsenal.

Rack upon rack of cheap Martini Henry ·450 rifles, a score of W.D. Lee-
Metfords that had survived the Anglo-Boer war, a lesser number of German
Mausers salvaged from his encounters with Askari across the Rovuma,
and a very few of the expensive hand-made doubles by Gibbs and Messrs
Greener of London. Not a single weapon had a serial number on it.
Above these, neatly stacked on the wooden shelves, were bulk packages of
cartridges, wrapped and soldered in lead foil—enough of them to fight a small
battle.

The room reeked with the slick, mineral smell of gun oil.

Flynn issued his recruits with Mausers, and set about instructing them in
the art of handling a rifle. Again he weeded out those who showed no aptitude
and he was left finally with eight men who could hit an elephant at fifty paces.
This group passed into the third and last period of training.

Many years previously, Mohammed had been recruited into the German
Askari. He had even won a medal during the Salito rebellion of 1904, and from
there had risen to the rank of sergeant and overseer of the officers' mess.
During a visit by the army auditor to Mbeya, where Mohammed was at that
time stationed, there had been discovered a stock discrepancy of some twenty
dozen bottles of schnapps, and a hole in the mess funds amounting to a little
over a thousand Reichsmarks. This was a hanging matter, and Mohammed
had resigned without ceremony from the Imperial army and reached the
Portuguese border by a series of forced marches. In Portuguese territory he
had met Flynn, and solicited and received employment from him. However,
he was still an authority on German army drill procedure and retained a
command of the language.

The recruits were handed over to him, for it was part of Flynn's
plans that they be able to masquerade as a squad of German Askari. For
days thereafter the camp at Lalapanzi reverberated to Mohammed's Teutonic
cries, as he goose-stepped about the lawns at the head of his band of
nearly naked troopers, with his fez set squarely on the grey wool of his
head.

This left Flynn free to make further preparations. Seated on the stoep of the
bungalow, he pored sweatily over his correspondence for many days. First
there was a letter to:

His Excellency, The Governor,
German Administration of East Africa,
Dar es Salaam.
Sir,
I enclose my account for damages, as follows, herewith:

1 Dhow (Market value)	£1,500 – –
10 Rifles	£200 – –
Various stores and provisions etcetera (too numerous to list)	£100 – –
Injury, suffering and hardships (estimated)	£200 – –
TOTAL	£2,000 – –

This claim arises from the sinking of the above-said dhow off the mouth of the Rufiji, July 10th, 1912, which was an act of piracy by your gunboat, the *Blücher*.

I would appreciate payment in gold, on or before September 25th, 1912, otherwise I will take the necessary steps to collect same personally.

Yours sincerely,
Flynn Patrick O'Flynn, Esq.

(Citizen of The United States of America)

After much heavy thought, Flynn had decided not to include a claim for the ivory as he was not too certain of its legality. Best not to mention it.

He had considered signing himself 'United States Ambassador to Africa', but had discarded the idea on the grounds that Governor Schee knew damned well that he was no such thing. However, there was no harm in reminding him of Flynn's nationality—it might make the old rogue hesitate before hanging Flynn out of hand if ever he got his hooks into him.

Satisfied that the only response to his demands would be a significant increase in Governor Schee's blood pressure, Flynn proceeded with his preparations to make good his threat of collecting the debt *personally*.

Flynn used this word lightly—he had long ago selected a representative debt collector in the form of Sebastian Oldsmith. It now remained to have him suitably outfitted for the occasion, and, armed with a tape-measure from Rosa's work-basket, Flynn visited Sebastian's sick bed. These days, visiting Sebastian was much like trying to arrange an interview with the Pope. Sebastian was securely under the maternal protection of Rosa O'Flynn.

Flynn knocked discreetly on the door of the guest bedroom, paused for a count of five, and entered.

'What do you want?' Rosa greeted him affectionately. She was sitting on the foot of Sebastian's bed.

'Hello, hello,' said Flynn, and then again lamely, 'Hello.'

'I suppose you're looking for a drinking companion,' accused Rosa.

'Good Lord, no!' Flynn was genuinely horrified by the accusation. What with Rosa's depredations his stock of gin was running perilously low, and he had no intention of sharing it with anyone. 'I just called in to see how he was doing.' Flynn transferred his attention to Sebastian. 'How you feeling, old Bassie boy?'

'Much better, thank you.' In fact, Sebastian was looking very chirpy indeed. Freshly shaved, dressed in one of Flynn's best night-shirts, he lay like a Roman emperor on clean sheets. On the low table beside his bed stood a vase of frangipani blooms, and there were other floral tributes standing about the room—all of them cut and carefully arranged by Rosa O'Flynn.

He was steadily putting on weight again as Rosa and Nanny stuffed food into him and colour was starting to drive the yellowish fever stains from his skin. Flynn felt a prickle of irritation in the way Sebastian was being pampered like a stud stallion, while Flynn himself was barely tolerated in his own home.

The metaphor which had come naturally into Flynn's mind, now sparked a further train of thought, and a sharper prickle of irritation. *Stud stallion!* Flynn looked at Rosa with attention, and noticed that the dress she wore was the white one with gauzy sleeves, that had belonged to her mother–a garment that Rosa usually kept securely locked away, a garment she had worn perhaps twice in her life. Furthermore, her feet, which were usually bare about the house, were now neatly clad in store-bought patent leather, and, by Jesus, she was wearing a sprig of bougainvillaea tucked into the shiny black slick of her hair. The tip of her long braid, which was usually tied carelessly with a thong of leather, flaunted a silk ribbon.

Now, Flynn O'Flynn was not a sentimental man but suddenly he recognized in his daughter a strange new glow, and a demure air that had never been there before, and within himself he became aware of an unusual sensation, so unfamiliar that he did not recognize it as paternal jealousy. He did, however, recognize that the sooner he sent Sebastian on his way, the safer it would be.

'Well, that's fine, Bassie,' he boomed genially. 'That's just fine. Now, I'm sending bearers down to Beira to pick up supplies, and I just thought they might as well get some clothes for you while they were there.'

'Well, thank you very much, Flynn.' Sebastian was touched by the kindness of his friend.

'Might as well do it properly.' Flynn produced his tape-measure with a flourish. 'We'll send your measurements down to old Parbhoo and he can tailor-make some stuff for you.'

'I say, that *is* jolly decent of you.'

And completely out of character, thought Rosa O'Flynn as she watched her father carefully noting the length of Sebastian's legs and arms, and the girth of his neck, chest, and waist.

'The boots and the hat will be a problem,' Flynn mused aloud when he had finished. 'But I'll find something.'

'And what do you mean by that, Flynn O'Flynn?' Rosa demanded suspiciously.

'Nothing, just nothing at all.' Hurriedly Flynn gathered his notes and his tape, and fled from further interrogation.

Some time later, Mohammed and the bearers returned from the shopping expedition to Beira, and he and Flynn immediately closeted themselves in secret conclave in the arsenal.

'Did you get it!' demanded Flynn eagerly.

'Five boxes of gin I left in the cave behind the waterfall at the top of the valley,' whispered Mohammed, and Flynn sighed with relief. 'But one bottle I brought with me.' Mohammed produced it from under his tunic. Flynn took it from him and drew the cork with his teeth, before spilling a little into the enamel mug that was standing ready.

'And the other purchases?'

'It was difficult–especially the hat.'

'But did you get it?' Flynn demanded.

'It was a direct intervention of Allah.' Mohammed refused to be hurried. 'In the harbour was a German ship, stopped at Beira on its way north to Dar es

Salaam. On the boat were three German officers. I saw them walking upon the deck.' Mohammed paused and cleared his throat portentously. 'That night a man who is my friend rowed me out to the ship, and I visited the cabin of one of the soldiers.'

'Where is it?' Flynn could not hold his patience. Mohammed stood up, went to the door of the rondavel, and called to one of the bearers. He returned and set a bundle on the table in front of Flynn. Grinning proudly, he waited while Flynn unwrapped the bundle.

'Good God Almighty,' breathed Flynn.

'Is it not beautiful?'

'Call Manali. Tell him to come here immediately.'

Ten minutes later Sebastian, whom Rosa had at last reluctantly placed on the list of walking wounded, entered the rondavel, to be greeted effusively by Flynn. 'Sit down, Bassie boy. I've got a present for you.'

Reluctantly, Sebastian obeyed, eyeing the covered object on the table. Flynn stood over it and whisked away the cloth. Then, with the same ceremony as the Archbishop of Canterbury placing the crown, he lifted the helmet above Sebastian's head and lowered it reverently.

On the summit a golden eagle cocked its wings on the point of flight and opened its beak in a silent squawk of menace, the black enamel of the helmet shone with a polished gloss, and the golden chain drooped heavily under Sebastian's chin.

It was indeed a thing of beauty. A thing of such presence that it completely overwhelmed Sebastian, enveloping his head to the bridge of his nose so that his eyes were just visible below the jutting brim.

'A few sizes too large,' Flynn conceded. 'But we can stuff some cloth into the crown to keep it up.' He backed away a few paces and cocked his head on one side as he examined the effect. 'Bassie boy, you'll slay them.'

'What's this for?' Sebastian asked in concern from under the steel helmet.

'You'll see. Just hold on a shake.' Flynn turned to Mohammed who was cooing with admiration in the doorway. 'The clothes?' he asked, and Mohammed beckoned imperiously to the bearers to bring in the boxes they had carried all the way from Beira.

Parbhoo, the Indian tailor, had obviously laboured with dedication and enthusiasm. The task set him by Flynn had touched the soul of the creative artist in him.

Ten minutes later, Sebastian stood self-consciously in the centre of the rondavel while Flynn and Mohammed circled him slowly, exclaiming with delight and self-congratulation.

Below the massive helmet, which was now propped high with a wad of cloth between steel and scalp, Sebastian was dressed in the sky-blue tunic and riding breeches. The cuffs of the jacket were ringed with yellow silk—a stripe of the same material ran down the outside of his breeches—and the high collar was covered with embroidered metal thread. Complete with spurs, the tall black boots pinched his toes so painfully that Sebastian stood pigeon-toed and blushed with bewilderment. 'I say, Flynn,' he pleaded, 'what's all this about?'

'Bassie boy.' Flynn laid a hand fondly on his shoulder. 'You're going to go in there and collect hut tax for . . .' he almost said *me*, but altered it quickly to '. . . us.'

'What is hut tax?'

'Hut tax is the annual sum of five shillings, paid by the headmen to the

German Governor for each hut in his village.' Flynn led Sebastian to the chair and seated him as gently as though he were pregnant. He lifted a hand to still Sebastian's further inquiries and protests. 'Yes, I know you don't understand. But I'll explain it to you carefully. Just keep your mouth shut and listen.' He sat down opposite Sebastian and leaned forward earnestly. 'Now! The Germans owe us for the dhow and that, like we agreed–right?'

Sebastian nodded, and the helmet slid forward over his eyes. He pushed it back.

'Well, you are going to go across the river with the gun-bearers dressed as Askari. You are going to visit each of the villages before the real tax-collector gets there and picks up the money that they owe us. Do you follow me so far?'

'Are you coming with me?'

'Now, how can I do that?' Me with my leg not properly healed yet?' Flynn protested impatiently. 'Besides that, every headman on the other side knows who I am. Not one of them has ever laid eyes on you before. You just tell them you're a new officer–straight out from Germany. One look at that uniform, and they'll pay up sharpish.'

'What happens if the real tax-collector has already been?'

'They don't start collecting until September usually–and then they start in the north and work down this way. You'll have plenty of time.'

Frowning below the rim of the helmet, Sebastian brought forward a series of objections–each one progressively weaker than its predecessor, and, one by one, Flynn annihilated them. Finally there was a long silence while Sebastian's brain ground to a standstill.

'Well?' Flynn asked. 'Are you going to do it?'

And the question was answered from an unexpected quarter in feminine, but not dulcet, tones. 'He is certainly *not* going to do it!'

Guiltily as small boys caught smoking in the school latrines, Flynn and Sebastian wheeled to face the door which had carelessly been left ajar.

Rosa's suspicions had been aroused by all the surreptitious activity around the rondavel, and when she had seen Sebastian join in, she had not the slightest qualms about listening outside the window. Her active intervention was not on ethical grounds. Rosa O'Flynn had acquired a rather elastic definition of honesty from her father. Like him, she believed that German property belonged to anybody who could get their hands on it. The fact that Sebastian was involved in a scheme based on dubious moral foundations in no way lowered her opinion of him–rather, in a sneaking sort of way, it heightened her estimate of him as a potential breadwinner. To date, this was the only area in which she had held misgivings about Sebastian Oldsmith.

From experience she knew that those of her father's business enterprises in which Flynn was not eager to participate personally always involved a great deal of risk. The thought of Sebastian Oldsmith dressed in a sky-blue uniform, marching across the Rovuma, and never coming back–roused in her the same instincts as those of a lioness shortly to be deprived of her cubs.

'He is certainly *not* going to do it,' she repeated, and then to Sebastian. 'Do you hear me? I forbid it. I forbid it absolutely.'

This was the wrong approach.

Sebastian had, in turn, acquired from his father very Victorian views on the rights and privileges of women. Mr Oldsmith, the senior, was a courteous domestic tyrant, a man whose infallibility had never been challenged by his wife. A man who regarded sex deviates, Bolsheviks, trade union organizers, and suffragettes, in that descending order of repugnance.

Sebastian's mother, a meek little lady with a perpetually harassed expression, would no more have contemplated *absolutely forbidding* Mr Oldsmith a course of action, than she would have contemplated denying the existence of God. Her belief in the divine rights of man had extended to her sons. From a very tender age Sebastian had grown accustomed to worshipful obedience, not only from his mother, but also from his large flock of sisters.

Rosa's present attitude and manner of speech came as a shock. It took him but a few seconds to recover and then he rose to his feet and adjusted the helmet. 'I beg your pardon?' he asked coldly.

'You heard me,' snapped Rosa. 'I'm not going to allow this.'

Sebastian nodded thoughtfully, and then hastily grabbed at the helmet as it threatened to spoil his dignity by blind-folding him again. Ignoring Rosa he turned to Flynn. 'I will leave as soon as possible—tomorrow?'

'It will take a couple more days to get organized,' Flynn demurred.

'Very well then.' Sebastian stalked from the room, and the sunlight lit his uniform with dazzling splendour.

With a triumphant guffaw, Flynn reached for the enamel mug at his elbow. 'You made a mess of that one,' he gloated, and then his expression changed to unease.

Standing in the doorway, Rosa O'Flynn's shoulders had sagged, the angry line of her lips drooped.

'Oh, come on now!' gruffed Flynn.

'He won't come back. You know what you are doing to him. You're sending him in there to die.'

'Don't talk silly. He's a big boy, he can look after himself.'

'Oh, I hate you. Both of you—I hate you both!' and she was gone, running across the yard to the bungalow.

22

In a red dawn Flynn and Sebastian stood together on the stoep of the bungalow, talking together quietly.

'Now listen, Bassie. I reckon the best thing you can do is send back the collection from each village, as you make it. No sense in carrying all that money round with you.' Tactfully Flynn refrained from pointing out that by following this procedure, in the event of Sebastian running into trouble half-way through the expedition, the profits to that time would be safe-guarded.

Sebastian was not really listening—he was more preoccupied with the whereabouts of Rosa O'Flynn. He had seen very little of her in the last few days.

'Now you listen to old Mohammed. He knows which are the biggest villages. Let him do the talking—those headmen are the biggest bunch of rogues you'll ever meet. They'll all plead poverty and famine, so you've got to be tough. Do you hear me? Tough, Bassie, tough!'

'Tough,' agreed Sebastian absent-mindedly, glancing surreptitiously into the windows of the bungalow for a glimpse of Rosa.

'Now another thing,' Flynn went on. 'Remember to keep moving fast. March until nightfall. Make your cooking fire, eat, and then march again in the dark before you camp. Never sleep at your first camp, that's asking for trouble. Then get away again before first light in the morning.' There were many other instructions, and Sebastian listened to them without attention. 'Remember the sound of gunfire carries for miles. Don't use your rifle except in emergency, and if you do fire a shot, then don't hang about afterwards. Now the route I've planned for you will never take you more than twenty miles beyond the Rovuma. At the first sign of trouble, you run for the river. If any of your men get hurt, leave them. Don't play hero, leave them and run like hell for the river.'

'Very well,' muttered Sebastian unhappily. The prospect of leaving Lalapanzi was becoming less attractive each minute. Where on earth was she?

'Now remember, don't let those headmen talk you out of anything. You might even have to . . .' Here Flynn paused to find the least offensive phraseology, '. . . you might even have to hang one or two of them.'

'Good God, Flynn. You're not serious.' Sebastian's full attention jerked back to Flynn.

'Ha! Ha!' Flynn laughed away the suggestion. 'I was joking, of course. But . . .' he went on wistfully, 'the Germans do it, and it gets results, you know.'

'Well, I'd better be on my way.' Sebastian changed the subject ostentatiously and picked up his helmet. He placed it upon his head and descended the steps to where his Askari, with rifles at the slope, were drawn up on the lawn. All of them, including Mohammed, were dressed in authentic uniform, complete with puttees and the little pillbox kepis. Sebastian had prudently refrained from asking Flynn how he had obtained these uniforms. The answer was evident in the neatly patched circular punctures in most of the tunics, and the faint brownish stain around each mend.

In single file, the blazing eagle on Sebastian's head-piece leading like a beacon, they marched past the massive solitary figure of Flynn O'Flynn on the veranda. Mohammed called for a salute and the response was enthusiastic, but ragged. Sebastian tripped on his spurs and with an effort, regained his equilibrium and plodded on gamely.

Shading his eyes against the glare, Flynn watched the gallant little column wind away down the valley towards the Rovuma river. Flynn's voice was without conviction as he spoke aloud, 'I hope to God he doesn't mess this one up.'

23

Once out of sight of the bungalow, Sebastian halted the column. Sitting beside the footpath, he sighed with relief as he removed the weight of the metal helmet from his head and replaced it with a sombrero of plaited grass, then he eased the spurred boots from his already aching feet, and slipped on a pair of rawhide sandals. He handed the discarded equipment to his personal bearer, stood up, and in his best Swahili ordered the march to continue.

Three miles down the valley the footpath crossed the stream above a tiny waterfall. It was a piece of shade where great trees reached out towards each other across the narrow watercourse. Clear water trickled and gurgled between a tumble of lichen-covered boulders, before jumping like white lace in the sunlight down the slippery black slope of the falls.

Sebastian paused on the bank and allowed his men to proceed. He watched them hop from boulder to boulder, the bearers balancing their loads without effort, and then scramble up the far bank and disappear into the dense river bush. He listened to their voices becoming fainter with distance, and suddenly he was sad and alone.

Instinctively he turned and looked back up the valley towards Lalapanzi, and the sense of loss was a great emptiness inside him. The urge to return burned up so strongly, that he took a step back along the bath before he could check himself.

He stood irresolute. The voices of his men were very faint now, muted by the dense vegetation, overlaid by the drowsy droning of insects, the wind murmur on the top branches of the trees, and the purl of falling water.

Then the soft rustle beside him, and he turned to it quickly. She stood near him and the sunlight through the leaves threw a golden dapple on her giving a sense of unreality, a fairy quality, to her presence.

'I wanted to give you something to take with you, a farewell present for you to remember,' she said softly. 'But there was nothing I could think of,' and she came forward, reached up to him with her arms and her mouth, and she kissed him.

24

Sebastian Oldsmith crossed the Rovuma river in a mood of dreamy goodwill towards all men.

Mohammed was worried about him. He suspected that Sebastian had suffered a malarial relapse and he watched him carefully for evidence of further symptoms.

Mohammed at the head of the column of Askari and bearers had reached the crossing place on the Rovuma, before he realized that Sebastian was missing. In wild concern he had taken two armed Askari with him and hurried back along the path through the thorn scrub and broken rock–expecting at any moment to find a pride of lions growling over Sebastian's dismembered corpse. They had almost reached the waterfall when they met Sebastian ambling benignly along the path towards them, an expression of ethereal contentment lighting his classic features. His magnificent uniform was now a little rumpled; there were fresh grass stains on the knees and elbows, and dead leaves and bits of dried grass clung to the expensive material. From this Mohammed deduced that Sebastian had either fallen, or in sickness had lain down to rest.

'Manali,' Mohammed cried in concern. 'Are you well?'

'Never better–never in all my life,' Sebastian assured him.

'You have been lying down,' Mohammed accused.

'Son of a gun,' Sebastian borrowed from the vocabulary of Flynn O'Flynn. 'Son of a gun, you can say that again–and then repeat it!' and he clapped Mohammed between the shoulder blades with such well-intentioned violence that it almost floored him. Since then, Sebastian had not spoken again, but every few minutes he would smile and shake his head in wonder. Mohammed was truly worried.

They crossed the Rovuma in hired canoes and camped that night on the far bank. Twice during the night Mohammed awoke, slipped out of his blanket, and crept across to Sebastian to check his condition. Each time Sebastian was sleeping easily and the silver moonlight showed just a suggestion of a smile on his lips.

In the middle of the next morning, Mohammed halted the column in thick cover and came back from the head to confer with Sebastian. 'The village of M'topo lies just beyond,' he pointed ahead. 'You can see the smoke from the fires.'

There was a greyish smear of it above the trees, and faintly a dog began yapping.

'Good. Let's go.' Sebastian had donned his eagle helmet and was struggling into his boots.

'First I will send the Askari to surround the village.'

'Why?' Sebastian looked up in surprise.

'Otherwise there will be nobody there when we arrive.' During his service with the German Imperial Army, Mohammed had been on tax expeditions before.

'Well–if you think it necessary,' Sebastian agreed dubiously.

Half an hour later Sebastian swaggered in burlesque of a German officer into the village of M'topo, and was dismayed by the reception he received. The lamentations of two hundred human beings made a hideous chorus for his entry. Some of them were on their knees and all of them were wringing their hands, smiting their breasts, or showing other signs of deep distress. At the far end of the village M'topo, the headman, waited under guard by Mohammed and two of his Askari.

M'topo was an old man, with a cap of pure white wool, and an emaciated body covered with a parchment of dry skin. One eye was glazed over with tropical ophthalmia, and he was clearly very agitated. 'I crawl on my belly before you, Splendid and Merciful Lord,' he greeted Sebastian, and prostrated himself in the dust.

'I say, that isn't necessary, you know,' murmured Sebastian.

'My poor village welcomes you,' whimpered M'topo. Bitterly he re-criminated himself for thus being taken unawares. He had not expected the tax expedition for another two months, and had taken no pains with the disposal of his wealth. Buried under the earthen floor of his hut was nearly a thousand silver Portuguese escudos and half again as many golden Deutsche Marks. The traffic of his villagers in dried fish, netted in the Rovuma river, was highly organized and lucrative.

Now he dragged himself pitifully to his old knees and signalled two of his wives to bring forward stools and gourds of palm wine.

'It has been a year of great pestilence, disease, and famine,' M'topo began his prepared speech, when Sebastian was seated and refreshed. The rest of it took fifteen minutes to deliver, and Sebastian's Swahili was now strong enough for him to follow the argument. He was deeply touched. Under the spell of palm wine and his new rosy outlook on life, he felt his heart going out to the old man.

While M'topo spoke, the other villagers had dispersed quietly and barricaded themselves in their huts. It was best not to draw attention to oneself when candidates for the rope were being selected. Now a mournful silence hung over the village, broken only by the mewling of an infant and the squabbling of a pair of mangy mongrels, contesting the ownership of a piece of offal.

'Manali,' impatiently Mohammed interrupted the old man's catalogue of misfortune. 'Let me search his hut.'

'Wait,' Sebastian stopped him. He had been looking about, and beneath the single baobab tree in the centre of the village he had noticed a dozen or so crude litters. Now he stood up and walked across to them.

When he saw what they contained, his throat contracted with horror. In each litter lay a human skeleton, the bones still covered with a thin layer of living flesh and skin. Naked men and women mixed indiscriminately, but their bodies so wasted that it was almost impossible to tell their sex. The pelvic girdles were gaunt basins of bone, elbows and knees great deformed knobs distorting the stick-like limbs, each rib standing out in clear definition, the faces were skulls whose lips had shrunk to expose the teeth in a perpetual sardonic grin. But the real horror was contained in the sunken eye cavities; the lids were fixed wide open—and the eyeballs glared like red marbles. There was no pupil nor iris, just those polished orbs the colour of blood.

Sebastian stepped back hurriedly, feeling his belly heave and the taste of it in his throat. Not trusting himself to speak, he beckoned for M'topo to come to him, and pointed at the bodies in the litters.

M'topo glanced at them without interest. They were so much part of the ordinary scene that for many days he had not consciously been aware of their existence. The village was situated on the edge of a tsetse fly belt, and since his childhood there had always been the sleeping sickness cases lying under the baobab tree, deep in the coma which always precedes death. He could not understand Sebastian's concern.

'When . . .?' Sebastian's voice faltered, and he swallowed before going on. 'When did these people last eat?' he asked.

'Not for a long time.' M'topo was puzzled by the question. Everybody knew that once the sleeping time came they never ate again.

Sebastian had heard of people dying of starvation. It happened in places like India, but here he was confronted with the actual fact. A revulsion of feeling swept over him. This was irrefutable proof that all M'topo had told him was true. This was famine as he had not believed really could exist—and he had been trying to extort money from these people!

Sebastian walked slowly back to his stool and sank down upon it. He removed the heavy helmet from his head, held it in his lap, and sat staring at his own feet. He was helpless with guilt and compassion.

Flynn O'Flynn had reluctantly provided Sebastian with one hundred escudos as travelling expenses to meet any emergency that might arise before he could make his first collection. Some of this had been expended on the hire of canoes to cross the Rovuma, but there was still eighty escudos left.

From his hip-pocket, Sebastian produced the tobacco pouch containing the money and counted out half of it. 'M'topo,' his voice was subdued. 'Take this money. Buy food for them.'

'Manali,' screeched Mohammed in protest. 'Manali. Do not do it.'

'Shut up!' Sebastian snapped at him, and prodded the handful of coins towards M'topo. 'Take it!'

M'topo stared at him as though he offered a live scorpion. It was as unnatural as though a man-eating lion had walked up and rubbed itself against his leg.

'Take it,' Sebastian insisted impatiently, and in disbelief, M'topo extended his cupped hands.

'Mohammed,' Sebastian stood up and replaced his helmet, 'we'll move on immediately to the next village.'

Long after Sebastian's column had disappeared into the bush again, old M'topo squatted alone, clutching the coins, too stunned to move. At last he roused himself and shouted for one of his sons.

'Go quickly to the village of Saali, who is my brother. Tell him that a madman comes to him. A German lord who comes to collect the hut tax and stays to offer gifts. Tell him . . .' here his voice broke as though he could not believe what he was about to say, '. . . tell him that this lord should be shown the ones who sleep, and that the madness will then come upon him, and he will give you forty escudos of the Portuguese. And, furthermore, there will be no hangings.'

'Saali, my uncle, will not believe these things.'

'No,' M'topo admitted. 'It is true that he will not believe. But tell him anyway.'

25

Saali received the message from his elder brother, and it induced in him a state of terror bordering on paralysis. M'topo, he knew, had a vicious sense of humour—and there was between them that matter of the woman Gita, a luscious little fourteen-year-old who had deserted the village of M'topo within two days of taking up her duties as M'topo's junior wife, on the grounds that he was impotent and smelled like an hyena. She was now a notable addition to Saali's household. Saali was convinced that the true interpretation of his brother's message was that the new German commissioner was a rampaging lion who would not be content with merely hanging a few of the old men but who might extend his attentions to Saali himself. Even should he escape the noose, he would be left destitute; his carefully accumulated hoard of silver, his six fine tusks of ivory, his goat herd, his dozen bags of white salt, the bar of copper, his two European-made axes, the bolts of trade cloth—all of his treasures gone! It required an heroic effort to rouse himself from the stupor of despair and make his few futile preparations for flight.

Mohammed's Askari caught him as he was heading for the bush at a trot, and when they led him back to meet Sebastian Oldsmith, the tears that coursed freely down his cheeks and dripped on to his chest were genuine.

Sebastian was very susceptible to tears. Despite the protests of Mohammed, Sebastian pressed upon Saali twenty silver escudos. It took Saali about twenty minutes to recover from the shock, at the end of which time he, in turn, shocked Sebastian profoundly by offering him on a temporary basis the unrestricted services of the girl, Gita. This young lady was witness to the offer made by her husband, and was obviously wholeheartedly in favour of it.

Sebastian set off again hurriedly, with his retinue straggling along behind him in a state of deep depression. Mohammed now had a bad case of the mutters.

Drums tap-tap-tapped, runners scurried along the network of footpaths that crossed and criss-crossed the bush; from hilltop to hilltop men called one to the other in the high-pitched wail that carries for miles. The news spread. Village after village buzzed with incredulous excitement, and then the inhabitants flocked out to meet the mad German commissioner.

By this time Sebastian was thoroughly enjoying himself. He was carried away with the pleasure of giving, delighted with these simple lovable people who welcomed him sincerely and pressed humble little gifts upon him. Here a scrawny fowl, there a dozen half-incubated eggs, a basin of sweet potatoes, a gourd of palm wine.

But Santa Claus's bag, or, more accurately, his tobacco pouch, was soon empty—and Sebastian was at a loss for some way to help alleviate the misery and poverty he saw in each village. He considered issuing indulgences from future tax . . . *the bearer is hereby excused from the payment of hut tax for five years* . . . but realized that this was a lethal gift. He shuddered at what Herman Fleischer might do to anybody he caught in possession of one of these.

Finally he struck on the solution. These people were starving. He would give them food. He would give them meat.

In fact, this was one of the most desirable commodities Sebastian could have offered. Despite the abundance of wild life, the great herds of game that spread across the plains and hills, these people were starved for protein. The primitive hunting methods they employed were so ineffectual, that the killing of a single animal was an event that happened infrequently, and then almost by accident. When the carcass was shared out among two or three hundred hungry mouths, there was only a few ounces of meat for each. Men and women would risk their lives in attempting to drive a pride of lions from their kill, for just a few mouthfuls of this precious stuff.

Sebastian's Askari joined in the sport with delight. Even old Mohammed perked up a little. Unfortunately, their marksmanship was about the same standard as Sebastian's own, and a day's hunting usually resulted in the expenditure of thirty or forty rounds of Mauser ammunition, and a bag of sometimes as little as one half-grown zebra. But there were good days also, like the memorable occasion when a herd of buffalo virtually committed suicide by running down the line of Askari. In the resulting chaos one of Sebastian's men was shot dead by his comrades, but eight full-grown buffalo followed him to the happy hunting grounds.

So Sebastian's tax tour proceeded triumphantly, leaving behind a trail of empty cartridge cases, racks of meat drying in the sun, full bellies, and smiling faces.

26

Three months after crossing the Rovuma river, Sebastian found himself back at the village of his good friend, M'topo. He had bypassed Saali's in order to avoid the offended Gita.

Sitting alone in the night within the hut that M'topo placed at his disposal, Sebastian was having his first misgivings. On the morrow, he would begin the return to Lalapanzi, where Flynn O'Flynn was waiting for him. Sebastian was acutely aware that from Flynn's point of view the expedition had not been a success—and Flynn would have a great deal to say on the subject. Once more Sebastian puzzled on the fates which took his best intentions, and manipulated them in such a manner that they became completely unrecognizable from the original.

Then his thoughts kicked off at a tangent. Soon, the day after tomorrow, if all went well, he would be back with Rosa. The deep yearning that had been his constant companion these last three months throbbed through Sebastian's whole body. Staring into the wood-fire on the hearth of the hut, it seemed as though the embers formed a picture of her face, and in his memory he heard her voice again.

'Come back, Sebastian. Come back soon.'

And he whispered the words aloud, watching her face in the fire. Gloating on each detail of it. He saw her smile, and her nose wrinkled a little, the dark eyes slanted upwards at the corners.

'Come back, Sebastian.'

The need of her was a physical pain so intense that he could hardly breathe, and his imagination reconstructed every detail of their parting beside the waterfall. Each subtle change and inflection of her voice, the very sound of her breathing, and the bitter salt taste of her tears upon his lips. He felt again the touch of her hands, her mouth—and through the woodsmoke that filled the hut, his nostrils flared at the warm woman smell of her body.

'I'm coming, Rosa. I'm coming back,' he whispered, and stood up restlessly from beside the fire. At that moment his attention was jerked back to the present by a soft scratching at the door of the hut.

'Lord. Lord.' He recognized M'topo's hoarse croaking.

'What is it?'

'We seek your protection.'

'What is the trouble?' Sebastian crossed to the door and lifted the cross-bar. 'What is it?'

In the moonlight M'topo stood with a skin blanket draped around his frail shoulders. Behind him a dozen of the villagers huddled in trepidation.

'The elephant are in our gardens. They will destroy them before morning. There will be nothing, not a single stalk of millet left standing.' He swung away and stood with his head cocked. 'Listen, you may hear them now.'

It was an eerie sound in the night, the high-pitched elephant squeal, and Sebastian's skin crawled. He could feel the hair on his forearms become erect.

'There are two of them.' M'topo's voice was a scratchy whisper. 'Two old bulls. We know them well. They came last season and laid waste our corn. They killed one of my sons who tried to drive them off.' In entreaty, the old man clawed hold of Sebastian's arm and hugged at it. 'Avenge my son, lord. Avenge my son for me, and save our millet that the children will not go hungry again this year.'

Sebastian responded to the appeal in the same manner that St George would have done.

In haste he buttoned his tunic and went to fetch his rifle. On his return he found his entire command armed to the teeth, and as eager for the hunt as a pack of foxhounds. Mohammed waited at their head.

'Lord Manali, we are ready.'

'Now, steady on, old chap.' Sebastian had no intention of sharing the glory. 'This is my shauri. Too many cooks, what?'

M'topo stood by, wringing his hands with impatience, listening alternately first to the distant sounds of the garden raiders feeding contentedly in his lands, and then to the undignified wrangling between Sebastian and his Askari, until at last he could bear it no longer. 'Lord, already half the millet is eaten. In an hour it will all be gone.'

'You're right,' Sebastian agreed, and turned angrily on his men. 'Shut up, all of you, shut up!'

They were unaccustomed to this tone of command from Sebastian, and it surprised them into silence.

'Only Mohammed shall accompany me. The rest of you go to your huts and stay there.'

It was a working compromise, Sebastian now had Mohammed as an ally. Mohammed turned on his comrades and scattered them before falling in beside Sebastian.

'Let us go.'

At the head of the main gardens, high on its stilts of poles, stood a rickety platform. This was the watch-tower from which, night and day, a guard was kept over the ripening millet. It was now deserted, the two young guards had left hurriedly at the first sight of the garden raiders. Kudu or waterbuck were one thing, a pair of bad-tempered old elephant bulls were another matter entirely.

Sebastian and Mohammed reached the watch-tower and paused beneath it. Quite clearly now they could hear the rustling and ripping sound of the millet stalks being torn up and trampled.

'Wait here,' whispered Sebastian, slinging his rifle over his shoulder, as he turned to the ladder beside him. He climbed slowly and silently to the platform, and from it, looked out over the gardens.

The moon was so brilliant as to throw sharply defined shadows below the tower and the trees. Its light was a soft silver that distorted distance and size, reducing all things to a cold homogeneous grey.

Beyond the clearing the forest rose like frozen smoke clouds, while the field of standing millet moved in the small night wind, rippling like the surface of a lake.

Humped big and darker grey, standing high above the millet, two great islands in the soft sea of vegetation, the old bulls grazed slowly. Although the nearest elephant was two hundred paces from the tower, the moon was so bright that Sebastian could see clearly as he reached forward with his trunk, coiled it about a clump of the leafy stalks and plucked them easily. Then swaying gently, rocking his massive bulk lazily from side to side, he beat the millet against his lifted foreleg to shake the clinging earth from the roots before lifting it and stuffing it into his mouth. The tattered banners of his ears flapping gently, an untidy tangle of millet leaves hanging from his lips between the long curved shafts of ivory, he moved on, feeding and trampling so that behind him he left a wide path of devastation.

On the open platform of the tower, Sebastian felt his stomach contracting, convulsing itself into a hard ball, and his hands on the rifle were unsteady; his breathing whistled softly in his own ears as the elephant thrill came upon him. Watching those two huge beasts, he found himself held motionless with an almost mystic sense of awe; a realization of his own insignificance, his presumption in going out against them, armed with this puny weapon of steel and wood. But beneath his reluctance was the tingle of tight nerves—that strange blend of fear and eagerness—the age-old lust of the hunter. He roused himself and climbed down to where Mohammed waited.

Through the standing corn that reached above their heads, stepping with care between the rows so that they disturb not a single leaf, they moved in towards the centre of the garden. Ears and eyes tuned to their finest limit, breathing controlled so that it did not match the wild pump of his heart, Sebastian homed in on the crackle and rustle made by the nearest bull.

Even though the millet screened him, he could feel the weak wash of the wind move his hair softly, and the first whiff of elephant smell hit him like an open-handed blow in the face. He stopped so suddenly that Mohammed almost bumped into him from behind. They stood crouching, peering ahead into the moving wall of vegetation. Sebastian felt Mohammed lean forward beside him, and heard his whisper breathed softer than the sound of the wind. 'Very close now.'

Sebastian nodded, and then swallowed jerkily. He could hear clearly the soft slithering scrape of leaves brushing against the rough hide of the old bull. It was feeding down towards them. They were standing directly in the path of its leisurely approach, at any moment now—at any moment!

Standing with the rifle lifted protectively, sweat starting to prickle his forehead and upper lip in the cool of the night, his eyes watering with the intensity of his gaze, Sebastian was suddenly aware of massive movement ahead of him. A solid shape through the bank of dancing leaves, and he looked up. High above him it loomed, black and big so that the night sky was blotted out by the spread of its ears, so near that he stood beneath the forward thrust of its tusks, and could see the trunk uncoil like a fat python and grope forward blindly towards him; and beneath it the mouth gaped a little, spilling leaves at the corners.

He lifted the rifle, pointed it upwards without aiming, almost touching the elephant's hanging lower lip with the muzzle, and he fired. The shot was a blunt burst of sound in the night.

The bullet angled up through the pink palate of the animal's mouth, up through the spongy bone of the skull; mushrooming and exploding, it tore into the fist-sized cell that contained the brain, and burst it into a grey jelly.

Had it passed four inches to either side, had it been deflected by one of the larger bones, Sebastian would have died before he had time to work the bolt of the Mauser, for he stood directly below the outstretched tusks and trunk. But the old bull reeled backwards from the shot, his trunk falling flabbily against his chest, his forelegs spreading, and his head unbalanced by long tusks sagged forwards, knees collapsed suddenly under him, and he fell so heavily that they heard the thump in the village half a mile away.

'Son of a gun!' gasped Sebastian, staring in disbelief at the dead mountain of flesh. 'I did it. Son of a gun, I did it!' Jubilation, a delirious release from fear and tension, mounted giddily within him. He lifted an arm to hit Mohammed across the back, but he froze in that attitude.

Like the shriek of steam escaping from a burst boiler, the other bull squealed in the moonlight near by. And they heard the crackling rush of his run in the corn.

'He's coming!' Sebastian looked frantically about him for the sound had no direction.

'No,' squawked Mohammed. 'He turns against the wind. First he seeks for the smell of us, and then he will come.' He grabbed Sebastian's arm and clung to him, while they listened to the elephant circling to get down-wind of them.

'Perhaps he will run,' whispered Sebastian.

'Not this one. He is old and evil-tempered, and he has killed men before. Now he will hunt us.' Mohammed pulled at Sebastian's arm. 'We must get into the open. In this stuff we will have no chance, he will be on top of us before we see him.'

They started to run. There is no more piquant sauce for fear than flying feet. Once he starts to run, even a brave man becomes a coward. Within twenty paces, both of them were in headlong flight towards the village. They ran without regard for stealth, fighting their way through the tangle of leaves and stalks, panting wildly. The noise of their flight blanketed the sounds made by the elephant, so they lost all idea of his whereabouts. This sharpened the spurs of terror that drove them, for at any moment he might loom over them.

At last they stumbled out into the open, and paused, panting, sweating heavily, heads swinging from side to side as they tried to place the second bull.

'There!' shouted Mohammed. 'He comes,' and they heard the shrill pig-squealing, the noisy rush of his charge through the millet.

'Run!' yelled Sebastian, still in the grip of panic, and they ran.

Around a freshly lit bonfire at the edge of the village, waited the rejected Askari and a hundred of M'topo's men. They waited in anxiety for they had heard the shot and the fall of the first bull—but since then, the squealing and shouting and crashing had left them in some doubt as to what was happening in the gardens.

This doubt was quickly dispelled as Mohammed, closely followed by Sebastian, came down the path towards them, giving a fair imitation of two dogs whose backsides had been dipped in turpentine. A hundred yards behind them the bank of standing millet burst open, and the second bull came out in full charge.

Immense in the great light, hump-backed, shambling in the deceptive speed of his run, streaming his huge ears, each squeal of rage enough to burst the eardrums—he bore down on the village.

'Get out! Run!' Sebastian's shouted warning was as wheezy as it was unnecessary. The waiting crowd was no longer waiting, it scattered like a shoal of sardines at the approach of a barracuda.

Men threw aside their blankets and ran naked; they fell over each other and ran headlong into trees. Two of them ran straight through the middle of the bonfire and emerged on the other side trailing sparks with live coals sticking to their feet. In a wailing hubbub they swept back through the village, and from each hut women with infants bundled under their arms, or slung over their backs, scurried out to join the terrified torrent of humanity.

Still making good time, Sebastian and Mohammed were passing the weaker runners among the villagers, while from behind, the elephant was gaining rapidly on all of them.

With the force and velocity of a great boulder rolling down a steep hillside, the bull reached the first hut of the village and ran into it. The flimsy structure of grass and light poles exploded, bursting asunder without diminishing the fury of the animal's charge. A second hut disintegrated, then a third, before the elephant caught the first human straggler.

She was an old woman, tottering on thin legs, the empty pouches of her breasts flopping against her wrinkled belly, a long monotonous wail of fear keening from the toothless pit of her mouth as she ran.

The bull uncoiled his trunk from his chest, lifted it high above the woman and struck her across the shoulder. The force of the blow crumpled her, bones snapped in her chest like old dry sticks, and she died before she hit the ground.

The next was a girl. Groggy with sleep, yet her naked body was silver-smooth and graceful in the moonlight, as she emerged from a hut into the path of the bull's charge. Lightly the thick trunk enfolded her, and then with an effortless flick threw her forty feet into the air.

She screamed, and the sound of the scream knifed through Sebastian's panic. He glanced over his shoulder in time to see the girl thrown high into the night sky. Her limbs were spread-eagled and she spun in the air like a cartwheel before she dropped back to earth—falling heavily so that the scream was cut off abruptly. Sebastian stopped running.

Deliberately the elephant knelt over the girl's feebly squirming body, and driving down with his tusks, impaled her through the chest. She hung from the shaft of ivory, squashed and broken, no longer recognizable as human, until the elephant shook his head irritably and threw her off.

It needed a sight as horrible as this to rally Sebastian's shattered nerves—to summon the reserves of his manhood from the far places that fear had scattered them. The rifle was still in his hands, he was shaking with fear and exertion; sweat had drenched his tunic and plastered his curly hair on to his forehead, and his breath sawed hoarsely in his throat. He stood irresolute, fighting the driving urge to run again.

The bull came on, and now his one tusk was painted glistening black with the girl's blood, and gouts of the same stuff were splattered across the bulging forehead and the bridge of his trunk. It was this that changed Sebastian's fear first to disgust, and then to anger.

He lifted the rifle and it weaved unsteadily in his hands. He sighted along the barrel and suddenly his vision snapped into sharp focus and his nerves stilled their clamour. He was a man again.

Coldly he moved the blob of the foresight on to the bull's head, holding it on the deep lateral crease at the root of the trunk, and he squeezed the trigger. The butt jumped solidly into his shoulder, the report stung his eardrums, but he saw the bullet strike exactly where he had aimed it—a spurt of dust from the crust of dried mud that caked the animal's head and the skin around it, twitched, the eyelids quivered shut for an instant, then blinked open again.

Without lowering the rifle Sebastian jerked the bolt open, and the empty case ejected crisply, pinging away into the dust. He levered another cartridge into the breech and held his aim into the massive head. Again he fired and the elephant staggered drunkenly. The ears which had been cocked half back, now fanned open and the head swung vaguely in his direction.

He fired again, and the bull winced as the bullet lanced into the bone and gristle of his head, then he turned and came for Sebastian—but there was a slackness, a lack of determination in his charge. Aiming now for the chest, handling the rifle with cold method, Sebastian fired again and again, leaning forward against the recoil of the rifle, sighting every shot with care, knowing that each of them was raking the chest cavity, tearing through lung and heart and liver.

And the bull broke his run into a shuffling, uncertain walk, losing direction, turning away from Sebastian to stand broadside, the barrel of his chest heaving against the agony of his torn vitals.

Sebastian lowered the rifle and with steady fingers pressed fresh cartridges down into the empty magazine. The bull groaned softly and from the tip of his trunk blood hosed up from the haemorrhaging lungs.

Without pity, cold in his anger, Sebastian lifted the reloaded rifle, and aimed for the dark cavity that nestled in the centre of the huge ear. The bullet struck with the sharp thwack of an axe swung against a tree trunk, and the elephant sagged and fell forward to the brain shot. His weight drove his tusks into the earth, burying them to the lip.

27

Four tons of meat delivered fresh to the very centre of the village was good value. The price paid was not exorbitant, M'topo decided. Three huts could be rebuilt in two days, and only four acres of millet had been destroyed. Furthermore, of the women who had died, one was very old and the other, although she was almost eighteen years old, had never conceived. There was a good reason, therefore, to believe she was barren and not a great loss to the community.

Warmed by the early sun, M'topo was a satisfied man. With Sebastian beside him, he sat on his carved wooden stool and grinned widely as he watched the fun.

Two dozen of his men, armed with short-handled, long-bladed spears, and divested of all clothing, were to act as butchers. They were gathered beside the mountainous carcass arguing good-naturedly as they waited for Mohammed and his four assistants to remove the tusks. Around them, in a wider circle, waited the rest of the villagers, and while they waited, they sang. A drum hammered out the rhythm for them, and the clap of hands and the stamp of feet confirmed it. The masculine bass was a foundation from which the clear, sweet soprano of the women soared, and sank, and soared again.

Beneath Mohammed's patiently chipping axe, first the one tusk and then the other were freed from the bone that held them, and, with two Askari staggering under the weight, they were carried to where Sebastian sat; and laid with ceremony at his feet.

It occurred to Sebastian that four big tusks carried home to Lalapanzi might in some measure mollify Flynn O'Flynn. They would at least cover the costs of the expedition. The thought cheered him up considerably, and he turned to M'topo. 'Old one, you may take the meat.'

'Lord.' In gratitude, M'topo clapped his hands at the level of his chest, and then turned to squawk an order at the waiting butchers.

A roar of excitement and meat hunger went up from the crowd as one of them scrambled up on to the carcass, and drove his spear through the thick grey hide behind the last rib. Then walking backwards, he drew it down towards the haunch and the razor steel sliced deep. Two others made the lateral incisions, opening a square flap—a trapdoor into the belly cavity from which the fat coils of the viscera bulged, pink and blue and glossy wet in the early morning sunlight. In mounting eagerness, four others dragged from the square hole the contents of the belly, and then, while Sebastian stared in disbelief, they wriggled into the opening and disappeared. He could hear their muffled shouts reverberating within the carcass as they competed for the prize of the liver. Within minutes one of them reappeared, clutching against his chest a slippery lump of tattered purple liver. Like a maggot, he came squirming out of the wound, painted over-all with a thick coating of dark red blood. It had matted in the woolly cap of his hair, and turned his face into a gruesome mask from which only his teeth and his eyes gleamed white. Carrying the mutilated liver, laughing in triumph, he ran through the crowd to where Sebastian sat.

The offering embarrassed Sebastian. More than that, it made his gorge rise, and he felt his stomach heave as it was thrust almost into his lap.

'Eat,' M'topo encouraged him. 'It will make you strong. It will sharpen the spear of your manhood. Ten, twenty women will not tire you.'

It was M'topo's opinion that Sebastian needed this type of tonic. He had heard from his brother Saali, and from the chiefs along the river, about Sebastian's lack of initiative.

'Like this.' M'topo cut a hunk of the liver and popped it into his mouth. He chewed heartily, and the juice wet his lips as he grinned in appreciation. 'Very good.' He thrust a piece into Sebastian's face. 'Eat.'

'No.' Sebastian's gorge pressed heavily on the back of his throat, and he stood up hurriedly. M'topo shrugged, and ate it himself. Then he shouted to the butchers to continue their work.

In a miraculously short space of time the huge carcass disintegrated under the blades of the spears and machetes. It was a labour in which the entire village joined. With a dozen strokes of the knife, a butcher would free a large hunk of flesh and throw it down to one of the women. She, in turn, would hack it into smaller pieces and pass these on to the children. Squealing with excitement, they would run with them to the hastily erected drying racks, deposit them, and come scampering back for more.

Sebastian had recovered from his initial revulsion and now he laughed to see how every mouth was busy, chewing as they worked and yet at the same time managing to emit a surprising volume of noise.

Among the milling feet the dogs snarled and yipped, and gulped the scraps. Without interrupting their feeding, they dodged the casual kicks and blows that were aimed at them.

Into the midst of this cosy, domestic scene entered Commissioner Herman Fleischer with ten armed Askari.

28

Herman Fleischer was tired and there were blisters on his feet from the series of forced marches that had brought him to M'topo's village.

A month before he had left his headquarters at Mahenge to begin the annual tax tour of his area. As was his custom, he had started in the northern province, and it had been an unusually successful expedition. The wooden chest with the rampant black eagle painted on its lid had grown heavier with each day's journey. Herman had amused himself by calculating how many more years' service in Africa would be necessary before he could resign and return home to Plaven and settle down on the estate he planned to buy. Three more years as fruitful as this, he decided, would be sufficient. It was a bitter shame that he had not been able to capture O'Flynn's dhow on the Rufiji thirteen months previously—that would have advanced his departure by a full twelve months. Thinking about it stirred his residual anger at that episode, and he placated it by doubling the hut tax on the next village he visited. This raised such a howl of protest from the village headman that Herman nodded at his sergeant of Askari, who began ostentatiously to unpack the rope from his saddlebag.

'O fat and beautiful bull elephant,' the headman changed his mind hastily. 'If you will wait but a little while, I will bring the money to you. There is a new hut, without lice or fleas, in which you may rest your lovely body, and I will send a young girl to you with beer for your thirst.'

'Good,' agreed Herman. 'While I rest, my Askari will stay with you.' He nodded to the sergeant to bind the chief, then waddled away to the hut.

The headman sent two of his sons to dig beneath a certain tree in the forest, and they returned an hour later with mournful faces, carrying a heavy skin bag.

Contentedly Herman Fleischer signed an official receipt for ninety per cent of the contents of the bag—Fleischer allowed himself a ten per cent handling fee—and the headman, who could not read a word of German, accepted it with relief.

'I will stay tonight in your village,' Herman announced. 'Send the same girl to cook my food.'

The runner from the south arrived in the night, and disturbed Herman Fleischer at a most inopportune moment. The news he carried was even more disturbing. From his description of the new German commissioner who was doing Herman's job for him in the southern province, and shooting up the countryside in the process, Herman immediately recognized the young Englishman whom he had last seen on the deck of a dhow in the Rufiji delta.

Leaving the bulk of his retinue, including the bearers of the tax chest, to follow him at their best speed, Herman mounted at midnight on his white donkey and, taking ten Askari with him, he rode southwards on a storm patrol.

Five nights later, in those still dark hours that precede the dawn, Herman was camped near the Rovuma river when he was awakend by his sergeant.

'What is it?' Grumpy with fatigue, Herman sat up and lifted the side of his mosquito net.

'We heard the sound of gunfire. A single shot.'

'Where?' He was instantly awake, and reaching for his boots.

'From the south, towards the village of M'topo on the Rovuma.'

Fully dressed now, Herman waited anxiously, straining his ears against the small sounds of the African night. 'Are you sure . . . ?' he began as he turned to his sergeant, but he did not finish. Faintly, but unmistakable in the darkness, they heard the pop, pop, pop, of a distant rifle—a pause and then another shot.

'Break camp,' bellowed Herman. 'Rasch! You black heathen. Rasch!'

The sun was well up by the time they reached M'topo's village. They came upon it suddenly through the gardens of tall millet that screened their approach. Herman Fleischer paused to throw out his Askari in a line of skirmishers before closing in on the cluster of huts, but when he reached the fringe, he stopped once more in surprise at the extraordinary spectacle which was being enacted in the open square of the village.

The dense knot of half-naked black people that swarmed over the remains of the elephant was perfectly oblivious of Herman's presence until at last he filled his lungs, and then emptied them again in a roar that carried over the hubbub of shouts and laughter. Instantly a vast silence fell upon the gathering, every head turned towards Herman, and from each head eyes bulged in horrified disbelief.

'Bwana Intambu,' a small voice broke the silence at last. 'Lord of the rope.' They knew him well.

'What . . . ?' Herman began, and then gasped in outrage as he noticed in the crowd a black man he had never seen before, dressed in the full uniform of German Askari. 'You!' he shouted, pointing an accusing finger, but the man whirled and ducked away behind the screen of blood-smeared black bodies. 'Stop him!' Herman fumbled with the flap of his holster.

Movement caught his eye and he turned to see another pseudo-Askari running away between the huts. 'There's another one! Stop him! Sergeant, Sergeant, get your men here!'

The initial shock that had held them frozen was now past, and the crowd broke and scattered. Once again, Herman Fleischer gasped in outrage as he saw, for the first time, a figure sitting on a carved native stool on the far side of the square. A figure in an outlandish uniform of bright but travel-stained blue, frogged with gold, his legs clad in high jackboots, and on his head the dress helmet of an illustrious Prussian regiment.

'Englishman!' Despite the disguise, Herman recognized him. He had finally succeeded in unbuttoning the flap of his holster, and now he withdrew his Luger. 'Englishman!' He repeated the insult and lifted the pistol.

With the quickness of mind for which he was noted, Sebastian sat bewildered by this unforeseen turn of events, but when Herman showed him the working end of the Luger, he realized that it was time to take his leave, and he attempted to leap nimbly to his feet. However, the spurs on his boots became entangled once more and he went backwards over the stool. The bullet hissed harmlessly through the empty space where he would have been standing.

'God damn!' Herman fired again, and the bullet kicked a burst of splinters out of the heavy wooden stool behind which Sebastian was lying. This second failure aroused in Herman Fleischer the blinding rage which spoiled his aim for the next two shots he fired, as Sebastian went on hands and knees around the corner of the nearest hut.

Behind the hut, Sebastian jumped to his feet and set off at a run. His main concern was to get out of the village and into the bush. In his ears echoed Flynn O'Flynn's advice.

'Make for the river. Go straight for the river.'

And he was so occupied with it that, when he charged around the side of the next hut, he could not check himself in time to avoid collision with one of Herman Fleischer's Askari, who was coming in the opposite direction. Both of them went down together in an untidy heap, and the steel helmet fell forward over Sebastian's eyes. As he struggled into a sitting position, he removed the helmet and found the man's woolly black head in front of him. It was ideally placed and Sebastian was holding the heavy helmet above it. With the strength of both his arms, he brought the helmet down again, and it clanged loudly against the Askari's skull. With a grunt the Askari sagged backwards and lay quietly in the dust. Sebastian placed the helmet over his sleeping face, picked up the man's rifle from beside him and got to his feet once more.

He stood crouching in the shelter of the hut while he tried to make sense of the chaos around him. Through the pandemonium set up by the panic-stricken villagers, who were milling about with all the purpose of a flock of sheep attacked by wolves, Sebastian could hear the bellowed commands of Herman Fleischer, and the answering shots of the German Askari. Rifle-fire cracked and whined, to be answered by renewed outbursts of screaming.

Sebastian's first impulse was to hide in one of the huts but he realized this would be futile. At the best it would only delay his capture.

No, he must get out of the village. But the thought of covering the hundred yards of open ground to the shelter of the nearest trees, while a dozen Askari shot at him, was most unattractive.

At this moment Sebastian became aware of an unpleasant warmth in his feet, and he looked down to find that he was standing in the live ashes of a cooking fire. The leather of his jackboots was already beginning to char and smoke. He stepped back hurriedly, and the smell of burning leather acted as a laxative for the constipation of his brain.

From the hut beside him he snatched a handful of thatch and stooped to thrust it into the fire. The dry grass burst into flame, and Sebastian held the torch to the wall of the hut. Instantly fire bloomed and shot upwards. With the torch in his hand, Sebastian ducked across the narrow opening to the next hut and set fire to that also.

'Son of a gun!' exulted Sebastian as great oily billows of smoke obscured the sun and limited his field of vision to ten paces.

Slowly he moved forward in the rolling cloud of smoke, setting fire to each hut he passed, and delighting in the frustrated bellows of Germanic rage he heard about him. Occasionally ghostly figures scampered past him in the acrid half-darkness but none of them paid him the slightest attention, and each time Sebastian relaxed the pressure of his forefinger on the trigger of the Mauser, and moved on.

He reached the last hut and paused there to gather himself for the final sprint across open ground to the edge of the millet garden. Through the eddying bank of smoke, the mass of dark green vegetation from which he had fled in terror not many hours before, now seemed as welcoming as the arms of his mother.

Movement near him in the smoke, and he swung the Mauser to cover it; he saw the square outline of a kepi and the sparkle of metal buttons, and his finger tightened on the trigger.

'Manali!'

'Mohammed! Good God, I nearly killed you.' Sebastian threw up the rifle barrel as he recognized him.

'Quickly! They are close behind me.' Mohammed snatched at his arm and dragged him forward. The jackboots pinched his toes and thumped like the hooves of a galloping buffalo as Sebastian ran. From the huts behind them a voice shouted urgently and, immediately afterwards, came the vicious crack of a Mauser and the shrill whinny of the ricochet.

Sebastian had a lead of ten paces on Mohammed as he plunged into the bank of leaves and millet stalks.

29

'What should we do now, Manali?' Mohammed asked, and the expression on the faces of the two other men echoed the question with pathetic trust. A benevolent chance had reunited Sebastian with the remnants of his command. During the flight through the millet gardens, with random rifle-fire clipping the leaves about their heads, Sebastian had literally fallen over these two. At the time they were engaged in pressing their bellies and their faces hard against the earth, and it had taken a number of lusty kicks with the jackboot to get them up and moving.

Since then Sebastian, mindful of Flynn's advice, had cautiously and circuitously led them down to the landing-place on the bank of the Rovuma. He arrived to find that Fleischer's Askari, by using the direct route and without the necessity of concealing themselves, had arrived before him. From the cover of the reed-banks Sebastian watched dejectedly, as they used an axe to knock the bottoms out of the dug-out canoes that were drawn up on the little white beach.

'Can we swim across?' he asked Mohammed in a whisper, and Mohammed's face crumpled with horror, as he considered the suggestion. Both of them peered out through the reeds across a quarter of a mile of deep water that flowed so fast, its surface was dimpled with tiny whirlpools.

'No,' said Mohammed with finality.

'Too far?' asked Sebastian hopelessly.

'Too far. Too fast. Too deep. Too many crocodiles,' agreed Mohammed, and in an unspoken, but mutual desire to get away from the river and the Askari, they crawled out of the reed-bank and crept away inland.

In the late afternoon they were lying up in a bushy gully about two miles from the river and an equal distance from M'topo's village.

'What should we do now, Manali?' Mohammed repeated his question, and Sebastian cleared his throat before answering.

'Well . . .' he said, and paused while his wide brow wrinkled in the agony of creative thought. Then it came to him with all the splendour of a sunrise. 'We'll just jolly well have to find some other way of getting across the river.' He said it with the air of a man well pleased with his own perspicacity. 'What do you suggest, Mohammed.'

A little surprised to find the ball returned so neatly into his own court, Mohammed remained silent.

'A raft?' hazarded Sebastian. The lack of tools, materials, and opportunity to build one was so obvious, that Mohammed did not deign to reply. He shook his head.

'No,' agreed Sebastian. 'Perhaps you are right.' Again the classic beauty of his features was marred by a scowl of concentration. At last he demanded, 'There are other villages along the river?'

'Yes,' Mohammed conceded. 'But the Askari will visit each of them and destroy the canoes. Also they will tell the headmen who we are, and threaten them with the rope.'

'But they cannot cover the whole river. It has a frontier of five or six hundred miles. We'll just keep walking until we find a canoe. It may take us a long time but we'll find one eventually.'

'If the Askari don't catch us first.'

'They'll expect us to stay close to the border. We'll make a detour well inland, and march for five or six days before we come back to the river again. We'll rest now and move tonight.'

Heading on a diagonal line of march away from the Rovuma and deeper into German territory, moving north-west along a well defined footpath, the four of them kept walking all that night. As the slow hours passed the pace flagged and twice Sebastian noticed one or other of his men wander off the path at an angle until suddenly they started and looked about in surprise, before hurrying back to join the others. It puzzled him and he meant to ask them what they were doing, but he was tired and the effort of speech was too great. An hour later he found the reason for their behaviour.

Plodding along with the movement of his legs become completely automatic, Sebastian was slowly overcome by a state of gentle well-being. He surrendered to it and let the warm, dark mists of oblivion wash over his mind.

The sting of a thorn branch across his cheek jerked him back to consciousness and he looked about in bewilderment. Ten yards away on his flank, Mohammed and the two gun-boys walked along the path in single file, their faces turned towards him with expressions of mild interest in the moonlight. It took some moments for Sebastian to realize that he had fallen asleep on his feet. Feeling a complete ass, he trotted back to take his place at the head of the line.

When the fat silver moon sank below the trees, they kept going by the faint glow of reflected light, but slowly that waned until the footpath hardly showed at their feet. Sebastian decided that dawn could be only an hour away and it was time to halt. He stopped and was about to speak when Mohammed's clutching hand on his shoulder prevented him.

'Manali!' There was a tone in Mohammed's whisper that cautioned him, and Sebastian felt his nerves jerk taut.

'What is it?' he breathed, protectively unslinging the Mauser.

'Look. There—ahead of us.'

Screwing up his eyes Sebastian searched the blackness ahead, and it was a long time before the faint ruddiness in the solid blanket of darkness registered itself upon the exhausted retinas of his eyes. 'Yes!' he whispered. 'What is it?'

'A fire,' breathed Mohammed. 'There is someone camped across the path in front of us.'

'Askari?' asked Sebastian.

'Perhaps.'

Peering at the ruby puddle of dying coals, Sebastian felt the hair on the back of his neck stir and come erect with alarm. He was fully awake now. 'We must go around them.'

'No. They will see our spoor in the dust of the path and they will follow us,' Mohammed demurred.

'What then?'

'First let me see how many there are.'

Without waiting for Sebastian's permission, Mohammed slipped away and disappeared into the night like a leopard. Five anxious minutes Sebastian waited. Once he thought he heard a scuffling sound but he was not certain. Mohammed's shape materialized again beside him. 'Ten of them,' he reported. 'Two Askari and eight bearers. One of the Askari sat guard by the fire. He saw me, so I killed him.'

'Good God!' Sebastian's voice rose higher. 'You did what?'

'I killed him. But do not speak so loud.'

'How?'

'With my knife.'

'Why?'

'Lest he kill me first.'

'And the other?'

'Him also.'

'You killed both of them?' Sebastian was appalled.

'Yes, and took their rifles. Now it is safe to go on. But the bearers have with them many cases. It comes to me that this party follows after Bwana Intambu, the German commissioner, and that they carry with them all his goods.'

'But you shouldn't have killed them,' protested Sebastian. 'You could have just tied them up or something.'

'Manali, you argue like a woman,' Mohammed snapped impatiently, and then went on with his original line of thought. 'Among the cases is one that by its size I think is the box for the tax money. The one Askari slept with his back against it as though to give it special care.'

'The tax money?'

'Yes.'

'Well, son of a gun!' Sebastian's scruples dissolved and in the darkness his expression was suddenly transformed into that of a small boy on Christmas morning.

They woke the German bearers by standing over them and prodding them with the rifle barrels. Then they hustled them out of their blankets and herded them into a small group, bewildered and shivering miserably in the chill of dawn. Wood was heaped on the fire; it burned up brightly, and by its light Sebastian examined the booty.

The one Askari had bled profusely from the throat on to the small wooden chest. Mohammed took him by the heels and dragged him out of the way, then used his blanket to wipe the chest clean.

'Manali,' he said with reverence. 'See the big lock. See the bird of the Kaiser painted on the lid . . .' He stooped over the chest and took a grip of the handles, '. . . but most of all, feel the weight of it!'

Among the other equipment around the fire, Mohammed found a thick coil of one-inch manila rope. A commodity which was essential equipment on any of Herman Fleischer's safaris. With it, Mohammed roped the bearers together, at waist level, allowing enough line between each of them to make concerted movement possible but preventing individual flight.

'Why are you doing that?' Sebastian asked with interest, through a mouthful of blood sausage and black bread. Most of the other boxes were filled with food, and Sebastian was breakfasting well and heartily.

'So they cannot escape.'

'We're not taking them with us—are we?'

'Who else will carry all this?' Mohammed asked patiently.

Five days later Sebastian was seated in the bows of a long dug-out canoe, with the charred soles of his boots set firmly on the chest that lay in the bilges. He was eating with relish a thick sandwich of polony and pickled onions, wearing a change of clean underwear and socks that were a few sizes too large, and there was clutched in his left hand an open bottle of Hansa beer—all these with the courtesy of Commissioner Fleischer.

The paddlers were singing with unforced gaiety, for the hiring fee that Sebastian had paid them would buy each of them a new wife at least.

Hugging the bank of the Rovuma on the Portuguese side, driven on by willing paddles and the eager current, in twelve hours they covered the distance that had taken Sebastian and his heavily-laden bearers five days on foot.

The canoe deposited Sebastian's party at the landing opposite M'topo's village, only ten miles from Lalapanzi. They walked that distance without resting and arrived after nightfall.

30

The windows of the bungalow were darkened, and the whole camp slept. After cautioning them to silence, Sebastian drew his depleted band up on the front lawn with the tax chest set prominently in front of them. He was proud of his success and wanted to achieve the appropriate mood for his home-coming. Having set the stage, he went up on to the stoep of the bungalow and tip-toed towards the front door with the intention of awakening the household by hammering upon it dramatically.

However, there was a chair on the stoep, and Sebastian tripped over it. He fell heavily. The chair clattered and the rifle slipped from his shoulder and rang on the stone flags.

Before Sebastian could recover his feet, the door was flung open and through it appeared Flynn O'Flynn in his night-shirt and armed with a double-barrelled shotgun. 'Caught you, you bastard!' he roared and lifted the shotgun.

Sebastian heard the click of the safety-catch and scrambled to his knees.

'Don't shoot! Flynn, it's me.'

The shotgun wavered a little. 'Who are you—and what do you want?'

'It's me—Sebastian.'

'Bassie?' Flynn lowered the shotgun uncertainly. 'It can't be. Stand up, let's have a look at you.'

Sebastian obeyed with alacrity.

'Good God,' Flynn swore in amazement. 'It *is* you. Good God! We heard that Fleischer caught you at M'topo's village a week ago. We heard he'd nobbled you for keeps!' He came forward with his right hand extended in welcome. 'You made it, did you? Well done, Bassie boy.'

Before Bassie could accept Flynn's hand, Rosa came through the doorway, brushed past Flynn, and almost knocked Sebastian down again. With her arms locked around his chest and her cheek pressed to his unshaven cheek, she kept repeating, 'You're safe! Oh Sebastian, you're safe.'

Acutely aware of the fact that Rosa wore nothing under the thin night-gown, and that everywhere he put his hands they came in contact with thinly-veiled warm flesh, Sebastian grinned sheepishly at Flynn over his shoulder.

'Excuse me,' he said.

His first two kisses were off target for she was moving around a lot. One caught her on the ear, the next on her eyebrow, but the third was right between the lips.

When at last they were forced to separate or suffocate, Rosa gasped, 'I thought you were dead.'

'All right, missie,' growled Flynn. 'You can go and put some clothes on now.'

Breakfast at Lalapanzi that morning was a festive affair. Flynn took advantage of his daughter's weakened condition and brought a bottle of gin to the table. Her protests were half-hearted, and later with her own hands she poured a little into Sebastian's tea to brace it.

They ate on the stoep in golden sunshine that filtered through the bougainvillaea creeper. A flock of glossy starlings hopped and chirruped on the lawns, and an oriel sang from the wild fig trees. All nature conspired to make Sebastian's victory feast a success, while Rosa and Nanny did their best from the kitchen—drawing upon the remains of Herman Fleischer's supplies that Sebastian had brought home with him.

Flynn O'Flynn's eyes were bloodshot and underhung with plum-coloured pouches, for he had been up all night counting the contents of the German tax chest and working out his accounts by the light of a hurricane lamp. Nevertheless, he was in a merry mood made merrier by the cups of fortified tea on which he was breakfasting. He joined warmly in the chorus of praise and felicitation to Sebastian Oldsmith that was being sung by Rosa O'Flynn.

'You turned up one for the book, so help me, Bassie,' he chortled at the end of the meal. 'I'd just love to hear how Fleischer is going to explain this one to Governor Schee. Oh, I'd love to be there when he tells him about the tax money—son of a gun, it'll nigh kill them both.'

'While you're on the subject of the money,' Rosa smiled at Flynn, 'have you worked out how much Sebastian's share comes to, Daddy?' Rosa only used Flynn's paternal title when she was extremely well-disposed towards him.

'That I have,' admitted Flynn, and the sudden shiftiness of his eyes aroused Rosa's suspicions. Her lips pursed a little.

'And how much is it?' she asked in the syrupy tone which Flynn recognized as the equivalent of the blood roar of a wounded lioness.

'Sure now, and who wants to be spoiling a lovely day with the talking of business?' Under pressure, Flynn exaggerated the brogue in his voice in the hope that Rosa would find it beguiling. A forlorn hope.

'How much?' demanded Rosa, and he told her.

There was a sickly silence. Sebastian paled under his sunburn and opened his mouth to protest. On the strength of his half share, he had the previous night made to Rosa O'Flynn a serious proposal, which she had accepted.

'Leave this to me, Sebastian,' she whispered and laid a restraining hand on his knees as she turned back to her father. 'You'll let us have a look at the accounts, won't you?' Still syrupy sweet.

'Sure and I will. They're all straight and square.'

The document that Flynn O'Flynn produced under the main heading, 'Joint Venture Between F. O'Flynn, Esq., S. Oldsmith, Esq., and Others. German East Africa. Period May 15th, 1913, to August 21st, 1913', showed that he belonged to an unorthodox school of accountancy.

The contents of the tax chest had been converted to English sterling at the rates laid down by Pear's Almanac for 1893. Flynn set great store by this particular publication.

From the gross proceeds of £4,652 18s 6d, Flynn had deducted his own fifty per cent share and the ten per cent of the other partners—the Portuguese Chef D'Post and the Governor of Mozambique. From the balance he had then deducted the losses incurred on the Rufiji expedition (for which see separate account addressed to German East African Administration). From there he had gone on to charge the expenses of the second expedition, not forgetting such items as:

To L. Parbhoo (Tailor)	£15	10 –
To One German Dress Helmet (say)	£5	10 –
To Five Uniforms (Askari) at £2 10–each	£12	10 –
To Five Mauser Rifles at £10—each	£50	– –
To Six Hundred and Twenty-Five Rounds 7mm Ammunition	£22	10 –
To Advance re travelling expenses, One Hundred Escudos made to S. Oldsmith, Esq.	£1	5 –

Finally, Sebastian's half share of the net losses amounted to a little under twenty pounds.

'Don't worry,' Flynn assured him magnanimously. 'I don't expect you to pay it now–we'll just deduct it from your share of the profits of the next expedition.'

'But, Flynn, I thought you said–well, I mean, you told me I had a half share.'

'And so you have, Bassie, and so you have.'

'You said we were equal partners.'

'You must have misunderstood me, boy. I said a half share–and that means after expenses. It's just a great pity there was such a large accumulated loss to bring forward.'

While they discussed this, Rosa was busy with a stub of indelible pencil on the reverse side of Flynn's account. Two minutes later she thrust the result across the breakfast table at Flynn. She said, 'And that's the way I work it out.'

Rosa O'Flynn was a student of the 'One-for-you-one-for-me' school, and her reckonings were much simpler than those of her father.

With a cry of anguish, Flynn O'Flynn lodged objection. 'You don't understand business.'

'But I recognize crookery when I see it,' Rosa flashed back.

'You'd call your old father a crook?'

'Yes.'

'I've a damn good mind to take the kiboko to you. You're not too big and uppity that I can't warm your tail up good.'

'You just try it!' said Rosa, and Flynn backpedalled.

'Anyway, what would Bassie do with all that money? It's not good for a youngster. It would spoil him.'

'He'd marry me with it. That's what he'd do with it.'

Flynn made a noise as though there was a fish-bone stuck in his throat, his face mottled over with emotion, and he swung ominously in Sebastian's direction. 'So!' he rasped. 'I thought so!'

'Now steady on, old chap,' Sebastian tried to soothe him.

'You come into my home and act like the king of bloody England. You try to fraudulently embezzle my money–but that's not enough! Oh no! That's not a bloody 'nough. You've also got to start tampering with my daughter just to round things off.'

'Don't be coarse,' said Rosa.

'That's rich–*don't be coarse*, she says, and just what exactly have you two been up to behind my back?'

Sebastian stood up from the breakfast table with dignity. 'I will not have you speak so of a lady in my presence, sir. Especially of the lady who has done me the great honour of consenting to become my wife.' He began unbuttoning his jacket. 'Will you step into the garden with me, and give me satisfaction?'

'Come along, then.' As Flynn lumbered out of his chair he made as if to pass Sebastian, but at the moment Sebastian's arms were behind him, still bound by the sleeves of his jacket as he attempted to shrug it off. Flynn side-stepped swiftly, paused a moment as he took his aim, and then drove his left fist into Sebastian's stomach.

'Oof!' said Sebastian, and leaned forward involuntarily to meet Flynn's other fist as it came up from the level of his knees. It took Sebastian between the eyes, and he changed direction abruptly and ran backwards across the veranda. The low wooden railing caught him behind the knees and he toppled slowly into the flower-beds below the stoep.

'You've killed him,' wailed Rosa, and picked up the heavy china tea-pot.

'I hope so,' said Flynn, and ducked as the pot flew towards his head, passed over it, and burst against the wall of the stoep, spraying tea and steam.

There was an ominous stirring among Rosa's flowers, and presently Sebastian's head emerged with blue hydrangea petals festively strewn in his hair and the skin around both eyes fast swelling and chameleoning to a creditable match with the petals. 'I say, Flynn. That wasn't fair,' he announced.

'He wasn't looking,' Rosa accused. 'You hit him before he was ready.'

'Well, he's looking now,' roared Flynn and went down the veranda stairs like a charging hippopotamus. From the hydrangeas, Sebastian rose to meet him and took up the classic stance of the ring fighter. 'Marquis of Queensberry rules?' he cautioned as Flynn closed in.

Flynn signified his rejection of the Marquis' code by kicking Sebastian on the shin. Sebastian yelped and hopped one-legged out of the flower-bed, while Flynn pursued him with a further series of lusty kicks. Placing his boot twice in succession into Sebastian's posterior, the third kick, however, missed and the force behind it was sufficient to throw Flynn on to his back. He sprawled on the lawn, and the pause while he scrambled to his knees, gave Sebastian respite to ready himself for the next round.

Both his eyes had puffed and he was experiencing discomfort from his rear end; nevertheless, he stood once again with his left arm extended and the right crossed over his chest. Glancing beyond Flynn, Sebastian saw his fiancée descending from the veranda. She was armed with a bread-knife.

'Rosa!' Sebastian was alarmed. It was clear that Rosa would not stop at patricide to protect her love. 'Rosa! What are you doing with that knife?'

'I'm going to stick him with it!'

'You'll do no such thing,' said Sebastian, but Flynn did not have the same faith in his daughter's restraint. Very hurriedly, he moved into a defensive position behind Sebastian. From there he listened with attention to the argument between Sebastian and Rosa. It took a full minute for Sebastian to persuade Rosa that her assistance was not necessary and that he was capable of handling the situation on his own. Reluctantly, Rosa retreated to the veranda.

'Thanks, Bassie,' said Flynn, and kicked him in his already bruised behind. It was extremely painful.

Very few people had ever seen Sebastian Oldsmith lose his temper. The last time it had happened was eight years previously; the two sixth-formers who had invoked it by forcing Sebastian's head into a toilet bowl and flushing the cistern, were both hospitalized for a short period.

This time there were more witnesses. Attracted by the cries and crash of breaking crockery, Flynn's entire following, including Mohammed and his Askari, had arrived from the compound and were assembled at the top of the lawn. They watched in breathless wonder.

From the grandstand of the veranda, Rosa, her eyes sparkling with that strange feminine ferocity that arises in even the mildest women when their man fights for them, exhorted Sebastian to even greater violence.

Like all great storms, it did not last long, and when it was over the silence was appalling. Flynn lay stretched full-length on the lawn. His eyes closed and his breathing snoring softly in his throat, and bursting from his nose in a froth of red bubbles.

Mohammed and five of his men carried him towards the bungalow. He lay massive on their shoulders with the bulge of his belly rising and falling softly, and an expression of unusual peace on his bloody face.

Standing alone on the lawn, Sebastian's features were contorted with savagery and his whole body shook as though he was in high fever. Then, watching them carry the huge, inert body, suddenly Sebastian's mood was past. His expression changed first to concern and then to gentle dismay. 'I say . . .' his voice was husky and he took a pace after them. 'You shouldn't have kicked me.' His hands opened helplessly, and he lifted them in a gesture of appeal. 'You shouldn't have done it.'

Rosa came down from the veranda and walked slowly towards him. She stopped and looked up at him, half in awe, half in glowing pride. 'You were magnificent,' she whispered. 'Like a lion.' She reached up with both arms around his neck, and before she kissed him she spoke again. 'I love you,' she said.

Sebastian had very little luggage to take with him. He was wearing everything he possessed. Rosa on the other hand, had boxes of it, enough to give full employment to the dozen bearers that were assembled on the lawn in front of the bungalow.

'Well,' murmured Sebastian, 'I suppose we should start moving.'

'Yes,' whispered Rosa, and looked at the gardens of Lalapanzi. Although she had suggested this departure, now that the time had come she was uncertain. This place had been her home since childhood. Here she had spun a cocoon that had shielded and protected her, and now that the time had come to emerge from it, she was afraid. She took Sebastian's arm, drawing strength from him.

'Don't you want to say goodbye to your father?' Sebastian looked down at her with the tender protectiveness that was such a new and delightful sensation for him.

Rosa hesitated a moment, and then realized that it would take very little to weaken her resolve. Her dutiful affection for Flynn, which at the moment was submerged beneath the tide of anger and resentment, could easily re-emerge should Flynn employ a little of his celebrated blarney. 'No,' she said.

'I suppose it's best,' Sebastian agreed. He glanced guiltily towards the bungalow where Flynn was, presumably, still lying in state–attended by the faithful Mohammed. 'But do you think he'll be all right? I mean, I did hit him rather hard, you know.'

'He'll be all right,' Rosa said without conviction, and tugged at his sleeve. Together they moved to take their places at the head of the little column of bearers.

Kneeling on the floor of the bedroom, below the window sill, peering with one swollen eye through a slit in the curtain, Flynn saw this decisive move. 'My God,' he whispered in concern. 'The young idiots are really leaving.'

Rosa O'Flynn was his last link with that frail little Portuguese girl. The one person in his life that Flynn had truly loved. Now that he was about to lose her also, Flynn was suddenly aware of his feelings for his daughter. The prospect of never seeing her again filled him with dismay.

As for Sebastian Oldsmith, here no sentiment clouded his reasoning. Sebastian was a valuable business asset. Through him, Flynn could put into operation a number of schemes that he had shelved as involving disproportionate personal risk. In these last few years Flynn had become increasingly aware of the depreciation that time and large quantities of raw spirit had wrought in his eyes and legs and nerves. Sebastian Oldsmith had eyes like a fish eagle, legs like a prize fighter, and no nerves at all that Flynn could discern. Flynn needed him.

Flynn opened his mouth and groaned. It was the throaty death rattle of an old bull buffalo. Peering through the curtain, Flynn grinned as he saw the young couple freeze, and stand tense and still in the sunlight. Their faces were turned towards the bungalow, and in spite of himself, Flynn had to admit they made a handsome pair; Sebastian tall above her with the body of a gladiator and the face of a poet; Rosa small beside him but with the full bosom and wide hips of womanhood. The slippery black cascade of her hair glowed in the sun, and her dark eyes were big with concern.

Flynn groaned again but softly this time. A breathless, husky sound, the last breath of a dying man, and instantly Rosa and Sebastian were running towards the bungalow. Her skirts gathered up above her knees, long legs flying, Rosa led Sebastian up on to the veranda.

Flynn had just sufficient time to return to his bed and compose his limbs and his face into the attitude of one fast sinking towards the abyss.

'Daddy!' Rosa leaned over him, and Flynn opened his eyes uncertainly. For a moment he did not seem to recognize her, then he whispered, 'My little girl,' so faintly she hardly caught the words.

'Oh, Daddy, what is it?' She knelt beside him.

'My heart.' His hand crawled up like a hairy spider across his belly and clutched weakly at his hairy chest. 'Like a knife. A hot knife.'

There was a terrible silence in the room, and then Flynn spoke again. 'I wanted to . . . give you my . . . blessing. I wish happiness for you . . . wherever you go.' The effort of speech was too much, and for a while he lay gasping. 'Think of your old Daddy sometimes. Say a prayer for him.'

A fat, shiny tear broke from the corner of Rosa's eye and slid down her cheek.

'Bassie, my boy.' Slowly Flynn's eyes sought him, found him, and focused with difficulty. 'Don't blame yourself for this. I was an old man anyway–I've had my life.' He panted a little and then went on painfully. 'Look after her. Look after my little Rosa. You are my son now. I've never had a son.'

'I didn't know . . . I had no idea that your heart . . . Flynn, I'm dreadfully sorry. Forgive me.'

Flynn smiled, a brave little smile that just touched his lips. He lifted his hand weakly and held it out towards Sebastian. While Sebastian clasped his hand, Flynn considered offering him the money that had been the cause of the dispute as a dying man's gift but he manfully restrained himself from such extravagance. Instead he whispered, 'I would like to have seen my grandson, but no matter. Goodbye, my boy.'

'You'll see him, Flynn. I promise you that. We'll stay, won't we, Rosa? We'll stay with him.'

'Yes, we'll stay,' said Rosa. 'We won't leave you, Daddy.'

'My children.' Flynn sank back and closed his eyes. Thank God, he hadn't offered the money. A peaceful little smile hovered around his mouth. 'You've made an old man very happy.'

31

Flynn made a strong come-back from the edge of death, so strong, in fact, that it aroused Rosa's suspicions. However, she let it pass for she was happy to have avoided the necessity of leaving Lalapanzi. In addition, there was another matter which was taking up a lot of her attention.

Since she had said goodbye to Sebastian at the start of his tax tour, Rosa had been aware of the cessation of certain womanly functions of her body. She consulted Nanny who, in turn, consulted the local nangane who, in his turn, opened the belly of a chicken, and consulted its entrails. His findings were conclusive, and Nanny reported back to Rosa, without disclosing the source of her information, for Little Long Hair had an almost blasphemous lack of faith in the occult.

Delighted, Rosa took Sebastian for a walk down the valley, and they reached the waterfall where it had all began, she stood on tip-toe, put both arms around his neck, and whispered in his ear. She had to repeat herself for her voice was muffled with breathless laughter.

'You're joking,' gasped Sebastian, and then blushed bright crimson.

'I'm not, you know.'

'Good grief,' said Sebastian; and then, groping for something more expressive, 'Son of a gun!'

'Aren't you pleased?' Rosa pouted playfully. 'I did it for you.'

'But we aren't even married.'

'That can be arranged.'

'And quickly, too,' agreed Sebastian. He grabbed her wrist. 'Come on!'

'Sebastian, remember my condition.'

'Good grief, I'm sorry.'

He took her back to Lalapanzi, handing her over the rough ground with as much care as though she was a case of sweating gelignite.

'What's the big hurry?' asked Flynn jovially at dinner that evening. 'I've got a little job for Bassie first. I want him to slip across the river . . .'

'No, you don't,' said Rosa. 'We're going to see the priest at Beira.'

'It would only take Bassie a couple of weeks. Then we could talk about it when he gets back.'

'We are going to Beira—tomorrow!'

'What's the rush?' Flynn asked again.

'Well, the truth is, Flynn, old boy . . .' Wriggling in his chair, colouring up vividly, Sebastian relapsed into silence.

'The truth is I'm going to have a baby,' Rosa finished for him.

'You're *what*?!' Flynn stared at her in horror.

'You said that you wanted to see your grandchild,' Rosa pointed out.

'But I didn't mean you to start work on it right away,' roared Flynn, and he rounded on Sebastian. 'You dirty young bugger!'

'Father, your heart!' Rosa restrained him. 'Anyway, don't pick on Sebastian, I did my share as well.'

'You shameless . . . You brazen little . . .'

Rosa reached behind the seat cushion where Flynn had hidden the gin bottle. 'Have a little of this—it will help calm you.'

They left for Beira the following morning. Rosa was carried in a maschille with Sebastian trotting beside it in anxious attendance, ready to help ease the litter over the fords and rough places, and to curse any of the bearers who stumbled.

When they left Lalapanzi, Flynn O'Flynn brought up the rear of the column, lying in his maschille with a square-faced bottle for company, scowling and muttering darkly about 'fornication' and 'sin'.

But both Rosa and Sebastian ignored him, and when they camped that night the two of them sat across the camp-fire from him, and whispered and laughed secretly together. They pitched their voices at such a tantalizing level that even by straining his ears, Flynn could not overhear their conversation. It infuriated him to such an extent that finally he made a loud remark about '. . . beating the hell out of the person who had repaid his hospitality by violating his daughter'.

Rosa said that she would give anything to see him try it *again*. In her opinion it would be better than a visit to the circus. And Flynn gathered his dignity and his gin bottle and stalked away to where Mohammed had laid out his bedding under a lean-to of thorn bushes.

During the dark hours before dawn they were visited by an old lion. He came with a rush from the darkness beyond the fire-light, grunting like an angry boar, the great black bush of his mane erect, snaking with incredible speed towards the huddle of blanket-wrapped figures about the fire.

Flynn was the only one not asleep. He had waited all night, watching Sebastian's reclining figure; just waiting for him to move across to the temporary thorn-bush shelter that gave Rosa privacy. Lying beside Flynn was his shotgun, double-loaded with big loopers, lion shot, and he had every intention of using it.

When the lion charged into the camp, Flynn sat up quickly and fired both barrels of the shotgun at point-blank range into the man-eater's head and chest, killing it instantly. But the momentum of its rush bowled it forward, sent it sliding full into Sebastian, and both of them rolled into the camp-fire.

Sebastian awoke to lion noises, and gunfire, and the violent collision of a big body into his, and red-hot coals sticking to various parts of his anatomy. With a single bound, and a wild cry, he threw off his blanket, came to his feet, and went into a such a lively song and dance routine, yodelling and high-kicking, and striking out at his imaginary assailants that Flynn was reduced to a jelly of helpless laughter.

The laughter, and the praise and thanks showered on him by Sebastian, Rosa, and the bearers, cleared the air.

'You saved my life,' said Sebastian soulfully.

'Oh Daddy, you're wonderful,' said Rosa. 'Thank you. Thank you,' and she hugged him.

The mantle of the hero felt snug and comfortable on Flynn's shoulders. He became almost human–and the improvement continued as each day's march brought him closer to the little Portuguese port of Beira, for Flynn greatly enjoyed his rare visits to civilization.

The last night they camped a mile from the outskirts of the town, and after a private conference with Flynn, old Mohammed went ahead armed with a small purse of escudos to make the arrangements for Flynn's formal entry on the morrow.

Flynn was up with the dawn, and while he shaved with care, and dressed in clean moleskin jacket and trousers, one of the bearers polished his boots with hippo fat, and two others scaled the tall bottle palm tree near the camp and cut fronds from its head.

All things being ready, Flynn ascended his maschille and lay back elegantly on the leopard-skin rugs. On each side of Flynn a bearer took his position, armed with a palm-frond, and began to fan him gently. Behind Flynn, in single file, followed other servants bearing tusks in ivory and the still-green lion skin. Behind this, with instructions from Flynn not to draw undue attention to themselves, followed Sebastian and Rosa, and the baggage bearers.

With a languid gesture such as might have been used by Nero to signal the start of a Roman circus, Flynn gave the order to move.

Along the rough road through the thick coastal bush, they came at last to Beira and entered the main street in procession.

'Good Lord,' Sebastian expressed his surprise when he saw the reception that awaited them, 'where did they all come from?'

Both sides of the street were lined with cheering crowds, mainly natives, but with here and there a Portuguese or an Indian trader come out of his shop to find the cause of the disturbance.

'Fini!' chanted the crowd, clapping their hands in unison. 'Bwana Mkuba! Great Lord! Slayer of elephant. Killer of lions!'

'I didn't realize that Flynn was so well regarded.' Sebastian was impressed.

'Most of them have never heard of him,' Rosa disillusioned him. 'He sent Mohammed in last night to gather a claque of about a hundred or so. Pays them one escudo each to come and cheer–they make so much noise that the entire population turns out to see what is going on. They fall for it every time.'

'What on earth does he go to so much trouble for?'

'Because he enjoys it. Just look at him!'

Lying in his maschille, graciously acknowledging the applause. Flynn was very obviously loving every minute of it.

The head of the procession reached the only hotel in Beira and halted. Madame da Souza, the portly, well-moustached widow who was the proprietress of the hotel, rushed down to welcome Flynn with a smacking kiss and usher him ceremoniously through the shabby portals. Flynn was the kind of customer she had always dreamed about.

When Rosa and Sebastian at last fought their way through the crowd into the hotel, Flynn was already seated at the bar counter and half-way through a tall glass of Laurentia beer. The man sitting on the stool beside his was the Governor of Mozambique's aide-de-camp, who had come to deliver His Excellency's invitation for Flynn O'Flynn to dine at Government House that evening. It was settlement day in the partnership of 'Flynn O'Flynn and Others'. His Excellency José De Clare Don Felezardo da Silva Marques had received from Governor Schee, in Dar es Salaam, an agitated report, in the form of an official protest and an extradition demand, of the success of the partnership's operations during the last few months—and His Excellency was delighted to see Flynn.

In fact, so pleased was His Excellency with the progress of the partnership's affairs, that he exercised his authority to waive the formalities required by law to precede a marriage under Portuguese jurisdiction. This saved a week, and the afternoon after their arrival in Beira, Rosa and Sebastian stood before the altar in the stucco and thatch cathedral, while Sebastian tried with little success to remember enough of his schoolroom Latin to understand just what he was getting himself into.

The wedding veil, that had belonged to Rosa's mother, was yellowed by many years of storage under tropical conditions, but it served well enough to keep off the flies which were always bad during the hot season in Beira.

Towards the end of the long ceremony, Flynn was so overcome by the heat, the gin he had taken at lunch, and an unusually fine flood of Irish feeling, that he began snuffling loudly. While he mopped at his eyes and nose with a grubby handkerchief, the Governor's aide-de-camp patted his shoulder soothingly and murmured encouragement.

The priest declared them husband and wife, and the congregation launched into a faltering rendition of the *Te Deum*. His voice quivering with emotion and alcohol, Flynn kept repeating, 'My little girl, my poor little girl.' Rosa lifted her veil and turned to Sebastian who immediately forgot his misgivings as to the form of the ceremony, and enfolded her enthusiastically in his arms.

Still maintaining his chorus of 'My little girl', Flynn was led away by the aide-de-camp to the hotel where the proprietress had prepared the wedding feast. In deference to Flynn O'Flynn's mood this started on a sombre note but as the champagne, which Madame da Souza had specially bottled the previous evening, started to do its work, so the tempo changed. Among his other actions, Flynn gave Sebastian a wedding present of ten pounds and poured a full glass of beer over the aide-de-camp's head.

When, later that evening, Rosa and Sebastian slipped away to the bridal suite above the bar, Flynn was giving lusty tongue in the chorus of 'They are jolly good fellows', Madame da Souza was seated on his lap, and over-flowing it in all directions. Every time Flynn pinched her posterior, great gusts of laughter made her shake like a stranded jellyfish.

Later the pleasure of Rosa and Sebastian's wedding-bed was disturbed by the fact that, in the bar-room directly below them, Flynn O'Flynn was shooting the bottles off the shelves with a double-barrelled elephant rifle. Every direct hit was greeted by thunderous applause from the other guests. Madame da Souza, still palpitating with laughter, sat in a corner of the bar-room dutifully making such entries in her notebook as, 'One bottle of Grandino London Dry Gin 14.50 escudos; one bottle Grandino French Cognac Five Star 14.50 escudos; one bottle Grandino Scotch whisky 30.00 escudos; 1 magnum Grandino French Champagne 75.90 escudos.' 'Grandino' was the brand-name of the house, and signified that the liquor each bottle contained had been brewed and bottled on the premises under the personal supervision of Madame da Souza.

Once the newly-wed couple realized that the uproar from the room below was sufficient to mask the protests of their rickety brass bedstead, they no longer grudged Flynn his amusements.

For everyone involved it was a night of great pleasure, a night to be looked back upon with nostalgia and wistful smiles.

32

Even at Flynn's prodigious rate of expenditure, his share of the profits from Sebastian's tax expedition lasted another two weeks.

During this period Rosa and Sebastian spent a little of their time wandering hand in hand through the streets and bazaars of Beira, or sitting, still hand in hand, on the beach and watching the sea. Their happiness radiated from them so strongly that it affected anyone who came within fifty feet of them. A worried stranger hurrying towards them along the narrow little street with his face creased in a frown would come under the spell; his pace would slacken, his step losing its urgency, the frown would smooth away to be replaced by an indulgent grin as he passed them. But mostly they remained closeted in the bridal suite above the bar—entering it in the early afternoon and not reappearing until early noon the following day.

Neither Rosa nor Sebastian had imagined such happiness could exist.

At the expiry of the two weeks Flynn was waiting for them in the bar-room as they came down to lunch. He hurried out to join them as they passed the door. 'Greetings! Greetings!' He threw an arm around each of their shoulders. 'And how are you this fine morning?' He listened without attention as Sebastian replied at length on how well he felt, how well Rosa was, and how well both of them had slept. 'Sure! Sure!' Flynn interrupted his rhapsodizing. 'Listen, Bassie, my boy, you remember that £10 I gave you?'

'Yes.' Sebastian was immediately wary.

'Let me have it back, will you?'

'I've spent it, Flynn.'

'You've *what*?' bellowed Flynn.

'I've spent it.'

'Good God Almighty! All of it? You've squandered ten pounds in as many days?' Flynn was horrified by his son-in-law's extravagance and Sebastian, who had honestly believed the money was his to do with as he wished, was very apologetic.

They left for Lalapanzi that afternoon. Madame da Souza had accepted Flynn's note of hand for the balance outstanding on his bill.

At the head of the column Flynn, broke to the wide, and nursing a burning hangover, was in evil temper. The line of bearers behind him, bedraggled and billious from two weeks spent in the flesh-pots, were in similar straits. At the rear of the doleful little caravan, Rosa and Sebastian chirruped and cooed together—an island of sunshine in the sea of gloom.

The months passed quickly at Lalapanzi during the monsoon of 1913. Gradually, as its girth increased, Rosa's belly became the centre of Lalapanzi. The pivot upon which the whole community turned. The debates in the servants' quarters, led by Nanny, the accepted authority, dealt almost exclusively with the contents thereof. All of them were hot for a man-child, although secretly Nanny cherished a treacherous hope that it might be another Little Long Hair.

Even Flynn, during the long months of enforced inactivity while the driving monsoon rains turned the land into a quagmire and the rivers into seething brown torrents, felt his grand-parental instincts stirred. Unlike Nanny, he had no doubts as to the unborn child's sex, and he decided to name it Patrick Flynn O'Flynn Oldsmith.

He conveyed his decision to Sebastian while the two of them were hunting for the pot in the kopjes above the homestead.

By dint of diligent application and practice, Sebastian's marksmanship had improved beyond all reasonable expectation. He had just demonstrated it. They were jump-shooting in thick cat-bush among the broken rock and twisted ravines of the kopjes. Constant rain had softened the ground and enabled them to move silently down-wind along one of the ravines. Flynn was fifty yards out on Sebastian's right, moving heavily but deceptively fast through the sodden grass and undergrowth.

The kudu were lying in dense cover below the lip of the ravine. Two young bulls, bluish-gold in colour, striped with thin chalk lines across the body, pendulant dewlaps heavily fringed with yellow hair, two and a half twists in each of the corkscrew horns—big as polo ponies but heavier. They broke left across the ravine when Flynn jumped them from their hide, and the intervening bush denied him a shot.

'Breaking your way, Bassie,' Flynn shouted and Sebastian took two swift paces around the bush in front of him, shook the clinging raindrops from his lashes, and slipped the safety-catch. He heard the tap of big horn against a branch, and the first bull came out of the ravine at full run across his front. Yet it seemed to float, unreal, intangible, through the blue-grey rain mist. It blended ghostlike into the background of dark rain-soaked vegetation, and the clumps of bush and the tree trunks between them made it an almost impossible shot. In the instant that the bull flashed across a gap between two clumps of buffalo thorn, Sebastian's bullet broke its neck a hand's width in front of the shoulder.

At the sound of the shot, the second bull swerved in dead run, gathered its forelegs beneath its chest, and went up in a high, driving leap over the thorn bush that stood in its path. Sebastian traversed his rifle smoothly without taking the butt from his shoulder, his right hand flicked the bolt open and closed, and he fired as a continuation of the movement.

The heavy bullet caught the kudu in mid-air and threw it sideways. Kicking and thrashing, it struck the ground and rolled down the bank of the ravine.

Whooping like a Red Indian, Mohammed galloped past Sebastian, brandishing a long knife, racing to reach the second bull and cut its throat before it died so that the dictates of the Koran might be observed.

Flynn ambled across to Sebastian. 'Nice shooting, Bassie boy. Salted and dried and pickled, there's meat there for a month.'

And Sebastian grinned in modest recognition of the compliment. Together they walked across to watch Mohammed and his gang begin paunching and quartering the big animals.

With the skill of a master tactician, Flynn chose this moment to inform Sebastian of the name he had selected for his grandson. He was not prepared for the fierce opposition he encountered from Sebastian. It seemed that Sebastian had expected to name the child Francis Sebastian Oldsmith. Flynn laughed easily, and then in his most reasonable and persuasive brogue he started pointing out to Sebastian just how cruel it would be to saddle the child with a name like that.

It was a lance in the pride of the Oldsmiths, and Sebastian rose to the

defence. By the time they returned to Lalapanzi, the discussion needed about
six hot words to reach the stage of single combat.
    Rosa heard them coming. Flynn's bellow carried across the lawns. 'I'll no
have my grandson called a pewling, milksop name like that!'
    'Francis is the name of kings and warriors and gentlemen!' cried Sebastian.
    'My aching buttocks, it is!'
    Rosa came out on to the wide veranda and stood there with her arms folded
over the beautiful bulge that housed the cause of the controversy.
    They saw her and started an undignified race across the lawns, each trying to
reach her first to enlist her support for their respective causes.
    She listened to the pleadings, a small and secret smile upon her lips, and
then said with finality, 'Her name will be Maria Rosa Oldsmith.'

Some time later Flynn and Sebastian were together on the veranda.
    Ten days before the last rains of the season had come roaring in from the
Indian Ocean and broken upon the unyielding shield of the continent. Now
the land was drying out; the rivers regained their sanity and returned,
chastened to the confines of their banks. New grass lifted from the red earth to
welcome the return of the sun. For this brief period the whole land was alive
and green; even the gnarled and crabbed thorn trees wore a pale fuzz of tender
leaves. Behind each pair of guinea-fowl that clinked and scratched on the
bottom lawns of Lalapanzi, there paraded a file of dappled chicks. Early that
morning a herd of eland had moved along the skyline across the valley, and
beside each cow had trotted a calf. Everywhere was new life, or the expectation
of new life.
    'Now, stop worrying!' said Flynn, as his impatient pacing brought him level
with Sebastian's chair.
    'I'm not worrying,' Sebastian said mildly. 'Everything will be all right.'
    'How do you know that?' challenged Flynn.
    'Well . . .'
    'You know the child could be stillborn, or something.' Flynn shook his
finger in Sebastian's face. 'It could have six fingers on each hand–how about
that? I heard about one that was born with . . .'
    While Flynn related a long list of horrors, Sebastian's expression of proud
and eager anticipation crumbled slowly. He rose from his chair and fell into
step beside Flynn. 'Have you got any gin left?' he asked hoarsely, glancing at
the shuttered windows of Rosa's bedroom. Flynn produced the bottle from the
inside pocket of his jacket.
    An hour later, Sebastian was hunched forward in his chair, clutching a half-
full tumbler of gin with both hands. He stared into it miserably. 'I don't know
what I'd do if it was born with . . .' He could not go on. He shuddered and
lifted the tumbler to his lips. At that instant a long, petulant wail issued from
the closed bedroom. Sebastian leapt as though he had been bayoneted from
behind, and spilled the gin down his shirt. His next leap was in the direction of
the bedroom, a direction which Flynn had also chosen. They collided heavily
and then set off together at a gallop along the veranda. They reached the locked
door and hammered upon it for admission. But Nanny, who had evicted them
in the first instance, still adamantly refused to lift the locking bar or to give
them any information as to the progress of the birthing. Her decision was
endorsed by Rosa.
    'Don't you dare let them in until everything is ready,' she whispered

huskily, and roused herself from the stupor of exhaustion, to help Nanny with washing and wrapping the infant.

When at last everything was ready, she lay propped on the pillows with her child held against her chest, and nodded to Nanny. 'Open the door,' she said.

The delay had confirmed Flynn's worst suspicions. The door flew open, and he and Sebastian fell into the room, wild with anxiety.

'Oh, thank God, Rosa. You're still alive!' Sebastian reached the bed and fell on his knees beside it.

'You check his feet,' instructed Flynn. 'I'll do his hands and head,' and before Rosa could prevent him, he had lifted the infant out of her arms.

'His fingers are all right. Two arms, one head,' Flynn muttered above Rosa's protests and the infant's muffled squawls of indignation.

'This end is fine. Just fine!' Sebastian spoke in rising relief and delight. 'He's beautiful, Flynn!' And he lifted the shawl that swaddled the child's body. His expression cracked and his voice choked. 'Oh, my God!'

'What's wrong?' Flynn asked sharply.

'You were right, Flynn. He's deformed.'

'What? Where?'

'There!' Sebastian pointed. 'He hasn't got a what-ye-ma-call-it,' and they both stared in horror.

It was many long seconds before they realized simultaneously that the tiny cleft was no deformity but very much as nature had intended it.

'It's a girl!' said Flynn in dismay.

'A girl!' echoed Sebastian, and quickly pulled down the shawl to preserve his daughter's modesty.

'It's a girl,' Rosa smiled, wan and happy.

'It's a girl,' cackled Nanny in triumph.

Maria Rosa Oldsmith had arrived without fuss and with the minimum of inconvenience to her mother, so that Rosa was on her feet again within twenty-four hours. All her other activities were conducted with the same consideration and dispatch. She cried once every four hours; a single angry howl which was cut off the instant the breast was thrust into her mouth. Her bowel movements were equally regular and of the correct volume and consistency, and the rest of her days and nights were devoted almost entirely to sleeping.

She was beautiful; without the parboiled, purple look of most new-borns; without the squashed-in pug features or the vague, squinty eyes.

From the curly cap of silk hair to the tips of her pink toes, she was perfection.

It took Flynn two days to recover from the disappointment of having been cheated out of a grandson. He sulked in the arsenal or sat solitary at the end of the veranda. On the second evening Rosa pitched her voice just high enough to carry the length of the veranda.

'Don't you think Maria looks just like Daddy—the same mouth and nose? Look at her eyes.'

Sebastian opened his mouth to deny the resemblance emphatically but closed it again, as Rosa kicked him painfully on the ankle.

'She is the image of him. There's no doubting who her grandfather is.'

'Well, I suppose . . . If you look closely,' Sebastian agreed unhappily.

At the end of the veranda, Flynn sat with his head cocked in an attitude of attention. Half an hour later Flynn had sidled up to the cradle and was studying the contents thoughtfully. By the following evening he had moved his chair alongside and was leading the discussion with such remarks as, 'There is quite a strong family resemblance. Look at those eyes—no doubt who her Granddaddy is!'

Interspersing his observations with warnings and instructions, 'Don't get so close, Bassie. You're breathing germs all over her.' 'Rosa, this child needs another blanket. When did she have her last feed?'

It was not long before he started bringing pressure to bear on Sebastian.

'You've got responsibilities now. Have you thought about that?'

'How do you mean, Flynn?'

'Just answer me this. What have you got in this world?'

'Rosa and Maria,' Sebastian answered promptly.

'Fine. That's just great! And how are you going to feed them and clothe them and . . . and look after them?'

Sebastian expressed himself well satisfied with the existing arrangements.

'I bet you are! It isn't costing you a thing. But I reckon it's about time you got up off your bum and did something.'

'Like what?'

'Like going and shooting some ivory.'

Three days later, armed and equipped for a full-scale poaching expedition, Sebastian led a column of gun-boys and bearers down the valley towards the Rovuma river.

Fourteen hours later, in the dusk of evening, he led them back.

'What in the name of all that's holy, are you doing back here?' Flynn demanded.

'I had this premonition.' Sebastian was sheepish.

'What premonition?'

'That I should come back,' muttered Sebastian.

He left again two days later. This time he actually crossed the Rovuma before the premonition over-powered him once more, and he came back to Rosa and Maria.

'Well,' Flynn sighed with resignation. 'I reckon I'll just have to go along with you and make sure you do it.' He shook his head. 'You've been a big disappointment to me, Bassie.' The biggest disappointment being the fact that he had hoped to have his granddaughter to himself for a few weeks.

'Mohammed,' he bellowed. 'Get my gear packed.'

33

Flynn sent his scouts across the river and when they reported back that the far bank was clear of German patrols, Flynn made the crossing.

This expedition was a far cry from Sebastian's amiable and aimless wandering in German territory. Flynn was a professional. They crossed in the night. They crossed in strictest silence and landed two miles downstream from M'topo's village. There was no lingering on the beach, but an urgent night march that began immediately and went on in grim silence until an hour before dawn; a march that took them fifteen miles inland from the river, and ended in a grove of elephant thorn, carefully chosen for the kopjes and ravines around it that afforded multiple avenues of escape in each direction.

Sebastian was impressed by the elaborate precautions that Flynn took before going into camp; the jinking and counter-marching, the careful sweeping of their spoor with brushes of dry grass, and the placing of sentries on the kopje above the camp.

During the ten days they waited there, not a single branch was broken from a tree, not a single axe-stroke swung to leave a tell-tale white blaze on the dark bush. The tiny night fire fed with dry trash and dead wood was carefully screened, and before dawn was smothered with sand so that not a wisp of smoke was left to mark them in the day.

Voices were never raised above conversational tones, and even the clatter of a bucket brought such a swift and ferocious reprimand from Flynn, that on all of them was a nervous awareness, an expectancy of danger, a tuning of the minds and bodies to action.

On the eighth night the scouts that Flynn had thrown out began drifting back to the camp. They came in with all the stealth and secrecy of night animals and huddled over the fire to tell what they had seen.

'. . . Last night three old bulls drank at the water-hole of the sick hyena. They carried teeth so, and so, and so . . .' showing the arm to measure the length of ivory, '. . . apart from them, ten cows left their feet in the mud, six of them young with calves. Yesterday, at the place where the hill of Inhosana breaks and turns its arms, I saw where another herd had crossed, moving towards the dawn; five young bulls, twenty-three cows, and . . .'

The reports were jumbled, unintelligible to Sebastian who did not carry a map of the land in his head. But Flynn, sitting beside the fire listening, fitted the fragments together and built them into an exact picture of how the game was moving. He saw that the big bulls were still separated from the breeding herds—that they lingered on the high ground while the cows had started moving back towards the swamps from which the floods had driven them, anxious to take their young away from the dangers that the savannah forests would offer once the dry season set in.

He noted the estimates of thickness and length of tusk. Immature ivory was hardly worth carrying home, good only for carving into billiard balls and piano keys. The market was glutted with it.

But on the other hand, a prime tusk, over one hundred pounds in weight, seven foot long, and twice the thickness of a fat woman's thigh, would fetch fifty shillings a pound avoirdupois.

An animal carrying such a tusk on each side of his face was worth four or five hundred pounds in good, gold sovereigns.

One by one Flynn discarded the possible areas in which he would hunt. This year there were no elephant in the M'bahora hills. There was good reason for this; thirty piles of great sun-bleached bones lay scattered along the ridge, marking the path that Flynn's rifles had followed two years before. The memory of gunfire was too fresh and the herds shunned that place.

There were no elephant on the Tabora escarpment. A blight had struck the groves of mapundu trees, and withered the fruit before it could ripen. Dearly the elephant loved mapundu berries and they had gone elsewhere to find them.

They had gone up to the Sania Heights, to Kilombera, and to the Salito hills.

Salito was an easy day's march from the German boma at Mahenge. Flynn struck it from his mental list.

As each of the scouts finished his report, Flynn asked the question which would influence his final decision.

'What of *Plough the Earth?*'

And they said, 'We saw nothing. We heard nothing.'

The last scout came in two days after the others. He looked sheepish and more than a little guilty.

'Where the hell have you been?' Flynn demanded, and the gun-boy had his excuse ready.

'Knowing that the great Lord Fini would ask of certain matters, I turned aside in my journey to the village of Yetu, who is my uncle. My uncle is a fundi. No wild thing walks, no lion kills, no elephant breaks a branch from a tree but my uncle knows of it. Thus I went to ask him of these matters.'

'Thy uncle is a famous fundi, he is also a famous breeder of daughters,' Flynn remarked drily. 'He breeds daughters the way the moon breeds stars.'

'Indeed, my uncle Yetu is a man of fame.' Hurriedly the scout went on to turn Flynn aside from his line of discussion. 'My uncle sends his greetings to the Lord Fini and bids me speak thus: "This season there are many fine elephants on the Sania Heights. They walk by twos and threes. With my own eyes I have seen twelve which show ivory as long as the shaft of a throwing spear, and I have seen signs of as many more." My uncle bids me speak further. "There is one among them of which the Lord Fini knows for he has asked of him many times. This one is a bull among great bulls. One who moves in such majesty that men have named him *Plough the Earth.*"'

'You do not bring a story from the honey-bird to cool my anger against you?' Flynn demanded harshly. 'Did you dream of *Plough the Earth* while you were ploughing the bellies of your uncle's many daughters?' His eagerness was soured by scepticism. Too many times he had followed wild stories in his pursuit of the great bull. He leaned forward across the fire to watch the gun-bearer's eyes as he replied, 'It is true, lord.' Flynn watched him carefully but found no hint of guilt in his face. Flynn grunted, rocked back on his hams, and lowered his gaze to the small flames of the camp-fire.

For his first ten years in Africa, Flynn had heard the legend of the elephant whose tusks were of such length that their points touched the ground and left a double furrow along his spoor. He had smiled at this story as he had at the story of the rhinoceros who fifty years before had killed an Arab slaver, and now wore around his horn a massive gold bangle studded with precious stones. They said the bangle had lodged there as he gored the Arab. There were a thousand other romantic tales come out of Africa; from Solomon's treasure to the legend of the elephants' graveyard, and Flynn believed none of them.

Then he saw a myth come alive. One evening, camped near the Zambesi in Portuguese territory, he had taken a bird-gun and walked along the bank hoping for a brace of sand-grouse. Two miles from the camp he had seen a flight of birds coming in to the water, fly fast as racing pigeons, whistling in on back-swept wings, and he had ducked into a thick bank of reeds and watched them come.

As they banked steeply overhead, dropping towards the sandbanks of the river, Flynn jumped to his feet and fired left and right, folding the lead bird and the second, so they crumpled in mid-air and tumbled, leaving a pale flurry of feathers to mark their fall.

But Flynn never saw the birds hit the ground. For, while the double blast of the shotgun still echoed along the river, the reed-bed below where he stood swayed and crashed and burst open, then an elephant came out into the open.

It was a bull elephant that stood fourteen feet high at the shoulder. An elephant so old that his ears were shredded to half their original size. The hide that covered his body hung in folds and deep wrinkles, baggy at the knees and the throat. The tuft of his tail long ago worn bald. The rheumy tears of great age staining his seared and dusty cheeks.

He came out of the reed-bed in a shambling, hump-backed run, and his head was tilted at an awkward, unnatural angle.

Flynn could hardly credit his vision when he saw the reason why the old bull cocked his head back in that fashion. From each side of the head extended two identical shafts of ivory, perfectly matched, straight as the columns of a Greek temple, with not an inch of taper from lip to bluntly rounded tip. They were stained to the colour of tobacco juice, fourteen long feet of ivory that would have touched the ground, if the elephant had carried his head relaxed.

As Flynn stood frozen in disbelief, the bull passed him by a mere fifty yards and lumbered on into the forest.

It took Flynn thirty minutes to get back to camp and exchange the bird-gun for the double-barrelled Gibbs, snatch up a water bottle, shout for his gun-boys, and return to the river.

He put Mohammed to the spoor. At first there were only the round pad marks in the dusty earth, smooth pad marks the size of a dustbin lid; the graining on the old bull's hooves had long been worn away. Then after five miles of flight there were other marks to follow. One each side of the spoor a double line scuffed through dead leaves and grass and soft earth where the tips of the tusks touched, and Flynn learned why the old bull was called *Plough the Earth.*

They lost the spoor on the third day in the rain, but a dozen times in the years since then, Flynn had followed and lost those double furrows, and once, through his binoculars, he had seen the old bull again, standing dozing beneath a grove of marula trees at a distance of three miles, his eroded old head propped up by the mythical tusks. When Flynn reached the spot on which he had seen the bull, it was deserted.

In all his life Flynn had never wanted anything with such obsessive passion as he wanted those tusks.

Now he sat silently staring into the camp-fire, remembering all these things, and the lust within him was tighter and more compelling than he had ever felt for a woman.

At last he looked up at the scout and said huskily, 'Tomorrow, with the first light, we will go to the village of Yetu, at Sania.'

A fly settled on Herman Fleischer's cheek and rubbed its front feet together in delight, as it savoured the prospect of drinking from the droplet of sweat that quivered precariously at the level of his ear lobe.

The Askari standing behind Herman's chair flicked the zebra tail switch with such skill, that not one of the long black hairs touched the Commissioner's face, and the fly darted away to take its place in the circuit that orbited around Herman's head.

Herman hardly noticed the interruption. He was sunk down in the chair; glowering at the two old men who squatted on the dusty parade ground below the veranda. The silence was a blanket that lay on them all in the stupefying heat. The two headmen waited patiently. They had spoken, and now they waited for the Bwana Mkuba to reply.

'How many have been killed?' Herman asked at last, and the senior of the two headmen answered.

'Lord, as many as the fingers of both your hands. But these are the ones of which we are certain, there may be others.'

Herman's concern was not for the dead, but their numbers would be a measure of the seriousness of the situation. Ritual murder was the first stage on the road to rebellion. It started with a dozen men meeting in the moonlight, dressed in cloaks of leopard skin, with designs of white clay painted on their faces. With the crude iron claws strapped to their hands, they would ceremoniously mutilate a young girl, and then devour certain parts of her body. This was harmless entertainment in Herman's view, but when it happened more frequently, it generated in the district a mood of abject terror. This was the climate of revolt. Then the leopard priests would walk through the villages in the night, walk openly in procession with the torches burning, and the men who lay shivering within the barricaded huts would listen to the chanted instructions from the macabre little procession—and they would obey.

It had happened ten years earlier at Salito. The priests had ordered them to resist the tax expedition that year. They had slaughtered the visiting Commissioner and twenty of his Askari, and they cut the bodies into small pieces with which they festooned the thorn trees.

Three months later a battalion of German infantry had disembarked at Dar es Salaam and marched to Salito. They burned the villages and they shot everything—men, women, children, chickens, dogs, and goats. The final casualty list could only be estimated, but the officer commanding the battalion boasted that they had killed two thousand human beings. He was probably exaggerating. Nevertheless, the Salito hills were still devoid of human life and habitation to this day. The whole episode was irritating and costly—and Herman Fleischer wanted no repetition of it during his term of office.

On the principle that prevention was better than cure, he decided to go down and conduct a few ritual sacrifices of his own. He humped himself forward in his chair, and spoke to his sergeant of Askari.

'Twenty men. We will leave for the village of Yetu, at Salito, tomorrow before dawn. Do not forget the ropes.'

34

On the Sania Heights, in the heat of the day, an elephant stood under the wide branches of a wild fig-tree. He was asleep on his feet but his head was propped up by two long columns of stained ivory. He slept as an old man sleeps, fitfully, never sinking very deep below the level of consciousness. Occasionally the tattered grey ears flapped, and each time a fine haze of flies rose around his head. They hung in the hot air and then settled again. The rims of the elephant's ears were raw where the flies had eaten down through the thick skin. The flies were everywhere. The humid green shade beneath the wild fig was murmurous with the sound of their wings.

Across the divide of the Sania Heights, four miles from the spot where the old bull slept, three men were moving up one of the bush-choked gulleys towards the ridge.

Mohammed was leading. He moved fast, half-crouched to peer at the ground, glancing up occasionally to anticipate the run of the spoor he was following. He stopped at a place where a grove of mapundu trees had carpeted the ground beneath them with a stinking, jellified mass of rotten berries. He looked back at the two white men and indicated the marks in the earth, and the pyramid of bright yellow dung that lay upon it. 'He stopped here for the first time in the heat, but it was not to his liking, and he has gone on.'

Flynn was sweating. It ran down his flushed jowls and dripped on to his already sodden shirt. 'Yes,' he nodded and a small cloudburst of sweat scattered from his head at the movement. 'He will have crossed the ridge.'

'What makes you so certain?' Sebastian spoke in the same sepulchral whisper as the others.

'The cool evening breeze will come from the east—he will cross to the other side of the ridge to wait for it.' Flynn spoke with irritation and wiped his face on the short sleeve of his shirt. 'Now, you just remember, Bassie. This is my elephant, you understand that? You try for it and, so help me God, I'll shoot you dead.'

Flynn nodded to Mohammed and they moved on up the slope, following the spoor that meandered between outcrops of grey granite and scrub.

The crest of the ridge was well defined, sharp as the spine of a starving ox. They paused below it, squatting to rest in the coarse brown grass. Flynn opened the binocular case that hung on his chest, lifted out the instrument, and began to polish the lens with a scrap of cloth.

'Stay here!' Flynn ordered the other two, then on his belly he wriggled up towards the skyline. Using the cover of a tree stump, he lifted his head cautiously and peered over.

Below him the Sania Heights fell away to a gentle slope, fifteen hundred feet and ten miles to the plain below. The slope was broken and crenellated, riven into a thousand gulleys and ravines, covered over-all with a mantle of coarse brown scrub and dotted with clumps of bigger trees.

Flynn settled himself comfortably on his elbows and lifted the binoculars to his eyes. Systematically he began to examine each of the groves below him.

'Yes!' he whispered aloud, wriggling a little on his belly, staring at the picture puzzle beneath the spread branches of the tree, a mile away. In the shade there were shapes that made no sense, a mass too diffuse to be the trunk of the tree.

He lowered the glasses and wiped away the sweat that clung in his eyebrows. He closed his eyes to rest them from the glare, then he opened them again, and lifted the glasses.

For two long minutes he stared before suddenly the puzzle made sense. The bull was standing half away from him, merging with the trunk of the wild fig, the head and half the body obscured by the lower branches of the tree—and what he had taken to be the stem of a lesser tree was, in fact, a tusk of ivory.

A spasm of excitement closed on his chest.

'Yes!' he said. 'Yes!'

Flynn planned his stalk with care, taking every precaution against the intervention of fate that twenty years of elephant hunting had taught him.

He had gone back to where Sebastian and Mohammed waited.

'He's there,' he told them.

'Can I come with you?' Sebastian pleaded.

'In a barrel you can,' snarled Flynn as he sat and pulled off his heavy boots to replace them with the light sandals that Mohammed produced from the pack.

'You stay here until you hear my shot. You so much as stick your nose over the ridge before that—and, so help me God, I'll shoot it off.'

While Mohammed knelt in front of Flynn and strapped the leather pads to his knees to protect them as he crawled over rock and thorn, Flynn fortified himself from the gin bottle. As he recorked it, he glowered at Sebastian again. 'That's a promise!' he said.

At the top of the ridge Flynn paused again with only his eyes lifted over the skyline, while he plotted his stalk, fixing in his memory a procession of landmarks—an ant-hill, an outcrop of white quartz, a tree festooned with weaver birds' nests—so that as he reached each of these he would know his exact position in relation to that of the elephant.

Then with the rifle cradled across the crook of his elbows he slid on his belly to begin the stalk.

Now, an hour after he had left the ridge, he saw before him through the grass a slab of granite like a headstone in an ancient cemetery. It stood square and weathered brown, and it was the end of the stalk.

He had marked it from the ridge as the point from which he would fire. It stood fifty yards from the wild fig tree, at a right angle from the old bull's position. It would give him cover as he rose to his knees to make the shot.

Anxious now, suddenly overcome with a premonition of disaster—sensing that somehow the cup would be dashed from his lips, the maid plucked from under him before the moment of fulfillment, Flynn started forward. Slithering towards the granite headstone, his face set hard in nervous anticipation, he reached the rock.

He rolled carefully on to his side and, holding the heavy rifle against his chest, he slipped the catch across and eased the rifle open, so that the click of the mechanism was muted. From the belt around his waist he selected two fat cartridges and examined the brass casings for tarnish or denting; with relief he saw the fingers that held them were steadier. He slipped the cartridges into the blank eyes of the breeches, and they slid home against the seatings with a soft metallic plong. And now his breathing was faintly ragged at the end of each inhalation. He closed the rifle, and with his thumb pushed the safety-catch forward into the 'fire' position.

His shoulder against the rough, sun-heated granite, he drew up his legs against his belly and rolled gently on to his knees. With his head bowed low and the rifle in his lap, he knelt behind the rock, and for the first time in an hour he lifted his head. He brought it up with inching deliberation. Slowly the crystalline texture of the granite passed before his eyes, then suddenly he looked across fifty yards of open ground at his elephant.

It stood broadside to him but the head was hidden by the leaves and branches of the wild fig. The brain shot was impossible from here. His eyes moved down on to the shoulder and he saw the outline of the bone beneath the thick grey skin. He picked out the point of the elbow and his eyes moved back into the barrel of the chest. He could visualize the heart pulsing softly there beneath the ribs, pink and soft and vital, throbbing like a giant sea anemone.

He lifted the rifle, and laid it across the rock in front of him. He looked along the barrels, and saw the blade of dry grass that was wound around the head of the foresight, obscuring it. He lowered the rifle and with his thumbnail picked away the shred of grass. Again he lifted and sighted.

The black blob of the foresight lay snugly in the deep, wide vee of the backsight, he moved the gun, riding the bead down across the old bull's shoulder then back on to the chest. It lay there ready to kill, and he took up the slack in the trigger, gently, lovingly, with his forefinger.

The shout was faint, a tiny sound in the drowsy immensity of the hot African air. It came from the high ground above him.

'Flynn!' and again, 'Flynn!'

In an explosive burst of movement under the wild fig tree, the old bull swung his body with unbelievable speed, his great tusks riding high, he went away from Flynn at an awkward shambling run, his flight covered by the trunk of the fig tree.

For stunned seconds, Flynn crouched behind the boulder, and with each second the chances of a shot dwindled. Flynn jumped to his feet and ran out to one side of the fig tree, opening his field of fire for a snap shot at the bull as he fled, a try for the spine where it curved down between the massive haunches to the tuftless tail.

Spiked agony stabbed up through the ball of his lightly shod foot, as he trod squarely on a three-inch buffalo thorn. Red-tipped, wickedly barbed, it buried its full length in his flesh, and he stumbled to his knees crying a protest at the pain.

Two hundred yards away, the old bull disappeared into one of the wooded ravines, and was gone.

'Flynn! Flynn!'

Sobbing in pain and frustration, his injured foot twisted up into his lap, Flynn sat in the grass and waited for Sebastian Oldsmith to come down to him.

'I'll let him get real close,' Flynn told himself. Sebastian was approaching with the long awkward strides of a man running downhill. He had lost his hat and the black tangled curls danced on his head at each stride. He was still shouting.

'I'll give it to him in the belly,' Flynn decided. 'Both barrels!' and he groped for the rifle that lay beside him.

Sebastian saw him and swerved in his run.

Flynn hefted the rifle. 'I warned him. I said I'd do it,' and his right hand settled around the pistol grip of the rifle, his forefinger instinctively hooking forward for the trigger.

'Flynn! Germans! A whole army of them, Just over the hill. Coming this way.'

'Christ!' said Flynn, immediately abandoning his homicidal intentions.

35

Lifting himself in the stirrups, Herman Fleischer reached behind to massage himself. His buttocks were of a plump, almost feminine, quantity and quality. After five hours in the saddle Herman longed to rest them. He had just crossed the ridge of the Sania Heights on his donkey, and it was cool here beneath the outspread branches of the wild fig tree. He flirted with the temptation, decided to indulge himself, and turned to give the order to the troop of twenty Askari who stood behind him. All of them were watching him avidly, anticipating the order that would allow them to throw themselves down and relax.

'Lazy dogs!' thought Herman as he scowled at them. He turned away from them, settled his aching posterior gently on to the saddle, and growled.

'Akwende! Let us go!' His heels thumped against the flanks of his donkey and it started forward at a trot.

From a crotch in the trunk of the fig tree ten feet above Herman's head, Flynn O'Flynn viewed his departure over the double barrels of his rifle. He watched the patrol wind away down the slope and drop from sight over a fold in the ground before he put up his gun.

'Phew! That was close.' Sebastian's voice came from the leafy mass above Flynn.

'If he'd touched one foot on the ground, I'd have blown his bloody head off,' said Flynn. He sounded as though he regretted missing the opportunity. 'All right, Bassie, get me down out of this frigging tree.'

Fully-dressed, except for his boots, Flynn sat against the base of the fig tree and proffered his right foot to Sebastian. '. . . I had him right there in my sights.'

'Who?' asked Sebastian.

'The elephant, you idiot. For the first time I had him cold. And then . . . Yeow! What the hell are you doing?'

'I'm trying to get the thorn out, Flynn.'

'Feels like you're trying to knock it in with a hammer.'

'I can't get a grip on it.'

'Use your teeth. That's the only way.' Flynn instructed, and Sebastian paled a little at the thought. He considered Flynn's foot. It was a large foot; corns on the toes, flakes of loose skin and other darker matter between them. Sebastian could smell it at a range of three feet. 'Couldn't you reach it with your own teeth, Flynn?' he hedged.

'You think I'm a goddamned contortionist?'

'Mohammed?' Sebastian's eyes lit up with relief as he turned on the little gun-bearer. In answer to the question Mohammed drew back his lips in a death's head grin, exposing his smooth, pink toothless gums. 'Yes,' agreed Sebastian. 'I see what you mean.' He returned his gaze to the foot, and studied it with sickened fascination. His Adam's apple bobbed as he swallowed.

'Get on with it,' said Flynn, and Sebastian stooped. There was a howl from Flynn, and Sebastian straightened up with the wet thorn gripped in his teeth. He spat it out explosively, and Mohammed handed him the gin bottle. Sebastian gargled from it loudly but when he lifted the bottle to his lips again, Flynn laid a restraining hand on his forearm. 'Now don't overdo it, Bassie boy,' he remonstrated mildly, retrieved the bottle, and placed it to his own mouth. It seemed to refuel Flynn's anger, for when he removed the bottle his voice had fire in it. 'That goddamn sneaking, sausage-eating slug. He spoiled the only chance I've ever had at that elephant.' He paused to breathe heavily. 'I'd like to do something really nasty to him, like . . . like. . . .' he searched for some atrocity to commit upon Herman Fleischer, and suddenly he found one. 'My God!' he said, and his scowl changed to a lovely smile. 'That's it!'

'What?' Sebastian was alarmed. He was certain that he would be selected as the vehicle of Flynn's revenge. 'What?' he repeated.

'We will go . . .' said Flynn, '. . . to Mahenge!'

'Good Lord, that's the German headquarters!'

'Yes,' said Flynn. 'With no Commissioner and no Askari to guard it! They've just passed us, heading in the opposite direction.'

36

They hit Mahenge two hours before dawn, in that time of utter darkness when mankind's vitality is at its lowest ebb. The defence put up by the corporal and five Askari whom Fleischer had left to guard his headquarters was hardly heroic. In fact, they were only half awakened by the lusty and indiscriminate use of Flynn's boot, and by the time they were fully conscious, they found themselves securely locked behind the bars of the jail-house. There was only one casualty. It was, of course, Sebastian Oldsmith, who, in the excitement, ran into a half-open door. It was fortunate, as Flynn pointed out, that he struck the door with his head, otherwise he may have done himself an injury. But as it was, he had recovered sufficiently by sunrise to watch the orgy of looting and vandalism in which Flynn and his gun-bearers indulged themselves.

They began in the office of the Commissioner. Built into the thick adobe wall of the room was an enormous iron safe.

'We will open that first,' decreed Flynn as he eyed it greedily. 'See if you can find some tools.'

Sebastian remembered the blacksmith shop at the end of the parade ground. He returned from there laden with sledge-hammers and crow-bars.

Two hours later they were sweating and swearing in an atmosphere heavy with plaster dust. They had torn the safe from the wall, and it lay in the centre of the floor. Three of Flynn's gun-boys were beating on it with sledge-hammers in a steadily diminishing display of enthusiasm, while Sebastian worked with a crow-bar at the hinge joints. He had succeeded in inflicting a few bright scratches upon the metal. Flynn was seated on the Commissioner's desk, steadily working himself into a fury of frustration; for the last hour his contribution to the assault on the safe had been limited to consuming half a bottle of schnapps that he had found in a drawer of the desk.

'It's no use, Flynn.' Sebastian's curls were slick with perspiration, and he licked at the blisters on the palms of his hands. 'We will just have to forget about it.'

'Stand back!' roared Flynn. 'I'll shoot the goddamned thing open.' He rose from the desk wild-eyed, his double-barrelled Gibbs clutched in his hands.

'Wait!' shouted Sebastian and he and the gun-bearers scattered for cover.

The detonations of the heavy rifle were thunderous in the confined space of the office; gun-smoke mingled with the plaster dust, and the bullets ricochetted off the metal of the safe, leaving long smears of lead upon it, before whining away to embed themselves in the floor, wall, and furniture.

This act of violence seemed to placate Flynn. He lost interest in the safe. 'Let's go and find something to eat,' he said mildly, and they trooped through to the kitchens.

Once Flynn had shot away the lock, Herman Fleischer's larder proved to be an Aladdin's cave of delight. The roof was hung with hams and polonies and sausages, there were barrels of pickled meats, stacks of fat round cheeses, cases of Hansa beer, cases of cognac, pyramids of canned truffles, asparagus tips, pâté, shrimps, mushrooms, olives in oil, and other rarities.

They stared at this profusion in awe, and then moved forward together. Each man to his own particular tastes, they fell upon Herman Fleischer's treasure house. The gun-boys rolled out a cask of pickled pork, Sebastian started with his hunting knife on the cans, while Flynn devoted himself to the case of Steinhager in the corner.

It took two hours of dedicated eating and drinking for them to reach saturation point.

'We'd better get ready to move on now.' Sebastian belched softly, and Flynn nodded owlish agreement, the movement spilling a little Steinhager down his bush jacket. He wiped at it with his hand and then licked his fingers.

'Yep! Best we are gone before Fleischer gets home.' He looked at Mohammed. 'Make up full loads of food for each of the bearers. What you can't carry away we'll dump in the latrine buckets.' He stood up carefully. 'I'll just have a look round, and make sure we haven't missed anything important,' and he went out through the door with unsteady dignity.

In Fleischer's office he stood for a minute regarding the invulnerable safe balefully. It was certainly much too heavy to carry away, and abandoning the notion with regret, he looked around for some outlet for his frustration.

There was a portrait of the Kaiser on the entrance wall, a colour print showing the Emperor in full dress, mounted on a magnificent cavalry charger. Flynn picked up an indelible pencil from the desk and walked across to the picture. With a dozen strokes of the pencil he drastically altered the relationship between horse and rider. Then, beginning to chuckle, he printed on the whitewashed wall below the picture, 'The Kaiser loves horses.'

This struck him as being such a pearl of wit, that he had to summon Sebastian and show it to him. 'That's what you call being subtle Bassie, boy. All good jokes are subtle.'

It seemed to Sebastian that Flynn's graffiti were as subtle as the charge of an enraged rhinoceros but he laughed dutifully. This encouraged Flynn to a further essay in humour. He had two of his gun-bearers carry in a bucket from the latrines, and under his supervision, they propped it above the half-open door of Herman Fleischer's bedroom.

An hour later, heavily laden with booty, the raiding party left Mahenge and began the first of a series of forced marches aimed at the Rovuma river.

37

In a state of mental confusion induced by a superfluity of adrenalin in the bloodstream, Herman Fleischer wandered through his ransacked boma. As he discovered each new outrage he regarded it with slitted eyes and laboured breathing. But first it was necessary to effect a jail-break in reverse in order to free his own captive Askari. When they emerged through the hole in the prison wall, Herman curtly ordered his sergeant to administer twenty strokes of the kiboko to each of them, as a token rebuke for their inefficiency. He stood by and drew a little comfort from the solid slap of the kiboko on bare flesh and the shrieks of the recipient.

However, the calming effect of the floggings evaporated when Herman entered the kitchen area of his establishment, and found that his larder of painstakingly accumulated foodstuffs was now empty. This nearly broke his spirit. His jowls quivered with self-pity, and from under his tongue saliva oozed in melancholic nostalgia. It would take a month to replace the sausages alone, heaven knew how long to replace the cheeses imported from the fatherland.

From the larder he went through to his office and found Flynn's subtleties. Herman's sense of humour was not equal to the occasion.

'Pig-swine, English bastard,' he muttered dejectedly, and a dark wave of despair and fatigue washed over him as he realized the futility of setting out in pursuit of the raiders. With two days start he could never hope to catch them before they reached the Rovuma. If only Governor Schee, who was so forthcoming with criticism, would allow him to cross the river one night with his Askari and visit the community at Lalapanzi. There would be no one left the following morning to make complaint to the Portuguese Government about breach of sovereignty.

Herman sighed. He was tired and depressed. He would go to his bed now and rest a while before supervising the tidying up of his headquarters. He left the office and plodded heavily along the stoep to his private quarters, and pushed open the door of his bedroom.

His bedroom temporarily uninhabitable. Herman reposed that night on the open stoep. But his sleep was disturbed by a dream in which he pursued Flynn O'Flynn across an endless plain without ever narrowing the gap between them, while above him circled two huge birds—one with the austere face of Governor Schee, and the other with the face of the young English bandit—at regular intervals these two voided their bowels on him. After the previous afternoon's experience the olfactory hallucinations which formed part of the dream were horribly realistic.

He was tactfully awakened by one of his household servants, and struggled up in bed with an ache behind his eyes and a foul taste in his mouth.

'What is it?' he growled.

'There is a bearer from Dodoma who brings a book with the red mark of the Bwana Mkuba upon it.'

Herman groaned. An envelope with Governor Schee's seal affixed to it usually meant trouble. Surely he could not so speedily have learnt about Flynn O'Flynn's latest escapade.

'Bring coffee!'

'Lord, there is no coffee. It was all stolen,' and Herman groaned again.

'Very well. Bring the messenger.' He would have to endure the ordeal of Governor Schee's rebukes without the fortifying therapy of a cup of coffee. He broke the seal and began to read:

August 4th, 1914
The Residency,
Dar es Salaam

To: The Commissioner (Southern Province).
At: Mahenge.
Sir,

It is my duty to inform you that a state of war now exists between the Empire and the Governments of England, France, Russia, and Portugal.

You are hereby appointed temporary Military Commander of the Southern Province of German East Africa, with orders to take whatever steps you deem necessary for the protection of our borders, and the confusion of the enemy.

In due course a military force, now being assembled at Dar es Salaam, will be dispatched to your area. But I fear that there will be a delay before this can be achieved.

In the meantime, you must operate with the force presently at your disposal.

There was more, much more, but Herman Fleischer read the detailed instructions with perfunctory attention. His headache was forgotten, the taste in his mouth unnoticed in the fierce surge of warrior passions that arose within him.

His chubby features puckered with smiles, he looked up from the letter, and spoke aloud. 'Ja, O'Flynn, now I will pay you for the bucket.'

He turned back to the first page of the letter, and his mouth formed the words as he read '. . . whatever steps you deem necessary for the protection of our borders, and the confusion of the enemy.'

At last. At last he had the order for which he had pleaded so many times. He shouted for his sergeant.

38

'Perhaps they will come home tonight.' Rosa Oldsmith looked up from the child's smock she was embroidering.

'Tonight or tomorrow, or the next day,' Nanny replied philosophically. 'There is no profit in guessing at the coming or going of men. They all have worms in their heads,' and she began again to rock the cradle, squatting beside it on the leopard-skin rugs like an animated mummy. The child snuffled a little in its sleep.

'I'm sure it will be tonight. I can feel it—something good is going to happen.' Rosa laid aside her sewing and crossed to the door that led out on to the stoep. In the last few minutes the sun had gone down below the trees, and the land was ghostly quiet in the brief African dusk.

Rosa went out on to the stoep, and hugging her arms across her chest at the chill of evening, she stared out down the darkening length of the valley. She stood there, waiting restlessly, and as the day passed swiftly into darkness, so her mood changed from anticipation to a formless foreboding.

Quietly, but with an edge to her voice, she called back into the room, 'Light the lamps please, Nanny.'

Behind her she heard the sounds of metal on glass, then the flare of a sulphur match, and a feeble yellow square of light was thrown out on to the veranda to fall around her feet.

The first puff of the night wind was cold on her bare arms. She felt the prickle of goose-flesh and she shivered unexpectedly.

But Rosa lingered, straining her eyes into the darkness until she could no longer see the shape of the fig trees at the bottom of the lawn. Then abruptly she turned away and went into the bungalow. She closed the door and slid the bolt across.

Later she woke. There was no moon outside and the room was dark. Beside her bed she could hear the soft, piglet sounds that little Maria made in her sleep.

Again the disquieting mood of the early evening returned to her and she lay in her bed, waiting and listening in the utter blackness, and the darkness bore down upon her so that she felt herself shrinking, receding, becoming remote from reality, small and lonely in the night.

In fear then she lifted the mosquito netting and groped for the cradle. The baby whimpered as she lifted her and brought her into the bed beside her, but

Rosa's arms quietened her and soon she slept against the breast, and the warmth of the tiny body stilled Rosa's own agitation.

The shouting woke her, and she opened her eyes with a surge of joy, for the shouts would be Sebastian's bearers. Before she was fully awake she had thrown aside the bedclothes, struggled out from under the mosquito netting, and was standing in her night-dress with the baby clasped to her chest.

It was then that she realized that the room was no longer in darkness. From the window into the yard it was lit by a red-gold glow that flared, and flickered, and faded.

The last tarnish of sleep was cleaned from her brain, so she could hear that the shouts from outside were not those of welcome, and on a lower key, there were other sounds—a whispering, rustling, and popping, that she could not identify.

She crossed to the window, moving slowly, with dread for what she might find, but before she reached it a scream froze her. It came from the kitchen yard, a scream that quivered on the air long after it had ended, a scream of terror and of pain.

'Merciful God!' she whispered, and forced herself to peer out.

The servants' quarters and the outhouses were on fire. From the thatch of each the flames stood up in writhing yellow columns, lighting the darkness.

There were men in the yard, many men, and all of them wore the khaki uniform of German Askari. Each of them carried a rifle, and the bayonet blades glittered in the glare of the flames.

'They have crossed the river—No, oh please God, no!' and Rosa hugged the baby to her, crouching down below the window sill.

The scream rang out again, but weaker now, and she saw a knot of four Askari crowded around something that squirmed in the dust of the yard. She heard their laughter, that excited laughter of men who kill for fun, as they stabbed down on the squirming thing with their bayonets.

At that moment another of the servants broke from the burning outbuildings and ran for the darkness beyond the circle of the flames. Shouting again, the Askari left the dying man and chased the other. They turned him like a pack of trained greyhounds coursing a gazelle, laughing and shouting in their excitement, and drove him back into the daylight glare of the flames.

Bewildered, surrounded, the servant stopped and looked wildly about him, his face with terror. Then the Askari swarmed over him, clubbing and hacking with their rifles.

'Oh, oh God, no,' Rosa's whisper sobbed in her throat, but she could not drag her eyes away.

Suddenly in the uproar she heard a new noise, a bull-bellow of authority. She could not understand the words for they were shouted in German but from around the angle of the bungalow appeared a white man, a massive man in the blue corduroy uniform of the German Colonial Service, with a slouch hat pulled low down on his head, and a pistol brandished in one hand. From the description that Sebastian had given her, she recognized the German Commissioner.

'Stop them!' Rosa did not speak aloud, the appeal was in her mind only. 'Please, stop them burning and killing.'

The white man was railing at his Askari, his face turned towards where Rosa crouched and she saw it was round and pink like that of an overweight baby. In the fire-light it glistened with a fine sheen of sweat.

'Stop them. Please stop them,' Rosa pleaded silently, but under the Commissioner's direction three of the Askari ran to where, in the excitement of the chase, they had dropped their torches of dry grass. While they lit them from the flaming out-buildings, the other Askari left the corpses of the two servants and spread out in a circle around the bungalow, facing inwards, with their rifles held at high port. Most of the bayonets were dulled with blood.

'I want Fini and the Singese–not bearers and gun-boys–I want the white men! Burn them out!' shouted Fleischer, but Rosa recognized only her father's name. She wanted to cry out that he was not here, that it was only her and the child.

The three Askari were running in towards the bungalow now, sparks and fire smeared back from the torches they carried. In turn each man checked his run, poised himself like a javelin thrower, then hurled his torch in a high, smoking arc towards the bungalow. Rosa heard them thump, thump, thump, on to the thatched roof above her.

'I must get my baby away, before the fire catches,' and she hurried across the room, out into the passage. It was dark here and she groped along the wall until she found the entrance to the main room. At the front door she fumbled with the bolts, and opened it a crack. Peering through to the fire-lit lawns beyond the stoep, she saw the dark forms of Askari waiting there also, and she drew back.

'The side windows of the kitchen,' she told herself. 'They're closest to the bush. That's the best chance,' and she stumbled back into the passage.

Above her now there was a sound like high wind and water, a rushing sound blending with the crackle of burning thatch, and the first taint of smoke stung her nostrils.

'If only I can reach the bush,' she whispered desperately, and the child in her arms began to cry.

'Hush, my darling, hush now,' but her voice was scratchy with fear. Maria seemed to sense it; her petulant whimperings changed to lusty, high-pitched yells and she struggled in Rosa's grasp.

From the side windows of the kitchen Rosa saw the familiar waiting figures of the Askari hovering at the edge of the fire-light. She felt despair catch her stomach in a cold grip and squeeze the resolve from her. Suddenly her legs were weak under her and her whole body was shaking.

From within the bungalow behind her there came a thunderous roar as part of the burning roof collasped. A blast of scalding air blew through the kitchen and the tall column of sparks and flames thrown up by the collapse lit the surroundings even more vividly. It showed another figure beyond the line of Askari, scampering in from the edge of the bush like a little black monkey, and Rosa heard Nanny's voice.

'Little Long Hair! Little Long Hair.' A plaintive, ancient wail.

Nanny had escaped into the bush during the first minutes of the attack. She had lain there watching until the roof of the bungalow fell in–then she could no longer contain herself. Insensible of her own danger, caring for nothing except her precious charges, she was coming back.

The Askari saw her also. Their rigid, well-spaced line crumpled as all of them ran to head her off. Suddenly the ground between Rosa and the edge of the bush was clear. Now there was a chance–just the smallest chance that she could get the child away. She flung the window open and dropped through it to the earth.

One moment she hesitated and glanced towards the confusion of running men away to her right hand. In that moment she saw one of the Askari catch up with the old woman and lunge forward with his bayonet. Nanny reeled from the force of the blow in her back. Involuntarily her arms were flung wide open, and for a fleeting second Rosa saw the point of the bayonet appear miraculously from the centre of her chest, as it impaled her.

Then Rosa was running towards the wall of bush and scrub fifty yards ahead of her, while Maria howled in her arms. The sound attracted the attention of the Askari. One of them shouted a warning, and then the whole pack was after her in full tongue.

Rosa's senses were overwrought by her terror, so finely tuned that it seemed the passage of time was lagging. Weighed down by the child, each pace she took dragged on for ever, as though she waded through waist-deep water. The long night-dress around her legs hampered her, and there was rough stone and thorn beneath her bare feet. The wall of bush ahead of her seemed to come no closer, and she ran with the cold hand of fear squeezing her chest and cramping her breathing.

Then into her line of vision from the side came a man, an Askari, a big man bounding towards her with the long loping gallop of a bull baboon, cutting across her line of flight, his open mouth an obscene pink pit in the shiny black of his face.

Rosa screamed and swung away from him. How she was running parallel to the edge of the bush and behind her she heard the slap of feet upon the earth, closing fast, and the babbling chorus of the pursuit.

A hand snatched at her shoulder, and she twisted away from it, feeling the stuff of her night-gown tear beneath the clutching fingers.

Blind with terror she stumbled a dozen paces back towards the burning homestead. She felt the vast waves of heat from it in her face and through her thin clothing—and then a rifle butt struck her in the small of the back, and a bright burst of agony paralysed her legs. She dropped to her knees, still holding Maria.

They ringed her, in a palisade of human bodies and gloating, blood-crazed faces.

The big one who had felled her with the rifle butt stooped over her and before she recognized his intention, he had snatched Maria from her arms and stepped back again.

He stood laughing, holding the child by the ankles, letting her swing head downwards, so her tiny face was suffused with blood, scarlet in the light of the flames.

'No, please, no!' Rosa crawled painfully towards the man. 'Give her back to me. My baby. Please give her back,' and she lifted her arms towards him.

The Askari dangled the child tantalizingly in front of her, retreating slowly as she crawled towards him. The others were laughing, hoarse sensual laughter, crowding around her, faces contorted with enjoyment, and polished ebony black with the sweat of excitement, as they jostled each other for a better view of the sport.

Then with a wild yell, the Askari swung Maria high, whirled her twice above his head as he pivoted to face the bungalow—and threw Maria up towards the burning roof.

The tiny body flew with the looseness of a rag doll through the air, her night-dress fluttered as she dropped and struck the roof, rolled awkwardly down the slope of it with her clothing blooming into instant flame, until she reached a weak spot in the burning thatch. It sucked Maria in like a fiery mouth and blew a belch of sparks as it swallowed her. At that instant Rosa heard the voice of her child for the last time. It was a sound she was never to forget.

For a moment the men about her were hushed, and then as though wind blew through trees, they moved a little with a sound that was half sigh, half moan.

Still kneeling, facing the burning building which was now a pyre, Rosa slumped forward and lifted her hands to cover her face as though in prayer.

The Askari who had thrown the child snatched up his rifle from where it lay at his feet and stood over her. He lifted it above his head the way a harpooner holds his steel with the point of the bayonet aimed at the base of Rosa's neck where her hair had fallen open to expose the pale skin.

In the moment that the Askari paused to take his aim, Herman Fleischer shot him in the back of the head with the Luger.

'Mad dog!' the Commissioner shouted at the Askari's corpse. 'I told you to take them alive.'

Then, breathing like an asthma case from the exertion of his run to intervene, he turned to Rosa.

'Fräulein, my apologies,' he doffed his slouch hat with ponderous courtesy, and spoke in German that Rosa did not understand. 'We do not make war on women and babies.'

She did not look up at him. She was crying quietly into her cupped hands.

39

'Early in the year for a bush fire,' Flynn muttered. He sat with an enamel mug cupped in his hands and blew steam from the hot coffee. His blanket had slid down to his waist.

Across the camp-fire from him Sebastian was also sitting in a muddle of bedding, and cooling his own pre-dawn mug of coffee. At Flynn's words he looked up from his labour, and out into the dark south.

False dawn had paled the sky just enough to define the hills below it as an undulating mass that seemed much closer than it was. That way lay Lalapanzi—and Rosa and Maria.

Without real interest Sebastian saw the radiated glow at one point along the spine of the ridge; a fan of pink light no larger than a thumbnail.

'Not a very big one,' he said.

'No,' agreed Flynn. 'Hope she doesn't spread though,' and he gulped noisily at his mug.

As Sebastian watched it idly, the glow diminished, shrinking into insignificance at the coming of the sun, and above it the stars paled also.

'We'd best get moving. It's a long day's march and we've wasted enough time on this trip already.'

'You're a regular bloody fire-eater when it comes to getting your home comforts.' Flynn feigned disinterest, yet secretly the thought of returning to his granddaughter had strong appeal. He hurried the coffee a little and scalded his tongue.

Sebastian was right. They had wasted a lot of time on the return trip from the Mahenge raid.

First, there was a detour to avoid a party of German Askari that one of the native headmen had warned them was at M'topo's village. They had trekked upstream for three days before finding a safe crossing, and a village willing to hire canoes.

Then there was the brush with the hippo which had cost them almost a week. As was usual practice, the four hired canoes, loaded to within a few inches of free-board with Flynn, Sebastian, their retinue, and loot, had slipped across the Rovuma and were hugging the Portuguese bank as they headed downstream towards the landing opposite M'topo's village when the hippo had disputed their passage.

She was an old cow hippo who a few hours earlier had given birth to her calf in a tiny island of reeds, separated from the south bank by twenty feet of lily-padded water. When the four canoes entered this channel in line astern with the paddlers chanting happily, she took it as a direct threat to her offspring and she threw a tantrum.

Two tons of hippo in a tantrum has the destructive force of a localized hurricane. Surfacing violently from under the leading canoe, she had thrown Sebastian, two gun-boys, four paddlers, and all their equipment, ten feet in the air. The canoe, rotted with beetle, had snapped in half and sunk immediately.

The mother hippo had then treated the three following canoes with the same consideration, and within the space of a few minutes, the canal was clogged with floating debris, and struggling, panic-stricken men. Fortunately they were no more than ten feet from the bank. Sebastian was first ashore. None of them, however, was very far behind him, and they all took off like the start of a cross-country race over the veld, when the hippo emerged from the river and signified that, not satisified with wrecking the flotilla, she intended chopping a few of them in half with her guillotine jaws.

A hundred yards later she abandoned the pursuit, and trotted back to the water, wiggling her little ears and snorting in triumph. Half a mile farther on the survivors had stopped running.

They camped there that night without food, bedding, or weapons, and the following morning, after a heated council of war, Sebastian was elected to return to the river and ascertain whether the hippo was still in control of the channel. He came back at high speed to report that she was.

Three more days they waited for the hippo and her calf to move away. During this time they suffered the miseries of cold nights and hungry days, but the greatest misery was inflicted on Flynn O'Flynn whose case of gin was under eight feet of water—and by the third morning he was threatening *delirium tremens* again. Just before Sebastian set off for his morning reconnaissance of the channel, Flynn informed him agitatedly that there were three blue scorpions sitting on his head. After the initial alarm, Sebastian went through the motions of removing the imaginary scorpions and stamping them to death, and Flynn was satisfied.

Sebastian returned from the river with the news that the hippo and her calf had evacuated the island, and it was now possible to begin salvage operations.

Protesting mildly and talking about crocodiles, Sebastian was stripped naked and coaxed into the water. On his first dive, he retrieved the precious case of gin.

'Bless you, my boy,' Flynn murmured fervently as he eased the cork out of a bottle.

By the following morning Sebastian had recovered nearly all their equipment and booty, without being eaten by crocodiles, and they set off for Lalapanzi on foot.

Now they were in their last camp before Lalapanzi, and Sebastian felt his impatience rising. He wanted to get home to Rosa and baby Maria. He should be home by evening.

'Come on, Flynn. Let's go.' He flicked the coffee grounds from his mug, threw aside his blanket, and shouted to Mohammed and the bearers who were huddled around the other fire.

'Safari! Let us march.'

Nine hours later, with the daylight around him, he breasted the last rise and paused at the top.

All that day eagerness had lengthened his stride, and he had left Flynn and the column of heavily laden bearers far behind.

Now he stood alone, and stared without comprehension at the smoke-blackened ruins of Lalapanzi from which a few thin tendrils of smoke still drifted.

'Rosa!' Her name was a harsh bellow of fear, and he ran wildly.

'Rosa!' he shouted as he crossed the scorched and trampled lawns.

'Rosa! Rosa! Rosa!' the echo from the kopje above the homestead shouted back.

'Rosa!' He saw something among the bushes at the edge of the lawn, and he ran to it. Old Nanny lying dead with the blood dried black on the floral stuff of her night-gown.

'Rosa!' He ran back towards the bungalow. The ash swirled in a warm mist around his legs as he crossed the stoep.

'Rosa!' His voice rang hollowly through the roofless shell of the house, as he stumbled over the fallen beams that littered the main room. The reek of burned cloth and hair and wood almost choked him, so that his voice was husky as he called again.

'Rosa!'

He found her in the burnt-out kitchen block and he thought she was dead. She was slumped against the cracked and blackened wall. Her night-gown was torn and scorched, and the snarled skeins of hair, that hid her face, were powdered with white wood ash.

'My darling. Oh, my darling.' He knelt beside her, and timidly touched her shoulder. Her flesh was warm and alive beneath his fingers, and he felt relief leap up into his throat, blocking it so he could not speak again. Instead, he brushed the tangle of hair from her face and looked at it.

Beneath the charcoal smears of dirt her skin was pale as grey marble. Her eyes, tight closed, were heavily underscored with blue, and rimmed with crusty red.

He touched her lips with the tips of his fingers, and she opened her eyes. But they looked beyond him; unseeing, dead eyes. They frightened him. He did not want to look into them, and he drew her head towards his shoulder.

There was no resistance in her. She lay against him quietly, and he pressed his face into her hair. Her hair was impregnated with the smell of smoke.

'Are you hurt?' he asked her in a whisper, not wanting to hear her answer. But she made no answer, lying inert in his arms.

'Tell me, Rosa. Speak to me. Where is Maria?'

At the mention of the child's name, she reacted for the first time. She began to tremble.

'Where is she?' more urgency in his voice now.

She rolled her head against his shoulder and looked across the floor of the room. He followed the direction of her gaze.

Near the far wall an area of the floor had been swept clear of debris and ash. Rosa had done it with her bare hands while the ash was still hot. Her fingers were blistered and burned raw in places, and her arms were black to the elbows. Lying in the centre of this cleared space was a small, charred thing.

'Maria?' Sebastian whispered, and Rosa shuddered against him.

'Oh, God,' he said, and lifted Rosa. Carrying her against his chest, he staggered from the ruins of the bungalow out into the cool, sweet evening air, but in his nostrils lingered the smell of smoke and burned flesh. He wanted to escape from it. He ran blindly along the path and Rosa lay unresisting in his arms.

40

The following day Flynn buried their dead on the kopje above Lalapanzi. He placed a thick slab of granite over the small grave that stood apart from the others, and when it was done he sent a bearer to the camp to fetch Rosa and Sebastian.

When they came, they found him standing alone by Maria's grave under the marula trees. His face was puffy and purply red. The thinning grey hair hung limply over his ears and forehead, like the wet feathers of an old rooster. His body looked as though it was melting. It sagged at the shoulders and the belly. Sweat had soaked through his clothing across the shoulders, and at the armpits and crotch. He was sick with drink and sorrow.

Sebastian stood beside Rosa, and the three of them took their silent farewell of the child.

'There is nothing else to do now.' Sebastian spoke huskily.

'Yes,' said Flynn. He stooped slowly and took a handful of the new earth from the grave. 'Yes, there is.' He crumbled the earth between his fingers. 'We still have to find the man who did this—and kill him.'

Beside Sebastian, Rosa straightened up. She turned to Sebastian, lifted her chin, and spoke for the first time since he had come home.

'Kill him!' she repeated softly.

PART II

41

With his hands clasped behind his back, and his chin thrust forward aggressively Rear-Admiral Sir Percy Howe sucked in his lower lip and nibbled it reflectively. 'What was our last substantiated sighting on *Blücher?*' he asked at last.

'A month ago, sir. Two days before the outbreak of war. Sighting reported by S.S. *Tygerberg*. Latitude 0° 27′ N. Longitude 52° 16′ E. Headed southwest; estimated speed, eighteen knots.'

'And a hell of a lot of good that does us,' Sir Percy interrupted his flagcaptain and glared at the vast Admiralty plot of the Indian Ocean. 'She could be back in Bremerhaven by now.'

'She could be, sir,' the flag-captain nodded, and Sir Percy glanced at him and permitted himself a wintry smile.

'But you don't believe that, do you, Henry?'

'No, sir, I don't. During the last thirty days, eight merchantmen had disappeared between Aden and Lourenço Marques. Nearly a quarter of a million tons of shipping. That's the *Blücher*'s work.'

'Yes, it's the *Blücher*, all right,' agreed the Admiral, and reached across the plot to pick up the black counter labelled '*Blücher*', that lay on the wide green expanse of the Indian Ocean.

A respectful silence held the personnel of the plotting room South Atlantic and Indian Oceans while they waited for the great man to reach his decision. It was a long time coming. He stood bouncing the '*Blücher*' in the palm of his right hand, his grey eyebrows erect like the spines of a hedgehog's back, as his forehead creased in thought. A full minute they waited.

'Refresh my memory of her class and commission.' Like most successful men Sir Percy would not hurry a decision when there was time to think, and the duty lieutenant who had anticipated his request, stepped forward with the German Imperial Navy list open at the correct page.

'"*Blücher*. Commissioned August 16th, 1905. 'B' Class heavy cruiser. Main armament, eight nine-inch guns. Secondary armament, six six-inch guns."'

The lieutenant finished his reading and waited quietly.

'Who is her captain?' Sir Percy asked, and the lieutenant consulted an addendum to the list.

'"Otto von Kleine (Count). Previously commanded the light cruiser *Sturm Vogel*."'·

'Yes,' said Sir Percy. 'I've heard of him,' and he replaced the counter on the plot, keeping his hand on it. 'A dangerous man to have here, south of Suez,' and he pushed the counter up towards the Red Sea and the entrance to the canal, where the tiny red shipping lanes amalgamated into a thick artery, '–or here,' and he pushed it down towards the Cape of Good Hope, around which were curved the same red threads that joined London to Australia and India. Sir Percy lifted his hand from the black counter and left it sitting menacingly upon the shipping lanes.

'What force have we deployed against him so far?' and in answer the flag-captain picked up a wooden pointer and touched in turn the red counters that were scattered about the Indian Ocean.

'*Pegasus* and *Renounce* in the north. *Eagle* and *Plunder* sweeping the southern waters, sir.'

'What further force can we spare, Henry?'

'Well, sir, *Orion* and *Bloodhound* are at Simonstown,' and he touched the nose of the African continent with the pointer.

'*Orion*–that's Manderson, isn't it?'

'Yes, sir.'

'And who has *Bloodhound*?'

'Little, sir.'

'Good,' Sir Percy nodded with satisfaction. 'A six-inch cruiser and a destroyer should be able to deal with *Blücher*,' and he smiled again. 'Especially with a hellion like Charles Little handling the *Bloodhound*. I played golf with him last summer–he damn nigh drove the sixteenth green at St Andrews!'

The flag-captain glanced at the Admiral and, on the strength of the destroyer captain's reputation, decided to permit himself an inanity. 'The young ladies of Cape Town will mourn his departure, sir.'

'We must hope that Kapitän zur See Otto von Kleine will mourn his arrival,' chuckled Sir Percy.

'Daddy likes you very much.'

'Your father is a man of exquisite good taste,' Commander the Honourable Charles Little conceded gallantly, and rolled his head to smile at the young lady who lay beside him on a rug, in the dappled shade beneath the pine trees.

'Can't you ever be serious?'

'Helen, my sweet, at times I can be deadly serious.'

'Oh, you!' and his companion blushed prettily as she remembered certain of Charles' recent actions, which would make her father hastily revise his judgement.

'I value your father's good opinion, but my chief concern is that you endorse it.'

The girl sat up slowly and while she stared at him her hands were busy, brushing the pine needles from the glorious tangle of her hair, readjusting the fastenings of her blouse, spreading the skirts of her riding-habit to cover sweet legs clad in dark, tall polished leather boots.

She stared at Charles Little and ached with the strength of her want. It was not a sensual need she felt, but an overpowering obsession to have this man as her very own. To own him in the same way as she already owned diamonds, and furs, and silk, and horses, and peacocks, and other beautiful things.

His body sprawled out on the rug with all the unconscious grace of a reclining leopard. A secret little smile tugged at the corners of his lips and his eyelids drooped to mask the sparkle of his eyes. His recent exertions had dampened the hair that flopped forward on to his forehead.

There was something satanical about him, an air of wickedness, and Helen decided it was the slant of the eyebrows and the way his ears lay flat against his temples, but were pointed like those of a satyr, yet they were pink and smooth as those of an infant.

'I think you have devil's ears,' she said, and then she blushed again, and scrambled to her feet avoiding Charles' arm that reached out for her. 'Enough of that!' she giggled and ran to the thoroughbred hunter that was tied near them in the forest. 'Come on,' she called as she mounted.

Charles stood up lazily and stretched. He tucked the tail of his shirt into his breeches, folded the rug on which they had lain, and went to his own horse.

At the edge of the pine forest, they checked their mounts and sat looking down over the Constania valley.

'Isn't it beautiful?' she said.

'It is indeed,' he agreed.

'I meant the view.'

'And so did I.' Twice in the six days he had known her, she had led him up this mountain and subjected him to the temptation. Below them lay six thousand acres of the richest land in all of Africa.

'When my brother Hubert was killed there was no one left to carry it on. Just my sister and I—and we are only girls. Poor Daddy isn't so well any more—he finds it such a strain.'

Charles let his eye move lazily from the great squat buttress of Table Mountain on their left, across the lush basin of vineyards below them, and then on to where the glittering wedge of False Bay drove into the mountains.

'Doesn't the homestead look lovely from here?' Helen drew his attention to the massive Dutch-gabled residence with its attendant outbuildings, grouped in servility behind it.

'I am truly impressed by the magnificence of the stud fee,' Charles murmured, purposely slurring the last two words, and the girl glanced at him in surprise, beginning to bridle.

'I beg your pardon?'

'It is truly magnificent scenery,' he amended. Her persistent efforts at ensnaring him were beginning to bore Charles. He had teased and avoided more artful huntresses.

'Charles,' she whispered. 'How would you like to live here. I mean, for ever?'

And Charles was shocked. This little provincial had no understanding whatsoever of the rules governing the game of flirtation. He was so shocked that he threw back his head and laughed.

When Charles laughed it sent shivers of delight through every woman within a hundred yards. It was a merry sound with underlying tones of sensuality. His teeth were very white against the sea-tan of his face, and the muscles of his chest and upper arms tensed into bold relief beneath the silk shirt he wore.

Helen was the only witness of this particular performance, and she was helpless as a sparrow in a hurricane. Eagerly she leaned across the space between their horses and touched his arm. 'You would like it, Charles. Wouldn't you?'

She did not know that Charles Little had a private income of twenty thousand pounds a year, that when his father died he would inherit the title

Viscount Sutherton and the estates that went with it. She did not know that one of those estates would swallow her father's own three times over; nor did she know that Charles had passed by willing young ladies with twice her looks, ten times her fortune, and a hundred times her breeding.

'You would, Charles. I know you would!'

So young, so vulnerable, that he stopped the flippant reply before it reached his lips.

'Helen,' he took her hand. 'I am a sea creature. We move with the wind and the waves,' and he lifted her hand to his lips.

A while she sat, feeling the warm pressure of his lips upon her flesh, and the burn of tears behind her eyes. Then she snatched her hand away, and wheeled her horse. She lifted the leather riding-crop and slashed the glossy black shoulder between her knees. Startled, the stallion jumped forward into a dead run back along the road towards the Constania valley.

Charles shook his head and grimaced with regret. He had not meant to hurt her. It had been an escapade, something to fill the waiting days while *Bloodhound* went through the final stages of her refit. But Charles had learned to harden himself to the ending of his adventures—to the tears and tragedy.

'Shame on you, you heartless cad,' he said aloud, and touching his mount with his heels ambled in pursuit of the galloping stallion.

He caught up with the stallion in the stable yards. A groom was walking it, and there were darker sweat patches on its coat, and the barrel of its chest still heaved with laboured breathing.

Helen was nowhere in sight, but her father stood at the stable gates—a big man, with a square-cut black beard picked out with grey.

'Enjoy your ride?'

'Thank you, Mr Uys.' Charles was noncommittal, and the older man glanced significantly at the blown stallion before going on.

'There's one of your sailors been waiting for you for an hour.'

'Where is he?' Charles' manner altered abruptly, became instantly businesslike.

'Here, sir.' From the deep shade of the stable doorway, a young seaman stepped out into the bright sunlight.

'What is it, man?' Impatiently Charles acknowledged his salute.

'Captain Manderson's compliments, sir, and you're to report aboard H.M.S. *Orion* with all possible speed. There's a motor car waiting to take you to the base, sir.'

'An untimely summons, Commander,' Uys gave his opinion lounging against the worked stone gateway. 'I fear we will see no more of you for a long time.'

But Charles was not listening. His body seemed to quiver with suppressed excitement, the way a good gun-dog reacts to the scent of the bird. 'Sailing orders,' he whispered, '—at last. At last!'

There was a heavy south-east swell battering Cape Point, so the sea spray wreathed the beam of the lighthouse on the cliffs above. A flight of malgas came in so high towards the land that they caught the last of the sun, and glowed pink above the dark water.

Bloodhound cleared Cape Hangklip and took the press of the South Atlantic on her shoulder, staggered from it with a welter of white water running waist-deep past her foredeck gun-turrets. Then in retaliation she hurled herself at

the next swell, and Charles Little on her bridge exulted at the vital movement
of the deck beneath his feet.

'Bring her round to oh-five-oh.'

'Oh-five-oh, sir,' repeated his navigating lieutenant.

'Revolutions for seventeen knots, pilot.'

Almost immediately the beat of the engines changed, and her action through
the water became more abandoned.

Charles crossed to the angle of the flimsy little bridge and looked back into
the dark, mountain-lined maw of False Bay. Two miles astern the shape of
H.M.S. *Orion* melted into the dying light.

'Come along, old girl. Do try and keep up,' murmured Charles Little with
the scorn that a destroyer man feels for any vessel that cannot cruise at twenty
knots. Then he looked beyond *Orion* at the land. Below the massif of Table
Mountain, near the head of the Constantia valley a single pink prick of light
showed.

'There'll be fog tonight, sir,' the pilot spoke at Charles' elbow, and Charles
turned without regret to peer over the bows into the gathering night.

'Yes, a good night for pirates.'

42

The fog condensed on the grey metal of the bridge, so the footplates were
slippery underfoot. It soaked into the overcoats of the men huddled against the
rail, and it dewed in minute pearls on the eyebrows and the beard of Kapitän
zur See Otto von Kleine. It gave him an air of derring-do, the reckless look of a
scholarly pirate.

Every few seconds Lieutenant Kyller glanced anxiously at his captain,
wondering when the order to turn would come. He hated this business of
creeping inshore in the fog, with a flood tide pushing them towards a hostile
coast.

'Stop all engines,' said von Kleine, and Kyller repeated the order to the helm
with alacrity. The muted throbbing died beneath their feet, and afterwards the
fog-blanketed air was heavy with a sepulchral hush.

'Ask masthead what he makes of the land.' Von Kleine spoke without
turning his head, and after a pause Kyller reported back.

'Masthead is in the fog. No visibility,' he paused. 'Foredeck reports fifty
fathoms shoaling rapidly.'

And von Kleine nodded. The sounding tended to confirm his estimate that
they were sitting five miles off the breakwater of Durban harbour. When the
morning wind swept the fog aside he hoped to see the low coastal hills of Natal
ahead of him, terraced with gardens and whitewashed buildings–but most of
all he hoped to see at least six British merchantmen anchored off the beach
waiting their turn to enter the congested harbour, plump and sleepy under the
protection of the shore batteries; unaware just how feeble was the protection
afforded by half a dozen obsolete ten-pounders manned by old men and boys
of the militia.

German naval intelligence had submitted a very detailed report of the
defences and conditions prevailing in Durban. After careful perusal of this
report, von Kleine had decided that he could trade certain betrayal of his exact

position to the English for such a rich prize. There was little actual risk involved. One pass across the entrance of the harbour at high speed, a single broadside for each of the anchored merchantmen, and he could be over the horizon again before the shore gunners had loaded their weapons.

The risk, of course, was in showing *Blücher* to the entire population of Durban city and thereby supplying the Royal Navy with its first accurate sighting since the declaration of war. Within minutes of his first broadside, the British squadrons, which were hunting him, would be racing in from all directions to block each of his escape routes. He hoped to counter this by swinging away towards the south, down into that watery wildnerness of wind and ice below latitude 40°, to the rendezvous with *Esther*, his supply ship. Then on to Australia or South America, as the opportunity arose.

He turned to glance at the chronometer above the ship's compass. Sunrise in three minutes, then they could expect the morning wind.

'Masthead reports the fog dispersing, sir.'

Von Kleine aroused himself, and looked out into the fog banks. They were moving now, twisting upon themselves in agitation at the warmth of the sun. 'All engines slow ahead together,' he said.

'Masthead,' warbled one of the voice-pipes in the battery in front of Kyller. 'Land bearing green four-oh. Range, ten thousand metres. A big headland.'

That would be the bluff above Durban, the massive whale-backed mountain that sheltered the harbour. But in the fog von Kleine had misjudged his approach; he was twice as far from the shore as he had intended.

'All engines full ahead together. New course. Oh-oh-six.' He waited for the order to be relayed to the helm before strolling across to the voice-pipes. 'Guns. Captain.'

'Guns,' the voice from far away acknowledged.

'I will be opening fire with high explosives in about ten minutes. The target will be massed merchant shipping on an approximate mark of three hundred degrees. Range, five thousand metres. You may fire as soon as you bear.'

'Mark three hundred degrees. Range, five thousand metres, sir,' repeated the pipe, and von Kleine snapped the voice-tube cover shut and returned to his original position, facing forward with his hands clasped loosely behind his back.

Below him the gun-turrets revolved ponderously and the long barrels lifted slightly, pointing out into the mist with impassive menace.

A burst of dazzling sunshine struck the bridge so fiercely that Kyller lifted his hand to shield his eyes, but it was gone instantly as the *Blücher* dashed into another clammy cold bank of fog. Then as though they had passed through a curtain on to a brilliantly lit stage, they came out into a gay summer's morning.

Behind them the fog rolled away in a sodden grey wall from horizon to horizon. Ahead rose the green hills of Africa, rimmed with white beach and surf and speckled with thousands of white flecks that were the buildings of Durban town. The scaffolding of the cranes along the harbour wall looked like derelict sets of gallows.

Humped on the smooth green mirror of water between them and the shore, lay four ungainly shapes looking like a troop of basking hippo. The British merchantmen.

'Four only,' muttered von Kleine in chagrin. 'I had hoped for more.'

The forty-foot barrels of the nine-inch guns moved restlessly, seeming to sniff for their prey, and the *Blücher* raced on, lifting a hissing white wave at her bows, vibrating and shuddering to the thrust of her engines as they built up to full speed.

'Masthead,' the voice-tube beside Kyller squawked urgently.

'Bridge,' said Kyller but the reply was lost in the deafening detonation of the first broadside, the long thunderous roll of heavy gunfire. He jumped involuntarily, taken unawares, and then quickly lifted the binoculars from his chest to train them on the British merchantmen.

All attention, every eye on the bridge was concentrated ahead, waiting for the fall of shot upon the doomed vessels.

In the comparative silence that followed the bellow of the broadside, a shriek from the masthead voice-pipe carried clearly.

'Warships! Enemy warships dead astern!'

'Starboard ten.' Von Kleine raised his voice a little louder than was his wont, and still under full power, *Blücher* swerved away from the land, leaning out from the turn, with her wake curved like an ostrich plume on the surface of the sea behind her, and ran for the shelter of the fog banks, leaving the rich prize of cargo shipping unscathed. On her bridge von Kleine and his officers were staring aft, the merchantmen forgotten as they search for this new threat.

'Two warships.' The masthead look-out was elaborating his sighting report. 'A destroyer and a cruiser. Bearing ninety degrees. Range, five-oh-seven-oh. Destroyer leading.'

In the spherical field of von Kleine's binoculars the neat little triangle of the leading destroyer's superstructure popped up above the horizon. The cruiser was not yet in sight from the bridge.

'If they'd been an hour later,' lamented Kyller, 'we'd have finished the business and . . .'

'What does masthead see of the cruiser?' von Kleine interrupted him impatiently. He had no time to mourn this chance of fate—his only concern was to evaluate the force that was pursuing him, and then make the decision whether to run, or to turn back and engage them immediately.

'Cruiser is a medium, six- or nine-inch. Either "O" class, or an "R". She's four miles behind her escort. Both ships still out of range.'

The destroyer was of no consequence; he could run down on her and blast her into a burning wreck, before her feeble little 4·7-inch guns were able to drop a shell within a mile of *Blücher*, but the cruiser was another matter entirely. To tackle her, *Blücher* would be engaging with her own class; victory would only be won after a severe mauling, and she was six thousand miles from the nearest friendly port where she could effect major repairs.

There was a further consideration. These two British ships might be the vanguard of a battle squadron. If he turned now and challenged action, engaged the cruiser in a single ship action, he might suddenly find himself pitted against imponderable odds. There could very well be another cruiser, or two, or three—even a battleship, below the southern horizon.

His duty and his orders dictated instant flight, avoiding action, and so prolonging *Blücher*'s fighting life.

'Enemy are streaming their colours, sir,' Kyller reported.

Von Kleine lifted his binoculars again. At the destroyer's masthead flew the tiny spots of white and red. This time he must leave the challenge to combat unanswered. 'Very well,' he said, and turned away to his stool in the corner of the bridge. He slumped into it and hunched his shoulders in thought. There were many interesting problems to occupy him, not least of them was how long he could run at full speed towards the north while his boilers devoured coal ravenously, and each minute widened the gap between *Blücher* and *Esther*.

He swivelled his stool and looked back over his stern. The destroyer was visible to the unaided eye now, and von Kleine frowned at it in irritation. She would yap at his heels like a terrier, clinging to him and shouting his course and speed across the ether to the hungry British squadrons, that must even now be closing with him from every direction. For days now he could expect to see her sitting in his wake.

43

'Come on! Come on!' Charles Little slapped his hand impatiently against the padded arm of his stool as he watched *Orion*.

For a night and a day he had watched her gaining on *Blücher* but so infinitesimally slowly that it required his range finder to confirm the gain every thirty minutes.

Orion's bows were unnaturally high, and the waves she lifted with the passage of her hull through the water were the white wings of a seagull in the tropical sunlight; for Manderson, her captain, had pumped out her forward fresh-water tanks and fired away half the shell and explosive propellent from her forward magazines. Every man whose presence in the front half of the ship was not essential to her operation had been ordered aft to stand on the open deck as human ballast—all this in an effort to lift *Orion*'s bows and to coax another inch of speed from the cruiser.

Now she faced the most dangerous hour of her life, for she was creeping within extreme range of *Blücher*'s terrible nine-inch armament, and, taking into account the discrepancy in their speeds, it would be another hour before she could bring her own six-inch guns to bear. During that time she would be under fire from *Blücher*'s after turrets and would have no answer to them.

It was heart-breaking for Charles to watch the chase, for *Bloodhound* had not once been asked to extend herself. Below there was a reserve of speed that would allow her to close with *Blücher* in fifty minutes of steaming—always provided she was not smashed into a fiery shambles long before.

Thus the three vessels fled towards the ever-receding northern horizon. The two long shapes of the cruisers flying arrow straight, solid columns of reeking smoke pouring from their triple funnels to besmear the gay, glittering surface of the sea with a long double bank of black that dispersed only slowly on the easterly breeze; while, like a water beetle, the diminutive *Bloodhound* circled out to the side of *Blücher* from where, when the time came, she could spot the fall of *Orion*'s shells more accurately and signal the corrections to her. But always *Bloodhound* tactfully kept outside the fifteen mile radius which marked the length of *Blücher*'s talons.

'We can expect *Blücher* to open fire at any moment now, sir,' the navigating lieutenant commented as he straightened up from the sextant, over which he had been measuring the angle subtended by the two cruisers.

Charles nodded in agreement. 'Yes. Von Kleine must try for a few lucky hits, even at that range.'

'This isn't going to be very pretty to watch.'

'We'll just have to sit tight, keep our fingers crossed, and hope old *Orion* can–' He stopped abruptly, and then jumped up from his stool. 'Hello! *Blücher*'s up to something!'

The silhouette of the German cruiser had altered drastically in the last few seconds. The gap between her funnels widened and now Charles could see the humped menace of her forward turrets.

'By God, she's altering course! The bloody bastard is bringing all his turrets to bear!'

Lieutenant Kyller studied his captain's face. In sleep there was an air of serenity about the man. It reminded Kyller of a painting he had seen in the cathedral at Nürnberg, a portrait of Saint Luke by Holbein. The same fine bone structure, the golden blond beard and moustache that framed the mobile and sensitive lips. He pushed the idea aside and leaned forward. Gently he touched von Kleine's shoulder.

'Captain. My Captain,' and von Kleine opened his eyes. They were smoky blue with sleep but his voice was crisp.

'What is it, Kyller?'

'The gunnery officer reports the enemy will be within range in fifteen minutes.

Von Kleine swivelled his stool and looked quickly about his ship. Above him the smoke poured from every funnel, and from the mouth of each stack a volcano of sparks and shimmering heat blew steadily. The paint had blistered and peeled from the metal of the funnels and they glowed red hot, even in the sunlight. *Blücher* was straining herself far beyond the limits her makers had set. God alone knew what injury this constant running at full speed was doing her, and von Kleine winced as he felt her tremble in protest beneath him.

He turned his eyes astern. The British cruiser was hull up on the horizon now. The difference in their speeds must be a small fraction of a knot, but *Blücher*'s superiority in fire power was enormous.

For a moment he allowed himself to ponder the arrogance of a nation that constantly, almost by choice, matched their men and ships against unnatural odds. Always they sent terriers to fight against wolfhounds. Then he smiled, you had to be English or mad, to understand the English.

He glanced out to starboard. The British destroyer had worked out on to his flank. It could do little harm from there.

'Very well, Kyller . . .' He stood as he spoke.

'Bridge–Engine Room,' the voice-tube squealed.

'Engine Room–Bridge.' Kyller turned to it,

'Our port main bearing is running red hot. I must shut down our port engine!'

The words struck von Kleine like a bucket of iced water thrown down his back. He leaped to the voice-tube.

'This is the Captain. I must have full power for another hour!'

'I can't do it, sir. Another fifteen minutes and the main drive shaft will seize up. God knows what damage it will do.'

For five seconds von Kleine hunched silently over the voice-tube. His mind raced. On one engine *Blücher* would lose ten knots on her speed. The enemy would be able to manœuvre about him freely–possibly hold off until nightfall and then . . . He must attack immediately; turn on them and press his attack home with all his armament.

'Give me full power for as long as you can,' he snapped, and then turning to the gunnery officer's tube, 'This is the Captain. I am turning four points to starboard, and will keep the enemy directly on our starboard beam for the next fifteen minutes. After that I will be forced to reduce speed. Open fire when you bear.' Von Kleine snapped the cover closed and turned to his yeoman of signals. 'Hoist the battle ensign!'

He spoke softly, without heat, but there were lights in his eyes like those in a blue sapphire.

44

'There she goes!' whispered Charles Little without lowering his glasses. Upon the black turrets of *Blücher* the gunfire gleamed and sparkled without sound. Quickly he traversed his glasses across the surface of the sea until he found *Orion*. She was plunging in eagerly, narrowing the gap very rapidly between herself and *Blücher*. In another seven minutes she would be able to return the German's fire.

Suddenly, a quarter of a mile ahead of her, there rose from the sea a series of tall columns, stately as the columns of a Greek temple, slender and beautiful, shining like white marble in the sun. Then slowly they dropped back.

'Short,' grunted the navigating lieutenant.

'Her guns are still cold,' Charles commented. 'Please God let old *Orion* get within range.'

Again *Blücher*'s shells fell short, and short again, but each time they were closer to the low bulk of *Orion*, and the next broadside dropped all around her, partially screening her with spray, and *Orion* started to zigzag.

'Another three minutes,' the navigating lieutenant spoke with tension making his voice husky.

At regular intervals of fifteen seconds the German salvoes fell around *Orion*—once within fifty feet of her bows so that as she tore into the standing columns of spray, they blew back over her and mingled with the black smoke of her funnels.

'Come on, old girl! Go in and get her. Go on! Go on!' Charles was gripping the rail in front of him and cheering like a maniac, all the dignity of his rank and his thirty-five years gone in the tense excitement of the battle. It had infected all of them on the bridge of the destroyer, and they capered and shouted with him.

'There she blows!' howled the lieutenant.

'She's opened fire!'

'Go it, *Orion*, go it!'

On *Orion*'s forward turrets gunfire sparkled, then again and again. The harsh roll of the broadsides carried to them against the light wind.

'Short,' groaned Charles. 'She's still out of range.'

'Short again!'

'Still short.'

Each time the call of shot was signalled by the chief yeoman at the Aldis lamp, and briefly acknowledged from *Orion*'s bridgeworks.

'Oh my God,' moaned Charles.

'She's hit!' echoed his lieutenant.

A flat yellow glare, like sheet lightning on a summer's day, lit *Orion*'s afterdeck, and almost immediately a ball of yellowish grey smoke enveloped her. Through it Charles saw her after-funnel sag drunkenly and hang back at an unnatural angle.

'She's holding on!'

Orion emerged from the shell smoke and dragged it after her like a funeral cloak, but her speed seemed unabated, and the regular salvoes burned briefly and brightly on her forward turrets.

'Now she's hitting,' exulted the lieutenant, and Charles turned quickly to see shell-fire burst on *Blücher*, and his wide grin split his face.

'Kill her! Kill her!' he roared, knowing that though *Blücher* was better armed yet she was as vulnerable as *Orion*. Her plating was egg-shell thin and the six-inch shells that crashed through it would be doing her terrible damage.

Now the two cruisers were pounding each other. The range was closing so rapidly that soon they must hit with every broadside. This was a contest from which only one ship, or neither of them, would emerge.

Charles was trying to estimate the damage that had been inflicted upon *Blücher* during the last few minutes. She was on fire forward. Sulphur-yellow flames poured from her, her upperworks were riven into a grotesque sculpture of destruction, and a pall of smoke enveloped her, so her profile was shadowy and vague, yet every fifteen seconds her turrets lit with those deadly little flashes.

Charles turned to assess the relative damage that *Orion* had suffered. He found and held her with his binoculars—and at that moment *Orion* ceased to exist.

Her boilers, pierced by high explosive shell, burst and tore her in half. A cloud of white steam spurted five hundred feet into the air, completely blanketing her. The steam hung for thirty seconds then sagged wearily, and rolled aside. *Orion* was gone. A wide circle of oil slick and floating debris marked her grave. The speed of her charge had run her clean under.

On the bridge of *Bloodhound*, the cheering strangled into deathly silence. The silence was not spoiled but rather accentuated by the mournful note of the wind in her rigging and the muted throb of her engines.

45

For eight long hours Charles Little had ridden his anger and his hatred, using the curb to hold it on the right side of madness, resisting the consuming and suicidal urge to hurl his ship at the German cruiser and die as *Orion* had died.

Immediately after the sinking of *Orion,* the *Blücher* had reduced speed sharply and turned due south. With her fires still raging, she had limped along like a gun-shot lion. The battle ensigns at her masthead were tattered by shrapnel and blackened by smoke.

As soon as she had passed, *Bloodhound* altered course and cruised slowly over the area of water that was still rainbowed by floating oil and speckled with wreckage. There were no survivors from *Orion*; all of them had died with her.

Bloodhound turned and and trailed after the crippled German cruiser, and hatred that emanated from the destroyer was of such strength that it should have reached out across the sea as a physical force and destroyed *Blücher*.

But as Charles Little stood at the rail of his bridge, he saw the smoke and flame upon *Blücher*'s decks reduce perceptibly every minute as her damage control teams fought it to a stand-still. The last wisp of smoke from her shrivelled.

'Fire's out,' said the pilot, and Charles made no answer. He had hoped that the flames would eat their way into one of *Blücher*'s magazines and blow her into the same oblivion into which she had sent *Orion*.

'But she isn't making more than six knots. *Orion* must have hit her in the engine room.' Hopefully the navigating lieutenant went on, 'My bet is that she's got major damage below. At this speed we can expect *Pegasus* and *Renounce* to catch up with us by midday tomorrow. Then *Blücher* will stand no chance!'

'Yes,' agreed Charles softly.

Summoned by *Bloodhound*'s frantic radio transmissions, *Pegasus* and *Renounce*, the two heavy cruisers of the northern squadron, were racing down the East African coast, cutting through the five hundred miles of water that separated them.

46

'Kyller. Ask the chief how he's making out.' Von Kleine was fretting beneath the calm set of his features. Night was closing, and in the darkness, even the frail little English destroyer was a danger to him. There was danger all around, danger must each minute be approaching from every quarter of the sea. He must have power on his port side engine before nightfall; it was a matter of survival; he must have speed to carry him south through the hunting packs of the British—south to where *Esther* waited to give him succour, to replace the shells he had fired away, to replenish his coal bunkers which were now dangerously depleted. Then once more *Blücher* would be a force to reckon with. But first he must have speed.

'Captain.' Kyller was beside him again. 'Commander Lochtkamper reports they have cleared the oil line to the main bearing. They have stripped the bearing and there is no damage to the shaft. He is fitting new half shells. The work is well advanced, sir.'

The words conjured up for von Kleine a picture of half-naked men, smeared to the elbows with black grease, sweating in the confined heat of the drive shaft tunnel as they worked. 'How much longer?' he asked.

'He promised full power on both engines within two hours, sir.'

Von Kleine sighed with relief, and glanced over his stern at the British destroyer that was shadowing him. He began to smile.

'I hope, my friend, that you are a brave man. I hope that when you see me increase speed, you will not be able to control your disappointment. I hope tonight you will try with your torpedoes, so that I can crush you, for your eyes always on me are a dangerous embarrassment.' He spoke so softly that his lips barely moved, then he turned back to Kyller. 'I want all the battle lights checked and reported.'

'Aye, aye, sir.'

Von Kleine crossed to the voice-tubes. 'Gunncry officer,' he said. 'I want "X" turret guns loaded with star shell and trained to maximum elevation . . .' He went on listing his preparations for night action and then he ended,

'. . . stand all your gun crews down. Let them eat and rest. From dusk action stations onwards they will be held in the first degree of readiness.'

'Commander, sir!'

The urgent call startled Commander Charles Little, and he spilled his mug of cocoa. This was the first period of rest he had allowed himself all day, and now it was interrupted within ten minutes. 'What is it?' He flung open the door of the chart room, and ran out on to the bridge.

'*Blücher* is increasing speed rapidly.'

'No!' It was too cruel a blow, and the exclamation of protest was wrung from Charles. He darted to the voice-pipe.

'Gunnery officer. Report your target.'

A moment's delay, and then the reply. 'Bearing mark, green oh-oh. Range, one-five-oh-five-oh. Speed, seventeen knots.'

It was true. *Blücher* was under full power again, with all her guns still operable. *Orion* had died in vain.

Charles wiped his mouth with the open palm of his hand, and felt the brittle stubble of his new beard rasp under his fingers. Beneath the tan, his face was sickly pale with strain and fatigue. There were smears of dark blue beneath his eyes, and in their corners were tiny lumps of yellow mucus. His eyes were bloodshot, and the wisp of hair that escaped from under the brim of his cap was matted on to his forehead by the salt spray, as he peered into the gathering dusk.

The fighting madness which had threatened all that day to overwhelm him, rose slowly from the depth of his belly and his loins. He no longer struggled to suppress it.

'Turn two points to starboard, pilot. All engines full ahead together.' The engine telegraph clanged, and *Bloodhound* pivoted like a polo pony. It would take her thirty minutes to work up to full speed, and by that time it would be dark.

'Sound action stations.' Charles wanted to attack in the hour of darkness before the moon came up. Through the ship the alarm bells thrilled, and without taking his eyes from the dark dot on the darkening horizon, Charles listened to the reports coming into the bridge, until the one for which he waited, 'Torpedo party closed up, sir!'

Now he turned and went to the voice-tube. 'Torps,' he said, 'I hope to give you a chance at *Blücher* with both port and starboard tubes. I am going to take you in as close as possible.'

The men grouped around Charles on the bridge listened to him say 'as close as possible', and knew that he had pronounced sentence of death upon·them.

Henry Sergent, the navigating lieutenant, was afraid. Stealthily he groped in the pocket of his overcoat until he found the little silver crucifix that Lynette had given him. It was warm from his own body heat. He held it tightly.

He remembered it hanging between her breasts on its silver chain, and the way she had lifted both hands to the back of her neck as she unclasped it. The chain had caught in the shiny cascade of hair as she had tried to free it, kneeling on the bed facing him. He had leaned forward to help her, and she had clung to him, pressing the warm smooth bulge of her pregnant stomach against him.

'God protect you, my darling husband,' she had whispered. 'Please God bring you back safely to us.'

And now he was afraid for her and the daughter he had never seen.

'Hold your course, damn you!' he snapped at Herbert Cryer, the helmsman. 'Aye, aye, sir,' Herbert Cryer replied with just a trace of injured innocence in his tone. No man could hold *Bloodhound* true when she hurled herself from swell to swell with such abandoned violence; she must yaw and throw her head that fraction before the helm could correct her. The reprimand was unjustified, uttered in fear and tension. 'Give it a flipping break, mate,' Herbert retorted silently. 'You're not the only one who is going to catch it. Tighten up the old arsehole like a bloody officer and a ruddy gentleman.'

In these wordless exchanges of repartee with his officers, Herbert Cryer was never bested. They were wonderful release for resentments and pent-up emotion, and now because he was also afraid, he became silently lyrical.

'Climb-aboard-Romeo's one way express to flipping glory.' Commander Little's reputation with the ladies had resulted in him being irreverently but affectionately baptized by his crew. 'Come along with us. We're off to shout at the devil, while Charlie kisses his daughter.'

Herbert glanced sideways at his commander and grinned. Fear made the grin wolfish, and Charles Little saw it and misinterpreted it. He read it as a mark of the same berserk fury that possessed him. The two of them grinned at each other for an instant in complete misunderstanding, before Herbert refocused his attention on *Bloodhound*'s next wild crabbing lunge.

Charles was afraid as well. He was afraid of finding a weakness in himself—but this was the fear that had walked at his right hand all his life, close beside him, whispering to him, 'Harder, try harder. You must do better, you must do it quicker, or bigger than they do, or they'll laugh at you. You mustn't fail—not in one thing, not for one moment, you mustn't fail. You mustn't fail!' This fear was the eternal companion and partner in every venture on which he embarked.

It had stood beside the thirteen-year-old Charles in a duck blind, while he fired a twelve gauge shotgun, and wept slowly fat tears of agony every time the recoil smashed into his bruised bicep and shoulder.

It had stooped over him as he lay in the mud hugging a broken collar bone. 'Get up!' it hissed at him. 'Get up!' It had forced him to his feet and led him back to the unbroken colt to mount again, and again, and again.

So conditioned was he to respond to its voice that when it crouched beside him now, twisted and misshapen on the footplates of the bridge, its presence almost tangible, and croaked so Charles alone could hear it, 'Prove it! Prove it!' there was only one course open to Charles Little; a peregrine stooping at a golden eagle, he took his ship in against the *Blücher*.

47

'The turn to starboard was a feint.' Otto von Kleine spoke with certainty, staring out to where the dusk had obliterated the frail silhouette of the English destroyer. 'Even now he is turning again to cross our stern. He will attack on our port side.'

'Captain, it could be the double bluff,' Kyller answered dubiously.

'No.' Von Kleine shook his golden beard. 'He must try to outline us against the last of the light from the sunset. He will attack from the east.' A moment longer he frowned in thought, as he anticipated his opponent's moves across the chessboard of the ocean. 'Kyller, plot me his course, assuming a speed of twenty-five knots, a turn four points to port three minutes after our last sighting, a run of fifteen miles across our stern, and then a turn of four points to starboard. If we hold our present course and speed, where will he be in relation to us, in ninety minutes' time?'

Working quickly, Kyller completed the problem. Von Kleine had been mentally checking every step of the calculation. 'Yes,' he agreed with Kyller's solution, and already he had formulated the orders for change of course and speed to place *Bloodhound* in ambush.

48

Under full power, *Bloodhound* threw a bow-wave ten feet high, and a wake that boiled out for a quarter of a mile behind her, a long faintly phosphorescent smear in the darkness.

Aboard *Blücher* a hundred pairs of eyes were straining out into the night, watching for that phosphorescence. Behind the battle lights on her upperworks men waited, in the dimly-lit turrets men waited, on the open bridge, at the masthead, deep in her belly, the crew of *Blücher* waited.

Von Kleine had reduced speed to lessen his own wake, and turned away from the land at an angle of forty-five degrees. He wanted to catch the Englishman on his starboard beam, out of torpedo range.

He stood peering out across the dark sea, with the fur-lined collar of his overcoat drawn up to his ears. The night was cool. The sea was a black immensity, vast as the sky that was lined in glowing ivory by the whorls and smears of the star patterns.

A dozen men saw it at the same instant; pale, ethereal, seeming to float upon the darkness of the sea like a plume of iridescent mist—the wake of the Englishman.

'Star shell!' Von Kleine snapped the order to the waiting guns. He was alarmed by the English destroyer's proximity. He had hoped to spot her at greater range.

High above the ocean, the star shells burst blue-white, so intensely bright as to sear the retina of the eye that looked directly at them. Beneath them the surface of the sea was polished ebony, sculptured and scooped with the pattern of the swells. The two ships were starkly and crisply lit, steaming on converging courses, already so close to each other that the mile-long, solid white beams of their battle lights jumped out to join, fumbling together like the hands of hesitant lovers.

In almost the same second both ships opened fire, but the banging of *Bloodhound*'s little 4·7-inch guns were lost in the bellow of the cruiser's broadside.

Blücher was firing over open sights with her guns depressed until the long barrels were horizontal to the surface of the sea. Her first salvo was aimed a fraction high, and the huge shells howled over *Bloodhound*'s open bridge.

The wind of their passage, the fierce draught of distrupted air they threw out, caught Charles Little and sent him reeling against the compass pinnacle. He felt the ribs below his armpit crack.

The command he shouted at the helm was hoarse with pain.

'Turn four points to port! Steer for the enemy!' and *Bloodhound* spun like a ballet dancer, and charged straight at *Blücher*.

The cruiser's next broadside was high again but now her secondary armament had joined in, and a four-pound shell from one of the quick-firing pom-poms burst on the director tower above *Bloodhound*'s bridge. It swept the exposed area with a buzzing hailstorm of shrapnel.

It killed the navigating lieutenant instantly, cutting away the top of his head as though it were the shell of a soft-boiled egg. He fell on the deck and splattered the footplates with the warm custard of his brains.

A piece of the red hot shell casing the size of a thumbnail entered the point of Herbert Cryer's right elbow and shattered the bone to splinters. He grasped at the shock and sprawled against the wheel.

'Hold her. Hold her true!' The order from Commander Little was blurred as the speech of a spastic. Herbert Cryer pulled himself up with his left hand spun the wheel to meet *Bloodhound*'s wild swing, but with his right arm hanging useless, his steering was clumsy and awkward.

'Steady her, man. Hold her steady!' Again that thick slurring voice, and Cryer was aware of Charles Little beside him, his hands on the helm, helping to hold *Bloodhound*'s frantic head.

'Aye, aye, sir.' Cryer glanced at his commander and gasped again. This time in horror. Razor-sharp steel had sliced off Charles Little's ear, then gone on to cut his cheek away, and expose the bone of his jaw and the white teeth that lined it. A flap of tattered flesh hung down on to his chest, and from a dozen severed blood vessels dark blood dripped and spurted and dribbled.

The two of them crouched wounded over the wheel, with the dead men at their feet, and aimed *Bloodhound* at the long low bulk of the German cruiser.

Now in the daylight glare of the star shells, the sea around them was thrashed and whipped into seething life by the cacophony of *Blücher*'s guns. Tall towers of white water rose briefly and majestically about them, then dropped back to leave the surface troubled and restless with foam.

And *Bloodhound* drove on until suddenly it seemed she had run into a cliff of solid granite. Beneath their feet, she jarred and bucked violently. A nine-inch shell had taken her full in the bows.

'Port full rudder.' Charles Little's voice was sloshy sounding, wet with the blood that filled his mouth, and together they spun the wheel to full left lock.

But *Bloodhound* was dying. The shell had split her bows wide open, torn her plating and fanned it open like the petals of a macabre orchid. The black night sea rushed through her. Already her bows were sinking, slumping wearily, lifting her stern so the rudder no longer had full purchase. But even in death she was trying desperately to obey. Slowly she swung, inchingly, achingly, she swung.

Charles Little left the helm and tottered towards the starboard rail. His legs were numb and heavy under him, and the weakness of his lost blood drummed in his ears. He reached the rail and clung there, peering down on the torpedo tubes that stood on the deck below him.

The tubes looked like a rack of fat cigars, and with weary jubilation Charles saw that there were men still tending them, crouching behind the sheet of armour plate, waiting for *Bloodhound* to turn and bring *Blücher* on to her starboard beam.

'Turn, old girl. Come on! That's it! Turn!' Charles croaked through the blood.

Another shell struck *Bloodhound*, and she heaved in mortal agony. Perhaps this movement, combined with a chance push of the sea swell, was enough to swing her those last few degrees.

There, full in the track of the torpedo tubes, lit by her own star shells and the gunfire from her turrets, a scant thousand yards across the black water, lay the German cruiser.

Charles heard the whoosh, whoosh, whoosh, whoosh, of the tubes as they fired. He saw the long sharklike shapes of the torpedoes leap out from the deck and strike the water, saw·the four white wakes arrowing away in formation, and behind him he heard the torpedo officer's triumphant shout, distorted by the voice-pipe.

'All four fired, and running true!'

Charles never saw his torpedoes strike, for one of *Blücher*'s nine-inch shells hit the bridgework three feet below him. For one brief unholy instant, he stood in the centre of a furnace as hot as the flames of the sun.

49

Otto von Kleine watched the English destroyer explode. Towering orange flames erupted from her, and a solid ball of black smoke spun upon itself, blooming on the dark ocean like a flower from the gardens of hell. The surface of the sea around her was dimpled by the fall of thrown debris and the cruiser's shells—for all of *Blücher*'s guns were still blazing.

'Cease fire,' he said, without taking his eyes from the awesome pageant of destruction that he had created.

Another salvo of star shell burst above, and von Kleine lifted his hand to his eyes and pressed his thumb and forefinger into the closed lids, shielding them from the stabbing brilliance of the light. It was finished, and he was tired.

He was tired, drained of nervous and physical energy, overwhelmed by the backwash of fatigue that followed these last two days and nights of ceaseless strain. And he was sad—sad for the brave men he had killed, and the terrible destruction he had wrought.

Still holding his eyes, he opened his mouth to give the order that would send *Blücher* once more thrashing southward, but before the words reached his lips, a wild shout from the lookout interrupted him.

'Torpedoes! Close on the starboard beam!'

Long seconds von Kleine hesitated. He had let his brain relax, let the numbness wash over it. The battle was over, and he had dropped back from the high pinnacle of alertness on which he had balanced these last desperate hours. It needed a conscious physical effort to call up his reserves, and during those seconds, the torpedoes fired by *Bloodhound* in her death throes were knifing in to revenge her.

At last von Kleine snapped the bonds of inertia that bound his mind. He leaped to the starboard rail of the bridge, and saw in the light of the star shells the pale phosphorescent·trails of the four torpedoes. Against the dark water they looked like the tails of meteors on a night sky.

'Full port rudder. All engines full astern together!' he shouted, his voice pitched high with consternation.

He felt his ship swerve beneath him, thrown violently over as the great propellers clawed at the sea to hold her from crossing the path of the torpedoes. Hopelessly he stood and reviled himself. *I should have anticipated this. I should have known the destroyer had fired.*

Helplessly he stood and watched the four white lines drawn swiftly across the surface towards him.

In the last moments he felt a fierce upward surge of hope. Three of the English torpedoes would miss. That was certain. They would cross *Blücher*'s bows as she side-stepped. And the fourth torpedo it was just possible would miss also.

His fingers upon the bridge rail clenched, until it felt as though they must press into the metal. His breath jammed in his throat and choked him.

Ponderously, *Blücher* swung her bows away. If he had given the order for the turn only five seconds earlier . . .

The torpedo struck *Blücher* five feet below the surface, on the very tip of her curved keel.

The explosion shot a mountain of white water one hundred and fifty feet into the air. It slammed *Blücher* back on to her haunches with such violence that Otto von Kleine and his officers were thrown heavily to the steel deck.

Von Kleine scrabbled to his knees and looked forward. A fine veil of spray, like pearl dust in the light of the star shells, hung over *Blücher*. As he watched, it subsided slowly.

All that night they struggled to keep *Blücher* afloat.

They sealed off her bows with the five-inch steel doors in the watertight bulkhead, and behind those doors they locked thirty German seamen whose battle stations were in the bows. At intervals during the frenzied activity of the night, von Kleine had visions of those men floating face-down in the flooded compartments.

While the pumps clanged throughout the ship to free her of the hundreds of tons of sea-water that washed through her, von Kleine left the bridge and, with his engineer commander and damage control officer, they listed the injuries that *Blücher* had received.

In the dawn they assembled grimly in the chart-room behind the bridge, and assessed their plight.

'What power can you give me, Lochtkamper?' von Kleine demanded of his engineer.

'I can give you as much as you ask.' A reddish-purple bruise covered half the engineer's face where he had been thrown against a steam cock-valve when the torpedo struck. 'But anything over five knots will carry away the watertight bulkheads forward. They will take the full brunt of the sea.'

Von Kleine swivelled his stool, and looked at the damage control officer. 'What repairs can you effect at sea?'

'None, sir. We have braced and propped the watertight bulkhead. We have patched and jammed the holes made by the British cruiser's guns. But I can do nothing about the underwater damage without a dry dock—or calm water where I can put divers over the side. We must enter a port.'

Von Kleine leaned back in his stool and closed his eyes to think.

The only friendly port within six thousand miles was Dar es Salaam, the capital of German East Africa, but he knew the British were blockading it. He discarded it from his list of possible refuges.

An island? Zanzibar?—The Seychelles?—Mauritius?—All hostile territories with no anchorage safe from bombardment by a British squadron.

A river mouth? The Zambezi? No, that was in Portuguese territory, navigable for only the first few miles of its length.

Suddenly he opened his eyes. There was one ideal haven situated in German territory, navigable even by a ship of *Blücher*'s tonnage for twenty miles. It was guarded from overland approach by formidable terrain, yet he could call upon the German Commissioner for stores and labour and protection.

'Kyller,' he said. 'Plot me a course for the Kikunya mouth of the Rufiji delta.'

Five days later the *Blücher* crawled painfully as a crippled centipede into the northernmost channel of the Rufiji delta. She was blackened with battle smoke, her riggings hung in tatters, and at a thousand places shell splinters had pierced her upperworks. Her bows were swollen and distorted, and the sea washed through her forward compartments and then boiled and spilled out of the ghastly rents in her plating.

As she passed between the forests of mangroves that lined the channel, they seemed to enfold her like welcoming arms.

Overside she lowered two picket boats and these darted ahead of her like busy little water beetles as they sounded the channel, and searched for a secure anchorage. Gradually *Blücher* wriggled and twisted her way deeper and deeper into the wilderness of the delta. At a place where the flood waters of the Rufiji had cut a deep bay between two islands, and formed a natural jetty on both sides, the *Blücher* came to rest.

50

Herman Fleischer wiped his face and neck with a hand towel and then looked at the sodden material. God, how he hated the Rufiji basin. As soon as he entered its humid and malodorous heat, a thousand tiny taps opened under his skin and out gushed the juices of his body.

The prospect of an extended stay aroused in him a dark resentment to all things, but especially to this young snob who stood beside him on the foredeck of the steam launch. Herman darted a glance at him now. Cool he looked, as though he were sauntering down Unter den Linden in June. The shimmering white of his tropical uniform was unwrinkled and dry, not like the thick corduroy that bunched damply at Herman's armpits and crotch. Mother of a dog, it would start the rash again; he could feel it beginning to itch and he scratched at it moodily, then checked his hand as he saw the lieutenant smile.

'How far are we from *Blücher*?' and then as an afterthought he used the lieutenant's surname without rank, 'How far, Kyller?' It was as well to keep reminding the man that as the equivalent of a full colonel, he far outranked him.

'Around the next bend, Commissioner.' Kyller's voice carried the lazy inflection that made Fleischer think of champagne and opera houses, of skiing parties and boar hunts.

'I hope that Captain von Kleine has made adequate preparation to defend her against enemy attack?'

'She is safe.' For the first time there was a brittle undertone to Kyller's reply, and Fleischer pounced on it. He sensed an advantage. For the last two days, ever since Kyller had met him at the confluence of the Ruhaha river, Herman had been needling him to find a weakness.

'Tell me, Kyller,' he dropped his voice to an intimate, confidential level. 'This is in strict confidence, of course, but do you really feel that Captain von Kleine is able to handle this situation? I mean, do you feel that someone else may have been able to reach a more satisfactory result?' Ah! Yes! That was it! Look at him flush, look at the anger stain those cool brown cheeks. For the first time the advantage was with Herman Fleischer.

'Commander Fleischer,' Kyller spoke softly but Herman exulted to hear his tone. 'Captain von Kleine is the most skilful, efficient, and courageous officer under whom I have had the honour to serve. He is, furthermore, a gentleman.'

'So?' Herman grunted. 'Then why is this paragon hiding in the Rufiji basin with his buttocks shot full of holes?' Then he threw back his head and guffawed in triumph.

'At another time, sir, and in different circumstances, I would ask you to withdraw those words.' Kyller turned from him and walked to the forward rail. He stood there staring ahead, while the launch chugged around another bend in the river, opening the same dreary vista of dark water and mangrove forest. Kyller spoke without turning his head. 'There is the *Blücher*,' he said.

There was nothing but the sweep of water and the massed fuzzy heads of the mangroves below a hump of higher ground upon the bank. The laughter faded from Herman's chubby face as he searched, then a small scowl replaced it as he realized that the lieutenant was baiting him. There was certainly no battle cruiser anchored in the waterway. 'Lieutenant . . .' he began angrily, then checked himself. The high ground was divided by a narrow channel, not more than a hundred yards wide, fenced in by the mangrove forest, but the channel was blocked by a shapeless and ungainly mound of vegetation. He stared at it uncomprehendingly until suddenly beneath the netting that was festooned with branches of mangroves, he saw the blurred outline of turrets and superstructure.

The camouflage had been laid with fascinating ingenuity. From a distance of three hundred yards the *Blücher* was invisible.

51

The bubbles came up slowly through the dark water as though it had the same viscosity as warm honey. They burst on the surface in a boiling white rash.

Captain von Kleine leaned across the foredeck rail of the *Blücher* and peered at the disturbance below him, with the absorption of a man attempting to read his own future in the murky mirror of the Rufiji waters. For almost two hours he had waited like this, drawing quietly on a succession of little black cheroots, occasionally easing his body into a more comfortable position.

Although his body was at rest, his brain was busy, endlessly reviewing his preparations and his plans. His preparations were complete, he had mentally listed them and found no omissions.

A party of six seamen had been dispatched fifteen miles downstream by picket boat to the entrance of the delta. They were encamped on a hummock of high ground above the channel to watch the sea for the British blockade squadron.

As *Blücher* crept up the channel she had sown the last of her globular multi-horned mines behind her. No British ship could follow her.

Remote as the chances of overload attack seemed, yet von Kleine had set up a system of defence around the *Blücher*. Half his seamen were ashore now, spread in a network to guard each of the possible approaches. Fields of fire had been cut through the mangroves for his Maxim guns. Crude fortifications of log and earth had been built and manned, communication lines set up, and he was ready.

After long discussions with his medical officer, von Kleine had issued orders to protect the health of his men. Orders for the purification of water, the disposal of sanitation and waste, for the issue of five grains of quinine daily to each man, and fifty other safeguards to health and morale.

He had ordered an inventory made of stocks of food and supplies, and he was satisfied that with care he could subsist for a further four months. Thereafter he would be reduced to fishing and hunting, and foraging.

He had dispatched Kyller upstream to make contact with the German Commissioner, and solicit his full co-operation.

Four days had been spent in hiding the *Blücher* under her camouflage, in setting up a complete workshop on the foredeck under sun awnings, so that the engineers could work in comparative comfort.

Now at last they had begun a full underwater appraisal of *Blücher*'s wounds.

Behind him he heard the petty officer pass an order to the team at the winch. 'Bring him up–slowly.'

The donkey engine spluttered into life, and the winch clattered and whined shrilly. Von Kleine stirred against the rail and focused his full attention on the water below him.

The heavy line and airpipe reeled in smoothly, then suddenly the surface bulged and the body of the diver was lifted dangling on the line. Black in shiny wet rubber, the three brass-bound cyclopean eyes of his helmet glaring, grotesque as a sea monster, he was swung inboard and lowered to the deck.

Two seamen hurried forward and unscrewed the bolts at the neck, lifted off the heavy helmet, and exposed the head of the engineering commander, Lochtkamper. The heavy face, flat and lined as that of a mastiff, was made heavier than usual by the thoughtful frown it now wore. He looked across at his captain and shook his head slightly.

'Come to my cabin when you are ready, Commander,' said von Kleine, and walked away.

'A small glass of cognac?' von Kleine suggested.

'I'd like that, sir.' Commander Lochtkamper looked out of place in the elegance of the cabin. The hands that accepted the glass were big, knuckles scarred and enlarged by constant violent contact with metal, the skin etched deeply with oil and engine filth. When he sank into the chair at his captain's invitation, his legs seemed to have too many knees.

'Well?' asked von Kleine, and Lochtkamper launched into his report. He spoke for ten minutes and von Kleine followed him slowly through the maze of technicalities where strange and irrelevant obscenities grew along the way. In moments of deep concentration such as these Lochtkamper fell back on the gutter idiom of his native Hamburg, and von Kleine was unable to suppress a smile when he learned that the copulator torpedo had committed a perversion on one of the main frames, springing the plating whose morals were definitely suspect. The damage sounded like that suffered in a brothel during a Saturday night brawl.

'Can you repair it?' von Kleine asked at last.

'It will mean cutting away all the obscenely damaged plating, lifting it to the deck, recutting it, welding and shaping it. But we will still be short of at least eight hundred obscene square feet of plate, sir.'

'A commodity not readily obtainable in the delta of the Rufiji river,' von Kleine mused.

'No, sir.'

'How long will it take you—if I can get the plating for you?'

'Two months, perhaps.'

'When can you start?'

'Now, sir.'

'Do it then,' said von Kleine, and Lochtkamper drained his glass, smacked his lips, and stood up. 'Very good cognac, sir,' he complimented his captain, and shambled out of the cabin.

52

Staring upward at the massive warship, Herman Fleischer surveyed the battle damage with the uncomprehending curiosity of a landsman. He saw the gaping ulcers where *Orion*'s shells had struck, the black blight where the flames had raged through her, the irregular rash with which the splinters had pierced and peppered her upperworks, and then he dropped his eyes to the bows. Work cradles were suspended a few feet above the water, and upon them clutters of seamen were illuminated by the crackling blue glare of the welding torches.

'God in heaven, what a beating!' He spoke with sadistic relish.

Kyller ignored the remark. He was directing the native helmsman of the launch to the landing ladder that had been rigged down the side of *Blücher*. Not even the presence of this sweaty peasant, Fleischer, could spoil his pleasure in this moment of homecoming. To Ernst Kyller, the *Blücher* was home in the deep sense of the word; it contained all that he valued in life, including the man for whom he bore a devotion surpassing the natural duty of a son to his father. He was savouring the anticipation of von Kleine's smile and words of commendation for another task well done.

'Ah, Kyller!' Von Kleine rose from behind his desk and moved around it to greet his lieutenant.

'Back so soon? Did you find Fleischer?'

'He is waiting outside, sir.'

'Good, good. Bring him in.'

Herman Fleischer paused in the companion-way and blinked suspiciously around the cabin. His mind was automatically converting the furnishings into Reichsmarks, the rugs were silk Teheran in blue and gold and red, the chairs were in dark buttoned leather, all the heavy furniture, including the panelling, was polished mahogany. The light fittings were worked in brass, the glasses in the liquor cabinet were sparkling diamond crystal flanked by a platoon of bottles that wore the uniforms of the great houses of Champagne and Alsace and the Rhine. There was a portrait in oils opposite the desk of two women, both beautiful golden women, clearly mother and daughter. The portholes were curtained with forest green velvet, corded and tasselled in gold.

Herman decided that the Count must be a rich man. He had a proper respect for wealth, and it showed in the way he stepped forward, drew himself up, brought his heels together sharply, and then creased his bulging belly in a bow.

'Captain. I came as soon as I received your message.'

'I am grateful, Commissioner.' Von Kleine returned the salutation. 'You will take refreshment?'

'A glass of beer, and . . .' Herman hesitated, he was certain that somewhere aboard *Blücher* there must be a treasure trove of rare foods, '. . . a bite to eat. I have not eaten since noon.'

It was now the middle of the afternoon. Von Kleine saw nothing unusual in a two-hour period of abstinence, yet he passed the word for his steward while he opened a bottle of beer for his guest.

'I must congratulate you on your victory over the two English warships, Captain. Magnificent, truly magnificent!'

Lying back in one of the leather chairs Fleischer was engaged in mopping his face and neck, and Kyller grinned cynically as he listened to this new tune.

'A victory that was dearly bought,' murmured von Kleine, bringing the glass to Fleischer's chair. 'And now I need your help.'

'Of course! You need only ask.'

Von Kleine went to his desk, sat down, and drew towards him a sheaf of notes. From their chamois leather case, he produced a pair of gold-rimmed spectacles and placed them on his nose.

'Commissioner . . .' he started, but at that moment he completely lost Fleischer's attention. For with a discreet knock the Captain's steward returned with a large, heavily laden carving-plate. He placed it on the table beside Fleischer's chair.

'Sweet Mother of God!' whispered Herman, his eyes glittering, and a fresh sweat of excitement breaking out on his upper lip.

'Smoked salmon!'

Neither von Kleine nor Kyller had ever been privileged to watch Herman eat before. They did so now in awed silence. This was a specialist working with skill and dedication. After a while von Kleine made another effort to attract Herman's attention by coughing and rustling his sheaf of notes, but the Commissioner's snufflings and small moans of sensual pleasure continued. Von Kleine glanced at his lieutenant and lifted a golden eyebrow, Kyller half smiled in embarrassment. It was like watching a man in orgasm, so intimate that von Kleine was obliged to light a cheroot and concentrate his attention on the portrait of his wife and daughter across the cabin.

A gusty sigh signalled Herman's climax, and von Kleine looked at him again. He sagged back in the chair, a vague and dreamy smile playing over the ruddy curves of his face. The plate was empty, and with the sweet sorrow of a man remembering a lost love, Herman dabbed a forefinger on to the last shred of pink flesh and lifted it to his mouth.

'That was the best salmon I have ever tasted.'

'I am pleased that you found it so.' Von Kleine's voice crackled a little. He felt nauseated by the exhibition.

'I wonder if I might trouble you for another glass of beer, Captain.'

Von Kleine nodded at Kyller, and the lieutenant went to refill Fleischer's glass.

'Commissioner. I need at least eight hundred square feet of $1\frac{1}{2}$-inch steel plate delivered to me here. I want it within six weeks,' von Kleine said, and Herman Fleischer laughed. He laughed the way a man laughs at a children's tale of fairies and witches, then suddenly he noticed von Kleine's eyes . . . and he stopped abruptly.

'Lying in Dar es Salaam harbour under British blockade is the steamer *Rheinlander*.' Von Kleine went on speaking softly and clearly. 'You will proceed there as fast as you can. I will send one of my engineers with you. He will beach the *Rheinlander* and dismantle her hull. You will then arrange to convey the plating to me here.'

'Dar es Salaam is one hundred kilometres away.' Herman was aghast.

'According to the Admiralty chart it is seventy-five kilometres,' von Kleine corrected him.

'The plating will weigh many tons!' he cried.

'In German East Africa there are many hundreds of thousands of indigents. I doubt not that you will be able to persuade them to serve as porters.'

'The route is impossible . . . and what is more, there is a band of enemy guerrillas operating in the area north of here. Guerrillas led by those same bandits that you allowed to escape from the dhow, off the mouth of this river.' In agitation Fleischer had risen from his chair and now he pointed a fat accusing forefinger at von Kleine. 'You allowed them to escape. Now they are ravaging the whole province. If I try to bring a heavily laden, slow moving caravan of porters down from Dar es Salaam, word will reach them before I have marched five kilometres. It's madness—I won't do it!'

'It seems then, that you have a choice.' Von Kleine smiled with his mouth only. 'The English marauders, or a firing party on the afterdeck of this ship.'

'What do you mean?' howled Fleischer.

'I mean that my request is no longer a request, it is now an order. If you defy it, I will immediately convene a court martial.'

Von Kleine drew his gold watch and checked the time.

'We should be able to dispose of the formalities and shoot you before dark. What do you think, Kyller?'

'It will be cutting things fine, sir. But I think we could manage it.'

53

When the Governor of Mozambique had offered Flynn a captaincy in the army of Portugal, there had been an ugly scene. Flynn felt strongly that he deserved at least the rank of colonel. He had suggested terminating their business relationship. The Governor had countered with an offer of major—and signalled to his aide-de-camp to refill Flynn's glass. Flynn had accepted both offers, but the one under protest. That was seven months ago, a few short weeks after the massacre at Lalapanzi.

Since then Flynn's army, a mixed bag of a hundred native troops, officered by himself, Sebastian, and Rosa Oldsmith, had been operating almost continually in German territory.

There had been a raid on the Songa railway siding where Flynn had burned five hundred tons of sugar, and nearly a thousand of millet that was in the warehouses awaiting shipment to Dar es Salaam, supplies badly needed by Governor Schee and Colonel Lettow von Vorbeck who were assembling an army in the coastal area.

There had been another brilliant success when they had ambushed and wiped out a band of thirty Askari at a river crossing. Flynn released the three hundred native recruits that the Askari were escorting, and advised them to get the hell back to their villages and forsake any ambitions of military glory—using the corpses of the Askari that littered the banks of the ford as tangible argument.

Apart from cutting every telegraph line, and blowing up the railway tracks they came across, three other raids had met with mixed results. Twice they had captured supply columns of bearers carrying in provisions to the massing German forces. Each time they had been forced to run as German reinforcements came up to drive them off. The third effort had been an abject failure, the ignominy of it being compounded by the fact that they had almost had the person of Commissioner Fleischer in their grasp.

Carried on the swift feet of the runners who were part of Flynn's intelligence system came the news that Herman Fleischer and a party of Askari had left Mahenge boma and marched to the confluence of the Ruhaha and Rufiji rivers. There they had gone aboard the steam launch and disappeared into the fastness of the Rufiji delta on a mysterious errand.

'What goes up must come down,' Flynn pointed out to Sebastian. 'And what goes down the Rufiji must come up again. We will go to the Ruhaha and wait for Herr Fleischer to return.'

For once there was no argument from either Sebastian or Rosa. Between the three of them it was understood without discussion that Flynn's army existed chiefly to act as the vehicle of retribution. They had made a vow over the grave of the child, and now they fought not so much from a sense of duty or patriotism, but from a burning desire for revenge. They wanted the life of Herman Fleischer in part payment for that of Maria Oldsmith.

They set out for the Ruhaha river. As happened so often these days, Rosa marched at the head of the column. There was only the long braid of dark hair hanging down her back to show she was a woman, for she was dressed in bush jacket and long khaki cotton trousers that concealed the feminine fullness of her hips. She stepped out long-legged, and from her shoulder the loaded Mauser hung on its strap and bumped lightly against her flank at each pace.

The change in her was so startling as to leave Sebastian bewildered. The new hard line of her mouth, her eyes that gave off the dark hot glow of a fanatic, the voice that had lost the underlying ripple of laughter. She spoke seldom, but when she did, Flynn and Sebastian were forced to hear her with respect. Sometimes listening to that flat deadly tone Sebastian could feel a prickle of horror under his skin.

They reached the landing-place and the jetty on the Ruhaha river and waited for the launch to return. It came three days later, heralding its approach by the soft chugging of its engine. When it came around the river bend, pushing briskly against the current, headed for the wooden jetty, they were lying in wait for it.

'There he is!' Sebastian's voice was thick with emotion as he recognized the plump grey-clad figure in the bows.

'The swine, oh, the bloody swine!' and he jerked the bolt of his rifle open then snapped it shut.

'Wait!' Rosa's hand closed on his wrist before he could lift the butt to his shoulder.

'I can get him from here!' protested Sebastian.

'No. I want him to see us. I want to tell him first. I want him to know why he must die.'

The launch swung in broadside to the current, losing its way, until it came in gently to nudge the jetty. Two of the Askari jumped ashore, laying back on the lines to hold her while the Commissioner disembarked.

Fleischer stood on the jetty for a minute, looking back down the river. This action should have warned Flynn, but he did not see its significance. Then the Commissioner shrugged slightly and trudged up the jetty towards the boat-house.

'Tell your men to drop their weapons into the river,' said Flynn in his best German as he stood up from the patch of reeds beside the jetty.

Herman Fleischer froze in mid-stride, but his belly quivered and his head turned slowly towards Flynn. His blue eyes seemed to spread until they filled his face, and he made a clucking noise in his throat.

'Tell them quickly, or I will shoot you through the stomach,' said Flynn, and Fleischer found his voice. He relayed Flynn's order to the Askari, and there were a series of splashes around the launch as it was obeyed.

Movement in the corner of his eye made Fleischer swing his head, and he was face to face with Rosa Oldsmith. Beyond her in a half circle stood Sebastian and a dozen armed Africans, but some instinct warned Fleischer that the woman was the danger. There was a merciless quality about her, some undefinable air of deadly purpose. It was to her he addressed his question.

'What do you want?' His voice was husky with apprehension.

'What did he say?' Rosa asked her father.

'He wants to know what you want.'

'Ask him if he remembers me.'

As he heard the question, Fleischer remembered her in her night-dress, kneeling in the fire-light, and with the memory came real fear.

'It was a mistake,' he whispered. 'The child! I did not order it.'

'Tell him . . .' said Rosa, 'tell him that I am going to kill him.' And her hands moved deliberately on the Mauser, slipping the safety-catch across, but her eyes never left his face.

'It was a mistake,' Herman repeated and he stepped backwards, lifting his hands to ward off the bullet that he knew must come.

At that moment Sebastian shouted behind Rosa, just one word.

'Look!'

Around the bend of the Ruhaha river, only two hundred yards from where they stood, another launch swept into view. It came silently, swiftly, and at its stubby masthead flew the ensign of the German Navy. There were men in crisp white uniforms clustered around the Maxim machine gun in its bows.

Flynn's party stared at it in complete disbelief. Its presence was as unbelievable as that of the Loch Ness monster in the Serpentine or a man-eating lion in St Paul's Cathedral, and in the long seconds they stood paralysed the launch closed in quickly on the jetty.

Herman Fleischer broke the spell. He opened his mouth and from the barrel of his chest issued a bellow that rang clearly across the water.

'Kyller, they are Englishmen!'

Then he moved, with three light steps he danced sideways, incredibly quickly he moved his gross body from under the threatening muzzle of Rosa's rifle and dived from the jetty into the dark green swirl of water below the boards.

The splash of his dive was immediately followed by the tack, tack, tack of the launch's machine gun—and the air was filled with the swishing crack of a hundred whips. The launch drove straight in towards them with the Maxim blazing on its prow. Around Flynn and Rosa and Sebastian the earth erupted in a rapid series of dust fountains, a ricochet howled dementedly, one of the gun-boys spun on his heels in a brief dervish dance and then sprawled down the bank, with his rifle clattering on the wooden boards of the jetty, and the frozen party on the bank exploded into violent movement. Flynn and his black troopers ducked and dodged away up the bank, but Rosa ran forward. She reached the edge of the jetty unscathed through the hailstorm of Maxim fire, there she checked and aimed the Mauser at the wallowing body of Herman Fleischer in the water below her.

'You killed my baby!' Rosa shrieked, and Fleischer looked up at her and knew he was about to die. A Maxim bullet struck the metal of the rifle, tearing it from Rosa's hands, and she staggered off balance, her arms windmilling as she tottered on the edge of the jetty.

Sebastian reached her as she fell. He caught her and swung her up on his shoulder, whirled with her and bounded away up the bank, running with all the reserves of his strength unlocked by the key of his terror.

With ten of the gun-boys Sebastian took the rearguard; for that day and the next they skirmished back along the line of the retreat, briefly holding each natural defensive point until the Germans brought up the Maxim gun. Then they dropped back, retreating slowly while Flynn and Rosa made a straight run of it. In the second night Sebastian broke contact with the pursuers and fled north towards the rendezvous at the stream below the ruins of Lalapanzi.

Forty-eight hours later he reached it. In the moonlight he staggered into the camp, and Rosa threw off her blankets and came running to him with a low joyous cry of greeting. She knelt before him, unlaced and gently drew off each of his boots. While Sebastian gulped the mug of coffee and hot gin that Flynn brewed for him, Rosa bathed and tended the blisters that had burst on his feet. Then she dried her hands, stood, and picked up her blankets.

'Come,' she said, and together they walked away along the bank of the stream. Behind a curtain of hanging creepers, on a nest of dry grass and blankets, while the jewelled night sky glowed above them, they gave each other the comfort of their bodies for the first time since the death of the child. Afterwards they slept entwined until the low sun woke them. Then they rose and went down the bank together naked into the stream. The water was cold when she splashed him, and she giggled like a little girl and ran through the shallows across the sandbank with the water bursting in a sparkling spray around her legs, drops of it glittering like sequins on her skin, her waist was the neck of a Venetian vase flaring down into full double rounds of her lower body.

He chased and caught her and they fell together and knelt facing each other, spluttering and laughing, and with each gust of laughter her bosom jumped and bounced. Sebastian leaned forward with the laughter drying in his throat and cupped them in his hands.

Instantly her own laughter ceased, she looked at him a moment, then suddenly her faced hardened and she struck his hands away.

'No!' she hissed at him, and jumping to her feet she waded to where her clothing lay on the bank. Swiftly she covered her femininity, and as she strapped the heavy bandolier of ammunition around her body the last soft memory of their loving was gone from her face.

54

It was that stinking Rufiji water, Herman Fleischer decided, and moved painfully in his maschille as another cramp took him.

The hot hand of dysentery that closed on his stomach added to his mood of dark resentment. His present discomfort was directly linked to the arrival of *Blücher* in his territory, the indignities he had experienced at the hands of her captain, the danger he had run into in his brush with the English bandits at the start of this expedition, and since then the constant gruelling work and ever-present fear of another attack, the nagging of the engineer whom von Kleine had placed over him—he hated everything to do with that cursed warship, he hated every man aboard her.

The jogging motion of the maschille bearers stirred the contents of his belly, making it gurgle and squeal. He would have to stop again, and he looked ahead for a suitable place in which to find privacy.

Ahead of him the caravan of porters was toiling along the shallow bottom of a valley between two sparsely wooded ridges of shale and broken rock.

The column was spread out in an untidy straggle half a mile long, for it comprised just under a thousand men.

In the van a hundred of them, stripped to loin-cloths and shiny with sweat, were wielding their long pangas on the scrub. The blades glinting as they rose and fell, the thudding of the blows muted in the lazy heat of afternoon. Working under the supervision of Gunther Raube, the young engineering officer from *Blücher,* they were cutting out the narrow track, widening it for the passage of the bulky objects that followed.

Dwarfing the men that swarmed around them, these four objects rolled slowly along, rocking and swaying over patches of uneven ground. Now and then halting as they came up against a tree stump or an outcrop of rock, before the animal exertions of two hundred black men could get them rolling again.

Three weeks previously they had beached the freighter *Rheinlander* in Dar es Salaam harbour and dismantled eight slabs of her plating. Then from the metal frames of her hull, Raube had shaped eight enormous wheel rims, fourteen feet in diameter, into each of these he had welded a sheet of $1\frac{1}{2}$-inch plating ten foot square. Using the freighter's bollards as axles, he had linked these eight discs in four pairs. Thus each of these contraptions looked like the wheel and axle assembly of a gigantic Roman chariot.

Herman Fleischer had made a swift recruitment tour, and secured nine hundred able-bodied volunteers from the town of Dar es Salaam and its outlying villages. These nine hundred were now engaged in trundling the four sets of wheels southward towards the Rufiji delta. While they worked, Herman's Askari stood by with loaded Mausers to discourage any of the volunteers from succumbing to an attack of homesickness; a malady which was fast reaching epidemic proportions, aggravated as it was by shoulders rubbed raw by contact with harsh sun-heated metal, and by palms whose outer layers of skin had been smeared away on the rough hemp ropes. They had been two weeks at their labours and they were still thirty torturous miles from the river.

Herman Fleischer squirmed again in his maschille as the amoebic dysentery gnawed at his guts.

'Mother of a pig!' he moaned, and then shouted at the bearers, 'Quickly, take me to those trees.' He pointed to a clump of wild ebony that smothered one of the side draws of the valley.

With alacrity, the maschille bearers swung off the path and trotted up the draw. Within the screen of wild ebony they paused while the Commissioner alighted from the hammock and hurried into the deepest recess of the bush to be alone. Then they threw themselves down with a communal sigh and gave themselves up to a session of African callisthenics.

When the Commissioner came out of retreat he was hungry. It was cool and restful in the shade, an ideal place to take his mid-afternoon snack. Raube would have to fend for himself for an hour or so. Herman nodded to his personal servant to set up the camp table and open the food box. His mouth was full of sausage when the first rifle shot clapped dully in the dusty dry air.

55

'Where is he? He must be here. The scouts said he was here. Can you see him?' Rosa Oldsmith spoke through lips that were chapped dry by sun and wind, white flakes of skin had come loose from the raw red patches of sunburn on her nose, and her eyes were bloodshot from the dust and the glare.

She lay on her stomach behind a bank of shale and coarse grass with the Mauser probing out in front of her.

'Can you see him?' she demanded again impatiently, turning her head towards her father.

Flynn grunted noncommittally, holding the binoculars to his eyes, panning them slowly down the length of the valley then back again to the head of the strange caravan.

'There is a white man there,' he said.

'Is it Fleischer, is it?'

'No,' doubtfully Flynn gave the negative.

'No, I don't think so.'

'Look for him. He must be there somewhere.'

'I wonder what the hell those things are.'

Flynn concentrated on the four huge sets of wheels. The lens of the binoculars magnified the heat distortion through the still air, making them change shape and size so that one second they were insignificant and the next they were monstrous.

'Look for Fleischer. Damn those things, look for Fleischer,' Rosa snapped at him.

'He's not with them.'

'He must be. He must be there.' Rosa rolled on her side and reached out to snatch the binoculars from Flynn's hands. Eagerly she scanned the long column that moved slowly towards them up the valley.

'He must be there. Please God, he must be there,' she whispered her hatred through cracked dry lips.

'We will have to attack soon. They are nearly in position now.'

'We must find Fleischer.' Desperately Rosa searched, her knuckles showing white through sun-brown skin as she clutched the binoculars.

'We can't let it go much longer. Sebastian is in position, he will be expecting my signal.'

'Wait! You must wait.'

'No. We can't let them get closer.' Flynn half lifted his body, and called softly.

'Mohammed! Are you ready?'

'We are ready.' The reply came from farther down the slope where the line of riflemen lay.

'Remember my words, oh, thou chosen of Allah. Kill the Askari first and the others will run.'

'Your words ring in my ears with the brightness and the beauty of golden bells,' Mohammed replied.

'Up yours!' said Flynn and unbuttoned the pocket flap of his tunic. He fumbled out the hand-mirror and held it slanted to catch the sun, deflecting a bright splinter of light towards the far slope of the valley. From the jumble of rock and bush there was an immediate answering flash as Sebastian acknowledged the signal.

'Ah!' Flynn breathed theatrical relief, 'I was afraid our Bassie might have fallen asleep over there.' And he picked up the Mauser from the rock in front of him.

'Wait,' pleaded Rosa. 'Please wait.'

'We can't. You know we can't—if Fleischer is down there then we'll get him. If he isn't, then waiting any longer isn't going to help us.'

'You don't care,' she accused. 'You have forgotten about Maria already.'

'No,' said Flynn. 'No, I haven't forgotten,' and he cuddled the Mauser into his shoulder. There was an Askari he had been watching. A big man who moved ahead of the column. Even at this range Flynn sensed that this man was dangerous. He moved with a leopard's slouching awareness, head cocked and alert.

Flynn picked him up in the notch of the rear sight and rode the pip down his body, aiming low to compensate for the downhill shot, taking him in the belly. He gathered the slack in the trigger, squeezing it up gently. The Mauser cracked viciously and the recoil jumped back into his shoulder.

Incredulously Flynn saw the bullet throw a jump of dust from the slope below the Askari. A clean miss at four hundred yards. from a carefully aimed shot—by Christ, he was getting old.

Frantically he worked the bolt of the rifle, but already the Askari had ducked for cover, unslinging his rifle as he disappeared into a bank of grey thorn bush, and Flynn's next shot ripped ineffectively into the coarse dry vegetation.

'Damn it to hell!' howled Flynn, and his voice was small in the storm of gunfire that blew around him. From both slopes all his riflemen were shooting down into the solid pack of humanity that clogged the valley floor.

For startled seconds the mass of native bearers stood quiescent under the lash of the Mausers, each man frozen in the attitude in which the attack had caught him; bent to the giant wheels, leaning forward against the ropes, panga raised to strike at a branch, or merely standing watching while others worked. Every head lifted to stare up at the slopes from which Flynn's hidden rifles menaced them, then with a sound like a rising wind a single voice climbed in a wail of terror, to be lost almost instantly in the babble from a thousand throats.

Without regard for Flynn's orders to single out only the armed Askari, his men were firing blindly into the mass of men around the wheels, bullets striking with a meaty thump, thump, thump, or whining from rock to inflict the ghastly secondary wounds of a ricochet.

Then the bearers broke. Flowing back like flood water along the valley, carrying the Askari whose khaki uniforms bobbed with them like driftwood in the torrent.

Beside Flynn in the donga, Rosa was firing also. Her hands on the rifle incongruously feminine, fingers long and sensitive working the bolt as though it were the shuttle of a loom, weaving death, her eyes slitted behind the gunsight, her lips barely moving as they formed the name which had become her battle hymn.

'Maria! Maria!' With each shot she said it softly.

As he fumbled a fresh clip of cartridges from his bandolier, Flynn glanced sideways at her. Even in this moment of hot excitement Flynn felt the prickle of disquiet as he saw his daughter's face. There was madness in her eyes, the madness of grief too long sustained, the madness of hatred too carefully nourished.

His rifle was loaded and he switched his attention back to the valley. The scene had changed. From the rush of fear-crazed bearers, the German, whom Flynn had earlier watched through the binoculars, was rallying a defence. With him was the big Askari, the one that Flynn had missed with his first shot. These two stood to hold the guards who were being carried away on the rush of panic-stricken bearers, stopping them, turning them back, pushing and shoving them into defensive cover around the four huge wheels. Now they were returning the fire of Flynn's men.

'Mohammed! Get that man! The white man—get him!' roared Flynn, and fired twice, missing with each shot. But his bullets passed so close that the German dodged back behind the metal shield of the nearest wheel.

'That's done it,' lamented Flynn, as his hopes of quick success faded. 'They're getting settled in down there. We are going to have to prise them loose.'

The prospect was unattractive. Flynn had found from experience that while every man in his motley band was a hero when firing from ambush, and a master in the art of strategic retreat, yet their weak suit was frontal assault, or any other manœuvre that involved exposure to the enemy. Of the hundred under his command, there were a dozen whom he could rely on to obey an order to attack. Flynn was understandably reluctant to issue such an order, for there are few situations more humiliating than bellowing, 'Charge!'—then having everybody look at you with a 'Who me? You must be joking!' expression.

Now he steeled himself to do it, aware that with every second the battle madness of his men was cooling and being replaced by sanity and caution. He filled his lungs and opened his mouth, but Rosa saved him.

She rolled and lifted her knees, coming on to her feet with one fluid motion whose continuation was a catlike leap that carried her over the shale bank and into the open. Boyish, big hipped, but graceful—the rifle across her hip, firing. Long hair streaming, long legs flying, she went down the slope.

'Rosa!' roared Flynn in consternation, and jumped up to chase her in an ungainly lumbering run like the charge of an old bull buffalo.

'Fini!' shouted Mohammed, and scampered after his master.

'My goodness!' Sebastian gasped where he lay on the opposite side of the valley. 'It's Rosa!' and in a completely reflex response he found himself on his feet and bounding down the rocky slope.

'Akwende!' yelled the man beside him, carried away in his excitement, and before any of them had time to think, fifty of them were up and following. After the first half-dozen paces they were committed, for once they had started to run down the steep incline they could not stop without falling flat on their faces, they could only accelerate.

Down both slopes of the valley, scrambling, sliding on loose stone, pell-mell through thorn bush, screaming, shouting, they poured down on the cluster of Askari around the wheels.

From opposite sides, Rosa and Sebastian were first to reach the perimeter of the German position. Their momentum carried them unscathed through the first line of the defenders, and then with the empty rifle in her hands Rosa ran chest to chest against the big Askari who rose from behind a boulder to meet her. She shrieked as he caught her, and the sound exploded with Sebastian's brain in a red burst of fury.

Twenty yards away Rosa struggled with the man, but she was helpless as a baby in his arms. He lifted her, changing his grip on her body, snatching her up above his head, steadying himself to hurl her down on to the pointed rock behind which he had hidden. There was such animal power in the bunched muscles of his arms, in the sweat-slimy neck, in the muscular straddled legs, that Sebastian knew that when he dashed Rosa against the rock he would kill her. Her spine, her ribs must shatter with the force of it; the soft vital organs within her trunk must bruise or burst.

Sebastian went for him. Brushing from his path two lesser men of the bewildered defenders, clubbing the Mauser in his hands because he could not fire for fear of hitting Rosa, silently saving his breath for physical effort, he crossed the distance that separated them and reached them in the moment that the Askari began the first downward movement of his arms.

'Aah!' A gusty grunt was forced up Sebastian's throat by the force with which he swung the rifle, he used it like an axe, swinging it low with the full weight of his body behind it. The blade of the butt hit the Askari across the small of his back, and within his body cavity the kidneys popped like overripe satsuma plums. He was dying as he toppled backwards. As he hit the ground Rosa fell on top of him, his body cushioning her fall.

Sebastian dropped the rifle and stooped to gather her in his arms, crouching over her protectively.

Around them Flynn led his men boiling over the defenders, swamping them, knocking the rifles from their hands and dragging them to their feet, laughing in awe of their own courageous assault, chattering in excitement and relief.

Sebastian was on the point of straightening up and lifting Rosa to her feet, he glanced around quickly to assure himself that all danger was past—and his breathing jammed in his throat.

Ten paces away, kneeling in the shadow of one of the huge steel wheels was the white officer. He was a young man, swarthy for a German, but with pale green eyes. The tropical white of his uniform was patchy with damp sweat stains, and smeared with dust; his cap was pushed back, the gold braid on its peak sparkling with incongruous gaiety, for beneath it the face was taut and angry, the mouth pulled tight by the clenched jaws.

There was a Luger pistol clutched in his right hand. He lifted it and aimed.

'No!' croaked Sebastian, clumsily trying to shield Rosa with his own body, but he knew the German was going to fire.

'Mädchen!' cried Sebastian in his schoolboy German. 'Nein shutzen dis ein Mädchen!' and he saw the change in the young officer's expression, the pale green glitter of his eyes softening as he responded automatically to the appeal to his chivalry. Yet still the Luger was levelled, and over it Sebastian and the officer stared at each other. All this in seconds, but the delay was enough. While the officer still hesitated, suddenly it was too late, for Flynn stood over him and pressed the muzzle of his rifle into the back of the German's neck.

'Drop it, me beauty. Else I'll shoot your tonsils clean out through your Adam's apple.'

56

Strewn along the floor of the valley were the loads dropped by the native bearers, in their anxiety to leave for far places and fairer climes. Many of the packs had burst open and all had been trampled in the rush, so the contents littered the ground and discarded clothing flapped in the lower branches of the thorn trees.

Flynn's men were looting, a pastime in which they demonstrated a marked aptitude and industry. Busy as jackals around a lion's kill they gleaned the spoils and bickered over them.

The German officer sat quietly against the metal wheel. In front of him stood Rosa; she had in her hand the Luger pistol. The two of them watched each other steadily and expressionlessly. To one side Flynn squatted and pored over the contents of the German's pocket. Beside him Sebastian was ready to give his assistance.

'He's a naval officer,' said Sebastian, looking at the German with interest. 'He's got an anchor on his cap badge.'

'Do me a favour, Bassie,' pleaded Flynn.

'Of course.' Sebastian was ever anxious to please.

'Shut up!' said Flynn, without looking up from the contents of the officer's wallet which he had piled on the ground in front of him. In his dealings with Flynn, Sebastian had built up a thick layer of scar tissue around his sensitivity. He went on without a change of tone or expression.

'I wonder what on earth a naval officer is doing in the middle of the bush—pushing these funny contraptions around.' Sebastian examined the wheel with interest, before addressing himself to the German. 'Bitte, was is das?' He pointed at the wheel. The young officer did not even glance at him. He was watching Rosa with almost hypnotic concentration.

Sebastian repeated his question and when he found that he was again ignored he shrugged slightly, and leaned across to lift a sheet of paper from the small pile in front of Flynn.

'Leave it,' Flynn slapped his hand away. 'I'm reading.'

'Can I look at this, then?' He touched a photograph.

'Don't lose it,' cautioned Flynn, and Sebastian held it in his lap and examined it. It showed three young men in white overalls and naval peaked caps. They were smiling broadly into the camera with their arms linked together. In the background loomed the superstructure of a warship, the gun-turrets showed clearly. One of the men in the photograph was their prisoner who now sat against the wheel.

Sebastian reversed the square of heavy cardboard and read the inscription on the back of it.

' "Bremerhaven. August 6th, 1911." '

Both Flynn and Sebastian were absorbed in their studies, and Rosa and the German were alone. Completely alone, isolated by an intimate relationship.

Gunther Raube was fascinated. Staring into the girl's face, he had never known this sensation of mingled dread and elation which she invoked within him. Though her expression was flat and neutral, he could sense in her a hunger and a promise. He knew that they were bound together by something he did not understand, between them there was something very important to happen. It excited him, he felt it crawling like a living thing in his loins, ghost-walking along his spine, and his breathing was cramped and painful. Yet there was fear with it, fear that was as cloying as warm olive oil in his belly.

'What is it?' he whispered huskily as a lover. 'I do not understand. Tell me.'

And he sensed that she could not understand his language, but his tone made something move in her eyes. They darkened like a cloud shadow on a green sea, and he saw she was beautiful. With a pang he thought how close he had been to firing the Luger she now held in her hand.

I might have killed her, and he wanted to reach out and touch her. Slowly he leaned forward, and Rosa shot him in the centre of his chest. The impact of the bullet threw him back against the metal frame of the wheel. He lay there looking at her.

Deliberately, each shot spaced, she emptied the magazine of the pistol. The Luger jumped and steadied and jumped again in her hand. Each blurt of gunfire shockingly loud, and the wounds appeared like magic on the white front of his shirt, beginning to weep blood as he slumped sideways, and he lay with his eyes still fastened on her face as he died.

The pistol clicked empty and she let it drop from her hand.

57

Sir Percy held the square of cardboard at arm's length to read the inscription on the back of it.

' "Bremerhaven. August 6th, 1911," ' he said. Across the desk from him his flag-captain sat uncomfortably on the edge of the hard-backed H.M. issue chair. His right hand reached for his pocket, checked, then withdrew guiltily.

'For God's sake, Henry. Smoke that damned thing if you must,' grunted Sir Percy.

'Thank you, sir.' Gratefully Captain Henry Green completed the reach for his pocket, brought out a gnarled briar, and began stuffing it with tobacco.

Laying aside the photograph, Sir Percy took up the bedraggled sheet of paper and studied the crude hand-drawn circles upon it, reading the descriptions that were linked by arrows to the circles. This sample of primitive art had been laboriously drawn by Flynn Patrick O'Flynn as an addendum to his report.

'You say this lot came in the diplomatic bag from the Embassy in Lourenço Marques?'

'That's right, sir.'

'Who is this fellow . . .' Sir Percy checked the name, 'Flynn Patrick O'Flynn?'

'It seems that he is a major in the Portuguese army, sir.'

'With a name like that?'

'You find these Irishmen everywhere, sir.' The captain smiled. 'He commands a group of scouts who raid across the border into German territory. They have built up something of a reputation for derring-do.'

Sir Percy grunted again, dropped the paper, clasped his hands behind his head, and stared across the room at the portrait of Lord Nelson.

'All right, Henry. Let's hear what you make of it.'

The captain held a flaring match to the bowl of his pipe and sucked noisily, waved the match to extinguish it, and spoke through wreaths of smoke.

'The photograph first. It showed three German engineering officers on the foredeck of a cruiser. The one in the centre was the man killed by the scouts.' He puffed again. 'Intelligence reports that the cruiser is a "B" class. Nine-inch guns in raked turrets.'

' "B" class?' asked Sir Percy. 'They only launched two vessels of that class.'

'*Battenburg* and *Blücher*, sir.'

'*Blücher!*' said Sir Percy softly.

'*Blücher!*' agreed Henry Green. 'Presumed destroyed in a surface action with His Majesty's ships *Bloodhound* and *Orion* off the east coast of Africa between 16th and 20th September.'

'Go on.'

'Well, this officer could have been a survivor from *Blücher* who was lucky enough to come ashore in German East Africa—and is now serving with von Vorbeck's army.'

'Still dressed in full naval uniform, trundling strange round objects about the continent?' asked Sir Percy sceptically.

'An unusual duty, I agree, sir.'

'Now what do you make of these things?' With one finger Sir Percy prodded Flynn's diagram in front of him.

'Wheels,' said Green.

'For what?'

'Transporting material.'

'What material?'

'Steel plate.'

'Now who would want steel plate on the east coast of Africa?' mused Sir Percy.

'Perhaps the captain of a damaged battle cruiser.'

'Let's go down into the plotting room.' Sir Percy heaved his bulk out of the chair, and headed for the door.

His shoulders hunched, massive jaw jutting, Admiral Howe brooded over the plot of the Indian Ocean.

'Where was this column intercepted?' he asked.

'Here, sir.' Green touched the vast map with the pointer. 'About fifteen miles south-east of Kibiti. It was moving southwards towards . . .' He did not finish the statement but let the tip of the marker slide down on to the complexity of islands that clustered about the mouth of the long black snake that was the Rufiji river.

'Admiralty plot for East Africa, please.' Sir Percy turned to the lieutenant in charge of the plot, and the lieutenant selected Volume II of the blue-jacketed books that lined the shelf on the far wall.

'What are the sailing directions for the Rufiji mouth?' demanded the Admiral, and the lieutenant began to read.

'*Ras Pombwe to Kikunya mouth, including Mto Rufiji and Rufiji delta* (*Latitude 8° 17′ S, Longitude 39° 20′ E*). For fifty miles the coast is a maze of low, swampy, mangrove-covered islands, intersected by creeks comprising the delta of Mto Rufiji. During the rainy season the whole area of the delta is frequently inundated.

'The coast of the delta is broken by ten large mouths, eight of which are connected at all times with Mto Rufiji.'

Sir Percy interrupted peevishly, 'What is all this *Mto* business?'

'Arabic word for "river", sir.'

'Well, why don't they say so? Carry on.'

'With the exception of *Simba Yranga mouth* and *Kikunya mouth*, all the other entrances are heavily shoaled and navigable only by craft drawing one metre or less.'

'Concentrate on those two then,' grunted Sir Percy, and the lieutenant turned the page.

'*Simba Uranga mouth*. Used by coasting vessels engaged in the timber trade. There is no defined bar and, in 1911, the channel was reported by the German Admiralty as having a low river level mean of ten fathoms.

'The channel is bifurcated by a wedge-shaped island, *Rufiji-yawake*, and both arms afford secure anchorage to vessels of large burden. However, holding ground is bad and securing to trees on the bank is more satisfactory. Floating islands of grass and weed are common.'

'All right!' Sir Percy halted the recitation, and every person in the plotting room looked expectantly at him. Sir Percy was glowering at the plot, breathing heavily through his nose. 'Where is *Blücher*'s plaque?' he demanded harshly.

The lieutenant went to the locker behind him, and came back with the black wooden disc he had removed from the plot two months previously. Sir Percy took it from him, and rubbed it slowly between thumb and forefinger. There was complete silence in the room.

Slowly Sir Percy leaned forward across the map and placed the disc with a click upon the glass top. They all stared at it. It sat sinister as a black cancer where the green land met the blue ocean.

'Communications!' grunted Sir Percy and the yeoman of signals stepped forward with his pad ready.

'Dispatch to Commodore Commanding Indian Ocean. Captain Joyce. H.M.S. *Renounce*. Maximum Priority. Message reads: Intelligence reports indicate high probability . . .'

58

'You know something, Captain Joyce, this is bloody good gin.' Flynn O'Flynn pointed the base of the glass at the ceiling, and in his eagerness to engulf the liquid, he did the same for the slice of lemon that the steward had placed in the glass. He gurgled like an air-locked geyser, his face changed swiftly to a deeper shade of red, then he expelled the lemon and with it a fine spray of gin and Indian tonic in a burst of explosive coughing.

'Are you all right?' Anxiously Captain Joyce leapt across the cabin and begun pounding Flynn between the shoulder-blades. He had visions of his key tool in the coming operation being asphyxiated before they had started.

'Pips!' gasped Flynn. 'Goddamned lemon pips.'

'Steward!' Captain Joyce called over his shoulder without interrupting the tattoo he was playing on Flynn's back. 'Bring the major a glass of water. Hurry!'

'Water?' wheezed Flynn in horror and the shock was sufficient to diminish the strength of his paroxysm.

The steward, who from experience could recognize a drinking man when he saw one, rose nobly to the occasion. He hurried across the cabin with a glass in his hand. A mouthful of raw spirit effected a near miraculous cure, Flynn lay back in his chair his face still bright purple but his breathing easing, and Joyce withdrew to the far side of the cabin to inhale with relief the moist warm tropical air that oozed sluggishly through the open porthole. After a close range whiff of Flynn's body smell, it was as sweet as a bunch of tulips.

Flynn had been in the field for six weeks, and during that time it had not occurred to him to change his clothing. He smelled like a Roquefort cheese.

There was a pause while everybody recovered their breath, then Joyce picked up where he had left off.

'I was saying, Major, how good it was of you to return so promptly to meet me here.'

'I came the moment I received your message. The runner was waiting for us in M'topo's village. I left my command camped south of the Rovuma, and pushed through in forced marches. A hundred and fifty miles in three days! Not bad going, hey?'

'Damn good show!' agreed Joyce, and looked across at the other two men in the cabin for confirmation. With the Portuguese Governor's aide-de-camp was a young army lieutenant. Neither of them could understand a word of English. The aide-de-camp was wearing a politely non-committal expression, and the lieutenant had loosened the top button of his tunic and was lolling on the cabin's day couch with a little black cigarette drooping from his lips. Yet he contrived to look as gracefully insolent as a matador.

'The English captain asks that you recommend me to the Governor for the Star of St Peter.' Flynn translated Captain Joyce's speech to the aide-de-camp. Flynn wanted a medal. He had been hounding the Governor for one these last six months.

'Will you please tell the English captain that I would be delighted to convey his written citation to the Governor.' The aide-de-camp smiled blandly. Through their business association he knew better than to take Flynn's translation literally. Flynn scowled at him, and Joyce sensed the strain in the cabin. He went on quickly.

'I asked you to meet me here to discuss a matter of very great importance.' He paused. 'Two months ago your scouts attacked a German supply column near the village of Kibiti.'

'That's right.' Flynn sat up in his chair. 'A hell of a fight. We fought like madmen. Hand-to-hand stuff.'

'Quite,' Joyce agreed quickly. 'Quite so. With this column was a German naval officer . . .'

'I didn't do it,' interjected Flynn with alarm. 'It wasn't me. He was trying to escape. You can't pin that one on me.'

Joyce looked startled.

'I beg your pardon.'

'He was shot trying to escape—and you try to prove different,' Flynn challenged him hotly.

'Yes, I know. I have a copy of your report. A pity. A great pity. We would dearly have liked to interrogate the man.'

'You calling me a liar?'

'Good Lord, Major O'Flynn. Nothing is further from my mind.' Joyce was finding that conversation with Flynn O'Flynn was similar to feeling your way blindfolded through a hawthorn bush. 'Your glass is empty, may I offer you a drink?'

Flynn's mouth was open to emit further truculent denials, but the offer of hospitality took him unawares and he subsided.

'Thank you. It's damn good gin, haven't tasted anything like it in years. I don't suppose you could spare a case or two?'

Again Joyce was startled.

'I'm sure the wardroom secretary will be able to arrange something for you.'

'Bloody good stuff,' said Flynn, and sipped at his recharged glass. Joyce decided on a different approach.

'Major O'Flynn, have you heard of a German warship, a cruiser, named *Blücher*?'

'Have I, hell!' bellowed Flynn with such vehemence that Joyce was left in no doubt that he had struck another jarring note. 'The bastard sank me!'

These words conjured up in the eye of Captain Joyce's mind a brief but macabre picture of a Flynn floating on his back, while a battle cruiser fired on him with nine-inch guns.

'Sank you?' asked Joyce.

'Rammed me! There I was sailing along in this dhow peaceful as anything, when up she comes and—bang, right up the arse.'

'I see,' murmured Joyce. 'Was it intentional?'

'You bloody tooting it was.'

'Why?'

'Well . . .' started Flynn, and then changed his mind. 'It's a long story.'

'Where did this happen?'

'About fifty miles off the mouth of the Rufiji river.'

'The Rufiji?' Joyce leaned forward eagerly. 'Do you know it? Do you know the Rufiji delta?'

'Do I know the Rufiji delta?' chuckled Flynn. 'I know it like you know the way to your own Thunder Box. I used to do a lot of business there before the war.'

'Excellent! Wonderful!' Joyce could not restrain himself from pursing his lips and whistling the first two bars of 'Tipperary'. From him this was expression of unadulterated joy.

'Yeah? What's so wonderful about that?' Flynn was immediately suspicious.

'Major O'Flynn. On the basis of your report, Naval Intelligence considers it highly probable that the *Blücher* is anchored somewhere in the Rufiji delta.'

'Who are you kidding? The *Blücher* was sunk months ago—everybody knows that.'

'Presumed sunk. She, and the two British warships that pursued her, disappeared off the face of the earth—or more correctly the ocean. Certain pieces of floating wreckage were recovered that indicated that a battle had been fought by the three ships. It was thought that all three had gone down.' Joyce paused and smoothed the grey wings of hair along his temples. 'But now it seems certain that *Blücher* was badly damaged during the engagement, and that she was holed up in the delta.'

'Those wheels! Steel plating for repairs!'

'Precisely, Major, precisely. But . . .' Joyce smiled at Flynn, '. . . thanks to you, they did not get the plating through.'

'Yes, they did.' Flynn growled a denial.

'They did?' demanded Joyce harshly.

'Yeah. We left them lying in the veld. My spies told me that after we had gone the Germans sent another party of bearers up and took them away.'

'Why didn't you prevent it?'

'What the hell for. They've got no value,' Flynn retorted.

'The enemy's insistence must have demonstrated their value.'

'Yeah. The enemy were so insistent they sent up a couple of Maxim guns with the second party. In my book the more Maxims there are guarding something, the less value it is.'

'Well, why didn't you destroy them while you had the chance?'

'Listen, friend, how do you reckon to destroy twenty tons of steel—swallow it perhaps?'

'Do you realize just what a threat this ship will be once it is seaworthy?' Joyce hesitated. 'I tell you now in strict confidence that there will be an invasion of German East Africa in the very near future. Can you imagine the havoc if *Blücher* were to slip out of the Rufiji and get among the troop convoys.'

'Yeah—all of us have got troubles.'

'Major.' The captain's voice was hoarse with the effect of checking his temper. 'Major. I want you to do a reconnaissance and locate the *Blücher* for us.'

'Is that so?' boomed Flynn. 'You want me to go galloping round in the delta when there's a Maxim behind every mangrove tree. It might take a year to search that delta, you've got no idea what it's like in there.'

'That won't be necessary.' Joyce swivelled his chair, he nodded at the Portuguese lieutenant. 'This officer is an aviator.'

'What's that mean?'

'He is a flyer.'

'Yeah? Is that so good? I did a bit of sleeping around when I was young—still get it up now and then.'

Joyce coughed.

'He flies an aircraft. A flying-machine.'

'Oh!' said Flynn. He was impressed. 'Jeez! is that so?' He looked at the Portuguese lieutenant with respect.

'With the co-operation of the Portuguese army I intend conducting an aerial reconnaissance of the Rufiji delta.'

'You mean flying over it in a flying-machine?'

'Precisely.'

'That's a bloody good idea.' Flynn was enthusiastic.

'When can you be ready?'

'What for?'

'For the reconnaissance.'

'Now hold on a shake, friend!' Flynn was aghast. 'You not getting me into one of those flying things.'

Two hours later they were still arguing on the bridge of H.M.S. *Renounce*, as Joyce conned her back towards the land to deposit Flynn and the two Portuguese on the beach from which his launch had picked them up that morning. The British cruiser steamed over a sea that was oil-slick calm and purple blue, and the land lay as a dark irregular line on the horizon.

'It is essential that someone who knows the delta flies with the pilot. He has just arrived from Portugal, besides which he will be fully occupied in piloting the machine. He must have an observer.' Joyce was trying again.

Flynn had lost all interest in the discussion, he was now occupied with weightier matters.

'Captain,' he started, and Joyce recognized the new tone of his voice and turned to him hopefully.

'Captain, that other business. What about it?'

'I'm sorry—I don't follow you.'

'That gin you promised me, what about it?'

Captain Arthur Joyce, R.N., was a man of gentle mien. His face was smooth and unlined, his mouth full but grave, his eyes thoughtful, the streaks of silver grey at his temples gave him dignity. There was only one pointer to his true temperament, his eyebrows grew in one solid continuous line across his face; they were as thick and furry across the bridge of his nose as they were above his eyes. Despite his appearance he was a man of dark and violent temper. Ten years on his own bridge, wielding the limitless power and authority of a Royal Naval Captain had not mellowed him, but had taught him how to use the curb on his temper. Since early that morning when he had first shaken Flynn O'Flynn's large hairy paw, Arthur Joyce had been exercising every bit of restraint he possessed—now he had exhausted it all.

Flynn found himself standing speechless beneath the full blaze of Captain Joyce's anger. In a staccato, low-pitched speech, Arthur Joyce told him his opinion of Flynn's courage, character, reliability, drinking habits, and sense of personal hygiene.

Flynn was shocked and deeply hurt.

'Listen . . .' he said.

'*YOU* listen,' said Joyce. 'Nothing will give me more pleasure than to see you leave this ship. And when you do so you can rest content in the knowledge that a full report of your conduct will go to my superiors—with copies to the Governor of Mozambique, and the Portuguese War Office.'

'Hold on!' cried Flynn. Not only was he going to leave the cruiser without the gin, but he could imagine that the wording of Joyce's report would ensure that he never got that medal. They might even withdraw his commission. In this moment of terrible stress the solution came to him.

'There is one man. *Only* one man who knows the delta better than I do. He's young, plenty of guts—and he's got eyes like a hawk.'

Joyce glared at him, breathing hard as he fought to check the headlong run of his rage.

'Who?' he demanded.

'My own son,' intoned Flynn, it sounded better than son-in-law.

'Will he do it?'

'He'll do it. I'll see to that,' Flynn assured him.

59

'It's as safe as a horse and cart,' boomed Flynn, he liked the simile, and repeated it.

'How safe is a horse and cart when it's up in the clouds?' asked Sebastian, without lowering his eyes from the sky.

'I'm disappointed in you, Bassie. Most young fellows would jump at this chance.' Flynn was literally in excellent spirits. Joyce had come through with three cases of best Beefeater gin. He sat on one of the gasoline drums that lay beneath the shade of the palm tree above the beach, around him in various attitudes of relaxation lay twenty of his scouts, for it was a drowsy, warm, and windless morning. A bright sun burned down from a clear sky, and the white sand was dazzling against the dark green of the sea. The low surf sighed softly against the beach, and half a mile out, a cloud of seabirds were milling and diving on a shoal of bait-fish. Their cries blending with the sound of the sea.

Even though they were a hundred miles north of the Rovuma mouth, deep in German territory, a holiday atmosphere prevailed. Heightened by anticipation of the imminent arrival of the flying-machine they were enjoying themselves—all of them except Sebastian and Rosa. They were holding each other's hands and looking into the southern sky.

'You must find it for us.' Rosa's voice was low, but not low enough to cover her intensity. For the last ten days, since Flynn had returned from his meeting with Joyce on board the *Renounce*, she had spoken of little else but the German warship. It had become another cup to catch the hatred that overflowed from her.

'I'll try,' said Sebastian.

'You must,' she said. 'You must.'

'Should be able to get a good view from up there. Like standing on a mountain—only with no mountain under you,' said Sebastian and he felt his skin crawl at the thought.

'Listen!' said Rosa.

'What?'

'Ssh!'

And he heard it, an insect drone that swelled and sank and swelled again. They heard it under the trees also, and some of them came out into the sun and stood peering towards the south.

Suddenly in the sky there was a flash of reflected sunlight off metal or glass, and a shout went up from the watchers.

It came in towards them, low on wobbly wings, the clatter of its engine rising to a crescendo, its shadow racing ahead of it along the white beach. The group of native scouts exploded in panic-stricken retreat, Sebastian dropped on his face in the sand, only Rosa stood unmoving as it roared a few feet over her head, and then rose and banked away in a curve out over the sea.

Sebastian stood up and sheepishly brushed sand from his bush-jacket, as the aircraft levelled in the sand down on to the hard-packed sand near the water's edge. The beat of its engine faded to a spluttering burble, and it waddled slowly towards them, the backwash of the propeller sending a misty plume of sand scudding out behind. The wings looked as though they were about to fall off.

'All right,' bellowed Flynn at his men who were standing well back in the palm grove. 'Get these drums down there.'

The pilot switched off the motor, and the silence was stunning. He climbed stiffly out of the cockpit on to the lower wing, dumpy and awkward in his thick leather jacket, helmet, and goggles. He jumped down on to the beach and shrugged out of the jacket, pulled off the helmet, and was revealed as the suave young Portuguese lieutenant.

'Da Silva,' he said offering his right hand as Sebastian ran forward to greet him. 'Hernandez da Silva.'

While Flynn and Sebastian supervised the refuelling of the aircraft, Rosa sat with the pilot under the palms, while he breakfasted on garlic polony and a bottle of white wine that he had brought with him—suitably exotic food for a dashing knight of the air.

Although his mouth was busy, the pilot's eyes were free and he used them on Rosa. Even at a distance of fifty yards Sebastian became aware with mounting disquiet that Rosa was suddenly a woman again. Where before there had been a lifted chin and the straightforward masculine gaze; now there were downcast eyes broken with quick bright glances and secret smiles, now there were soft rose colours that glowed and faded beneath the sunbrowned skin of her cheeks and neck. She touched her hair with a finger, pushing a strand back behind her ear. She tugged at the front of her bush-jacket to straighten it, then drew her long khaki-clad legs up sideways beneath her as she sat in the sand. The pilot's eyes followed the movement. He wiped the neck of the wine bottle on his sleeve, and then with a flourish offered it to Rosa.

Rosa murmured her thanks and accepted the bottle to sip at it delicately. With the freckles across her cheeks and the skin peeling from her nose she looked as fresh and as innocent as a little girl, Sebastian thought.

The Portuguese lieutenant on the other hand looked neither fresh nor innocent. He was handsome, if you liked the slimy continental type with that slightly jaded tom cat look. Sebastian decided that there was something obscenely erotic about that little black moustache, that lay upon his upper lip and accentuated the cherry-pink lips beneath.

Watching him take the bottle back from Rosa and lift it towards her in salutation before drinking, Sebastian was overcome with two strong desires. One was to take the wine bottle and thrust it down the lieutenant's throat, the other was to get him into the flying-machine and away from Rosa just as quickly as was possible.

'Paci. Paci,' he growled at Mohammed's gang who were slopping gasoline into the funnel on the upper wing. 'Get a move on, for cat's sake!'

'Get your clobber into this thing, Bassie, and stop giving orders—you know it just confuses everybody.'

'I don't know where to put it—you'd better tell that greaser to come and show me. I can't speak his language.'

'Put it in the front cockpit—the observer's cockpit.'

'Tell that damned Portuguese to come here.' Sebastian dug in stubbornly. 'Tell him to leave Rosa alone and come here.'

Rosa followed the pilot to the aircraft and the expression of awed respect on her face, as she listened to him throwing out orders in Portuguese, infuriated Sebastian. The ritual of starting the aircraft completed, it stood clattering and quivering on the beach, and the pilot waved imperiously at Sebastian from the cockpit to come aboard.

Instead he went to Rosa and took her possessively in his arms.

'Do you love me?' he asked.

'What?' she shouted above the bellow of the engine.

'Do you love me?' he roared.

'Of course I do, you fool,' she shouted back and smiled up into his face before going up on tip-toe to kiss him while the slipstream of the propeller howled around them. Her embrace had passion in it that had not been there these many months, and Sebastian wondered sickly how much of it had been engendered by an outside agency.

'You can do that when you get back.' Flynn prised him loose from Rosa's grip, and boosted him up into the cockpit. The machine jerked forward and Sebastian clutched desperately to retain his balance, then glanced back. Rosa was waving and smiling, he was not certain if the smile was directed at him or at the helmeted head in the cockpit behind him, but his jealousy was swamped by the primeval instinct of survival.

Clutching with both hands at the sides of the cockpit, even his toes curling in their boots as though to grip the floor-boards of the cockpit, Sebastian stared ahead.

The beach disappeared beneath the fuselage in a solid white blur; the palm trees whipped past on one side, the sea on the other; the wind tore at his face and the tears streamed back along his cheeks, the machine bumped and bucked and bounced, and then leaped upwards under him, dropped back to bounce once more and then was airborne. The earth fell away gently beneath them as they soared, and Sebastian's spirits soared with them. His misgivings melted away.

Sebastian remembered at last to pull the goggles down over his eyes to protect them from the stinging wind, and godlike he looked down through them at a world that was small and tranquil.

When at last he looked back over his shoulder at the pilot, this strange and wonderful shared experience of immortality had lifted him above the petty passions of mere men, and they smiled at each other.

The pilot pointed out over the right wing tip, and Sebastian followed the direction of his arm.

Far, far out on the crenellated blue blanket of the sea, tiny beneath vast fluffy piles of thunderhead cloud, he saw the grey shape of the British cruiser *Renounce* with the pale white feather of its wake fanning on the surface of the ocean behind it.

He nodded and smiled at his companion. Again the pilot pointed, this time ahead.

Still misty in the blue haze of distance, haphazard as the unfitted pieces of a jigsaw puzzle, the islands of the Rufiji delta were spilled and scattered between ocean and mainland.

In the rackety little cockpit, Sebastian squatted over his pack and took from it binoculars, pencil, and map-case.

60

It was hot. Moist itchy hot. Even in the shade beneath the festooned camouflage-nets the decks of *Blücher* were smothered with hot sticky waves of swamp air. The sweat that oozed and trickled down the glistening bodies of the half-naked men who slaved on her foredeck gave them no relief, for the air was too humid to evaporate the moisture. They moved like sleep-walkers, with slow mechanical determination, manhandling the thick sheet of steel plate into its slings beneath the high arm of the crane.

Even the flow of obscenity from the lips of Lochtkamper, the engineering commander, had dried up like a spring in drought season. He worked with his men, like them stripped to the waist, and the tattoos on his upper arms and across his chest heaved and bulged as they rode on an undulating sea of muscles.

'Rest,' he grunted; and they straightened up from their labour, mouths gaping as they sucked in the stale air, massaging aching backs, glowering at the sheet of steel with true hatred.

'Captain.' Lochtkamper became aware of von Kleine for the first time. He stood against the forward gun-turret, tall in full whites, the blond beard half concealing the cross of black enamel and silver that hung at his throat. Lochtkamper crossed to him.

'It goes well?' von Kleine asked, and the engineer shook his head.

'Not as well as I had hoped.' He wiped one huge hand across his forehead, leaving a smudge of grease and rust scale on his own face. 'Slow,' he said. 'Too slow.'

'You have encountered difficulties?'

'Everywhere,' growled the engineer, and he looked around at the heat mist and the mangroves, at the sluggish black waters and the mud banks. 'Nothing works here—the welding equipment, the winch engines, even the men—everything sickens in this obscene heat.'

'How much longer?'

'I do not know, Captain. I truly do not know.'

Von Kleine would not press him. If any man could get *Blücher* seaworthy, it would be this man. When Lochtkamper slept at all, it was here on the foredeck, curled like a dog on a mattress thrown on the planking. He slept a few exhausted hours amid the whine and groan of the winches, the blue hissing glare of the welding torches, and the drum splitting hammering of the riveters, then he was up again bullying, leading, coaxing, and threatening.

'Another three weeks,' Lochtkamper estimated reluctantly. 'A month at the most—if all goes as it does now.'

They were both silent, standing together, two men from different worlds drawn together by a common goal, united by respect for each other's ability.

A mile up the channel, movement caught their attention. It was one of the launches returning to the cruiser, yet it looked like a hayrick under its bulky cargo. It came slowly against the sluggish current, sitting so low in the water that only a few inches of freeboard showed, while its load was a great shaggy hump on which sat a dozen black men.

Von Kleine and Lochtkamper watched it approaching.

'I still do not know about that obscene wood, Captain.' Lochtkamper shook his big untidy head again. 'It is so soft, so much ash, it could clog the furnace.'

'There is nothing else we can do,' von Kleine reminded him.

When *Blüther* entered the Rufiji, her coal-bunkers were almost empty. There was enough fuel for perhaps four thousand miles of steaming. Hardly enough to carry her in a straight run down into latitude 45° south, where her mother ship, *Esther*, waited to refuel her, and fill her magazines with shell.

There was not the faintest chance of obtaining coal. Instead von Klein had set Commissioner Fleischer and his thousand native porters to cutting cordwood from the forests, that grew at the apex of the delta. It was a duty that Commissioner Fleischer had opposed with every argument and excuse he could muster. He felt that in delivering safety to Captain von Kleine the steel plating from Dar es Salaam, he had discharged any obligation that he might have towards the *Blücher*. His eloquence availed him not at all—Lochtkamper had fashioned two hundred primitive axe heads from the steel plate, and von Kleine had sent Lieutenant Kyller up-river with Fleischer to help him keep his enthusiasm for wood-cutting burning brightly.

For three weeks now, the *Blücher*'s launches had been plying steadily back and forth. Up to the present they had delivered some five hundred tons of timber. The problem was finding storage for this unwieldy cargo once the coal-bunkers were filled.

'We will have to begin deck loading the cordwood soon,' von Kleine muttered, and Lochtkamper opened his mouth to reply when the alarm bells began to clamour an emergency, and the loudhailer boomed.

'Captain to the bridge. Captain to the bridge.'

Von Kleine turned and ran.

On the companion ladder he collided with one of his lieutenants. They caught at each other for balance and the lieutenant shouted into von Kleine's face.

'Captain—an aircraft. Flying low. Coming this way. Portuguese markings.'

'Damn it to hell!' Von Kleine pushed past him, and bounded up the ladder. He burst on to the bridge, panting.

'Where is it?' he shouted.

The officer of the watch dropped his binoculars and turned to von Kleine with relief.

'There it is, sir!' He pointed through a hole in the tangled screen of camouflage that hung like a veranda roof over the bridge.

Von Kleine snatched the binoculars from him, as he trained them on the distant winged shape in the mist haze above the mangroves, he issued his orders.

'Warn the men ashore. Everybody under cover,' he barked. 'All guns trained to maximum elevation. Pom-poms loaded with shrapnel. Machine gun crews closed up—but no firing until my orders.'

He held the aircraft in the round field of the field glasses.

'Portuguese, all right,' he grunted; the green and red insignia showed clearly against the brown body of the aircraft.

'She's searching . . .' The aircraft was sweeping back and forth, banking over and turning back at the end of each leg of her search pattern, like a farmer ploughing a field. Von Kleine could make out the head and shoulders of a man crouched forward in the squat round nose of the aircraft. '. . . Now we'll find out how effective is our camouflage.'

So the enemy have guessed at last. They must have reported the convoy of steel plate—or perhaps the chopping of the cordwood has alerted them, he thought, watching the aircraft tacking slowly towards him. *We could not hope to go undetected for ever—but I did not expect them to send an aircraft.*

Then suddenly the thought struck him so hard that he gasped with the danger of it. He whirled and ran to the forward rail of the bridge and peered out through the camouflage net.

Still half a mile distant, trundling slowly down the centre of the channel with the wide rippling V of her wake spread on the current behind her, clumsy as a pregnant hippo with her load of cordwood, the launch was aimed straight at *Blücher*. From the air she would be as conspicuous as a fat tick on a white sheet.

'The launch . . .' shouted von Kleine, '. . . hail her. Order her to run for the bank—get her under cover:'

But he knew it was useless. By the time she was within hail, it would be too late. He thought of ordering his forward turrets to fire on the launch and sink her—but discarded the idea immediately, the fall of shell would immediately draw the enemy's attention.

Impatiently he stood gripping the rail of the bridge, and mouthing his anger and his frustration at the approaching launch.

61

Sebastian hung over the edge of the cockpit. The wind buffeted him, flapping his jacket wildly about his body, whipping his hair into a black tangle. With his usual dexterity Sebastian had managed to drop the binoculars overboard. They were the property of Flynn Patrick O'Flynn, and Sebastian knew that he would be expected to pay for them. This spoiled Sebastian's enjoyment of the flight to some extent, he already owed Flynn a little over three hundred pounds. Rosa would have something to say also. However, the loss of the binoculars was no handicap, the aircraft was flying too low and was so unstable that the unaided eye was much more effective.

From a height of five hundred feet the mangrove forest looked like a fluffy overstuffed mattress, a sickly fever green in colour, with the channels and the waterways between them dark gunmetal veins that flashed the sunlight back like a heliograph. The clouds of white egrets that rose in alarm as the aircraft approached looked like drifts of torn paper scraps. A fish eagle hung suspended in silent flight ahead of them, the wide span of its wings flared at the tips like the fingers of a hand, It dipped away, sliding past the aircraft's wing tip so close, that Sebastian saw the fierce yellow eyes in its white hooded head.

Sebastian laughed with delight, and then grabbed at the side of the cockpit to steady himself, as the machine rocked violently under him. This was the pilot's method of attracting Sebastian's attention, and Sebastian wished he would think up some other way of doing it.

He looked back angrily shouting in the howl of wind and engine.

'Watch it! You stupid dago.'

Da Silva was gesticulating wildly, his pink mouth working under the black moustache, his eyes wild behind the panes of his goggles, his right hand stabbing urgently out over the starboard wing.

Sebastian saw it immediately on the wide waterway, the launch was so glaringly conspicuous that he wondered why he had not seen it before, then he recalled that his attention had been concentrated on the terrain directly beneath the aircraft—and he excused himself.

Yet there was little to justify da Silva's excitement, he thought. This was no battle cruiser, it was a tiny vessel of perhaps twenty-five feet. Quickly he ran his eyes down the channel, following it to the open sea in the blue distance. It was empty.

He glanced back at the pilot and shook his head. But da Silva's excitement had, if anything, increased. He was making another frenzied hand-signal that Sebastian could not understand. To save argument Sebastian nodded in agreement, and instantly the machine dropped away under him so that Sebastian's belly was left behind and he clutched desperately at the side of the cockpit once more.

In a shallow turning dive, da Silva took the machine down and then levelled out with the landing-wheels almost brushing the tops of the mangroves. They rushed towards the channel, and as the last mangroves whipped away under them da Silva eased the nose down still farther and they dropped to within a few feet of the surface of the water. It was a display of fine flying that was completely wasted on Sebastian. He was cursing da Silva quietly, his eyes starting from their sockets.

A mile ahead of them across the open water bobbed the over-laden launch. It was only a few feet below their own level, and they raced towards it with the wash of the propeller blowing a squall of ripples across the surface behind them.

'My God!' The blasphemy was wrung from Sebastian in his distress. 'He's going to fly right into it!'

It was an opinion that seemed to be shared by the crew of the launch. As the machine roared in on them, they began to abandon ship. Sebastian saw two men leap from the high piled load of timber and hit the water with small white splashes.

At the last second da Silva lifted the plane and they hopped over the launch. For a fleeting instant Sebastian stared at a range of fifteen feet into the face of the German naval officer who crouched down over the tiller bar at the stern of the launch. They were then past and climbing sharply, banking and turning back.

Sebastian saw the launch had rounded to, and that her crew were clambering aboard and splashing around her sides. Once more the aircraft dropped towards the channel, but da Silva had throttled back and the engine was burbling under half power. He levelled out fifty feet above the water, and flew sedately, keeping away from the launch and well towards the northern side of the channel.

'What are you doing?' Sebastian mouthed the question at da Silva. In reply the pilot made a sweeping gesture with his right hand at the thick bank of mangroves alongside.

Puzzled, Sebastian stared into the mangroves. What was the fool doing, surely he didn't think that . . .

There was a hump of high ground on the bank, a hump that rose perhaps one hundred and fifty feet above the level of the river. They came up to it.

Like a hunter following a wounded buffalo, moving carelessly through thin scattered bush which could not possibly give cover to such a large animal, and then suddenly coming face to face with it—so close, that he sees the minute detail of crenellation on the massive bosses of the horns, sees the blood dripping from moist black nostrils, and the dull furnace glare of the piggy little eyes–in the same fashion Sebastian found the *Blücher*.

She was so close he could see the pattern of rivets on her plating, the joints in the planking of her foredeck, the individual strands of the canopy of camouflage netting spread over her. He saw the men on her bridge, and the gun-crews behind the pom-poms and the Maxim machine guns on the balconies of her upperworks. From her squatting turrets her big guns gaped at him with hungry mouths, revolving to follow the flight of the machine.

She was monstrous, grey, and sinister among the mangroves, crouching in her lair, and Sebastian cried aloud in surprise and alarm, a sound without shape or coherence, and at the same moment the engine of the aeroplane bellowed in full power as da Silva thrust the throttle wide and hauled the joystick back into his crotch.

As the aircraft rocketed upwards, the deck of the *Blücher* erupted in a thunderous volcano of flame. Flame flew in great bell-shaped ejaculations from the muzzles of her nine-inch guns. Flame spat viciously from the multi-barrelled pom-poms and the machine guns on her upperworks.

Around the little aircraft the air boiled and hissed, disrupted, churned into violent turbulence by the passage of the big shells.

Something struck the plane, and she was whirled upwards like a burning leaf from a garden bonfire. Wing over wing she rolled, her engine surging wildly, her rigging groaning and creaking at the strain.

Sebastian was flung forward, the bridge of his nose cracked against the edge of the cockpit and instantly twin jets of blood spurted from his nostrils to douse the front of his jacket.

The machine stood on her tail, propeller clawing ineffectively at the air, engine wailing in over rev. Then she dropped away on one wing and one side swooped sickeningly downwards.

Da Silva fought her, feeling the sloppiness of the stall in her controls come alive again as she regained air-speed. The fluffy tops of the mangroves rushed up to meet him, and desperately he tried to ease her off. She was trying to respond, the fabric wrinkling along her wings as they flexed to the enormous pressure. He felt her lurch again as she touched the top branches, heard above the howl of the engine the faint crackling brush of the vegetation against her belly. Then suddenly, miraculously, she was clear; flying straight and level, climbing slowly up and away from the hungry swamp.

She was sluggish and heavy, and there was something loose under her. It banged and thumped and slapped in the slip-stream, jarring the whole fuselage. Da Silva could not dare to manœuvre her. He held her on the course she had chosen, easing her nose slightly upwards, slowly gaining precious altitude.

At a thousand feet he brought her round in a wide gentle turn to the south, and banging and thumping, one wing heavy, she staggered drunkenly through the sky towards her rendezvous with Flynn O'Flynn.

62

Flynn stood up with slow dignity from where he had been leaning against the bole of the palm tree.

'Where are you going?' Rosa opened her eyes and looked up at him.

'To do something you can't do for me.'

'That's the third time in an hour!' Rosa was suspicious.

'That's why they call it the East African quickstep,' said Flynn, and moved off ponderously into the undergrowth. He reached the lantana bush, and looked around carefully. He couldn't trust Rosa not to follow him. Satisfied, he dropped to his knees and dug with his hands in the loose sand.

With the air of an old-time pirate unearthing a chest of doubloons, he lifted the bottle from its grave, and withdrew the cork.

The neck of the bottle was in his mouth, when he heard the muted beat of the returning aircraft. The bottle stayed there a while longer, Flynn's Adam's apple pulsing up and down his throat as he swallowed, but his eyes swivelled upwards and creased in concentration.

With a sigh of intense pleasure he recorked, and laid the bottle once more to rest, kicked sand over it, and set course for the beach.

'Can you see them?' he shouted the question at Rosa as he came down through the palms. She was standing out in the open. Her head was thrown back so that the long braid of her hair hung down to her waist behind. She did not answer him, but the set of her expression was hard and strained with anxiety. The men standing about her were silent also, held by an expectant dread.

Flynn looked up and saw it coming in like a wounded bird, the engine stuttering and surging irregularly, streaming a long bluish streak of oily smoke from the exhaust manifold, the wings rocking crazily, and a loose tangle of wreckage hanging and swinging under the belly where one of the landing-wheels had been shot away.

It sagged wearily towards the beach, the broken beat of the engine fading so they could hear the whisper of the wind in her rigging.

The single landing-wheel touched down on the hard sand and for fifty yards she ran true, then with a jerk she toppled sideways. The port wing bit into the sand, slewing her towards the edge of the sea, the tail came up and over. There was a crackling, ripping, tearing sound; and in a dust storm of flying sand she cartwheeled, stern over stem.

The propeller tore into the beach, disintegrating in a blur of flying splinters, and from the forward cockpit a human body was flung clear, spinning in the air so that the outflung limbs were the spokes of a wheel. It fell with a splash in the shallow water at the edge of the beach, while the aircraft careened onwards, tearing herself to pieces. A lower wing broke off—the guy wires snapping with a sound like a volley of musketry. The body of the machine slowed as it hit the water, skidding to a standstill on its back, with the surf washing around it. Da Silva hung motionless in the cockpit, suspended upside down by his safety-straps, his arms dangling.

The next few seconds of silence were appalling.

'Help the pilot! I'll get Sebastian.' Rosa broke it at last. Mohammed and the two Askari ran with her towards where Sebastian was lying awash, a piece of flotsam at the water's edge.

'Come on!' Flynn shouted at the men near him, and lumbered through the soft fluffy sand towards the wreck. They never reached it.

There was a concussion, a vast disturbance in the air that sucked at their eardrums, as the gasoline ignited in explosive combustion. The machine and the surface of the sea about it were instantly transformed into a roaring, raging sheet of flame.

They backed away from the heat. The flames were dark red laced with satanic black smoke, and they ate the canvas skin from the body of the aircraft, exposing the wooden framework beneath.

In the heart of the flames da Silva still hung in his cockpit, a blackened monkey-like shape as his clothing burned. Then the fire ate through the straps of his harness and he dropped heavily into the shallow water, hissing and sizzling as the flames were quenched.

The fire was still smouldering by the time Sebastian regained consciousness, and was able to lift himself on one elbow. Muzzily he stared down the beach at the smoking wreckage. The shadows of the palms lay like the stripes of a tiger on the sand that the low evening sun had softened to a dull gold.

'Da Silva?' Sebastian's voice was thick and slurred. His nose was broken and squashed across his face. Although Rosa had wiped most of the blood away, there were still little black crusts of it in his nostrils and at the corners of his mouth. Both his eyes were slits in the swollen plum-coloured bruises that bulged from the sockets.

'No!' Flynn shook his head. 'He didn't make it.'

'Dead?' whispered Sebastian.

'We buried him back in the bush.'

'What happened?' asked Rosa. 'What on earth happened out there?' She sat close beside him, protective as a mother over her child. Slowly Sebastian turned his head to look at her.

'We found the *Blücher*,' he said.

63

Captain Arthur Joyce, R.N., was a happy man. He stooped over his cabin desk, his hands placed open and flat on either side of the spread Admiralty chart. He glowed with satisfaction as he looked down at the hand-drawn circle in crude blue pencil as though it were the signature of the President of the Bank of England on a cheque for a million sterling.

'Good!' he said. 'Oh, very good,' and he pursed his lips as though he were about to whistle 'Tipperary'. Instead he made a sucking sound, and smiled across at Sebastian. Behind his flattened nose and blue-ringed eyes, Sebastian smiled back at him.

'A damn good show, Oldsmith!' Joyce's expression changed, the little lights of recognition sparkled suddenly in his eyes. 'Oldsmith?' he repeated. 'I say, didn't you open the bowling for Sussex in the 1911 cricket season?'

'That's right, sir.'

'Good Lord!' Joyce beamed at him. 'I'll never forget your opening over to Yorkshire in the first match of the season. You dismissed Graham and

Penridge for two runs–two for two, hey?'

'Two for two, it was.' Sebastian liked this man.

'Fiery stuff! And then you made fifty-five runs?'

'Sixty-five,' Sebastian corrected him. 'A record ninth wicket partnership with Clifford Dumont of–one hundred and eighty-six!'

'Yes! Yes! I remember it well. Fiery stuff! You were damned unlucky not to play for England.'

'Oh, I don't know about that,' said Sebastian in modest agreement.

'Yes, you were.' Joyce pursed his lips again. '*Damned* unlucky.'

Flynn O'Flynn had not understood a word of this. He was thrashing around in his chair like an old buffalo in a trap, bored to the point of pain. Rosa Oldsmith had understood no more than he had, but she was fascinated. It was clear that Captain Joyce knew of some outstanding accomplishment of Sebastian's, and if a man like Joyce knew of it–then Sebastian was famous. She felt pride swell in her chest and she smiled on Sebastian also.

'I didn't know, Sebastian. Why didn't you tell me?' She glowed warmly at him.

'Some other time,' Joyce interrupted quickly. 'Now we must get on with this other business.' And he returned his attention to the chart on the desk.

'Now I want you to cast your mind back. Shut your eyes and try to see it again. Every detail you can remember, every little detail–it might be important. Did you see any signs of damage?'

Obediently Sebastian closed his eyes, and was surprised at how vividly the acid of fear had engraved the picture of *Blücher* on his mind.

'Yes,' he said. 'There were holes in her. Hundreds of holes, little black ones. And at the front end–the bows–there were trapezes hanging down on ropes, near the water. You know the kind that they use when they paint a high building . . .'

Joyce nodded at his secretary to record every word of it.

64

The single fan suspended over the table in the wardroom hummed quietly, the blades stirred the air that was moist and warm as the bedding of a malarial patient.

Except for the soft clink of cutlery on china, the only other sound was that of Commissioner Fleischer drinking his soup. It was thick, green pea soup, scalding hot, so that Fleischer found it necessary to blow heavily on each spoonful before ingesting it with a noise, not of the same volume as, but with the delicate tonal quality of, a flushing water closet. During the pause while he crumbled a slice of black bread into his soup, Fleischer looked across the board at Lieutenant Kyller.

'So you did not find the enemy flying-machine, then?'

'No.' Kyller went on fiddling with his wine glass without looking up. For forty-eight hours he and his patrols had searched the swamps and channels and mangrove forests for the wreckage of the aircraft. He was exhausted and covered with insect bites.

'Ja,' Fleischer nodded solemnly. 'It fell only a short way but it did not hit the trees. I was sure of that. I have seen sand-grouse do the same thing sometimes when you shoot them with a shotgun. Pow! They come tumbling down like this . . .' He fluttered his hand in the air, letting it fall towards his soup, '. . . then suddenly they do this.' The hand took flight again in the direction of the Commander (Engineering) Lochtkamper's rugged Neanderthal face. They all watched it.

'The little bird flies away home. It was bad shooting from so close,' said Fleischer, and ended the demonstration by picking up his spoon, and the moist warm silence once more gripped the wardroom.

Commander Lochtkamper stoked his mouth as though it were one of his furnaces. The knuckles of both his hands were knocked raw by contact with steel plate and wire rope. Even when Fleischer's hand had flown into his face, he had not been distracted from his thoughts. His mind was wholly occupied with steel and machinery, weights and points of balance. He wanted to achieve twenty degrees of starboard list on *Blücher*, so that a greater area of her bottom would be exposed to his welders. This meant displacing one thousand tons of dead weight. It seemed an impossibility—unless we flood the port magazines, he thought, and take the guns from their turrets and move them. Then we could rig camels under her . . .

'It was not bad shooting,' said the gunnery lieutenant. 'She was flying too close, the rate of track was . . .' He broke off, wiped the side of his long pointed nose with his forefinger, and regarded balefully the sweat that came away on it. This fat peasant would not understand, he would not waste energy in explaining the technicalities. He contented himself with repeating, 'It was not bad shooting.'

'I think we must accept that the enemy machine has returned safely to her base,' said Lieutenant Kyller. 'Therefore we can expect the enemy to mount some form of offensive action against us in the very near future.' Kyller enjoyed a position of privilege in the wardroom. No other of the junior officers would have dared to express his opinions so freely. Yet none of them would have made as much sense as Kyller. When he spoke his senior officers listened, if not respectfully, at least attentively. Kyller had passed out sword of honour cadet from Bremerhaven Naval Academy in 1910. His father was a Baron, a personal friend of the Kaiser's, and an Admiral of the Imperial Fleet. Kyller was wardroom favourite, not only because of his dark good looks and courteous manners—but also because of his appetite for hard work, his meticulous attention to detail, and his ready mind. He was a good officer to have aboard—a credit to the ship.

'What can the enemy do?' Fleischer asked with scorn. He did not share the general opinion of Ernst Kyller. 'We are safe here—what can he do?'

'A superficial study of naval history will reveal, sir, that the English can be expected to do what you least expect them to do. And that they will do it, quickly, efficiently, and with iron purpose.' Kyller scratched the lumpy red insect bites behind his left ear.

'Bah!' said Fleischer, and sprayed a little pea soup with the violence of his disgust. 'The English are fools and cowards—at the worst, they will skulk off the mouth of the river. They would not dare come in here after us.'

'I have no doubt that time will prove you correct, sir.' This was Kyller's phrase of violent disagreement with a senior officer, and from experience Captain von Kleine and his commanders recognized it. They smiled a little.

'This soup is bitter,' said Fleischer, satisfied that he had carried the argument. 'The cook has used seawater in it.'

The accusation was so outrageous, that even von Kleine looked up from his plate.

'Please do not let our humble hospitality delay you, Herr Commissioner. You must be anxious to return up-river to your wood-cutting duties.'

And Fleischer subsided quickly, hunching over his food. Von Kleine transferred his gaze to Kyller.

'Kyller, you will not be returning with the Herr Commissioner. I am sending Ensign Proust with him this trip. You will be in command of the first line of defence that I plan to place at the mouth of the delta, in readiness for the English attack. You will attend the conference in my cabin after this meal, please.'

'Thank you, sir.' His voice was husky with gratitude for the honour his captain was conferring upon him. Von Kleine looked from him to his gunnery lieutenant.

'You also, please, Guns. I want to relieve you of your beloved upper deck pom-poms.'

'You mean to take them off their mountings, sir?' the gunnery lieutenant asked, looking at von Kleine dolefully over his long doleful nose.

'I regret the necessity,' von Kleine told him sympathetically.

65

'Well, Henry. We were right. *Blücher*'s there.'

'Unfortunately, sir.'

'Two heavy cruisers tied up indefinitely on blockade service.' Admiral Sir Percy thrust out his lower lip lugubriously as he regarded the plaques of *Renounce* and *Pegasus* on the Indian Ocean plot. 'There is work for them elsewhere.'

'There is, at that,' agreed Henry Green.

'That request of Joyce's for two motor torpedo-boats . . .'

'Yes, sir?'

'We must suppose he intends mounting a torpedo attack into the delta.'

'It looks like it, sir.'

'It might work—worth a try anyway. What can we scratch together for him?'

'There is a full squadron at Bombay, and another at Aden, sir.'

For five seconds, Sir Percy Howe reviewed the meagre forces with which he was expected to guard two oceans. With this new submarine menace, he could not detach a single ship from the approaches to the Suez Canal—it would have to be Bombay. 'Send him an MTB from the Bombay squadron.'

'He asked for two, sir.'

'Joyce knows full well that I only let him have half of anything he requests. He always doubles up.'

'What about this recommendation for a decoration, sir?'

'The fellow who spotted the *Blücher*?'

'Yes, sir.'

'A bit tricky—Portuguese irregular and all that sort of thing.'

'He's a British subject, sir.'

'Then he shouldn't be with the dagos,' said Sir Percy. 'Leave it over until the operation is completed. We'll think about it after we've sunk the *Blücher*.'

66

The sunset was blood and roses, nude pink and tarnished gold as the British blockade squadron stood in towards the land.

Renounce led with the commodore's pennant flying at her masthead. In the smooth wide road of her wake, *Pegasus* slid over the water. Their silhouettes were crisp and black against the garish colours of the sunset. There was something prim and old-maidish about the lines of a heavy cruiser–none of the solid majesty of a battleship, nor the jaunty devil-may-care rake of a destroyer.

Close in under *Pegasus*'s beam, screened by her hull from the land, like a cygnet swimming beside the swan, rode the motor torpedo-boat.

Even in this light surface chop she was taking in water. Each wave puffed up over her bows and then streamed back greenish and cream along the decks. The spray rattled against the thin canvas that screened the open bridge.

Flynn O'Flynn crouched behind the screen and cursed the vaunting ambition that had led him to volunteer as pilot for this expedition. He glanced across at Sebastian who stood in the open wing of the bridge, behind the canvas-shrouded batteries of Lewis guns. Sebastian was grinning as the warm spray flew back into his face and trickled down his cheeks.

Joyce had recommended Sebastian for a Distinguished Service Order. This was almost more than Flynn could bear. He wanted one also. He had decided to go along now for that reason alone. Therefore Sebastian was directly to blame for Flynn's present discomfort, and Flynn felt a small warmth of satisfaction as he looked at the flattened, almost negroid contours of Sebastian's new nose. The young bastard deserved it, and he found himself wishing further punishment on his son-in-law.

'Distinguished Service Order and all . . .' he grunted. 'A half-trained chimpanzee could have done what he did. Yet who was it who found the wheels in the first place? No, Flynn Patrick, there just ain't no justice in this world, but we'll show the sons of bitches this time . . .'

His thoughts were interrupted by the small bustle of activity on the bridge around him. An Aldis lamp was winking from the high dark bulk of *Renounce* ahead of them.

The lieutenant commanding the torpedo-boat spelled the message aloud.

'Flag to YN2. D . . . P departure point. Good luck.' He was a dumpy amorphous figure in his duffle coat with the collar turned up. 'Thanks a lot, old chap–and one up your pipe also. No, Signaller, don't make that.' He went on quickly, 'YN2 to flag. Acknowledged!' Then turning to the engine voice-pipe. 'Both engines stop,' he said.

The beat of her engines faded away, and she wallowed in the trough of the next wave. *Renounce* and *Pegasus* sailed on sedately, leaving the tiny vessel rolling crazily in the turbulence of their wakes. A lonely speck five miles off the mouth of the Rufiji delta, too far off for the shorewatchers to see her in the fading evening light.

67

Lieutenant Ernst Kyller watched through his binoculars as the two British cruisers turned in succession away from the land, and coalesced with the darkness that fell so swiftly over the ocean and the land. They were gone.

'Every day it is the same.' Kyller let the binoculars fall against his chest and pulled his watch from the pocket of his tunic. 'Fifteen minutes before sunset, and again fifteen minutes before sun-up they sail past to show us that they are still waiting.'

'Yes, sir,' agreed the seaman who was squeezed into the crow's nest beside Kyller.

'I will go down now. Moon comes up at 11.44 tonight—keep awake.'

'Yes, sir.'

Kyller swung his legs over the side and groped with his feet for the rungs of the rope ladder. Then he climbed down the palm tree to the beach fifty feet below. By the time he reached it the light had gone, and the beach was a vague white blur down to the green lights of phosphorus in the surf.

The sand crunched like sugar under his boots as he set off to where the launch was moored. As he walked, his mind was wholly absorbed with the details of his defence system.

There were only two of the many mouths of the Rufiji, up which the English could attack. They were separated by a low wedge-shaped island of sand and mud and mangrove. It was on the seaward side of this island that Kyller had sited the four-pounder pom-poms taken from their mountings on *Blücher*'s upper deck.

He had sunk a raft of logs into the soft mud to give them a firm foundation on which to stand, and he had cut out the mangroves so they commanded an arc of fire across both channels. His searchlights he sited with equal care—so they could sweep left or right without blinding his gunners.

From Commander Lochtkamper he had solicited a length of four-inch steel hawser. This was rather like an unrehabilitated insolvent raising an unsecured loan from a money-lender, for Commander Lochtkamper was not easily parted from his stores. Far up river Ensign Proust had diverted some of his axemen to felling fifty giant African mahogany trees. They had floated the trunks down on the tide; logs the size of the columns of a Greek temple. With these and the cable Kyller had fashioned a boom that stretched across both channels, an obstacle so formidable that it would rip the belly out of even a heavy cruiser coming down on it at speed.

Not satisfied with this, for Kyller had highly developed the Teutonic capacity for taking infinite pains, he lifted the fat globular mines with their sinister horns that *Blücher* had sown haphazardly behind her on her journey up-river. These he rearranged into neat geometrical ranks behind his log boom, a labour that left his men almost prostrated with nervous exhaustion.

This work had taken ten days to complete, and immediately Kyller had begun building observation posts. He placed them on every hump of high ground that commanded a view of the ocean, he built them in the tops of the palm trees, and on the smaller islands that stood out at sea. He arranged a system of signals with his observers—flags and heliographs for the day, skyrockets for the night.

During the hours of darkness, two whale boats rowed steadily back and forth along the log boom, manned by seamen who slapped steadily and sulkily at the light cloud of mosquitoes that haloed their heads, and made occasional brief but vitriolic statements about Lieutenant Kyller's ancestry, present worth, and future prospects.

At 2200 hours on the night of June 16th, 1915, the British motor torpedo-boat YN2 crept with both engines running dead slow into the centre of Lieutenant Kyller's elaborate reception arrangements.

68

After the clean cool air on the open sea, the smell was like entering the monkey-house of London Zoo. The land masked the breeze, and the frolic of the surface chop died away. As the torpedo-boat groped its way into the delta, the miasma of the swamps spread out to meet her.

'My God, that smell.' Sebastian twitched his flattened nose. 'It brings back pleasant memories.'

'Lovely, isn't it?' agreed Flynn.

'We must be almost into the channel.' Sebastian peered into the night, sensing rather than seeing the loom of the mangroves ahead and on either hand.

'I don't know what the hell I'm doing on this barge,' grunted Flynn. 'This is raving bloody madness. We've got more chance of catching a clap than finding our way up to where *Blücher* is anchored.'

'Faith! Major O'Flynn, and shame on ye!' The commander of the torpedo-boat exclaimed in his best music-hall brogue. 'We put our trust in you and the Lord.' His tone changed and he spoke crisply to the helmsman beside him. 'Lay her off a point to starboard.'

The long nose of the boat, with the torpedo tubes lying like a rack of gigantic champagne bottles on her foredeck, swung fractionally. The commander cocked his head to listen to the whispered soundings relayed from the leadsman in the bows.

'Twelve fathoms,' he repeated thoughtfully. 'So far so good.' Then he turned back to Flynn.

'Now, Major, I heard you shooting the blarney to Captain Joyce about how well you know this river, I think your exact words were, "Like you know the way to your own Thunder Box." You don't seem so certain about it any longer. Why is that?'

'It's dark,' said Flynn sulkily.

'My, so it is. But that shouldn't fluster an old river pilot like you.'

'Well, it sure as hell does.'

'If we get into the channel and lay up until the moon rises, would that help?'

'It wouldn't do any harm.'

That exchange seemed to exhaust the subject and for a further fifteen minutes the tense silence on the bridge was spoiled only by the commander's quiet orders to the helm, as he kept his ship within the ten fathom line of the channel.

Then Sebastian made a contribution.

'I say, there's something dead ahead of us.'

A patch of deeper darkness in the night; a low blurred shape that showed against the faint sheen of the star reflections on the surface. A reef perhaps? No, there was a splash alongside it as an oar dipped and pulled.

'Guard boat!' said the commander, and stooped to the voice-pipe. 'Both engines full ahead together.'

The deck canted sharply under their feet as the bows lifted, the whisper of the engines rose to a dull bellow and the torpedo-boat plunged forward like a bull at the cape.

'Hold on! I'm going to ram it.' The commander's voice was pitched at conversational level, and a hubbub of shouts broke out ahead, oars splashed frantically as the guard boat tried to pull out of their line of charge.

'Steer for them,' said the commander pleasantly, and the helmsman put her over a little.

Flash and crack, flash and crack, someone in the guard boat fired a rifle just as the torpedo-boat struck her. It was a glancing blow, taken on her shoulder, that spun the little whale boat aside, shearing off the protruding oars with a crackling popping sound.

She scraped down the gunwhale of the torpedo-boat, and then she was left astern and rocking wildly as the larger vessel surged ahead.

Then abruptly it was no longer dark. From all around them sparkling trails of fire shot into the sky and burst in balls of blue, that lit it all with an eerie flickering glow.

'Sky rockets, be Jesus. Guy Fawkes, Guy,' said the commander.

They could see the banks of mangrove massed on either hand, and ahead of them the double mouths of the two channels.

'Steer for the southern channel.' This time the commander lifted his voice a little, and the ship plunged onward, throwing out white wings of water from under her bows, bucking and jarring as she leapt over the low swells pushed up by the outflowing tide, so the men on the bridge hung on to the hand rail to steady themselves.

Then all of them gasped together in the pain of seared eye-balls as a solid shaft of dazzling white light struck them. It leapt out from the dark wedge of land that divided the two channels, and almost immediately two other searchlights on the outer banks of the channels joined in the hunt. Their beams fastened on the ship like the tentacles of a squid on the carcass of a flying fish.

'Get those lights!' this time the commander shouted the order at the gunners behind the Lewis guns at the corners of the bridge. The tracer that hosed out in a gentle arc towards the base of the searchlight beams was anaemic and pinkly pale, in contrast to the brilliance they were trying to quench.

The torpedo-boat roared on into the channel.

Then there was another sound. A regular thump, thump, thump like the working of a distant water pump. Lieutenant Kyller had opened up with his quick firing pom-pom.

The four-pound tracer emanated from the dark blob of the island. Seeming to float slowly towards the torpedo-boat, but gaining speed as it approached, until it flashed past with the whirr of a rocketing pheasant.

'Jesus!' said Flynn as though he meant it. He sat down hurriedly on the deck and began to unlace his boots.

Still held in the cold white grip of the searchlights, the torpedo-boat roared on with four-pounder shell streaking around her, and bursting in flurries of spray on the surface near her. The long dotted tendrils of tracer from her own Lewis guns still arched out in delicate lines towards the shore, and suddenly they had effect.

The beam of one of the searchlights snapped off as a bullet shattered the glass, for a few seconds the filaments continued to glow dull red as they burned themselves out.

In the relief from the blinding glare, Sebastian could see ahead, and he saw a sea serpent. It lay across the channel, undulating in the swells, bellied from bank to bank by the push of the tide, showing its back at the top of the swells and then ducking into the troughs; long and sinuous and menacing, Lieutenant Kyller's log boom waited to welcome them.

'Good God, what's that?'

'Full port rudder!' the commander bellowed. 'Both engines full astern together.'

And before the ship could answer her helm or the drag of her propellers, she ran into a log four feet thick and a hundred feet long. A log as unyielding as a reef of solid granite that stopped her dead in the water and crunched in her bows.

The men in the well of her bridge were thrown into a heap of tangled bodies on the deck. A heap from which the bull figure of Flynn Patrick O'Flynn was the first to emerge. On stockinged feet he made for the side of the ship.

'Flynn, where are you going?' Sebastian shouted after him

'Home,' said Flynn.

'Wait for me.' Sebastian scrambled to his knees.

The engines roaring in reverse pulled the torpedo-boat back off the log boom, her plywood hull crackling and squeaking, but she was mortally wounded. She was sinking with a rapidity that amazed Sebastian. Already her cockpit was flooding.

'Abandon ship,' shouted the commander.

'You damned tooting,' said Flynn O'Flynn and leaped in an untidy tangle of arms and legs into the water.

Like a playful seal the torpedo-boat rolled over on its side, and Sebastian jumped. Drawing his breath while he was in the air, steeling himself against the cold of the water.

He was surprised at how warm it was.

69

From the bridge of H.M.S. *Renounce,* the survivors looked like a cluster of bedraggled water rats. In the dawn they floundered and splashed around the edge of the balloon of stained and filthy water where the Rufiji had washed them out, like the effluent from the sewer outlet of a city. *Renounce* found them before the sharks did, for there was no blood. There was one broken leg, a fractured collar bone, and a few cracked ribs—but miraculously there was no blood. So from a crew of fourteen, *Renounce* recovered every man—including the two pilots.

They came aboard with their hair matted, their faces streaked, and their eyes swollen and inflamed with engine oil. With a man on either hand to guide them, leaving a trail of malodorous Rufiji water across the deck, they shuffled down to the sick-bay, a sodden and sorrowful-looking assembly of humanity.

'Well,' said Flynn O'Flynn, 'if we don't get a medal for *that*, then I'm going back to my old job—and the hell with them.'

'That,' said Captain Arthur Joyce, sitting hunched behind his desk, 'was not a roaring success.' He showed no inclination to whistle 'Tipperary.'

'It wasn't even a good try, sir,' agreed the torpedo-boat commander. 'The Boche had everything ready to throw at our heads.'

'A log boom'—Joyce shook his head—'good Lord, they went out with the Napoleonic War!' He said it in a tone that implied that he was a victim of unfair play.

'It was extraordinarily effective, sir.'

'Yes, it must have been.' Joyce sighed. 'Well, at the very least we have established that an attack up the channel is not practical.'

'During the few minutes before the tide swept us away from the boom I looked beyond it, and I saw what I took to be a mine. I think it certain that the Boche have laid a minefield beyond the boom, sir.'

'Thank you, Commander,' Joyce nodded. 'I will see to it that their Lordships receive a full account of your conduct. I consider it excellent.' Then he went on. 'I would value your opinion of Major O'Flynn and his son—do you think they are reliable men?'

'Well . . .' the commander hesitated, he did not want to be unfair, '—they can both swim and the young one seems to have good eyesight. Apart from that I am not really in a position to give a judgement.'

'No, I don't suppose you are. Still I wish I knew more about them. For the next phase in this operation I am going to rely quite heavily on them.' He stood up. 'I think I will talk to them now.'

You mean you actually want someone to go on board *Blücher*!' Flynn was appalled.

'I have explained to you, Major, how important it is for me to know exactly what state she is in. I must be able to estimate when she is likely to break out of the delta. I must know how much time I have.'

'Madness,' whispered Flynn. 'Stark raving bloody madness.' He stared at Joyce in disbelief.

'You have told me how well organized is your intelligence system ashore, of the reliable men who work for you. Indeed it is through you that we know that the Germans are cutting cordwood and taking it aboard. We know that they have recruited an army of native labourers and are using them not only for wood-cutting, but also for heavy work aboard the *Blücher*.'

'So?' Into that single word Flynn put a wealth of caution.

'One of your men could infiltrate the labour gangs and get aboard *Blücher*.'

And Flynn perked up immediately; he had anticipated that Joyce would suggest that Flynn Patrick O'Flynn should personally conduct a survey of *Blücher*'s damage.

'It might be done.' There was a lengthy pause while Flynn considered every aspect of the business. 'Of course, Captain, my men aren't fighting patriots like you and I. They work for money. They are . . .' Flynn searched for the word. 'They are . . .'

'Mercenaries?'

'Yes,' said Flynn. 'That's exactly what they are.'

'Hmmm,' said Joyce. 'You mean they would want payment?'

'They'd want a big dollop of lolly—and you can't blame them, can you?'

'The person you send would have to be a first-class man.'

'He would be,' Flynn assured him.

'On behalf of His Majesty's Government, I could undertake to purchase a complete and competent report on the disposition of the German cruiser *Blücher*, for the sum of . . .' he thought about it a moment, '. . . one thousand pounds.'

'Gold?'

'Gold,' agreed Joyce.

'That would cover it nicely.' Flynn nodded, then allowed his eyes to move across the cabin to where Sebastian and Rosa sat side by side on the day couch. They were holding hands, and showing more interest in each other than in the bargainings of Flynn and Captain Joyce.

It was a good thing, Flynn decided, that the Wakamba tribe from which Commissioner Fleischer had recruited the majority of his labour force, effected clean-shaven pates. It would be impossible for a person of European descent to dress his straight hair to resemble the woollen cap of an African.

It was also a good thing about the M'senga tree. From the bark of the M'senga tree the fishermen of Central Africa decocted a liquid in which they soaked their nets. It toughened the fibres of the netting, and it also stained the skin. Once Flynn had dipped his finger into a basin of the stuff, and despite constant scrubbing, it was fifteen days before the black stain faded.

It was finally a good thing about Sebastian's nose. Its new contours were decidedly negroid.

70

'A thousand pounds!' said Flynn O'Flynn as though it were a benediction, and he scooped another mugful of the black liquid and poured it over Sebastian Oldsmith's clean-shaven scalp. 'Think of it, Bassie, me lad, a thousand pounds! Your half share of that is five hundred. Why! You'll be in a position to pay me back every penny you owe me. You'll be out of debt at last.'

They were camped on the Abati river, one of the tributaries of the Rufiji. Six miles downstream was Commissioner Fleischer's wood-cutting camp.

'It's money for jam,' opined Flynn. He was sitting comfortably in a riempie chair beside the galvanized iron tub, in which Sebastian Oldsmith squatted with his knees drawn up under his chin. Sebastian had the dejected look of a spaniel taking a bath in flea shampoo. The liquid in which he sat was the colour and viscosity of strong Turkish coffee and already his face and body were a dark purply chocolate colour.

'Sebastian isn't interested in the money,' said Rosa Oldsmith. She knelt beside the tub and, tenderly as a mother bathing her infant, she was ladling the M'senga juice over Sebastian's shoulders and back.

'I know, I know!' Flynn agreed quickly. 'We are all doing our duty. We all remember little Maria—may the Lord bless and keep her tiny soul. But the money won't hurt us either.'

Sebastian closed his eyes as another mugful cascaded over his head.

'Rub it into the creases round your eyes—and under your chin,' said Flynn, and Sebastian obeyed. 'Now, let's go over it again, Bassie, so you don't get it all balled up. One of Mohammed's cousins is boss-boy of the gang loading the timber into the launches. They are camped on the bank of the Rufiji. Mohammed will slip you in tonight, and tomorrow his cousin will get you on to one of the launches going down with a load for *Blücher*. All you've got to do is keep your eyes open. Joyce just wants to know what work they are doing to repair her; whether or not they've got the boilers fired; things like that. You understand?'

Sebastian nodded glumly.

'You'll come back up-river tomorrow evening, slip out of camp soon as it's dark, and meet us here. Simple as a pimple, right?'

'Right,' murmured Sebastian.

'Right then. Out you get and dry off.'

As the wind from the uplands blew over his naked body, the purply tint of the dye faded into a matt chocolate. Rosa had modestly moved away into the grove of Marula trees behind the camp. Every few minutes Flynn came across to Sebastian and touched his skin.

'Coming along nicely,' he said, and, 'Nearly done,' and, 'Jeez, you look better than real.' Then finally in Swahili, 'Right, Mohammed, mark his face.'

Mohammed squatted in front of Sebastian with a tiny gourd of cosmetics; a mixture of animal fat and ash and ochre. With his fingers he daubed Sebastian's cheeks and nose and forehead with the tribal patterns. His head held on one side in artistic concentration, making soft clucking sounds of concentration as he worked, until at last Mohammed was satisfied.

'He is ready.'

'Get the clothes,' said Flynn. This was an exaggeration. Sebastian's attire could hardly be called clothing.

A string of bark around his neck from which was suspended a plugged duiker horn filled with snuff, a cloak of animal skin that smelled of woodsmoke and man-sweat, draped over his shoulders.

'It stinks!' said Sebastian cringing from contact with the garment. 'And it's probably got lice.'

'The real thing,' agreed Flynn jovially. 'All right, Mohammed, show him how to fit the istopo—the hat.'

'I don't have to wear that also,' Sebastian protested, staring in horror as Mohammed came towards him, grinning.

'Of course you've got to wear it.' Impatiently Flynn brushed aside his protest.

The hat was a hollow six-inch length cut from the neck of a calabash gourd. An anthropologist would have called it a penis-sheath. It had two purposes; firstly to protect the wearer from the scratches of thorns and the bites of insect pests, and secondly as a boost to his masculinity.

Once in position it looked impressive, enhancing Sebastian's already considerable muscular development.

Rosa said nothing when she returned. She took one long startled look at the hat and then quickly averted her gaze, but her cheeks and neck flared bright scarlet.

'For God's sake, Bassie. Act like you proud of it. Stand up straight and take your hands away.' Flynn coached his son-in-law.

Mohammed knelt to slip the rawhide sandals on to Sebastian's feet, and then hand him the small blanket roll tied with a bark string. Sebastian slung it over one shoulder then picked up the long-handled throwing-spear.

Automatically he grounded the butt and leaned his weight on the shaft; lifting his left leg and placing the sole of his foot against the calf of his right leg, he stood in the stork posture of rest.

In every detail he was a Wakamba tribesman.

'You'll do,' said Flynn.

71

In the dawn little wisps of river mist swirled around Commissioner Fleischer's legs as he came down the bank and on to the improvised jetty of logs.

He ran his eyes over the two launches, checking the ropes that held down the cargoes of timber. The launches sat low in the water, their exhausts puttering and blowing pale blue smoke that drifted away across the slick surface of the river.

'Are you ready?' he called to his sergeant of Askari.

'The men are eating, Bwana Mkuba.'

'Tell them to hurry,' growled Fleischer. It was a futile order and he stepped to the edge of the jetty, unbuttoning his trousers. He urinated noisily into the river, and the circle of men who squatted around the three-legged pot on the jetty watched him with interest, but without interrupting their breakfast.

With leather cloaks folded around their shoulders against the chill air off the water, they reached in turn into the pot and took a handful of the thick white maize porridge, moulding it into a mouth-size ball and then with the thumb forming a cup in the ball, dipping the ball into the smaller enamel dish and filling the depression with the creamy yellow gravy it contained, a tantalizing mixture of stewed catfish and tree caterpillars.

It was the first time that Sebastian had tasted this delicacy. He sat with the others and imitated their eating routine, forcing himself to place a lump of the spiced maize meal in his mouth. His gorge rose and gagged him, it tasted like fish oil and new-mown grass, not really offensive—it was just the thought of those fat yellow caterpillars. But had he been eating ham sandwiches, his appetite would not have been hearty.

His stomach was cramped with apprehension. He was a spy. A word from one of his companions, and Commissioner Fleischer would shout for the hanging ropes. Sebastian remembered the men he had seen in the monkey-bean tree on the bank of this same river, he remembered the flies clustered on their swollen, lolling tongues. It was not a mental picture conducive to enjoyment of breakfast.

Now, pretending to eat, he watched Commissioner Fleischer instead. It was the first time he had done so at leisure. The bulky figure in grey corduroy uniform, the pink-boiled face with pale golden eyelashes, the full petulant lips, the big freckled hands, all these revolted him. He felt his uneasiness swamped by a revival of the emotions that had possessed him as he stood beside the newly filled grave of his daughter on the heights above Lalapanzi.

'Black pig-animals,' shouted Herman Fleischer in Swahili, as he rebuttoned his clothing. 'That is enough! You do nothing but eat and sleep. It is time now for work.' He waddled across the logs of the jetty, into the little circle of porters. His first kick sent the three-legged pot clattering, his second kick caught Sebastian in the back and threw him forward on to his knees.

'Rasch!' He aimed another kick at one of them, but it was dodged, and the porters scattered to the launches.

Sebastian scrambled up. He had been kicked only once before in his life, and Flynn O'Flynn had learned not to do it again. For Sebastian there was nothing so humiliating as the contact of another man's foot against his person, also it had hurt.

Herman Fleischer had turned away to chivvy the others, so he did not see the hatred nor the way that Sebastian snarled at him, crouching like a leopard. Another second and he would have been on him. He might have killed Fleischer before the Askari shot him down—but he never made the attempt.

A hand on his arm. Mohammed's cousin beside him, his voice very low.

'Come! Let it pass. They will kill us also.'

And when Fleischer turned back the two of them had gone to the launch.

On the run down-river, Sebastian huddled with the others. Like them, drawing his cloak over his head to keep off the sun, but unlike them, he did not sleep. Through half-hooded eyes he was still watching Herman Fleischer, and his thoughts were hate-ugly.

Even with the current, the run in the deep-laden launches took almost four hours, and it was noon before they chugged around the last bend in the channel and turned in towards the mangrove forests.

Sebastian saw Herman Fleischer swallow the last bite of sausage and carefully repack the remainder into his haversack. He stood up and spoke to the man at the rudder, and both of them peered ahead.

'We have arrived,' said Mohammed's cousin, and removed his cloak from over his head. The little huddle of porters stirred into wakefulness and Sebastian stood up with them.

This time he knew what to look for, and he saw the muzzy silhouette of the *Blücher* skulking under her camouflage. From low down on the water she looked mountainous, and Sebastian's spine tingled as he remembered when last he had seen her from this angle, driving down to ram them with those axe-sharp bows. But now she floated awry, listing heavily.

'The boat leans over to one side.'

'Yes,' agreed Mohammed's cousin. 'The allemand wanted it so. There had been a great carrying of goods within her, they have moved everything to make the boat lean over.'

'Why?'

The man shrugged and pointed with his chin. 'They have lifted her belly from the water, see how they work with fire on the holes in her skin.'

Tiny as beetles, men swarmed on the exposed hull, and even in the bright glare of midday, the welding torches flared and sparkled with blue-white flame. The new plating was conspicuous in its coat of dull brown oxide paint, against the battleship-grey of the original hull.

As the launch approached, Sebastian studied the work carefully. He could see that it was nearing completion, the welders were running closed the last seams in the new plating. Already there were painters covering the oxide red with the matt grey final coat.

The pock marks of the shell splinters in her upperworks had been closed, and here again men hung on the flimsy trapezes of rope and planks, their arms lifting and falling as they plied the paint brushes.

An air of bustle and intent activity gripped the *Blücher*. Everywhere men moved about fifty different tasks, while the uniforms of the officers were restless white spots roving about her decks.

'They have closed all the holes in her belly?' Sebastian asked.

'All of them,' Mohammed's cousin confirmed. 'See how she spits out the water that was in her womb.' And he pointed again with his chin. From a dozen outlet vents, *Blücher*'s pumps were expelling solid streams of brown water as she emptied the flooded compartments.

'There is smoke from her chimneys,' Sebastian exclaimed, as he noticed for the first time the faint shimmer of heat at the mouths of her stacks.

'Yes. They have built fires in the iron boxes deep inside her. My brother Walaka works there now. He is helping to tend the fires. At first the fires were small, but each day they feed them higher.'

Sebastian nodded thoughtfully, he knew it took time to heat cold furnaces without cracking the linings of fireclay.

The launch nosed in and bumped against the cliff-high side of the cruiser.

'Come,' said Mohammed's cousin. 'We will climb up and work with the gangs carrying the wood down into her. You will see more up there.'

A new wave of dread flooded over Sebastian. He didn't want to go up there among the enemy. But already his guide was scrambling up the catwalk that hung down *Blücher*'s flank.

Sebastian adjusted his penis-sheath, hitched up his cloak, took a deep breath, and followed him.

72

'Sometimes it goes like that. In the beginning everything is an obscene shambles; nothing but snags and accidents and delays. Then suddenly everything drops into place and the job is finished.' Standing under the awning on the foredeck, Commander (Engineering) Lochtkamper was a satisfied man, as he looked around the ship. 'Two weeks ago it looked as though we would still be messing around when the war was over—but now!'

'You have done well,' von Kleine understated the facts. 'Again you have justified my confidence. But now I have another task to add to your burdens.'

'What is it, Captain?' Lochtkamper kept his voice noncommittal, but there was a wariness in his eyes.

'I want to alter the ship's profile—change it to resemble that of a British heavy cruiser.'

'How?'

'A dummy stack abaft the radio office. Canvas on a wooden frame. Then mask "X" turret, and block in the dip of our waist. It we run into the British blockade squadron in the night, it may give us the few extra minutes that will make the difference between success or failure.' Von Kleine spoke again as he turned away, 'Come, I will show you what I mean.'

Lochtkamper fell in beside him and they started aft, an incongruous pair; the engineer swaddled in soiled overalls, long arms dangling, shambling along beside his captain like a trained ape. Von Kleine tall over him, his tropical whites crisp and sterile, hands clasped behind his back and golden beard bowed forward on to his chest, leaning slightly against the steeply canted angle of the deck.

He spoke carefully. 'When can I sail, Commander? I must know precisely.

Is the work so far advanced that you can say with certainty?'

Lochtkamper was silent, considering his reply as they picked their way side by side through the milling jostle of seamen and native porters.

'I will have full pressure on my boilers by tomorrow night, another day after that to complete the work on the hull, two more days to adjust the trim of the ship and to make the alterations to the superstructure,' he mused aloud. Then he looked up. Von Kleine was watching him. 'Four days,' he said. 'I will be ready in four days.'

'Four days. You are certain of that?'

'Yes.'

'Four days,' repeated von Kleine, and he stopped in mid-stride to think. This morning he had received a message from Governor Schee in Dar es Salaam, a message relayed from the Admiralty in Berlin. Naval Intelligence reported that three days ago a convoy of twelve troopships, carrying Indian and South African infantry, had left Durban harbour. Their destination was not known, but it was an educated guess that the British were about to open a new theatre of war. The campaign in German West Africa had been brought to a swift and decisive conclusion by the South Africans. Botha and Smuts had launched a double-pronged offensive, driving in along the railroads to the German capital of Windhoek. The capitulation of the German West African army had released the South African forces for work elsewhere. It was almost certain that those troopships were trundling up the east coast at this very moment, intent on a landing at one of the little harbours that dotted the coast of East Africa. Tanga perhaps, or Kilwa Kvinje—possibly even Dar es Salaam itself.

He must have his ship seaworthy and battle-ready to break out through the blockade squadron, and destroy that convoy.

'The big job will be readjusting the ship's trim. There is much to be done. Stores to be manhandled, shell from the magazines, the guns remounted . . .' Lochtkamper interrupted his thoughts, 'We will need labour.'

'I will order Fleischer to bring all his forced labour down to assist with the work,' von Kleine muttered. 'But we must sail in four days. The moon will be right on the night of the thirtieth, we must break out then.' The saintly face was ruffled by the force of his concentration, he paced slowly, the golden beard sunk on his chest as he formulated his plans, speaking aloud. 'Kyller has buoyed the channel. He must start clearing the minefield at the entrance. We can cut the boom at the last moment—and the current will sweep it aside.'

They had reached the waist of the cruiser. Von Kleine was so deep in his thoughts that it took Lochtkamper's restraining hand on his arm, to return him to reality.

'Careful, sir.'

With a start von Kleine looked up. They had walked into a knot of African porters. Wild tribesmen, naked beneath their filthy leather cloaks, faces daubed with yellow ochre. They were manhandling the faggots of cordwood that were coming aboard from the launch that lay alongside *Blücher*. One of the heavy bundles was suspended from the boom of the derrick, it was swaying twenty feet above the deck and von Kleine had been about to walk under it. Lochtkamper's warning stopped him.

While he waited for them to clear away the faggot, von Kleine idly watched the native gang of workers.

One of the porters caught his attention. He was taller than his companions, his body sleeker, lacking the bunched and knotty muscles. His legs also were sturdier and finely moulded. The man lifted his head from his labours, and von Kleine looked into his face. The features were delicate; the lips not as full as, the forehead broader and deeper than, the typical African.

But it was the eyes that jerked von Kleine's attention back from the troop convoy. They were brown, dark brown and shifty. Von Kleine had learned to recognize guilt in the faces of his subordinates, it showed in the eyes. This man was guilty. It was only an instant that von Kleine saw it, then the porter dropped his gaze and stooped to take a grip on the bundle of timber. The man worried him, left him feeling vaguely uneasy, he wanted to speak to him—question him. He started towards him.

'Captain! Captain!' Commissioner Fleischer had come puffing up the catwalk from the launch, plump and sweaty he was pawing von Kleine's arm.

'I must speak with you, Captain.'

'Ah, Commissioner,' von Kleine greeted him coolly, trying to avoid the damp paw. 'One moment, please. I wish to . . .'

'It is a matter of the utmost importance. Ensign Proust . . .'

'In a moment, Commissioner.' Von Kleine pulled away, but Fleischer was determined. He stepped in front of von Kleine, blocking his path.

'Ensign Proust, the cowardly little prig . . .' and von Kleine found himself embroiled in a long report about Ensign Proust's lack of respect for the dignity of the Commissioner. He had been insubordinate, he had argued with Herr Fleischer, and further he had told Herr Fleischer that he considered him 'fat'.

'I will speak to Proust,' said von Kleine. It was a trivial matter and he wanted no part of it. The Commander Lochtkamper was beside them. Would the Captain speak to the Herr Commissioner about the labour for the landing of ballast? They fell into a long discussion and while they talked, the gang of porters lugged the bundle of timber aft and were absorbed by the bustling hordes of workmen.

Sebastian was sweating with fright; trembling, giddy with fright. Clearly he had sensed the German officer's suspicions. Those cold blue eyes had burned like dry ice. Now he stooped under his load, trying to shrink himself into insignificance, trying to overcome the grey clammy sense of dread that threatened to crush him.

'He saw you,' wheezed Mohammed's cousin, shuffling along beside Sebastian.

'Yes.' Sebastian bent lower. 'Is he still watching?'

The old man glanced back over his shoulder.

'No. He speaks with the Mafuta, the fat one.'

'Good.' Sebastian felt a lift of relief. 'We must get back on the launch.'

'The loading is almost finished, but we must first speak with my brother. He waits for us.'

They turned the corner of the aft gun-turrets. On the deck was a mountain of cordwood. Stacked neatly and lashed down with rope. Black men swarmed over it, between them spreading a huge green tarpaulin over the wood pile.

They reached the wood pile and added the faggots they carried to the stack. Then, in the custom of Africa, they paused to rest and talk. A man clambered down from the wood pile to join them, a sprightly old gentleman with woolly grey hair, impeccably turned out in cloak and penis-sheath. Mohammed's cousin greeted him with courteous affection, and they took snuff together.

'This man is my brother,' he told Sebastian. 'His name is Walaka. When he was a young man he killed a lion with a spear. It was a big lion with a black mane.' To Sebastian this information seemed to be slightly irrelevant, his fear of discovery was making him nervously impatient. There were Germans all around them, big blond Germans bellowing orders as they chivvied on the labour gangs, Germans looking down on them from the tall superstructure above them, Germans elbowing them aside as they passed. Sebastian found it difficult to concentrate.

His two accomplices were involved in a family discussion. It seemed that Walaka's youngest daughter had given birth to a fine son, but that during his absence a leopard had raided Walaka's village and killed three of his goats. The new grandson did not seem to compensate Walaka for the loss of his goats. He was distressed.

'Leopards are the excrement of dead lepers,' he said, and would have enlarged on the subject but Sebastian interrupted him.

'Tell me of the things you have seen on this canoe. Say swiftly, there is little time. I must go before the Allemand comes for all of us with the ropes.'

Mention of the ropes brought the meeting to order, and Walaka launched into his report.

There were fires burning in the iron boxes in the belly of the canoe. Fires of such heat that they pained the eye when the door of the box was opened, fires with a breath like that of a hundred bush fires, fires that consumed . . .

'Yes, yes.' Sebastian cut short the lyrical description. 'What else?'

There had been a great carrying of goods, moving of them to one side of the canoe to make it lean in the water. They had carried boxes and bales, unbolted machinery and guns. See how they had been moved. They had taken from the rooms under her roof a great quantity of the huge bullets, also the white bags of powder for the guns and placed them in other rooms on the far side.

'What else?'

There was more, much more to tell. Walaka enthused about meat which came out of little tins, of lanterns that burned without wick, flame, or oil, of great wheels that spun, and boxes of steel that screamed and hummed, of clean fresh water that gushed from the mouths of long rubber snakes, sometimes cold and at other times hot as though it had been boiled over a fire. There were marvels so numerous that it confused a man.

'These things I know. Is there nothing else that you have seen?'

Indeed there was. The Allemand had shot three native porters, lining them up and covering their eyes with strips of white cloth. The men had jumped and wriggled and fallen in a most comical fashion, and afterwards the Germans had washed the blood from the deck with water from the long snakes. Since then none of the other porters had helped themselves to blankets and buckets and other small movables—the price was exorbitant.

Walaka's description of the execution had a chilling effect on Sebastian. He had done what he had come to do and now his urge to leave *Blücher* became overpowering. It was helped on by a German petty officer who joined the group uninvited.

'You lazy black baboons,' he bellowed. 'This is not a bloody Sunday-school outing—move, you swine, move!' And his boots flew. Led by Mohammed's cousin they left Walaka without farewell and scampered back along the deck. Just before they reached the entry port, Sebastian checked. The two German officers stood where he had left them, but now they were looking up at the high smoke stacks. The tall officer with the golden beard was describing sweeping motions with his outstretched hand, talking while the stocky one listened intently.

Mohammed's cousin scurried past them and disappeared over the side into the launch, leaving Sebastian hesitant and reluctant to run the gauntlet of those pale blue eyes.

'Manali, come quickly. The boat swims, you will be left!' Mohammed's cousin called from down below, his voice faint but urgent above the chug of the launch's engine.

Sebastian started forward again, his stomach a cold lump under his ribs. A dozen paces and he had reached the entry port.

The German officer turned and saw him. He challenged with raised voice, and came towards Sebastian, one arm outstretched as though to hold him.

Sebastian whirled and dived down the catwalk. Below him the launch was casting off her lines, water churning back from her propeller.

Sebastian reached the grating at the bottom of the catwalk. There was a gap of ten feet between him and the launch. He jumped, hung for a moment in the air, then hit the gunwhale of the launch. His clutching fingers found a grip while his legs dangled in the warm water.

Mohammed's cousin caught his shoulder and dragged him aboard. They tumbled together in a heap on the deck of the launch.

'Bloody kaffir,' said Herman Fleischer and stooped to cuff them both heavily around the ears. Then he went back to his seat in the stern, and Sebastian smiled at him with something close to affection. After those deadly blue eyes, Herman Fleischer seemed as dangerous as a teddy-bear.

Then he looked back at *Blücher*. The German officer stood at the top of the catwalk, watching them as they drew away, and set a course upstream. Then he turned away from the rail and disappeared.

73

Sebastian sat on the day couch in the master cabin of H.M.S. *Renounce*, he sagged against the arm-rest and fought off the grey waves of exhaustion that washed over his mind.

He had not slept in thirty hours. After his escape from *Blücher* there had been the long launch journey up-river during which he had remained awake and jittery with the after-effects of tension.

After disembarking he had sneaked out of Fleischer's camp, avoiding the Askari guards, and trotted through the moonlight to meet Flynn and Rosa.

A hurried meal, and then all three of them had mounted on bicycles supplied with the compliments of the Royal Navy, and ridden all night along a rough elephant path to where they had left a canoe hidden among the reeds on the bank of one of the Rufiji tributaries.

In the dawn they had paddled out of one of the unguarded channels of the delta and made their rendezvous with the little whaler from H.M.S. *Renounce*.

Two long days of activity without rest, and Sebastian was groggy. Rosa sat beside him on the couch. She leaned across and touched his arm, her eyes dark with concern. Neither of them were taking any part in the conference in which the other persons in the crowded cabin were deeply involved.

Joyce sat as chairman, and beside him an older heavier man with bushy grey eyebrows and a truculent jaw, hair brushed in streaks across his pate in an ineffectual attempt to conceal his baldness. This was Armstrong, Captain of H.M.S. *Pegasus*, the other cruiser of the blockade squadron.

'Well, it looks as though *Blücher* has made good her damage, then. If she has fired her boilers, we can expect her to break out any day now—von Kleine would not burn up good fuel to keep his stokers warm.' He said it with relish, a fighting man anticipating a good hard fight. 'There's a message I'd like to give her from *Bloodhound* and *Orion*—an old account to settle.'

But Joyce also had a message, one that had its origin at the desk of Admiral Sir Percy Howe, Commander-in-Chief, South Atlantic and Indian Oceans. In part this message read:

'The safety of your squadron considered secondary to containing *Blücher*. Risk involved in delaying until *Blücher* leaves the delta before engaging her is too high. Absolutely imperative that she be either destroyed or blocked at her present anchorage. Consequences of *Blücher* running blockade and attacking the troop convoy conveying landing forces to invasion of Tanga will be catastrophic. Efforts being made to send you two tramp steamers to act as block ships, but failing their arrival, and failing also effective offensive action against *Blücher* before July 30th, 1915, you are hereby ordered to scuttle *Renounce* and *Pegasus* in the channel of the Rufiji to block *Blücher*'s exit.'

It was a command that left Captain Arthur Joyce sick with dread. To scuttle his splendid ships—a thought as repulsive and loathsome as that of incest, of patricide, of human sacrifice. Today was July 26th, he had four days in which to find an alternative before the order became effective.

'She'll come out at night, of course, bound to!' Armstrong's voice was thick with battle lust. 'This time she'll not have an old girl and a baby like *Orion* and *Bloodhound* to deal with.' His tone changed slightly. 'We'll have to look lively. New moon in three days so *Blücher* will have dark nights. There could be a change in the weather ' Armstrong was looking a little worried now, '. . . we'll have to tighten up . . .'

'Read this,' said Joyce, and passed the flimsy to Armstrong. He read it.

'My God!' he gasped. 'Scuttle. Oh, my God!'

'There are two channels that *Blücher* could use.' Joyce spoke softly. 'We would have to block both of them—*Renounce* and *Pegasus*!'

'Jesus God!' swore Armstrong in horror. 'There must be another way.'

'I think there is,' said Joyce, and looked across at Sebastian. 'Mr Oldsmith,' he spoke gently, 'would it be possible for you to get on board the German cruiser once again?'

There were tiny lumps of yellow mucus in the corner of Sebastian's bloodshot eyes, but the stain that darkened his skin concealed the rings of fatigue under them.

'I'd rather not, old chap.' He ran his hand thoughtfully over his shaven scalp and the stubble of new hair rasped under his fingers. 'It was one of the most unpleasant hours of my life.'

'Quite,' said Captain Joyce. 'Quite so! I wouldn't have asked you, had I not considered it to be of prime importance.' Joyce paused and pursed his lips to whistle softly the first bar of Chopin's 'Funeral March', then he sighed and shook his head. 'If I were to tell you that you alone have it in your power to save both the cruisers of this squadron from destruction and to protect the lives of fifteen thousand British soldiers and seamen—how would you answer then?'

Glumly, Sebastian sagged back against the couch and closed his eyes.
'Can I have a few hours sleep first?'

74

It was exactly the size of a box of twenty-five Monte Cristo Havana Cigars, for that had been its contents before *Renounce*'s chief engine room artificer and the gunnery lieutenant had set to work on it.

It lay on the centre of Captain Joyce's desk, while the artificer explained its purpose to the respectful audience that stood around him.

'It's verra simple,' started the artificer in an accent that was as bracing as the fragrance of heather and highland whisky.

'It would have to be . . .' commented Flynn O'Flynn, '. . . for Bassie to understand it.'

'All you do is lift the lid.' The artificer suited action to the words, and even Flynn craned forward to examine the contents of the cigar box. Packed neatly into it were six yellow sticks of gelignite, looking like candles wrapped in grease-proof paper. There was also the flat dry cell battery from a bull's eye lantern, and a travelling-clock in a pigskin case. All of these were connected by loops and twists of fine copper wire. Engraved into the metal of the clock base were the words:

> To my dear husband Arthur,
> With love,
> Iris.
> Christmas 1914

Captain Arthur Joyce stilled a sentimental pang of regret with the thought that Iris would understand.

'Then . . .' said the artificer, clearly enjoying the hold he had on his audience, '. . . you wind the knob on the clock.' He touched it with his forefinger, '. . . close the lid,' he closed it, '. . . wait twelve hours, and—Boom!' The enthusiasm with which the Scotsman simulated an explosion blew a fine spray of spittle across the desk, and Flynn withdrew hurriedly out of range.

'Wait twelve hours?' asked Flynn, dabbing at the droplets on his cheeks. 'Why so long?'

'I ordered a twelve-hour delay on the fusing of the charge.' Joyce answered the question. 'If Mr Oldsmith is to gain access to the *Blücher*'s magazines, he will have to infiltrate the native labour gangs engaged in transferring the explosives. Once he is a member of the gang he might find difficulty in extricating himself and getting away from the ship after he had placed the charge. I am sure that Mr Oldsmith would be reluctant to make this attempt unless we could ensure that there is time for him to escape from *Blücher*, when his efforts . . . ah,' he sought the correct phraseology, ' . . . ah . . . come to fruition.' Joyce was pleased with this speech, and he turned to Sebastian for endorsement. 'Am I correct in my assumption, Mr Oldsmith?'

Not to be outdone in verbosity, Sebastian pondered his reply for a second. Five hours of deathlike sleep curled in Rosa's arms had refreshed his body and sharpened his wit to the edge of a Toledo steel blade.

'Indubitably,' he replied, and beamed in triumph.

75

They sat together in the time when the sun was dying and bleeding on the clouds. They sat together on a kaross of monkey skin in a thicket of wild ebony, at the head of one of the draws that wrinkled down into the valley of the Rufiji. They sat in silence. Rosa bent forward over her needlework, as she stitched a concealed pocket into the filthy cloak of leather that lay across her lap. The pocket would hold the cigar box. Sebastian watched her, and his eyes upon her were a caress. She pulled the last stitch tight, knotted it, then leaned forward to bite the thread.

'There!' she said. 'It's finished.' And looked up into his eyes.

'Thank you,' said Sebastian. They sat together quietly and Rosa reached out to touch his shoulder. The muscle under the black stained skin was rubber hard, and warm.

'Come,' she said and drew his head down to her so that their cheeks touched, and they held each other while the last light faded. The African dusk thickened the shadows in the wild ebony, and down the draw a jackal yipped plaintively.

'Are you ready?' Flynn stood near them, a dark bulky figure, with Mohammed beside him.

'Yes.' Sebastian looked up at him.

'Kiss me,' whispered Rosa, 'and come back safely.'

Gently Sebastian broke from her embrace. He stood tall above her, and draped the cloak over his naked body. The cigar box hung heavily between his shoulder blades.

'Wait for me,' he said, and walked away.

Flynn Patrick O'Flynn moved restlessly under his single blanket and belched. Heartburn moved acid sour in his throat, and he was cold. The earth under him had long since lost the warmth it had sucked from yesterday's sun. A small slice of the old moon gave a little silver light to the night.

Unsleeping he lay and listened to the soft sound of Rosa sleeping near him. The sound irritated him, he lacked only an excuse to waken her and make her talk to him. Instead he reached into the haversack that served as his pillow and his fingers closed round the cold smooth glass of the bottle.

A night-bird hooted softly down the draw, and Flynn released the bottle and sat up quickly. He placed two fingers between his lips and repeated the night-bird's cry.

Minutes later Mohammed drifted like a small black ghost into camp and came to squat beside Flynn's bed.

'I see you, Fini.'

'You I see also, Mohammed. It went well?'

'It went well.'

'Manali has entered the camp of the Allemand?'

'He sleeps now beside the man who is my cousin, and in the dawn they will go down the Rufiji, to the big boat of the Allemand once again.'

'Good!' grunted Flynn. 'You have done well.'

Mohammed coughed softly to signify that there was more to tell.

'What is it?' Flynn demanded.

'When I had seen Manali safely into the care of my cousin, I came back along the valley and . . .' he hesitated, '. . . perhaps it is not fitting to speak of such matters at a time when our Lord Manali goes unarmed and alone into the camp of the Allemand.'

'Speak,' said Flynn.

'As I walked without sound, I came to a place where this valley falls down to the river called Abati. You know the place?'

'Yes, about a mile down the draw from here.'

'That is the place.' Mohammed nodded. 'It was here that I saw something move in the night. It was as though a mountain walked.'

A sliver of ice was thrust down Flynn's spine, and his breathing snagged painfully in his throat.

'Yes?' he breathed.

'It was a mountain armed with teeth of ivory that grew from its face to touch the ground as it walked.'

'*Plough the Earth.*' Flynn whispered the name, and his hand fell on to the rifle that lay loaded beside his bed.

'It was that one.' Mohammed nodded again. 'He feeds quietly, moving towards the Rufiji. But the voice of a rifle would carry down to the ears of the Allemand.'

'I won't fire,' whispered Flynn. 'I just want to have a look at him. I just want to see him again.' And the hand on the rifle shook like that of a man in high fever.

76

The sun pushed up and sat fat and fiery as molten gold, on the hills of the Rufiji basin. Its warmth lifted streamers of mist from the swamps and reed-beds that bounded the Abati river, and they smoked like the ashes of a dying fire.

Under the fever trees the air was still cool with the memory of the night, but the sun sent long yellow shafts of light probing through the branches to disperse and warm it.

Three old eland bulls came up from the river, bigger than domestic cattle, light bluey-brown in colour with faint chalk stripes across the barrel of their bodies, they walked in single file, heavy dewlaps swinging, thick stubby horns held erect, and the tuft of darker hair on their foreheads standing out clearly. They reached the grove of fever trees and the lead bull stopped, suddenly alert. For long seconds they stood absolutely still, staring into the open palisade of fever tree trunks where the light was still vague beneath the canopy of interlaced leaves and branches.

The lead bull blew softly through his nostrils, and swung off the game path that led into the grove. Stepping lightly for such large animals, the three eland skirted the grove and moved away to blend into the dry thorn scrub higher up the slope.

'He is in there,' whispered Mohammed. 'The eland saw him, and turned aside.'

'Yes,' agreed Flynn. 'It is such a place as he would choose to lie up for the day.' He sat in the crotch of a M'banga tree, wedged securely ten feet above the ground, and peered across three hundred yards of open grassland at the dense stand of fever trees. The hands that held the binoculars to his eyes were unsteady with gin and excitement, and he was sweating, a droplet broke from his hair-line and slid down his cheek, tickling like an insect. He brushed it away.

'A wise man would leave him, and walk away even as the eland did.' Mohammed gave his opinion. He leaned against the base of the tree, holding Flynn's rifle across his chest. Flynn did not reply. He peered through the binoculars, swinging them slowly in an arc as he searched.

'He must be deep among the trees, I cannot see him from here.' And he loosened his leg grip from the crotch and clambered down to where Mohammed waited. He took his rifle and checked the load.

'Leave him, Fini,' Mohammed urged softly. 'There is no profit in it. We cannot carry the teeth away.'

'Stay here,' said Flynn.

'Fini, the Allemand will hear you. They are close–very close.'

'I will not shoot,' said Flynn. 'I must see him again–that is all. I will not shoot.'

Mohammed took the gin bottle from the haversack and handed it to him. Flynn drank.

'Stay here,' he repeated, his voice husky from the burn of the raw spirit.

'Be careful, Fini. He is an old one of evil temper–be careful.' Mohammed watched Flynn start out across the clearing. He walked with slow deliberation of a man who goes in good time to a meeting that has long been prearranged. He reached the grove of fever trees and walked on into them without checking.

Plough the Earth was sleeping on his feet. His little eyes closed tightly in their wrinkled pouches. Tears had oozed in a long dark stain down his cheeks, and a fine haze of midges hovered about them. Tattered as battle-riven banners on a windless day, his ears lay back against his shoulders. His tusks were crutches that propped up the gnarled old head, and his trunk hung down between them, grey and slack and heavy.

Flynn saw him, and picked his way towards him between the trunks of the fever trees. The setting had an unreal quality, for the light effect of the low sun through the branches was golden beams reflected in shimmering misty green from the leaves of the fever trees. The grove was resonant with the whine of cicada beetles.

Flynn circled out until he was head on to the sleeping elephant, and then he moved in again. Twenty paces from him Flynn stopped. He stood with his feet set apart, the rifle held ready across one hip, and his head thrown back as he looked up at the unbelievable bulk of the old bull.

Up to this moment Flynn still believed that he would not shoot. He had come only to look at him once more, but it was as futile as an alcoholic who promised himself just one taste. He felt the madness begin at the base of his spine, hot and hard it poured into his body, filling him as though he were a container. The level rose to his throat and he tried to check it there, but the rifle was coming up. He felt the butt in his shoulder. Then he heard with surprise a voice, a voice that rang clearly through the grove and instantly stilled the whine of the cicadas. It was his own voice, crying out in defiance of his conscious resolve.

'Come on, then,' he shouted. And the old elephant burst from massive quiescence into full charge. It came down on him like a dynamited cliff of black rock. He saw it over the open rear sight of his rifle, saw it beyond the minute pip of the foresight that rode unwaveringly in the centre of the old bull's bulging brow—between the eyes, where the crease of skin at the base of its trunk was a deep lateral line.

The shot was thunderous, shattering into a thousand echoes against the boles of the fever trees. The elephant died in the fullness of his run. Legs buckled, and he came toppling forward, carried by his own momentum, a loose avalanche of flesh and bone and long ivory.

Flynn turned aside like a matador from the run of the bull, three quick dancing steps and then one of the tusks hit him. It took him across the hip with a force that hurled him twenty feet, the rifle spinning from his hands so that as he fell and rolled in the soft bed of loose trash and leaf mould, his lower body twisted away from his trunk at an impossible angle. His brittle old bones had broken like china; the ball of the femur snapping off in its socket, his pelvis fracturing clean through.

Lying face down, Flynn was mildly surprised that there was no pain. He could feel the jagged edges of bone rasping together deep in his flesh at his slightest movement, but there was no pain.

Slowly, pulling himself forward on his elbows so that his legs slithered uselessly after him, he crawled towards the carcass of the old bull.

He reached it, and with one hand stroked the yellow shaft of ivory that had crippled him.

'Now,' he whispered, fondling the smoothly polished tusk the way a man might touch his firstborn son. 'Now, at last you are mine.'

And then the pain started, and he closed his eyes and cowered down, huddled beneath the hillock of dead and cooling flesh that had been *Plough the Earth*. The pain buzzed in his ears like cicada beetles, but through it he heard Mohammed's voice.

'Fini. It was not wise.'

He opened his eyes and saw Mohammed's monkey face puckered with concern.

'Call Rosa,' he croaked. 'Call Little Long Hair. Tell her to come.'

Then he closed his eyes again, and rode the pain. The tempo of the pain changed constantly—first it was drums, tom-toms that throbbed and beat within him. Then it was the sea, long undulating swells of agony. Then again it was night, cold black night that chilled him so he shivered and moaned—and the night gave way to the sun. A great fiery ball of pain that burned and shot out lances of blinding light that burst against his clenched eyelids. Then the drums began again.

Time was of no significance. He rode the pain for a minute and a million years, then through the beat of the drums of agony he heard movement near him. The shuffle of feet through the dead leaves, the murmur of voices that were not part of his consuming anguish.

'Rosa,' Flynn whispered, 'you have come!'

He rolled his head and forced his eyelids open.

Herman Fleischer stood over him. He was grinning. His face flushed as a rose petal, fresh sweat clinging in his pale eyebrows, breathing quickly and heavily with exertion as though he had been running, but he was grinning.

'So!' he wheezed. 'So!'

The shock of his presence was muted for Flynn by the haze of pain in which he lay. There were smears of dust dulling the gloss of Fleischer's jackboots, and dark patches of sweat had soaked through the thick grey corduroy tunic at the armpits. He held a Luger pistol in his right hand and with his left hand he pushed the slouch hat to the back of his head.

'Herr Flynn!' he said and chuckled. It was the fat infectious chuckle of a healthy baby.

Mildly Flynn wondered how Fleischer had found him so quickly in the broken terrain and thick bush. The shot would have alerted him, but what had led him directly to the grove of fever trees?

Then he heard a rustling fluting rush in the air above him, and he looked upwards. Through the lacework of branches he saw the vultures spiralling against the aching blue of the sky. They turned and dipped on spread black wings, cocking their heads sideways in flight to look down with bright beady eyes on the elephant carcass.

'Ja! The birds. We followed the birds.'

'Jackals always follow the birds,' whispered Flynn, and Fleischer laughed. He threw back his head and laughed with genuine delight.

'Good. Oh, ja. That is good.' And he kicked Flynn. He swung the jackboot lazily into Flynn's body, and Flynn shrieked. The laughter died instantly in Fleischer's throat, and he bent quickly to examine Flynn.

He noticed for the first time how his lower body was grotesquely twisted and distorted. And he dropped to his knees beside him. Gently he touched Flynn's forehead, and deep concern flashed across his chubby features at the clammy cold feeling of the skin.

'Sergeant!' There was a desperate edge to his voice now. 'This man is badly injured. He will not last long. Be quick! Get the rope! We must hang him before he loses consciousness.'

77

Rosa awoke in the dawn and found that she was alone. Beside Flynn's personal pack, his discarded blanket had been carelessly flung aside. His rifle was gone.

She was not alarmed, not at first. She guessed that he had gone into the bush on one of his regular excursions to be alone while he drank his breakfast. But an hour later when he had not returned she grew anxious. She sat with her rifle across her lap, and every bird noise or animal scuffle in the ebony thicket jarred her nerves.

Another hour and she was fretting. Every few minutes she stood up and walked to the edge of the clearing to listen. Then she went back to sit and worry.

Where on earth was Flynn? Why had Mohammed not returned? What had happened to Sebastian? Was he safe, or had he been discovered? Had Flynn gone to assist him? Should she wait here, or follow them down the draw?

Her eyes haunted, her mouth hard set with doubts, she sat and twisted the braid of her hair around one finger in a nervously restless gesture.

Then Mohammed came. Suddenly he appeared out of the thicket beside her, and Rosa jumped up with a low cry of relief. The cry died in her throat as she saw his face.

'Fini!' he said. 'He is hurt. The great elephant has broken his bones and he lies in pain. He asks for you.'

Rosa stared at him, appalled, not understanding.

'An elephant?'

'He followed *Plough the Earth*, the great elephant, and killed him. But in dying the elephant struck him, breaking him.'

'The fool. Oh, the fool!' Rosa whispered. 'Now of all times. With Sebastian in danger, he must . . .' And then she caught herself and broke off her futile lament. 'Where is he, Mohammed? Take me to him.'

Mohammed led along one of the game paths. Rosa ran behind him. There was no time for caution, no thought of it as they hurried to find Flynn. They came to the stream of the Abati, and swung off the path, staying on the near bank. They plunged through a field of arrow grass, skirted around a tiny swamp and ran on into a stand of buffalo thorn. As they emerged on the far side Mohammed stopped abruptly and looked at the sky.

The vultures turned in a high wheel against the blue, like debris in a lazy whirlwind. The spot above which they circled lay half a mile ahead.

'Daddy!' Rosa choked on the word. In an instant all the hardness accumulated since that night at Lalapanzi disappeared from her face.

'Daddy!' she said again, and then she ran in earnest. Brushing past Mohammed, throwing her rifle aside so it clattered on the earth, she darted out of the buffalo thorn and into the open.

'Wait, Little Long Hair. Be careful.' Mohammed started after her. In his agitation he stepped carelessly, fully on to a fallen twig from the buffalo thorn. There was a worn spot on the sole of his sandal, and three inches of cruel red-tipped thorn drove up through it and buried in his foot.

For a dozen paces he struggled on after Rosa, hopping on one leg, flapping his arms to maintain his balance and calling, but not too loudly.

'Wait! Be careful, Little Long Hair.'

But she took not the least heed, and went away from him, leaving him at last to sink down and tend to his wounded foot.

She crossed the open ground before the fever tree grove with the slack, blundering steps of exhaustion. Running silently, saving her breath for the effort of reaching her father. She ran into the grove, and a drop of perspiration fell into her eye, blurring her vision so she staggered against one of the trunks. She recovered her balance and ran on into the midst of them.

She recognized Herman Fleischer instantly. She had run almost against his chest, and his huge body towered over her. She screamed with shock and twisted away from the bear-like arms outspread to clutch her.

Two of the native Askari who were working over the crude litter on which lay Flynn O'Flynn, jumped up. As she ran they closed on her from either side, the way a pair of trained greyhounds will course a hare. They caught her between them, and dragged her struggling and screaming to where Herman Fleischer waited.

'Ah, so!' Fleischer nodded pleasantly in greeting. 'You have come in time for the fun.' Then he turned to his sergeant. 'Have them tie the woman.'

Rosa's screams penetrated the light mists of insensibility that screened Flynn's brain. He stirred on the litter, muttering incoherently, rolling his head from side to side, then he opened his eyes and focused them with difficulty. He saw her struggling between the Askari and he snapped back into full consciousness.

'Leave her!' he roared. 'Call those bloody animals off. Leave her, you murderous bloody German bastard.'

'Good!' said Herman Fleischer. 'You are awake now.' Then he lifted his voice above Flynn's bellows. 'Hurry, Sergeant, tie the woman—and get the rope up.'

While they secured Rosa, one of the Askari shinned up the smooth yellow trunk of a fever tree. With his bayonet he hacked the twigs from the thick horizontal branch above their heads. The sergeant threw the end of the rope up to him, and at the second attempt the Askari caught it and passed it over the branch. Then he dropped back to earth.

There was a hangman's knot fixed in the rope, ready for use.

'Set the knot,' said Fleischer, and the sergeant went to where Flynn lay. With poles cut from a small tree they had rigged a combination litter and splints. The poles had been laid down Flynn's flanks from ankle to armpit, with bark strips they had bound them firmly so that Flynn's body was held rigidly as that of an Egyptian mummy, only his head and neck were free.

The sergeant stooped over him, and Flynn fell silent, watching him venomously. As his hands came down with the noose to loop it over Flynn's head, Flynn moved suddenly. He darted his head forward like a striking adder and fastened his teeth in the man's wrist. With a howl the sergeant tried to pull away, but Flynn held on, his head jerking and wrenching as the man struggled.

'Fool,' grunted Fleischer, and strode over to the litter. He lifted his foot and placed it on Flynn's lower body. As he brought his weight down on it Flynn stiffened and gasped with pain, releasing the Askari's wrist.

'Do it this way.' Fleischer lunged forward and took a handful of Flynn's hair, roughly he yanked Flynn's head forward. 'Now, the rope quickly.'

The Askari dropped the noose over Flynn's head and drew the slip-knot tight until it lay snugly under Flynn's ear.

'Good.' Fleischer stepped back. 'Four men on the rope,' he ordered. 'Gently. Do not jerk the rope. Walk away with it slowly. I don't want to break his neck.'

Rosa's hysteria had stilled into cold horror as she watched the preparations for the execution, and now she found her voice again.

'Please,' she whispered. 'He's my father. Please don't. Oh no, please don't.'

'Hush, girl,' roared Flynn. 'You'd not shame me now by pleading with this fat bag of pus.' He swivelled his head, his eyes rolled towards the four Askari who stood ready with the rope end. 'Pull! You black sons of bitches. Pull! And damn you. I'll beat you to hell, and speak to the devil so he'll have you castrated and smeared with pig's fat.'

'You heard what Fini told you,' smiled Fleischer at his Askari. 'Pull!'

And they walked backwards in single file, shuffling through the dead leaves, leaning against the rope.

The litter lifted slowly at one end, came upright and then left the ground.

Rosa turned away and clenched her eyelids tight closed, but her hands were bound so she could not stop her ears, she could not keep out the sounds that Flynn Patrick O'Flynn made as he died.

When at last there was silence, Rosa was shivering. Hard spasms that shuddered through her whole body.

'All right,' said Herman Fleischer. 'That's it. Bring the woman. We can get back to camp in time for lunch if we hurry.'

When they were gone, the litter and its contents still hung in the fever tree. Swinging a little and turning slowly on the end of the rope. Near it lay the carcass of the elephant, and a vulture planed down slowly and made a flapping ungainly landing in the top branches of the fever tree. It sat hunched and suspicious, then suddenly squawked and launched again into noisy flight, for it had seen the man coming.

The little old man limped slowly into the grove. He stopped beside the dead elephant and looked up at the man who had been his master and his friend.

'Go in peace, Fini!' said Mohammed.

78

The alleyway was a narrow low-roofed corridor, the bulkheads were painted a pale grey that glistened in the harsh light of the electric globes set in small wire cages at regular intervals along the roof.

At the end of the corridor, a guard stood outside the heavy watertight door in the bulkhead that led through into the handling room of the forward magazine. The guard wore only a thin white singlet and white flannel trousers, but his waist was belted in a blancoed webbing from which hung a sheathed bayonet, and there was a Mauser rifle slung from his shoulder.

From his position he could look into the handling room, and he could keep the full length of the alleyway under surveillance.

A double file of Wakamba tribesmen filled the alleyway, living chains along one of which passed the cordite charges; along the other the nine-inch shells.

The Africans worked with the stoical indifference of draught animals, turning to grip the ugly cylindro-conical shells, hugging a hundred and twenty pounds' weight of steel and explosive to their chests while they moved it on to the next man in the chain.

The cordite charges, each wrapped in thick paper, were not so weighty and moved more swiftly along their line. Each man bobbed and swung as he handled his load, so it seemed that the two ranks were sets in a complicated dance pattern.

From this mass of moving humanity rose clouds of warm body odour, that filled the alleyway and defeated the efforts of the air-conditioning fans.

Sebastian felt sweat trickling down his chest and back under the leather cloak, he felt also the tug of weight within the folds of the cloak each time he swung to receive a fresh cordite charge from his neighbour.

He stood just outside the door of the handling room, and each time he passed a charge through, he looked into the interior of the magazine where another gang was at work, packing the charges into the shelves that lined the bulkheads, and easing the nine-inch shells into their steel racks. Here there was another armed guard.

The work had been in progress since early that morning, with a half-hour's break at noon, so the German guards had relaxed their vigilance. They were restless in anticipation of relief. The one in the magazine was a fat middle-aged man who at intervals during the day had broken the monotony by releasing sudden ear-splitting posterior discharges of gas. With each salvo he had clapped the nearest African porter on the back and shouted happily.

'Have a bite at that one!' or, 'Cheer up—it doesn't smell.'

But at last he also was deflated. He slouched across the handling room, and leaned against the angle of the door to address his colleague in the alleyway.

'It's hot as hell, and smells like a zoo. These savages stink.'

'You've been doing your share.'

'I'll be glad when it's finished.'

'It's cooler in the magazine with the fans running—you are all right.'

'Jesus, I'd like to sit down for a few minutes.'

'Better not, Lieutenant Kyller is on the prowl.'

This exchange was taking place within a few feet of Sebastian. He followed the German conversation with more ease now that he had been able to exercise his rusty vocabulary, but he kept his head down in a renewed burst of energy. He was worried. In a short while the day's shift would end and the African porters would be herded on deck and into the launches to be transported to their camp on one of the islands. None of the native labour force were allowed to spend the night aboard *Blücher*.

He had waited since noon for an opportunity to enter the magazine and place the time charge. But he had been frustrated by the activities of the two German guards. It must be nearly seven o'clock in the evening now. It would have to be soon, very soon. He glanced once more into the magazine, and he caught the eye of Walaka, Mohammed's cousin. Walaka stood by the cordite shelves, supervising the packing, and now he shrugged at Sebastian in eloquent helplessness.

Suddenly there was a thud of a heavy object being dropped to the deck, and a commotion of shouts in the alleyway behind Sebastian. He glanced round quickly. One of the bearers had fainted in the heat and fallen with a shell in his arms, the shell had rolled and knocked down another man. Now there was a milling confusion clogging the alleyway. The two guards moved forward, forcing their way into the press of black bodies, shouting hoarsely and clubbing with the rifle butts. It was the opportunity for which Sebastian had waited.

He stepped over the threshold of the magazine, and went to Walaka beside the cordite shelves.

'Send one of your men to take my place,' he whispered, and reaching up into the folds of his cloak he brought out the cigar box.

With his back towards the door of the magazine, using the cloak as a screen to hide his movements, he slipped the catch of the box and opened the lid.

His hands trembled with haste and nervous agitation as he fumbled with the winder of the travelling-clock. It clicked, and he saw the second hand begin its endless circuit of the dial. Even over the shouts and scuffling in the alleyway, the muted ticking of its mechanism seemed offensively loud to Sebastian. Hastily he shut the lid and glanced guiltily over his shoulder at the doorway. Walaka stood there, and his face was sickly grey with the tension of imminent discovery, but he nodded to Sebastian, a signal that the guards were still occupied without.

Reaching up to the nearest shelf, Sebastian wedged the cigar box between two of the paper-wrapped cylinders of cordite. Then he packed others over it, covering it completely.

He stood back and found with surprise that he was panting, his breathing whistling in his throat, and his legs felt as though they would collapse under him. He could feel the little drops of sweat prickling on his shaven head. In the white electric light they shone like glass beads on his velvety, black-stained skin.

'Is it done?' Walaka croaked beside him.

'It is done,' Sebastian croaked back at him, and suddenly he was overcome with a driving compulsion to be out of this steel room, out of this box-packed room with the ingredients of violent death and destruction; out of the stifling press of bodies that had surrounded him all day. A dreadful thought seized his imagination, suppose the artificer had erred in his assembly of the time charge, suppose that even now the battery was heating the wires of the detonator and bringing them to explosion point. He felt panic as he looked around wildly at the tons of cordite and shell around him. He wanted to run, to fight his way out and up into the open air. He made the first move, and then froze.

The commotion in the alleyway had subsided miraculously, and now only one voice was raised. It came from just outside the doorway, using the curt inflection of authority. Sebastian had heard that voice repeatedly during that long day, and he had come to dread it. It heralded danger.

'Get them back to work immediately,' snapped Lieutenant Kyller as he stepped over the threshold into the magazine. He drew a gold watch from the pocket of his tunic and read the time. 'It is five minutes after seven. There is still almost half an hour before you knock off.' He tucked the watch away, and swept the magazine with a gaze that missed no detail. He was a tall young man, immaculate in his tropical whites. Behind him the two guards were hurriedly straightening their dishevelled uniforms and trying to look efficient and intelligent.

'Yes, sir,' they said in unison.

For a moment Kyller's eyes rested on Sebastian. It was probably because Sebastian was the finest physical specimen among the bearers, he stood taller than the rest of them—as tall as Kyller himself. But Sebastian felt his interest was deeper. He felt that Kyller was searching beneath the stain on his skin, that he was naked of disguise beneath those eyes. He felt that Kyller would remember him, had marked him down in his memory.

'That shelf.' Kyller turned away from Sebastian and crossed the magazine. He went directly to the shelf on which Sebastian had placed his time charge, and he patted the cordite cylinders that Sebastian had handled. They were slightly awry. 'Have it repacked immediately,' said Kyller.

'Right away, sir,' said the fat guard.

Again Kyller's eyes rested on Sebastian. It seemed that he was about to speak, then he changed his mind. He stooped through the doorway and disappeared.

Sebastian stood stony still, appalled by the order that Kyller had given. The fat guard grimaced sulkily.

'Christ, that one is a busy bastard.' And he glared at the cordite shelf. 'There's nothing wrong there.' He crossed to it and fiddled ineffectually. After a moment he asked the guard at the door. 'Has Kyller gone yet?'

'Yes. He's gone down the companion-way into the sick-bay.'

'Good!' grunted the fat one. 'I'm damned if I'm going to waste half an hour repacking this whole batch.' He hunched his shoulders, and screwed up his face with effort. There was a bagpipe squeal, and the guard relaxed and grinned. 'That one was for Lieutenant Kyller, God bless him!'

79

Darkness was falling, and with it the temperature dropped a few degrees into the high eighties and created an illusion that the faint evening breeze was chilly. Sebastian hugged his cloak around his body, and shuffled along in the slow column of native labourers that dribbled over the side of the German battle cruiser into the waiting launches.

He was exhausted both in body and in mind from the strain of the day's labour in the magazine, so that he went down the catwalk and took his place in the whaler, moving in a state of stupor. When the boat shoved off and puttered up the channel towards the labour camp on the nearest island, Sebastian looked back at *Blücher* with the same dumb stare as the men who squatted beside him on the floorboards of the whaler. Mechanically he registered the fact that Commissioner Fleischer's steam launch was tied up alongside the cruiser.

'Perhaps the fat swine will be aboard when the whole lot blows to hell,' he thought wearily. 'I can at least hope for that.'

He had no way of knowing who else Herman Fleischer had taken aboard the cruiser with him. Sebastian had been below decks toiling in the handling room of the magazine when the launch arrived from up-river, and Rosa Oldsmith had been ushered up the catwalk by the Commissioner in person.

'Come along, Mädchen. We will take you to see the gallant captain of this fine ship.' Fleischer puffed jovially as he mounted the steps behind her. 'I am sure there are many interesting things that you can tell him.'

Bedraggled and exhausted with grief, pale with the horror of her father's death, and with cold hatred for the man who had engineered it, Rosa stumbled as she stepped from the catwalk on to the deck. Her hands were still bound in front of her so she could not check herself. She fell forward, letting herself fall uncaring, and with mild surprise felt hands hold and steady her.

She looked up at the man who had caught her, and in her confusion of mind she thought it was Sebastian. He was tall and dark and his hands were strong. Then she saw the peaked uniform cap with its golden insignia, and she jerked away from him in revulsion.

'Ah! Lieutenant Kyller.' Commissioner Fleischer spoke behind her. 'I have brought you a visitor—a lovely lady.'

'Who is she?' Kyller was appraising Rosa. Rosa could not understand a word that was spoken. She stood in quiet acceptance, her whole body drooping.

'This . . .' answered Fleischer proudly, '. . . is the most dangerous young lady in the whole of Africa. She is one of the leaders of the gang of English bandits that raided the column bringing down the steel plate from Dar es Salaam. It was she who shot and killed your engineer. I captured her and her father this morning. Her father was the notorious O'Flynn.'

'Where is he?' Kyller snapped.

'I hanged him.'

'You hanged him?' demanded Kyller. 'Without trial?'

'No trial was necessary.'

'Without interrogating him?'

'I brought in the woman for interrogation.'

Kyller was angry now, his voice crackled with it.

'I will leave it to Captain von Kleine to judge the wisdom of your actions,' and he turned to Rosa; his eyes dropped to her hands, and, with an exclamation of concern, he took her by the wrist.

'Commissioner Fleischer, how long has this woman been bound?'

Fleischer shrugged. 'I could take no chances on her escaping.'

'Look at this!' Kyller indicated Rosa's hands. They were swollen, the fingers puffy and blue, sticking out stiffly, dead-looking and useless.

'I could take no chances.' Fleischer bridled at the implied criticism.

'Give me your knife,' Kyller snapped at the petty officer in charge of the gangway, and the man produced a large clasp knife. He opened it and handed it to the lieutenant.

Carefully Kyller ran the blade between Rosa's wrists and sawed at the rope. As he bonds dropped away Rosa cried out in pain of fresh blood flowing into her hands.

'You will be lucky if you have not done her permanent damage,' Kyller muttered furiously as he massaged Rosa's bloated hands.

'She is a criminal. A dangerous criminal,' growled Fleischer.

'She is a woman, and therefore deserving of your consideration. Not of this barbarous treatment.'

'She will hang.'

'Her crimes she will answer for, in due course—but until she has stood trial she will be treated as a woman.'

Rosa did not understand the harsh German argument that raged around her. She stood quietly and her eyes were fastened on the knife in Lieutenant Kyller's hand. The hilt brushed her fingers as he worked to restore the circulation of her blood. The blade was long and silver bright, she had seen how keen was its edge by the way in which it had cut through the rope. As she stared at it, it seemed to her fevered fancy that there were two names engraved in the steel of the blade. The names of the two persons she had loved. The names of her father and her child.

With an effort she tore her gaze from the knife and looked at the man she hated. Fleischer had come close up to her, as though to take her away from Lieutenant Kyller's attention. His face was flushed with anger and the fold of flesh under his chin wobbled flabbily as he argued.

Rosa flexed her fingers. They were still numb and stiff, but she could feel the strength flowing back into them. She let her gaze drop down to Fleischer's belly.

It jutted out round and full, soft-looking under the grey corduroy tunic, and again her fevered imagination formed a picture of the blade going into that belly. Slipping in silently, smoothly, burying itself to the hilt, and then drawing upwards to open the flesh like a pouch. The picture was so vivid that Rosa shuddered with the intense sensual pleasure of it.

Kyller was completely occupied with Fleischer. He felt the girl's fingers slide into the cupped palm of his right hand, but before he could pull away she had scooped the knife deftly from his grip. He lunged at her, but she pirouetted lightly away from him. Her knife hand dropped and then darted forward, driven by the full weight of her body at the bulging belly of Herman Fleischer.

Rosa thought that because he was fat he would be slow. She expected him to be stunned by the unexpected attack, to stand and take the knife in his vitals.

Herman Fleischer was fully alert before she even started her thrust. He was fast as a striking mamba, and strong beyond credibility. He did not make the mistake of intercepting the knife with his bare hands. Instead he struck her right shoulder with a clenched fist the size of a carpenter's mallet. The force of the blow knocked her sideways, deflecting the blade from its target. Her arm from the shoulder downwards was paralysed, and the knife flew from her hand and slithered away across the deck.

'Ja!' roared Fleischer triumphantly. 'Ja! So! Now you see how I was right to tie the bitch. She is vicious, dangerous.'

And he lifted the huge fist to smash it into Rosa's face as she crouched, hugging her hurt shoulder, and sobbing with pain and disappointment.

'Enough!' Kyller stepped between them. 'Leave her.'

'She must be tied up like an animal—she is dangerous,' bellowed Fleischer, but Kyller put a protective arm around Rosa's bowed shoulders.

'Petty Officer,' he said. 'Take this woman to the sick-bay. Have Surgeon Commander Buchholz see to her. Guard her carefully, but be gentle with her. Do you hear me?' And they took her away below.

'I must see Captain von Kleine,' Fleischer demanded. 'I must make a full report to him.'

'Come,' said Kyller, 'I will take you to him.'

80

Sebastian lay on his side beside the smoky little fire with his cloak draped over him. Outside he heard the night sounds of the swamp, the faint splash of a fish or a crocodile in the channel, the clink and boom of the tree frogs, the singing of insects, and the lap and sigh of wavelets on the mud bank below the hut.

The hut was one of twenty crude open-sided shelters that housed the native labour force. The earth floor was thickly strewn with sleeping bodies. The sound of their breathing was a restless murmur, broken by the cough and stir of dreamers.

Despite his fatigue, Sebastian was not sleeping, he could not relax from the state of tension in which he had been held all that day. He thought of the little travelling-clock ticking away in its nest of high explosive, measuring out the minutes and the hours, and then his mind side-stepped and went to Rosa. The muscles of his arms tightened with longing. Tomorrow, he thought, tomorrow I will see her and we will go away from this stinking river. Up into the sweet air of the highlands. Again his mind jumped. Seven o'clock, seven o'clock tomorrow morning and it will be over. He remembered Lieutenant Kyller's voice as he stood in the doorway of the magazine with the gold watch in his hand. '. . . The time is five minutes past seven . . .' he had said. So that Sebastian knew to within a few minutes when the time fuse would explode.

He must stop the porters going aboard *Blücher* in the morning. He had impressed on old Walaka that they must refuse to turn out for the next day's shift. They must . . .

'Manali! Manali!' his name was whispered close by in the gloom, and Sebastian lifted himself on one elbow. In the flickering light from the fire there was a shadowy figure, crawling on hands and knees across the earthen floor, and searching the faces of the sleeping men.

'Manali, where are you?'

'Who is it?' Sebastian answered softly, and the man jumped up and scurried to where he lay.

'It is I, Mohammed.'

'Mohammed?' Sebastian was startled. 'Why are you here? You should be with Fini at the camp on the Abati.'

'Fini is dead.' Mohammed's whisper was low with sorrow, so low that Sebastian thought he had misunderstood.

'What? What did you say?'

'Fini is dead. The Allemand came with the ropes. They hung him in the fever trees beside the Abati, and when he was dead they left him for the birds.'

'What talk is this?' Sebastian demanded.

'It is true,' mourned Mohammed. 'I saw it, and when the Allemand had gone, I cut the rope and brought him down. I wrapped him in my own blanket and buried him in an ant-bear hole.'

'Dead? Flynn dead? It isn't true!'

'It is true, Manali.' In the red glow of the camp-fire Mohammed's face was old and raddled and gaunt. He licked his lips. 'There is more, Manali. There is more to tell.'

But Sebastian was not listening. He was trying to force his mind to accept the reality of Flynn's death, but it baulked. It would not accept the picture of Flynn swinging at the rope's end, Flynn with the rope burns at his throat and his face swollen and empurpled, Flynn wrapped in a dirty blanket and crammed into an ant-bear hole. Flynn dead? No! Flynn was too big, too vital–they could not kill Flynn.

'Manali, hear me.'

Sebastian shook his head, bemused, denying it. It could not be true.

'Manali, the Allemand, they have taken Little Long Hair. They have bound her with ropes and taken her.'

Sebastian winced, and jerked away as though he had been struck open-handed across the face.

'No!' He tried to close his mind against the words.

'They caught her this morning early as she went to Fini. They took her down-river in the small boat, and she is now on the great ship of the Allemand.'

'*Blücher?* Rosa is aboard *Blücher?*'

'Yes. She is there.'

'No. Oh, God, *no!*'

In five hours *Blücher* would blow up. In five hours Rosa would die. Sebastian swung his head and looked out into the night, he looked through the open side of the hut, down the channel to where *Blücher* lay at her moorings half a mile away. There was a dim glow of light across the water from the hooded lanterns on *Blücher*'s main deck. But her form was indistinguishable against the dark mass of the mangroves. Between her and the island, the channel was a smooth expanse of velvety blackness on which the reflections of the stars were scattered sequins of light.

'I must go to her,' said Sebastian. 'I cannot let her die there alone.' His voice gathered strength and resolve. 'I cannot let her die. I'll tell the Germans where to find the charge–I'll tell them . . .' Then he faltered. 'I can't. No, I can't. I'd be a traitor then, but, but . . .'

He threw aside his cloak.

'Mohammed, how did you come here? Did you bring the canoe? Where is it?'

Mohammed shook his head. 'No. I swam. My cousin brought me close to the island in the canoe, but he has gone away. We could not leave the canoe here, lest the Askari find it. They would have seen the canoe.'

'There isn't a boat on the island—nothing,' muttered Sebastian. The Germans were careful to guard against deserters. Each night the labour force was marooned on the island—and the Askari patrolled the mud banks.

'Mohammed, hear me now,' Sebastian reached across and laid his hand on the man's shoulders. 'You are my friend. I thank you that you have come to tell me these things.'

'You are going to Little Long Hair?'

'Yes.'

'Go in peace, Manali.'

'Take my place here, Mohammed. When the guards count tomorrow morning, you will stand for me.' Sebastian tightened his grip on the bony shoulder. 'Stay in peace, Mohammed.'

His blackened body blending into the darkness, Sebastian crouched beneath the spread branches of a clump of pampa scrub, and the Askari guard almost brushed against him as he passed. The Askari slouched along with his rifle slung so that the barrel stood up behind his shoulder. The constant patrolling had beaten a path around the circumference of the island, the guard followed it mechanically. Half asleep on his feet, completely unaware of Sebastian's presence. He stumbled in the darkness and swore sleepily, and moved on.

Sebastian crossed the path on his hands and knees, then stretched out on his belly into a reptilian slither as he reached the mud bank. Had he tried to walk across it, the glutinous mud would have sucked so loudly around his feet that every guard within a hundred yards would have heard him.

The mud coated his chest and belly and legs with its coldly loathsome, clinging oiliness, and the reek of it filled his nostrils so he gagged. Then he was into the water. The water was blood warm, he felt the tug of the current and the bottom dropped away beneath him. He swam to the side, careful that neither legs nor arms should break the surface. His head alone showed, like the head of a swimming otter, and he felt the mud washing off his body.

He swam across the current, guided by the distant glimmer of *Blücher*'s deck lights. He swam slowly, husbanding his strength, for he knew he would need all of it later.

His mind was filled with layers of awareness. The lowest layer was a lurking undirected terror of the dark water in which he swam, his dangling legs were vulnerable to the scaly predators which infested the Rufiji river. The current must be carrying his scent down to them. Soon they would come hunting up to find him. But he kept up the easy stroke of arms and legs. It was a chance, one chance of the many he was taking and he tried to ignore it and grapple with the practical problems of his attempt. When he reached *Blücher*, how was he to get aboard her? Her sides were fifty feet high, and the catwalks were the only means of access. These were both heavily guarded. It was a problem without solution, and yet he harried it.

Over this was a thick layer of hopeless sorrow. Sorrow for Flynn.

But the uppermost layer was thickest, strongest. Rosa, Rosa, and Rosa.

He found with surprise that he was saying it aloud.

'Rosa!' with each forward thrust of his body through the water.

'Rosa!' each time he drew breath.

'Rosa!' as his legs kicked out and pushed him towards the *Blücher*.

He did not know what he would do if he reached her. Perhaps there was some half-formed idea of escaping with her, of fighting his way out of *Blücher* with his woman. Getting her away before that moment when the ship would vanish in a holocaust of flame. He did not know, but he swam on quietly.

Then he was under *Blücher*'s side. The towering mass of steel blotted out the starry night sky, and he stopped swimming and hung in the warm water looking up at her.

There were small sounds. The hum of machinery within her, the faint clang of metal struck against metal, the low guttural murmur of voices at her gangway, the thump of a rifle butt against the wooden deck, the soft wash of water around the hull—and then a closer, clearer sound, a regular creak and tap, creak and tap.

He swam in towards the hull, searching for the source of this new sound. It came from near the bows, creak and tap. The creak of rope, and the tap of wood against the steel hull. He saw it then, just above his head. He almost cried out with joy.

The cradles! The platforms still suspended above the water on which the welders and the painters had worked.

He reached up and gripped the wooden edge and drew himself on to the platform. He rested a few seconds and then began to climb the rope. Hand over hand, gripping the rope between the insides of his bare feet, he went up.

His head came level with the deck and he hung there, searching carefully. Fifty yards away he saw two seamen at the gangway. Neither was looking his way.

At intervals the hooded lanterns threw puddles of yellow light upon the deck, but there were concealing shadows beyond them. It was dark around the base of the forward gun-turrets, and there were piles of material, abandoned welding equipment, heaps of rope and canvas in the shadows which would hide him when he had crossed the deck.

Once more he checked the two guards at the gangway, their backs were turned to him.

Sebastian filled his lungs and steeled himself to act. Then with one fluid movement he drew himself up and rolled over the side. He landed lightly on his feet and darted across the exposed deck into the shadows. He ducked down behind a pile of canvas and rope netting, and struggled to control his breathing. He could feel his legs trembling violently under him, so he sat down on the planking and huddled against the protecting pile of canvas. River water trickled from his shaven pate over his forehead and into his eyes. He wiped it away.

'Now what?' He was aboard *Blücher*, but what should he do next?

Where would they hold Rosa? Was there some sort of guard-room for prisoners? Would they put her in one of the officer's cabins? The sick-bay?

He knew roughly where the sick-bay was located. While he was working in the magazine he had heard the one German guard say, 'He has gone down the companion-way to the sick-bay.'

It must be somewhere just below the forward magazine—oh, God! If they had her there she would be almost at the centre of the explosion.

He came up on his knees, and peered over the pile of canvas. It was lighter now. Through the screen of camouflage netting, he could see the night sky had paled a little in the east. Dawn was not far off. The night had passed so swiftly, morning was on its way, and there were but a few scant hours before the hands of the travelling-clock completed their journey, and made the electrical connection that would seal the *Blücher*'s fate, and the fate of all those aboard her.

He must move. He rose slowly and then froze. The guards at the gangway had come to attention. They stood stiffly with their rifles at the slope, and into the light stepped a tall, white-clad figure.

There was no mistaking him. It was the officer that Sebastian had last seen in the forward magazine. Kyller, they had called him, Lieutenant Kyller.

Kyller acknowledged the salutes of the two guards, and he spoke with them a while. Their voices were low and indistinct. Kyller saluted again, and then left them. He came down the deck towards the bows; he walked briskly, and his face below the peak of his cap was in darkness.

Sebastian crouched down again, only his eyes lifted above the piled canvas. He watched the officer and he was afraid.

Kyller stopped in mid-stride. He half stooped to look at the deck at his feet, and then in the same movement, straightened with his right hand dropping to the holstered pistol on his belt.

'Guard!' he bellowed. 'Here! At the double!'

On the holystoned white planking, the wet footprints that Sebastian had left behind him glittered in the lantern light. Kyller started in the direction that they led, coming directly towards Sebastian's hiding-place.

The boots of the two guards pounded heavily along the deck. They had unslung their rifles as they ran to join Kyller.

'Someone has come aboard here. Spread out and search . . .' Kyller shouted at them, as he closed in on Sebastian.

Sebastian panicked. He jumped up and ran, trying to reach the corner of the gun-turret.

'There he is!' Kyller's voice. 'Stop! Stop or I'll fire.'

Sebastian ran. His legs driving powerfully, his elbows pumping, head down, bare feet slapping on the planking, he raced through shadow.

'Stop!' Kyller was balanced on the balls of his feet, legs braced, right shoulder thrust forward and right arm outflung in the classic stance of the pistol marksman. The arm dropped slowly and then kicked up violently, as the shot spouted from the Luger in a ball of yellow flame. The bullet spanged against the plating of the turret and then glanced off in whining ricochet.

Sebastian felt the wind of the bullet pass his head and he jinked his run. The corner of the turret was very close, and he dodged towards it.

Then Kyller's next shot blurted loudly in the night, and simultaneously something struck Sebastian a heavy blow under his left shoulder-blade. It threw him forward off balance and he reeled against the turret, his hands scrabbled at the smooth steel without finding purchase. His body flattened against the side of the turret, so that the blood from the exit hole that the bullet had torn in his breast sprayed on to the pale grey, painted turret.

His legs buckled and he slid down, slowly, still trying to find purchase with the hooked claws of his fingers, so that as his knees touched the deck he was in the attitude of devout prayer. Forehead pressed against the turret, kneeling, arms spread high and wide.

Then the arms sank down, and he slid sideways, collapsed on to the deck, and rolled on to his back.

Kyller came and stood over him. The pistol hanging slackly in the hand at his side.

'Oh, my God,' there was genuine regret in Kyller's voice. 'It's only one of the porters. Why did the fool run! I wouldn't have fired if he had stood.'

Sebastian wanted to ask him where Rosa was. He wanted to explain that Rosa was his wife, that he loved her, and that he had come to find her.

He concentrated his vision on Kyller's face as it hung over him, and he summoned his school-boy German, marshalling the sentences in his mind.

But as he opened his mouth the blood welled up in his throat and choked him. He coughed, racking, and the blood bubbled through his lips in a pink froth.

'Lung shot!' said Kyller, and then to the guards as they came up, 'Get a stretcher. Hurry. We must take him down to the sick-bay.'

81

There were twelve bunks in *Blücher*'s sick-bay, six down each side of the narrow cabin. In eight of them lay German seamen; five malaria cases and three men injured in the work of repairing her bows.

Rosa Oldsmith was in the bunk farthest from the door. She lay behind a movable screen, and a guard sat outside the screen. He wore a pistol at his belt and was wholly absorbed in a year-old variety magazine, the cover of which depicted a buxom blonde woman in a black corset and high boots, with a horse whip in her one hand.

The cabin was brightly lit and smelled of antiseptic. One of the malarial cases was in delirium, and he laughed and shouted. The medical orderly moved along the rows of bunks carrying a metal tray from which he administered the morning dosages of quinine. The time was 5 a.m.

Rosa had slept only intermittently during the night. She lay on top of the blankets and she wore a striped towelling dressing-gown over the blue flannel night-gown. The gown was many sizes too large and she had rolled back the cuffs of the sleeves. Her hair was loose on the pillows, and damp at the temples with sweat. Her face was pale and drawn, with bluish smudges of fatigue under her eyes, and her shoulder ached dully where Fleischer had struck her.

She was awake now. She lay staring up at the low roof of the cabin, playing over in her mind fragments from the happenings of the last twenty-four hours.

She recalled the interrogation with Captain von Kleine. He had sat opposite her in his luxuriously furnished cabin, and his manner had been kindly, his voice gentle, pronouncing the English words with blurring of the consonants and a hardening of the vowel sounds. His English was good.

'When did you last eat?' he asked her.

'I am not hungry,' she replied, making no attempt to conceal her hatred. Hating them all—this handsome, gentle man, the tall lieutenant who stood beside him, and Herman Fleischer who sat across the cabin from her, with his knees spread apart to accommodate the full hang of his belly.

'I will send for food.' Von Kleine ignored her protest and rang for his steward. When the food came, she could not deny the demands of her body and she ate, trying to show no enjoyment. The sausage and pickles were delicious, for she had not eaten since the previous noon.

Courteously von Kleine turned his attention to a discussion with Lieutenant Kyller until she had finished, but when the steward removed the empty tray he came back to her.

'Herr Fleischer tells me you are the daughter of Major O'Flynn, the commander of the Portuguese irregulars operating in German territory?'

'I was until he was hanged, murdered! He was injured and helpless. They tied him to a stretcher . . .' Rosa flared at him, tears starting in her eyes.

'Yes,' von Kleine stopped her, 'I know. I am not pleased. That is now a matter between myself and Commissioner Fleischer. I can only say that I am sorry. I offer you my condolence.' He paused and glanced at Herman Fleischer. Rosa could see by the angry blue of his eyes that he meant what he said.

'But now there are some questions I must ask you . . .'

Rosa had planned her replies, for she knew what he would ask. She replied frankly and truthfully to anything that did not jeopardize Sebastian's attempt to place the time fuse aboard *Blücher*.

What were she and Flynn doing when they were captured? Keeping the *Blücher* under surveillance. Waiting to signal her departure to the blockading cruisers.

How did the British know that Blücher was in the Rufiji? The steel plate, of course. Then confirmation by aerial reconnaissance.

Were they contemplating offensive action against Blücher? No, they would wait until she sailed.

What was the strength of the blockade squadron? Two cruisers that she had seen, she did not know if there were other warships waiting over the horizon.

Von Kleine phrased his questions carefully, and listened attentively to her replies. For an hour the interrogation continued, until Rosa was yawning openly, and her voice was slurred with exhaustion. Von Kleine realized that there was nothing to be learned from her, all she had told him he already knew or had guessed.

'Thank you,' he finished. 'I am keeping you aboard my ship. There will be danger here, for soon I will be going out to meet the British warships. But I believe that it will be better for you than if I handed you over to the German administration ashore.' He hesitated a moment and glanced at Commissioner Fleischer. 'In every nation there are evil men, fools and barbarians. Do not judge us all by one man.'

With distaste at her own treachery, Rosa found that she could not hate this man. A weary smile tugged her mouth and she answered him.

'You are kind.'

'Lieutenant Kyller will see you to the hospital. I am sorry I can offer you no better quarters, but this is a crowded vessel.'

When she had gone, von Kleine lit a cheroot and while he tasted its comforting fragrance, he allowed his eyes to rest on the portrait of the two golden women across the cabin. Then he sat up in his chair and his voice had lost its gentleness as he spoke to the man who lolled on the couch.

'Herr Fleischer, I find it difficult to express fully my extreme displeasure at your handling of this affair . . .'

After a night of fitful sleep, Rosa lay on her hospital bunk behind the screen and she thought of her husband. If things had gone well Sebastian must by now have placed the time charge and escaped from *Blücher*. Perhaps he was already on his way to the rendezvous on the Abati river. If this were so, then she would not see him again. It was her one regret. She imagined him in his ludicrous disguise, and she smiled a little. Dear lovable Sebastian. Would he ever know what had happened to her? Would he know that she had died with those whom she hated? She hoped that he would never know—that he would never torture himself with the knowledge that he had placed the instrument of her death with his own hands.

I wish I could see him just once more to tell him that my death is unimportant beside the death of Herman Fleischer, beside the destruction of this German warship. I wish only that when the time comes, I could see it. I wish there were some way I could know the exact time of the explosion so I could tell Herman Fleischer a minute before, when it is too late for him to escape, and watch him. Perhaps he would blubber, perhaps he would scream with fear. I would like that. I would like that very much.

The strength of her hatred was such that she could no longer lie still. She sat up and tied the belt of her gown around her waist. She was filled with a restless itchy exhilaration. It would be today—she felt sure—sometime today she would slake this burning thirst for vengeance that had tormented her for so long.

She threw her legs over the side of the bunk and pulled open the screen. The guard dropped his magazine and started up from his chair, his hand dropping to the pistol at his hip.

'I will not harm you . . .' Rosa smiled at him, '. . . not yet!'

She pointed to the door which led into the tiny shower cabinet and toilet. The guard relaxed and nodded acquiescence. He followed her as she crossed the cabin.

Rosa walked slowly between the bunks, looking at the sick men that lay in them.

'All of you,' she thought happily. 'All of you!'

She slid the tongue of the lock across, and was alone in the bathroom. She undressed, and leaned across the wash-basin to the small mirror set above it. She could see the reflection of her head and shoulders. There was a purple and red bruise spreading down from her neck and staining the white swell of her right breast. She touched it tenderly with her finger-tips.

'Herman Fleischer,' she said the name gloatingly, 'it will be today—I promise you that. Today you will die.'

And then suddenly she was crying.

'I only wish you could burn as my baby burned—I wish you could choke and swing on the rope as my father did.' And the tears fell fat and slow, sliding down her cheeks to drop into the basin. She started to sob, dry convulsive gasps of grief and hatred. She turned blindly to the shower cabinet, and turned both taps full on so that the rush of the water would cover the sound of her weeping. She did not want them to hear it.

Later, when she had bathed her face and body and combed her hair and dressed again, she unlocked the door and stepped through it. She stopped abruptly and through puffy reddened eyes tried to make sense of what was happening in the sick-bay.

It was crowded. The surgeon was there, two orderlies, four German seamen, and the young lieutenant. All of them hovered about the stretcher that was being manœuvred between the bunks. There was a man on the stretcher, she could see his form under the single grey blanket that covered him, but Lieutenant Kyller's back obscured her view of the man's face. There was blood on the blanket, and a brown smear of blood on the sleeve of Kyller's white tunic.

She moved along the bulkhead of the cabin and craned her head to see around Kyller, but at that moment one of the orderlies leaned across to swab the mouth of the man on the stretcher with a white cloth. The cloth obscured the wounded man's face. Bright frothy blood soaked through the material, and the sight of it nauseated Rosa. She averted her gaze and slipped away towards her own bunk at the end of the cabin. She reached the screen, and behind her somebody groaned. It was a low delirious groan, but the sound of it stopped Rosa instantly. She felt as though something within her chest was swelling to stifle her. Slowly, fearfully, she turned back.

They were lifting the man from the stretcher to lay him on an empty bunk. The head lolled sideways, and beneath its stain of bark juice Rosa saw that dear, well loved face.

'Sebastian!' she cried, and she ran to him, pushing past Kyller, throwing herself on to the blanket-draped body, trying to get her arms around him to hug him.

'Sebastian! What have they done to you!'

82

'Sebastian! Sebastian!' Rosa leaned across him and held her mouth to his ear.

'Sebastian!' She called his name quietly but urgently, then brushed his forehead with her lips. The skin was cold and damp.

He lay on his back with the bed clothes turned back to his waist. His chest was swathed in bandages, and his breathing sawed and gurgled.

'Sebastian. It's Rosa. It's Rosa. Wake up, Sebastian. Wake up, it's Rosa.'

'Rosa?' At last her name had reached him. He whispered it painfully, wetly, and fresh blood stained his lips.

Rosa had been on the edge of despair. Two hours she had been sitting beside him. Since the surgeon had finished dressing the wound, she had sat with him—touching him, calling to him. This was the first sign of recognition he had given her.

'Yes! Yes! It's Rosa. Wake up, Sebastian.' Her voice lifted with relief.

'Rosa?' His eyelashes trembled.

'Wake up.' She pinched his cold cheek and he winced. His eyelids fluttered open.

'Rosa?' on a shallow, sawing breath.

'Here, Sebastian. I'm here.' His eyes rolled in their sockets, searching, trying desperately to focus.

'Here,' she said, leaning over him and taking his face between her hands. She looked into his eyes.

'Here, my darling, here!'

'Rosa!' His lips convulsed into a dreadful parody of a smile.

'Sebastian, did you set the bomb?'

His breathing changed, hoarser, and his mouth twitched with the effort.

'Tell them,' he whispered.

'Tell them what?'

'Seven. Must stop it.'

'Seven o'clock?'

'Don't–want–you–'

'Will it explode at seven o'clock?'

'You–' It was too much and he coughed.

'Seven o'clock? Is that it, Sebastian?'

'You will . . .' He squeezed his eyes closed, putting all his strength into the effort of speaking. 'Please. Don't die. Stop it.'

'Did you set it for seven o'clock?' In her impatience she tugged his head towards her. 'Tell me, for God's sake, tell me!'

'Seven o'clock. Tell them–tell them.'

Still holding him, she looked at the clock set high up on the bulkhead of the sick-bay.

On the white dial, the ornate black hands stood at fifteen minutes before the hour.

'Don't die, please don't die,' mumbled Sebastian.

She hardly heard the pain-muted pleading. A fierce surge of triumph lifted her–she knew the hour. The exact minute. Now she could send for Herman Fleischer, and have him with her.

Gently she laid Sebastian's head back on the pillow. On the table below the clock she had seen a pad and pencil among the bottles and jars, and trays of instruments. She went to it, and while the guard watched her suspiciously she scribbled a note.

Captain,
  My husband is conscious. He has a message of vital importance for Commissioner Fleischer. He will speak to no one but Commissioner Fleischer. The message could save your ship.
                                                                            Rosa Oldsmith

She folded the sheet of paper and pushed it into the guard's hand.

'For the Captain. Captain.'

'Kapitan,' repeated the guard. 'Jawohl.' And he went to the door of the sick-bay. She saw him speak with the second guard outside the door, and then pass him the note.

Rosa sank down on the edge of Sebastian's bunk. She ran her hand tenderly over his shaven head. The new hair was stiff and bristly under her fingers.

'Wait for me. I'm coming with you, my darling. Wait for me.'

But he had lapsed back into unconsciousness. Crooning softly, she gentled him. Smiling to herself, happily, she waited for the minute hand of the clock to creep up to the zenith of the dial.

83

Captain Arthur Joyce had personally supervised the placing of the scuttling charges. Perhaps, long ago, another man had felt the way he did–hearing the command spoken from the burning bush, and knowing he must obey.

The charges were small, but laid in twenty places against the bare plating, they would rip *Renounce*'s belly out of her cleanly. The watertight bulkhead had been opened to let the water rush through her. The magazines had all of them been flooded to minimize the danger of explosion. The furnaces had been damped down, and he had blown the pressure on his boilers–retaining a head of steam, just sufficient to take *Renounce* in on her last run into the channel of the Rufiji.

The cruiser had been stripped of her crew. Twenty men left aboard her to handle the ship. The rest of them transhipped aboard *Pegasus*.

Joyce was going to attempt to force the log boom, take *Renounce* through the minefield, and sink her higher up, where the double mouth of the channel merged into a single thoroughfare.

If he succeeded he would effectively have blocked *Blücher*, and sacrificed a single ship.

If he failed, if *Renounce* sank in the minefield before she reached the confluence of the two channels, then Armstrong would have to take *Pegasus* in and scuttle her also. On his bridge Joyce sat hunched in his canvas deck chair, looking out at the land; the green line of Africa which the morning sun lit in harsh golden brilliance.

Renounce was running parallel to the coast, five miles off shore. Behind her *Pegasus* trailed like a mourner at a funeral.

'06.45 hours, sir.' The officer of the watch saluted.

'Very well.' Joyce roused himself. Until this moment he had hoped. Now the time had come and *Renounce* must die.

'Yeoman of Signals,' he spoke quietly, 'make this signal with *Pegasus* number "Plan A Effective".' This was the code that *Renounce* was to stand in for the channel. 'Stand by to pick up survivors.'

'*Pegasus* acknowledges, sir.'

Joyce was glad that Armstrong has not sent some inane message such as 'Good luck'. A curt acknowledgement, that was as it should be.

'All right, Pilot,' he said, 'take us in, please.'

84

It was a beautiful morning and a flat sea. The captain of the escort destroyer wished it were not, he would have forfeited a year's seniority for a week of fog and rain.

As his ship tore down the line of transports to administer a rebuke to the steamer at the end of the column for not keeping proper station, he looked out at the western horizon. Visibility was perfect, a German masthead would be able to pick out this convoy of fat sluggish transports at a distance of thirty miles.

Twelve ships, fifteen thousand men–and *Blücher* could be out. At any moment she could come hurtling up over the horizon, with those long nine-inch guns blazing. The thought gave him the creeps. He jumped up from his stool, and crossed to the port rail of his bridge to glower at the convoy.

Close alongside wallowed one of the transports. They were playing cricket on her afterdeck. As he watched, a sun-bronzed giant of a South African clad only in short khaki pants swung the bat and cleanly he heard the crack as it struck the ball. The ball soared up and dropped into the sea with a tiny splash.

'Oh, good shot, sir!' applauded the lieutenant who stood beside the captain.

'This is not the members' enclosure at Lords, Mr Parkinson,' snarled the destroyer captain. 'If you have nothing to occupy you, I can find duties for you.'

The lieutenant retired hurt, and the captain glanced along the line of troopships.

'Oh, no!' he groaned. Number Three was making smoke again. Ever since leaving Durban harbour Number Three had been giving periodic impersonations of Mount Vesuvius. It would be a give-away to the look-out at *Blücher*'s masthead.

He reached for his megaphone, ready to hurl the most scathing reprimand he could master at Number Three as he passed her.

'This is worse than being a teacher in a kindergarten. They'll break me yet.' And he lifted the megaphone to his lips as Number Three came abreast.

The infantry men that lined the troopships' rail cheered his eloquence to the echo.

'The fools. Let them cheer *Blücher* when she comes,' growled the captain and crossed the bridge to gaze apprehensively into the west where Africa lay just below the horizon.

'Strength to *Renounce* and *Pegasus*.' He made the wish fervently. 'God grant they hold *Blücher*. If she gets through . . .'

85

'It's no use, Bwana. They won't move,' the sergeant of Askari reported to Ensign Proust.

'What is the trouble?' demanded Proust.

'They say there is a bad magic on the ship. They will not go to her today.'

Proust looked over the mass of black humanity. They squatted sullenly among the huts and palm trees, rank upon rank of them, huddled in their cloaks, faces closed and secretive.

Drawn up on the mud beaches of the island were two motor launches, ready to ferry the bearers downstream to the day's labour aboard *Blücher*. The German seamen tending the launches were watching with interest this charade of dumb rebellion, and Ensign Proust was very conscious of their attention.

Proust was at the age where he had an iron-clad faith in his own sagacity, the dignity of a patriarch, and pimples.

He was, in other words, nineteen years of age.

It was clear to him that these native tribesmen had embarked on their present course of action for no other reason than to embarrass Ensign Proust. It was a direct and personal attack on his standing and authority.

He lifted his right hand to his mouth and began to feed thoughtfully on his fingernails. His rather prominent Adam's apple moved in sympathy with the working of his jaws. Suddenly he realized what he was doing. It was a habit he was trying to cure, and he jerked his hand away and linked it with its mate behind his back, in a faithful imitation of Captain Otto von Kleine, a man whom he held in high admiration. It had hurt him deeply when Lieutenant Kyller had greeted his request for permission to grow a beard like Captain von Kleine's with ribald laughter.

Now he sank his bare chin on to his chest and began to pace solemnly up and down the small clearing above the mud bank. The sergeant of Askari waited respectfully with his men drawn up behind him for Ensign Proust to reach a decision.

He could send one of the launches back to *Blücher*, to fetch Commissioner Fleischer. After all, this was really the Herr Commissioner's shauri (Proust had taken to using odd Swahili words like an old African hand). Yet he realized that to call for Fleischer would be an admission that he was unable to handle the situation. Commissioner Fleischer would jeer at him, Commissioner Fleischer had shown an increasing tendency to jeer at Ensign Proust.

'No,' he thought, flushing so that the red spots on his skin were less noticeable, 'I will not send for that fat peasant.' He stopped pacing and addressed himself to the sergeant of Askari.

'Tell them . . .' he started, and his voice squeaked alarmingly. He adjusted the timbre to a deep throaty rumble, 'Tell them I take a very serious view of this matter.'

The sergeant saluted, did a showy about-face with much feet stamping, and passed on Ensign Proust's message in loud Swahili. From the dark ranks of bearers there was no reaction whatsoever, not so much as a raised eyebrow. The crews of the launches were more responsive. One of them laughed.

Ensign Proust's Adam's apple bobbed, and his ears chameleoned to the colour of a good burgundy.

'Tell them that it is *mutiny*!' The last word squeaked again, and the sergeant hesitated while he groped for the Swahili equivalent. Finally he settled for:

'Bwana Heron is very angry.' Proust had been nicknamed for his pointed nose and long thin legs. The tribesmen bore up valiantly under this intelligence.

'Tell them I will take drastic steps.'

Now, thought the sergeant, he is making sense. He allowed himself literary licence in his translation.

'Bwana Heron says that there are trees on this island for all of you–and he has sufficient rope.'

A sigh blew through them, soft and restless as a small wind in a field of wheat. Heads turned slowly until they were all looking at Walaka.

Reluctantly Walaka stood up to reply. He realized that it was foolhardy to draw attention to himself when there was talk of ropes in the air, but the damage had already been done. The hundreds of eyes upon him had singled him out to the Allemand. Bwana Intanbu always hanged the man that everyone looked at.

Walaka began to speak. His voice had the soothing quality of a rusty gate squeaking in the wind. It went on and on, as Walaka attempted a one-man filibust.

'What is he talking about?' demanded Ensign Proust.

'He is talking about leopards,' the sergeant told him.

'What is he saying about them?'

'He says, among other things, that they are the excrement of dead lepers.'

Proust looked stunned, he had expected Walaka's speech to have at least some bearing on the business in hand. He rallied gamely.

'Tell him that he is a wise old man, and that I look to him to lead the others to their duties.'

And the sergeant gazed upon Walaka sternly.

'Bwana Heron says that you, Walaka, are the son of a diseased porcupine and that you feed on offal with the vultures. He says further that you he has chosen to lead the others in the dance of the rope.'

Walaka stopped talking. He sighed in resignation and started down towards the waiting launch. Five hundred men stood up and followed him.

The two vessels chugged sedately down to *Blücher*'s moorings. Standing in the bows of the leading launch with his hands on his hips, Ensign Proust had the proud bearing of a Viking returning from a successful raid.

'I understand these people,' he would tell Lieutenant Kyller. 'You must pick out their leader and appeal to his sense of duty.'

He took his watch from his breast pocket.

'Fifteen minutes to seven,' he murmured. 'I'll have them aboard on the hour.' He turned and smiled fondly at Walaka who squatted miserably beside the wheel-house.

'Good man, that! I'll bring his conduct to Lieutenant Kyller's attention.'

86

Lieutenant Ernst Kyller shrugged out of his tunic and sat down on his bunk. He held the tunic in his lap and fingered the sleeve. The smear of blood had dried, and as he rubbed the material between his thumb and forefinger, the blood crumbled and flaked.

'He should not have run. I had to shoot.'

He stood up and hung the tunic in the little cupboard at the head of his bunk. Then he took his watch from the pocket and sat down again to wind it.

'Fifteen minutes to seven.' He noted the time mechanically, and laid the gold hunter on the flap table beside the bunk. Then he lay back and arranged the pillows under his head, he crossed his still-booted feet and regarded them dispassionately.

'He came aboard to try and rescue his wife. It was the natural thing to do. But that disguise—the shaven head, and stained skin—that must have been carefully thought out. It must have taken time to arrange.'

Kyller closed his eyes. He was tired. It had been a long and eventful watch. Yet there was something nagging him, a feeling that there was an important detail that he had overlooked, a detail of vital—no, of deadly importance.

Within two minutes of the girl's recognition of the wounded man, Kyller and the surgeon commander had established that he was not a native, but a white man disguised as one.

Kyller's English was sketchy, but he had understood the girl's cries of love and concern and accusation.

'You've killed him also. You've killed them all. My baby, my father—and now my husband. You murderers, you filthy murdering swines!'

Kyller grimaced and pressed his knuckles into his aching eyes. Yes, he had understood her.

When he had reported to Captain von Kleine, the captain had placed little importance on the incident.

'Is the man conscious?'

'No, sir.'

'What does the surgeon say his chances are?'

'He will die. Probably before midday.'

'You did the right thing, Kyller.' Von Kleine touched his shoulder in a show of understanding. 'Do not reproach yourself. It was your duty.'

'Thank you, sir.'

'You are off watch now. Go to your cabin and rest—that is an order. I want you fresh and alert by nightfall.'

'Is it tonight then, sir?'

'Yes. Tonight we sail. The minefield has been cleared and I have given the order for the boom to be destroyed. The new moon sets at 11.47. We will sail at midnight.'

But Kyller could not rest. The girl's face, pale, smeared with her tears, haunted him. The strangled breathing of the dying man echoed in his ears, and that nagging doubt scratched against his nerves.

There was something he must remember. He flogged his tired brain, and it balked.

Why was the man disguised? If he came as soon as he had heard that his wife was a prisoner he would not have had time to effect the disguise.

Where had the man been when Fleischer had captured his wife? He had not been there to protect her. Where had he been? It must have been somewhere near at hand.

Kyller rolled on to his stomach and pressed his face into the pillow. He must rest. He must sleep now for tonight they would go out to break through the blockading English warships.

A single ship against a squadron. Their chances of slipping through unchallenged were small. There would be a night action. His imagination was heightened by fatigue, and behind his closed eyelids he saw the English cruisers, lit by the flashes of their own broadsides as they closed with *Blücher*. The enemy intent on vengeance. The enemy in overwhelming strength. The enemy strong and freshly provisioned, their coal-bunkers glutted, their magazines crammed with shell, their crews uncontaminated by the fever miasma of the Rufiji.

Against them a single ship with her battle damage hastily patched, half her men sick with malaria, burning green cord-wood in her furnaces, her fire-power hampered by the desperate shortage of shell.

He remembered the tiers of empty shell racks, the depleted cordite shelves in the forward magazine.

The magazine? That was it? The magazine! It was something about the magazine that he must remember. That was the thing that had been nagging him. The magazine!

'Oh, my God!' he shouted in horror. In one abrupt movement he had leapt from his prone position on the bunk to stand in the centre of his cabin.

The skin on his bare upper arms prickled with goose-flesh.

That was where he had seen the Englishman before. He had been with the labour party—in the forward magazine.

He would have been there for one reason only—sabotage.

Kyller burst from his cabin, and raced, half dressed, along the corridor.

'I must get hold of Commander Lochtkamper. We'll need a dozen men—strong men—stokers. There are tons of explosive to move, we'll have to handle it all to find whatever the Englishman placed there. Please, God, give us time. Give us time!'

87

Captain Otto von Kleine bit the tip from the end of his cheroot, and removed a flake of tobacco from the tip of his tongue with thunb and forefinger. His steward held a match for him and von Kleine lit the cheroot. At the wardroom table, the chairs of Lochtkamper, Kyller, Proust, and one other were empty.

'Thank you, Schmidt,' he said through the smoke. He pushed his chair back and stretched out his legs, crossing his ankles and laying his shoulders against the padded back-rest. The breakfast had not been of gourmet standard; bread without butter, fish taken from the river and strong with the taste of the mud, washed down with black unsweetened coffee. Nevertheless, Herr Fleischer seemed to be enjoying it. He was beginning his third plateful.

Von Kleine found his appreciative snuffling distracting. This would be the last period of relaxation that von Kleine could anticipate in the next many days. He wanted to savour it along with his cheroot, the wardroom was not the place to do so. Apart from the gusto with which the Herr Commissioner was demolishing his breakfast, and the smell of fish—there was a mood among his officers that was almost tangible. This was the last day and it was heavy with the prospect of what the night might bring. They were all of them edgy and tense. They ate in silence, keeping their attention on their plates, and it was obvious that most of them had slept badly. Von Kleine decided to finish his cheroot alone in his cabin. He stood up.

'Excuse me please, gentlemen.'

A polite murmur, and von Kleine turned to leave.

'Yes, Schmidt. What is it?' His steward was standing deferentially in his path.

'For you, sir.'

Von Kleine clamped the cheroot between his teeth and took the note in both hands, screwing up his eyes against the blue spiral of tobacco smoke. He frowned.

This woman, and the man she claimed was her husband, worried him. They were a drain on the attention which he should be devoting entirely to the problem of getting *Blücher* ready for tonight. Now this message—what could she mean by 'could save your ship'? He felt a prickle of apprehension.

He swung around.

'Herr Commissioner, a moment of your time, please.'

Fleischer looked up from his food with a smear of grease on his chin.

'Ja?'

'Come with me.'

'I will just finish . . .'

'Immediately, please.' And to avert argument von Kleine stomped out of the wardroom, leaving Herman Fleischer in terrible indecision, but he was a man for the occasion, he took the remaining piece of fish on his plate and put it in his mouth. It was a tight fit, but he still found space for the half cup of coffee as well. Then he scooped up a slice of bread and wiped his plate hurriedly. With the bread in his hand he lumbered after von Kleine.

He was still masticating as he entered the sick-bay behind von Kleine. He stopped in surprise.

The woman sat on one of the bunks. She had a cloth in her hand and with it she wiped the mouth of a black man who lay there. There was blood on the cloth. She looked up at Fleischer. Her expression was soft with compassion and sorrow, but it changed the moment she saw Fleischer. She stood up quickly.

'Oh, thank God, you've come,' she cried with joy as though she were greeting a dear friend. Then incongruously she looked up at the clock.

Keeping warily away from her, Fleischer worked his way around to the opposite side of the bunk by which she stood. He leaned over and studied the face of the dying man. There was something very familiar about it. He chewed stolidly as he puzzled over it. It was the association with the woman that triggered his memory.

He made a choking sound, and bits of half chewed bread flew from his mouth.

'Captain!' he shouted, 'this is one of them—one of the English bandits.'

'I know,' said von Kleine.

'Why wasn't I told? This man must be executed immediately. Even now it might be too late. Justice will be cheated.'

'Please, Herr Commissioner. The woman has an important message for you.'

'This is monstrous. I should have been told . . .'

'Be still,' snapped von Kleine. Then to Rosa, 'You sent for me? What is it you have to tell us?'

With one hand Rosa was stroking Sebastian's head, but she was looking up at the clock.

'You must tell Herr Fleischer that the time is one minute before seven.'

'I beg your pardon?'

'Tell him exactly as I say it.'

'Is this a joke?'

'Tell him, quickly. There is very little time.'

'She says the time is one minute to seven' von Kleine rattled out the translation. Then in English, 'I have told him.'

'Tell him that at seven o'clock he will die.'

'What is the meaning of that?'

'Tell him first. Tell him!' insisted Rosa.

'She says that you will die at seven o'clock.' And Fleischer interrupted his impatient gobbling over the prone form of Sebastian. He stared at the woman for a moment, then he giggled uncertainly.

'Tell her I feel very well,' he said, and laughed again, 'better than this one here.' He prodded Sebastian. 'Ja, much better.' And his laughter came full and strong, booming in the confined space of the sick-bay.

'Tell him my husband has placed a bomb in this ship, and it will explode at seven o'clock.'

'Where?' demanded von Kleine.

'Tell him first.'

'If this is true you are in danger also—where is it?'

'Tell Fleischer what I said.'

'There is a bomb in the ship.' And Fleischer stopped laughing.

'She is lying,' he spluttered. 'English lies.'

'Where is the bomb?' von Kleine had grasped Rosa's arm.

'It is too late,' Rosa smiled complacently. 'Look at the clock.'

'Where is it?' Von Kleine shook her wildly in his agitation.

'In the *magazine*! The forward magazine.'

'In the *magazine*! Sweet merciful Jesus!' von Kleine swore in German, and turned for the door.

'The magazine?' shouted Fleischer and started after him. 'It is impossible—it can't be.' But he was running, wildly, desperately, and behind him he heard Rosa Oldsmith's triumphant laughter.

'You are dead. Like my baby—dead, like my father. It is too late to run, much too late!'

88

Von Kleine went up the companion-way steps three at a time. He came out into the alleyway that led to the magazine, and stopped abruptly.

The alleyway was almost blocked by a mountain of cordite charges thrown haphazard from the magazine by a knot of frantically busy stokers.

'What are you doing?' he shouted.

'Lieutenant Kyller is looking for a bomb.'

'Has he found it?' Von Kleine demanded as he brushed past them.

'Not yet, sir.'

Von Kleine paused again in the entrance to the magazine. It was a shambles. Led by Kyller, men were tearing at the stacks of cordite, sweeping them from the shelves, ransacking the magazine.

Von Kleine jumped forward to help.

'Why didn't you send for me?' he asked as he reached up to the racks above his head.

'No time, sir,' grunted Kyller beside him.

'How did you know about the bomb?'

'It's a guess—I could be wrong, sir.'

'You're right! The woman told us. It's set for seven o'clock.'

'Help us God! Help us!' pleaded Kyller, and hurled himself at the next shelf.

'It could be anywhere—anywhere!' Captain von Kleine worked like a stevedore, knee-deep in spilled cylinders of cordite.

'We should clear the ship. Get the men off.' Kyller attacked the next rack.

'No time. We've got to find it.'

Then in the uproar there was a small sound, a muffled tinny buzz. The alarm bell of a travelling-clock.

'There!' shouted Kyller. 'That's it!' And he dived across the magazine at the same moment as von Kleine did. They collided and fell, but Kyller was up instantly, dragging himself on to his feet with hands clawing at the orderly rack of cordite cylinders.

The buzz of the clock seemed to roar in his ears. He reached out and his hands fell on the smoothly paper wrapped parcel of death, and at that instant the two copper terminals within the leather case of the clock that had been creeping infinitesimally slowly towards each other for the past twelve hours, made contact.

Electricity stored in the dry cell battery flowed through the circuit, reached the hair-thin filament in the detonator cap, and heated it white-hot. The detonator fired, transferring its energy into the sticks of gelignite that were packed into the cigar box. The wave of explosion leapt from molecule to molecule with the speed of light so that the entire contents of *Blücher*'s magazine were consumed in one hundredth part of a second. With it were consumed Lieutenant Kyller and Captain von Kleine and the men about them.

In the centre of that fiery holocaust they burned to vapour.

The blast swept through *Blücher*. Downwards through two decks with a force that blew the belly out of her as easily as popping a paper bag, down through ten fathoms of water to strike the bottom of the river and the shock wave bounced up to raise fifteen-foot waves along the surface.

It blew sideways through *Blücher*'s watertight bulkheads, crumpling and tearing them like silver paper.

It caught Rosa Oldsmith as she lay across Sebastian's chest, hugging him. She did not even hear it come.

It caught Herman Fleischer just as he reached the deck, and shredded him to nothingness.

It swept through the engine room and burst the great boilers, releasing millions of cubic feet of scalding steam to race through the ship.

It blew upwards through the deck, lifting the forward gun-turret off its seating, tossing the hundreds of tons of steel high in a cloud of steam and smoke and debris.

It killed every single human being aboard. It did more that merely kill them, it reduced them to gas and minute particles of flesh or bone. Then still unsatisfied, its fury unabated, it blew outwards from *Blücher*'s shattered hulk, a mighty wind that tore the branches from the mangrove forest and stripped it of leaves.

It lifted a column of smoke and flame writhing and twisting into the bright morning sky above the Rufiji delta, and the waves swept across the river as though from the eye of a hurricane.

They overwhelmed the two launches that were approaching *Blücher*, pouring over them and capsizing them, swirling them over and over and spilling their human cargo into the frightened frothing water.

And the shock waves rolled on across the delta to burst thunderously against the far hills, or to dissipate out on the vastness of the Indian Ocean.

They passed over the British cruiser *Renounce* as she entered the channel between the mangroves. They rolled overhead like giant cannon-balls across the roof of the sky.

Captain Arthur Joyce leapt to the rail of his bridge, and he saw the column of agonized smoke rise from the swamps ahead of him. A grotesque living thing, unbelievable in its size, black and silver and shot through with flame.

'They've done it!' shouted Arthur Joyce. 'By Jove, they've done it!'

He was shaking; his whole body juddering, his face white as ice, and his eyes which he could not drag from that spinning column of destruction that rose into the sky, filled slowly with tears. He let them overflow his eyelids and run unashamedly down his cheeks.

89

Two old men walked into a grove of fever trees that stood on the south bank of the Abati river. They stopped beside a pile of gargantuan bones from which the scavengers had picked the flesh, leaving them scattered and white.

'The tusks are gone,' said Walaka.

'Yes,' agreed Mohammed, 'the Askari came back and stole them.'

Together they walked on through the fever trees and then they stopped again. There was a low mound of earth at the edge of the grove. Already it had settled and new grass was growing upon it.

'He was a man,' said Walaka.

'Leave me, my cousin. I will stay here a while.'

'Stay in peace, then,' said Walaka, and settled the string of his blanket roll more comfortably over his shoulder before he walked on.

Mohammed squatted down beside the grave. He sat there unmoving all that day. Then in the evening Mohammed stood up and walked away towards the south.